MORE O. HENRY

BOOKS BY

O. HENRY

"The time is coming, let us hope, when the whole English-speaking world will recognise in O. Henry one of the greatest masters of modern fiction."

THE FOUR MILLION
THE TRIMMED LAMP
SIXES AND SEVENS
STRICTLY BUSINESS
ROADS OF DESTINY
CABBAGES AND KINGS
HEART OF THE WEST
THE GENTLE GRAFTER
OPTIONS
WHIRLIGIGS
THE VOICE OF THE CITY
ROLLING STONES
WAIFS AND STRAYS

The O. Henry
Omnibus Volumes

THE BEST OF O. HENRY
MORE O. HENRY
and
THE O. HENRY ENCORE

—

HODDER & STOUGHTON

MORE

O. HENRY

One Hundred more
of the Master Stories
introduced by

JAMES HILTON

First Edition	. .	*November 1933*
Reprinted	. .	*September 1938*
Reprinted	. .	*March 1941*

INTRODUCTION

AFTER *The Best of O. Henry*, Sapper's finely-chosen hundred from the 270 stories left to the world by the great American yarn-spinner, a second volume was inevitable. Now it comes, under the plain and exciting title—*More O. Henry*, and every O. Henry enthusiast will know what *that* means.

It means, of course, *More* of the *Best*. O. Henry's work was like that. All his stories reach a high and an amazingly well-sustained level of excellence; they are a range of mountains in which the appearance of peaks is largely a matter of the reader's mind's-eye-view. Sapper, in his introduction to the first collection, put the point very wisely when he said: "With certain obvious exceptions I believe you could take the titles of all his stories, put them in a hat, and leave the draw to chance." Whether such a method has been adopted in making this new volume I do not know, but I do know that the result is as wholly admirable as if a selection-committee of professors had sat in solemn conclave for six months. Perhaps even more admirable. At any rate, it is safe enough to pick winners with a pin when there are no losers in the list.

Here, then, are the second hundred, to be savoured with joy by new and old readers alike, and to which any prefatory remarks are almost as superfluous as a lecture on vitamins before dinner at the Savoy. For O. Henry needs no introduction; the world has long ago realized that he is one of its great short-story craftsmen. The really unique thing is that he wears his greatness so lightly. Some writers are just great enough to make their readers feel small; but O. Henry isn't that sort. He gives himself no airs; he deals out his stuff, and it is his readers who feel grand about it. You can enjoy him irrespective of age, erudition, or height of brow, because his yarns are much more than *very* good; they are *jolly* good.

William Sydney Porter (to give the author his real name) would have been sixty-six this year—younger, in fact, than many of the current big names in literature. Unfortunately, he died nearly a quarter of a century ago, in 1910; which, by all that is logical and mathematical, ought to put him into that remote and moribund category "pre-War." Now the odd thing is that O. Henry simply won't go into that category. His work is neither remote nor moribund; on the contrary, it has a curious quality of seeming more up to date to-day (for us on this side of the Atlantic, at least) than it did a generation ago. Not only do his stories possess all the sparkle and verbal liveliness which we are apt to think of as post-War; but a few years' experience of talking-films has made us more at home with the language. Even occasional slang-terms and topical allusions that are still unfamiliar have an air of being too new, rather than too old, for us to comprehend. When, for instance, we read that a certain character knew something "as well as the cat in the City Hall knows an O'Sullivan," we may not see the point immediately, but it is fun trying to think it out. And, since most of these O. Henry-isms *can* be thought out, what better way is there to "brush up your American?"

The stories, too, are full of an intensely modern quality to which one can only give the not very adequate word, speed. They get off the mark like a supercharged Bentley, and at the end of the first sentence are usually as far advanced as the average story after a couple of pages. By the time you get to that clinching last paragraph in which O. Henry so often scores his most surprising effects, you will probably find yourself thinking: "By Jove, *this* is a fine story—*that* was!"

Literary pundits of the future will doubtless give the work of O. Henry a keen analysis, tracing and examining his affinities with Mark Twain, Stephen Leacock, and our own glorious Wodehouse. The subject will be a suitable one for a research degree thesis in, say, the year 2033. For us in these days, who are not compelled to take things so learnedly, it is enough to say that O. Henry's humour, though it has kinships, is chiefly endowed with a flavour of its own. Take this, for example: "When Jacob first began to compare the eyes of needles with the camels in the Zoo, he decided upon organized charity." Got it? Good—and even if you haven't yet, you will.

But wit and wisecracks are nowhere near the sum-total of the man. There are many deeper qualities. He did not have a particularly happy life—certainly not a particularly easy one. After working on a ranch and in a drug-store, he found success late—*too* late for one doomed to die at the age of forty-three after years of ill-health. It is not surprising that he had his sombre moments, and at these times he could write stories (such as "A Fog in Santone" in this collection) in which wit and humour are transmuted into a passionate, pitiful irony. O. Henry's sympathies were all for the underdog; and in this connection it is well to realize that his America was much more like the America of 1933 than of 1929. It was a period of unemployment, of poverty and riches in close contrast, and of intense commercial rivalries. About one of his characters, O. Henry writes: "He originated the discovery that bread was made from flour and not from wheat futures." Whether that sounded an up-to-date remark when it first appeared I have no means of telling; but it certainly has a stop-press flavour to-day.

These, perhaps, have been enough remarks for any middleman to interpose between Demand and Supply. Just one final thought obtrudcs—had O. Henry lived, what would Hollywood have done with him, and what would he have done with Hollywood? There is so much in his work that reminds one of Disney and Lubitsch—his agility of mind, his swiftness in getting to the point, his ironic sensitiveness, the brilliant fecundity of his plot-making, and—above all—his hatred of bunk. To some of the big film-companies his genius would probably be worth to-day as many dollars a month as he earned in an entire lifetime.

Which is just the sort of idea that O. Henry himself might have turned into a short story. He knew, as well as anyone who ever lived, the exceeding queerness of life; and if you turn over the page and read on, you will find and enjoy a hundred proofs of it.

LIST OF STORIES

*

I: THE VOICE OF THE CITY

TWENTY-FIVE years ago the school children used to chant their lessons. The manner of their delivery was a singsong recitative between the utterance of an Episcopal minister and the drone of a tired sawmill. I mean no disrespect. We must have lumber and sawdust.

I remember one beautiful and instructive little lyric that emanated from the physiology class. The most striking line of it was this:

"The shin-bone is the long-est bone in the hu-man bod-y."

What an inestimable boon it would have been if all the corporeal and spiritual facts pertaining to man had thus been tunefully and logically inculcated in our youthful minds! But what we gained in anatomy, music and philosophy was meagre.

The other day I became confused. I needed a ray of light. I turned back to those school days for aid. But in all the nasal harmonies we whined forth from those hard benches I could not recall one that treated of the voice of agglomerated mankind.

In other words, of the composite vocal message of massed humanity.

In other words, of the Voice of a Big City.

Now, the individual voice is not lacking. We can understand the song of the poet, the ripple of the brook, the meaning of the man who wants $5 until next Monday, the inscriptions on the tombs of the Pharaohs, the language of flowers, the "step lively" of the conductor, and the prelude of the milk cans at 4 a.m. Certain large-eared ones even assert that they are wise to the vibrations of the tympanum produced by concussion of the air emanating from Mr. H. James. But who can comprehend the meaning of the voice of the city?

I went out for to see.

First, I asked Aurelia. She wore white Swiss and a hat with flowers on it, and ribbons and ends of things fluttered here and there.

"Tell me," I said, stammeringly, for I have no voice of my own, "what does this big—er—enormous—er—whopping city say? It must have a voice of some kind. Does it ever speak to you? How do you interpret its meaning? It is a tremendous mass, but it must have a key."

"Like a Saratoga trunk?" asked Aurelia.

"No," said I. "Please do not refer to the lid. I have a fancy that every city has a voice. Each one has something to say to the one who can hear it. What does the big one say to you?"

"All cities," said Aurelia, judicially, "say the same thing. When they get through saying it there is an echo from Philadelphia. So, they are unanimous."

"Here are 4,000,000 people," said I, scholastically, "compressed upon an island, which is mostly lamb surrounded by Wall Street water. The conjunction of so many units into so small a space must result in an identity—or, or rather a homogeneity—that finds its oral expression through a common channel. It is, as you might say, a consensus of translation, concentrating in a crystallized, general idea which reveals itself in what may be termed the Voice of the City. Can you tell me what it is?"

Aurelia smiled wonderfully. She sat on the high stoop. A spray of insolent ivy bobbed against her right ear. A ray of impudent moonlight flickered upon her nose. But I was adamant, nickel-plated.

"I must go and find out," I said, "what is the Voice of this city. Other cities have voices. It is an assignment. I must have it. New York," I continued, in a rising tone, "had better not hand me a cigar and say: 'Old man, I can't talk for publication.' No other city acts in that way. Chicago says, unhesitatingly, 'I will'; Philadelphia says, 'I should'; New Orleans says, 'I used to'; Louisville says, 'Don't care if I do'; St. Louis says, 'Excuse me'; Pittsburg says, 'Smoke up.' Now, New York——"

Aurelia smiled.

"Very well," said I, "I must go elsewhere and find out."

I went into a palace, tile-floored, cherub-ceilinged, and square with the cop. I put my foot on the brass rail and said to Billy Magnus, the best bartender in the diocese:

"Billy, you've lived in New York a long time—what kind of a song-and-dance does this old town give you? What I mean is, doesn't the gab of it seem to kind of bunch up and slide over the bar to you in a sort of amalgamated tip that hits off the burg in a kind of an epigram with a dash of bitters and a slice of——"

"Excuse me a minute," said Billy, "somebody's punching the button at the side door."

He went away; came back with an empty tin bucket; again vanished with it full; returned and said to me:

"That was Mame. She rings twice. She likes a glass of beer for supper. Her and the kid. If you ever saw that little skeesicks of mine brace up in his high chair and take his beer and—— But, say, what was yours? I get kind of excited when I hear them two rings—was it the baseball score or gin fizz you asked for?"

"Ginger ale," I answered.

I walked up to Broadway. I saw a cop on the corner. The cops take kids up, women across, and men in. I went up to him.

"If I'm not exceeding the spiel limit," I said, "let me ask you. You see New York during its vocative hours. It is the function of you and your brother cops to preserve the acoustics of the city. There must be a civic voicc that is intelligible to you. At night during your lonely rounds you must have heard it. What is the epitome of its turmoil and shouting? What does the city say to you?"

"Friend," said the policeman, spinning his club, "it don't say nothing. I get my orders from the man higher up. Say, I guess you're all right. Stand here for a few minutes and keep an eye open for the roundsman."

The cop melted into the darkness of the side-street. In ten minutes he had returned.

"Married last Tuesday," he said, half gruffly. "You know how they are. She comes to that corner at nine every night for a—comes to say 'hello!' I generally manage to be there. Say, what was it you asked me a bit ago—what's doing in the city? Oh, there's a roof-garden or two just opened, twelve blocks up."

I crossed a crow's-foot of street-car tracks, and skirted the edge of an umbrageous park. An artificial Diana, gilded, heroic, poised, wind-ruled, on the tower, shimmered in the clear light of her namesake in the sky. Along came my poet, hurrying, hatted, haired, emitting dactyls, spondees and dactylis. I seized him.

"Bill," said I (in the magazine he is Cleon), "give me a lift. I am on an assignment to find out the Voice of the city. You see, it's a special order. Ordinarily a symposium comprising the views of Henry Clews, John J. Sullivan, Edwin Markham, May Irwin and Charles Schwab would be about all. But this is a different matter. We want a broad, poetic, mystic vocalization of the city's soul and meaning. You are the very chap to give me a hint. Some years ago a man got at the Niagara Falls and gave us its pitch. The note was about two feet below the lowest G on the piano. Now, you can't put New York into a note unless it's better indorsed than that. But give me an idea of what it would say if it should speak. It is bound to be a mighty and far-reaching utterance. To arrive at it we must take the tremendous crash of the chords of the day's traffic, the laughter and music of the night, the solemn tones of Dr. Parkhurst, the rag-time, the weeping, the stealthy hum of cab-wheels, the shout of the press agent, the tinkle of fountains on the roof-gardens, the hullabaloo of the strawberry vendor and the covers of *Everybody's Magazine*, the whispers of the lovers in the parks—all these sounds must go into your Voice—not combined, but mixed, and of the mixture an essence made; and of the essence an extract —an audible extract, of which one drop shall form the thing we seek."

"Do you remember," asked the poet, with a chuckle, "that California girl we met at Stiver's studio last week? Well, I'm on my way to see her. She repeated that poem of mine, 'The Tribute of Spring,' word for word. She's the smartest proposition in this town just at present. Say, how does this confounded tie look? I spoiled four before I got one to set right."

"And the Voice that I asked you about?" I inquired.

"Oh, she doesn't sing," said Cleon. "But you ought to hear her recite my 'Angel of the Inshore Wind.' "

I passed on. I cornered a newsboy, and he flashed at me prophetic pink papers that outstripped the news by two revolutions of the clock's longest hand.

"Son," I said, while I pretended to chase coins in my penny pocket, "doesn't it sometimes seem to you as if the city ought to be able to talk? All these ups and downs and funny business and queer things happening every day—what would it say, do you think, if it could speak?"

"Quit yer kiddin'," said the boy. "Wot paper yer want? I got no time to waste. It's Mag's birthday, and I want thirty cents to git her a present."

Here was no interpreter of the city's mouthpiece. I bought a paper, and consigned its undeclared treaties, its premeditated murders and unfought battles to an ash can.

Again I repaired to the park and sat in the

moon shade. I thought and thought, and wondered why none could tell me what I asked for.

And then, as swift as light from a fixed star, the answer came to me. I arose and hurried—hurried as so many reasoners must, back around my circle. I knew the answer, and I hugged it in my breast as I flew, fearing lest some one would stop me and demand my secret.

Aurelia was still on the stoop. The moon was higher and the ivy shadows were deeper. I sat at her side, and we watched a little cloud tilt at the drifting moon and go asunder, quite pale and discomfited.

And then, wonder of wonders and delight of delights! our hands somehow touched, and our fingers closed together and did not part.

After half an hour Aurelia said, with that smile of hers:

"Do you know, you haven't spoken a word since you came back!"

"That," said I, nodding wisely, "is the Voice of the City."

II: ART AND THE BRONCO

OUT of the wilderness had come a painter. Genius, whose coronations alone are democratic, had woven a chaplet of chaparral for the brow of Lonny Briscoe. Art, whose divine expression flows impartially from the finger-tips of a cowboy or a dilettante emperor, had chosen for a medium the Boy Artist of the San Saba. The outcome, seven feet by twelve of besmeared canvas, stood, gilt-framed, in the lobby of the Capitol.

The legislature was in session; the capital city of that great Western state was enjoying the season of activity and profit that the congregation of the solons bestowed. The boarding-houses were corralling the easy dollars of the gamesome law-makers. The greatest state in the West, an empire in area and resources, had arisen and repudiated the old libel of barbarism, law-breaking, and blood-shed. Order reigned within her borders. Life and property were as safe there, sir, as anywhere among the corrupt cities of the effete East. Pillow-shams, churches, strawberry feasts and *habeas corpus* flourished. With impunity might the tenderfoot ventilate his "stovepipe" or his theories of culture. The arts and sciences received nurture and subsidy. And, therefore, it behooved the legislature of this great state to makc appropriation for the purchase of Lonny Briscoe's immortal painting.

Rarely has the San Saba country contributed to the spread of the fine arts. Its sons have excelled in the solider graces, in the throw of the lariat, the manipulation of the esteemed ·45, the intrepidity of the one-card draw, and the nocturnal stimulation of towns from undue lethargy; but, hitherto, it had not been famed as a stronghold of æsthetics. Lonny Briscoe's brush had removed that disability. Here, among the limestone rocks, the succulent cactus, and the drought-parched grass of that arid valley, had been born the Boy Artist. Why he came to woo art is beyond postulation. Beyond doubt, some spore of the afflatus must have sprung up within him in spite of the desert soil of San Saba. The tricksy spirit of creation must have incited him to attempted expression, and then have sat hilarious among the white-hot sands of the valley, watching its mischievous work. For Lonny's picture, viewed as a thing of art, was something to have driven away dull care from the bosoms of the critics.

The painting—one might almost say panorama—was designed to portray a typical Western scene, interest culminating in a central animal figure, that of a stampeding steer, life-size, wild-eyed, fiery, breaking away in a mad rush from the herd that, close-ridden by a typical cowpuncher, occupied a position somewhat in the right background of the picture. The landscape presented fitting and faithful accessories. Chaparral, mesquit, and pear were distributed in just proportions. A Spanish dagger-plant, with its waxen blossoms in a creamy aggregation as large as a water-bucket, contributed floral beauty and variety. The distance was undulating prairie, bisected by stretches of the intermittent streams peculiar to the region lined with the rich green of live-oak and water-elm. A richly mottled rattlesnake lay coiled beneath a pale green clump of prickly pear in the foreground. A third of the canvas was ultramarine and lake white—the typical Western sky and the flying clouds, rainless and feathery.

Between two plastered pillars in the commodious hallway near the door of the chamber of representatives stood the painting. Citizens and law-makers passed there by twos and groups and sometimes crowds to gaze upon it. Many—perhaps a majority of them—had lived the prairie life and recalled easily the familiar scene. Old cattlemen stood, reminiscent and candidly pleased, chatting with brothers of former camps and trails of the days it brought back to mind. Art critics were few in the town, and there was heard none of that jargon of colour, perspective, and feeling such as the East loves to use as a curb and a rod to the pretensions of the artist. 'Twas a great picture, most of them agreed, admiring the gilt frame—larger than any they had ever seen.

Senator Kinney was the picture's champion and sponsor. It was he who so often stepped forward and asserted, with the voice of a bronco-buster, that it would be a lasting blot, sir, upon the name of this great state if it should decline to recognize in a proper manner the genius that had so brilliantly transferred to imperishable canvas a scene so typical of the great sources of our state's wealth and prosperity, land—and—er—livestock.

Senator Kinney represented a section of the state in the extreme West—400 miles from the San Saba country—but the true lover of art is not limited by metes and bounds. Nor was Senator Mullens, representing the San Saba country, lukewarm in his belief that the state should purchase the painting of his constituent. He was advised that the San Saba country was unanimous in its admiration of the great painting by one of its own denizens. Hundreds of connoisseurs had straddled their broncos and ridden miles to view it before its removal to the capital. Senator Mullens desired re-election, and he knew the importance of the San Saba vote. He also knew that with the help of Senator Kinney—who was a power in the legislature—the thing could be put through. Now, Senator Kinney had an irrigation bill that he wanted passed for the benefit of his own section, and he knew Senator Mullens could render him valuable aid and information, the San Saba country already enjoying the benefits of similar legislation. With these interests happily dovetailed, wonder at the sudden interest in art at the state capital must, necessarily, be small. Few artists have uncovered their first picture to the world under happier auspices than did Lonny Briscoe.

Senators Kinney and Mullens came to an understanding in the matters of irrigation and art while partaking of long drinks in the café of the Empire Hotel.

"H'm!" said Senator Kinney, "I don't know. I'm no art critic, but it seems to me the thing won't work. It looks like the worst kind of a chromo to mc. I don't want to cast any reflections upon the artistic talent of your constituent, Senator, but I, myself, wouldn't give six bits for the picture—without the frame. How are you going to cram a thing like that down the throat of a legislature that kicks about a little item in the expense bill of six hundred and eighty-one dollars for rubber erasers for only one term? It's wasting time. I'd like to help you, Mullens, but they'd laugh us out of the Senate chamber if we were to try it."

"But you don't get the point," said Senator Mullens, in his deliberate tones, tapping Kinney's glass with his long forefinger. "I have my own doubts as to what the picture is intended to represent, a bullfight or a Japanese allegory, but I want this legislature to make an appropriation to purchase. Of course, the subject of the picture should have been in the state historical line, but it's too late to have the paint scraped off and changed. The state won't miss the money and the picture can be stored away in a lumber-room where it won't annoy anyone. Now, here's the point to work on, leaving art to look after itself—the chap that painted the picture is the grandson of Lucien Briscoe."

"Say it again," said Kinney, leaning his head thoughtfully. "Of the old, original Lucien Briscoe?"

"Of him. 'The man who,' you know. The man who carved the state out of the wilderness. The man who settled the Indians. The man who cleaned out the horse thieves. The man who refused the crown. The state's favourite son. Do you see the point now?"

"Wrap up the picture," said Kinney. "It's as good as sold. Why didn't you say that at first, instead of philandering along about art. I'll resign my seat in the Senate and go back to chain-carrying for the county surveyor the day I can't make this state buy a picture calcimined by a grandson of Lucien Briscoe. Did you ever hear of a special appropriation for the purchase of a home for the daughter of One-Eyed Smothers? Well, that went through like a motion to adjourn, and old One-Eyed never killed half as many Indians as Briscoe did. About what figure had you and the calciminer agreed upon to sandbag the treasury for?"

"I thought," said Mullens, "that maybe five hundred——"

"Five hundred!" interrupted Kinney, as he hammered on his glass for a lead pencil and looked around for a waiter. "Only five hundred for a red steer on the hoof delivered by a grandson of Lucien Briscoe! Where's your state pride, man! Two thousand is what it'll be. You'll introduce the bill and I'll get up on the floor of the Senate and wave the scalp of every Indian old Lucien ever murdered. Let's see, there was something else proud and foolish he did, wasn't there? Oh yes; he declined all emoluments and benefits he was entitled to. Refused his head-right and veteran donation certificates. Could have been governor, but wouldn't. Declined a pension. Now's the state's chance to pay up. It'll have to take the picture, but then it deserves some punishment for keeping the Briscoe family waiting so long. We'll bring this thing up about the middle of the month, after the tax bill is settled. Now, Mullens, you send over, as soon as you can, and get me the figures on the cost of those irrigation ditches and the statistics about the increased production per acre. I'm going to need you when that bill of mine comes up. I reckon we'll be able to pull along pretty well together that session and maybe others to come, eh, Senator?"

Thus did fortune elect to smile upon the Boy Artist of the San Saba. Fate had already done her share when she arranged his atoms in the cosmogony of creation as the grandson of Lucien Briscoe.

The original Briscoe had been a pioneer both as to territorial occupation and in certain acts prompted by a great and simple heart. He had been one of the first setters and crusaders against the wild forces of nature, the savage and the shallow politician. His name and memory were revered equally with any upon the list comprising Houston, Boone, Crockett, Clark, and Green. He had lived simply, independently, and unvexed by ambition. Even a less shrewd man than Senator Kinney could have prophesied that his state would hasten to honour and reward his grandson, come out of the chaparral at even so late a day.

And so, before the great picture by the door of the chamber of representatives, at frequent times for many days, could be found the breezy, robust form of Senator Kinney and be heard his clarion voice reciting the past deeds of Lucien Briscoe in connection with the handiwork of his grandson. Senator Mullen's work was more subdued in sight and sound, but directed along identical lines.

Then, as the day for the introduction of the bill for appropriation draws nigh, up from the San Saba country rides Lonny Briscoe and a loyal lobby of cowpunchers, bronco-back, to boost the cause of art and glorify the name of friendship, for Lonny is one of them, a knight of stirrup and chaparreras, as handy with the lariat and ·45 as he is with brush and palette.

On a March afternoon the lobby dashed, with a whoop, into town. The cowpunchers had adjusted their garb suitably from that prescribed for the range to the more conventional requirements of town. They had conceded their leather chaparreras and transferred their six-shooters and belts from their persons to the horns of their saddles. Among them rode Lonny, a youth of twenty-three, brown, solemn-faced, ingenuous, bow-legged, reticent, bestriding Hot Tamales, the most sagacious cow-pony west of the Mississippi. Senator Mullens had informed him of the bright prospects of the situation; had even mentioned—so great was his confidence in the capable Kinney—the price that the state would, in all likelihood, pay. It seemed to Lonny that fame and fortune were in his hands.

Certainly, a spark of the divine fire was in the little brown centaur's breast, for he was counting the two thousand dollars as but a means to future development of his talent. Some day he would paint a picture even greater than this—one, say, twelve feet by twenty, full of scope and atmosphere and action.

During the three days that yet intervened before the coming of the date fixed for the introduction of the bill the centaur lobby did valiant service. Coatless, spurred, weather-tanned, full of enthusiasm expressed in bizarre terms, they loafed in front of the painting with tireless zeal. Reasoning not unshrewdly, they estimated that their comments upon its fidelity to nature would be received as expert evidence. Loudly they praised the skill of the painter whenever there were ears near to which such evidence might be profitably addressed. Lem Perry, the leader of the claque, had a somewhat set speech, being uninventive in the construction of new phrases.

"Look at that two-year-old, now," he would say, waving a cinnamon-brown hand toward the salient point of the picture. "Why, dang my hide, the critter's alive. I can jest hear him, 'lumpety-lump,' a-cuttin' away from the herd, pretendin' he's skeered. He's a mean scamp, that there steer. Look at his eyes a-wallin' and his tail a-wavin'. He's true and nat'ral to life. He's jest hankerin' fur a cow-pony to round him up and send him scootin' back to the bunch. Dang my hide! jest look at that tail of his 'n a-wavin'. Never knowed a steer to wave his tail any other way, dang my hide if I did."

Jud Shelby, while admitting the excellence of the steer, resolutely confined himself to open admiration of the landscape, to the end that the entire picture received its meed of praise.

"That piece of range," he declared, "is a dead ringer for Dead Hoss Valley. Same grass, same lay of the land, same old Whipperwill Creek skally-hootin' in and out of them motts of timber. Them buzzards on the left is circlin' 'round over Sam Kildrake's old paint hoss that killed hisself over-drinkin' on a hot day. You can't see the hoss for that mott of ellums on the creek, but he's thar. Anybody that was goin' to look for Dead Hoss Valley and come across this picture, why, he'd jest light off 'n his bronco and hunt a place to camp."

Skinny Rogers, wedded to comedy, conceived a complimentary little piece of acting that never failed to make an impression. Edging quite near to the picture, he would suddenly, at favourable moments, emit a piercing and awful "Yi-yi!" leap high and away, coming down with a great stamp of heels and whirring of rowels upon the stone-flagged floor.

"Jeeming Christopher!"—so ran his lines—"thought that rattler was a gin-u-ine one. Ding baste my skin if I didn't. Seemed to me I heard him rattle. Look at the blamed, unconverted insect a-layin' under that pear. Little more, and somebody would a-been snake-bit."

With these artful dodges, contributed by Lonny's faithful coterie, with the sonorous Kinney perpetually sounding the picture's merits, and with the solvent prestige of the pioneer Briscoe covering it like a precious varnish, it seemed that the San Saba country could not fail to add a reputation as an art centre to its well-known superiority in steer-roping contests and achievements with the precarious busted flush. Thus was created for the picture an atmosphere, due rather to externals than to the artist's brush, but through it the people seemed to gaze with more of admiration. There was a magic in the name of Briscoe that counted high against faulty technique and crude colouring. The old Indian fighter and wolf slayer would have smiled grimly in his happy hunting-grounds had he known that his dilettante ghost was thus figuring as an art patron two generations after his uninspired existence.

Came the day when the Senate was expected to pass the bill of Senator Mullens appropriating two thousand dollars for the purchase of the picture. The gallery of the Senate chamber was early preempted by Lonny and the San Saba lobby. In the front row of chairs they sat, wild-haired, self-conscious, jingling, creaking, and rattling, subdued by the majesty of the council hall.

The bill was introduced, went to the second reading, and then Senator Mullens spoke for it dryly, tediously, and at length. Senator Kinney then arose, and the welkin seized the bell-rope preparatory to ringing. Oratory was at that time a living thing ; the world had not quite come to measure its questions by geometry and the multiplication table. It was the day of the silver tongue, the sweeping gesture, the decorative apostrophe, the moving peroration.

The Senator spoke. The San Saba contingent sat, breathing hard, in the gallery, its disordered hair hanging down to its eyes, its sixteen-ounce hats shifted restlessly from knee to knee. Below, the distinguished Senators either lounged at their desks with the abandon of proven statesmanship or maintained correct attitudes indicative of a first term.

Senator Kinney spoke for an hour. History was his theme—history mitigated by patriotism and sentiment. He referred casually to the picture in the outer hall—it was unnecessary, he said, to dilate upon its merits—the Senators had seen for themselves. The painter of the picture was the grandson of Lucien Briscoe. Then came the word-pictures of Briscoe's life set forth in thrilling colours. His rude and venturesome life, his simple-minded love for the commonwealth he helped to upbuild, his contempt for rewards and praise, his extreme and sturdy independence, and the great services he had rendered the state. The subject of the oration was Lucien Briscoe; the painting stood in the background, serving simply as a means, now happily brought forward, through which the state might bestow a tardy recompense upon the descendant of its favourite son. Frequent enthusiastic applause from the Senators testified to the well reception of the sentiment.

The bill passed without an opposing vote. To-morrow it would be taken up by the House. Already was it fixed to glide through that body on rubber tyres. Blandford, Grayson, and Plummer, all wheel-horses and orators, and provided with plentiful memoranda concerning the deeds of pioneer Briscoe, had agreed to furnish the motive power.

The San Saba lobby and its protégé stumbled awkwardly down the stairs and out into the Capitol yard. Then they herded closely and gave one yell of triumph. But one of them—Buck-Kneed Summers it was—hit the key with the thoughtful remark:

"She cut the mustard," he said, "all right. I reckon they're goin' to buy Lon's steer. I ain't right much on the parlyment'ry, but I gather that's what the signs added up. But she seems to me, Lonny, the argyment ran principal to grandfather, instead of paint. It's reasonable calculatin' that you want to be glad you got the Briscoe brand on you, my son."

That remark clinched in Lonny's mind an unpleasant, vague suspicion to the same effect. His reticence increased, and he gathered grass from the ground, chewing it pensively. The picture as a picture had been humiliatingly absent from the Senator's arguments. The painter had been held up as a grandson, pure and simple. While this was gratifying on certain lines, it made art look little and slab-sided. The Boy Artist was thinking.

The hotel Lonny stopped at was near the Capitol. It was near to the one o'clock dinner-hour when the appropriation had been passed by the Senate. The hotel clerk told Lonny that a famous artist from New York had arrived in town that day and was in the hotel. He was on his way westward to New Mexico to study the effect of sunlight upon the ancient walls of the Zuñis. Modern stone reflects light. Those ancient building materials absorb it. The artist wanted this effect in a picture he was painting and was travelling two thousand miles to get it.

Lonny sought this man out after dinner and told his story. The artist was an unhealthy man, kept alive by genius and indifference to life. He went with Lonny to the Capitol and stood there before the picture. The artist pulled his beard and looked unhappy.

should like to have your sentiments," said Lonny, "just as they run out of the pen."

"It's the way they'll come," said the painter man. "I took three different kinds of medicine before dinner—by the tablespoonful. The taste still lingers. I am primed for telling the truth. You want to know if the picture is, or if it isn't?"

"Right," said Lonny. "Is it wool or cotton? Should I paint some more or cut it out and ride herd a-plenty?"

"I heard the rumour during pie," said the artist, "that the state is about to pay you two thousand dollars for this picture."

"It's passed the Senate," said Lonny, "and the House rounds it up to-morrow."

"That's lucky," said the pale man. "Do you carry a rabbit's foot?"

"No," said Lonny, "but it seems I had a grandfather. He's considerable mixed up in the colour scheme. It took me a year to paint that picture. Is she entirely awful or not? Some say, now, that that steer's tail ain't badly drawed. They think it's proportioned nice. Tell me."

The artist glanced at Lonny's wiry figure and nut-brown skin. Something stirred him to a passing irritation.

"For Art's sake, son," he said, fractiously, "don't spend any more money for paint. It isn't a picture at all. It's a gun. You hold up the state with it, if you like, and get your two thousand, but don't get in front of any more canvas. Live under it. Buy a couple of hundred ponies with the money—I'm told they're that cheap—and ride, ride, ride. Fill your lungs and eat and sleep and be happy. No more pictures. You look healthy.

That's genius. Cultivate it." He looked at his watch. "Twenty minutes to three. Four capsules and one tablet at three. That's all you wanted to know, isn't it?"

At three o'clock the cowpunchers rode up for Lonny, bringing Hot Tamales, saddled. Traditions must be observed. To celebrate the passing of the bill by the Senate the gang must ride wildly through the town, creating uproar and excitement. Liquor must be partaken of, the suburbs shot up, and the glory of the San Saba country vociferously proclaimed. A part of the programme had been carried out in the saloons on the way up.

Lonny mounted Hot Tamales, the accomplished little beast prancing with fire and intelligence. He was glad to feel Lonny's bowlegged grip against his ribs again. Lonny was his friend, and he was willing to do things for him.

"Come on, boys," said Lonny, urging Hot Tamales into a gallop with his knees. With a whoop, the inspired lobby tore after him through the dust. Lonny led his cohorts straight for the Capitol. With a wild yell, the gang endorsed his now evident intention of riding into it. Hooray for San Saba.

Up the six broad, limestone steps clattered the broncos of the cowpunchers. Into the resounding hallway they pattered, scattering in dismay those passing on foot. Lonny, in the lead, shoved Hot Tamales direct for the great picture. At that hour a downpouring, soft light from the second-story windows bathed the big canvas. Against the darker background of the hall the painting stood out with valuable effect. In spite of the defects of the art you could almost fancy that you gazed out upon a landscape. You might well flinch a step from the convincing figure of the life-sized steer stampeding across the grass. Perhaps it thus seemed to Hot Tamales. The scene was in his line. Perhaps he only obeyed the will of his rider. His ears pricked up; he snorted. Lonny leaned forward in the saddle and elevated his elbows, wing-like. Thus signals the cowpuncher to his steed to launch himself full speed ahead. Did Hot Tamales fancy he saw a steer, red and cavorting that should be headed off and driven back to herd? There was a fierce clatter of hoofs, a rush, a gathering of steely flank muscles, a leap to the jerk of the bridle rein, and Hot Tamales, with Lonny bending low in the saddle to dodge the top of the frame, ripped through the great canvas like a shell from a mortar, leaving the cloth hanging in ragged shreds about a monstrous hole.

Quickly Lonny pulled up his pony, and rounded the pillars. Spectators came running, too astounded to add speech to the commotion. The sergeant-at-arms of the House came forth, frowned, looked ominous, and then grinned. Many of the legislators crowded out to observe the tumult. Lonny's cowpunchers were stricken to silent horror by his mad deed.

Senator Kinney happened to be among the earliest to emerge. Before he could speak Lonny leaned in his saddle as Hot Tamales pranced, pointed his squirt at the Senator, and said calmly:

"That was a fine speech you made to-day, mister, but you might as well let up on that 'propriation business. I ain't askin' the state to give me nothin'. I thought I had a picture to sell to it, but it wasn't one. You said a heap of things about Grandfather

Briscoe that makes me kind of proud I'm his grandson. Well, the Briscoes ain't takin' presents from the state yet. Anybody can have the frame that wants it. Hit her up, boys."

Away scuttled the San Saba delegation out of the hall, down the steps, along the dusty street.

Half-way to the San Saba country they camped that night. At bedtime Lonny stole away from the camp-fire and sought Hot Tamales, placidly eating grass at the end of his stake rope. Lonny hung upon his neck, and his art aspirations went forth for ever in one long, regretful sigh. But as he thus made renunciation his breath formed a word or two.

"You was the only one, Tamales, what seen anything in it. It *did* look like a steer, didn't it, old hoss?"

III: A CHAPARRAL CHRISTMAS GIFT

THE original cause of the trouble was about twenty years in growing.

At the end of that time it was worth it.

Had you lived anywhere within fifty miles of Sundown Ranch you would have heard of it. It possessed a quantity of jet-black hair, a pair of extremely frank, deep-brown eyes, and a laugh that rippled across the prairie like the sound of a hidden brook. The name of it was Rosita McMullen; and she was the daughter of old man McMullen of the Sundown Sheep Ranch.

There came riding on red roan steeds—or, to be more explicit, on a paint and a flea-bitten sorrel—

two wooers. One was Madison Lane, and the other was the Frio Kid. But at that time they did not call him the Frio Kid, for he had not earned the honours of special nomenclature. His name was simply Johnny McRoy.

It must not be supposed that these two were the sum of the agreeable Rosita's admirers. The bronchos of a dozen others champed their bits at the long hitching-rack of the Sundown Ranch. Many were the sheep's-eyes that were cast in those savannas that did not belong to the flocks of Dan McMullen. But of all the cavaliers, Madison Lane and Johnny McRoy galloped far ahead, wherefore they are to be chronicled.

Madison Lane, a young cattleman from the Nueces country, won the race. He and Rosita were married one Christmas day. Armed, hilarious, vociferous, magnanimous, the cowmen and the sheepmen, laying aside their hereditary hatred, joined forces to celebrate the occasion.

Sundown Ranch was sonorous with the cracking of jokes and sixshooters, the shine of buckles and bright eyes, the outspoken congratulations of the herders of kine.

But while the wedding feast was at its liveliest there descended upon it Johnny McRoy, bitten by jealousy, like one possessed.

"I'll give you a Christmas present," he yelled shrilly at the door, with his ·45 in his hand. Even then he had some reputation as an offhand shot.

His first bullet cut a neat underbit in Madison Lane's right ear. The barrel of his gun moved an inch. The next shot would have been the bride's had not Carson, a sheepman, possessed a mind with triggers somewhat well oiled and in repair. The guns of the wedding party had been hung, in their belts, upon nails in the wall when they sat at table, as a concession to good taste. But Carson, with great promptness, hurled his plate of roast venison and frijoles at McRoy, spoiling his aim. The second bullet, then, only shattered the white petals of a Spanish dagger flower suspended two feet above Rosita's head.

The guests spurned their chairs and jumped for their weapons. It was considered an improper act to shoot the bride and groom at a wedding. In about six seconds there were twenty or so bullets due to be whizzing in the direction of Mr. McRoy.

"I'll shoot better next time," yelled Johnny; "and there'll be a next time." He backed rapidly out the door.

Carson, the sheepman, spurred on to attempt further exploits by the success of his plate-throwing, was first to reach the door. McRoy's bullet from the darkness laid him low.

The cattlemen then swept out upon him, calling for vengeance, for, while the slaughter of a sheepman has not always lacked condonement, it was a decided misdemeanour in this instance. Carson was innocent; he was no accomplice at the matrimonial proceedings; nor had anyone heard him quote the line "Christmas comes but once a year" to the guests.

But the sortie failed in its vengeance. McRoy was on his horse and away, shouting back curses and threats as he galloped into the concealing chaparral.

That night was the birthnight of the Frio Kid. He became the "bad man" of that portion of the State. The rejection of his suit by Miss McMullen turned him to a dangerous man. When officers went after him for the shooting of Carson, hc killed two of them, and entered upon the life of an outlaw. He became a marvellous shot with either hand. He would turn up in towns and settlements, raise a quarrel at the slightest opportunity, pick off his man and laugh at the officers of the law. He was so cool, so deadly, so rapid, so inhumanly bloodthirsty that none but faint attempts were ever made to capture him. When he was at last shot and killed by a little one-armed Mexican who was nearly dead himself from fright, the Frio Kid had the deaths of eighteen men on his head. About half of these were killed in fair duels depending upon the quickness of the draw. The other half were men whom he assassinated from absolute wantonness and cruelty.

Many tales are told along the border of his impudent courage and daring. But he was not one of the breed of desperadoes who have seasons of generosity and even of softness. They say he never had mercy on the object of his anger. Yet at this and every Christmastide it is well to give each one credit, if it can be done, for whatever speck of good he may have possessed. If the Frio Kid ever did a kindly act or felt a throb of generosity in his heart it was once at such a time and season, and this is the way it happened.

One who has been crossed in love should never breathe the odour from the blossoms of the ratama tree. It stirs the memory to a dangerous degree.

One December in the Frio country there was a ratama tree in full bloom, for the winter had been as warm as springtime. That way rode the Frio Kid and his satellite and co-murderer, Mexican Frank. The Kid reined in his mustang, and sat in his saddle, thoughtful and grim, with dangerously narrowing eyes. The rich, sweet scent touched him somewhere beneath his ice and iron.

"I don't know what I've been thinking about, Mex," he remarked in his usual mild drawl, "to have forgot all about a Christmas present I got to give. I'm going to ride over to-morrow night and shoot Madison Lane in his own house. He got my girl—Rosita would have had me if he hadn't cut into the game. I wonder why I happened to overlook it up to now?"

"Ah, shucks, Kid," said Mexican, "don't talk foolishness. You know you can't get within a mile of Mad Lane's house to-morrow night. I see old man Allen day before yesterday, and he says Mad is going to have Christmas doings at his house. You remember how you shot up the festivities when Mad was married, and about the threats you made? Don't you suppose Mad Lane'll kind of keep his eye open for a certain Mr. Kid? You plumb make me tired, Kid, with such remarks."

"I'm going," repeated the Frio Kid, without heat, "to go to Madison Lane's Christmas doings and kill him. I ought to have done it a long time ago. Why, Mex, just two weeks ago I dreamed me and Rosita was married instead of her and him; and we was living in a house, and I could see her smiling at me, and—oh! h——l, Mex, he got her; and I'll get him—yes, sir, on Christmas Eve he got her, and then's when I'll get him."

"There's other ways of committing suicide," advised Mexican. "Why don't you go and surrender to the sheriff."

"I'll get him," said the Kid.

Christmas Eve fell as balmy as April. Perhaps

there was a hint of far-away frostiness in the air, but it tingled like seltzer, perfumed faintly with late prairie blossoms and the mesquite grass.

When night came the five or six rooms of the ranch-house were brightly lit. In one room was a Christmas tree, for the Lanes had a boy of three, and a dozen or more guests were expected from the nearer ranches.

At nightfall Madison Lane called aside Jim Belcher and three other cowboys employed on his ranch.

"Now, boys," said Lane, "keep your eyes open. Walk around the house and watch the road well. All of you know the 'Frio Kid,' as they call him now, and if you see him, open fire on him without asking any questions. I'm not afraid of his coming around, but Rosita is. She's been afraid he'd come in on us every Christmas since we were married."

The guests had arrived in buckboards and on horseback, and were making themselves comfortable inside.

The evening went along pleasantly. The guests enjoyed and praised Rosita's excellent supper, and afterward the men scattered in groups about the rooms or on the broad "gallery," smoking and chatting.

The Christmas tree, of course, delighted the youngsters, and above all were they pleased when Santa Claus himself in magnificent white beard and furs appeared and began to distribute the toys.

"It's my papa," announced Billy Sampson, aged six. "I've seen him wear 'em before."

Berkly, a sheepman, an old friend of Lane, stopped Rosita as she was passing by him on the gallery, where he was sitting smoking.

"Well, Mrs. Lane," said he, "I suppose by this

Christmas you've gotten over being afraid of that fellow McRoy, haven't you? Madison and I have talked about it, you know."

"Very nearly," said Rosita, smiling, "but I am still nervous sometimes. I shall never forget that awful time when he came so near to killing us."

"He's the most cold-hearted villain in the world," said Berkly. "The citizens all along the border ought to turn out and hunt him down like a wolf."

"He has committed awful crimes," said Rosita, "but—I—don't—know. I think there is a spot of good somewhere in everybody. He was not always bad—that I know."

Rosita turned into the hallway between the rooms. Santa Claus, in muffling whiskers and furs, was just coming through.

"I heard what you said through the window, Mrs. Lane," he said. "I was just going down in my pocket for a Christmas present for your husband. But I've left one for you, instead. It's in the room to your right."

"Oh, thank you, kind Santa Claus," said Rosita brightly.

Rosita went into the room, while Santa Claus stepped into the cooler air of the yard.

She found no one in the room but Madison.

"Where is my present that Santa said he left for me in here?" she asked.

"Haven't seen anything in the way of a present," said her husband, laughing, "unless he could have meant me."

The next day Gabriel Radd, the foreman of the X O Ranch, dropped into the post-office at Loma Alta.

"Well, the Frio Kid's got his dose of lead at last," he remarked to the postmaster.

"That's so? How'd it happen?"

"One of old Sanchez's Mexican sheep-herders did it!—think of it! the Frio Kid killed by a sheep-herder! The Greaser saw him riding along past his camp about twelve o'clock last night, and was so skeered that he up with a Winchester and let him have it. Funniest part of it was that the Kid was dressed all up with white Angora-skin whiskers and a regular Santy Claus rig-out from head to foot. Think of the Frio Kid playing Santy!"

IV: PSYCHE AND THE PSKYSCRAPER

IF you are a philosopher you can do this thing: you can go to the top of a high building, look down upon your fellow-men 300 feet below, and despise them as insects. Like the irresponsible black waterbugs on summer ponds, they crawl and circle and hustle about idiotically without aim or purpose. They do not even move with the admirable intelligence of ants, for ants always know when they are going home. The ant is of a lowly station, but he will often reach home and get his slippers on while you are left at your elevated station.

Man, then, to the housetopped philosopher, appears to be but a creeping, contemptible beetle. Brokers, poets, millionaires, bootblacks, beauties, hod-carriers and politicians become little black specks dodging bigger black specks in streets no wider than your thumb.

From this high view the city itself becomes degraded to an unintelligible mass of distorted buildings and impossible perspectives; the revered ocean is a duck pond; the earth itself a lost golf ball. All the minutiæ of life are gone. The philosopher gazes into the infinite heavens above him, and allows his soul to expand to the influence of his new view. He feels that he is the heir to Eternity and the child of Time. Space, too, should be his by the right of his immortal heritage, and he thrills at the thought that some day his kind shall traverse those mysterious aerial roads between planet and planet. The tiny world beneath his feet upon which this towering structure of steel rests as a speck of dust upon a Himalayan mountain—it is but one of a countless number of such whirling atoms. What are the ambitions, the achievements, the paltry conquests and loves of those restless black insects below compared with the serene and awful immensity of the universe that lies above and around their insignificant city?

It is guaranteed that the philosopher will have these thoughts. They have been expressly compiled from the philosophies of the world and set down with the proper interrogation point at the end of them to represent the invariable musings of deep thinkers on high places. And when the philosopher takes the elevator down his mind is broader, his heart is at peace, and his conception of the cosmogony of creation is as wide as the buckle of Orion's summer belt.

But if your name happened to be Daisy, and you worked in an Eighth Avenue candy store and lived in a little cold hall bedroom, five feet by eight, and earned $6 per week and ate ten-cent lunches and were nineteen years old, and got up at 6.30 and worked till nine, and never had studied philosophy, maybe things wouldn't look that way to you from the top of a skyscraper.

Two sighed for the hand of Daisy the unphilosophical. One was Joe, who kept the smallest store in New York. It was about the size of a tool-box of the D.P.W., and was stuck like a swallow's nest against a corner of a down-town skyscraper. Its stock consisted of fruit, candies, newspapers, song books, cigarettes, and lemonade in season. When stern winter shook his congealed locks and Joe had to move himself and the fruit inside, there was exactly room in the store for the proprietor, his wares, a stove the size of a vinegar cruet, and one customer.

Joe was not of the nation that keeps us for ever in a furore with fugues and fruit. He was a capable American youth who was laying by money, and wanted Daisy to help him spend it. Three times he had asked her.

"I got money saved up, Daisy," was his love song; "and you know how bad I want you. That store of mine ain't very big, but——"

"Oh, ain't it?" would be the antiphony of the unphilosophical one. "Why, I heard Wanamaker's was trying to get you to sublet part of your floor-space to them for next year."

Daisy passed Joe's corner every morning and evening.

"Hallo, Two-by-Four!" was her usual greeting. "Seems to me your store looks emptier. You must have sold a package of chewing gum."

"Ain't much room in here, sure," Joe would answer, with his slow grin, "except for you, Daise. Me and the store are waitin' for you whenever you'll take us. Don't you think you might before long?"

"Store!"—a fine scorn was expressed by Daisy's uptilted nose—"sardine box! Waitin' for me, you say? Gee! you'd have to throw out about a hundred pounds of candy before I could get inside of it, Joe."

"I wouldn't mind an even swap like that," said Joe, complimentary.

Daisy's existence was limited in every way. She had to walk sideways between the counter and the shelves in the candy store. In her own hall bedroom cosiness had been carried close to cohesiveness. The walls were so near to one another that the paper on them made a perfect babel of noise. She could light the gas with one hand and close the door with the other without taking her eyes off the reflection of her own brown pompadour in the mirror. She had Joe's picture in a gilt frame on the dresser, and sometimes—but her next thought would always be of Joe's funny little store tacked like a soap-box to the corner of that great building, and away would go her sentiment in a breeze of laughter.

Daisy's other suitor followed Joe by several months. He came to board in the house where she lived. His name was Dabster, and he was a philosopher. Though young, attainments stood out upon him like continental labels on a Passaic (N.J.) suit-case. Knowledge he had kidnapped from cyclopedias and handbooks of useful information; but as for wisdom, when she passed he was left sniffing in the road without so much as the number of her motor-car. He could and would tell you the proportion of water and muscle-making properties of peas and veal, the shortest verse in the Bible, the number of pounds of shingle nails required to fasten 256 shingles laid four inches to the weather, the population of Kankakee, Ill., the theories of Spinoza, the name of Mr. H. McKay Twombly's second hall footman, the length of the Hoosac Tunnel, the best time to set a hen, the salary of the railway post-office messenger between Driftwood and Red Bank Furnace, Pa., and the number of bones in the foreleg of a cat.

This weight of learning was no handicap to Dabster. His statistics were the sprigs of parsley with which he garnished the feast of small talk that he would set before you if he conceived that to be your taste. And again he used them as breastworks in foraging at the boarding-house. Firing at you a volley of figures concerning the weight of a lineal foot of bar-iron $5 \times 2\frac{3}{4}$ inches, and the average annual rainfall at Fort Snelling, Minn., he would transfix with his fork the best piece of chicken on the dish while you were trying to rally sufficiently to ask him weakly why does a hen cross the road.

Thus, brightly armed, and further equipped with a measure of good looks, of a hair-oily, shopping-district-at-three-in-the-afternoon kind, it seems that Joe, of the Lilliputian emporium, had a rival worthy of his steel. But Joe carried no steel. There wouldn't have been room in his store to draw it if he had.

One Saturday afternoon, about four o'clock, Daisy and Mr. Dabster stopped before Joe's booth. Dabster wore a silk hat, and—well, Daisy was a woman, and that hat had no chance to get back in its box until Joe had seen it. A stick of pineapple chewing gum was the ostensible object of the call.

Joe supplied it through the open side of his store. He did not pale or falter at sight of the hat.

"Mr. Dabster's going to take me on top of the building to observe the view," said Daisy, after she had introduced her admirers. "I never was on a skyscraper. I guess it must be awful nice and funny up there."

"H'm!" said Joe.

"The panorama," said Mr. Dabster, "exposed to the gaze from the top of a lofty building is not only sublime, but instructive. Miss Daisy has a decided pleasure in store for her."

"It's windy up there, too, as well as here," said Joe. "Are you dressed warm enough, Daise?"

"Sure thing! I'm all lined," said Daisy, smiling slyly at his clouded brow. "You look just like a mummy in a case, Joe. Ain't you just put in an invoice of a pint of peanuts or another apple? Your store looks awful overstocked."

Daisy giggled at her favourite joke; and Joe had to smile with her.

"Your quarters are somewhat limited, Mr.—er—er——," remarked Dabster, "in comparison with the size of this building. I understand the area of its side to be about 340 by 100 feet. That would make you occupy a proportionate space as if half of Beloochistan were placed upon a territory as large as the United States east of the Rocky Mountains, with the Province of Ontario and Belgium added."

"Is that so, sport?" said Joe genially. "You are Weisenheimer on figures, all right. How many square pounds of baled hay do you think a jackass could eat if he stopped brayin' long enough to keep still a minute and five-eighths?"

A few minutes later Daisy and Mr. Dabster stepped from an elevator to the top floor of the skyscraper. Then up a short steep stairway and out upon the roof. Dabster led her to the parapet so she could look down at the black dots moving in the street below.

"What are they?" she asked, trembling. She had never been on a height like this before.

And then Dabster must needs play the philosopher on the tower, and conduct her soul forth to meet the immensity of space.

"Bipeds," he said solemnly. "See what they become even at the small elevation of 340 feet—mere crawling insects going to and fro at random."

"Oh, they ain't anything of the kind," exclaimed Daisy suddenly—"they're folks! I saw an automobile. Oh, gee! are we that high up?"

"Walk over this way," said Dabster.

He showed her the great city lying like an orderly array of toys far below, starred here and there, early as it was, by the first beacon lights of the winter afternoon. And then the bay and sea to the south and east vanishing mysteriously into the sky.

"I don't like it," declared Daisy, with troubled blue eyes. "Say we go down."

But the philosopher was not to be denied his opportunity. He would let her behold the grandeur of his mind, the half-nelson he had on the infinite, and the memory he had for statistics. And then she would never more be content to buy chewing gum at the smallest store in New York. And so he began to prate of the smallness of human affairs, and how that even so slight a removal from earth made man and his works look like the tenth part of a dollar thrice computed. And that one should consider the sidereal system and the maxims of Epictetus and be comforted.

"You don't carry me with you," said Daisy. "Say, I think it's awful to be up so high that folks look like fleas. One of them we saw might have been Joe. Why, Jiminy! we might as well be in New Jersey! Say, I'm afraid up here!"

The philosopher smiled fatuously.

"The earth," said he, "is itself only as a grain of wheat in space. Look up there."

Daisy gazed upward apprehensively. The short day was spent and the stars were coming out above.

"Yonder star," said Dabster, "is Venus, the evening star. She is 66,000,000 miles from the sun."

"Fudge!" said Daisy, with a brief flash of spirit, "where do you think I come from—Brooklyn? Susie Price, in our store—her brother sent her a ticket to go to San Francisco—that's only three thousand miles."

The philosopher smiled indulgently.

"Our world," he said, "is 91,000,000 miles from the sun. There are eighteen stars of the first magnitude that are 211,000 times further from us than the sun is. If one of them should be extinguished it would be three years before we would see its light go out. There are six thousand stars of the sixth magnitude. It takes thirty-six years for the light of one of them to reach the earth. With an eighteen-foot telescope we can see 43,000,000 stars, including those of the thirteenth magnitude, whose light takes 2,700 years to reach us. Each of these stars——"

"You're lyin'," cried Daisy angrily. "You're tryin' to scare me. And you have; I want to go down!"

She stamped her foot.

"Arcturus——" began the philosopher soothingly, but he was interrupted by a demonstration out of the vastness of the nature that he was endeavouring to portray with his memory instead of his heart. For to the heart-expounder of nature the stars were set in the firmament expressly to give soft light to lovers wandering happily beneath them; and if you stand tiptoe some September night with your sweetheart on your arm you can almost touch them with your hand. Three years for their light to reach us, indeed!

Out of the west leaped a meteor, lighting the roof of the skyscraper almost to midday. Its fiery parabola was limned against the sky toward the east. It hissed as it went, and Daisy screamed.

"Take me down," she cried vehemently, "you—you mental arithmetic!"

Dabster got her to the elevator, and inside of it. She was wild-eyed, and she shuddered when the express made its debilitating drop.

Outside the revolving door of the skyscraper the philosopher lost her. She vanished; and he stood, bewildered, without figures or statistics to aid him.

Joe had a lull in trade, and by squirming among his stock succeeded in lighting a cigarette and getting one cold foot against the attenuated stove.

The door was burst open, and Daisy, laughing, crying, scattering fruit and candies, tumbled into his arms.

"Oh, Joe, I've been up on the skyscraper. Ain't it cosy and warm and homelike in here! I'm ready for you, Joe, whenever you want me."

V: THE RENAISSANCE AT CHARLEROI

GRANDEMONT CHARLES was a little Creole gentleman, aged thirty-four, with a bald spot on the top of his head and the manners of a prince. By day he was a clerk in a cotton broker's office in one of those cold, rancid mountains of oozy brick, down near the levee in New Orleans. By night, in his three-story-high *chambre garnier* in the old French Quarter he was again the last male descendant of the Charles family, that noble house that had lorded it in France, and had pushed its way smiling, rapiered, and courtly into Louisiana's early and brilliant days. Of late years the Charleses had subsided into the more republican but scarcely less royally carried magnificence and ease of plantation life along the Mississippi. Perhaps Grandemont was even Marquis de Brassé. There was that title in the family. But a Marquis on seventy-five dollars per month! *Vraiment!* Still, it has been done on less.

Grandemont had saved out of his salary the sum of six hundred dollars. Enough, you would say, for any man to marry on. So, after a silence of two years on that subject, he re-opened that most hazardous question to Mlle. Adèle Fauquier, riding down to Meade d'Or, her father's plantation. Her answer was the same that it had been any time during the last ten years: "First find my brother, Monsieur Charles."

This time he had stood before her, perhaps discouraged by a love so long and hopeless, being dependent upon a contingency so unreasonable, and demanded to be told in simple words whether she loved him or no.

Adèle looked at him steadily out of her grey eyes that betrayed no secrets, and answered, a little more softly:

"Grandemont, you have no right to ask that question unless you can do what I ask of you. Either bring back brother Victor to us or the proof that he died."

Somehow, though five times thus rejected, his heart was not so heavy when he left. She had not denied that she loved. Upon what shallow waters can the bark of passion remain afloat! Or, shall we play the doctrinaire, and hint that at thirty-four the tides of life are calmer and cognizant of many sources instead of but one—as at four-and-twenty?

Victor Fauquier would never be found. In those early days of his disappearance there was money to the Charles name, and Grandemont had spent the dollars as if they were picayunes in trying to find the lost youth. Even then he had had small hope of success, for the Mississippi gives up a victim from its oily tangles only at the whim of its malign will.

A thousand times had Grandemont conned in his mind the scene of Victor's disappearance. And, at each time that Adèle had set her stubborn but pitiful alternative against his suit, still clearer it repeated itself in his brain.

The boy had been the family favourite: daring, winning, reckless. His unwise fancy had been captured by a girl on the plantation—the daughter of an overseer. Victor's family was in ignorance of the intrigue, as far as it had gone. To save them the inevitable pain that his course promised,

Grandemont strove to prevent it. Omnipotent money smoothed the way. The overseer and his daughter left, between a sunset and dawn, for an undesignated bourne. Grandemont was confident that this stroke would bring the boy to reason. He rode over to Meade d'Or to talk with him. The two strolled out of the house and grounds, crossed the road, and, mounting the levee, walked its broad path while they conversed. A thunder-cloud was hanging, imminent, above, but, as yet, no rain fell. At Grandemont's disclosure of his interference in the clandestine romance, Victor attacked him, in a wild and sudden fury. Grandemont, though of slight frame, possessed muscles of iron. He caught the wrists amid a shower of blows descending upon him, bent the lad backward and stretched him upon the levee path. In a little while the gust of passion was spent, and he was allowed to rise. Calm now, but a powder mine where he had been but a whiff of the tantrums, Victor extended his hand toward the dwelling-house of Meade d'Or.

"You and they," he cried, "have conspired to destroy my happiness. None of you shall ever look upon my face again."

Turning, he ran swiftly down the levee, disappearing in the darkness. Grandemont followed as well as he could, calling to him, but in vain. For longer than an hour he pursued the search. Descending the side of the levee, he penetrated the rank density of weeds and willows that undergrew the trees until the river's edge, shouting Victor's name. There was never an answer, though once he thought he heard a bubbling scream from the dun waters sliding past. Then the storm broke, and he returned to the house drenched and dejected.

There he explained the boy's absence sufficiently, he thought, not speaking of the tangle that had led to it, for he hoped that Victor would return as soon as his anger had cooled. Afterward, when the threat was made good and they saw his face no more, he found it difficult to alter his explanations of that night, and there clung a certain mystery to the boy's reasons for vanishing as well as to the manner of it.

It was on that night that Grandemont first perceived a new and singular expression in Adèle's eyes whenever she looked at him. And through the years following that expression was always there. He could not read it, for it was born of a thought she would never otherwise reveal.

Perhaps, if he had known that Adèle had stood at the gate on that unlucky night, where she had followed, lingering, to await the return of her brother and lover, wondering why they had chosen so tempestuous an hour and so black a spot to hold converse—if he had known that a sudden flash of lightning had revealed to her sight that short, sharp struggle as Victor was sinking under his hands, he might have explained everything, and she——

I know not what she would have done. But one thing is clear—there was something besides her brother's disappearance between Grandemont's pleadings for her hand and Adèle's "yes." Ten years had passed, and what she had seen during the space of that lightning flash remained an indelible picture. She had loved her brother, but was she holding out for the solution of that mystery or for the "Truth"? Women have been known to reverence it, even as an abstract principle. It is said there have been a few who, in the matter of their affections, have considered a life to be a small thing as compared with a lie. That I do not know. But, I wonder, had Grandemont cast himself at her feet crying that his hand had sent Victor to the bottom of that inscrutable river, and that he could no longer sully his love with a lie, I wonder if—I wonder what she would have done!

But, Grandemont Charles, Arcadian little gentleman, never guessed the meaning of that look in Adèle's eyes; and from this last bootless payment of his devoirs he rode away as rich as ever in honour and love, but poor in hope.

That was in September. It was during the first winter month that Grandemont conceived his idea of the *renaissance*. Since Adèle would never be his, and wealth without her were useless trumpery, why need he add to that hoard of slowly harvested dollars? Why should he even retain that hoard?

Hundreds were the cigarettes he consumed over his claret, sitting at the little polished tables in the Royal Street cafés while thinking over his plan. By and by he had it perfect. It would cost, beyond doubt, all the money he had, but—*le jeu vaut la chandelle*—for some hours he would be once more a Charles of Charleroi. Once again should the nineteenth of January, that most significant day in the fortunes of the house of Charles, be fittingly observed. On that date the French king had seated a Charles by his side at table; on that date Armand Charles, Marquis de Brassé, landed, like a brilliant meteor, in New Orleans; it was the date of his mother's wedding; of Grandemont's birth. Since Grandemont could remember until the breaking up of the family that anniversary had been the synonym for feasting, hospitality, and proud commemoration.

Charleroi was the old family plantation, lying some twenty miles down the river. Years ago the estate had been sold to discharge the debts of its too-bountiful owners. Once again it had changed hands, and now the must and mildew of litigation had settled upon it. A question of heirship was in the courts, and the dwelling house of Charleroi, unless the tales told of ghostly powdered and laced Charleses haunting its unechoing chambers were true, stood uninhabited.

Grandemont found the solicitor in chancery who held the keys pending the decision. He proved to be an old friend of the family. Grandemont explained briefly that he desired to rent the house for two or three days. He wanted to give a dinner at his old home to a few friends. That was all.

"Take it for a week—a month, if you will," said the solicitor; "but do not speak to me of rental." With a sigh he concluded: "The dinners I have eaten under that roof, *mon fils*!"

There came to many of the old, established dealers in furniture, china, silverware, decorations and household fittings at their stores on Canal, Chartres, St. Charles, and Royal Streets, a quiet young man with a little bald spot on the top of his head, distinguished manners, and the eye of a connoisseur, who explained what he wanted. To hire the complete and elegant equipment of a dining-room, hall, reception-room, and cloak-rooms.

The goods were to be packed and sent, by boat, to the Charleroi landing, and would be returned within three or four days. All damage or loss to be promptly paid for.

Many of those old merchants knew Grandemont by sight, and the Charleses of old by association. Some of them were of Creole stock and felt a thrill of responsive sympathy with the magnificently indiscreet design of this impoverished clerk who would revive but for a moment the ancient flame of glory with the fuel of his savings.

"Choose what you want," they said to him. "Handle everything carefully. See that the damage bill is kept low, and the charges for the loan will not oppress you."

To the wine merchants next; and here a doleful slice was lopped from the six hundred. It was an exquisite pleasure to Grandemont once more to pick among the precious vintages. The champagne bins lured him like the abodes of sirens, but these he was forced to pass. With his six hundred he stood before them as a child with a penny stands before a French doll. But he bought with taste and discretion of other wines—Chablis, Moselle, Château d'Or, Hockheimer, and port of right age and pedigree.

The matter of the cuisine gave him some studious hours until he suddenly recollected André—André, their old *chef*—the most sublime master of French Creole cookery in the Mississippi Valley. Perhaps he was yet somewhere about the plantation. The solicitor had told him that the place was still being cultivated, in accordance with a compromise agreement between the litigants.

On the next Sunday after the thought Grandemont rode, horseback, down to Charleroi. The big, square house with its two long ells looked blank and cheerless with its closed shutters and doors.

The shrubbery in the yard was ragged and riotous. Fallen leaves from the grove littered the walks and porches. Turning down the lane at the side of the house, Grandemont rode on to the quarters of the plantation hands. He found the workers just streaming back from church, careless, happy, and bedecked in gay yellows, reds and blues.

Yes, André was still there: his wool a little greyer; his mouth as wide; his laughter as ready as ever. Grandemont told him of his plan, and the old *chef* swayed with pride and delight. With a sigh of relief, knowing that he need have no further concern until the serving of that dinner was announced, he placed in André's hands a liberal sum for the cost of it, giving *carte blanche* for its creation.

Among the blacks were also a number of the old house servants. Absalom, the former major-domo, and a half-dozen of the younger men, once waiters and attachés of the kitchen, pantry, and other domestic departments, crowded around to greet "*M'shi Grande.*" Absalom guaranteed to marshal, of these, a corps of assistants that would perform with credit the serving of the dinner.

After distributing a liberal largess among the faithful, Grandemont rode back to town well pleased. There were many other smaller details to think of and provide for, but eventually the scheme was complete, and now there remained only the issuance of the invitations to his guests.

Along the river within the scope of a score of miles dwelt some half-dozen families with whose princely hospitality that of the Charleses had been contemporaneous. They were the proudest and most august of the old regime. Their small circle had been a brilliant one; their social relations close and warm; their house full of rare welcome and discriminating bounty. Those friends, said Grandemont, should once more, if never again, sit at Charleroi on a nineteenth of January to celebrate the festal day of his house.

Grandemont had his cards of invitation engraved. They were expensive, but beautiful. In one particular their good taste might have been disputed; but the Creole allowed himself that one feather in the cap of his fugacious splendour. Might he not be allowed, for the one day of the *renaissance*, to be "Grandemont du Puy Charles, of Charleroi"? He sent the invitations out early in January so that the guests might not fail to receive due notice.

At eight o'clock on the morning of the nineteenth, the lower-coast steamboat, *River Belle*, gingerly approached the long-unused landing at Charleroi. The bridge was lowered, and a swarm of the plantation hands streamed along the rotting pier, bearing ashore a strange assortment of freight. Great shapeless bundles and bales and packets swathed in cloths and bound with ropes; tubs and urns of palms, evergreens, and tropical flowers; tables, mirrors, chairs, couches, carpets, and pictures—all carefully bound and padded against the dangers of transit.

Grandemont was among them, the busiest there. To the safe conveyance of certain large hampers eloquent with printed cautions to delicate handling he gave his superintendence, for they contained the fragile china and glassware. The dropping of one of those hampers would have cost him more than he could have saved in a year.

The last article unloaded, the *River Belle* backed off and continued her course downstream. In less than an hour everything had been conveyed to the house. And came then Absalom's task, directing the placing of the furniture and wares. There was plenty of help, for that day was always a holiday at Charleroi, and the negroes did not suffer the old traditions to lapse. Almost the entire population of the quarters volunteered their aid. A score of piccaninnies were sweeping at the leaves in the yard. In the big kitchen at the rear André was lording it with his old-time magnificence over his numerous sub-cooks and scullions. Shutters were flung wide; dust spun in clouds; the house echoed to voices and the tread of busy feet. The prince had come again, and Charleroi woke from its long sleep.

The full moon, as she rose across the river that night and peeped above the levee, saw a sight that had been long missing from her orbit. The old plantation house shed a soft and alluring radiance from every window. Of its two score rooms only four had been refurnished—the large reception-chamber, the dining-hall, and two smaller rooms for the convenience of the expected guests. But lighted wax candles were set in the windows of every room.

The dining-hall was the *chef d'œuvre*. The long table, set with twenty-five covers, sparkled like a winter landscape with its snowy napery and china and the icy gleam of crystal. The chaste beauty of the room had required small adornment. The polished floor burned to a glowing ruby with the reflection of candle-light. The rich wainscoting reached half-way to the ceiling. Along and above this had been set the relieving lightness of a few water-colour sketches of fruit and flower.

The reception-chamber was fitted in a simple but elegant style. Its arrangement suggested nothing of the fact that on the morrow the room would again be cleared and abandoned to the dust and the spider. The entrance hall was imposing with palms and ferns and the light of an immense candelabrum.

At seven o'clock Grandemont, in evening dress, with pearls—a family passion—in his spotless linen, emerged from somewhere. The invitations had specified eight as the dining hour. He drew an arm-chair upon the porch, and sat there, smoking cigarettes and half dreaming.

The moon was an hour high. Fifty yards back from the gate stood the house, under its noble grove. The road ran in front, and then came the grass-grown levee and the insatiate river beyond. Just above the levee-top a tiny red light was creeping down and a tiny green one was creeping up. Then the passing steamers saluted, and the hoarse din startled the drowsy silence of the melancholy lowlands. The stillness returned, save for the little voices of the night—the owl's recitative, the capriccio of the crickets, the concerto of the frogs in the grass. The piccaninnies and the dawdlers from the quarters had been dismissed to their confines, and the mêlée of the day was reduced to an orderly and intelligent silence. The six coloured waiters, in their white jackets, paced, cat-footed, about the table, pretending to arrange where all was beyond betterment. Absalom, in black and shining pumps, posed, superior, here and there where the lights set off his grandeur. And Grandemont rested in his chair, waiting for his guests.

He must have drifted into a dream—and an extravagant one—for he was master of Charleroi and Adèle was his wife. She was coming out to him now; he could hear her steps; he could feel her hand upon his shoulder——

"*Pardon moi, M'shi Grande*"—it was Absalom's hand touching him, it was Absalom's voice, speaking the patois of the blacks—"but it is eight o'clock."

Eight o'clock. Grandemont sprang up. In the moonlight he could see the row of hitching-posts outside the gate. Long ago the horses of the guests should have stood there. They were vacant.

A chanted roar of indignation, a just, waxing bellow of affront and dishonoured genius came from André's kitchen, filling the house with rhythmic protest. The beautiful dinner, the pearl of a dinner, the little excellent superb jewel of a dinner! But one moment more of waiting, and not even the thousand thunders of black pigs of the quarters would touch it!

"They are a little late," said Grandemont calmly. "They will come soon. Tell André to hold back dinner. And ask him if, by some chance, a bull from the pastures has broken, roaring, into the house."

He seated himself again to his cigarettes. Though he had said it, he scarcely believed Charleroi would entertain company that night. For the first time in history the invitation of a Charles had been ignored. So simple in courtesy and honour was Grandemont, and, perhaps, so serenely confident in the prestige of his name, that the most likely reasons for his vacant board did not occur to him.

Charleroi stood by a road travelled daily by people from those plantations whither his invitations had gone. No doubt even on the day before the sudden reanimation of the old house they had driven past and observed the evidences of long desertion and decay. They had looked at the corpse of Charleroi and then at Grandemont's invitations, and though the puzzle or tasteless hoax or whatever the thing meant left them perplexed, they would not seek its solution by the folly of a visit to that deserted house.

The moon was now above the grove and the yard was pied with deep shadows save where they lightened in the tender glow of outpouring candle-light. A crisp breeze from the river hinted at the possibility of frost when the night should have become older. The grass at one side of the steps was specked with the white stubs of Grandemont's cigarettes. The cotton-broker's clerk sat in his chair with the smoke spiralling above him. I doubt that he once thought of the little fortune he had so impotently squandered. Perhaps it was compensation enough for him to sit thus at Charleroi for a few retrieved hours. Idly his mind wandered in and out many fanciful paths of memory. He smiled to himself as a paraphrased line of Scripture strayed into his mind: "A certain *poor* man made a feast."

He heard the sound of Absalom coughing a

note of summons. Grandemont stirred. This time he had not been asleep—only drowsing.

"Nine o'clock, *M'shi Grande*," said Absalom in the uninflected voice of a good servant who states a fact unqualified by personal opinion.

Grandemont rose to his feet. In their time all the Charleses had been proven, and they were gallant losers.

"Serve dinner," he said calmly. And then he checked Absalom's movement to obey, for something clicked the gate latch and was coming down the walk toward the house. Something that shuffled its feet and muttered to itself as it came. It stopped in the current of light at the foot of the steps and spake, in the universal whine of the gadding mendicant.

"Kind sir, could you spare a poor, hungry man, out of luck, a little to eat? And to sleep in the corner of a shed? For"—the thing concluded, irrelevantly—"I can sleep now. There are no mountains to dance reels in the night; and the copper kettles are all scoured bright. The iron band is still around my ankle, and a link if it is your desire I should be chained."

It set a foot upon the step and drew up the rags that hung upon the limb. Above the distorted shoe, caked with the dust of a hundred leagues, they saw the link and the iron band. The clothes of the tramp were wreaked to piebald tatters by sun and rain and wear. A mat of brown, tangled hair and beard covered his head and face, out o which his eyes stared distractedly. Grandemont noticed that he carried in one hand a white, square card.

"What is that?" he asked.

"I picked it up, sir, at the side of the road." The vagabond handed the card to Grandemont. "Just a little to eat, sir. A little parched corn, a *tortilla*, or a handful of beans. Goat's meat I cannot eat. When I cut their throats they cry like children."

Grandemont held up the card. It was one of his own invitations to dinner. No doubt some one had cast it away from a passing carriage after comparing it with the tenantless house of Charleroi.

"From the hedges and highways bid them come," he said to himself, softly smiling. And then to Absalom: "Send Louis to me."

Louis, once his own body-servant, came promptly, in his white jacket.

"This gentleman," said Grandemont, "will dine with me. Furnish him with bath and clothes. In twenty minutes have him ready and dinner served."

Louis approached the disreputable guest with the suavity due to a visitor to Charleroi, and spirited him away to inner regions.

Promptly, in twenty minutes, Absalom announced dinner, and, a moment later, the guest was ushered into the dining-hall where Grandemont waited, standing, at the head of the table. The attentions of Louis had transformed the stranger into something resembling the polite animal. Clean linen and an old evening suit that had been sent down from town to clothe a waiter had worked a miracle with his exterior. Brush and comb had partially subdued the wild disorder of his hair. Now he might have passed for no more extravagant a thing than one of those *poseurs* in art and music who affect such oddity of guise. The man's countenance, and demeanour, as he approached the table, exhibited nothing of the awkwardness or confusion to be expected from his Arabian Nights change. He allowed Absalom to seat him at Grandemont's right hand with the manner of one thus accustomed to be waited upon.

"It grieves me," said Grandemont, "to be obliged to exchange names with a guest. My own names is Charles."

"In the mountains," said the wayfarer, "they call me Gringo. Along the roads they call me Jack."

"I prefer the latter," said Grandemont. "A glass of wine with you, Mr. Jack."

Course after course was served by the supernumerous waiters. Grandemont, inspired by the results of André's exquisite skill in cookery and his own in the selection of wines, became the model host, talkative, witty, and genial. The guest was fitful in conversation. His mind seemed to be sustaining a succession of waves of dementia followed by intervals of comparative lucidity. There was the glassy brightness of recent fever in his eyes. A long course of it must have been the cause of his emaciation and weakness, his distracted mind, and the dull pallor that showed even through the tan of wind and sun.

"Charles," he said to Grandemont—for thus he seemed to interpret his name—"you never saw the mountains dance, did you?"

"No, Mr. Jack," answered Grandemont gravely, "the spectacle has been denied me. But I assure you, I can understand it must be a diverting sight. The big ones, you know, white with snow on the tops, waltzing—*décolleté*, we may say."

"You first scour the kettles," said Mr. Jack, leaning toward him excitedly, "to cook the beans in the morning, and you lie down on a blanket and keep quite still. Then they come out and dance for you. You would go out and dance with them but you are chained every night to the centre pole of the hut. You believe the mountains dance, don't you, Charlie?"

"I contradict no traveller's tales," said Grandemont, with a smile.

Mr. Jack laughed loudly. He dropped his voice to a confidential whisper.

"You are a fool to believe it," he went on. "They don't really dance. It's the fever in your head. It's the hard work and the bad water that does it. You are sick for weeks and there is no medicine. The fever comes on every evening, and then you are as strong as two men. One night the *compañia* are lying drunk with *mescal*. They have brought back sacks of silver dollars from a ride, and they drink to celebrate. In the night you file the chain in two and go down the mountain. You walk for miles—hundreds of them. By and by the mountains are all gone, and you come to the prairies. They do not dance at night; they are merciful, and you sleep. Then you come to the river, and it says things to you. You follow it down, down, but you can't find what you are looking for."

Mr. Jack leaned back in his chair, and his eyes slowly closed. The food and wine had steeped him in a deep calm. The tense strain had been smoothed from his face. The languor of repletion was claiming him. Drowsily he spoke again.

"It's bad manners—I know—to go to sleep—

at table—but—that was—such a good dinner—Grande, old fellow."

Grande! The owner of the name started and set down his glass. How should this wretched tatterdemalion whom he had invited, Caliph-like, to sit at his feast know his name?

Not at first, but soon, little by little, the suspicion, wild and unreasonable as it was, stole into his brain. He drew out his watch with hands that almost balked him by their trembling, and opened the back case. There was a picture there —a photograph fixed to the inner side.

Rising, Grandemont shook Mr. Jack by the shoulder. The weary guest opened his eyes. Grandemont held the watch.

"Look at this picture, Mr. Jack. Have you ever——"

"*My sister Adèle!*"

The vagrant's voice rang loud and sudden through the room. He started to his feet, but Grandemont's arms were about him, and Grandemont was calling him "Victor! Victor Fauquier! *Merci, merci, mon Dieu!*"

Too far overcome by sleep and fatigue was the lost one to talk that night. Days afterward, when the tropic *calentura* had cooled in his veins, the disordered fragments he had spoken were completed in shape and sequence. He told the story of his angry flight, of toils and calamities on sea and shore, of his ebbing and flowing fortune in southern lands, and of his latest peril when, held a captive, he served menially in a stronghold of bandits in the Sonora Mountains of Mexico. And of the fever that seized him there, and his escape and delirium, during which he strayed, perhaps led by some marvellous instinct, back to the river on whose bank he had been born. And of the proud and stubborn thing in his blood that had kept him silent through all those years, clouding the honour of one, though he knew it not, and keeping apart two loving hearts. "What a thing is love!" you may say. And if I grant it, you shall say, with me: "What a thing is pride!"

On a couch in the reception chamber Victor lay, with a dawning understanding in his heavy eyes and peace in his softened countenance. Absalom was preparing a lounge for the transient master of Charleroi, who, to-morrow, would be again the clerk of a cotton broker, but also——

"To-morrow," Grandemont was saying, as he stood by the couch of his guest, speaking the words with his face shining as must have shone the face of Elijah's charioteer when he announced the glories of that heavenly journey—"To-morrow I will take you to Her."

VI: THE WHIRLIGIG OF LIFE

JUSTICE-OF-THE-PEACE BENAJA WIDDUP sat in the door of his office smoking his elder-stem pipe. Half-way to the zenith the Cumberland range rose blue-grey in the afternoon haze. A speckled hen swaggered down the main street of the "settlement," cackling foolishly.

Up the road came a sound of creaking axles, and then a slow cloud of dust, and then a bull-cart bearing Ransie Bilbro and his wife. The cart stopped at the Justice's door, and the two climbed down.

Ransie was a narrow six feet of sallow brown skin and yellow hair. The imperturbability of the mountains hung upon him like a suit of armour. The woman was calicoed, angled, snuff-brushed, and weary with unknown desires. Through it all gleamed a faint protest of cheated youth unconscious of its loss.

The Justice of the Peace slipped his feet into his shoes, for the sake of dignity, and moved to let them enter.

"We-all," said the woman, in a voice like the wind blowing through pine boughs, "wants a divo'ce." She looked at Ransie to see if he noted any flaw or ambiguity or evasion or partiality or self-partisanship in her statement of their business.

"A divo'ce," repeated Ransie, with a solemn nod. "We-all can't git along together nohow. It's lonesome enough fur to live in the mount'ins when a man and a woman keers fur one another. But when she's a-spittin' like a wildcat or a-sullenin' like a hoot-owl in the cabin, a man ain't got no call to live with her."

"When he's a no-'count varmint," said the woman, without any especial warmth, "a-traipsin' along of scalawags and moonshiners and a-layin' on his back pizen 'ith co'n whisky, and a-pesterin' folks with a pack o' hungry, triflin' houn's to feed!"

"When she keeps a-throwin' skillet lids," came Ransie's antiphony, "and slings b'ilin' water on the best coon-dog in the Cumberlands, and sets herself agin' cookin' a man's victuals, and keeps him awake o' nights accusin' him of a sight of doin's!"

"When he's al'ays a-fightin' the revenues, and gits a hard name in the mount'ins fur a mean man, who's gwine to be able fur to sleep o' nights?"

The Justice of the Peace stirred deliberately to his duties. He placed his one chair and a wooden stool for his petitioners. He opened his book of statutes on the table and scanned the index. Presently he wiped his spectacles and shifted his inkstand.

"The law and the statutes," said he, "air silent on the subjeck of divo'ce as fur as the jurisdiction of this co't air concerned. But, accordin' to equity and the Constitution and the golden rule, it's a bad barg'in that can't run both ways. If a justice of the peace can marry a couple, it's plain that he is bound to be able to divo'ce 'em. This here office will issue a decree of divo'ce and abide by the decision of the Supreme Co't to hold it good."

Ransie Bilbro drew a small tobacco-bag from his trousers pocket. Out of this he shook upon the table a five-dollar note. "Sold a b'arskin and two foxes fur that," he remarked. "It's all the money we got."

"The regular price of a divo'ce in this co't," said the Justice, "air five dollars." He stuffed the bill into the pocket of his homespun vest with a deceptive air of indifference. With much bodily toil and mental travail he wrote the decree upon half a sheet of foolscap, and then copied it upon the other. Ransie Bilbro and his wife listened to his reading of the document that was to give them freedom:

"Know all men by these presents that Ransie Bilbro and his wife, Ariela Bilbro, this day personally appeared before me and promises that hereinafter they will neither love, honour, nor obey each other, neither for better nor worse, being of sound mind and body, and accept summons for divorce according to the peace and dignity of the State. Herein fail not, so help you God. Benaja Widdup, justice of the peace in and for the county of Piedmont, State of Tennessee."

The Justice was about to hand one of the documents to Ransie. The voice of Ariela delayed the transfer. Both men looked at her. Their dull masculinity was confronted by something sudden and unexpected in the woman.

"Judge, don't you give him that air paper yit. 'Tain't all settled, nohow. I got to have my rights first. I got to have my ali-money. 'Tain't no kind of a way to do fur a man to divo'ce his wife 'thout her havin' a cent fur to do with. I'm a-layin' off to be a-goin' up to brother Ed's up on Hogback Mount'n. I'm bound fur to hev a pa'r of shoes and some snuff and things besides. Ef Ranse kin affo'd a divo'ce, let him pay me ali-money."

Ransie Bilbro was stricken to dumb perplexity. There had been no previous hint of alimony. Women were always bringing up startling and unlooked-for issues.

Justice Benaja Widdup felt that the point demanded judicial decision. The authorities were also silent on the subject of alimony. But the woman's feet were bare. The trail to Hogback Mountain was steep and flinty.

"Ariela Bilbro," he asked, in official tones, "how much did you 'low would be good and sufficient ali-money in the case befo' the co't."

"I 'lowed," she answered, "fur the shoes and all, to say five dollars. That ain't much fur ali-money, but I reckon that'll git me up to brother Ed's."

"The amount," said the Justice, "air not onreasonable. Ransie Bilbro, you air ordered by the co't to pay the plaintiff the sum of five dollars befo' the decree of divo'ce air issued."

"I hain't no mo' money," breathed Ransie heavily. "I done paid you all I had."

"Otherwise," said the Justice, looking severely over his spectacles, "you air in contempt of co't."

"I reckon if you gimme till to-morrow," pleaded the husband, "I mout be able to rake or scrape it up somewhars. I never looked for to be a-payin' no ali-money."

"The case air adjourned," said Benaja Widdup, "till to-morrow, when you-all will present yo'selves and obey the order of the co't. Followin' of which the decrees of divo'ce will be delivered." He sat down in the door and began to loosen a shoestring.

"We mout as well go down to Uncle Ziah's," decided Ransie, "and spend the night." He climbed into the cart on one side, and Ariela climbed in on the other. Obeying the flap of his rope, the little red bull slowly came around on a tack, and the cart crawled away in the nimbus arising from its wheels.

Justice-of-the-Peace Benaja Widdup smoked his elder-stem pipe. Late in the afternoon he got his weekly paper and read it until the twilight dimmed its lines. Then he lit the tallow candle on his table, and read until the moon rose, marking the time for supper. He lived in the double log cabin on the slope near the girdled poplar. Going home to supper he crossed a little branch darkened by a laurel thicket. The dark figure of a man stepped from the laurels and pointed a rifle at his breast. His hat was pulled down low, and something covered most of his face.

"I want yo' money," said the figure, "'thout any talk. I'm gettin' nervous, and my finger's a-wabblin' on this here trigger."

"I've only got f-f-five dollars," said the Justice, producing it from his vest pocket.

"Roll it up," came the order, "and stick it in the end of this here gun-bar'l."

The bill was crisp and new. Even fingers that were clumsy and trembling found little difficulty in making a spill of it and inserting it (this with less ease) into the muzzle of the rifle.

"Now I reckon you kin be goin' along," said the robber.

The Justice lingered not on his way.

The next day came the little red bull, drawing the cart to the office door. Justice Benaja Widdup had his shoes on, for he was expecting the visit. In his presence Ransie Bilbro handed to his wife a five-dollar bill. The official's eye sharply viewed it. It seemed to curl up as though it had been rolled and inserted into the end of a gun-barrel. But the Justice refrained from comment. It is true that other bills might be inclined to curl. He handed each one a decree of divorce. Each stood awkwardly silent, slowly folding the guarantee of freedom. The woman cast a shy glance full of constraint at Ransie.

"I reckon you'll be goin' back up to the cabin," she said, "along 'ith the bull-cart. There's bread in the tin box settin' on the shelf. I put the bacon in the b'ilin'-pot to keep the hounds from gittin' it. Don't forget to wind the clock to-night."

"You air a-goin' to your brother Ed's?" asked Ransie, with fine unconcern.

"I was 'lowin' to get along up thar afore night. I ain't sayin' as they'll pester theyselves any to make me welcome, but I hain't nowhar else fur to go.

It's a right smart ways, and I reckon I better be goin'. I'll be a-sayin' good-bye, Ranse—that is, if you keer fur to say so."

"I don't know as anybody's a hound dog," said Ransie, in a martyr's voice, "fur to not want to say good-bye—'less you air so anxious to git away that you don't want me to say it."

Ariela was silent. She folded the five-dollar bill and her decree carefully, and placed them in the bosom of her dress. Benaja Widdup watched the money disappear with mournful eyes behind his spectacles.

And then with his next words he achieved rank (as his thoughts ran) with either the great crowd of the world's sympathizers or the little crowd of its great financiers.

"Be kind o' lonesome in the old cabin to-night, Ranse," he said.

Ransie Bilbro stared out at the Cumberlands, clear blue now in the sunlight. He did not look at Ariela.

"I 'low it might be lonesome," he said; "but when folks gits mad and wants a divo'ce, you can't make folks stay."

"There's others wanted a divo'ce," said Ariela, speaking to the wooden stool. "Besides, nobody don't want nobody to stay."

"Nobody never said they didn't."

"Nobody never said they did. I reckon I better start on now to brother Ed's."

"Nobody can't wind that old clock."

"Want me to go back along 'ith you in the cart and wind it fur you, Ranse?"

The mountaineer's countenance was proof against emotion. But he reached out a big hand and enclosed Ariela's thin brown one. Her soul peeped out once through her impassive face, hallowing it.

"Them hounds shan't pester you no more," said Ransie. "I reckon I been mean and low down. You wind that clock, Ariela."

"My heart hit's in that cabin, Ranse," she whispered, "along 'ith you. I ain't a-goin' to git mad no more. Le's be startin', Ranse, so's we kin git home by sundown."

Justice-of-the-Peace Benaja Widdup interposed as they started for the door, forgetting his presence.

"In the name of the State of Tennessee," he said, "I forbid you-all to be a-defyin' of its laws and statutes. This co't is mo' than willin' and full of joy to see the clouds of discord and misunderstandin' rollin' away from two lovin' hearts, but it air the duty of the co't to p'eserve the morals and integrity of the State. The co't reminds you that you air no longer man and wife, but air divo'ced by regular decree, and as such air not entitled to the benefits and 'purtenances of the mattermonal estate."

Ariela caught Ransie's arm. Did those words mean that she must lose him now when they had just learned the lesson of life?

"But the co't air prepared," went on the Justice, "fur to remove the disabilities set up by the decree of divo'ce. The co't air on hand to perform the solemn ceremony of marri'ge, thus fixin' things up and enablin' the parties in the case to resume the honour'ble and elevatin' state of mattermony which they desires. The fee fur performin' said ceremony will be, in this case, to wit, five dollars."

Ariela caught the gleam of promise in his words. Swiftly her hand went to her bosom. Freely as an alighting dove the bill fluttered to the Justice's table. Her sallow cheek coloured as she stood hand in hand with Ransie and listened to the reuniting words.

Ransie helped her into the cart, and climbed in beside her. The little red bull turned once more, and they set out, hand-clasped, for the mountains.

Justice-of-the-Peace Benaja Widdup sat in his door and took off his shoes. Once again he fingered the bill tucked down in his vest pocket. Once again he smoked his elder-stem pipe. Once again the speckled hen swaggered down the main street of the "settlement," cackling foolishly.

VII: A MADISON SQUARE ARABIAN NIGHT

TO Carson Chalmers, in his apartment near the square, Phillips brought the evening mail. Besides the routine correspondence there were two items bearing the same foreign postmark.

One of the incoming parcels contained a photograph of a woman. The other contained an interminable letter, over which Chalmers hung, absorbed, for a long time. The letter was from another woman; and it contained poisoned barbs, sweetly dipped in honey, and feathered with innuendoes concerning the photographed woman.

Chalmers tore this letter into a thousand bits and began to wear out his expensive rug by striding back and forth upon it. Thus an animal from the jungle acts when it is caged, and thus a caged man acts when he is housed in a jungle of doubt.

By and by the restless mood was overcome. The rug was not an enchanted one. For sixteen feet he could travel along it; three thousand miles was beyond its power to aid.

Phillips appeared. He never entered; he invariably appeared, like a well-oiled genie.

"Will you dine here, sir, or out?" he asked.

"Here," said Chalmers, "and in half an hour." He listened glumly to the January blasts making an æolian trombone of the empty street.

"Wait," he said to the disappearing genie. "As I came home across the end of the square I saw many men standing there in rows. There was one mounted upon something, talking. Why do these men stand in rows, and why are they there?"

"They are homeless men, sir," said Phillips. "The man standing on the box tries to get lodging for them for the night. People come around to listen and give him money. Then he sends as many as the money will pay for to some lodging-house. That is why they stand in rows; they get sent to bed in order as they come."

"By the time dinner is served," said Chalmers, "have one of those men here. He will dine with me."

"W-w-which——" began Phillips, stammering for the first time during his service.

"Choose one at random," said Chalmers. "You might see that he is reasonably sober—and a certain amount of cleanliness will not be held against him. That is all."

It was an unusual thing for Carson Chalmers to play the Caliph. But on that night he felt the inefficacy of conventional antidotes to melancholy. Something wanton and egregious, something high-flavoured and Arabian, he must have to lighten his mood.

On the half-hour Phillips had finished his duties as slave of the lamp. The waiters from the restaurant below had whisked aloft the delectable dinner. The dining-table, laid for two, glowed cheerily in the glow of the pink-shaded candles.

And now Phillips, as though he ushered a cardinal—or held in charge a burglar—wafted in the shivering guest who had been haled from the line of mendicant lodgers.

It is a common thing to call such men wrecks; if the comparison be used here it is the specific one of a derelict come to grief through fire. Even yet some flickering combustion illuminated the drifting hulk. His face and hands had been recently washed—a rite insisted upon by Phillips as a memorial to the slaughtered conventions. In the candle-light he stood, a flaw in the decorous fitting of the apartment. His face was a sickly white, covered almost to the eyes with a stubble the shade of a red Irish setter's coat. Phillips' comb had failed to control the pale brown hair, long matted and conformed to the contour of a constantly worn hat. His eyes were full of a hopeless, tricky defiance like that seen in a cur's that is cornered by his tormentors. His shabby coat was buttoned high, but a quarter-inch of redeeming collar showed above it. His manner was singularly free from embarrassment when Chalmers rose from his chair across the round dining-table.

"If you will oblige me," said the host, "I shall be glad to have your company at dinner."

"My name is Plumer," said the highway guest, in harsh and aggressive tones. "If you're like me, you like to know the name of the party you're dining with."

"I was going to say," continued Chalmers somewhat hastily, "that mine is Chalmers. Will you sit opposite?"

Plumer, of the ruffled plumes, bent his knees for Phillips to slide the chair beneath him. He had an air of having sat at attended boards before. Phillips set out the anchovies and olives.

"Good!" barked Plumer; "going to be in courses, is it? All right, my jovial ruler of Bagdad. I'm your Scheherezade all the way to the tooth-picks. You're the first Caliph with a genuine Oriental flavour I've struck. What luck! And I was forty-third in the line. I finished counting just as your welcome emissary arrived to bid me to the feast. I had about as much chance of getting a bed to-night as I have of being the next Prime Minister. How will you have the sad story of my life, Mr. Al Raschid—a chapter with each course, or the whole edition with the cigars and coffee?"

"The situation does not seem a novel one to you," said Chalmers, with a smile.

"By the chin-whiskers of the prophet—no!" answered the guest. "New York's as full of cheap Haroun al Raschids as Bagdad is of fleas. I've been held up for my story with a loaded meal pointed at my head twenty times. Catch anybody in New York giving you something for nothing! They spell curiosity and charity with the same set of building blocks. Lots of 'em will stake you to a dime and chopsuey; and a few of 'em will play Caliph to the tune of a top sirloin; but every one of 'em will stand over you till they screw your autobiography out of you with footnotes, appendix and unpublished fragments. Oh, I know what to do when I see victuals coming toward me in little old Bagdad-on-the-Subway. I strike the asphalt three times with my forehead and get ready to spiel yarns for my supper. I claim descent from the late Tommy Tucker, who was forced to hand out vocal harmony for his predigested wheaterina and spoop-ju."

"I do not ask your story," said Chalmers. "I tell you frankly that it was a sudden whim that prompted me to send for some stranger to dine with me. I assure you you will not suffer through any curiosity of mine."

"Oh, fudge!" exclaimed the guest, enthusiastically tackling his soup; "I don't mind it a bit. I'm a regular Oriental magazine with a red cover and the leaves cut when the Caliph walks abroad. In fact, we fellows in the bed-line have a sort of union rate for things of this sort. Somebody's always stopping and wanting to know what brought us down so low in the world. For a sandwich and a glass of beer I tell 'em that drink did it. For corned beef and cabbage and a cup of coffee I give 'em the hard-hearted-landlord—six-months-in-the-hospital-lost-job story. A sirloin steak and a quarter for a bed gets the Wall Street tragedy of the swept-away fortune and the gradual descent. This is the first spread of this kind I've stumbled against. I haven't got a story to fit it. I'll tell you what, Mr. Chalmers, I'm going to tell you the truth for this, if you'll listen to it. It'll be harder for you to believe than the made-up ones."

An hour later the Arabian guest lay back with a sigh of satisfaction while Phillips brought the coffee and cigars and cleared the table.

"Did you ever hear of Sherrard Plumer?" he asked, with a strange smile.

"I remember the name," said Chalmers. "He was a painter, I think, of a good deal of prominence a few years ago."

"Five years," said the guest. "Then I went down like a chunk of lead. I'm Sherrard Plumer! I sold the last portrait I painted for $2,000. After that I couldn't have found a sitter for a gratis picture."

"What was the trouble?" Chalmers could not resist asking.

"Funny thing," answered Plumer grimly. "Never quite understood it myself. For a while I swam like a cork. I broke into the swell crowd and got commissions right and left. The newspapers called me a fashionable painter. Then the funny things began to happen. Whenever I finished a picture people would come to see it, and whisper and look queerly at one another.

"I soon found out what the trouble was. I had a knack of bringing out in the face of a portrait the hidden character of the original. I don't know how I did it—I painted what I saw—but I know it did me. Some of my sitters were fearfully enraged and refused their pictures. I painted the portrait of a very beautiful and popular society dame. When it was finished her husband looked at it with a peculiar expression of his face, and the next week he sued for divorce.

"I remember one case of a prominent banker who sat to me. While I had his portrait on exhibition in my studio an acquaintance of his came in to look at it. 'Bless me,' says he, 'does he really look like that?' I told him it was considered a faithful likeness. 'I never noticed that expression about his eyes before,' said he; 'I think I'll drop downtown and change my bank account.' He did drop down, but the bank account was gone and so was Mr. Banker.

"It wasn't long till they put me out of business. People don't want their secret meannesses shown up in a picture. They can smile and twist their own faces and deceive you, but the picture can't. I couldn't get an order for another picture, and I had to give up. I worked as a newspaper artist for awhile, and then for a lithographer, but my work with them got me into the same trouble. If I drew from a photograph my drawing showed up characteristics and expressions that you couldn't find in the photo, but I guess they were in the original, all right. The customers raised lively rows, especially the women, and I never could hold a job long. So I began to rest my weary head upon the breast of Old Booze for comfort. And pretty soon I was in the free-bed line and doing oral fiction for handouts among the food-bazaars. Does the truthful statement weary thee, O Caliph? I can turn on the Wall Street disaster stop if you prefer, but that requires a tear, and I'm afraid I can't hustle one up after that good dinner."

"No, no," said Chalmers earnestly, "you interest me very much. Did all your portraits reveal some unpleasant trait, or were there some that did not suffer from the ordeal of your peculiar brush?"

"Some? Yes," said Plumer. "Children generally, a good many women and a sufficient number of men. All people aren't bad, you know. When they were all right the pictures were all right. As I said, I don't explain it, but I'm telling you facts."

On Chalmers' writing-table lay the photograph that he had received that day in the foreign mail. Ten minutes later he had Plumer at work making a sketch from it in pastels. At thc end of an hour the artist rose and stretched wearily.

"It's done," he yawned. "You'll excuse me for being so long. I got interested in the job. Lord! but I'm tired. No bed last night you know. Guess it'll have to be good night now, O Commander of the Faithful!"

Chalmers went as far as the door with him and slipped some bills into his hand.

"Oh! I'll take 'em," said Plumer. "All that's included in the fall. Thanks. And for the very good dinner. I shall sleep on feathers to-night and dream of Bagdad. I hope it won't turn out to be a dream in the morning. Farewell, most excellent Caliph!"

Again Chalmers paced restlessly upon his rug. But his beat lay as far from the table whereon lay the pastel sketch as the room would permit. Twice, thrice, he tried to approach it, but failed. He could see the dun and gold and brown of the colours, but there was a wall about it built by his fears that kept him at a distance. He sat down and tried to calm himself. He sprang up and rang for Phillips.

"There is a young artist in this building," he said, "—a Mr. Reineman—do you know which is his apartment?"

"Top floor, front, sir," said Phillips.

"Go up and ask him to favour me with his presence here for a few minutes."

Reineman came at once. Chalmers introduced himself.

"Mr. Reineman," said he, "there is a little pastel

sketch on yonder table. I would be glad if you will give me your opinion of it as to its artistic merits and as a picture."

The young artist advanced to the table and took up the sketch. Chalmers half turned away, leaning upon the back of a chair.

"How—do—you—find it?" he asked slowly.

"As a drawing," said the artist, "I can't praise it enough. It's the work of a master—bold and fine and true. It puzzles me a little; I haven't seen any pastel work near as good in years."

"The face, man—the subject—the original—what would you say of that?"

"The face," said Reineman, "is the face of one of God's own angels. May I ask who——"

"My wife!" shouted Chalmers, wheeling and pouncing upon the astonished artist, gripping his hand and pounding his back. "She is travelling in Europe. Take that sketch, boy, and paint the picture of your life from it and leave the price to me."

VIII: THE HIGHER ABDICATION

CURLY the tramp sidled toward the free-lunch counter. He caught a fleeting glance from the bar-tender's eye, and stood still, trying to look like a business man who had just dined at the Menger and was waiting for a friend who had promised to pick him up in his motor-car. Curly's histrionic powers were equal to the impersonation; but his make-up was wanting.

The bar-tender rounded the bar in a casual way,

looking up at the ceiling as though he was pondering some intricate problem of kalsomining, and then fell upon Curly so suddenly that the roadster had no excuses ready. Irresistibly, but so composedly that it seemed almost absentmindedness on his part, the dispenser of drinks pushed Curly to the swinging doors and kicked him out, with a nonchalance that almost amounted to sadness. That was the way of the South-west.

Curly arose from the gutter leisurely. He felt no anger or resentment toward his ejector. Fifteen years of tramphood spent out of the twenty-two years of his life had hardened the fibres of his spirit. The slings and arrows of outrageous fortune fell blunted from the buckler of his armoured pride. With especial resignation did he suffer contumely and injury at the hands of bar-tenders. Naturally, they were his enemies; and unnaturally, they were often his friends. He had to take his chances with them. But he had not yet learned to estimate these cool, languid, South-western knights of the bung-starter, who had the manners of an Earl of Pawtucket, and who, when they disapproved of your presence, moved you with the silence and dispatch of a chess automaton advancing a pawn.

Curly stood for a few moments in the narrow, mesquite-paved street. San Antonio puzzled and disturbed him. Three days he had been a non-paying guest of the town, having dropped off there from a box car of an I. & G.N. freight, because Greaser Johnny had told him in Des Moines that the Alamo City was manna fallen, gathered, cooked, and served free with cream and sugar. Curly had found the tip partly a good one. There was hospitality in plenty of a careless, liberal, irregular sort. But the town itself was a weight upon his spirits after his experience with the rushing, business-like, systematized cities of the North and East. Here he was often flung a dollar, but too frequently a good-natured kick would follow it. Once a band of hilarious cowboys had roped him on Military Plaza and dragged him across the black soil until no respectable rag-bag would have stood sponsor for his clothes. The winding, doubling streets, leading nowhere, bewildered him. And then there was a little river, crooked as a pot-hook, that crawled through the middle of the town, crossed by a hundred little bridges so nearly alike that they got on Curly's nerves. And the last bar-tender wore a number nine shoe.

The saloon stood on a corner. The hour was eight o'clock. Homefarers and outgoers jostled Curly on the narrow stone sidewalk. Between the buildings to his left he looked down a cleft that proclaimed itself another thoroughfare. The alley was dark except for one patch of light. Where there was light there were sure to be human beings. Where there were human beings after nightfall in San Antonio there might be food, and there was sure to be drink. So Curly headed for the light.

The illumination came from Schwegel's Café. On the sidewalk in front of it Curly picked up an old envelope. It might have contained a cheque for a million. It was empty; but the wanderer read the address, "Mr. Otto Schwegel," and the name of the town and State. The postmark was Detroit.

Curly entered the saloon. And now in the light it could be perceived that he bore the stamp of many years of vagabondage. He had none of the tidiness of the calculating and shrewd professional tramp. His wardrobe represented the cast-off specimens of half a dozen fashions and eras. Two factories had combined their efforts in providing shoes for his feet. As you gazed at him there passed through your mind vague impressions of mummies, wax figures, Russian exiles, and men lost on desert islands. His face was covered almost to his eyes with a curly brown beard that he kept trimmed short with a pocket-knife, and that had furnished him with his *nom de route*. Light blue eyes, full of sullenness, fear, cunning, impudence, and fawning, witnessed the stress that had been laid upon his soul.

The saloon was small, and in its atmosphere the odours of meat and drink struggled for the ascendency. The pig and the cabbage wrestled with hydrogen and oxygen. Behind the bar Schwegel laboured with an assistant whose epidermal pores showed no signs of being obstructed. Hot wienerwurst and sauerkraut were being served to purchasers of beer. Curly shuffled to the end of the bar, coughed hollowly, and told Schwegel that he was a Detroit cabinet-maker out of a job.

It followed as the night the day that he got his schooner and lunch.

"Was you acquainted maybe mit Heinrich Strauss in Detroit?" asked Schwegel.

"Did I know Heinrich Strauss?" repeated Curly affectionately. "Why, say, 'Bo, I wish I had a dollar for every game of pinocle me and Heine has played on Sunday afternoons."

More beer and a second plate of steaming food was set before the diplomat. And then Curly, knowing to a fluid-drachm how far a "confidence" game would go, shuffled out into the unpromising street.

And now he began to perceive the inconveniences of this stony Southern town. There was none of the outdoor gaiety and brilliancy and music that provided distraction even to the poorest in the cities of the North. Here, even so early, the gloomy, rock-walled houses were closed and barred against the murky dampness of the night. The streets were mere fissures through which flowed grey wreaths of river mist. As he walked he heard laughter and the chink of coin and chips behind darkened windows, and music coming from every chink of wood and stone. But the diversions were selfish; the day of popular pastimes had not yet come to San Antonio.

But at length Curly, as he strayed, turned the sharp angle of another lost street and came upon a rollicking band of stockmen from the outlying ranches celebrating in the open in front of an ancient wooden hotel. One great roisterer from the sheep country who had just instigated a movement toward the bar, swept Curly in like a stray goat with the rest of his flock. The princes of kine and wool hailed him as a new zoological discovery, and uproariously strove to preserve him in the diluted alcohol of their compliments and regards.

An hour afterward Curly staggered from the hotel bar-room dismissed by his fickle friends, whose interest in him had subsided as quickly as it had risen. Full—stoked with alcoholic fuel and cargoed with food, the only question remaining to disturb him was that of shelter and bed.

A drizzling, cold Texas rain had begun to fall—an endless, lazy, unintermittent downfall that lowered the spirits of men and raised a reluctant steam from the warm stones of the streets and houses. Thus comes the "norther" dousing gentle spring and amiable autumn with the chilling salutes and adieux of coming and departing winter.

Curly followed his nose down the first tortuous street into which his irresponsible feet conducted him. At the lower end of it, on the bank of the serpentine stream, he perceived an open gate in a cemented rock wall. Inside he saw camp fires and a row of low wooden sheds built against three sides of the enclosing wall. He entered the enclosure. Under the sheds many horses were champing at their oats and corn. Many wagons and buckboards stood about with their teams' harness thrown carelessly upon the shafts and doubletrees. Curly recognized the place as a wagon-yard, such as is provided by merchants for their out-of-town friends and customers. No one was in sight. No doubt the drivers of those wagons were scattered about the town "seeing the elephant and hearing the owl." In their haste to become patrons of the town's dispensaries of mirth and good cheer the last ones to depart must have left the great wooden gate swinging open.

Curly had satisfied the hunger of an anaconda and the thirst of a camel, so he was neither in the mood nor the condition of an explorer. He zigzagged his way to the first wagon that his eyesight distinguished in the semi-darkness under the shed. It was a two-horse wagon with a top of white canvas. The wagon was half filled with loose piles of wool sacks, two or three great bundles of grey blankets, and a number of bales, bundles, and boxes. A reasoning eye would have estimated the load at once as ranch supplies, bound on the morrow for some outlying hacienda. But to the drowsy intelligence of Curly they represented only warmth and softness and protection against the cold humidity of the night. After several unlucky efforts, at last he conquered gravity so far as to climb over a wheel and pitch forward upon the best and warmest bed he had fallen upon in many a day. Then he became instinctively a burrowing animal, and dug his way like a prairie-dog down among the sacks and blankets, hiding himself from the cold air as snug and safe as a bear in his den. For three nights sleep had visited Curly only in broken and shivering doses. So now, when Morpheus condescended to pay him a call, Curly got such a strangle hold on the mythological old gentleman that it was a wonder that anyone else in the whole world got a wink of sleep that night.

Six cowpunchers of the Cibolo Ranch were waiting around the door of the ranch store. Their ponies cropped grass near by, tied in the Texas fashion—which is not tied at all. Their bridle reins had been dropped to the earth, which is a more effectual way of securing them (such is the power of habit and imagination) than you could devise out of a half-inch rope and a live oak tree.

These guardians of the cow lounged about, each with a brown cigarette paper in his hand, and gently but unceasingly cursed Sam Revell, the storekeeper. Sam stood in the door, snapping the red elastic bands on his pink madras shirtsleeves and looking down affectionately at the only pair of tan shoes within a forty-mile radius. His offence had been serious, and he was divided between humble apology and admiration for the beauty of his raiment. He had allowed the ranch stock of "smoking" to become exhausted.

"I thought sure there was another case of it under the counter, boys," he explained. "But it happened to be catterdges."

"You've sure got a case of happenedicitis," said Poky Rodgers, fence rider of the Largo Verde *potrero*. "Somebody ought to happen to give you a knock on the head with the butt end of a quirt. I've rode in nine miles for some tobacco; and it don't appear natural and seemly that you ought to be allowed to live."

"The boys was smokin' cut plug and dried mesquite leaves mixed when I left," sighed Mustang Taylor, horse wrangler of the Three Elm camp. "They'll be lookin' for me back by nine. They'll be settin' up, with their papers ready to roll a whiff of the real thing before bedtime. And I've got to tell 'em that this pink-eyed, sheep-headed, sulphur-footed, shirt-waisted son of a calico broncho, Sam Revell, hasn't got no tobacco on hand."

Gregorio Falcon, Mexican vaquero and best thrower of the rope on the Cibolo, pushed his heavy, silver-embroidered straw sombrero back upon his thicket of jet black curls, and scraped the bottoms of his pockets for a few crumbs of the precious weed.

"Ah, Don Samuel," he said reproachfully, but with his touch of Castilian manners, "escuse me. Dthey say dthe jackrabbeet and dthe sheep have dthe most leetle *sesos*—how you call dthem—brain-es? Ah don' believe dthat, Don Samuel—escuse me. Ah dthink people w'at don' keep esmokin' tobacco, dthey—bot you weel escuse me, Don Samuel."

"Now, what's the use of chewin' the rag, boys," said the untroubled Sam, stooping over to rub the toes of his shoes with a red and yellow handkerchief. "Ranse took the order for some more smokin' to San Antone with him Tuesday. Pancho rode Ranse's hoss back yesterday; and Ranse is goin' to drive the wagon back himself. There wa'n't much of a load—just some woolsacks and blankets and nails and canned peaches and a few things we was out of. I look for Ranse to roll in to-day sure. He's an early starter and a hell-to-split driver, and he ought to be here not far from sundown."

"What plugs is he drivin'?" asked Mustang Taylor, with a smack of hope in his tones.

"The buckboard greys," said Sam.

"I'll wait a spell, then," said the wrangler. "Them plugs eat up a trail like a road-runner swallowin' a whip snake. And you may bust me open a can of greengage plums, Sam, while I'm waitin' for somethin' better."

"Open me some yellow clings," ordered Poky Rodgers, "I'll wait, too."

The tobaccoless punchers arranged themselves comfortably on the steps of the store. Inside Sam chopped open with a hatchet the tops of the cans of fruit.

The store, a big, white wooden building like a barn, stood fifty yards from the ranch-house. Beyond it were the horse corrals; and still farther the wool-sheds and the brush-topped shearing-pens—for the Rancho Cibolo raised both cattle and sheep. Behind the store, at a little distance, were the grass-thatched *jacals* of the Mexicans who bestowed their allegiance upon the Cibolo.

The ranch-house was composed of four large rooms, with plastered adobe walls, and a two-room wooden ell. A twenty-feet-wide "gallery" circumvented the structure. It was set in a grove of immense live oaks and water-elms near a lake—a long, not very wide, and tremendously deep lake in which at nightfall great gars leaped to the surface and plunged with the noise of hippopotamuses frolicking at their bath. From the trees hung garlands and massive pendants of the melancholy grey moss of the South. Indeed, the Cibolo ranch-house seemed more of the South than of the West. It looked as if old "Kiowa" Truesdell might have brought it with him from the lowlands of Mississippi when he came to Texas with his rifle in the hollow of his arm in '55.

But, though he did not bring the family mansion, Truesdell did bring something in the way of a family inheritance that was more lasting than brick or stone. He brought one end of the Truesdell-Curtis family feud. And when a Curtis bought the Rancho de los Olmos, sixteen miles from the Cibolo, there were lively times on the pear flats and in the chaparral thickets of the South-west. In those days Truesdell cleaned the brush of many a wolf and tiger cat and Mexican lion; and one or two Curtises fell heirs to notches on his rifle stock. Also he buried a brother with a Curtis bullet in him on the bank of the lake at Cibolo. And then the Kiowa Indians made their last raid upon the ranches between the Frio and the Rio Grande, and Truesdell at the head of his rangers rid the earth of them to the last brave, earning his sobriquet. Then came prosperity in the form of waxing herds and broadening lands. And then old age and bitterness, when he sat, with his great mane of hair as white as the Spanish-dagger blossoms and his fierce, pale blue eyes, on the shaded gallery at Cibolo, growling like the pumas that he had slain. He snapped his fingers at old age; the bitter taste to life did not come from that. The cup that stuck at his lips was that his only son Ransom wanted to marry a Curtis, the last youthful survivor of the other end of the feud.

For a while the only sounds to be heard at the store were the rattling of the tin spoons and the gurgling intake of the juicy fruits by the cow-punchers, the stamping of the grazing ponies, and the singing of a doleful song by Sam as he contentedly brushed his stiff auburn hair for the twentieth time that day before a crinkly mirror.

From the door of the store could be seen the irregular, sloping stretch of prairie to the south, with its reaches of light green, billowy mesquite flats in the lower places, and its rises crowned with nearly black masses of short chaparral. Through the mesquite flat wound the ranch road that, five miles away, flowed into the old government trail to San Antonio. The sun was so low that the gentlest elevation cast its grey shadow miles into the green-gold sea of sunshine.

That evening ears were quicker than eyes.

The Mexican held up a tawny finger to still the scraping of tin against tin.

"One waggeen," said he, "cross dthe Arroyo Hondo. Ah hear dthe wheel. Verree rockee place, dthe Hondo."

"You've got good ears, Gregorio," said Mustang Taylor. "I never heard nothin' but the song-bird in the bush and the zephyr skallyhootin' across the peaceful dell."

In ten minutes Taylor remarked: "I see the

dust of a wagon risin' right above the fur end of the flat."

"You have verree good eyes, señor," said Gregorio, smiling.

Two miles away they saw a faint cloud dimming the green ripples of the mesquites. In twenty minutes they heard the clatter of the horses' hoofs: in five minutes more the grey plugs dashed out of the thicket whickering for oats and drawing the light wagon behind them like a toy.

From the *jacals* came a cry of: "*El Amo! El Amo!*" Four Mexican youths raced to unharness the greys. The cowpunchers gave a yell of greeting and delight.

Ranse Truesdell, driving, threw the reins to the ground and laughed.

"It's under the wagon sheet, boys," he said. "I know what you're waiting for. If Sam lets it run out again we'll use them yellow shoes of his for a target. There's two cases. Pull 'em out and light up. I know you all want a smoke."

After striking dry country Ranse had removed the wagon sheet from the bows and thrown it over the goods in the wagon. Six pairs of hasty hands dragged it off and grabbled beneath the sacks and blankets for the cases of tobacco.

Long Collins, tobacco messenger from the San Gabriel outfit, who rode with the longest stirrups west of the Mississippi, delved with an arm like the tongue of a wagon. He caught something harder than a blanket and pulled out a fearful thing—a shapeless, muddy bunch of leather tied together with wire and twine. From its ragged end, like the head and claws of a disturbed turtle, protruded human toes.

"Who-ee!" yelled Long Collins. "Ranse, are you a-packin' around of corpuses? Here's a—howlin' grasshopper's!"

Up from his long slumber popped Curly, like some vile worm from its burrow. He clawed his way out and sat blinking like a disreputable, drunken owl. His face was as bluish-red and puffed and seamed and cross-lined as the cheapest round steak of the butcher. His eyes were swollen slits; his nose a pickled beet; his hair would have made the wildest thatch of a Jack-in-the-box look like the satin poll of a Cléo de Mérode. The rest of him was scarecrow done to the life.

Ranse jumped down from his seat and looked at his strange cargo with wide-open eyes.

"Here, you maverick, what are you doing in my wagon? How did you get in there?"

The punchers gathered around in delight. For the time they had forgotten tobacco.

Curly looked around him slowly in every direction. He snarled like a Scotch terrier through his ragged beard.

"Where is this?" he rasped through his parched throat. "It's a damn farm in an old field. What'd you bring me here for—say? Did I say I wanted to come here? What are you Reubs rubberin' at—hey? G'wan or I'll punch some of yer faces."

"Drag him out, Collins," said Ranse.

Curly took a slide and felt the ground rise up and collide with his shoulder-blades. He got up and sat on the steps of the store shivering from outraged nerves, hugging his knees and sneering. Taylor lifted out a case of tobacco and wrenched off its top. Six cigarettes began to glow, bringing peace and forgiveness to Sam.

"How'd you come in my wagon?" repeated Ranse, this time in a voice that drew a reply.

Curly recognized the tone. He had heard it used by freight brakemen and large persons in blue carrying clubs.

"Me?" he growled. "Oh, was you talkin' to me? Why, I was on my way to the Menger, but my valet had forgot to pack my pajamas. So I crawled into that wagon in the wagon-yard—see? I never told you to bring me out to this bloomin' farm—see?"

"What is it, Mustang?" asked Poky Rodgers, almost forgetting to smoke in his ecstasy. "What do it live on?"

"It's a galliwampus, Poky," said Mustang. "It's the thing that hollers 'willi-walloo' up in ellum tree in the low grounds of night. I don't know if it bites."

"No, it ain't, Mustang," volunteered Long Collins. "Them galliwampuses has fins on their backs, and eighteen toes. This here is a hicklesnifter. It lives under the ground and eats cherries. Don't stand so close to it. It wipes out villages with one stroke of its prehensile tail."

Sam, the cosmopolite, who called bar-tenders in San Antone by their first name, stood in the door. He was a better zoologist.

"Well, ain't that a Willie for your whiskers?" he commented. "Where'd you dig up the hobo, Ranse? Goin' to make an auditorium for inbreviates out of the ranch?"

"Say," said Curly, from whose panoplied breast all shafts of wit fell blunted. "Any of you kiddin' guys got a drink on you? Have your fun. Say, I've been hittin' the stuff till I don't know straight up."

He turned to Ranse. "Say, you shanghaied me on your d——d old prairie schooner—did I tell you to drive me to a farm? I want a drink. I'm goin' all to little pieces. What's doin'?"

Ranse saw that the tramp's nerves were racking him. He dispatched one of the Mexican boys to the ranch-house for a glass of whisky. Curly gulped it down; and into his eyes came a brief, grateful glow—as human as the expression in the eye of a faithful setter dog.

"Thanky, boss," he said quietly.

"You're thirty miles from a railroad, and forty miles from a saloon," said Ranse.

Curly fell back weakly against the steps.

"Since you are here," continued the ranchman, "come along with me. We can't turn you out on the prairie. A rabbit might tear you to pieces."

He conducted Curly to a large shed where the ranch vehicles were kept. There he spread out a canvas cot and brought blankets.

"I don't suppose you can sleep," said Ranse, "since you've been pounding your ear for twenty-four hours. But you can camp here till morning. I'll have Pedro fetch you up some grub.

"Sleep!" said Curly. "I can sleep a week. Say, sport, have you got a coffin nail on you?"

Fifty miles had Ransom Truesdell driven that day. And yet this is what he did.

Old "Kiowa" Truesdell sat in his great wicker chair reading by the light of an immense oil lamp. Ranse laid a bundle of newspapers fresh from town at his elbow.

"Back, Ranse?" said the old man, looking up.

"Son," old "Kiowa" continued, "I've been thinking all day about a certain matter that we have talked about. I want you to tell me again. I've lived for you. I've fought wolves and Indians and worse white men to protect you. You never had any mother that you can remember. I've taught you to shoot straight, ride hard, and live clean. Later on I've worked to pile up dollars that'll be yours. You'll be a rich man, Ranse, when my chunk goes out. I've made you. I've licked you into shape like a leopard cat licks its cubs. You don't belong to yourself—you've got to be a Truesdell first. Now, is there to be any more nonsense about this Curtis girl?"

"I'll tell you once more," said Ranse slowly. "As I am a Truesdell and as you are my father, I'll never marry a Curtis."

"Good boy," said old "Kiowa." "You'd better go get some supper."

Ranse went to the kitchen at the rear of the house. Pedro, the Mexican cook, sprang up to bring the food he was keeping warm in the stove.

"Just a cup of coffee, Pedro," he said, and drank it standing. And then—

"There's a tramp on a cot in the wagon-shed. Take him something to eat. Better make it enough for two."

Ranse walked out toward the *jacals*. A boy came running.

"Manuel, can you catch Vaminos, in the little pasture, for me?"

"Why not, señor? I saw him near the *puerta* but two hours past. He bears a drag-rope."

"Get him and saddle him as quick as you can."

"*Prontito, señor.*"

Soon, mounted on Vaminos, Ranse leaned in the

saddle, pressed with his knees, and galloped eastward past the store, where sat Sam trying his guitar in the moonlight.

Vaminos shall have a word Vaminos the good dun horse. The Mexicans, who have a hundred names for the colours of a horse, called him *gruyo*. He was a mouse-coloured, slate-coloured, flea-bitten roan-dun, if you can conceive it. Down his back from his mane to his tail went a line of black. He would live for ever; and surveyors have not laid off as many miles in the world as he could travel in a day.

Eight miles east of the Cibolo ranch-house Ranse loosened the pressure of his knees, and Vaminos stopped under a big ratama tree. The yellow ratama blossoms showered fragrance that would have undone the roses of France. The moon made the earth a great concave bowl with a crystal sky for a lid. In a glade five jackrabbits leaped and played together like kittens. Eight miles farther east shone a faint star that appeared to have dropped below the horizon. Night riders, who often steered their course by it, knew it to be the light in the Rancho de los Olmos.

In ten minutes Yenna Curtis galloped to the tree on her sorrel pony Dancer. The two leaned and clasped hands heartily.

"I ought to have ridden nearer your home," said Ranse. "But you never will let me."

Yenna laughed. And in the soft light you could see her strong white teeth and fearless eyes. No sentimentality there, in spite of the moonlight, the odour of the ratamas, and the admirable figure of Ranse Truesdell, the lover. But she was there, eight miles from her home, to meet him.

"How often have I told you, Ranse," she said, "that I am your half-way girl? Always half-way."

"Well?" said Ranse, with a question in his tones.

"I did," said Yenna, with almost a sigh. "I told him after dinner when I thought he would be in a good humour. Did you ever wake up a lion, Ranse, with the mistaken idea that he would be a kitten? He almost tore the ranch to pieces. It's all up. I love my daddy, Ranse, and I'm afraid—I'm afraid of him, too. He ordered me to promise that I'd never marry a Truesdell. I promised. That's all. What luck did you have?"

"The same," said Ranse slowly. "I promised him that his son would never marry a Curtis. Somehow I couldn't go against him. He's mighty old. I'm sorry, Yenna."

The girl leaned in her saddle and laid one hand on Ranse's, on the horn of his saddle.

"I never thought I'd like you better for giving me up," she said ardently, "but I do. I must ride back now, Ranse. I slipped out of the house and saddled Dancer myself. Good night, neighbour."

"Good night," said Ranse. "Ride carefully over them badger holes."

They wheeled and rode away in opposite directions. Yenna turned in her saddle and called clearly—

"Don't forget I'm your half-way girl, Ranse."

"Damn all family feuds and inherited scraps," muttered Ranse vindictively to the breeze as he rode back to the Cibolo.

Ranse turned his horse into the small pasture and went to his own room. He opened the lowest drawer of an old bureau to get out the packet of letters that Yenna had written him one summer when she had gone to Mississippi for a visit. The drawer stuck, and he yanked at it savagely—as a man will. It came out of the bureau, and bruised both his shins—as a drawer will. An old, folded yellow letter without an envelope fell from somewhere—probably from where it had lodged in one of the upper drawers. Ranse took it to the lamp and read it curiously.

Then he took his hat and walked to one of the Mexican *jacals*.

"Tia Juana," he said, "I would like to talk with you a while."

An old, old Mexican woman, white-haired and wonderfully wrinkled, rose from a stool.

"Sit down," said Ranse, removing his hat and taking the one chair in the *jacal*. "Who am I, Tia Juana?" he asked, speaking Spanish.

"Don Ransom, our good friend and employer. Why do you ask?" answered the old woman wonderingly.

"Tia Juana, who am I?" he repeated, with his stern eyes looking into hers.

A frightened look came in the old woman's face. She fumbled with her black shawl.

"Who am I, Tia Juana?" said Ranse once more.

"Thirty-two years I have lived on the Rancho Cibolo," said Tia Juana. "I thought to be buried under the coma mott beyond the garden before these things should be known. Close the door, Don Ransom, and I will speak. I see in your face that you know."

An hour Ranse spent behind Tia Juana's closed

door. As he was on his way back to the house Curly called to him from the wagon-shed.

The tramp sat on his cot, swinging his feet and smoking.

"Say, sport," he grumbled. "This is no way to treat a man after kidnappin' him. I went up to the store and borrowed a razor from that fresh guy and had a shave. But that ain't all a man needs. Say—can't you loosen up for about three fingers more of that booze? I never asked you to bring me to your d——d farm."

"Stand up out here in the light," said Ranse, looking at him closely.

Curly got up sullenly and took a step or two.

His face, now shaven smooth, seemed transformed. His hair had been combed, and it fell back from the right side of his forehead with a peculiar wave. The moonlight charitably softened the ravages of drink; and his aquiline, well-shaped nose and small, square cleft chin almost gave distinction to his looks.

Ranse sat on the foot of the cot and looked at him curiously.

"Where did you come from—have you got any home or folks anywhere?"

"Me? Why, I'm a dook," said Curly. "I'm Sir Reginald—oh, cheese it. No; I don't know anything about my ancestors. I've been a tramp ever since I can remember. Say, old pal, are you going to set 'em up again to-night or not?"

"You answer my questions and maybe I will. How did you come to be a tramp?"

"Me?" answered Curly. "Why, I adopted that profession when I was an infant. Case of had to. First thing I can remember, I belonged to a big, lazy hobo called Beefsteak Charley. He sent me around to houses to beg. I wasn't hardly big enough to reach the latch of a gate."

"Did he ever tell you how he got you?" asked Ranse.

"Once when he was sober he said he bought me for an old six-shooter and six bits from a band of drunken Mexican sheep-shearers. But what's the diff? That's all I know."

"All right," said Ranse. "I reckon you're a maverick for certain. I'm going to put the Rancho Cibolo brand on you. I'll start you to work in one of the camps to-morrow."

"Work!" sniffed Curly disdainfully. "What do you take me for? Do you think I'd chase cows, and hop-skip-and-jump around after crazy sheep like that pink and yellow guy at the store says these Reubs do? Forget it."

"Oh, you'll like it when you get used to it," said Ranse. "Yes, I'll send you up one more drink by Pedro. I think you'll make a first-class cowpuncher before I get through with you."

"Me?" said Curly. "I pity the cows you set me to chaperon. They can go chase themselves. Don't forget my nightcap, please, boss."

Ranse paid a visit to the store before going to the house. Sam Revell was taking off his tan shoes regretfully and preparing for bed.

"Any of the boys from the San Gabriel camp riding in early in the morning?" asked Ranse.

"Long Collins," said Sam briefly. 'For the mail."

"Tell him," said Ranse, "to take that tramp out to camp with him and keep him till I get there."

Curly was sitting on his blankets in the San

Gabriel camp cursing talentedly when Ranse Truesdell rode up and dismounted on the next afternoon. The cowpunchers were ignoring the stray. He was grimy with dust and black dirt. His clothes were making their last stand in favour of the conventions.

Ranse went up to Buck Rabb, the camp boss and spoke briefly.

"He's a plumb buzzard," said Buck. "He won't work, and he's the low-downest passel of inhumanity I ever see. I didn't know what you wanted done with him, Ranse, so I just let him set. That seems to suit him. He's been condemned to death by the boys a dozen times, but I told 'em maybe you was savin' him for torture."

Ranse took off his coat.

"I've got a hard job before me, Buck, I reckon, but it has to be done. I've got to make a man out of that thing. That's what I've come to camp for."

He went up to Curly.

"Brother," he said, "don't you think if you had a bath it would allow you to take a seat in the company of your fellow-men with less injustice to the atmosphere."

"Run away, farmer," said Curly sardonically. "Willie will send for nursey when he feels like having his tub."

The *charco*, or water hole, was twelve yards away. Ranse took one of Curly's ankles and dragged him like a sack of potatoes to the brink. Then with the strength and sleight of a hammer-thrower he hurled the offending member of society far into the lake.

Curly crawled out and up the bank spluttering like a porpoise.

Ranse met him with a piece of soap and a coarse towel in his hands.

"Go to the other end of the lake and use this," he said. "Buck will give you some dry clothes at the wagon."

The tramp obeyed without protest. By the time supper was ready he had returned to camp. He was hardly to be recognized in his new blue shirt and brown duck clothes. Ranse observed him out of the corner of his eye.

"Lordy, I hope he ain't a coward," he was saying to himself. "I hope he won't turn out to be a coward."

His doubts were soon allayed. Curly walked straight to where he stood. His light blue eyes were blazing.

"Now I'm clean," he said meaningly, "maybe you'll talk to me. Think you've got a picnic here, do you? You clodhoppers think you can run over a man because you know he can't get away. All right. Now, what do you think of that?"

Curly planted a stinging slap against Ranse's left cheek. The print of his hand stood out a dull red against the tan.

Ranse smiled happily.

The cowpunchers talk to this day of the battle that followed.

Somewhere in his restless tour of the cities Curly had acquired the art of self-defence. The ranchman was equipped only with the splendid strength and equilibrium of perfect health and the endurance conferred by decent living. The two attributes nearly matched. There were no formal rounds. At last the fibre of the clean liver prevailed. The last time Curly went down from one of the ranchman's awkward but powerful blows he remained on the grass, but looking up with an unquenched eye.

Ranse went to the water-barrel and washed the red from a cut on his chin in the stream from the faucet.

On his face was a grin of satisfaction.

Much benefit might accrue to educators and moralists if they could know the details of the curriculum of reclamation through which Ranse put his waif during the month that he spent in the San Gabriel camp. The ranchman had no fine theories to work out—perhaps his whole stock of pedagogy embraced only a knowledge of horse-breaking and a belief in heredity.

The cowpunchers saw that their boss was trying to make a man out of the strange animal that he had sent among them; and they tacitly organized themselves into a faculty of assistants. But their system was their own.

Curly's first lesson stuck. He became on friendly and then on intimate terms with soap and water. And the thing that pleased Ranse most was that his "subject" held his ground at each successive higher step. But the steps were sometimes far apart.

Once he got at the quart bottle of whisky kept sacredly in the grub tent for rattlesnake bites, and spent sixteen hours on the grass, magnificently drunk. But when he staggered to his feet his first move was to find his soap and towel and start for the *charco*. And once, when a treat came from the ranch in the form of a basket of fresh tomatoes and young onions, Curly devoured the entire consignment before the punchers reached the camp at supper-time.

And then the punchers punished him in their own way. For three days they did not speak to him, except to reply to his own questions or remarks. And they spoke with absolute and unfailing politeness. They played tricks on one another; they pounded one another hurtfully and affectionately; they heaped upon one another's heads friendly curses and obloquy; but they were polite to Curly. He saw it, and it stung him as much as Ranse hoped it would.

There came a night that brought a cold, wet norther. Wilson, the youngest of the outfit, had lain in camp two days, ill with a fever. When Joe got up at daylight to begin breakfast he found Curly sitting asleep against a wheel of the grub wagon with only a saddle blanket around him, while Curly's blankets were stretched over Wilson to protect him from the rain and wind.

Three nights after that Curly rolled himself in his blanket and went to sleep. Then the other punchers rose up softly and began to make preparations. Ranse saw Long Collins tie a rope to the horn of a saddle. Others were getting out their six-shooters.

"Boys," said Ranse, "I'm much obliged. I was hoping you would. But I didn't like to ask."

Half a dozen six-shooters began to pop—awful yells rent the air—Long Collins galloped wildly across Curly's bed, dragging the saddle after him. That was merely their way of gently awaking their victim. Then they hazed him for an hour, carefully and ridiculously, after the code of cow camps. Whenever he uttered protest they held him stretched over a roll of blankets and thrashed him woefully with a pair of leather leggings.

And all this meant that Curly had won his spurs, that he was receiving the puncher's accolade. Never more would they be polite to him. But he would be their "pardner" and stirrup-brother, foot to foot.

When the fooling was ended all hands made a raid on Joe's big coffee-pot by the fire for a Java night-cap. Ranse watched the new knight carefully to see if he understood and was worthy. Curly limped with his cup of coffee to a log and sat upon it. Long Collins followed and sat by his side. Buck Rabb went and sat at the other. Curly—grinned.

And then Ranse furnished Curly with mounts and saddle and equipment, and turned him over to Buck Rabb, instructing him to finish the job.

Three weeks later Ranse rode from the ranch into Rabb's camp, which was then in Snake Valley. The boys were saddling for the day's ride. He sought out Long Collins among them.

"How about that bronco?" he asked.

Long Collins grinned.

"Reach out your hand, Ranse Truesdell," he said, "and you'll touch him. And you can shake his'n, too, if you like, for he's plumb white and there's none better in no camp."

Ranse looked again at the clear-faced, bronzed, smiling cowpuncher who stood at Collins's side. Could that be Curly? He held out his hand, and Curly grasped it with the muscles of a broncobuster.

"I want you at the ranch," said Ranse.

"All right, sport," said Curly heartily. "But I want to come back again. Say, pal, this is a dandy farm. And I don't want any better fun than hustlin' cows with this bunch of guys. They're all to the merry-merry."

At the Cibolo ranch-house they dismounted. Ranse bade Curly wait at the door of the living-room. He walked inside. Old "Kiowa" Truesdell was reading at a table.

"Good morning, Mr. Truesdell," said Ranse.

The old man turned his white head quickly.

"How is this?" he began. "Why do you call me 'Mr.——'?"

When he looked at Ranse's face he stopped, and the hand that held his newspaper shook slightly.

"Boy," he said slowly, "how did you find it out?"

"It's all right," said Ranse, with a smile. "I made Tia Juana tell me. It was kind of by accident, but it's all right."

"You've been like a son to me," said old "Kiowa," trembling.

"Tia Juana told me all about it," said Ranse. "She told me how you adopted me when I was knee-high to a puddle duck out of a wagon train of prospectors that was bound West. And she told me how the kid—your own kid, you know—got lost or was run away with. And she said it was the same day that the sheep-shearers got on a bender and left the ranch."

"Our boy strayed from the house when he was two years old," said the old man. "And then along came these emigrant wagons with a youngster they didn't want; and we took you. I never intended you to know, Ranse. We never heard of our boy again."

"He's right outside, unless I'm mighty mistaken," said Ranse, opening the door and beckoning.

Curly walked in.

No one could have doubted. The old man and the young had the same sweep of hair, the same nose, chin, line of face, and prominent light blue eyes.

Old "Kiowa" rose eagerly.

Curly looked about the room curiously. A puzzled expression came over his face. He pointed to the wall opposite.

"Where's the tick-tock?" he asked absent-mindedly.

"The clock," cried old "Kiowa" loudly. "The eight-day clock used to stand there. Why——"

He turned to Ranse, but Ranse was not there.

Already a hundred yards away, Vaminos, the good flea-bitten dun, was bearing him eastward like a racer through dust and chaparral toward the Rancho de los Olmos.

IX: CHURCH WITH AN OVERSHOT-WHEEL

LAKELANDS is not to be found in the catalogues of fashionable summer resorts. It lies on a low spur of the Cumberland range of mountains on a little tributary of the Clinch River. Lakelands proper is a contented village of two dozen houses situated on a forlorn, narrow-gauge railroad line. You wonder whether the railroad lost itself in the pine woods and ran into Lakelands from fright and loneliness, or whether Lakelands got lost and huddled itself along the railroad to wait for the cars to carry it home.

You wonder again why it was named Lakelands. There are no lakes, and the lands about are too poor to be worth mentioning.

Half a mile from the village stands the Eagle

House, a big, roomy old mansion run by Josian Rankin for the accommodation of visitors who desire the mountain air at inexpensive rates. The Eagle House is delightfully mismanaged. It is full of ancient instead of modern improvements, and it is altogether as comfortably neglected and pleasingly disarranged as your own home. But you are furnished with clean rooms and good and abundant fare: yourself and the piny woods must do the rest. Nature has provided a mineral spring, grape-vine swings, and croquet—even the wickets are wooden. You have Art to thank only for the fiddle-and-guitar music twice a week at the hop in the rustic pavilion.

The patrons of the Eagle House are those who seek recreation as a necessity, as well as a pleasure. They are busy people, who may be likened to clocks that need a fortnight's winding to ensure a year's running of their wheels. You will find students there from the lower towns, now and then an artist, or a geologist absorbed in construing the ancient strata of the hills. A few quiet families spend the summers there; and often one or two tired members of that patient sisterhood known to Lakelands as "school marms."

A quarter of a mile from the Eagle House was what would have been described to its guests as "an object of interest" in the catalogue, had the Eagle House issued a catalogue. This was an old, old mill that was no longer a mill. In the words of Josiah Rankin, it was "the only church in the United States, sah, with an overshot-wheel; and the only mill in the world, sah, with pews and a pipe organ." The guests of the Eagle House attended the old mill church each Sabbath, and heard the preacher liken the purified Christian to bolted flour ground to usefulness between the millstones of experience and suffering.

Every year about the beginning of autumn there came to the Eagle House one Abram Strong, who remained for a time an honoured and beloved guest. In Lakelands he was called "Father Abram" because his hair was so white, his face so strong and kind and florid, his laugh so merry, and his black clothes and broad hat so priestly in appearance. Even new guests after three or four days' acquaintance gave him this familiar title.

Father Abram came a long way to Lakelands. He lived in a big, roaring town in the North-west where he owned mills, not little mills with pews and an organ in them, but great, ugly, mountain-like mills that the freight trains crawled around all day like ants around an ant-heap. And now you must be told about Father Abram and the mill that was a church, for their stories run together.

In the days when the church was a mill, Mr. Strong was the miller. There was no jollier, dustier, busier, happier miller in all the land than he. He lived in a little cottage across the road from the mill. His hand was heavy, but his toll was light, and the mountaineers brought their grain to him across many weary miles of rocky roads.

The delight of the miller's life was his little daughter, Aglaia. That was a brave name, truly, for a flaxen-haired toddler; but the mountaineers love sonorous and stately names. The mother had encountered it somewhere in a book, and the deed was done. In her babyhood Aglaia herself repudiated the name, as far as common use went, and persisted in calling herself "Dums." The miller and his wife often tried to coax from Aglaia the source of this mysterious name, but without results. At last they arrived at a theory. In the little garden behind the cottage was a bed of rhododendrons in which the child took a peculiar delight and interest. It may have been that she perceived in "Dums" a kinship to the formidable name of her favourite flowers.

When Aglaia was four years old she and her father used to go through a little performance in the mill every afternoon, that never failed to come off, the weather permitting. When supper was ready her mother would brush her hair and put on a clean apron and send her across to the mill to bring her father home. When the miller saw her coming in the mill door he would come forward, all white with the flour dust, and wave his hand and sing an old miller's song that was familiar in those parts and ran something like this:

> The wheel goes round,
> The grist is ground,
> The dusty miller's merry.
> He sings all day,
> His work is play,
> While thinking of his dearie.

Then Aglaia would run to him laughing, and call: "Da-da, come take Dums home"; and the miller would swing her to his shoulder and march over to supper, singing the miller's song. Every evening this would take place.

One day, only a week after her fourth birthday, Aglaia disappeared. When last seen she was plucking wild flowers by the side of the road in front of the cottage. A little while later her mother went out to see that she did not stray too far away' and she was already gone.

Of course, every effort was made to find her. The neighbours gathered and searched the woods and the mountains for miles around. They dragged every foot of the mill race and the creek for a long distance below the dam. Never a trace of her did they find. A night or two before there had been a family of wanderers camped in a grove near by. It was conjectured that they might have stolen the child; but when their wagon was overtaken and searched she could not be found.

The miller remained at the mill for nearly two years; and then his hope of finding her died out. He and his wife moved to the North-west. In a few years he was the owner of a modern mill in one of thc important milling cities in that region. Mrs. Strong never recovered from the shock caused by the loss of Aglaia, and two years after they moved away the miller was left to bear his sorrow alone.

When Abram Strong became prosperous he paid a visit to Lakelands and the old mill. The scene was a sad one for him, but he was a strong man, and always appeared cheery and kindly. It was then that he was inspired to convert the old mill into a church. Lakelands was too poor to build one; and the still poorer mountaineers could not assist. There was no place of worship nearer than twenty miles.

The miller altered the appearance of the mill as little as possible. The big overshot-wheel was left in its place. The young people who came to church used to cut their initials in its soft and slowly decaying wood. The dam was partly destroyed, and the clear mountain stream rippled unchecked down its rocky bed. Inside the mill the changes were greater. The shafts and millstones and belts and pulleys were, of course, all removed. There were two rows of benches with aisles between, and a little raised platform and pulpit at one end. On three sides overhead was a gallery containing seats, and reached by a stairway inside. There was also an organ—a real pipe organ—in the gallery, that was the pride of the congregation of the Old Mill Church. Miss Phœbe Summers was the organist. The Lakelands boys proudly took turns at pumping it for her at each Sunday's service. The Rev. Mr. Banbridge was the preacher, and rode down from Squirrel Gap on his old white horse without ever missing a service. And Abram Strong paid for everything. He paid the preacher five hundred dollars a year; and Miss Phœbe two hundred dollars.

Thus, in memory of Aglaia, the old mill was converted into a blessing for the community in which she had once lived. It seemed that the brief life of the child had brought about more good than the threescore years and ten of many. But Abram Strong set up yet another monument to her memory.

Out from his mills in the North-west came the "Aglaia" flour, made from the hardest and finest wheat that could be raised. The country soon found out that the "Aglaia" flour had two prices. One was the highest market price, and the other was—nothing.

Wherever there happened a calamity that left people destitute—a fire, a flood, a tornado, a strike, or a famine, there would go hurrying a generous consignment of the "Aglaia" at its "nothing" price. It was given away cautiously and judiciously, but it was freely given, and not a penny could the hungry ones pay for it. There got to be a saying that whenever there was a disastrous fire in the poor districts of a city the fire chief's buggy reached the scene first, next the "Aglaia" flour wagon, and then the fire engines.

So this was Abram Strong's other monument to Aglaia. Perhaps to a poet the theme may seem too utilitarian for beauty; but to some the fancy will seem sweet and fine that the pure, white, virgin flour, flying on its mission of love and charity, might be likened to the spirit of the lost child whose memory it signalized.

There came a year that brought hard times to the Cumberlands. Grain crops everywhere were light, and there were no local crops at all. Mountain floods had done much damage to property. Even game in the woods was so scarce that the hunters brought hardly enough home to keep their folk alive. Especially about Lakelands was the rigour felt.

As soon as Abram Strong heard of this his messages flew; and the little narrow-gauge cars began to unload "Aglaia" flour there. The miller's orders were to store the flour in the gallery of the Old Mill Church; and that every one who attended the church was to carry home a sack of it.

Two weeks after that Abram Strong came for his yearly visit to the Eagle House, and became "Father Abram" again.

That season the Eagle House had fewer guests than usual. Among them was Rose Chester. Miss Chester came to Lakelands from Atlanta, where she worked in a department store. This was the first vacation outing of her life. The wife of the store manager had once spent a summer at the Eagle House. She had taken a fancy to Rose, and had persuaded her to go there for her three weeks' holiday. The manager's wife gave her a letter to Mrs. Rankin, who gladly received her in her own charge and care.

Miss Chester was not very strong. She was about twenty, and pale and delicate from an indoor life. But one week of Lakelands gave her a brightness and spirit that changed her wonderfully. The time was early September when the Cumberlands are at their greatest beauty. The mountain foliage was growing brilliant with autumnal colours; one breathed aerial champagne, the nights were deliciously cool, causing one to snuggle cosily under the warm blankets of the Eagle House.

Father Abram and Miss Chester became great friends. The old miller learned her story from Mrs. Rankin, and his interest went out quickly to the slender, lonely girl who was making her own way in the world.

The mountain country was new to Miss Chester. She had lived many years in the warm, flat town of Atlanta; and the grandeur and variety of the Cumberlands delighted her. She was determined to enjoy every moment of her stay. Her little hoard of savings had been estimated so carefully in connection with her expenses that she knew almost to a penny what her very small surplus would be when she returned to work.

Miss Chester was fortunate in gaining Father Abram for a friend and companion. He knew every road and peak and slope of the mountains near Lakelands. Through him she became acquainted with the solemn delight of the shadowy, tilted aisles of the pine forests, the dignity of the bare crags, the crystal, tonic mornings, the dreamy, golden afternoons full of mysterious sadness. So her health improved, and her spirits grew light. She had a laugh as genial and hearty in its feminine way as the famous laugh of Father Abram. Both of them were natural optimists; and both knew how to present a serene and cheerful face to the world.

One day Miss Chester learned from one of the guests the history of Father Abram's lost child. Quickly she hurried away and found the miller seated on his favourite rustic bench near the chalybeate spring. He was surprised when his little friend slipped her hand into his, and looked at him with tears in her eyes.

"Oh, Father Abram," she said, "I'm so sorry! I didn't know until to-day about your little daughter. You will find her yet some day.—Oh, I hope you will."

The miller looked down at her with his strong, ready smile.

"Thank you, Miss Rose," he said, in his usual cheery tones. "But I do not expect to find Aglaia. For a few years I hoped that she had been stolen by vagrants, and that she still lived; but I have lost that hope. I believe that she was drowned."

"I can understand," said Miss Chester, "how the doubt must have made it so hard to bear. And yet you are so cheerful and so ready to make other people's burdens light. Good Father Abram!"

"Good Miss Rose!" mimicked the miller, smiling. "Who thinks of others more than you do?"

A whimsical mood seemed to strike Miss Chester.

"Oh, Father Abram," she cried, "wouldn't it

be grand if I should prove to be your daughter? Wouldn't it be romantic? And wouldn't you like to have me for a daughter?"

"Indeed, I would," said the miller, heartily. "If Aglaia had lived I could wish for nothing better than for her to have grown up to be just such a little woman as you are. Maybe you are Aglaia," he continued, falling in with her playful mood; "can't you remember when we lived at the mill?"

Miss Chester fell swiftly into serious meditation. Her large eyes were fixed vaguely upon something in the distance. Father Abram was amused at her quick return to seriousness. She sat thus for a long time before she spoke.

"No," she said at length, with a long sigh. "I can't remember anything at all about a mill. I don't think that I ever saw a flour mill in my life until I saw your funny little church. And if I were your little girl I would remember it, wouldn't I? I'm so sorry, Father Abram."

"So am I," said Father Abram, humouring her. "But if you cannot remember that you are my little girl, Miss Rose, surely you can recollect being some one else's. You remember your own parents, of course."

"Oh, yes; I remember them very well—especially my father. He wasn't a bit like you, Father Abram. Oh, I was only making believe. Come, now, you've rested long enough. You promised to show me thc pool where you can see the trout playing this afternoon. I never saw a trout."

Late one afternoon Father Abram set out for the old mill alone. He often went to sit and think of the old days when he lived in the cottage across the road. Time had smoothed away the sharpness of his grief until he no longer found the memory of those times painful. But whenever Abram Strong sat in the melancholy September afternoons on the spot where "Dums" used to run in every day with her yellow curls flying, the smile that Lakelands always saw upon his face was not there.

The miller made his way slowly up the winding, steep road. The trees crowded so close to the edge of it that he walked in their shade, with his hat in his hand. Squirrels ran playfully upon the old rail fence at his right. Quails were calling to their young broods in the wheat stubble. The low sun sent a torrent of pale gold up the ravine that opened to the west. Early September!—it was within a few days only of the anniversary of Aglaia's disappearance.

The old overshot-wheel, half covered with mountain ivy, caught patches of the warm sunlight filtering through the trees. The cottage across the road was still standing, but it would doubtless go down before the next winter's mountain blasts. It was overrun with morning glory and wild gourd vines, and the door hung by one hinge.

Father Abram pushed open the mill door, and entered softly. And then he stood still, wondering. He heard the sound of some one within, weeping inconsolably. He looked, and saw Miss Chester sitting in a dim pew, with her head bowed upon an open letter that her hands held.

Father Abram went to her, and laid one of his strong hands firmly upon hers. She looked up, breathed his name, and tried to speak further.

"Not yet, Miss Rose," said the miller, kindly.

"Don't try to talk yet. There's nothing as good for you as a nice, quiet little cry when you are feeling blue."

It seemed that the old miller, who had known so much sorrow himself, was a magician in driving it away from others. Miss Chester's sobs grew easier. Presently she took her little plain-bordered handkerchief and wiped away a drop or two that had fallen from her eyes upon Father Abram's big hand. Then she looked up and smiled through her tears. Miss Chester could always smile before her tears had dried, just as Father Abram could smile through his own grief. In that way the two were very much alike.

The miller asked her no questions; but by and by Miss Chester began to tell him.

It was the old story that always seems so big and important to the young, and that brings reminiscent smiles to their elders. Love was the theme, as may be supposed. There was a young man in Atlanta, full of all goodness and the graces, who had discovered that Miss Chester also possessed these qualities above all other people in Atlanta or anywhere else from Greenland to Patagonia. She showed Father Abram the letter over which she had been weeping. It was a manly, tender letter, a little superlative and urgent, after the style of love letters written by young men full of goodness and the graces. He proposed for Miss Chester's hand in marriage at once. Life, he said, since her departure for a three-weeks' visit, was not to be endured. He begged for an immediate answer; and if it were favourable he promised to fly, ignoring the narrow-gauge railroad, at once to Lakelands.

"And now where does the trouble come in?" asked the miller when he had read the letter.

"I cannot marry him," said Miss Chester.

"Do you want to marry him?" asked Father Abram.

"Oh, I love him," she answered, "but——" Down went her head and she sobbed again.

"Come, Miss Rose," said the miller; "you can give me your confidence. I do not question you, but I think you can trust me."

"I do trust you," said the girl. "I will tell you why I must refuse Ralph. I am nobody; I haven't even a name; the name I call myself is a lie. Ralph is a noble man. I love him with all my heart, but I can never be his."

"What talk is this?" said Father Abram. "You said that you remember your parents. Why do you say you have no name? I do not understand."

"I do remember them," said Miss Chester. "I remember them too well. My first recollections are of our life somewhere in the far South. We moved many times to different towns and states. I have picked cotton, and worked in factories, and have often gone without enough food and clothes. My mother was sometimes good to me; my father was always cruel, and beat me. I think they were both idle and unsettled.

"One night when we were living in a little town on a river near Atlanta they had a great quarrel. It was while they were abusing and taunting each other that I learned—oh, Father Abram, I learned that I didn't even have the right to be—don't you understand? I had no right even to a name; I was nobody.

"I ran away that night. I walked to Atlanta

and found work. I gave myself the name of Rose Chester, and have earned my own living ever since. Now you know why I cannot marry Ralph—and oh, I can never tell him why."

Better than any sympathy, more helpful than pity, was Father Abram's depreciation of her woes.

"Why, dear, dear! is that all?" he said. "Fie, fie! I thought something was in the way. If this perfect young man is a man at all he will not care a pinch of bran for your family tree. Dear Miss Rose, take my word for it, it is yourself he cares for. Tell him frankly, just as you have told me, and I'll warrant that he will laugh at your story, and think all the more of you for it."

"I shall never tell him," said Miss Chester, sadly. "And I shall never marry him nor any one else. I have not the right."

But they saw a long shadow come bobbing up the sunlit road. And then came a shorter one bobbing by its side; and presently two strange figures approached the church. The long shadow was made by Miss Phœbe Summers, the organist, come to practise. Tommy Teague, aged twelve, was responsible for the shorter shadow. It was Tommy's day to pump the organ for Miss Phœbe, and his bare toes proudly spurned the dust of the road.

Miss Phœbe, in her lilac-spray chintz dress, with her accurate little curls hanging over each ear. curtsied low to Father Abram, and shook her curls ceremoniously at Miss Chester. Then she and her assistant climbed the steep stairway to the organ loft.

In the gathering shadows below, Father Abram and Miss Chester lingered. They were silent;

Aglaia looked up at him with a tender smile.

"I want to ask him to wait," she said. "I have just found my father, and I want it to be just we two for awhile. I want to tell him he will have to wait."

X: PHILANTHROMATHEMATICS

"I SEE that the cause of Education has received the princely gift of more than fifty millions of dollars," said I.

I was gleaning the stray items from the evening papers while Jeff Peters packed his briar pipe with plug cut.

"Which same," said Jeff, "calls for a new deck, and a recitation by the entire class in philanthromathematics."

"Is that an allusion?" I asked.

"It is," said Jeff. "I never told you about the time when me and Andy Tucker was philanthropists, did I? It was eight years ago in Arizona. Andy and me was out in the Gila mountains with a two-horse wagon prospecting for silver. We struck it, and sold out to parties in Tucson for $25,000. They paid our cheque at the bank in silver—a thousand dollars in a sack. We loaded it in our wagon and drove east a hundred miles before we recovered our presence of intellect. Twenty-five thousand dollars don't sound like so much when you're reading the annual report of the Pennsylvania Railroad or listening to an actor talking about his salary; but when you can raise up a wagon sheet and kick around with your boot-heel and hear every one of 'em ring against another it makes you feel like you was a night-and-day bank with the clock striking twelve.

"The third day out we drove into one of the most specious and tidy little towns that Nature or Rand and McNally ever turned out. It was in the foothills, and mitigated with trees and flowers and about 2,000 head of cordial and dilatory inhabitants. The town seemed to be called Floresville, and Nature had not contaminated it with many railroads, fleas or Eastern tourists.

"Me and Andy deposited our money to the credit of Peters and Tucker in the Esperanza Savings Bank, and got rooms at the Skyview Hotel. After supper we lit up, and sat out on the gallery and smoked. Then was when the philanthropy idea struck me. I suppose every grafter gets it some time.

"When a man swindles the public out of a certain amount he begins to get scared and wants to return part of it. And if you'll watch close and notice the way his charity runs you'll see that he tries to restore it to the same people he got it from. As a hydrostatical case, take, let's say, A. A made his millions selling oil to poor students who sit up nights studying political economy and methods for regulating the trusts. So, back to the universities and colleges goes his conscience dollars.

"There's B got his from the common labouring man that works with his hands and tools. How's he to get some of the remorse fund back into their overalls?

" 'Aha!' says B, 'I'll do it in the name of Education. I've skinned the labouring man,' says he to himself, 'but, according to the old proverb, "Charity covers a multitude of skins." '

"So he puts up eighty million dollars' worth of libraries; and the boys with the dinner pail that builds 'em gets the benefit.

" 'Where's the books?' asks the reading public.

" 'I dinna ken,' says B. 'I offered ye libraries; and there they are. I suppose if I'd given ye preferred steel trust stock instead ye'd have wanted the water in it set out in cut-glass decanters. Hoot, for ye!'

"But, as I said, the owning of so much money was beginning to give me philanthropitis. It was the first time me and Andy had ever made a pile big enough to make us stop and think how we got it.

" 'Andy,' says I, 'we're wealthy—not beyond the dreams of average; but in our humble way we are comparatively as rich as Greasers. I feel as if I'd like to do something for as well as to humanity.'

" 'I was thinking the same thing, Jeff,' says he. 'We've been gouging the public for a long time with all kinds of little schemes from selling self-igniting celluloid collars to flooding Georgia with Hoke Smith presidential campaign buttons. I'd like, myself, to hedge a bet or two in the graft game if I could do it without actually banging the cymbalines in the Salvation Army or teaching a Bible class by the Bertillon system.'

" 'What'll we do?' says Andy. 'Give free grub to the poor or send a couple of thousand to George Cortelyou?'

" 'Neither,' says I. 'We've got too much money to be implicated in plain charity; and we haven't got enough to make restitution. So, we'll look about for something that's about half-way between the two.'

"The next day in walking around Floresville we see on a hill a big red-brick building that appears to be disinhabited. The citizens speak up and tell us that it was begun for a residence several years before by a mine-owner. After running up the house he finds he only had $2.80 left to furnish it with, so he invests that in whisky and jumps off the roof on a spot where he now requiescats in pieces.

"As soon as me and Andy saw that building the same idea struck both of us. We would fix it up with lights and penwipers and professors, and put an iron dog and statues of Hercules and Father John on the lawn, and start one of the finest free educational institutions in the world right there.

"So we talks it over to the prominent citizens of Floresville, who falls in fine with the idea. They give a banquet in the engine-house to us, and we make our bow for the first time as benefactors to the cause of progress and enlightenment. Andy makes an hour-and-a-half speech on the subject of irrigation in Lower Egypt, and we have a moral tune on the phonograph and pineapple sherbet.

"Andy and we didn't lose any time in philanthropping. We put every man in town that could tell a hammer from a step-ladder to work on the building, dividing it up into class-rooms and lecture halls. We wire to 'Frisco for a car-load of desks, footballs, arithmetics, penholders, dictionaries, chairs for the professors, slates, skeletons, sponges, twenty-seven cravenetted gowns and caps for the senior class, and an open order for all the truck that goes with a first-class university. I took it on myself to put up a campus and a curriculum on the list; but the telegraph operator must have got the words wrong, being an ignorant man, for when the goods come we found a can of peas and a currycomb among 'em.

"While the weekly paper was having chalk-plate cuts of me and Andy we wired an employment agency in Chicago to express us f.o.b., six professors immediately—one English literature, one up-to-date dead languages, one chemistry, one political economy—democrat preferred—one logic, and one wise to painting, Italian and music, with union card. The Esperanza bank guaranteed salaries, which was to run between $800 and $800.50.

"Well, sir, we finally got in shape. Over the front door was carved the words: 'The World's University; Peters & Tucker, Patrons and Proprietors.' And when September the first got a cross-mark on the calendar, the come-ons begun to roll in. First the faculty got off the tri-weekly express from Tucson. They was mostly young, spectacled and red-headed, with sentiments divided between ambition and food. Andy and me got 'em billeted on the Floresvillains and then laid for the students.

"They came in bunches. We had advertised the University in all the State papers, and it did us good to see how quick the country responded. Two hundred and nineteen husky lads ageing along from 18 up to chin-whiskers answered the clarion call of free education. They ripped open that town, sponged the seams, turned it, lined it with new mohair; and you couldn't have told it from Harvard or Goldfields at the March term of court.

"They marched up and down the streets waving flags with the World's University colours—ultramarine and blue—and they certainly made a lively place of Floresville. Andy made 'em a speech from the balcony of the Skyview Hotel, and the whole town was out celebrating.

"In about two weeks the professors got the students disarmed and herded into classes. I don't believe there's any pleasure equal to being a philanthropist. Me and Andy bought high silk hats and pretended to dodge the two reporters of the *Floresville Gazette*. The paper had a man to kodak us whenever we appeared on the street, and ran our pictures every week over the column headed 'Educational Notes.' Andy lectured twice a week at the University; and afterwards I would rise and tell a humorous story. Once the *Gazette* printed my pictures with Abe Lincoln on one side and Marshall P. Wilder on the other.

"Andy was as interested in philanthropy as I was. We used to wake up of nights and tell each other new ideas for booming the University.

" 'Andy,' says I to him one day, 'there's something we overlooked. The boys ought to have dromedaries.'

" 'What's that?' Andy asks.

" 'Why, something to sleep in, of course,' says I. 'All colleges have 'em.'

" 'Oh, you mean pajamas,' says Andy.

" 'I do not,' says I. 'I mean dromedaries.' But I never could make Andy understand; so we never ordered 'em. Of course, I meant them long bedrooms in colleges where the scholars sleep in a row.

"Well, sir, the World's University was a success. We had scholars from five States and territories, and Floresville had a boom. A new shooting gallery and a pawnshop and two more saloons started;

and the boys got up a college yell that went this way:

> "Raw, raw, raw,
> Done, done, done,
> Peters, Tucker,
> Lots of fun.
> Bow-wow-wow,
> Haw-hee-haw,
> World University,
> Hip, hurrah!

"The scholars was a fine lot of young men, and me and Andy was as proud of 'em as if they belonged to our own family.

"But one day about the last of October Andy comes to me and asks if I have any idea how much money we had left in the bank. I guesses about sixteen thousand. 'Our balance,' says Andy, 'is $821.62.'

" 'What!' says I, with a kind of a yell. 'Do you mean to tell me that them infernal clod-hopping, dough-headed, pup-faced, goose-brained, gate-stealing, rabbit-eared sons of horse thieves have soaked us for that much?'

" 'No less,' says Andy.

" 'Then, to Helvetia with philanthropy,' says I.

" 'Not necessarily,' says Andy. 'Philanthropy,' says he, 'when run on a good business basis is one of the best grafts going. I'll look into the matter and see if it can't be straightened out.'

"The next week I am looking over the pay-roll of our faculty when I run across a new name—Professor James Darnley McCorkle, chair of mathematics; salary $100 per week. I yells so loud that Andy runs in quick.

" 'What's this?' says I. 'A professor of mathematics at more than $5,000 a year? How did this happen? Did he get in through the window and appoint himself?'

" 'I wired to 'Frisco for him a week ago,' says Andy. 'In ordering the faculty we seemed to have overlooked the chair of mathematics.'

" 'A good thing we did,' says I. 'We can pay his salary two weeks, and then our philanthropy will look like the ninth hole on the Skibo golf links.'

" 'Wait a while,' says Andy, 'and see how things turn out. We have taken up too noble a cause to draw out now. Besides, the further I gaze into the retail philanthropy business the better it looks to me. I never thought about investigating it before. Come to think of it now,' goes on Andy, 'all the philanthropists I ever knew had plenty of money. I ought to have looked into that matter long ago, and located which was the cause and which was the effect.'

"I had confidence in Andy's chicanery in financial affairs, so I left the whole thing in his hands. The University was flourishing fine, and me and Andy kept our silk hats shined up, and Floresville kept on heaping honours on us like we was millionaires instead of almost busted philanthropists.

"The students kept the town lively and prosperous. Some stranger came to town and started a faro bank over the Red Front livery stable, and began to amass money in quantities. Me and Andy strolled up one night and piked a dollar or two for sociability. There were about fifty of our students there drinking rum punches and shoving high stacks of blues and reds about the table as the dealer turned the cards up.

" 'Why, dang it, Andy,' says I, 'these free-school-hunting, gander-headed, silk-socked little sons of sap-suckers have got more money than you and me ever had. Look at the rolls they're pulling out of their pistol pockets!"

" 'Yes,' says Andy, 'a good many of them are sons of wealthy miners and stockmen. It's very sad to see 'em wasting their opportunities this way.'

"At Christmas all the students went home to spend the holidays. We had a farewell blow-out at the University, and Andy lectured on 'Modern Music and Prehistoric Literature of the Archipelagos.' Each one of the faculty answered to toasts, and compared me and Andy to Rockefeller and the Emperor Marcus Autolycus. I pounded on the table and yelled for Professor McCorkle; but it seems he wasn't present on the occasion. I wanted a look at the man that Andy thought could earn $100 a week in philanthropy that was on the point of making an assignment.

"The students all left on the night train; and the town sounded as quiet as the campus of a correspondence school at midnight. When I went to the hotel I saw a light in Andy's room, and I opened the door and walked in.

"There sat Andy and the faro dealer at a table dividing a two-foot high stack of currency in thousand-dollar packages.

" 'Correct,' says Andy. 'Thirty-one thousand apiece. Come in, Jeff,' says he. 'This is our share of the profits of the first half of the scholastic term of the World's University, incorporated and philanthropated. Are you convinced now,' says Andy, 'that philanthropy when practised in a business way is an art that blesses him who gives as well as him who receives?'

" 'Great!' says I, feeling fine. 'I'll admit you are the doctor this time.'

" 'We'll be leaving on the morning train,' says Andy. 'You'd better get your collars and cuffs and Press clippings together.'

" 'Great!' says I. 'I'll be ready. But, Andy,' says I, 'I wish I could have met that Professor James Darnley McCorkle before we went. I had a curiosity to know that man.'

" 'That'll be easy,' says Andy, turning around to the faro dealer.

" 'Jim,' says Andy, 'shake hands with Mr. Peters.' "

XI: EXTRADITED FROM BOHEMIA

FROM near the village of Harmony, at the foot of the Green Mountains, came Miss Medora Martin to New York with her colour-box and easel.

Miss Medora resembled the rose which the autumnal frosts had spared the longest of all her sister blossoms. In Harmony, when she started alone to the wicked city to study art, they said she was a mad, reckless, headstrong girl. In New York, when she first took her seat at a West Side boarding-house table, the boarders asked: "Who is the nice-looking old maid?"

Medora took heart, a cheap hall bedroom, and two art lessons a week from Professor Angelini, a retired barber who had studied his profession in a Harlem dancing academy. There was no one to set her right, for here in the big city they do it unto all of us. How many of us are badly shaved daily and taught the two-step imperfectly by ex-pupils of Bastien Le Page and Gérôme? The most pathetic sight in New York—except the manners of the rush-hour crowds—is the dreary march of the hopeless army of Mediocrity. Here Art is no benignant goddess, but a Circe who turns her wooers into mewing Toms and Tabbies who linger about the doorsteps of her abode, unmindful of the flying brickbats and boot-jacks of the critics. Some of us creep back to our native villages to the skim-milk of "I told you so"; but most of us prefer to remain in the cold courtyard of our mistress's temple, snatching the scraps that fall from her divine table d'hôte. But some of us grow weary at last of the fruitless service. And then there are two fates open to us. We can get a job driving a grocer's wagon, or wc can get swallowed up in the Vortex of Bohemia. The latter sounds good; but the former really pans out better. For when the grocer pays us off we can rent a dress-suit and—the capitalized system of humour describes it best—Get Bohemia on the Run.

Miss Medora chose the Vortex, and thereby furnishes us with our little story.

Professor Angelini praised her sketches excessively. Once when she had made a neat study of a horse-chestnut tree in the park he declared she would become a second Rosa Bonheur. Again—a great artist has his moods—he would say cruel and cutting things. For example, Medora had spent an afternoon patiently sketching the statue and the architecture at Columbus Circle. Tossing it aside with a sneer, the professor informed her that Giotto had once drawn a perfect circle with one sweep of his hand.

One day it rained, the weekly remittance from

Harmony was overdue, Medora had a headache, the professor had tried to borrow two dollars from her, her art dealer had sent back all her water-colours unsold, and—Mr. Binkley asked her out to dinner.

Mr. Binkley was the gay boy of the boarding-house. He was forty-nine, and owned a fish-stall in a down-town market. But after six o'clock he wore an evening suit and whooped things up connected with the beaux arts. The young men said he was an "Indian." He was supposed to be an accomplished habitué of the inner circles of Bohemia. It was no secret that he had once loaned $10 to a young man who had had a drawing printed in *Puck*. Often has one thus obtained his entrée into the charmed circle, while the other obtained both his entrée and roast.

The other boarders enviously regarded Medora as she left at Mr. Binkley's side at nine o'clock. She was as sweet as a cluster of dried autumn grasses in her pale blue—oh—er—that very thin stuff—in her pale blue Comstockized silk waist and box-pleated voile skirt, with a soft pink glow on her thin cheeks and the tiniest bit of rouge powder on her face, with her handkerchief and room key in her brown walrus, pebble-grain hand-bag.

And Mr. Binkley looked imposing and dashing with his red face and grey moustache, and his tight dress-coat, that made the back of his neck roll up just like a successful novelist's.

They drove in a cab to the Café Terence just off the most glittering part of Broadway, which, as every one knows, is one of the most popular and widely patronized, jealously exclusive Bohemian resorts in the city.

Down between the rows of little tables tripped Medora, of the Green Mountains, after her escort. Thrice in a lifetime may woman walk upon clouds—once when she trippeth to the altar, once when she first enters Bohemian halls, the last when she marches back across her first garden with the dead hen of her neighbour in her hand.

There was a table set, with three or four about it. A waiter buzzed around it like a bee, and silver and glass shone upon it. And, preliminary to the meal, as the prehistoric granite strata heralded the protozoa, the bread of Gaul, compounded after the formula of the recipe for the eternal hills, was there set forth to the hand and tooth of a long-suffering city, while the gods lay beside their nectar and home-made biscuits and smiled, and the dentists leaped for joy in their gold-lcafy dcns.

The eye of Binkley fixed a young man at his table with the Bohemian gleam, which is a compound of the look of the Basilisk, the shine of a bubble of Würzburger, the inspiration of genius, and the pleading of a pan-handler.

The young man sprang to his feet. "Hello, Bink, old boy!" he shouted. "Don't tell me you were going to pass our table. Join us—unless you've another crowd on hand."

"Don't mind, old chap," said Binkley, of the fish-stall. "You know how I like to butt up against the fine arts. Mr. Vandyke—Mr. Madder—er—Miss Martin, one of the elect also in art—er——"

The introduction went around. There were also Miss Elise and Miss 'Toinette. Perhaps they were models, for they chattered of the St. Regis decorations and Henry James—and they did it not badly.

Medora sat in transport. Music—wild, intoxicating music made by troubadours direct from a rear basement room in Elysium—set her thoughts to dancing. Here was a world never before penetrated by her warmest imagination or any of the lines controlled by Harriman. With the Green Mountains' external calm upon her she sat, her soul flaming in her with the fire of Andalusia. The tables were filled with Bohemia. The room was full of the fragrance of flowers—both mille and cauli. Questions and corks popped; laughter and silver rang; champagne flashed in the pail, wit flashed in the pan.

Vandyke ruffled his long, black locks, disarranged his careless tie, and leaned over to Madder.

"Say, Maddy," he whispered, feelingly, "sometimes I'm tempted to pay this Philistine his ten dollars and get rid of him."

Madder ruffled his long, sandy locks and disarranged his careless tie.

"Don't think of it, Vandy," he replied. "We are short, and Art is long."

Medora ate strange viands and drank elderberry wine that they poured in her glass. It was just the colour of that in the Vermont home. The waiter poured something in another glass that seemed to be boiling, but when she tasted it it was not hot. She had never felt so light-hearted before. She thought lovingly of the Green Mountain farm and its fauna. She leaned, smiling, to Miss Elise.

"If I were at home," she said, beamingly, "I could show you the cutest little calf!"

"Nothing for you in the White Lane," said Miss Elise. "Why don't you pad?"

The orchestra played a wailing waltz that Medora had learned from the hand-organs. She followed the air with nodding head in a sweet soprano hum. Madder looked across the table at her, and wondered in what strange waters Binkley had caught her in his seine. She smiled at him, and they raised glasses and drank of the wine that boiled when it was cold. Binkley had abandoned art, and was prating of the unusual spring catch of shad. Miss Elise arranged the palette-and-maul-stick tiepin of Mr. Vandyke. A Philistine at some distant table was maundering volubly either about Jerome or Gérôme. A famous actress was discoursing excitably about monogrammed hosiery. A hose clerk from a department store was loudly proclaiming his opinions of the drama. A writer was abusing Dickens. A magazine editor and a photographer were drinking a dry brand at a reserved table. A 36-25-42 young lady was saying to an eminent sculptor: "Fudge for your Prax Italys! Bring one of your Venus Anno Dominis down to Cohen's and see how quick she'd be turned down for a cloak model. Back to the quarries with your Greeks and Dagos!"

Thus went Bohemia.

At eleven Mr. Binkley took Medora to the boarding-house and left her, with a society bow, at the foot of the hall stairs. She went up to her room and lit the gas.

And then, as suddenly as the dreadful genie arose in vapour from the copper vase of the fisherman, arose in that room the formidable shape of the New England Conscience. The terrible thing that Medora had done was revealed to her in its full enormity. She had sat in the presence of the ungodly, and looked upon the wine both when it was red and effervescent.

At midnight she wrote this letter:

"Mr. Beriah Hoskins, Harmony, Vermont.

"Dear Sir,—Henceforth consider me as dead to you for ever. I have loved you too well to blight your career by bringing into it my guilty and sin-stained life. I have succumbed to the insidious wiles of this wicked world, and have been drawn into the Vortex of Bohemia. There is scarcely any depth of glittering iniquity that I have not sounded. It is hopeless to combat my decision. There is no rising from the depths to which I have sunk. Endeavour to forget me. I am lost for ever in the fair but brutal maze of awful Bohemia. Farewell.

"Once Your Medora."

On the next day Medora formed her resolutions. Beelzebub, flung from heaven, was no more cast down. Between her and the apple blossoms of Harmony there was a fixed gulf. Flaming cherubim warded her from the gates of her lost paradise. In one evening, by the aid of Binkley and Mumm, Bohemia had gathered her into its awful midst.

There remained to her but one thing—a life of brilliant but irremediable error. Vermont was a shrine that she never would dare to approach again. But she would not sink—there were great and compelling ones in history upon whom she would model her meteoric career—Camille, Lola Montez, Royal Mary, Zaza—such a name as one of these would that of Medora Martin be to future generations.

For two days Medora kept her room. On the third she opened a magazine at the portrait of the King of Belgium, and laughed sardonically. If that far-famed breaker of women's hearts should cross her path, he would have to bow before her cold and imperious beauty. She would not spare the old or the young. All America—all Europe should do homage to her sinister but compelling charm.

As yet she could not bear to think of the life she had once desired—a peaceful one in the shadow of the Green Mountains with Beriah at her side, and orders for expensive oil paintings coming in by each mail from New York. Her one fatal misstep had shattered that dream.

On the fourth day Medora powdered her face and rouged her lips. Once she had seen Carter in "Zaza." She stood before the mirror in a reckless attitude and cried: "*Zut! zut!*" She rhymed it with "nut," but with the lawless word Harmony seemed to pass away for ever. The Vortex had her. She belonged to Bohemia for evermore. And never would Beriah——

The door opened and Beriah walked in.

" 'Dory," said he, "what's all that chalk and pink stuff on your face, honey?"

Medora extended an arm.

"Too late," she said, solemnly. "The die is cast. I belong in another world. Curse me if you will—it is your right. Go, and leave me in the path I have chosen. Bid them all at home never to mention my name again. And sometimes, Beriah, pray for me when I am revelling in the gaudy but hollow pleasures of Bohemia."

"Get a towel, 'Dory," said Beriah, "and wipe that paint off your face. I came as soon as I got your letter. Them pictures of yours ain't amounting to anything. I've got tickets for both of us back on the evening train. Hurry and get your things in your trunk."

"Fate was too strong for me, Beriah. Go while I am strong to bear it."

"How do you fold this easel, 'Dory?—now begin to pack, so we have time to eat before train time. The maples is all out in full-grown leaves, 'Dory—you just ought to see 'em!"

"Not this early, Beriah?"

"You ought to see 'em, 'Dory; they're like an ocean of green in the morning sunlight."

"Oh, Beriah!"

On the train she said to him suddenly:

"I wonder why you came when you got my letter."

"Oh, shucks!" said Beriah. "Did you think you could fool me? How could you be run away to that Bohemia country like you said when your letter was postmarked New York as plain as day?"

XII: CHERCHEZ LA FEMME

ROBBINS, reporter for the *Picayune*, and Dumars, of *L'Abeille*—the old French newspaper that has buzzed for nearly a century—were good friends, well proven by years of ups and downs together. They were seated where they had a habit of meeting—in the little, Creole-haunted café of Madame Tibault, in Dumaine Street. If you know the place, you will experience a thrill of pleasure in recalling it to mind. It is small and dark, with six little polished tables, at which you may sit and drink the best coffee in

New Orleans, and concoctions of absinthe equal to Sazerac's best. Madame Tibault, fat and indulgent, presides at the desk, and takes your money. Nicolette and Mémé, madame's nieces, in charming bib aprons, bring the desirable beverages.

Dumars, with true Creole luxury, was sipping his absinthe, with half-closed eyes, in a swirl of cigarette smoke. Robbins was looking over the morning *Pic.*, detecting, as young reporters will, the gross blunders in the make-up, and the envious blue-pencilling his own stuff had received. This item, in the advertising columns, caught his eye, and with an exclamation of sudden interest he read it aloud to his friend.

Public Auction.—At three o'clock this afternoon there will be sold to the highest bidder all the common property of the Little Sisters of Samaria, at the home of the Sisterhood, in Bonhomme Street. The sale will dispose of the building, ground, and the complete furnishings of the house and chapel, without reserve.

This notice stirred the two friends to a reminiscent talk concerning an episode in their journalistic career that had occurred about two years before. They recalled the incidents, went over the old theories, and discussed it anew from the different perspective time had brought.

There were no other customers in the café. Madame's fine ear had caught the line of their talk, and she came over to their table—for had it not been her lost money—her vanished twenty thousand dollars—that had set the whole matter going?

The three took up the long-abandoned mystery, threshing over the old, dry chaff of it. It was in the chapel of this house of the Little Sisters of Samaria that Robbins and Dumars had stood during that eager, fruitless news search of theirs, and looked upon the gilded statue of the Virgin.

"Thass so, boys," said madame, summing up. "Thass ver' wicked man, M'sieur Morin. Everybody shall be cert' he steal those money I plaze in his hand for keep safe. Yes. He's boun' spend that money, somehow." Madame turned a broad and comprehensive smile upon Dumars. "I ond'stand you, M'sieur Dumars, those day you come ask me fo' tell ev'ything I know 'bout M'sieur Morin. Ah! yes, I know most time when those men lose money you say '*Cherchez la femme*'—there is somewhere the woman. But not for M'sieur Morin. No, boys. Before he shall die, he is like one saint. You might's well, M'sieur Dumars, go try find those money in those statue of Virgin Mary that M'sieur Morin present at those *p'tite sœurs*, as try find one *femme*."

At Madame Tibault's last words, Robbins started slightly and cast a keen, sidelong glance at Dumars. The Creole sat, unmoved, dreamily watching the spirals of his cigarette smoke.

It was then nine o'clock in the morning and, a few minutes later, the two friends separated, going different ways to their day's duties. And now follows the brief story of Madame Tibault's vanished thousands:

New Orleans will readily recall to mind the circumstances attendant upon the death of Mr. Gaspard Morin, in that city. Mr. Morin was an artistic goldsmith and jeweller in the old French Quarter, and a man held in the highest esteem. He belonged to one of the oldest French families, and was of some distinction as an antiquary and historian. He was a bachelor, about fifty years of age. He lived in quiet comfort at one of those rare old hostelries in Royal Street. He was found in his rooms, one morning, dead from unknown causes.

When his affairs came to be looked into, it was found that he was practically insolvent, his stock of goods and personal property barely—but nearly enough to free him from censure—covering his liabilities. Following came the disclosure that he had been intrusted with the sum of twenty thousand dollars by a former upper servant in the Morin family, one Madame Tibault, which she had received as a legacy from relatives in France.

The most searching scrutiny by friends and the legal authorities failed to reveal the disposition of the money. It had vanished, and left no trace. Some weeks before his death, Mr. Morin had drawn the entire amount, in gold coin, from the bank where it had been placed while he looked about (he told Madame Tibault) for a safe investment. Therefore, Mr. Morin's memory seemed doomed to bear the cloud of dishonesty, while madame was, of course, disconsolate.

Then it was that Robbins and Dumars, representing their respective journals, began one of those pertinacious private investigations which, of late years, the press has adopted as a means to glory and the satisfaction of public curiosity.

"*Cherchez la femme*," said Dumars.

"That's the ticket!" agreed Robbins. "All roads

lead to the eternal feminine. We will find the woman."

They exhausted the knowledge of the staff of Mr. Morin's hotel, from the bell-boy down to the proprietor. They gently, but inflexibly, pumped the family of the deceased as far as his cousins twice removed. They artfully sounded the employees of the late jeweller, and dogged his customers for information concerning his habits. Like bloodhounds they traced every step of the supposed defaulter, as nearly as might be, for years along the limited and monotonous paths he had trodden.

At the end of their labours, Mr. Morin stood an immaculate man. Not one weakness that might be served up as a criminal tendency, not one deviation from the path of rectitude, not even a hint of a predilection for the opposite sex, was found to be placed to his debit. His life had been as regular and austere as a monk's; his habits, simple and unconcealed. Generous, charitable, and a model in propriety, was the verdict of all who knew him.

"What, now?" asked Robbins, fingering his empty notebook.

"*Cherchez la femme*," said Dumars, lighting a cigarette. "Try Lady Bellairs."

This piece of femininity was the race-track favourite of the season. Being feminine, she was erratic in her gaits, and there were a few heavy losers about town who had believed she could be true. The reporters applied for information.

Mr. Morin? Certainly not. He was never even a spectator at the races. Not that kind of a man. Surprised the gentleman should ask.

"Shall we throw it up?" suggested Robbins, "and let the puzzle department have a try?"

"*Cherchez la femme*," hummed Dumars, reaching for a match. "Try the Little Sisters of What-d'-you-call-'em."

It had developed, during the investigation, that Mr. Morin had held this benevolent order in particular favour. He had contributed liberally toward its support and had chosen its chapel as his favourite place of private worship. It was said that he went there daily to make his devotions at the altar. Indeed, toward the last of his life his whole mind seemed to have fixed itself upon religious matters, perhaps to the detriment of his worldly affairs.

Thither went Robbins and Dumars, and were admitted through the narrow doorway in the blank stone wall that frowned upon Bonhomme Street. An old woman was sweeping the chapel. She told them that Sister Félicité, the head of the order, was then at prayer at the altar in the alcove. In a few moments she would emerge. Heavy, black curtains screened the alcove. They waited.

Soon the curtains were disturbed, and Sister Félicité came forth. She was tall, tragic, bony, and plain-featured, dressed in the black gown and severe bonnet of the sisterhood.

Robbins, a good rough-and-tumble reporter, but lacking the delicate touch, began to speak.

They represented the press. The lady had, no doubt, heard of the Morin affair. It was necessary, in justice to that gentleman's memory, to probe the mystery of the lost money. It was known that he had come often to this chapel. Any information, now, concerning Mr. Morin's habits, tastes, the friends he had, and so on, would be of value in doing him posthumous justice.

Sister Félicité had heard. Whatever she knew would be willingly told, but it was very little. Monsieur Morin had been a good friend to the order, sometimes contributing as much as a hundred dollars. The sisterhood was an independent one, depending entirely upon private contributions for the means to carry on its charitable work. Mr. Morin had presented the chapel with silver candlesticks and an altar cloth. He came every day to worship in the chapel, sometimes remaining for an hour. He was a devout Catholic, consecrated to holiness. Yes, and also in the alcove was a statue of the Virgin that he had himself modelled, cast, and presented to the order. Oh, it was cruel to cast a doubt upon so good a man!

Robbins was also profoundly grieved at the imputation. But, until it was found what Mr. Morin had done with Madame Tibault's money, he feared the tongue of slander would not be stilled. Sometimes—in fact, very often—in affairs of the kind there was—er—as the saying goes—er—a lady in the case. In absolute confidence, now—if—perhaps——

Sister Félicité's large eyes regarded him solemnly.

"There was one woman," she said, slowly, "to whom he bowed—to whom he gave his heart."

Robbins fumbled rapturously for his pencil.

"Behold the woman!" said Sister Félicité, suddenly, in deep tones.

She reached a long arm and swept aside the curtain of the alcove. In there was a shrine, lit to a glow of soft colour by the light pouring through a stained-glass window. Within a deep niche in the bare stone wall stood an image of the Virgin Mary, the colour of pure gold.

Dumars, a conventional Catholic, succumbed to the dramatic in the act. He bowed his head for an instant and made the sign of the cross. The somewhat abashed Robbins, murmuring an indistinct apology, backed awkwardly away. Sister Félicité drew back the curtain, and the reporters departed.

On the narrow stone sidewalk of Bonhomme Street, Robbins turned to Dumars, with unworthy sarcasm.

"Well, what next? Churchy law fem?"

"Absinthe," said Dumars.

With the history of the missing money thus partially related, some conjecture may be formed of the sudden idea that Madame Tibault's words seemed to have suggested to Robbins's brain.

Was it so wild a surmise—that the religious fanatic had offered up his wealth—or, rather, Madame Tibault's—in the shape of a material symbol of his consuming devotion? Stranger things have been done in the name of worship. Was it not possible that the lost thousands were moulded into that lustrous image? That the goldsmith had formed it of the pure and precious metal, and set it there, through some hope of a perhaps disordered brain to propitiate the saints and pave the way to his own selfish glory?

That afternoon, at five minutes to three, Robbins entered the chapel door of the Little Sisters of Samaria. He saw, in the dim light, a crowd of perhaps a hundred people gathered to attend the sale. Most of them were members of various religious orders, priests, and churchmen, come to purchase the paraphernalia of the chapel, lest they fall into desecrating hands. Others were business men and agents come to bid upon the reality. A clerical-looking brother had volunteered to wield the hammer, bringing to the office of auctioneer the anomaly of choice diction and dignity of manner.

A few of the minor articles were sold, and then two assistants brought forward the image of the Virgin.

Robbins started the bidding at ten dollars. A stout man, in an ecclesiastical garb, went to fifteen. A voice from another part of the crowd raised to twenty. The three bid alternately, raising by bids of five, until the offer was fifty dollars. Then the stout man dropped out, and Robbins, as a sort of *coup de main*, went to a hundred.

"One hundred and fifty," said the other voice.

"Two hundred," bid Robbins, boldly.

"Two-fifty," called his competitor, promptly.

The reporter hesitated for the space of a lightning flash, estimating how much he could borrow from the boys in the office, and screw from the business manager from his next month's salary.

"Three hundred," he offered.

"Three-fifty," spoke up the other, in a louder voice—a voice that sent Robbins diving suddenly through the crowd in its direction, to catch Dumars, its owner, ferociously by the collar.

"You unconverted idiot!" hissed Robbins, close to his ear—"pool!"

"Agreed!" said Dumars coolly. "I couldn't raise three hundred and fifty dollars with a search-warrant, but I can stand half. What you come bidding against me for?"

"I thought I was the only fool in the crowd," explained Robbins.

No one else bidding, the statue was knocked down to the syndicate at their last offer. Dumars remained with the prize, while Robbins hurried forth to wring from the resources and credit of both the price. He soon returned with the money, and the two musketeers loaded their precious package into a carriage and drove with it to Dumars's room, in old Chartres Street, near by. They lugged it, covered with a cloth, up the stairs, and deposited it on a table. A hundred pounds it weighed, if an ounce, and at that estimate, according to their calculation, if their daring theory were correct, it stood there, worth twenty thousand golden dollars.

Robbins removed the covering, and opened his pocket-knife.

"*Sacré!*" muttered Dumars, shuddering. "It is the Mother of Christ. What would you do?"

"Shut up, Judas!" said Robbins, coldly. "It's too late for you to be saved now."

With a firm hand, he chipped a slice from the shoulder of the image. The cut showed a dull, greyish metal, with a thin coating of gold leaf.

"Lead!" announced Robbins, hurling his knife to the floor—"gilded!"

"To the devil with it!" said Dumars, forgetting his scruples. "I must have a drink."

Together they walked moodily to the café of Madame Tibault, two squares away.

It seemed that madame's mind had been stirred that day to fresh recollections of the past services of the two young men in her behalf.

"You mustn't sit by those table," she interposed,

as they were about to drop into their accustomed seats. "Thass so, boys. But no. I mek you come at this room, like my *très bons amis*. Yes. I goin' mek for you myself one *anisette* and one *café royale* ver' fine. Ah! I lak treat my fren' nize. Yes. Plis come in this way."

Madame led them into the little back room, into which she sometimes invited the especially favoured of her customers. In two comfortable arm-chairs, by a big window that opened upon the courtyard, she placed them, with a low table between. Bustling hospitably about, she began to prepare the promised refreshments.

It was the first time the reporters had been honoured with admission to the sacred precincts. The room was in dusky twilight, flecked with gleams of the polished, fine woods and burnished glass and metal that the Creoles love. From the little courtyard a tiny fountain sent in an insinuating sound of trickling waters, to which a banana plant by the window kept time with its tremulous leaves.

Robbins, an investigator by nature, sent a curious glance roving about the room. From some barbaric ancestor, madame had inherited a *penchant* for the crude in decoration.

The walls were adorned with cheap lithographs—florid libels upon nature, addressed to the taste of the *bourgeoisie*—birthday cards, garish newspaper supplements, and specimens of art-advertising calculated to reduce the optic nerve to stunned submission. A patch of something unintelligible in the midst of the more candid display puzzled Robbins, and he rose and took a step nearer, to interrogate it at closer range. Then he leaned weakly against the wall, and called out:

"Madame Tibault! Oh, madame! Since when—oh! since when have you been in the habit of papering your walls with five thousand dollar United States four per cent. gold bonds? Tell me—is this a Grimm's fairy tale, or should I consult an oculist?"

At his words Madame Tibault and Dumars approached.

"H'what you say?" said madame, cheerily. "H'what you say, M'sieur Robbin'? *Bon!* Ah! those nize li'l peezes papier! One tam I think those w'at you call calendair, wiz ze li'l day of mont' below. But no. Those wall is broke in those plaze, M'sieur Robbin', and I plaze those li'l peezes papier to conceal ze crack. I did think the couleur harm'nize so well with the wall papier. Where I get them from? Ah, yes, I remem' ver' well. One day M'sieur Morin, he come at my houze—thass 'bout one mont' before he shall die—thass 'long 'bout tam he promise fo' inves' those money fo' me. M'sieur Morin, he leave thoze li'l peezes papier in those table, and say ver' much 'bout money thass hard for me to ond'stan. *Mais* I never see those money again. Thass ver' wicked man, M'sieur Morin. H'what you call those peezes papier, M'sieur Robbin'—*bon!*"

Robbins explained.

"There's your twenty thousand dollars, with coupons attached," he said, running his thumb around the edge of the four bonds. "Better get an expert to peel them off for you. Mister Morin was all right. I'm going out to get my ears trimmed."

He dragged Dumars by the arm into the outer room. Madame was screaming for Nicolette and

Mémé to come and observe the fortune returned to her by M'sieur Morin, that best of men, that saint in glory.

"Marsy," said Robbins, "I'm going on a jamboree. For three days the esteemed *Pic.* will have to get along without my valuable services. I advise you to join me. Now, that green stuff you drink is no good. It stimulates thought. What we want to do is to forget to remember. I'll introduce you to the only lady in this case that is guaranteed to produce the desired results. Her name is Belle of Kentucky, twelve-year-old Bourbon. In quarts. How does the idea strike you?"

"*Allons!*" said Dumars. "*Cherchez la femme.*"

XIII: THE PRIDE OF THE CITIES

SAID Mr. Kipling, "The cities are full of pride, challenging each to each." Even so.

New York was empty. Two hundred thousand of its people were away for the summer. Three million eight hundred thousand remained as caretakers and to pay the bills of the absentees. But the two hundred thousand are an expensive lot.

The New Yorker sat at a roof-garden table, ingesting solace through a straw. His panama lay upon a chair. The July audience was scattered among vacant seats as widely as outfielders when the champion batter steps to the plate. Vaudeville happened at intervals. The breeze was cool from the bay; around and above—everywhere except on the stage—were stars. Glimpses were to be had of waiters, always disappearing, like startled chamois. Prudent visitors who had ordered refreshments by 'phone in the morning were now being served. The New Yorker was aware of certain drawbacks to his comfort, but content beamed softly from his rimless eye-glasses. His family was out of town. The drinks were warm; the ballet was suffering from lack of both tune and talcum—but his family would not return until September.

Then up into the garden stumbled the man from Topaz City, Nevada. The gloom of the solitary sightseer enwrapped him. Bereft of joy through loneliness, he stalked with a widower's face through the halls of pleasure. Thirst for human companionship possessed him as he panted in the metropolitan draught. Straight to the New Yorker's table he steered.

The New Yorker, disarmed and made reckless by the lawless atmosphere of a roof garden, decided upon utter abandonment of his life's traditions. He resolved to shatter with one rash, dare-devil, impulsive, hair-brained act the conventions that had hitherto been woven into his existence. Carrying out this radical and precipitous inspiration he nodded slightly to the stranger as he drew nearer the table.

The next moment found the man from Topaz City in the list of the New Yorker's closest friends. He took a chair at the table, he gathered two others for his feet, he tossed his broad-brimmed hat upon a fourth, and told his life's history to his new-found pard.

The New Yorker warmed a little, as an apartment house furnace warms when the strawberry season begins. A waiter who came within hail in an unguarded moment was captured and paroled on an errand to the Doctor Wiley experimental station. The ballet was now in the midst of a musical vagary, and danced upon the stage programmed as Bolivian peasants, clothed in some portions of its anatomy as Norwegian fisher maidens, in others as ladies-in-waiting of Marie Antoinette, historically denuded in other portions so as to represent sea nymphs, and presenting the *tout ensemble* of a social club of Central Park West housemaids at a fish fry.

"Been in the city long?" inquired the New Yorker, getting ready the exact tip against the waiter's coming with large change from the bill.

"Me?" said the man from Topaz City. "Four days. Never in Topaz City, was you?"

"I!" said the New Yorker. "I was never farther west than Eighth Avenue. I had a brother who died on Ninth, but I met the cortège at Eighth. There was a bunch of violets on the hearse, and the undertaker mentioned the incident to avoid mistake. I cannot say that I am familiar with the West."

"Topaz City," said the man who occupied four chairs, "is one of the finest towns in the world."

"I presume that you have seen the sights of the metropolis," said the New Yorker. "Four days is not a sufficient length of time in which to view even our most salient points of interest, but one can possibly form a general impression. Our architectural supremacy is what generally strikes visitors to our city most forcibly. Of course you have seen our Flatiron Building. It is considered——"

"Saw it," said the man from Topaz City. "But

you ought to come out our way. It's mountainous, you know, and the ladies all wear short skirts for climbing and——"

"Excuse me," said the New Yorker, "but that isn't exactly the point. New York must be a wonderful revelation to a visitor from the West. Now, as to our hotels——"

"Say," said the man from Topaz City, "that reminds me—there were sixteen stage robbers shot last year within twenty miles of——"

"I was speaking of hotels," said the New Yorker. "We lead Europe in that respect. And as far as our leisure class is concerned we are far——"

"Oh, I don't know," interrupted the man from Topaz City. "There were twelve tramps in our jail when I left home. I guess New York isn't so——"

"Beg pardon, you seem to misapprehend the idea. Of course, you visited the Stock Exchange and Wall Street, where the——"

"Oh, yes," said the man from Topaz City as he lighted a Pennsylvania stogie, "and I want to tell you that we've got the finest town marshal west of the Rockies. Bill Rainer, he took in five pick-pockets out of the crowd when Red Nose Thompson laid the corner stone of his new saloon. Topaz City don't allow——"

"Have another Rhine wine and seltzer," suggested the New Yorker. "I've never been West, as I said; but there can't be any place out there to compare with New York. As to the claims of Chicago, I——"

"One man," said the Topazite—"one man only has been murdered and robbed in Topaz City in the last three——"

"Oh, I know what Chicago is," interposed the New Yorker. "Have you been up Fifth Avenue to see the magnificent residences of our mil——"

"Seen 'em all. You ought to know Reub Stegall, the assessor of Topaz. When old man Tilbury, that owns the only two-story house in town, tried to swear his taxes from $6,000 down to $450·75, Reub buckled on his forty-five and went down to see——"

"Yes, yes, but speaking of our great city—one of its greatest features is our superb police department. There is no body of men in the world that can equal it for——"

"That waiter gets around like a Langley flying-machine," remarked the man from Topaz City, thirstily. "We've got men in our town, too, worth $400,000. There's old Bill Withers and Colonel Metcalf and——"

"Have you seen Broadway at night?" asked the New Yorker, courteously. "There are few streets in the world that can compare with it. When the electrics are shining and the pavements are alive with two hurrying streams of elegantly clothed men and beautiful women attired in the costliest costumes that wind in and out in a close maze of expensively——"

"Never knew but one case in Topaz City," said the man from the West. "Jim Bailey, our mayor, had his watch and chain and $235 in cash taken from his pocket while——"

"That's another matter," said the New Yorker. "While you are in our city you should avail yourself of every opportunity to see its wonders. Our rapid transit system——"

"If you was out in Topaz," broke in the man

from there, "I could show you a whole cemetery full of people that got killed accidentally. Talking about mangling folks up! why, when Berry Rogers turned loose that old double-barrelled shot-gun of his loaded with slugs at anybody——"

"Here, waiter!" called the New Yorker. "Two more of the same. It is acknowledged by every one that our city is the centre of art, and literature, and learning. Take, for instance, our after-dinner speakers. Where else in the country would you find such wit and eloquence as emanate from Depew and Ford, and——"

"If you take the papers," interrupted the Westerner, "you must have read of Pete Webster's daughter. The Websters live two blocks north of the court-house in Topaz City. Miss Tillie Webster, she slept forty days and nights without waking up. The doctors said that——"

"Pass the matches, please," said the New Yorker. "Have you observed the expedition with which new buildings are being run up in New York? Improved inventions in steel framework and——"

"I noticed," said the Nevadian, "that the statistics of Topaz City showed only one carpenter crushed by falling timbers last year, and he was caught in a cyclone."

"They abuse our sky line," continued the New Yorker, "and it is likely that we are not yet artistic in the construction of our buildings. But I can safely assert that we lead in pictorial and decorative art. In some of our houses can be found masterpieces in the way of paintings and sculpture. One who has the entrée to our best galleries will find——"

"Back up," exclaimed the man from Topaz City.

"There was a game last month in our town in which $90,000 changed hands on a pair of——"

"Ta-romt-tara!" went the orchestra. The stage curtain, blushing pink at the name "Asbestos" inscribed upon it, came down with a slow midsummer movement. The audience trickled leisurely down the elevator and stairs.

On the sidewalk below, the New Yorker and the man from Topaz City shook hands with alcoholic gravity. The elevated crashed raucously, surface cars hummed and clanged, cabmen swore, newsboys shrieked, wheels clattered ear-piercingly. The New Yorker conceived a happy thought, with which he aspired to clinch the pre-eminence of his city.

"You must admit," said he, "that in the way of noise New York is far ahead of any other——"

"Back to the everglades!" said the man from Topaz City. "In 1900, when Sousa's band and the repeating candidate were in our town you couldn't——"

The rattle of an express wagon drowned the rest of the words.

XIV: ROSES, RUSES AND ROMANCE

RAVENEL—Ravenel, the traveller, artist and poet, threw his magazine to the floor. Sammy Brown, broker's clerk, who sat by the window, jumped.

"What is it, Ravvy?" he asked. "The critics been hammering your stock down?"

"Romance is dead," said Ravenel, lightly. When

Ravenel spoke lightly he was generally serious. He picked up the magazine and fluttered its leaves.

"Even a Philistine, like you, Sammy," said Ravenel, seriously (a tone that insured him to be speaking lightly), "ought to understand. Now, here is a magazine that once printed Poe and Lowell and Whitman and Bret Harte and Du Maurier and Lanier and—well, that gives you the idea. The current number has this literary feast to set before you: an article on the stokers and coal bunkers of battleships, an exposé of the methods employed in making liverwurst, a continued story of a Standard Preferred International Baking Powder deal in Wall Street, a 'poem' on the bear that the President missed, another 'story' by a young woman who spent a week as a spy making overalls on the East Side, another 'fiction' story that reeks of the 'garage' and a certain make of automobile. Of course, the title contains the words 'Cupid' and 'Chauffeur'—an article on naval strategy illustrated with cuts of the Spanish Armada, and the new Staten Island ferry-boats; another story of a political boss who won the love of a Fifth Avenue belle by blackening her eye and refusing to vote for an iniquitous ordinance (it doesn't say whether it was in the Street Cleaning Department or Congress), and nineteen pages by the editors bragging about the circulation. The whole thing, Sammy, is an obituary on Romance."

Sammy Brown sat comfortably in the leather arm-chair by the open window. His suit was a vehement brown with visible checks, beautifully matched in shade by the ends of four cigars that his vest pocket poorly concealed. Light tan were his shoes, grey his socks, sky-blue his apparent linen, snowy and high and adamantine his collar, against which a black butterfly had alighted and spread his wings. Sammy's face—least important—was round and pleasant and pinkish, and in his eyes you saw no haven for fleeing Romance.

That window of Ravenel's apartment opened upon an old garden full of ancient trees and shrubbery. The apartment-house towered above one side of it; a high brick wall fended it from the street; opposite Ravenel's window an old, old mansion stood, half-hidden in the shade of the summer foliage. The house was a castle besieged. The city howled and roared and shrieked and beat upon its double doors, and shook white, fluttering cheques above the wall, offering terms of surrender. The grey dust settled upon the trees; the siege was pressed hotter, but the drawbridge was not lowered. No further will the language of chivalry serve. Inside lived an old gentleman who loved his home and did not wish to sell it. That is all the romance of the besieged castle.

Three or four times every week came Sammy Brown to Ravenel's apartment. He belonged to the poet's club, for the former Browns had been conspicuous, though Sammy had been vulgarized by Business. He had no tears for departed Romance. The song of the ticker was the one that reached his heart, and when it came to matters equine and batting scores he was something of a pink edition. He loved to sit in the leather arm-chair by Ravenel's window. And Ravenel didn't mind particularly. Sammy seemed to enjoy his talk; and then the broker's clerk was such a perfect embodiment of modernity and the day's sordid praticality, that Ravenel rather liked to use him as a scapegoat.

"I'll tell you what's the matter with you," said Sammy, with the shrewdness that business had taught him. "The magazine has turned down some of your poetry stunts. That's why you are sore at it."

"That would be a good guess in Wall Street or in a campaign for the presidency of a woman's club," said Ravenel, quietly. "Now, there is a poem—if you will allow me to call it that—of my own in this number of the magazine."

"Read it to me," said Sammy, watching a cloud of pipe-smoke he had just blown out the window.

Ravenel was no greater than Achilles. No one is. There is bound to be a spot. The Somebody-or-Other must take hold of us somewhere when she dips us in the Something-or-Other that makes us invulnerable. He read aloud this verse in the magazine:

THE FOUR ROSES.

"One rose I twined within your hair—
(White rose, that spake of worth);
And one you placed upon your breast—
(Red rose, love's seal of birth).
You plucked another from its stem—
(Tea rose, that means for aye);
And one you gave—that bore for me
The thorns of memory."

"That's a crackerjack," said Sammy, admiringly.

"There are five more verses," said Ravenel, patiently sardonic. "One naturally pauses at the end of each. Of course——"

"Oh, let's have the rest, old man," shouted Sammy, contritely, "I didn't mean to cut you off. I'm not much of a poetry expert, you know. I never saw a poem that didn't look like it ought to have terminal facilities at the end of every verse. Reel off the rest of it."

Ravenel sighed, and laid the magazine down. "All right," said Sammy, cheerfully, "we'll have it next time. I'll be off now. Got a date at five o'clock."

He took a last look at the shaded green garden and left, whistling in an off key an untuneful air from a roofless farce comedy.

The next afternoon Ravenel, while polishing a ragged line of a new sonnet, reclined by the window overlooking the besieged garden of the unmercenary baron. Suddenly he sat up, spilling two rhymes and a syllable or two.

Through the trees one window of the old mansion could be seen clearly. In its window, draped in flowing white, leaned the angel of all his dreams of romance and poesy. Young, fresh as a drop of dew, graceful as a spray of clematis, conferring upon the garden hemmed in by the roaring traffic the air of a princess's bower, beautiful as any flower sung by poet—thus Ravenel saw her for the first time. She lingered for a while, and then disappeared within, leaving a few notes of a birdlike ripple of song to reach his entranced ears through the rattle of cabs and the snarling of the electric cars.

Thus, as if to challenge the poet's flaunt at romance and to punish him for his recreancy to the undying spirit of youth and beauty, this vision had dawned upon him with a thrilling and accusive power. And so metabolic was the power, that in an instant the atoms of Ravenel's entire world were redistributed. The laden drays that passed the house in which she lived rumbled a deep double-bass to the tune of love. The newsboys' shouts were the notes of singing birds; that garden was the pleasance of the Capulets; the janitor was an ogre; himself a knight, ready with sword, lance or lute.

Thus does romance show herself amid forests of brick and stone when she gets lost in the city and there has to be sent out a general alarm to find her again.

At four in the afternoon Ravenel looked out across the garden. In the window of his hopes were set four small vases, each containing a great, full-blown rose—red and white. And, as he gazed, she leaned above them, shaming them with her loveliness and seeming to direct her eyes pensively toward his own window. And then, as though she had caught his respectful, but ardent regard, she melted away, leaving the fragrant emblems on the window-sill.

Yes, emblems!—he would be unworthy if he had not understood. She had read his poem, "The Four Roses"; it had reached her heart; and this was its romantic answer. Of course, she must know that Ravenel, the poet, lived across her garden. His picture, too, she must have seen in the magazines. The delicate, tender, modest, flattering message could not be ignored.

Ravenel noticed beside the roses a small flowering-pot containing a plant. Without shame he brought his opera-glasses and employed them from the cover of his window-curtain. A nutmeg geranium!

With the true poetic instinct he dragged a book of useless information from his shelves, and tore open the leaves at "The Language of Flowers."

"Geranium, Nutmeg—I expect a meeting."

So! Romance never does things by halves. If she comes back to you she brings gifts and her knitting, and will sit in your chimney-corner if you will let her.

And now Ravenel smiled. The lover smiles when he thinks he has won. The woman who loves ceases to smile with victory. He ends a battle; she begins hers. What a pretty idea to set the four roses in her window for him to see! She must have a sweet, poetic soul. And now to contrive the meeting.

A whistling and slamming of doors preluded the coming of Sammy Brown.

Ravenel smiled again. Even Sammy Brown was shone upon by the far-flung rays of the renaissance. Sammy, with his ultra clothes, his horseshoe pin, his plump face, his trite slang, his uncomprehending admiration of Ravenel—the broker's clerk made an excellent foil to the new, bright, unseen visitor to the poet's sombre apartment.

Sammy went to his old seat by the window, and looked out over the dusty green foliage in the garden. Then he looked at his watch, and rose hastily.

"By grabs!" he exclaimed. "Twenty after four! I can't stay, old man; I've got a date at 4.30."

"Why did you come, then," asked Ravenel, with sarcastic jocularity, "if you had an engagement at that time? I thought you business men kept better account of your minutes and seconds than that."

Sammy hesitated in the doorway and turned pinker.

"Fact is, Ravvy," he explained, as to a customer whose margin is exhausted, "I didn't know I had it till I came. I'll tell you, old man—there's a dandy girl in that old house next door that I'm dead gone on. I put it straight—we're engaged. The old man says 'nit'—but that don't go. He keeps her pretty close. I can see Edith's window from yours here. She gives me a tip when she's going shopping, and I meet her. It's 4.30 to-day. Maybe I ought to have explained sooner, but I know it's all right with you—so long."

"How do you get your 'tip,' as you call it?" asked Ravenel, losing a little spontaneity from his smile.

"Roses," said Sammy, briefly. "Four of 'em to-day. Means four o'clock at the corner of Broadway and Twenty-third."

"But the geranium?" persisted Ravenel, clutching at the end of flying Romance's trailing robe.

"Means half-past," shouted Sammy from the hall. "See you to-morrow."

XV: THE MARQUIS AND MISS SALLY

WITHOUT knowing it, Old Bill Bascom had the honour of being overtaken by fate the same day with the Marquis of Borodale.

The Marquis lived in Regent Square, London. Old Bill lived on Limping Doe Creek, Hardeman County, Texas. The cataclysm that engulfed the Marquis took the form of a bursting bubble known as the Central and South American Mahogany and Caoutchouc Monopoly. Old Bill's Nemesis was in the no less perilous shape of a band of civilized Indian cattle thieves from the Territory who ran off his entire herd of four hundred head, and shot Old Bill dead as he trailed after them. To even up the consequences of the two catastrophes, the Marquis, as soon as he found that all he possessed would pay only fifteen shillings in the pound of his indebtedness, shot himself.

Old Bill left a family of six motherless sons and daughters, who found themselves without even a red steer left to eat, or a red cent to buy one with.

The Marquis left one son, a young man who had come to the States and established a large and well stocked ranch in the Panhandle of Texas. When this young man learned the news he mounted his pony and rode to town. There he placed everything he owned except his horse, saddle, Winchester, and fifteen dollars in his pockets, in the hands of his lawyers, with instructions to sell and forward the proceeds to London to be applied to the payment of his father's debts. Then he mounted his pony and rode southward.

One day, arriving about the same time, but by different trails, two young chaps rode up to the Diamond-Cross ranch, on the Little Piedra, and asked for work. Both were dressed neatly and sprucely in cowboy costume. One was a straight-set fellow, with delicate handsome features, short brown hair, and smooth face, sunburned to a golden brown. The other applicant was stouter and broad-shouldered, with fresh red complexion, somewhat freckled, reddish curling hair, and a rather plain face, made attractive by laughing eyes and a pleasant mouth.

The superintendent of the Diamond-Cross was of the opinion that he could give them work. In fact, word had reached him that morning that the camp cook—a most important member of the outfit—had straddled his broncho and departed, being unable to withstand the fire of fun and practical jokes of which he was, ex-officio, the legitimate target.

"Can either of you cook?" asked the superintendent.

"I can," said the reddish-haired fellow, promptly. "I've cooked in camp quite a lot. I'm willing to take the job until you've got something else to offer."

"Now, that's the way I like to hear a man talk," said the superintendent, approvingly. "I'll give you a note to Saunders, and he'll put you to work."

Thus the names of John Bascom and Charles Norwood were added to the pay-roll of the Diamond-Cross. The two left for the round-up camp immediately after dinner. Their directions were simple, but sufficient: "Keep down the arroyo for fifteen miles till you get there." Both being strangers from afar, young, spirited, and thus thrown together by chance for a long ride, it is likely that the comradeship that afterward existed so strongly between them began that afternoon as they meandered along the little valley of the Canada Verda.

They reached their destination just after sunset. The main camp of the round-up was comfortably located on the bank of a long water-hole, under a fine mott of timber. A number of small A tents pitched upon grassy spots and the big wall tent for provisions showed that the camp was intended to be occupied for a considerable length of time.

The round-up had ridden in but a few moments before, hungry and tired, to a supperless camp. The boys were engaged in an emulous display of anathemas supposed to fit the case of the absconding cook. While they were unsaddling and hobbling their ponies, the new-comers rode in and inquired for Pink Saunders. The boss of the round-up came forth and was given the superintendent's note.

Pink Saunders, though a boss during working hours, was a humorist in camp, where everybody, from cook to superintendent, is equal. After reading the note he waved his hand toward the camp and shouted, ceremoniously, at the top of his voice: "Gentlemen, allow me to present to you the Marquis and Miss Sally."

At the words both the new arrivals betrayed confusion. The newly employed cook started, with a surprised look on his face, but, immediately recollecting that "Miss Sally" is the generic name for the male cook in every west Texas cow camp, he recovered his composure with a grin at his own expense.

His companion showed little less discomposure, even turning angrily, with a bitten lip, and reaching for his saddle pommel, as if to remount his pony; but "Miss Sally" touched his arm and said, laughingly, "Come now, Marquis; that was quite a compliment from Saunders. It's that distinguished air of yours and aristocratic nose that made him call you that."

He began to unsaddle, and the Marquis, restored to equanimity, followed his example. Rolling up his sleeves, Miss Sally sprang for the grub wagon, shouting:

"I'm the new cook, b'thunder! Some of you chaps rustle a little wood for a fire, and I'll guarantee you a hot square meal inside of thirty minutes." Miss Sally's energy and good-humour, as he ransacked the grub wagon for coffee, flour, and bacon, won the good opinion of the camp instantly.

And also, in days following, the Marquis, after becoming better acquainted, proved to be a cheerful, pleasant fellow, always a little reserved, and taking no part in the rough camp frolics; but the boys gradually came to respect this reserve—which fitted the title Saunders had given him—and even to like him for it. Saunders had assigned him to a place holding the herd during the cuttings. He proved to be a skilful rider and as good with the lariat or in the branding pen as most of them.

The Marquis and Miss Sally grew to be quite close comrades. After supper was over, and everything cleaned up, you would generally find them together, Miss Sally smoking his brier-root pipe, and the Marquis plaiting a quirt or scraping rawhide for a new pair of hobbles.

The superintendent did not forget his promise to keep an eye on the cook. Several times, when visiting the camp, he held long talks with him. He seemed to have taken a fancy to Miss Sally. One afternoon he rode up, on his way back to the ranch from a tour of the camps, and said to him:

"There'll be a man here in the morning to take your place. As soon as he shows up you come to the ranch. I want you to take charge of the ranch accounts and correspondence. I want somebody that I can depend upon to keep things straight when I'm away. The wages'll be all right. The Diamond-Cross'll hold its end up with a man who'll look after its interests."

"All right," said Miss Sally, as quietly as if he had expected the notice all along. "Any objections to my bringing my wife down to the ranch?"

"You married?" said the superintendent, frowning a little. "You didn't mention it when we were talking."

"Because I'm not," said the cook. "But I'd like

to be. Thought I'd wait till I got a job under roof. I couldn't ask her to live in a cow camp."

"Right," agreed the superintendent. "A camp isn't quite the place for a married man—but—well, there's plenty of room at the house, and if you suit us as well as I think you will you can afford it. You write to her to come on."

"All right," said Miss Sally again, "I'll ride in as soon as I am relieved to-morrow."

It was a rather chilly night, and after supper the cow-punchers were lounging about a big fire of dried mesquite chunks.

Their usual exchange of jokes and repartee had dwindled almost to silence, but silence in a cow camp generally betokens the brewing of mischief.

Miss Sally and the Marquis were seated upon a log, discussing the relative merits of the lengthened or shortened stirrup in long-distance riding. The Marquis arose presently and went to a tree near by to examine some strips of rawhide he was seasoning for making a lariat. Just as he left a little puff of wind blew some scraps of tobacco from a cigarette that Dry-Creek Smithers was rolling, into Miss Sally's eyes. While the cook was rubbing at them, with tears flowing, "Phonograph" Davis—so called on account of his strident voice—arose and began a speech.

"Fellers and citizens! I desire to perpound a interrogatory. What is the most grievious spectacle what the human mind can contemplate?"

A volley of answers responded to his question.

"A busted flush!"

"A Maverick when you ain't got your branding-iron!"

"Yourself!"

"The hole in the end of some other feller's gun!"

"Shet up, you ignoramuses," said old Taller, the fat cow-puncher. "Phony knows what it is. He's waitin' for to tell us."

"No, fellers and citizens," continued Phonograph.

"Them spectacles you've e-numerated air shore grievious, and way up yonder close to the so-lution, but they ain't it. The most grievious spectacle air that"—he pointed to Miss Sally, who was still rubbing his streaming eyes—"a trustin' and a inveegled female a-weepin' tears on account of her heart bein' busted by a false deceiver. Air we men or air we catamounts to gaze upon the blightin' of our Miss Sally's affections by a a-risto-crat, which has come among us with his superior beauty and his glitterin' title to give the weeps to the lovely critter we air bound to pertect? Air we goin' to act like men, or air we goin' to keep on eatin' soggy chuck from her cryin' so plentiful over the bread-pan?"

"It's a gallopin' shame," said Dry-Creek, with a sniffle. "It ain't human. I've noticed the varmint a-palaverin' round her frequent. And him a Marquis! Ain't that a title, Phony?"

"It's somethin' like a king," the Brushy Creek Kid hastened to explain, "only lower in the deck. Guess it comes in between the Jack and the ten-spot."

"Don't miscontruct me," went on Phonograph, "as undervaluatin' the a-ristocrats. Some of 'em air proper people and can travel right along with the Watson boys. I've herded some with 'em myself. I've viewed the elephant with the Mayor of Fort Worth, and I've listened to the owl with the gen'ral passenger agent of the Katy, and they can keep up with the percession from where you laid the chunk. But when a Marquis monkeys with the innocent affections of a cook-lady, may I inquire what the case seems to call for?"

"The leathers," shouted Dry-Creek Smithers.

"You hearn 'er, Charity!" was the Kid's form of corroboration.

"We've got your company," assented the cow-punchers, in chorus.

Before the Marquis realized their intention, two of them seized him by each arm and led him up to the log. Phonograph Davis, self-appointed to carry out the sentence, stood ready, with a pair of stout leather leggings in his hands.

It was the first time they had ever laid hands on the Marquis during their somewhat rude sports.

"What are you up to?" he asked, indignantly, with flashing eyes.

"Go easy, Marquis," whispered Rube Fellows, one of the boys that held him. "It's all in fun. Take it good-natured and they'll let you off light. They're only goin' to stretch you over the log an tan you eight or ten times with the leggin's. 'Twon't hurt much."

The Marquis, with an exclamation of anger, his white teeth gleaming, suddenly exhibited a surprising strength. He wrenched with his arms so violently that the four men were swayed and dragged many yards from the log. A cry of anger escaped him, and then Miss Sally, his eyes cleared of the tobacco, saw, and he immediately mixed with the struggling group.

But at that moment a loud "Hallo!" rang in their ears, and a buckboard drawn by a team of galloping mustangs spun into the camp-fire's circle of light. Every man turned to look, and what they saw drove from their minds all thoughts of carrying out Phonograph Davis's rather time-worn contribution to the evening's amusement. Bigger game than the Marquis was at hand, and his captors released him and stood staring at the approaching victim.

The buckboard and team belonged to Sam Holly, a cattleman from the Big Muddy. Sam was driving, and with him was a stout smooth-faced man, wearing a frock coat and a high silk hat. That was the county judge, Mr. Dave Hackett, candidate for re-election. Sam was escorting him about the county, among the camps, to shake up the sovereign voters.

The men got out, hitched the team to a mesquite, and walked toward the fire.

Instantly every man in camp, except the Marquis, Miss Sally, and Pink Saunders, who had to play host, uttered a frightful yell of assumed terror and fled on all sides into the darkness.

"Heavens alive!" exclaimed Hackett, "are we as ugly as that? How do you do, Mr. Saunders? Glad to see you again. What are you doing to my hat, Holly?"

"I was afraid of this hat," said Sam Holly, meditatively. He had taken the hat from Hackett's head and was holding it in his hand, looking dubiously around at the shadows beyond the firelight where now absolute stillness reigned. "What do you think, Saunders?"

Pink grinned.

"Better elevate it some," he said, in the tone of one giving disinterested advice. "The light ain't none too good. I wouldn't want it on my head."

Holly stepped upon the hub of a hind wheel of the grub wagon, and hung the hat upon a limb of a live-oak. Scarcely had his foot touched the ground when the crash of a dozen six-shooters split the air, and the hat fell to the ground riddled with bullets.

A hissing noise was heard as if from a score of rattlesnakes, and now the cow-punchers emerged on all sides from the darkness, stepping high, with ludicrously exaggerated caution, and "hist"-ing to one another to observe the utmost prudence in approaching. They formed a solemn wide circle about the hat, gazing at it in manifest alarm, and seized every few moments by little stampedes of panicky flight.

"It's the varmint," said one in awed tones, "that flits up and down in the low grounds at night, saying, 'Willie-wallo!' "

"It's the venemous Kypootum," proclaimed another. "It stings after it's dead, and hollers after it's buried."

"It's the chief of the hairy tribe," said Phonograph Davis. "But it's stone dead, now, boys."

"Don't you believe it," demurred Dry-Creek. "It's only 'possumin'.' It's the dreaded High-gollacum fantod from the forest. There's only one way to destroy its life."

He led forward Old Taller, the 240-pound cow-puncher. Old Taller placed the hat upright on the ground and solemnly sat upon it, crushing it as flat as a pancake.

Hackett had viewed these proceedings with wide-open eyes. Sam Holly saw that his anger was rising, and said to him:

"Here's where you win or lose, Judge. There

are sixty votes on the Diamond Cross. The boys are trying your mettle. Take it as a joke, and I don't think you'll regret it." And Hackett saw the point and rose to the occasion.

Advancing to where the slayers of the wild beast were standing above its remains and declaring it to be at last defunct, he said, with deep earnestness:

"Boys, I must thank you for this gallant rescue. While driving through the arroyo that cruel monster that you have so fearlessly and repeatedly slaughtered sprang upon us from the tree tops. To you I shall consider that I owe my life, and also, I hope, re-election to the office for which I am again a candidate. Allow me to hand you my card."

The cow-punchers, always so sober-faced while engaged in their monkey-shines, relaxed into a grin of approval.

But Phonograph Davis, his appetite for fun not yet appeased, had something more up his sleeve.

"Pardner," he said, addressing Hackett with grave severity, "many a camp would be down on you for turnin' loose a pernicious varmint like that in it; but, bein' as we all escaped without loss of life, we'll overlook it. You can play square with us if you'll do it."

"How's that?" asked Hackett suspiciously.

"You're authorized to perform the sacred rights and lefts of mattermony, air you not?"

"Well, yes," replied Hackett. "A marriage ceremony conducted by me would be legal."

"A wrong air to be righted in this here camp," said Phonograph, virtuously. "A aristocrat have slighted a 'umble but beautchoos female wat's pinin' for his affections. It's the jooty of the camp to drag forth the haughty descendant of a hundred—

or maybe a hundred and twenty-five—earls, even so at the p'int of a lariat, and jine him to the weepin' lady. Fellows! round up Miss Sally and the Marquis, there's goin' to be a weddin'."

This whim of Phonograph's was received with whoops of appreciation. The cow-punchers started to apprehend the principals of the proposed ceremony.

"Kindly prompt me," said Hackett, wiping his forehead, though the night was cool, "how far this thing is to be carried. And might I expect any further portions of my raiment to be mistaken for wild animals and killed?"

"The boys are livelier than usual to-night," said Saunders. "The ones they are talking about marrying are two of the boys—a herd rider and the cook. It's another joke. You and Sam will have to sleep here to-night anyway; p'rhaps you'd better see 'em through with it. Maybe they'll quiet down after that."

The matchmakers found Miss Sally seated on the tongue of the grub wagon, calmly smoking his pipe. The Marquis was leaning idly against one of the trees under which the supply tent was pitched.

Into this tent they were both hustled, and Phonograph, as master of ceremonies, gave orders for the preparations.

"You, Dry-Creek and Jimmy, and Ben and Taller—hump yourselves to the wildwood and rustle flowers for the blow-out—mesquite'll do—and get that Spanish dagger blossom at the corner of the horse corral for the bride to pack. You, Limpy, get out that red and yaller blanket of your'n for Miss Sally's skyirt. Marquis, you'll do 'thout fixin'; nobody don't ever look at the groom."

During their absurd preparation, the two principals were left alone for a few moments in the tent. The Marquis suddenly showed wild perturbation.

"This foolishness must not go on," he said, turning to Miss Sally a face white in the light of the lantern hanging to the ridge-pole.

"Why not?" said the cook, with an amused smile. "It's fun for the boys; and they've always let you off pretty light in their frolics. I don't mind it."

"But you don't understand," persisted the Marquis, pleadingly. "That man is county judge, and his acts are binding. I can't—oh, you don't know——"

The cook stepped forward and took the Marquis's hands.

"Sally Bascom," he said, "I KNOW!"

"You know!" faltered the Marquis, trembling. "And you—want to——"

"More than I ever wanted anything. Will you —here come the boys!"

The cow-punchers crowded in, laden with armfuls of decorations.

"Perfidous coyote!" said Phonograph, sternly, addressing the Marquis. "Air you willing to patch up the damage you've did this ere slab-sided but trustin' bunch o' calico by single-footin' easy to the altar, or will we have to rope ye, and drag you thar?"

The Marquis pushed back his hat, and leaned jauntily against some high-piled sacks of beans. His cheeks were flushed, and his eyes were shining.

"Go on with the rat killin'," said he.

A little while after a procession approached the tree under which Hackett, Holly, and Saunders were sitting smoking.

Limpy Walker was in the lead, extracting a doleful tune from his concertina. Next came the bride and groom. The cook wore the gorgeous Navajo blanket tied around his waist and carried in one hand the waxen-white Spanish dagger blossom as large as a peck-measure and weighing fifteen pounds. His hat was ornamented with mesquite branches and yellow ratama blooms. A resurrected mosquito bar served as a veil. After them stumbled Phonograph Davis, in the character of the bride's father, weeping into a saddle blanket with sobs that could be heard a mile away. The cow-punchers followed by twos, loudly commenting upon the bride's appearance in a supposed imitation of the audiences at fashionable weddings.

Hackett rose as the procession halted before him, and after a little lecture upon matrimony, asked:

"What are your names?"

"Sally and Charles," answered the cook.

"Join hands, Charles and Sally."

Perhaps there never was a stranger wedding. For, wedding it was, though only two of those present knew it.

When the ceremony was over, the cow-punchers gave one yell of congratulation and immediately abandoned their foolery for the night. Blankets were unrolled, and sleep became the paramount question.

The cook (divested of his decorations) and the Marquis lingered for a moment in the shadow of the grub wagon. The Marquis leaned her head against his shoulder.

"I didn't know what else to do," she was saying. "Father was gone, and we kids had to rustle. I had helped him so much with the cattle that I thought I'd turn cowboy. There wasn't anything else I could make a living at. I wasn't much stuck on it though, after I got here, and I'd have left only——"

"Only what?"

"You know. Tell me something. When did you first—what made you——"

"Oh, it was as soon as we struck the camp, when Saunders bawled out 'The Marquis and Miss Sally!' I saw how rattled you got at the name, and I had my sus——"

"Cheeky!" whispered the Marquis. "And why should you think that I thought he was calling me 'Miss Sally'?"

"Because," answered the cook, calmly, "I was the Marquis. My father was the Marquis of Borodale. But you'll excuse that, won't you, Sally? It really isn't my fault, you know."

XVI: SUPPLY AND DEMAND

FINCH keeps a hats-cleaned-by-electricity-while-you-wait establishment, nine feet by twelve, in Third Avenue. Once a customer, you are always his. I do not know his secret process, but every four days your hat needs to be cleaned again.

Finch is a leathern, sallow, slow-footed man, between twenty and forty. You would say he had been brought up a bushelman in Essex Street. When business is slack he likes to talk, so I had my hat cleaned even oftener than it deserved, hoping Finch might let me into some of the secrets of the sweat-shops.

One afternoon I dropped in and found Finch alone. He began to anoint my headpiece de Panama with his mysterious fluid that attracted dust and dirt like a magnet.

"They say the Indians weave 'em under water," said I, for a leader.

"Don't you believe it," said Finch. "No Indian or white man could stay under water that long. Say, do you pay much attention to politics? I see in the paper something about a law they've passed called 'the law of supply and demand.' "

I explained to him as well as I could that the reference was to a politico-economical law and not to a legal statute.

"I didn't know," said Finch. "I heard a good deal about it a year or so ago, but in a one-sided way."

"Yes," said I, "political orators use it a great deal. In fact, they never give it a rest. I suppose you heard some of those cart-tail fellows spouting on the subject over here on the east side."

"I heard it from a king," said Finch—"the white king of a tribe of Indians in South America."

I was interested but not surprised. The big city is like a mother's knee to many who have strayed far and found the roads rough beneath their uncertain feet. At dusk they come home and sit upon the doorstep. I know a piano player in a cheap café who has shot lions in Africa, a bell-boy who fought in the British army against the Zulus, an express-driver whose left arm had been cracked like a lobster's claw for a stewpot of Patagonian cannibals when the boat of his rescuers hove in sight. So a hat-cleaner who has been a friend of a king did not oppress me.

"A new band?" asked Finch, with his dry, barren smile.

"Yes," said I, "and half an inch wider." I had had a new band five days before.

"I meets a man one night," said Finch, beginning his story—"a man brown as snuff, with money in every pocket, eating schweiner-knuckel in Schlagel's. That was two years ago, when I was a hose-cart driver for No. 98. His discourse runs to the subject of gold. He says that certain mountains in a country down South that he calls Gaudymala is full of it. He says the Indians wash it out of the streams in plural quantities.

" 'Oh, Geronimo!' says I. 'Indians! There's no Indians in the South,' I tell him, 'except Elks, Maccabees, and the buyers for the fall dry-goods trade. The Indians are all on the reservations,' says I.

" 'I'm telling you this with reservations,' says he. They ain't Buffalo Bill Indians; they're squattier and more pedigreed. They call 'em Inkers and Aspics, and they was old inhabitants when Mazuma was king of Mexico. They wash the gold out of the mountain streams,' says the brown man, 'and fill quills with it; and then they empty 'em into red jars till they are full; and then they pack it in buckskin sacks of one arroba each—an arroba is twenty-five pounds—and store it in a stone house, with an engraving of a idol with marcelled hair, playing a flute, over the door.'

" 'How do they work off this unearth increment?' I asks.

" 'They don't,' says the man. 'It's a case of "Ill fares the land with the great deal of velocity where wealth accumulates and there ain't any reciprocity." '

"After this man and me got through our conversation which left him dry of information, I shook hands with him and told him I was sorry I couldn't believe him. And a month afterward I landed on the coast of this Gaudymala with $1,300 that I had been saving up for five years. I thought I knew what Indians liked, and I fixed myself accordingly. I loaded down four pack-mules with red woollen blankets, wrought-iron pails, jewelled side-combs for the ladies, glass necklaces, and safety-razors. I hired a black mozo, who was supposed to be a mule-driver and an interpreter too. It turned out that he could interpret mules all right, but he drove the English language much too hard. His name sounded like a Yale key when you push it in wrong side up, but I called him McClintock, which was close to the noise.

"Well, this gold village was forty miles up in the mountains, and it took us nine days to find it. But one afternoon McClintock led the other mules and myself over a rawhide bridge stretched across a precipice five thousand feet deep, it seemed to me. The hoofs of the beasts drummed on it just like before George M. Cohan makes his first entrance on the stage.

"This village was built of mud and stone, and had no streets. Some few yellow-and-brown persons popped their heads out-of-doors, looking about like Welsh rabbits with Worcester sauce on 'em. Out of the biggest house, that had a kind of porch around it, steps a big white man, red as a beet in colour, dressed in fine tanned deerskin clothes, with a gold chain around his neck, smoking a cigar. I've seen United States Senators of his style of features and build, also head-waiters and cops.

"He walks up and takes a look at us, while McClintock disembarks and begins to interpret to the lead mule while he smokes a cigarette.

" 'Hello, Buttinsky,' said the fine man to me. 'How did you get in the game? I didn't see you buy any chips. Who gave you the keys of the city?'

" 'I'm a poor traveller,' says I. 'Especially muleback. You'll excuse me. Do you run a hack line or only a bluff?'

" 'Segregate yourself from your pseudo-equine quadruped,' says he, 'and come inside.'

"He raises a finger, and a villager runs up.

" 'This man will take care of your outfit,' says he, 'and I'll take care of you.'

"He leads me into the biggest house, and sets out the chairs and a kind of a drink thc colour of milk. It was the finest room I ever saw. The stone walls was hung all over with silk shawls, and there was red and yellow rugs on the floor, and jars of red pottery and Angora goat skins, and enough bamboo furniture to misfurnish half a dozen seaside cottages.

" 'In the first place,' says the man, 'you want to know who I am. I'm sole lessee and proprietor of this tribe of Indians. They call me the Grand Yacuma, which is to say King or Main Finger of the bunch. I've got more power here than a chargé d'affaires, a charge of dynamite, and a charge account at Tiffany's combined. In fact, I'm the Big Stick, with as many extra knots on it as there is on the record run of the *Lusitania*. Oh, I read the papers now and then,' says he. 'Now, let's hear your entitlements,' he goes on, 'and the meeting will be open.'

" 'Well,' says I, 'I am known as one W. D. Finch. Occupation, capitalist. Address, 541 East Thirty-second——'

" 'New York,' chips in the Noble Grand. 'I know,' says he, grinning. 'It ain't the first time you've seen it go down on the blotter. I can tell by the way you hand it out. Well, explain "capitalist." '

"I tells this boss plain what I come for and how I come to came.

" 'Gold-dust?' says he, looking as puzzled as a baby that got a feather stuck on its molasses finger. 'That's funny. This ain't a gold-mining country. And you invested all your capital on a stranger's story? Well, well! These Indians of mine—they are the last of the tribe of Peches—are simple as children. They know nothing of the purchasing power of gold. I'm afraid you've been imposed on,' says he.

" 'Maybe so,' says I, 'but it sounded pretty straight to me.'

" 'W. D.,' says the King, all of a sudden, 'I'll give you a square deal. It ain't often I get to talk to a white man, and I'll give you a show for your money. It may be these constituents of mine have a few grains of gold-dust hid away in their clothes. To-morrow you may get out these goods you've brought up and see if you can make any sales. Now, I'm going to introduce myself unofficially. My name is Shane—Patrick Shane. I own this tribe of Peche Indians by right of conquest—single handed and unafraid. I drifted up here four years ago, and won 'em by my size and complexion and nerve. I learned their language in six weeks—it's easy; you simply emit a string of consonants as long as your breath holds out and then point at what you're asking for.

" 'I conquered 'em, spectacularly,' goes on King Shane, 'and then I went at 'em with economical politics, law, sleight-of-hand, and a kind of New England ethics and parsimony. Every Sunday, or as near as I can guess at it, I preach to 'em in the council-house (I'm the council) on the law of supply and demand. I praise supply and knock demand. I use the same text every time. You wouldn't think, W. D.,' says Shane, 'that I had poetry in me, would you?'

" 'Well,' says I, 'I wouldn't know whether to call it poetry or not.'

" 'Tennyson,' says Shane, 'furnishes the poetic gospel I preach. I always considered him the boss poet. Here's the way the text goes:

"For, not to admire, if a man could learn it, were more
Than to walk all day like a Sultan of old in a garden of spice."

" 'You see, I teach 'em to cut out demand—that supply is the main thing. I teach 'em not to desire anything beyond their simplest needs. A little mutton, a little cocoa, and a little fruit brought up from the coast—that's all they want to make 'em happy. I've got 'em well trained. They make their own clothes and hats out of a vegetable fibre and straw, and they're a contented lot. It's a great thing,' winds up Shane, 'to have made a people happy by the incultivation of such simple institutions.'

"Well, the next day, with the King's permission, I has the McClintock open up a couple of sacks of my goods in the little plaza of the village. The Indians swarmed around by the hundred and looked the bargain-counter over. I shook red blankets at 'em, flashed finger-rings and ear-bobs, tried pearl necklaces and side-combs on the women, and a line of red hosiery on the men. 'Twas no use. They looked on like hungry graven images, but I never made a sale. I asked McClintock what was the trouble. Mac yawned three or four times, rolled a cigarette, made one or two confidential side remarks to a mule, and then condescended to inform me that the people had no money.

"Just then up strolls King Patrick, big and red, and royal as usual, with the gold chain over his chest and his cigar in front of him.

" 'How's business, W. D.?' he asks.

" 'Fine,' says I. 'It's a bargain-day rush. I've got one more line of goods to offer before I shut up shop. I'll try 'em with safety-razors. I've got two gross that I bought at a fire sale.'

"Shane laughs till some kind of mameluke or private secretary he carries with him has to hold him up.

" 'O my sainted Aunt Jerusha!' says he, 'ain't you one of the Babes in the Goods, W. D.? Don't you know that no Indians ever shave? They pull out their whiskers instead.'

" 'Well,' says I, 'that's just what these razors would do for 'em—they wouldn't have any kick coming if they used 'em once.'

"Shane went away, and I could hear him laughing a block, if there had been any block.

" 'Tell 'em,' says I to McClintock, 'it ain't money I want—tell 'em I'll take gold-dust. Tell 'em I'll allow 'em sixteen dollars an ounce for it in trade. That's what I'm out for—the dust.'

"Mac interprets, and you'd have thought a

squadron of cops had charged the crowd to disperse it. Every uncle's nephew and aunt's niece of 'em faded away inside of two minutes.

"At the royal palace that night me and the King talked it over.

" 'They've got the dust hid out somewhere,' says I, 'or they wouldn't have been so sensitive about it.'

" 'They haven't,' says Shane. 'What's this gag you've got about gold? You been reading Edward Allan Poe? They ain't got any gold.'

" 'They put it in quills,' says I, 'and then they empty it in jars, and then into sacks of twenty-five pounds each. I got it straight.'

" 'W. D.,' says Shane, laughing and chewing his cigar, 'I don't often see a white man, and I feel like putting you on. I don't think you'll get away from here alive, anyhow, so I'm going to tell you. Come over here.'

"He draws aside a silk fibre curtain in a corner of the room and shows me a pile of buckskin sacks.

" 'Forty of 'em,' says Shane. 'One arroba in each one. In round numbers, $220,000 worth of gold-dust you see there. It's all mine. It belongs to the Grand Yacuma. They bring it all to me. Two hundred and twenty thousands dollars—think of that, you glass-bead peddler,' says Shane—'and all mine.'

" 'Little good it does you,' says I, contemptuously and hatefully. 'And so you are the government depository of this gang of moneyless money-makers? Don't you pay enough interest on it to enable one of your depositors to buy an Augusta (Maine) Pullman carbon diamond worth $200 for $4.85?'

" 'Listen,' says Patrick Shane, with the sweat

coming out on his brow. 'I'm confident with you, as you have, somehow, enlisted my regards. Did you ever,' he says, 'feel the avoirdupois power of gold—not the troy weight of it, but the sixteen-ounces-to-the-pound force of it?'

"'Never,' says I. 'I never take in any bad money.'

"Shane drops down on the floor and throws his arms over the sacks of gold-dust.

"'I love it,' says he. 'I want to feel the touch of it day and night. It's my pleasure in life. I come in this room, and I'm a king and a rich man. I'll be a millionaire in another year. The pile's getting bigger every month. I've got the whole tribe washing out the sands in the creeks. I'm the happiest man in the world, W. D. I just want to be near this gold, and know it's mine and it's increasing every day. Now, you know,' says he, 'why my Indians wouldn't buy your goods. They can't. They bring all the dust to me. I'm their king. I've taught 'em not to desire or admire. You might as well shut up shop.'

"'I'll tell you what you are,' says I. 'You're a plain, contemptible miser. You preach supply and you forget demand. Now, supply,' I goes on, 'is never anything but supply. On the contrary,' says I, 'demand is a much broader syllogism and assertion. Demand includes the rights of our women and children, and charity and friendship, and even a little begging on the street corners. They've both got to harmonize equally. And I've got a few things up my commercial sleeve yet,' says I, 'that may jostle your preconceived ideas of politics and economy.'

"The next morning I had McClintock bring up

another mule-load of goods to the plaza and open it up. The people gathered around the same as before.

"I got out the finest line of necklaces, bracelets, haircombs, and earrings that I carried, and had the women put 'em on. And then I played trumps.

"Out of my last pack I opened up a half gross of hand-mirrors, with solid tinfoil backs, and passed 'em around among the ladies. That was the first introduction of looking-glasses among the Peche Indians.

"Shane walks by with his big laugh.

" 'Business looking up any?' he asks.

" 'It's looking at itself right now,' says I.

"By and by a kind of a murmur goes through the crowd. The women had looked into the magic crystal and seen that they were beautiful, and was confiding the secret to the men. The men seemed to be urging the lack of money and the hard times just before the election, but their excuses didn't go.

"Then was my time.

"I called McClintock away from an animated conversation with his mules and told him to do some interpreting.

" 'Tell 'em,' says I, 'that gold-dust will buy for them these befitting ornaments for kings and queens of the earth. Tell 'em the yellow sand they wash out of the waters for the High Sanctified Yacomay and Chop Suey of the tribe will buy the precious jewels and charms that will make them beautiful and preserve and pickle them from evil spirits. Tell 'em the Pittsburg banks are paying four per cent. interest on deposits by mail, while this get-rich-frequently custodian of the public funds ain't even paying attention. Keep telling 'em, Mac,' says I, 'to let the gold-dust family do their work. Talk to 'em like a born anti-Bryanite,' says I. 'Remind 'em that Tom Watson's gone back to Georgia,' says I.

"McClintock waves his hand affectionately at one of his mules, and then hurls a few stickfuls of minion type at the mob of shoppers.

"A gutta-percha Indian man, with a lady hanging on his arm, with three strings of my fish-scale jewellery and imitation marble beads around her neck, stands up on a block of stone and makes a talk that sounds like a man shaking dice in a box to fill aces and sixes.

" 'He says,' says McClintock, 'that the people not know that gold-dust will buy their things. The women very mad. The Grand Yacuma tell them it no good but for keep to make bad spirits keep away.'

" 'You can't keep bad spirits away from money,' says I.

" 'They say,' goes on McClintock, 'the Yacuma fool them. They raise plenty row.'

" 'Going! Going!' says I. 'Gold-dust or cash takes the entire stock. The dust weighed before you, and taken at sixteen dollars the ounce—the highest price on the Gaudymala coast.'

"Then the crowd disperses all of a sudden, and I don't know what's up. Mac and me packs away the hand-mirrors and jewellery they had handed back to us, and we had the mules back to the corral they had set apart for our garage.

"While we was there we hear great noises of shouting, and down across the plaza runs Patrick Shane, hotfoot, with his clothes ripped half off, and scratches on his face like a cat had fought him hard for every one of its lives.

" 'They're looting the treasury, W. D.,' he sings out. 'They're going to kill me and you, too. Unlimber a couple of mules at once. We'll have to make a getaway in a couple of minutes.'

" 'They've found out,' says I, 'the truth about the law of supply and demand.'

" 'It's the women, mostly,' says the King. 'And they used to admire me so!'

" 'They hadn't seen looking-glasses then,' says I.

" 'They've got knives and hatchets,' says Shane; 'hurry!'

" 'Take that roan mule,' says I. 'You and your law of supply! I'll ride the dun, for he's two knots per hour the faster. The roan has a stiff knee, but he may make it,' says I. 'If you'd included reciprocity in your political platform I might have given you the dun,' says I.

"Shane and McClintock and me mounted our mules and rode across the rawhide bridge just as the Peches reached the other side and began firing stones and long knives at us. We cut the thongs that held up our end of the bridge and headed for the coast."

A tall, bulky policeman came into Finch's shop at that moment and leaned an elbow on the showcase. Finch nodded at him friendly.

"I heard down at Casey's," said the cop, in rumbling, husky tones, "that there was going to be a picnic of the Hat-Cleaners' Union over at Bergen Beach, Sunday. Is that right?"

"Sure," said Finch. "There'll be a dandy time."

"Gimme five tickets," said the cop, throwing a five-dollar bill on the showcase.

"Why," said Finch, "ain't you going it a little too——"

"Go to h——!" said the cop. "You got 'em to sell, ain't you? Somebody's got to buy 'em. Wish I could go along."

I was glad to see Finch so well thought of in his neighbourhood.

And then in came a wee girl of seven, with dirty face and pure blue eyes and a smutched and insufficient dress.

"Mumma says," she recited shrilly, "that you must give me eighty cents for the grocer and nineteen for the milkman and five cents for me to buy hokey-pokey with—but she didn't say that," the elf concluded, with a hopeful but honest grin.

Finch shelled out the money, counting it twice, but I noticed that the total sum that the small girl received was one dollar and four cents.

"That's the right kind of a law," remarked Finch as he carefully broke some of the stitches of my hatband so that it would assuredly come off within a few days—"the law of supply and demand. But they've both got to work together. I'll bet," he went on, with his dry smile, "she'll get jelly beans with that nickel—she likes 'em. What's supply if there's no demand for it?"

"Whatever became of the King?" I asked, curiously.

"Oh, I might have told you," said Finch. "That was Shane came in and bought the tickets. He came back with me, and he's on the force now."

XVII: AN ADJUSTMENT OF NATURE

IN an art exhibition the other day I saw a painting that had been sold for $5,000. The painter was a young scrub out of the West named Kraft, who had a favourite food and a pet theory. His pabulum was an unquenchable belief in the Unerring Artistic Adjustment of Nature. His theory was fixed around corned-beef hash with poached egg. There was a story behind the picture, so I went home and let it drip out of a fountain-pen. The idea of Kraft—but that is not the beginning of the story.

Three years ago Kraft, Bill Judkins (a poet), and I took our meals at Cypher's, on Eighth Avenue. I say "took." When we had money, Cypher got it "off of" us, as he expressed it. We had no credit; we went in, called for food and ate it. We paid or we did not pay. We had confidence in Cypher's sullenness and smouldering ferocity. Deep down in his sunless soul he was either a prince, a fool, or an artist. He sat at a worm-eaten desk, covered with files of waiters' checks so old that I was sure the bottomest one was for claims that Hendrik Hudson had eaten and paid for. Cypher had the power, in common with Napoleon III and the goggle-eyed perch, of throwing a film over his eyes, rendering opaque the windows of his soul. Once when we left him unpaid, with egregious excuses, I looked back and saw him shaking with inaudible laughter behind his film. Now and then we paid up back scores.

But the chief thing at Cypher's was Milly. Milly was a waitress. She was a grand example of

Kraft's theory of the Artistic Adjustment of Nature. She belonged, largely, to waiting, as Minerva did to the art of scrapping, or Venus to the science of serious flirtation. Pedestalled and in bronze she might have stood with the noblest of her heroic sisters as "Liver-and-Bacon Enlivening the World." She belonged to Cypher's. You expected to see her colossal figure loom through that reeking blue cloud of smoke from frying fat just as you expect the Palisades to appear through a drifting Hudson River fog. There amid the steam of vegetables and the vapours of acres of "ham and," the crash of crockery, the clatter of steel, the screaming of "short orders," the cries of the hungering and all the horrid tumult of feeding man, surrounded by swarms of the buzzing winged beasts bequeathed us by Pharaoh, Milly steered her magnificent way like some great liner cleaving among the canoes of howling savages.

Our Goddess of Grub was built on lines so majestic that they could be followed only with awe. Her sleeves were always rolled above her elbows. She could have taken us three musketeers in her two hands and dropped us out of the window. She had seen fewer years than any of us, but she was of such superb Evehood and simplicity that she mothered us from the beginning. Cypher's store of eatables she poured out upon us with royal indifference to price and quantity, as from a cornucopia that knew no exhaustion. Her voice rang like a great silver bell; her smile was many-toothed and frequent; she seemed like a yellow sunrise on mountain-tops. I never saw her but I thought of the Yosemite. And yet, somehow, I could never think of her as existing outside of Cypher's. There Nature had placed her, and she had taken root and grown mightily. She seemed happy, and took her few poor dollars on Saturday nights with the flushed pleasure of a child that receives an unexpected donation.

It was Kraft who first voiced the fear that each of us must have held latently. It came up apropos, of course, of certain questions of art at which we were hammering. One of us compared the harmony existing between a Haydn symphony and pistache ice-cream to the exquisite congruity between Milly and Cypher's.

"There is a certain fate hanging over Milly," said Kraft, "and if it overtakes her she is lost to Cypher's and to us."

"She will grow fat?" asked Judkins fearsomely.

"She will go to night school and become refined?" I ventured anxiously.

"It is this," said Kraft, punctuating in a puddle of spilled coffee with a stiff forefinger. "Cæsar had his Brutus—the cotton has its bollworm, the chorus girl has her Pittsburger, the summer boarder has his poison ivy, the hero has his Carnegie medal, art has its Morgan, the rose has its——"

"Speak," I interrupted, much perturbed. "You do not think that Milly will begin to lace?"

"One day," concluded Kraft solemnly, "there will come to Cypher's for a plate of beans a millionaire lumberman from Wisconsin, and he will marry Milly."

"Never!" exclaimed Judkins and I, in horror.

"A lumberman," repeated Kraft hoarsely.

"And a millionaire lumberman!" I sighed despairingly.

"From Wisconsin!" groaned Judkins.

We agreed that the awful fate seemed to menace her. Few things were less improbable. Milly, like some vast virgin stretch of pine woods, was made to catch the lumberman's eye. And well we knew the habits of the Badgers, once fortune smiled upon them. Straight to New York they hie, and lay their goods at the feet of the girl who serves them beans in a beanery. Why, the alphabet itself connives. The Sunday newspaper's head-liner's work is cut for him.

"Winsome Waitress Wins Wealthy Wisconsin Woodsman."

For awhile we felt that Milly was on the verge of being lost to us.

It was our love of the unerring Artistic Adjustment of Nature that inspired us. We could not give her over to a lumberman, doubly accursed by wealth and provincialism. We shuddered to think of Milly, with her voice modulated and her elbows covered, pouring tea in the marble teepee of a tree murderer. No! In Cypher's she belonged —in the bacon smoke, the cabbage perfume, the grand, Wagnerian chorus of hurled iron-stone china and rattling casters.

Our fears must have been prophetic, for on that same evening the wildwood discharged upon us Milly's preordained confiscator—our fee to adjustment and order. But Alaska and not Wisconsin bore the burden of the visitation.

We were at our supper of beef stew and dried apples when he trotted in as if on the heels of a dog-team, and made one of the mess at our table. With the freedom of the camps he assaulted our ears and claimed the fellowship of men lost in the wilds of a hash-house. We embraced him as a specimen, and in three minutes we had all but died for one another as friends.

He was rugged and bearded and wind-dried. He had just come off the "trail," he said, at one of the North River ferries. I fancied I could see the snow-dust of Chilcoot yet powdering his shoulders. And then he strewed the table with the nuggets, stuffed ptarmigans, bead work and seal pelts of the returned Klondiker, and began to prate to us of his millions.

"Bank drafts for two millions," was his summing up, "and a thousand a day piling up from my claims. And now I want some beef stew and canned peaches. I never got off the train since I mushed out of Seattle, and I'm hungry. The stuff the niggers feed you on Pullmans don't count. You gentlemen order what you want."

And then Milly loomed up with a thousand dishes on her bare arm—loomed up big and white and pink and awful as Mount Saint Elias—with a smile like day breaking in a gulch. And the Klondiker threw down his pelts and nuggets as dross, and let his jaw fall half-way, and stared at her. You could almost see the diamond tiaras on Milly's brow and the hand-embroidered silk Paris gowns that he meant to buy for her.

At last the bollworm had attacked the cotton—the poison ivy was reaching out its tendrils to entwine the summer boarder—the millionaire lumberman, thinly disguised as the Alaskan miner, was about to engulf our Milly and upset Nature's adjustment.

Kraft was the first to act. He leaped up and pounded the Klondiker's back. "Come out and drink," he shouted. "Drink first and eat afterward." Judkins seized one arm and I the other. Gaily, roaringly, irresistibly, in jolly-good-fellow style, we dragged him from the restaurant to a café, stuffing his pockets with his embalmed birds and indigestible nuggets.

There he rumbled a roughly good-humoured protest. "That's the girl for my money," he declared. "She can eat out of my skillet the rest of her life. Why, I never see such a fine girl. I'm going back there and ask her to marry me. I guess she won't want to sling hash any more when she sees the pile of dust I've got."

"You'll take another whisky and milk now," Kraft persuaded, with Satan's smile. "I thought you up-country fellows were better sports."

Kraft spent his puny store of coin at the bar and then gave Judkins and me such an appealing look that we went down to the last dime we had in toasting our guest.

Then, when our ammunition was gone and the Klondiker, still somewhat sober, began to babble again of Milly, Kraft whispered into his ear such a polite, barbed insult relating to people who were miserly with their funds, that the miner crashed down handful after handful of silver and notes, calling for all the fluids in the world to drown the imputation.

Thus the work was accomplished. With his own guns we drove him from the field. And then we had him carted to a distant small hotel and put to bed with his nuggets and baby seal-skins stuffed around him.

"He will never find Cypher's again," said Kraft. "He will propose to the first white apron he sees in a dairy restaurant to-morrow. And Milly—I mean the Natural Adjustment—is saved!"

And back to Cypher's went we three, and, finding customers scarce, we joined hands and did an Indian dance with Milly in the centre.

This, I say, happened three years ago. And about that time a little luck descended upon us three, and we were enabled to buy costlier and less wholesome food than Cypher's. Our paths separated, and I saw Kraft no more and Judkins seldom.

But, as I said, I saw a painting the other day that was sold for $5,000. The title was "Boadicea," and the figure seemed to fill all out-of-doors. But of all the picture's admirers who stood before it, I believe I was the only one who longed for Boadicea to stalk from her frame, bringing me corned-beef hash with poached egg.

I hurried away to see Kraft. His satanic eyes were the same, his hair was worse tangled, but his clothes had been made by a tailor.

"I didn't know," I said to him.

"We've bought a cottage in the Bronx with the money," said he. "Any evening at seven."

"Then," said I, "when you led us against the lumberman—the—Klondiker—it wasn't altogether on account of the Unerring Artistic Adjustment of Nature?"

"Well, not altogether," said Kraft, with a grin.

XVIII: HELPING THE OTHER FELLOW

"But can thim that helps others help thimselves?"
—*Mulvaney*.

I

THIS is the story that William Trotter told me on the beach at Aguas Frescas while I waited for the gig of the captain of the fruit steamer *Andador*, which was to take me aboard. Reluctantly I was leaving the Land of Always Afternoon. William was remaining, and he favoured me with a condensed oral autobiography as we sat on the sands in the shade cast by the Bodega Naçional.

As usual, I became aware that the Man from Bombay had already written the story; but as he had compressed it to an eight-word sentence, I have become an expansionist, and have quoted his phrase above, with apologies to him and best regards to *Terence*.

II

"Don't you ever have a desire to go back to the land of derby hats and starched collars?" I asked him. "You seem to be a handy man and a man of action," I continued, "and I am sure I could find you a comfortable job somewhere in the States."

Ragged, shiftless, barefooted, a confirmed eater of the lotos, William Trotter had pleased me much, and I hated to see him gobbled up by the tropics.

"I've no doubt you could," he said, idly splitting thc bark from a section of sugar-cane. "I've no doubt you could do much for me. If every man could do as much for himself as he can for others, every country in the world would be holding millenniums instead of centennials."

There seemed to be pabulum in W. T.'s words. And then another idea came to me.

I had a brother in Chicopee Falls who owned manufactories—cotton, or sugar, or A.A. sheetings, or something in the commercial line. He was vulgarly rich, and therefore reverenced art. The artistic temperament of the family was monopolized at my birth. I knew that Brother James would honour my slightest wish. I would demand from him a position in cotton, sugar, or sheetings for William Trotter—something, say, at two hundred a month or thereabouts. I confided my beliefs and made my large propositions to William. He had pleased me much, and he was ragged.

While we were talking, there was a sound of firing guns—four or five, rattlingly, as if by a squad. The cheerful noise came from the direction of the cuartel, which is a kind of makeshift barracks for the soldiers of the republic.

"Hear that?" said William Trotter. "Let me tell you about it.

"A year ago I landed on this coast with one solitary dollar. I have the same sum in my pocket to-day. I was second cook on a tramp fruiter; and they marooned me here early one morning, without benefit of clergy, just because I poulticed the face of the first mate with cheese omelette at dinner. The fellow had kicked because I'd put horseradish in it instead of cheese.

"When they threw me out of the yawl into three feet of surf, I waded ashore and sat down under a palm-tree. By and by a fine-looking white man with a red face and white clothes, genteel as possible, but somewhat under the influence, came and sat down beside me.

"I had noticed there was a kind of a village back of the beach, and enough scenery to outfit a dozen moving-picture shows. But I thought, of course, it was a cannibal suburb, and I was wondering whether I was to be served with carrots or mushrooms. And, as I say, this dressed-up man sits beside me, and we become friends in the space of a minute or two. For an hour we talked, and he told me all about it.

"It seems that he was a man of parts, conscientiousness, and plausibility, besides being educated and a wreck to his appetites. He told me all about it. Colleges had turned him out, and distilleries had taken him in. Did I tell you his name? It was Clifford Wainwright. I didn't exactly catch the cause of his being cast away on that particular stretch of South America; but I reckon it was his own business. I asked him if he'd ever been second cook on a tramp fruiter, and he said no; so that concluded my line of surmises. But he talked like the encyclopedia from 'A—Berlin' to 'Trilo—Zyria.' And he carried a watch—a silver arrangement with works, and up to date within twenty-four hours, anyhow.

" 'I'm pleased to have met you,' says Wainwright. 'I'm a devotee to the great joss Booze; but my ruminating facilities are unrepaired,' says he—or words to that effect. 'And I hate,' says he, 'to see fools trying to run the world.'

" 'I never touch a drop,' says I, 'and there are many kinds of fools; and the world runs on its own apex, according to science, with no meddling from me.'

" 'I was referring,' says he, 'to the president of this republic. His country is in a desperate condition. Its treasury is empty, it's on the verge of war with Nicamala, and if it wasn't for the hot weather the people would be starting revolutions in every town. Here is a nation,' goes on Wainwright, 'on the brink of destruction. A man of intelligence could rescue it from its impending doom in one day by issuing the necessary edicts and orders. President Gomez knows nothing of statesmanship or policy. Do you know Adam Smith?'

" 'Lemme see,' says I. 'There was a one-eared man named Smith in Fort Worth, Texas, but I think his first name was——'

" 'I am referring to the political economist,' says Wainwright.

" 'S'mother Smith, then,' says I. 'The one I speak of never was arrested.'

"So Wainwright boils some more with indignation at the insensibility of people who are not corpulent to fill public positions; and then he tells me he is going out to the president's summer palace, which is four miles from Aguas Frescas, to instruct him in the art of running steam-heated republics.

" 'Come along with me, Trotter,' says he, 'and I'll show you what brains can do.'

" 'Anything in it?' I asks.

" 'The satisfaction,' says he, 'of redeeming a country of two hundred thousand population from ruin back to prosperity and peace.'

" 'Great,' says I. 'I'll go with you. I'd prefer to eat a live broiled lobster just now; but give me liberty as second choice if I can't be in at the death.'

"Wainwright and me permeates through the town, and he halts at a rum-dispensary.

" 'Have you any money?' he asks.

" 'I have,' says I, fishing out my silver dollar. 'I always go about with adequate sums of money.'

" 'Then we'll drink,' says Wainwright.

" 'Not me,' says I. 'Not any demon rum or any of its ramifications for mine. It's one of my non-weaknesses.'

" 'It's my failing,' says he. 'What's your particular soft point?'

" 'Industry,' says I, promptly. 'I'm hard-working, diligent, industrious, and energetic.'

" 'My dear Mr. Trotter,' says he, 'surely I've known you long enough to tell you you are a liar. Every man must have his own particular weakness, and his own particular strength in other things. Now, you will buy me a drink of rum, and we will call on President Gomez.' "

III

"Well, sir," Trotter went on, "we walks the four miles out, through a virgin conservatory of palms and ferns and other roof-garden products, to the president's summer White House. It was blue, and reminded you of what you see on the stage in the third act, which they describe as 'same as the first,' on the programmes.

"There was more than fifty people waiting outside the iron fence that surrounded the house and grounds. There was generals and agitators and épergnes in gold-laced uniforms, and citizens in diamonds and Panama hats—all waiting to get an audience with the Royal Five-Card Draw. And in a kind of a summer-house in front of the mansion we could see a burnt-sienna man eating breakfast out of gold dishes and taking his time. I judged that the crowd outside had come out for their morning orders and requests, and was afraid to intrude.

"But C. Wainwright wasn't. The gate was open, and he walked inside and up to the president's table as confident as a man who knows the head waiter in a fifteen-cent restaurant. And I went with him, because I had only seventy-five cents, and there was nothing else to do.

"The Gomez man rises from his chair, and looks, coloured man as he was, like he was about to call out for a corporal of the guard, post number one.

But Wainwright says some phrases to him in a peculiarly lubricating manner; and the first thing you know we was all three of us seated at the table, with coffee and rolls and iguana cutlets coming as fast as about ninety peons could rustle 'em.

"And then Wainwright begins to talk; but the president interrupts him.

" 'You Yankees,' says he, polite, 'assuredly take the cake for assurance, I assure you'—or words to that effect. He spoke English better than you or me. 'You've had a long walk,' says he, 'but it's nicer in the cool morning to walk than to ride. May I suggest some refreshments?' says he.

" 'Rum,' says Wainwright.

" 'Gimme a cigar,' says I.

"Well, sir, the two talked an hour, keeping the generals and equities all in their good uniforms waiting outside the fence. And while I smoked, silent, I listened to Clifford Wainwright making a solid republic out of the wreck of one. I didn't follow his arguments with any special collocation of international intelligibility, but he had Mr. Gomez's attention glued and riveted. He takes out a pencil and marks the white linen tablecloth all over with figures and estimates and deductions. He speaks more or less disrespectfully of import and export duties and custom-house receipts and taxes and treaties and budgets and concessions and such truck that politics and government require; and when he gets through the Gomez man hops up and shakes his hand and says he's saved the country and the people.

" 'You shall be rewarded,' says the president.

" 'Might I suggest another—rum?' says Wainwright.

" 'Cigar for me—darker brand,' says I.

"Well, sir, the president sent me and Wainwright back to the town in a victoria hitched to two flea-bitten selling-platers—but the best the country afforded.

"I found out afterwards that Wainwright was a regular beachcomber—the smartest man on the whole coast, but kept down by rum. I liked him.

"One day I inveigled him into a walk out a couple of miles from the village, where there was an old grass hut on the bank of a little river. While he was sitting on the grass, talking beautiful of the wisdom of the world that he had learned in books, I took hold of him easy and tied his hands and feet together with leather thongs that I had in my pocket.

" 'Lie still,' says I, 'and meditate on the exigencies and irregularities of life till I get back.'

"I went to a shack in Aguas Frescas where a mighty wise girl named Timotea Carrizo lived with her mother. The girl was just about as nice as you ever saw. In the States she would have been called a brunette; but she was better than a brunette—I should say she was what you might term an écru shade. I knew her pretty well. I told her about my friend Wainwright. She gave me a double handful of bark—calisaya, I think it was—and some more herbs that I was to mix with it, and told me what to do. I was to make tea of it and give it to him, and keep him from rum for a certain time. And for two weeks I did it. You know, I liked Wainwright. Both of us was broke; but Timotea sent us goat-meat and plantains and tortillas every day; and at last I got the curse of drink lifted from Clifford Wainwright. He lost his taste for it. And in the cool of the evening him and me would sit on the roof of Timotea's mother's hut, eating harmless truck like toffee and rice and stewed crabs, and playing the accordion.

"About that time President Gomez found out that the advice of C. Wainwright was the stuff he had been looking for. The country was pulling out of debt, and the treasury had enough boodle in it for him to amuse himself occasionally with the night-latch. The people were beginning to take their two-hour siestas again every day—which was the surest sign of prosperity.

"So down from the regular capital he sends for Clifford Wainwright and makes him his private secretary at twenty thousand Peru dollars a year. Yes, sir—so much. Wainwright was on the water-wagon—thanks to me and Timotea—and he was soon in clover with the government gang. Don't forget what done it—calisaya bark with them other herbs mixed—make a tea of it, and give a cupful every two hours. Try it yourself. It takes away the desire.

"As I said, a man can do a lot more for another party than he can for himself. Wainwright, with his brains, got a whole country out of trouble and on its feet; but what could he do for himself? And without any special brains, but with some nerve and common sense, I put him on his feet because I never had the weakness that he did—nothing but a cigar for mine, thanks. And——"

Trotter paused. I looked at his tattered clothes and at his deeply sunburnt, hard, thoughtful face.

"Didn't Cartwright ever offer to do anything for you?" I asked.

"Wainwright," corrected Trotter. "Yes, he offered me some pretty good jobs. But I'd have had to leave Aguas Frescas; so I didn't take any of 'em up. Say, I didn't tell you much about that girl—Timotea. We rather hit it off together. She was as good as you find 'em anywhere—Spanish, mostly, with just a twist of lemon-peel on top. What if they did live in a grass hut and went bare-armed?

"A month ago," went on Trotter, "she went away. I don't know where to. But——"

"You'd better come back to the States," I insisted. "I can promise you positively that my brother will give you a position in cotton, sugar, or sheetings—I am not certain which."

"I think she went back with her mother," said Trotter, "to the village in the mountains that they come from. Tell me, what would this job you speak of pay?"

"Why," said I, hesitating over commerce, "I should say fifty or a hundred dollars a month—maybe two hundred."

"Ain't it funny," said Trotter, digging his toes in the sand, "what a chump a man is when it comes to paddling his own canoe? I don't know. Of course, I'm not making a living here. I'm on the bum. But—well, I wish you could have seen that Timotea. Every man has his own weak spot."

The gig from the *Andador* was coming ashore to take out the captain, purser, and myself, the lone passenger. "I'll guarantee," said I confidently, "that my brother will pay you seventy-five dollars a month."

"All right, then," said William Trotter. "I'll——"

But a soft voice called across the blazing sands. A girl, faintly lemon-tinted, stood in the Calle Real and called. She was bare-armed—but what of that?

"It's her!" said William Trotter, looking. "She's come back! I'm obliged, but I can't take the job. Thanks, just the same. Ain't it funny how we can't do nothing for ourselves, but we can do wonders for the other fellow? You was about to get me with your financial propositions; but we've all got our weak points. Timotea's mine. And, say!" Trotter had turned to leave, but he retraced the step or two that he had taken. "I like to have left you without saying good-bye," said he. "It kind of rattles you when they go away unexpected for a month and come back the same way. Shake hands. So long! Say, do you remember them gunshots we heard a while ago up at the cuartel? Well, I knew what they was, but I didn't mention it. It was Clifford Wainwright being shot by a squad of soldiers against a stone wall for giving away secrets of state to that Nicamala republic. Oh, yes, it was rum that did it. He backslided and got his. I guess we all have our weak points, and can't do much toward helping ourselves. Mine's waiting for me. I'd have liked to have that job with your brother, but—we've all got our weak points. So long!"

IV

A big black Carib carried me on his back through the surf to the ship's boat. On the way the purser handed me a letter that he had brought for me at the last moment from the post office in Aguas Frescas. It was from my brother. He requested me to meet him at the St. Charles Hotel in New Orleans and accept a position with his house—in either cotton, sugar, or sheetings, and with five thousand dollars a year as my salary.

When I arrived at the Crescent City I hurried away—far away from the St. Charles to a dim *chambre garnie* in Bienville Street. And there, looking down from my attic window from time to time at the old, yellow, absinthe house across the street, I wrote this story to buy my bread and butter.

"Can thim that helps others help thimselves?"

XIX: THE CALIPH AND THE CAD

SURELY there is no pastime more diverting than that of mingling, incognito, with persons of wealth and station. Where else but in those circles can one see life in its primitive, crude state, unhampered by the conventions that bind the dwellers in a lower sphere?

There was a certain Caliph of Bagdad who was accustomed to go down among the poor and lowly for the solace obtained from the relation of their tales and histories. Is it not strange that the humble and poverty-stricken have not availed themselves of the pleasure they might glean by donning diamonds and silks and playing Caliph among the haunts of the upper world?

There was one who saw the possibilities of thus turning the tables on Haroun al Raschid. His name was Corny Brannigan, and he was a truck driver for a Canal Street importing firm. And if you read further you will learn how he turned upper Broadway into Bagdad and learned something about himself that he did not know before.

Many people would have called Corny a snob—preferably by means of a telephone. His chief interest in life, his chosen amusement, and his sole diversion after working hours, was to place himself in juxtaposition—since he could not hope to mingle—with people of fashion and means.

Every evening after Corny had put up his team and dined at a lunch-counter that made immediateness a speciality, he would clothe himself in evening raiment as correct as any you will see in the palm rooms. Then he would betake himself to that ravishing, radiant roadway devoted to Thespis, Thaïs, and Bacchus.

For a time he would stroll about the lobbies of the best hotels, his soul steeped in blissful content. Beautiful women, cooing like doves, but feathered like birds of Paradise, flicked him with their robes as they passed. Courtly gentlemen attended them, gallant and assiduous. And Corny's heart within him swelled like Sir Lancelot's, for the mirror spoke to him as he passed and said: "Corny, lad, there's not a guy among 'em that looks a bit the sweller than yerself. And you drivin' of a truck and them swearin' off their taxes and playin' the red in art galleries with the best in the land!"

And the mirrors spake the truth. Mr. Corny Brannigan had acquired the outward polish, if nothing more. Long and keen observation of polite society had gained for him its manner, its genteel air, and—most difficult of acquirement—its repose and ease.

Now and then in the hotels Corny had managed conversation and temporary acquaintance with substantial, if not distinguished, guests. With many of these he had exchanged cards, and the ones he received he carefully treasured for his own use later. Leaving the hotel lobbies, Corny would stroll leisurely about, lingering at the theatre entrance, dropping into the fashionable restaurants as if seeking some friend. He rarely patronized any of these places; he was no bee come to suck honey, but a butterfly flashing his wings among the flowers whose calyces held no sweets for him. His wages were not large enough to furnish him with more than the outside garb of the gentleman. To have been one of the beings he so cunningly imitated, Corny Brannigan would have given his right hand.

One night Corny had an adventure. After absorbing the delights of an hour's lounging in the principal hotels along Broadway, he passed up into the stronghold of Thespis. Cab drivers hailed him as a likely fare, to his prideful content. Languishing eyes were turned upon him as a hopeful source of lobsters and the delectable, ascendant globules of effervescence. These overtures and unconscious compliments Corny swallowed as manna, and hoped Bill, the off horse, would be less lame in the left forefoot in the morning.

Beneath a cluster of milky globes of electric light Corny paused to admire the sheen of his low-cut patent leather shoes. The building occupying the angle was a pretentious café. Out of this came a couple, a lady in a white, cobwebby evening gown, with a lace wrap like a wreath of mist thrown over it, and a man, tall, faultless, assured—too assured. They moved to the edge of the sidewalk and halted. Corny's eye, ever alert for "pointers" in "swell" behaviour, took them in with a sidelong glance.

"The carriage is not here," said the lady. "You ordered it to wait?"

"I ordered it for nine-thirty," said the man. "It should be here now."

A familiar note in the lady's voice drew a more especial attention from Corny. It was pitched in a key well known to him. The soft electric shone upon her face. Sisters of sorrow have no quarters fixed for them. In the index to the book of breaking hearts you will find that Broadway follows very soon after the Bowery. This lady's face was sad, and her voice was attuned with it. They waited, as if for the carriage. Corny waited too, for it was out of doors, and he was never tired of accumulating and profiting by knowledge of gentlemanly conduct.

"Jack," said the lady, "don't be angry. I've done everything I could to please you this evening. Why do you act so?"

"Oh, you're an angel," said the man. "Depend upon woman to throw the blame upon a man."

"I'm not blaming you. I'm only trying to make you happy."

"You go about it in a very peculiar way."

"You have been cross with me all the evening without any cause."

"Oh, there isn't any cause except—you make me tired."

Corny took out his card case and looked over his collection. He selected one that read: "Mr. White, of Kensington, London." This card he had inveigled from a tourist at the King Edward Hotel. Corny stepped up to the man and presented it with a correctly formal air.

"May I ask why I am selected for the honour?" asked the lady's escort.

Now, Mr. Corny Brannigan had a very wise habit of saying little during his imitations of the

Caliph of Bagdad. The advice of Lord Chesterfield, "Wear a black coat and hold your tongue," he believed in without having heard. But now speech was demanded and required of him.

"No gent," said Corny, "would talk to a lady like you done. Fie upon you, Willie ! Even if she happens to be your wife you ought to have more respect for your clothes than to chin her back that way. Maybe it ain't my butt-in, but it goes, anyhow—you strike me as bein' a whole lot to the wrong."

The lady's escort indulged in more elegantly expressed but fetching repartee. Corny, eschewing his truck driver's vocabulary, retorted as nearly as he could in polite phrases. Then diplomatic relations were severed; there was a brief but lively set-to with other than oral weapons, from which Corny came forth easily victor.

A carriage dashed up, driven by a tardy and solicitous coachman.

"Will you kindly open the door for me?" asked the lady. Corny assisted her to enter, and took off his hat. The escort was beginning to scramble up from the sidewalk.

"I beg your pardon, ma'am," said Corny, "if he's your man."

"He's no man of mine," said the lady. "Perhaps he—but there's no chance of his being now. Drive home, Michael. If you care to take this—with my thanks."

Three red roses were thrust through the carriage window into Corny's hand. He took them, and the hand for an instant; and then the carriage sped away.

Corny gathered his foe's hat and began to brush the dust from his clothes.

"Come along," said Corny, taking the other man by the arm.

His late opponent was yet a little dazed by the hard knocks he had received. Corny led him carefully into a saloon three doors away.

"The drinks for us," said Corny, "me and my friend."

"You're a queer feller," said the lady's late escort—"lick a man and then want to set 'em up."

"You're my best friend," said Corny exultantly. "You don't understand? Well, listen. You just put me wise to somethin'. I been playin' gent a long time, thinkin' it was just the glad rags I had and nothin' else. Say—you're a swell, ain't you? Well, you trot in that class, I guess. I don't; but I found out one thing—I'm a gentleman, by ——, and I know it now. What'll you have to drink?"

XX: CUPID À LA CARTE

"THE dispositions of woman," said Jeff Peters, after various opinions on the subject had been advanced, "run, regular, to diversions. What a woman wants is what you're out of. She wants more of a thing when it's scarce. She likes to have souvenirs of things that never happened. She likes to be reminded of things she never heard of. A one-sided view of objects is disjointing to the female composition.

" 'Tis a misfortune of mine, begotten by nature and travel," continued Jeff, looking thoughtfully between his elevated feet at the grocery stove, "to look deeper into some subjects than most people do. I've breathed gasoline smoke talking to street crowds in nearly every town in the United States. I've held 'em spellbound with music, oratory, sleight of hand, and prevarications, while I've sold 'em jewellery, medicine, soap, hair tonic, and junk of other nominations. And during my travels, as a matter of recreation and expiation, I've taken cognisance some of women. It takes a man a lifetime to fall out about one particular woman; but if he puts in, say, ten years, industrious and curious, he can acquire the general rudiments of the sex. One lesson I picked up was when I was working the West with a line of Brazilian diamonds and a patent fire kindler just after my trip from Savannah down through the cotton belt with Dalby's Anti-explosive Lamp Oil Powder. 'Twas when the Oklahoma country was in first bloom. Guthrie was rising in the middle of it like a lump of self-raising dough. It was a boom town of the regular kind—you stood in line to get a chance to wash your face; if you ate over ten minutes you had a lodging bill added on; if you slept on a plank at night they charged it to you as board the next morning.

"By nature and doctrines I am addicted to the habit of discovering choice places wherein to feed. So I looked around and found a proposition that exactly cut the mustard. I found a restaurant tent just opened up by an outfit that had drifted in on the tail of the boom. They had knocked together a box house, where they lived and did the cooking, and served the meals in a tent pitched against the side. That tent was joyful with placards on it calculated to redeem the world-worn pilgrim from the sinfulness of boarding-houses and pick-me-up hotels. 'Try Mother's Home-Made Biscuits,' 'What's the Matter with Our Apple Dumplings and Hard Sauce?' 'Hot Cakes and Maple Syrup Like You Ate When a Boy,' 'Our Fried Chicken Never Was Heard to Crow'—there was literature doomed to please the digestions of man! I said to myself that mother's wandering boy should munch there that night. And so it came to pass. And there is where I contracted my case of Mame Dugan.

"Old Man Dugan was six feet by one of Indiana loafer, and he spent his time sitting on his shoulder-blades in a rocking-chair in the shanty memorializing the great corn-crop failure of '86. Ma Dugan did the cooking, and Mame waited on the table.

"As soon as I saw Mame I knew there was a mistake in the census reports. There wasn't but one girl in the United States. When you come to specifications it isn't easy. She was about the size of an angel, and she had eyes, and ways about her. When you come to the kind of a girl she was, you'll find a belt of 'em reaching from the Brooklyn Bridge west as far as the courthouse in Council Bluffs, Ia. They earn their own living in stores, restaurants, factories, and offices. They're descended straight from Eve, and they're the crowd that's got woman's rights, and if a man wants to dispute it he's in line to get one of them against his jaw. They're chummy and honest and free and tender and sassy, and they look life straight in the eye. They've met man face to face, and discovered that he's a poor creature. They've dropped to it that the reports in the Seaside Library about his being a fairy prince lack confirmation.

"Mame was that sort. She was full of life and

fun, and breezy; she passed the repartee with the boarders quick as a wink; you'd have smothered laughing. I am disinclined to make excavations into the insides of a personal affection. I am glued to the theory that the diversions and discrepancies of the indisposition known as love should be as private a sentiment as a toothbrush. 'Tis my opinion that the biographies of the heart should be confined with the historical romances of the liver to the advertising pages of the magazines. So, you'll excuse the lack of an itemized bill of my feelings toward Mame.

"Pretty soon I got a regular habit of dropping into the tent to eat at irregular times when there wasn't so many around. Mame would sail in with a smile, in a black dress and white apron, and say: 'Hallo, Jeff—why don't you come at meal-time? Want to see how much trouble you can be, of course. Friedchickenbeefsteakporkpiechopshamandeggspotpie'—and so on. She called me Jeff, but there was no significations attached. Designations was all she meant. The front names of any of us she used as they came to hand. I'd eat about two meals before I left, and string 'em out like a society spread where they change plates and wives, and josh one another festively between bites. Mame stood for it, pleasant, for it wasn't up to her to take any canvas off the tent by declining dollars just because they were chipped in after meal-times.

"It wasn't long until there was another fellow named Ed Collier got the between-meals affliction, and him and me put in bridges between breakfast and dinner, and dinner and supper, that made a three-ringed circus of that tent, and Mame's turn as waiter a continuous performance. That Collier man was saturated with designs and contrivings. He was in well-boring or insurance or claim-jumping, or something—I've forgotten which. He was a man well lubricated with gentility, and his words were such as recommended you to his point of view. So, Collier and me infested the grub tent with care and activity. Mame was level full of impartiality. 'Twas like a casino hand the way she dealt out her favours—one to Collier and one to me and one to the board, and not a card up her sleeve.

"Me and Collier naturally got acquainted, and gravitated together some on the outside. Divested of his stratagems, he seemed to be a pleasant chap, full of an amiable sort of hostility.

" 'I notice you have an affinity for grubbing in the banquet hall after the guests have fled,' says I to him one day, to draw his conclusions.

" 'Well, yes,' says Collier, reflecting; 'the tumult of a crowded board seems to harass my sensitive nerves.'

" 'It exasperates mine some, too,' says I. 'Nice little girl, don't you think?'

" 'I see,' says Collier, laughing. 'Well, now that you mention it, I have noticed that she doesn't seem to displease the optic nerve.'

" 'She's a joy to mine,' says I, 'and I'm going after her. Notice is hereby served.'

" 'I'll be as candid as you,' admits Collier, 'and if the drug stores don't run out of pepsin I'll give you a run for your money that'll leave you a dyspeptic at the wind-up.'

"So Collier and me begins the race; the grub department lays in new supplies; Mame waits on us, jolly and kind and agreeable, and it looks like an even break, with Cupid and the cook working overtime in Dugan's restaurant.

"'Twas one night in September when I got Mame to take a walk after supper when the things were all cleared away. We strolled out a distance and sat on a pile of lumber at the edge of town. Such opportunities was seldom, so I spoke my piece, explaining how the Brazilian diamonds and the fire kindler were laying up sufficient treasure to guarantee the happiness of two, and that both of 'em together couldn't equal the light from somebody's eyes, and that the name of Dugan should be changed to Peters, or reasons why not would be in order.

"Mame didn't say anything right away. Directly she gave a kind of shudder, and I began to learn something.

"'Jeff,' she says, 'I'm sorry you spoke. I like you as well as any of them, but there isn't the man in the world I'd ever marry, and there never will be. Do you know what a man is in my eye? He's a tomb. He's a sarcophagus for the interment of Beefsteakporkchopsliver'nbaconhamandeggs. He's that and nothing more. For two years I've watched men eat, eat, eat, until they represent nothing on earth to me but ruminant bipeds. They're absolutely nothing but something that goes in front of a knife and fork and plate at the table. They're fixed that way in my mind and memory. I've tried to overcome it, but I can't. I've heard girls rave about their sweethearts, but I never could understand it. A man and a sausage grinder and a pantry awake in me exactly the same sentiments. I went to a matinée once to see an actor the girls were crazy about. I got interested enough to wonder whether he liked his steak rare, medium, or well done, and his eggs over or straight up. That was all. No, Jeff; I'll marry no man and see him sit at the breakfast-table and eat, and come back to dinner and eat, and happen in again at supper to eat, eat, eat.'

" 'But, Mame,' says I, 'it'll wear off. You've had too much of it. You'll marry some time, of course. Men don't eat always.'

" 'As far as my observation goes, they do. No, I'll tell you what I'm going to do.' Mame turns, sudden, to animation and bright eyes. 'There's a girl named Susie Foster in Terre Haute, a chum of mine. She waits in the railroad eating-house there. I worked two years in a restaurant in that town. Susie has it worse than I do, because the men who eat at railroad stations gobble. They try to flirt and gobble at the same time. Whew! Susie and I have it all planned out. We're saving our money, and when we get enough we're going to buy a little cottage and five acres we know of, and live together, and grow violets for the Eastern market. A man better not bring his appetite within a mile of that ranch.'

" 'Don't girls ever——' I commenced, but Mame heads me off, sharp.

" 'No, they don't. They nibble a little bit sometimes; that's all.'

" 'I thought the confect——'

" 'For goodness' sake, change the subject,' says Mame.

"As I said before, that experience put me wise that the feminine arrangement ever struggles after deceptions and illusions. Take England—beef made her; wieners elevated Germany; Uncle Sam owes his greatness to fried chicken and pie, but the young ladies of the Shetalkyou schools, they'll never believe it. Shakespeare, they allow, and Rubinstein, and the Rough Riders is what did the trick.

" 'Twas a situation calculated to disturb. I couldn't bear to give up Mame; and yet it pained me to think of abandoning the practice of eating. I had acquired the habit too early. For twenty-seven years I had been blindly rushing upon my fate, yielding to the insidious lures of that deadly monster, food. It was too late. I was a ruminant biped for keeps. It was lobster salad to a doughnut that my life was going to be blighted by it.

"I continued to board at the Dugan tent, hoping that Mame would relent. I had sufficient faith in true love to believe that since it has often outlived the absence of a square meal it might, in time, overcome the presence of one. I went on ministering to my fatal vice, although I felt that each time I shoved a potato into my mouth in Mame's presence I might be burying my fondest hopes.

"I think Collier must have spoken to Mame and got the same answer, for one day he orders a cup of coffee and a cracker, and sits nibbling the corner of it like a girl in the parlour, that's filled up in the kitchen, previous, on cold roast and fried cabbage. I caught on and did the same, and maybe we thought we'd made a hit! The next day we tried it again, and out comes old man Dugan fetching in his hands the fairy viands.

" 'Kinder off yer feed, ain't ye, gents?' he asks, fatherly and some sardonic. 'Thought I'd spell

Mame a bit, seein' the work was light, and my rheumatiz can stand the strain.'

"So back me and Collier had to drop to the heavy grub again. I noticed about that time that I was seized by a most uncommon and devastating appetite. I ate until Mame must have hated to see me darken the door. Afterward I found out that I had been made the victim of the first dark and irreligious trick played on me by Ed Collier. Him and me had been taking drinks together up town regular, trying to drown our thirst for food. That man had bribed about ten bar-tenders to always put a big slug of Appletree's Anaconda Appetite Bitters in every one of my drinks. But the last trick he played me was hardest to forget.

"One day Collier failed to show up at the tent. A man told me he left town that morning. My only rival now was the bill of fare. A few days before he left Collier had presented me with a two-gallon jug of fine whisky which he said a cousin had sent him from Kentucky. I now have reason to believe that it contained Appletree's Anaconda Appetite Bitters almost exclusively. I continued to devour tons of provisions. In Mame's eyes I remained a mere biped, more ruminant than ever.

"About a week after Collier pulled his freight there came a kind of side-show to town, and hoisted a tent near the railroad. I judged it was a sort of fake museum and curiosity business. I called to see Mame one night, and Ma Dugan said she and Thomas, her younger brother, had gone to the show. That same thing happened for three nights that week. Saturday night I caught her on the way coming back, and got to sit on the steps a while and talk to her. I noticed she looked different. Her eyes were softer, and shiny like. Instead of a Mame Dugan to fly from the voracity of man and raise violets, she seemed to be a Mame more in line as God intended her, approachable, and suited to bask in the light of the Brazilians and the Kindler.

" 'You seem to be right smart inveigled,' says I, 'with the Unparalleled Exhibition of the World's Living Curiosities and Wonders.'

" 'It's a change,' says Mame.

" 'You'll need another,' says I, 'if you keep on going every night.'

" 'Don't be cross, Jeff,' says she, 'it takes my mind off business.'

" 'Don't the curiosities eat?' I ask.

" 'Not all of them. Some of them are wax.'

" 'Look out, then, that you don't get stuck,' says I, kind of flip and foolish.

"Mame blushed. I didn't know what to think about her. My hopes raised some that perhaps my attentions had palliated man's awful crime of visibly introducing nourishment into his system. She talked some about the stars, referring to them with respect and politeness, and I drivelled a quantity about united hearts, homes made bright by true affection, and the Kindler. Mame listened without scorn, and I says to myself, 'Jeff, old man, you're removing the hoodoo that has clung to the consumer of victuals; you're setting your heel upon the serpent that lurks in the gravy bowl.'

"Monday night I drop around. Mame is at the Unparalleled Exhibition with Thomas.

" 'Now, may the curse of the forty-one seven-sided sea cooks,' says I, 'and the bad luck of the nine impenitent grasshoppers rest upon this self-same side-show at once and for ever more. Amen. I'll go to see it myself to-morrow night and investigate its baleful charm. Shall man that was made to inherit the earth be bereft of his sweetheart first by a knife and fork and then by a ten-cent circus?'

"The next night before starting out for the exhibition tent I inquire and find out that Mame is not at home. She is not at the circus with Thomas this time, for Thomas waylays me in the grass outside of the grub tent with a scheme of his own before I had time to eat supper.

" 'What'll you give me, Jeff,' says he, 'if I tell you something?'

" 'The value of it, son,' I says.

" 'Sis is stuck on a freak,' says Thomas, 'one of the side-show freaks. I don't like him. She does. I overheard 'em talking. Thought maybe you'd like to know. Say, Jeff, does it put you wise two dollars' worth? There's a target rifle up town that——'

"I frisked my pockets and commenced to dribble a stream of halves and quarters into Thomas's hat. The information was of the pile-driver system of news, and it telescoped my intellects for a while. While I was leaking small change and smiling foolish on the outside, and suffering disturbances internally, I was saying, idiotically and pleasantly—

" 'Thank you, Thomas—thank you—er—a freak, you said, Thomas. Now, could you make out the monstrosity's entitlements a little clearer, if you please, Thomas?'

" 'This is the fellow,' says Thomas, pulling out a yellow handbill from his pocket and shoving it under my nose. 'He's the Champion Faster of the Universe, I guess that's why Sis got soft on him. He don't eat nothing. He's going to fast forty-nine days. This is the sixth. That's him.'

"I looked at the name Thomas pointed out—'Professor Eduardo Collieri.' 'Ah!' says I, in admiration, 'that's not so bad, Ed Collier. I give you credit for the trick. But I don't give you the girl until she's Mrs. Freak.'

"I hit the sod in the direction of the show. I came up to the rear of the tent, and, as I did so, a man wiggled out like a snake from under the bottom of the canvas, scrambled to his feet, and ran into me like a locoed bronco. I gathered him by the neck and investigated him by the light of the stars. It is Professor Eduardo Collieri, in human habiliments, with a desperate look in one eye and impatience in the other.

" 'Hallo, Curiosity,' says I. 'Get still a minute and let's have a look at your freakship. How do you like being the willopus-wallopus or the bim-bam from Borneo, or whatever name you are denounced by in the side-show business?'

" 'Jeff Peters,' says Collier, in a weak voice. 'Turn me loose, or I'll slug you one. I'm in the extremest kind of a large hurry. Hands off!'

" 'Tut, tut, Eddie,' I answers, holding him hard; 'let an old friend gaze on the exhibition of your curiousness. It's an eminent graft you fell onto, my son. But don't speak of assaults and battery, because you're not fit. The best you've got is a lot of nerve and a mighty empty stomach.' And so it was. The man was as weak as a vegetarian cat.

" 'I'd argue this case with you, Jeff,' says he,

regretful in his style, 'for an unlimited number of rounds if I had half an hour to train in and a slab of beefsteak two feet square to train with. Curse the man, I say, that invented the art of going foodless. May his soul in eternity be chained up within two feet of a bottomless pit of red-hot hash. I'm abandoning the conflict, Jeff; I'm deserting to the enemy. You'll find Miss Dugan inside contemplating the only living mummy and the informed hog. She's a fine girl, Jeff. I'd have beat you if I could have kept up the grubless habit a little while longer. You'll have to admit that the fasting dodge was aces up for a while. I figured it out that way. But, say, Jeff, it's said that love makes the world go around. Let me tell you, the announcement lacks verification. It's the wind from the dinner horn that does it. I love that Mame Dugan. I've gone six days without food in order to coincide with her sentiments. Only one bite did I have. That was when I knocked the tattooed man down with a war club and got a sandwich he was gobbling. The manager fined me all my salary; but salary wasn't what I was after. 'Twas that girl. I'd give my life for her, but I'd endanger my immortal soul for a beef stew. Hunger is a horrible thing, Jeff. Love and business and family and religion and art and patriotism are nothing but shadows of words when a man's starving!'

"In such language Ed Collier discoursed to me, pathetic. I gathered the diagnosis that his affections and his digestions had been implicated in a scramble and the commissary had won out. I never disliked Ed Collier. I searched my internal admonitions of suitable etiquette to see if I could find a remark of a consoling nature, but there was none convenient.

" 'I'd be glad, now,' says Ed, 'if you'll let me go. I've been hard hit, but I'll hit the ration supply harder. I'm going to clean out every restaurant in town. I'm going to wade waist deep in sirloins and swim in ham and eggs. It's an awful thing, Jeff Peters, for a man to come to this pass—to give up his girl for something to eat—it's worse than that man Esau, that swapped his copyright for a partridge—but then, hunger's a fierce thing. You'll excuse me, now, Jeff, for I smell a pervasion of ham frying in the distance, and my legs are crying out to stampede in that direction.'

" 'A hearty meal to you, Ed Collier,' I says to him, 'and no hard feelings. For myself, I am projected to be an unseldom eater, and I have condolence for your predicaments.'

"There was a sudden big whiff of frying ham smell on the breeze; and the champion Faster gives a snort and gallops off in the dark toward fodder.

"I wish some of the cultured outfit that are always advertising the extenuating circumstances of love and romance had been there to see. There was Ed Collier, a fine man full of contrivances and flirtations, abandoning the girl of his heart and ripping out into the contiguous territory in the pursuit of sordid grub. 'Twas a rebuke to the poets and a slap at the best-paying element of fiction. An empty stomach is a sure antidote to an overfull heart.

"I was naturally anxious to know how far Mame was infatuated with Collier and his stratagems. I went inside the Unparalleled Exhibition, and there she was. She looked surprised to see me, but unguilty.

"'It's an elegant evening outside,' says I. 'The coolness is quite nice and gratifying, and the stars are lined out, first class, up where they belong. Wouldn't you shake these by-products of the animal kingdom long enough to take a walk with a common human who never was on a programme in his life?'

"Mame gave a sort of sly glance around, and I knew what that meant.

"'Oh,' says I, 'I hate to tell you; but the curiosity that lives on wind has flew the coop. He just crawled out under the tent. By this time he has amalgamated himself with half the delicatessen truck in town.'

"'You mean Ed Collier?' says Mame.

"'I do,' I answers; 'and a pity it is that he has gone back to crime again. I met him outside the tent, and he exposed his intentions of devastating the food crop of the world. 'Tis enormously sad when one's ideal descends from his pedestal to make a seventeen-year locust of himself.'

"Mame looked me straight in the eye until she had corkscrewed my reflections.

"'Jeff,' says she, 'it isn't quite like you to talk that way. I don't care to hear Ed Collier ridiculed. A man may do ridiculous things, but they don't look ridiculous to the girl he does 'em for. That was one man in a hundred. He stopped eating just to please me. I'd be hardhearted and ungrateful if I didn't feel kindly toward him. Could you do what he did?'

"'I know,' says I, seeing the point, 'I'm condemned. I can't help it. The brand of the consumer is upon my brow. Mrs. Eve settled that business for me when she made the dicker with the snake. I fell from the fire into the frying-pan. I guess I'm the Champion Feaster of the Universe.' I spoke humble, and Mame mollified herself a little.

" 'Ed Collier and I are good friends,' she said, 'the same as me and you. I gave him the same answer I did you—no marrying for me. I liked to be with Ed and talk with him. There was something mighty pleasant to me in the thought that here was a man who never used a knife and fork, and all for my sake.'

" 'Wasn't you in love with him?' I asks, all injudicious. 'Wasn't there a deal on for you to become Mrs. Curiosity?'

"All of us do it sometimes. All of us get jostled out of the line of profitable talk now and then. Mame put on that little lemon *glacé* smile that runs between ice and sugar, and says, much too pleasant: 'You're short on credentials for asking that question, Mr. Peters. Suppose you do a forty-nine-day fast, just to give you ground to stand on, and then maybe I'll answer it.'

"So, even after Collier was kidnapped out of the way by the revolt of his appetite, my own prospects with Mame didn't seem to be improved. And then business played out in Guthrie.

"I had stayed too long there. The Brazilians I had sold commenced to show signs of wear, and the Kindler refused to light up right frequent on wet mornings. There is always a time, in my business, when the star of success says, 'Move on to the next town.' I was travelling by wagon at that time so as not to miss any of the small towns; so I hitched up a few days later and went down to tell Mame good-bye. I wasn't abandoning the game; I intended running over to Oklahoma City and work it for a week or two. Then I was coming back to institute fresh proceedings against Mame.

"What do I find at the Dugans' but Mame all conspicuous in a blue travelling dress, with her little trunk at the door. It seems that sister Lottie Bell, who is a typewriter in Terre Haute, is going to be married next Thursday, and Mame is off for a week's visit to be an accomplice at the ceremony. Mame is waiting for a freight wagon that is going to take her to Oklahoma, but I condemns the freight wagon with promptness and scorn, and offers to deliver the goods myself. Ma Dugan sees no reason why not, as Mr. Freighter wants pay for the job; so, thirty minutes later, Mame and I pull out in my light spring wagon with white canvas cover, and head due south.

"That morning was of a praiseworthy sort. The breeze was lively, and smelled excellent of flowers and grass, and the little cotton-tail rabbits entertained themselves with skylarking across the road. My two Kentucky bays went for the horizon until it come sailing in so fast you wanted to dodge it like a clothes-line. Mame was full of talk and rattled on like a kid about her old home and her school pranks and the things she liked and the hateful ways of those Johnson girls just across the street, 'way up in Indiana. Not a word was said about Ed Collier or victuals or such solemn subjects. About noon Mame looks and finds that the lunch she had put up in a basket had been left behind. I could have managed quite a coltation, but Mame didn't seem to be grieving over nothing to eat, so I made no lamentations. It was a sore subject with me, and I ruled provender in all its branches out of my conversation.

"I am minded to touch light on explanations how I came to lose the way. The road was dim and well grown with grass; and there was Mame by my side confiscating my intellects and attention. The excuses are good or they are not, as they may appear to you. But I lost it, and at dusk that afternoon, when we should have been in Oklahoma City, we were seesawing along the edge of nowhere in some undiscovered river bottom, and the rain was falling in large, wet bunches. Down there in the swamps we saw a little log house on a small knoll of high ground. The bottom grass and the chaparral and the lonesome timber crowded all around it. It seemed to be a melancholy little house, and you felt sorry for it. 'Twas that house for the night, the way I reasoned it. I explained to Mame, and she leaves it to me to decide. She doesn't become galvanic and prosecuting, as most women would, but she says it's all right; she knows I didn't mean to do it.

"We found the house was deserted. It had two empty rooms. There was a little shed in the yard where beasts had once been kept. In a loft of it was a lot of old hay. I put my horses in there and gave them some of it, for which they looked at me sorrowful, expecting apologies. The rest of the hay I carried into the house by armfuls, with a view to accommodations. I also brought in the patent kindler and the Brazilians, neither of which are guaranteed against the action of water.

"Mame and I sat on the wagon seats on the

floor, and I lit a lot of the kindler on the hearth, for the night was chilly. If I was any judge, that girl enjoyed it. It was a change for her. It gave her a different point of view. She laughed and talked, and the kindler made a dim light compared to her eyes. I had a pocketful of cigars, and as far as I was concerned there had never been any fall of man. We were at the same old stand in the Garden of Eden. Out there somewhere in the rain and the dark was the river of Zion, and the angel with the flaming sword had not yet put up the keep-off-the-grass sign. I opened up a gross or two of the Brazilians and made Mame put them on—rings, brooches, necklaces, ear-drops, bracelets, girdles, and lockets. She flashed and sparkled like a million-dollar princess until she had pink spots in her cheeks and almost cried for a looking-glass.

"When it got late I made a fine bunk on the floor for Mame with the hay and my lap robes and blankets out of the wagon, and persuaded her to lie down. I sat in the other room burning tobacco and listening to the pouring rain and meditating on the many vicissitudes that come to a man during the seventy years or so immediately preceding his funeral.

"I must have dozed a little before morning, for my eyes were shut, and when I opened them it was daylight, and there stood Mame with her hair all done up neat and correct, and her eyes bright with admiration of existence.

" 'Gee whiz, Jeff!' she exclaims, 'but I'm hungry. I could eat a——'

"I looked up and caught her eye. Her smile went back in and she gave me a cold look of suspicion. Then I laughed, and laid down on the floor to laugh easier. It seemed funny to me. By nature and geniality I am a hearty laugher, and I went the limit. When I came to, Mame was sitting with her back to me, all contaminated with dignity.

" 'Don't be angry, Mame,' I says, 'for I couldn't help it. It's the funny way you've done up your hair. If you could only see it!'

" 'You needn't tell stories, sir,' said Mame, cool and advised. 'My hair is all right. I know what you were laughing about. Why, Jeff, look outside,' she winds up, peeping through a chink between the logs. I opened the little wooden window and looked out. The entire river bottom was flooded, and the knob of land on which the house stood was an island in the middle of a rushing stream of yellow water a hundred yards wide. And it was still raining hard. All we could do was to stay there till the dove brought in the olive branch.

"I am bound to admit that conversations and amusements languished during that day. I was aware that Mame was getting a too prolonged one-sided view of things again, but I had no way to change it. Personally, I was wrapped up in a desire to eat. I had hallucinations of hash and visions of ham, and I kept saying to myself all the time, 'What'll you have to eat, Jeff?—what'll you order, now, old man, when the waiter comes?' I picks out to myself all sorts of favourites from the bill of fare, and imagines them coming. I guess it's that way with all very hungry men. They can't get their cogitations trained on anything but something to eat. It shows that the little table with the broken-legged caster and the imitation Worcester sauce and the napkin covering up the coffee stains is the paramount issue, after all, instead of the question of immortality or peace between nations.

"I sat there, musing along, arguing with myself quite heated as to how I'd have my steak—with mushrooms or *à la créole*. Mame was on the other seat, pensive, her head leaning on her hand. 'Let the potatoes come home-fried,' I states in my mind, 'and brown the hash in the pan, with nine poached eggs on the side.' I felt, careful, in my own pockets to see if I could find a peanut or a grain or two of pop-corn.

"Night came on again with the river still rising and the rain still falling. I looked at Mame and I noticed that desperate look on her face that a girl always wears when she passes an ice-cream lair. I knew that poor girl was hungry—maybe for the first time in her life. There was that anxious look in her eye that a woman has only when she has missed a meal or feels her skirt coming unfastened in the back.

"It was about eleven o'clock or so on the second night when we sat, gloomy, in our shipwrecked cabin. I kept jerking my mind away from the subject of food, but it kept flopping back again before I could fasten it. I thought of everything good to eat I had ever heard of. I went away back in my kidhood and remembered the hot biscuit sopped in sorghum and bacon gravy with partiality and respect. Then I trailed along up the years, pausing at green apples and salt, flap-jacks and maple, lye hominy, fried chicken Old Virginia style, corn on the cob, spare-ribs and sweet potato pie, and wound up with Georgia Brunswick stew, which is the top notch of good things to eat, because it comprises 'em all.

"They say a drowning man sees a panorama of his whole life pass before him. Well, when a man's starving he sees the ghost of every meal he ever ate set out before him, and he invents new dishes that would make the fortune of a chef. If somebody would collect the last words of men who starved to death they'd have to sift 'em mighty fine to discover the sentiment, but they'd compile into a cook book that would sell into the millions.

"I guess I must have had my conscience pretty well inflicted with culinary meditations, for, without intending to do so, I says, out loud, to the imaginary waiter, 'Cut it thick, with the French fried, and six, soft-scrambled, on toast.'

"Mame turned her head quick as a wink. Her eyes were sparkling and she smiled sudden.

" 'Medium done for me,' she rattles out, 'with the Juliennes. Oh, Jeff, wouldn't it be glorious! And then I'd like to have a half fry, and a little chicken curried with rice, and a cup custard with ice cream, and——'

" 'Go easy,' I interrupts; 'where's the chicken liver pie, and the kidney *sauté* on toast, and the roast lamb, and——'

" 'Oh,' cuts in Mame, all excited, 'with mint sauce, and the turkey salad, and stuffed olives, and raspberry tarts, and——'

" 'Keep it going,' says I. 'Hurry up with the fried squash, and the hot corn pone with sweet milk, and don't forget the apple dumpling with hard sauce, and the cross-barred dewberry pie——'

"Yes, for ten minutes we kept up that kind of

restaurant repartee. We ranges up and down and backward and forward over the main trunk lines and the branches of the victual subject, and Mame leads the game, for she is apprised in the ramifications of grub, and the dishes she nominates aggravates my yearnings. It seems that there is set up a feeling that Mame will line up friendly again with food. It seems that she looks upon the obnoxious science of eating with less contempt than before.

"The next morning we find that the flood has subsided. I geared up the bays, and we splashed out through the mud, some precarious, until we found the road again. We were only a few miles wrong, and in two hours we were in Oklahoma City. The first thing we saw was a big restaurant sign, and we piled into there in a hurry. Here I finds myself sitting with Mame at table, with knives and forks and plates between us, and she not scornful, but smiling with starvation and sweetness.

"'Twas a new restaurant and well stocked. I designated a list of quotations from the bill of fare that made the waiter look out toward the wagon to see how many more might be coming.

"There we were, and there was the order being served. 'Twas a banquet for a dozen, but we felt like a dozen. I looked across the table at Mame and smiled, for I had recollections. Mame was looking at the table like a boy looks at his first stem-winder. Then she looked at me, straight in the face, and two big tears came in her eyes. The waiter was gone after more grub.

"'Jeff,' she says, soft like, 'I've been a foolish girl. I've looked at things from the wrong side.

I never felt this way before. Men get hungry every day like this, don't they? They're big and strong, and they do the hard work of the world, and they don't eat just to spite silly waiter girls in restaurants, do they, Jeff? You said once—that is, you asked me—you wanted me to—well, Jeff, if you still care—I'd be glad and willing to have you always sitting across the table from me. Now give me something to eat, quick, please.'

"So, as I've said, a woman needs to change her point of view now and then. They get tired of the same old sights—the same old dinner-table, washtub, and sewing machine. Give 'em a touch of the various—a little travel and a little rest, a little tomfoolery along with the tragedies of keeping house, a little petting after the blowing-up, a little upsetting and jostling around—and everybody in the game will have chips added to their stack by the play."

XXI: ACCORDING TO THEIR LIGHTS

SOMEWHERE in the depths of the big city, where the unquiet dregs are for ever being shaken together, young Murray and the Captain had met and become friends. Both were at the lowest ebb possible to their fortunes; both had fallen from at least an intermediate Heaven of respectability and importance, and both were typical products of the monstrous and peculiar social curriculum of their overweening and bumptious civic Alma Mater.

The Captain was no longer a captain. One of

those sudden moral cataclysms that sometimes sweep the city had hurled him from a high and profitable position in the Police Department, ripping off his badge and buttons and washing into the hands of his lawyers the solid pieces of real estate that his frugality had enabled him to accumulate. The passing of the flood left him low and dry. One month after his dishabilitation a saloon-keeper plucked him by the neck from his free-lunch counter as a tabby plucks a strange kitten from her nest, and cast him asphaltward. This seems low enough. But after that he acquired a pair of cloth-top, button Congress gaiters and wrote complaining letters to the newspapers. And then he fought the attendant at the Municipal Lodging House who tried to give him a bath. When Murray first saw him he was holding the hand of an Italian woman who sold apples and garlic on Essex Street, and quoting the words of a song-book ballad.

Murray's fall had been more Luciferian, if less spectacular. All the pretty, tiny little kickshaws of Gotham had once been his. The megaphone man roars out at you to observe the house of his uncle on a grand and revered avenue. But there had been an awful row about something, and the prince had been escorted to the door by the butler, which, in said avenue, is equivalent to the impact of the avuncular shoe. A weak Prince Hal, without inheritance or sword, he drifted downward to meet his humourless Falstaff, and to pick the crusts of the streets with him.

One evening they sat on a bench in a little downtown park. The great bulk of the Captain, which starvation seemed to increase—drawing irony instead of pity to his petitions for aid—was heaped against the arm of the bench in a shapeless mass. His red face, spotted by tufts of vermilion, week-old whiskers and topped by a sagging white straw hat, looked, in the gloom, like one of those structures that you may observe in a dark Third Avenue window, challenging your imagination to say whether it be something recent in the way of ladies' hats or a strawberry short-cake. A tight-drawn belt—last relic of his official spruceness—made a deep furrow in his circumference. The Captain's shoes were buttonless. In a smothered bass he cursed his star of ill-luck.

Murray, at his side, was shrunk into his dingy and ragged suit of blue serge. His hat was pulled low; he sat quiet and a little indistinct, like some ghost that had been dispossessed.

"I'm hungry," growled the Captain—"by the top sirloin of the Bull of Bashan, I'm starving to death. Right now I could eat a Bowery restaurant clear through to the stovepipe in the alley. Can't you think of nothing, Murray? You sit there with your shoulders scrunched up, giving an imitation of Reginald Vanderbilt driving his coach—what good are them airs doing you now? Think of some place we can get something to chew."

"You forget, my dear Captain," said Murray, without moving, "that our last attempt at dining was at my suggestion."

"You bet it was," groaned the Captain, "you bet your life it was. Have you got any more like that to make—hey?"

"I admit we failed," sighed Murray. "I was sure Malone would be good for one more free lunch after the way he talked baseball with me the last time I spent a nickel in his establishment."

"I had this hand," said the Captain, extending the unfortunate member—"I had this hand on the drumstick of a turkey and two sardine sandwiches when them waiters grabbed us."

"I was within two inches of the olives," said Murray. "Stuffed olives. I haven't tasted one in a year."

"What'll we do?" grumbled the Captain. "We can't starve."

"Can't we?" said Murray quietly. "I'm glad to hear that. I was afraid we could."

"You wait here," said the Captain, rising heavily and puffily to his feet. "I'm going to try to make one more turn. You stay here till I come back, Murray. I won't be over half an hour. If I turn the trick I'll come back flush."

He made some elephantinc attempts at smartening his appearance. He gave his fiery moustache a heavenward twist; he dragged into sight a pair of black-edged cuffs, deepened the crease in his middle by tightening his belt another hole, and set off, jaunty as a zoo rhinoceros, across the south end of the park.

When he was out of sight Murray also left the park, hurrying swiftly eastward. He stopped at a building whose steps were flanked by two green lights.

"A police captain named Maroney," he said to the desk sergeant, "was dismissed from the force after being tried under charges three years ago. I believe sentence was suspended. Is this man wanted now by the police?"

"Why are ye asking?" inquired the sergeant, with a frown.

"I thought there might be a reward standing,"

explained Murray easily. "I know the man well. He seems to be keeping himself pretty shady at present. I could lay my hands on him at any time. If there should be a reward——"

"There's no reward," interrupted the sergeant shortly. "The man's not wanted. And neither are ye. So, get out. Ye are frindly with um, and ye would be selling um. Out with ye quick, or I'll give ye a start."

Murray gazed at the officer with serene and virtuous dignity.

"I would be simply doing my duty as a citizen and gentleman," he said severely, "if I should assist the law in laying hold of one of its offenders."

Murray hurried back to the bench in the park. He folded his arms, and shrank within his clothes to his ghost-like presentment.

Ten minutes afterward the Captain arrived at the rendezvous, windy and thunderous as a dog-day in Kansas. His collar had been torn away; his straw hat had been twisted and battered; his shirt with oxblood stripes split to the waist. And from head to knee he was drenched with some vile and ignoble greasy fluid that loudly proclaimed to the nose its component leaven of garlic and kitchen stuff.

"For Heaven's sake, Captain," sniffed Murray, "I doubt that I would have waited for you if I had suspected you were so desperate as to resort to swill barrels. I——"

"Cheese it," said the Captain harshly. "I'm not hogging it yet. It's all on the outside. I went around on Essex and proposed marriage to that Catrina that's got the fruit shop there. Now, that business could be built up. She's a peach as far as a Dago could be. I thought I had that senoreena mashed sure last week. But look what she done to me! I guess I got too fresh. Well, there's another scheme queered."

"You don't mean to say," said Murray, with infinite contempt, "that you would have married that woman to help yourself out of your disgraceful troubles!"

"Me?" said the Captain. "I'd marry the Empress of China for one bowl of chop suey. I'd commit murder for a plate of beef stew. I'd steal a wafer from a waif. I'd be a Mormon for a bowl of chowder."

"I think," said Murray, resting his head on his hands, "that I would play Judas for the price of one drink of whisky. For thirty pieces of silver I would——"

"Oh, come now!" exclaimed the Captain in dismay. "You wouldn't do that, Murray? I always thought that Kike's squeal on his boss was about the lowest-down play that ever happened. A man that gives his friend away is worse than a pirate."

Through the park stepped a large man scanning the benches where the electric light fell.

"Is that you, Mac?" he said, halting before the derelicts. His diamond stickpin dazzled. His diamond-studded fob chain assisted. He was big and smooth and well-fed. "Yes, I see it's you," he continued. "They told me at Mike's that I might find you over here. Let me see you a few minutes, Mac."

The Captain lifted himself with a grunt of alacrity. If Charlie Finnegan had come down in the bottomless pit to seek him there must be something doing. Charlie guided him by an arm into a patch of shadow.

"You know, Mac," he said, "they're trying Inspector Pickering on graft charges."

"He was my inspector," said the Captain.

"O'Shea wants the job," went on Finnegan. "He must have it. It's for the good of the organization. Pickering must go under. Your testimony will do it. He was your 'man higher up' when you were on the force. His share of the boodle passed through your hands. You must go on the stand and testify against him."

"He was——" began the Captain.

"Wait a minute," said Finnegan. A bundle of yellowish stuff came out of his inside pocket. "Five hundred dollars in it for you. Two-fifty on the spot and the rest——"

"He was my friend, I say," finished the Captain. "I'll see you and the gang, and the city, and the party in the flames of Hades before I'll take the stand against Dan Pickering. I'm down and out; but I'm no traitor to a man that's been my friend." The Captain's voice rose and boomed like a split trombone. "Get out of this park, Charlie Finnegan, where us thieves and tramps and boozers are your betters; and take your dirty money with you."

Finnegan drifted out by another walk. The Captain returned to his seat.

"I couldn't avoid hearing," said Murray, drearily. "I think you are the biggest fool I ever saw."

"What would you have done?" asked the Captain.

"Nailed Pickering to the cross," said Murray.

"Sonny," said the Captain, huskily and without heat. "You and me are different. New York is divided into two parts—above Forty-second Street, and below Fourteenth. You come from the other part. We both act according to our lights."

An illuminated clock above the trees retailed the information that it lacked the half-hour of twelve. Both men rose from the bench and moved away together as if seized by the same idea. They left the park, struck through a narrow cross street, and came into Broadway, at this hour as dark, echoing and depeopled as a by-way in Pompeii.

Northward they turned; and a policeman who glanced at their unkempt and slinking figures withheld the attention and suspicion that he would have granted them at any other hour and place. For on every street in that part of the city other unkempt and slinking figures were shuffling and hurrying toward a converging point—a point that is marked by no monument save that groove on the pavement worn by tens of thousands of waiting feet.

At Ninth Street a tall man wearing an opera hat alighted from a Broadway car and turned his face westward. But he saw Murray, pounced upon him and dragged him under a street light. The Captain lumbered slowly to the corner, like a wounded bear, and waited, growling.

"Jerry!" cried the hatted one. "How fortunate! I was to begin a search for you to-morrow. The old gentleman has capitulated. You're to be restored to favour. Congratulate you. Come to the office in the morning and get all the money you want. I've liberal instructions in that respect."

"And the little matrimonial arrangement?" said Murray, with his head turned sidewise.

"Why—er—well, of course, your uncle understands—expects that the engagement between you and Miss Vanderhurst shall be——"

"Good night!" said Murray, moving away.

"You madman!" cried the other, catching his arm. "Would you give up two millions on account of——"

"Did you ever see her nose, old man?" asked Murray solemnly.

"But listen to reason, Jerry. Miss Vanderhurst is an heiress, and——"

"Did you ever see it?"

"Yes, I admit that her nose isn't——"

"Good night!" said Murray. "My friend is waiting for me. I am quoting him when I authorize you to report that there is 'nothing doing.' Good night."

A wriggling line of waiting men extended from a door in Tenth Street far up Broadway, on the outer edge of the pavement. The Captain and Murray fell in at the tail of the quivering millipede.

"Twenty feet longer than it was last night," said Murray, looking up at his measuring angle of Grace Church.

"Half an hour," growled the Captain, "before we get our punk."

The city clocks began to strike twelve; the Bread Line moved forward slowly, its leathern feet sliding on the stones with the sound of a hissing serpent, as they who had lived according to their lights closed up in the rear.

XXII: THE GIRL AND THE GRAFT

THE other day I ran across my old friend, Ferguson Pogue. Pogue is a conscientious grafter of the highest type. His headquarters is the Western Hemisphere, and his line of business is anything from speculating in town lots on the Great Staked Plains to selling wooden toys in Connecticut, made by hydraulic pressure from nutmegs ground to a pulp.

Now and then when Pogue has made a good haul he comes to New York for a rest. He says the jug of wine and loaf of bread and Thou in the wilderness business is about as much rest and pleasure to him as sliding down the bumps at Coney would be to President Taft. "Give me," says Pogue, "a big city for my vacation. Especially New York. I'm not much fond of New Yorkers, and Manhattan is about the only place on the globe where I don't find any."

While in the metropolis Pogue can always be found at one of two places. One is a little second-hand bookshop on Fourth Avenue, where he reads books about his hobbies, Mahometanism and taxidermy. I found him at the other—his hall bedroom in Eighteenth Street—where he sat in his stocking feet trying to pluck "The Banks of the Wabash" out of a small zither. Four years he has practised this tune without arriving near enough to cast the longest trout line to the water's edge. On the dresser lay a blued-steel Colt's forty-five and a tight roll of tens and twenties large enough around to belong to the spring rattlesnake-story class. A chambermaid with a room-cleaning air fluttered near by in the hall, unable to enter or to flee, scandalized by the stocking feet, aghast at the Colt's, yet powerless, with her metropolitan instincts, to remove herself beyond the magic influence of the yellow-hued roll.

I sat on his trunk while Ferguson Pogue talked. No one could be franker or more candid in his conversation. Beside his expression the cry of Henry James for lacteal nourishment at the age of one month would have seemed like a Chaldean cryptogram. He told me stories of his profession with pride, for he considered it an art. And I was curious enough to ask him whether he had known any women who followed it.

"Ladies?" said Pogue, with Western chivalry. "Well, not to any great extent. They don't amount to much in special lines of graft, because they're all so busy in general lines. What? Why, they have to. Who's got the money in the world? The men. Did you ever know a man to give a woman a dollar without any consideration? A man will shell out his dust to another man free and easy and gratis. But if he drops a penny in one of the machines run by the Madam Eve's Daughters' Amalgamated Association and the pineapple chewing-gum don't fall out when he pulls the lever you can hear him kick to the superintendent four blocks away. Man is the hardest proposition a woman has to go up against. He's a low-grade one, and she has to work overtime to make him pay. Two times out of five she's salted. She can't put in crushers and costly machinery. He'd notice 'em and be on to the game. They have to pan out what they get, and it hurts their tender hands. Some of 'em are natural sluice troughs and can carry out $1,000 to the ton. The dry-eyed ones have to depend on signed letters, false hair, sympathy, the kangaroo walk, cowhide whips, ability to cook, sentimental juries, conversational powers, silk underskirts, ancestry, rouge, anonymous letters, violet sachet powders, witnesses, revolvers, pneumatic forms, carbolic acid, moonlight, cold cream and the evening newspapers."

"You are outrageous, Ferg," I said. "Surely there is none of this 'graft,' as you call it, in a perfect and harmonious matrimonial union!"

"Well," said Pogue, "nothing that would justify you every time in calling up Police Headquarters and ordering out the reserves and a vaudeville manager on a dead run. But it's this way: Suppose you're a Fifth Avenue millionaire, soaring high, on the right side of copper and cappers.

"You come home at night and bring a $9,000,000 diamond brooch to the lady who's staked you for a claim. You hand it over. She says, 'Oh George!' and looks to see if it's backed. She comes up and kisses you. You've waited for it. You get it. All right. It's graft.

"But I'm telling you about Artemisia Blye. She was from Kansas and she suggested corn in all of its phases. .Her hair was as yellow as the silk; her form was as tall and graceful as a stalk in the low grounds during a wet summer; her eyes were as big and startling as bunions, and green was her favourite colour.

"On my last trip into the cool recesses of your sequestered city, I met a human named Vaucross. He was worth—that is, he had a million. He told me he was in business on the street. 'A sidewalk merchant?' says I, sarcastic. 'Exactly,' says he. 'Senior partner of a paving concern.'

"I kind of took to him. For this reason, I met him on Broadway one night when I was out of heart, luck, tobacco and place. He was all silk hat, diamonds and front. He was all front. If you had gone behind him you would have only looked yourself in the face. I looked like a cross between Count Tolstoy and a June lobster. I was out of luck. I had—but let me lay my eyes on that dealer again.

"Vaucross stopped and talked to me a few minutes and then he took me to a high-toned restaurant to eat dinner. There was music, and then some Beethoven, and Bordelaise sauce, and cussing in French, and frangipangi, and some hauteur and cigarettes. When I am flush I know them places.

"I declare, I must have looked as bad as a magazine artist, sitting there without any money and my hair all rumpled like I was booked to read a chapter from *Elsie's School Days* at a Brooklyn Bohemian smoker. But Vaucross treated me like a bear-hunter's guide. He wasn't afraid of hurting the waiter's feelings.

" 'Mr. Pogue,' he explains to me, 'I am using you.'

" 'Go on,' says I; 'I hope you don't wake up.'

"And then he tells me, you know, the kind of man he was. He was a New Yorker. His whole ambition was to be noticed. He wanted to be conspicuous. He wanted people to point him out and bow to him, and tell others who he was. He said it had been the desire of his life always. He didn't have but a million, so he couldn't attract attention by spending money. He said he tried to get into public notice one time by planting a little public square on the east side with garlic for free use of the poor; but Carnegie heard of it, and covered it over at once with a library in the Gaelic language. Three times he had jumped in the way of automobiles; but the only result was five broken ribs and a notice in the papers that an unknown man, five feet ten, with four amalgam-filled teeth, supposed to be the last of the famous Red Leary gang, had been run over.

" 'Ever try the reporters?' I asked him.

" 'Last month,' says Mr. Vaucross, 'my expenditure for lunches to reporters was $124.80.'

" 'Get anything out of that?' I asks.

" 'That reminds me,' says he; 'add $8.50 for pepsin. Yes, I got indigestion.'

" 'How am I supposed to push along your scramble for prominence?' I inquires. 'Contrast?'

" 'Something of that sort to-night,' says Vaucross. 'It grieves me; but I am forced to resort to eccentricity.' And here he drops his napkin in his soup and rises up and bows to a gent who is devastating a potato under a palm across the room.

" 'The Police Commissioner,' says my climber, gratified. " 'Friend,' says I, in a hurry, 'have ambitions but don't kick a rung out of your ladder. When you use me as a stepping-stone to salute the police you spoil my appetite on the grounds that I may be degraded and incriminated. Be thoughtful.'

"At the Quaker City squab *en casserole* the idea about Artemisia Blye comes to me.

" 'Suppose I can manage to get you in the papers,' says I—'a column or two every day in all of 'em and your picture in most of 'em for a week. How much would it be worth to you?'

" 'Ten thousand dollars,' says Vaucross, warm

in a minute. 'But no murder,' says he; 'and I won't wear pink pants at a cotillon.'

" 'I wouldn't ask you to,' says I. 'This is honourable, stylish and uneffeminate. Tell the waiter to bring a *demi tasse* and some other beans, and I will disclose to you the *opus moderandi*.'

"We closed the deal an hour later in the rococo rouge et noise room. I telegraphed that night to Miss Artemisia in Salina. She took a couple of photographs and an autograph letter to an elder in the Fourth Presbyterian Church in the morning, and got some transportation and $80. She stopped in Topeka long enough to trade a flashlight interior and a valentine to the vice-president of a trust company for a mileage book and a package of five-dollar notes with $250 scrawled on the band.

"The fifth evening after she got my wire she was waiting, all *décolletée* and dressed up, for me and Vaucross to take her to dinner in one of these New York feminine apartment houses where a man can't get in unless he plays bezique and smokes depilatory powder cigarettes.

" 'She's a stunner,' says Vaucross when he saw her. 'They'll give her a two-column cut sure.'

"This was the scheme the three of us concocted. It was business straight through. Vaucross was to rush Miss Blye with all the style and display and emotion he could for a month. Of course, that amounted to nothing as far as his ambitions were concerned. The sight of a man in a white tie and patent-leather pumps pouring greenbacks through the large end of a cornucopia to purchase nutriment and heartsease for tall, willowy blondes in New York is as common a sight as blue turtles in delirium tremens. But he was to write her love letters—

the worst kind of love letters, such as your wife publishes after you are dead—every day. At the end of the month he was to drop her and she would bring suit for $100,000 for breach of promise.

"Miss Artemisia was to get $10,000. If she won the suit that was all; and if she lost she was to get it, anyhow. There was a signed contract to that effect.

"Sometimes they had me out with 'em, but not often. I couldn't keep up to their style. She used to pull out his notes and criticize them like bills of lading.

" 'Say, you!' she'd say. 'What do you call this—Letter to a Hardware Merchant from His Nephew on Learning that His Aunt Has Nettlerash? You Eastern duffers know as much about writing love letters as a Kansas grasshopper does about tugboats. "My dear Miss Blye!"—wouldn't that put pink icing and a little red sugar bird on your bridal cake? How long do you expect to hold an audience in a court-room with that kind of stuff? You want to get down to business, and call me "Tweedlums Babe" and "Honeysuckle," and sign yourself "Mama's Own Big Bad Puggy Wuggy Boy" if you want any limelight to concretrate upon your sparse grey hairs. Get sappy.'

"After that Vaucross dipped his pen in the indelible tabasco. His notes read like something or other in the original. I could see a jury sitting up, and women tearing one another's hats to hear 'em read. And I could see piling up for Mr. Vaucross as much notoriousness as Archbishop Cranmer or the Brooklyn Bridge or cheese-on-salad ever enjoyed. He seemed mighty pleased at the prospects.

"They agreed on a night; and I stood on Fifth

Avenue outside a solemn restaurant and watched 'em. A process-server walked in and handed Vaucross the papers at his table. Everybody looked at 'em; and he looked as proud as Cicero. I went back to my room and lit a five-cent cigar, for I knew the $10,000 was as good as ours.

"About two hours later somebody knocked at my door. There stood Vaucross and Miss Artemisia, and she was clinging—yes, sir, clinging—to his arm. And they tells me they'd been out and got married. And they articulated some trivial cadences about love and such. And they laid down a bundle on the table and said 'Good night' and left.

"And that's why I say," concluded Ferguson Pogue, "that a woman is too busy occupied with her natural vocation and instinct of graft such as is given her for self-preservation and amusement to make any great success in special lines."

"What was in the bundle that they left?" I asked, with my usual curiosity.

"Why," said Ferguson, "there was a scalper's railroad ticket as far as Kansas City and two pairs of Mr. Vaucross's old pants."

XXIII: BLIND MAN'S HOLIDAY

ALAS for the man and for the artist with the shifting point of perspective! Life shall be a confusion of ways to the one; the landscape shall rise up and confound the other. Take the case of Lorison. At one time he appeared to himself to be the feeblest of fools; at another he conceived that he followed ideals so fine that the world was not yet ready to accept them. During one mood he cursed his folly; possessed by the other, he bore himself with a serene grandeur akin to greatness; in neither did he attain the perspective.

Generations before, the name had been "Larsen." His race had bequeathed him its fine-strung, melancholy temperament, its saving balance of thrift and industry.

From his point of perspective he saw himself an outcast from society, for ever to be a shady skulker along the ragged edge of respectability; a denizen *des trois-quartz de monde*, that pathetic spheroid lying between the *haut* and the *demi*, whose inhabitants envy each of their neighbours, and are scorned by both. He was self-condemned to this opinion, as he was self-exiled, through it, to this quaint Southern city a thousand miles from his former home. Here he had dwelt for longer than a year, knowing but few, keeping in a subjective world of shadows which was invaded at times by the perplexing bulks of jarring realities. Then he fell in love with a girl whom he met in a cheap restaurant, and his story begins.

The Rue Chartres, in New Orleans, is a street of ghosts. It lies in the quarter where the Frenchman, in his prime, set up his translated pride and glory; where, also, the arrogant don had swaggered, and dreamed of gold and grants and ladies' gloves. Every flagstone has its grooves worn by footsteps going royally to the wooing and the fighting. Every house has a princely heartbreak; each doorway its untold tale of gallant promise and slow decay.

By night the Rue Chartres is now but a murky fissure, from which the groping wayfarer sees, flung against the sky, the tangled filigree of Moorish iron balconies. The old houses of monsieur stand yet, indomitable against the century, but their essence is gone. The street is one of ghosts to whomsoever can see them.

A faint heartbeat of the street's ancient glory still survives in a corner occupied by the Café Carabine d'Or. Once men gathered there to plot against kings, and to warn presidents. They do so yet, but they are not the same kind of men. A brass button will scatter these; those would have set their faces against an army. Above the door hangs the signboard, upon which has been depicted a vast animal of unfamiliar species. In the act of firing upon this monster is represented an unobtrusive human levelling an obtrusive gun, once the colour of bright gold. Now the legend above the picture is faded beyond conjecture; the gun's relation to the title is a matter of faith; the menaced animal, wearied of the long aim of the hunter, has resolved itself into a shapeless blot.

The place is known as "Antonio's," as the name, white upon the red-lit transparency, and gilt upon the windows, attests. There is a promise in "Antonio"; a justifiable expectancy of savoury things in oil and pepper and wine, and perhaps an angel's whisper of garlic. But the rest of the name is "O'Riley." Antonio O'Riley!

The Carabine d'Or is an ignominious ghost of the Rue Chartres. The café where Bienville and Conti dined, where a prince has broken bread, is become a "family ristaurant."

Its customers are working men and women, almost to a unit. Occasionally you will see chorus girls from the cheaper theatres, and men who follow avocations subject to quick vicissitudes; but at

Antonio's—name rich in Bohemian promise, but tame in fulfilment—manners debonair and gay are toned down to the "family" standard. Should you light a cigarette, mine host will touch you on the "arrum" and remind you that the proprieties are menaced. "Antonio" entices and beguiles from fiery legend without, but "O'Riley" teaches decorum within.

It was at this restaurant that Lorison first saw the girl. A flashy fellow with a predatory eye had followed her in, and had advanced to take the other chair at the little table where she stopped, but Lorison slipped into the seat before him. Their acquaintance began, and grew, and now for two months they had sat at the same table each evening, not meeting by appointment, but as if by a series of fortuitous and happy accidents. After dining, they would take a walk together in one of the little city parks, or among the panoramic markets where exhibits a continuous vaudeville of sights and sounds. Always at eight o'clock their steps led them to a certain street corner, where she prettily but firmly bade him good night and left him. "I do not live far from here," she frequently said, "and you must let me go the rest of the way alone."

But now Lorison had discovered that he wanted to go the rest of the way with her, or happiness would depart, leaving him on a very lonely corner of life. And at the same time that he made the discovery, the secret of his banishment from the society of the good laid its finger in his face and told him it must not be.

Man is too thoroughly an egoist not to be also an egotist; if he love, the object shall know it. During a lifetime he may conceal it through stress of expediency and honour but it shall bubble from his dying lips, though it disrupt a neighbourhood. It is known, however, that most men do not wait so long to disclose their passion. In the case of Lorison, his particular ethics positively forbade him to declare his sentiments, but he must needs dally with the subject, and woo by innuendo at least.

On this night, after the usual meal at the Carabine d'Or, he strolled with his companion down the dim old street toward the river.

The Rue Chartres perishes in the old Place d'Armes. The ancient Cabildo, where Spanish justice fell like hail, faces it, and the Cathedral, another provincial ghost, overlooks it. Its centre is a little, iron-railed park of flowers and immaculate gravelled walks, where citizens take the air of evenings. Pedestalled high above it, the general sits his cavorting steed, with his face turned stonily down the river toward English Turn, whence come no more Britons to bombard his cotton bales.

Often the two sat in this square, but to-night Lorison guided her past the stone-stepped gate, and still riverward. As they walked, he smiled to himself to think that all he knew of her—except that he loved her—was her name, Norah Greenway, and that she lived with her brother. They had talked about everything except themselves. Perhaps her reticence had been caused by his.

They came, at length, upon the levee, and sat upon a great, prostrate beam. The air was pungent with the dust of commerce. The great river slipped yellowly past. Across it Algiers lay, a longitudinous black bulk against a vibrant electric haze sprinkled with exact stars.

The girl was young and of the piquant order.

A certain bright melancholy pervaded her; she possessed an untarnished, pale prettiness doomed to please. Her voice, when she spoke, dwarfed her theme. It was the voice capable of investing little subjects with a large interest. She sat at ease, bestowing her skirts with the little womanly touch, serene as if the begrimed pier were a summer garden. Lorison poked the rotting boards with his cane.

He began by telling her that he was in love with some one to whom he durst not speak of it. "And why not?" she asked, accepting swiftly his fatuous presentation of a third person of straw. "My place in the world," he answered, "is none to ask a woman to share. I am an outcast from honest people; I am wrongly accused of one crime, and am, I believe, guilty of another."

Thence he plunged into the story of his abdication from society. The story, pruned of his moral philosophy, deserves no more than the slightest touch. It is no new tale, that of the gambler's declension. During one night's sitting he lost, and then had imperilled a certain amount of his employer's money, which, by accident, he carried with him. He continued to lose, to the last wager, and then began to gain, leaving the game winner to a somewhat formidable sum. The same night his employer's safe was robbed. A search was had; the winnings of Lorison were found in his room, their total forming an accusative nearness to the sum purloined. He was taken, tried and, through incomplete evidence, released, smutched with the sinister *devoirs* of a disagreeing jury.

"It is not in the unjust accusation," he said to the girl, "that my burden lies, but in the knowledge that from the moment I staked the first dollar of the firm's money I was a criminal—no matter whether I lost or won. You see why it is impossible for me to speak of love to her."

"It is a sad thing," said Norah, after a little pause, "to think what very good people there are in the world."

"Good?" said Lorison.

"I was thinking of this superior person whom you say you love. She must be a very poor sort of creature."

"I do not understand."

"Nearly," she continued, "as poor a sort of creature as yourself."

"You do not understand," said Lorison, removing his hat and sweeping back his fine, light hair. "Suppose she loved me in return, and were willing to marry me. Think, if you can, what would follow. Never a day would pass but she would be reminded of her sacrifice. I would read a condescension in her smile, a pity even in her affection, that would madden me. No. The thing would stand between us for ever. Only equals should mate. I could never ask her to come down upon my lower plane."

An arc light faintly shone upon Lorison's face. An illumination from within also pervaded it. The girl saw the rapt, ascetic look; it was the face either of Sir Galahad or Sir Fool.

"Quite starlike," she said, "is this unapproachable angel. Really too high to be grasped."

"By me, yes."

She faced him suddenly. "My dear friend, would you prefer your star fallen?" Lorison made a wide gesture.

"You push me to the bald fact," he declared;

"you are not in sympathy with my argument. But I will answer you so. If I could reach my particular star, to drag it down, I would not do it; but if it were fallen, I would pick it up, and thank Heaven for the privilege."

They were silent for some minutes. Norah shivered, and thrust her hands deep into the pockets of her jacket. Lorison uttered a remorseful exclamation.

"I'm not cold," she said. "I was just thinking. I ought to tell you something. You have selected a strange confidante. But you cannot expect a chance acquaintance, picked up in a doubtful restaurant, to be an angel."

"Norah!" cried Lorison.

"Let me go on. You have told me about yourself. We have been such good friends. I must tell you now what I never wanted you to know. I am—worse than you are. I was on the stage. . . . I sang in the chorus. . . . I was pretty bad, I guess. . . . I stole diamonds from the prima donna . . . they arrested me. . . . I gave most of them up, and they let me go. . . . I drank wine every night . . . a great deal. . . . I was very wicked, but——"

Lorison knelt quickly by her side and took her hands.

"Dear Norah!" he said exultantly. "It is you, it is you I love! You never guessed it, did you? 'Tis you I meant all the time. Now I can speak. Let me make you forget the past. We have both suffered; let us shut out the world, and live for each other. Norah, do you hear me say I love you?"

"In spite of——"

"Rather say because of it. You have come out

of your past noble and good. Your heart is an angel's. Give it to me."

"A little while ago you feared the future too much to even speak."

"But for you; not for myself. Can you love me?"

She cast herself, wildly sobbing, upon his breast.

"Better than life—than truth itself—than everything."

"And my own past," said Lorison, with a note of solicitude—"can you forgive and——"

"I answered you that," she whispered, "when I told you I loved you." She leaned away, and looked thoughtfully at him. "If I had not told you about myself, would you have—would you——"

"No," he interrupted; "I would never have let you know I loved you. I would never have asked you this—Norah, will you be my wife?"

She wept again.

"Oh, believe me; I am good now—I am no longer wicked! I will be the best wife in the world. Don't think I am—bad any more. If you do I shall die, I shall die!"

While he was consoling her, she brightened up, eager and impetuous. "Will you marry me to-night?" she said. "Will you prove it that way? I have a reason for wishing it to be to-night. Will you?"

Of one of two things was this exceeding frankness the outcome: either of importunate brazenness or of utter innocence. The lover's perspective contained only the one.

"The sooner," said Lorison, "the happier I shall be."

"What is there to do?" she asked. "What do you have to get? Come! You should know."

Her energy stirred the dreamer to action.

'A city directory first," he cried gaily, "to find where the man lives who gives licences to happiness. We will go together and rout him out. Cabs, cars, policemen, telephones and ministers shall aid us."

"Father Rogan shall marry us," said the girl, with ardour. "I will take you to him."

An hour later the two stood at the open doorway of an immense, gloomy brick building in a narrow and lonely street. The licence was tight in Norah's hand.

"Wait here a moment," she said, "till I find Father Rogan."

She plunged into the black hallway, and the lover was left standing, as it were, on one leg, outside. His impatience was not greatly taxed. Gazing curiously into what seemed the hallway to Erebus, he was presently reassured by a stream of light that bisected the darkness, far down the passage. Then he heard her call, and fluttered lampward, like the moth. She beckoned him through a doorway into the room whence emanated the light. The room was bare of nearly everything except books, which had subjugated all its space. Here and there little spots of territory had been reconquered. An elderly, bald man, with a superlatively calm, remote eye, stood by a table with a book in his hand, his finger still marking a page. His dress was sombre and appertained to a religious order. His eye denoted an acquaintance with the perspective.

"Father Rogan," said Norah, "this is *he*."

"The two of ye," said Father Rogan, "want to get married?"

They did not deny it. He married them. The

ceremony was quickly done. One who could have witnessed it, and felt its scope, might have trembled at the terrible inadequacy of it to rise to the dignity of its endless chain of results.

Afterward the priest spake briefly, as if by rote, of certain other civil and legal addenda that either might or should, at a later time, cap the ceremony. Lorison tendered a fee, which was declined, and before the door closed after the departing couple Father Rogan's book popped open again where his finger marked it.

In the dark hall Norah whirled and clung to her companion, tearful.

"Will you never, never be sorry?"

At last she was reassured.

At the first light they reached upon the street, she asked the time, just as she had each night. Lorison looked at his watch. Half-past eight.

Lorison thought it was from habit that she guided their steps toward the corner where they always parted. But, arrived there, she hesitated, and then released his arm. A drug store stood on the corner, its bright, soft light shone upon them.

"Please leave me here as usual to-night," said Norah sweetly. "I must—I would rather you would. You will not object? At six to-morrow evening I will meet you at Antonio's. I want to sit with you there once more. And then—I will go where you say." She gave him a bewildering, bright smile, and walked swiftly away.

Surely it needed all the strength of her charm to carry off this astounding behaviour. It was no discredit to Lorison's strength of mind that his head began to whirl. Pocketing his hands, he rambled vacuously over to the druggist's windows, and began assiduously to spell over the names of the patent medicines therein displayed.

As soon as he had recovered his wits, he proceeded along the street in an aimless fashion. After drifting for two or three squares, he flowed into a somewhat more pretentious thoroughfare, a way much frequented by him in his solitary ramblings. For here was a row of shops devoted to traffic in goods of the widest range of choice—handiworks of art, skill and fancy, products of nature and labour from every zone.

Here, for a time, he loitered among the conspicuous windows, where was set, emphasized by congested floods of light, the cunningest spoil of the interiors. There were few passers, and of this Lorison was glad. He was not of the world. For a long time he had touched his fellow-man only at the gear of a levelled cog-wheel—at right angles, and upon a different axis. He had dropped into a distinctly new orbit. The stroke of ill fortune had acted upon him, in effect, as a blow delivered upon the apex of a certain ingenious toy, the musical top, which, when thus buffeted while spinning, gives forth, with scarcely retarded motion, a complete change of key and chord.

Strolling along the pacific avenue, he experienced a singular, supernatural calm, accompanied by an unusual activity of brain. Reflecting upon recent affairs, he assured himself of his happiness in having won for a bride the one he had so greatly desired, yet he wondered mildly at his dearth of active emotion. Her strange behaviour in abandoning him without valid excuse on his bridal eve aroused in him only a vague and curious speculation. Again he found himself contemplating, with complaisant serenity, the incidents of her somewhat lively career. His perspective seemed to have been queerly shifted.

As he stood before a window near a corner, his ears were assailed by a waxing clamour and commotion. He stood close to the window to allow passage to the cause of the hubbub—a procession of human beings, which rounded the corner and headed in his direction. He perceived a salient hue of blue and a glitter of brass about a central figure of dazzling white and silver, and a ragged wake of black, bobbing figures.

Two ponderous policemen were conducting between them a woman dressed as if for the stage, in a short, white, satiny skirt reaching to the knees, pink stockings, and a sort of sleeveless bodice bright with relucent, armour-like scales. Upon her curly, light hair was perched, at a rollicking angle, a shining tin helmet. The costume was to be instantly recognized as one of those amazing conceptions to which competition has harried the inventors of the spectacular ballet. One of the officers bore a long cloak upon his arm, which, doubtless, had been intended to veil the candid attractions of their effulgent prisoner, but, for some reason, it had not been called into use, to the vociferous delight of the tail of the procession.

Compelled by a sudden and vigorous movement of the woman, the parade halted before the window by which Lorison stood. He saw that she was young, and, at the first glance, was deceived by a sophistical prettiness of her face, which waned before a more judicious scrutiny. Her look was bold and reckiess, and upon her countenance, where yet the contours of youth survived, were the fingermarks of old age's credentialed courier, Late Hours.

The young woman fixed her unshrinking gaze upon Lorison, and called to him in the voice of the wronged heroine in straits:

"Say! You look like a good fellow; come and put up the bail, won't you? I've done nothing to get pinched for. It's all a mistake. See how they're treating me! You won't be sorry, if you'll help me out of this. Think of your sister or your girl being dragged along the streets this way! I say, come along now, like a good fellow."

It may be that Lorison, in spite of the unconvincing bathos of this appeal, showed a sympathetic face, for one of the officers left the woman's side, and went over to him.

"It's all right, sir," he said, in a husky, confidential tone; "she's the right party. We took her after the first act at the Green Light Theatre, on a wire from the chief of police of Chicago. It's only a square or two to the station. Her rig's pretty bad, but she refused to change clothes—or, rather," added the officer, with a smile, "to put on some. I thought I'd explain matters to you so you wouldn't think she was being imposed upon."

"What is the charge?" asked Lorison.

"Grand larceny. Diamonds. Her husband is a jeweller in Chicago. She cleaned his show case of the sparklers, and skipped with a comic-opera troupe."

The policeman, perceiving that the interest of the entire group of spectators was centred upon himself and Lorison—their conference being regarded as a possible new complication—was fain to prolong the situation—which reflected his own importance—by a little after-piece of philosophical comment.

"A gentleman like you, sir," he went on affably,

"would never notice it, but it comes in my line to observe what an immense amount of trouble is made by that combination—I mean the stage, diamonds and light-headed women who aren't satisfied with good homes. I tell you, sir, a man these days and nights wants to know what his women-folks are up to."

The policeman smiled a good night, and returned to the side of his charge, who had been intently watching Lorison's face during the conversation, no doubt for some indication of his intention to render succour. Now, at the failure of the sign, and at the movement made to continue the ignominious progress, she abandoned hope, and addressed him thus, pointedly:

"You damn chalk-faced quitter! You was thinking of giving me a hand, but you let the cop talk you out of it the first word. You're a dandy to tie to. Say, if you ever get a girl, she'll have a picnic. Won't she work you to the queen's taste! Oh, my!" She concluded with a taunting, shrill laugh that rasped Lorison like a saw. The policemen urged her forward; the delighted train of gaping followers closed up the rear; and the captive Amazon, accepting her fate, extended the scope of her maledictions so that none in hearing might seem to be slighted.

Then there came upon Lorison an overwhelming revulsion of his perspective. It may be that he had been ripe for it, but the abnormal condition of mind in which he had for so long existed was already about to revert to its balance; however, it is certain that the events of the last few minutes had furnished the channel, if not the impetus, for the change.

The initial determining influence had been so

small a thing as the fact and manner of his having been approached by the officer. That agent had, by the style of his accost, restored the loiterer to his former place in society. In an instant he had been transformed from a somewhat rancid prowler along the fishy side streets of gentility into an honest gentleman, with whom even so lordly a guardian of the peace might agreeably exchange the compliments.

This, then, first broke the spell, and set thrilling in him a resurrected longing for the fellowship of his kind, and the rewards of the virtuous. To what end, he vehemently asked himself, was this fanciful self-accusation, this empty renunciation, this moral squeamishness through which he had been led to abandon what was his heritage in life, and not beyond his deserts? Tcchnically, he was uncondemned; his sole guilty spot was in thought rather than deed, and cognizance of it unshared by others. For what good, moral or sentimental, did he slink, retreating like the hedgehog from his owu shadow, to and fro in this musty Bohemia that lacked even the picturesque?

But the thing that struck home and set him raging was the part played by the Amazonian prisoner. To the counterpart of that astounding belligerent—identical at least, in the way of experience—to one, by her own confession, thus far fallen, had he, not three hours since, been united in marriage. How desirable and natural it had seemed to him then, and how monstrous it seemed now! How the words of diamond thief number two yet burned in his ears: "If you ever get a girl, she'll have a picnic." What did that mean but that women instinctively knew him for one they could hoodwink? Still again, there reverberated the policeman's sapient contribution to his agony: "A man these days and nights wants to know what his women-folks are up to." Oh, yes, he had been a fool; he had looked at things from the wrong standpoint.

But the wildest note in all the clamour was struck by pain's forefinger, jealousy. Now, at least, he felt that keenest sting—a mounting love unworthily bestowed. Whatever she might be, he loved her; he bore in his own breast his doom. A grating, comic flavour to his predicament struck him suddenly, and he laughed creakingly as he swung down the echoing pavement. An impetuous desire to act, to battle with his fate, seized him. He stopped upon his heel, and smote his palms together triumphantly. His wife was—where? But there was a tangible link; an outlet more or less navigable, through which his derelict ship of matrimony might yet be safely towed—the priest!

Like all imaginative men with pliable natures, Lorison was, when thoroughly stirred, apt to become tempestuous. With a high and stubborn indignation upon him, he retraced his steps to the intersecting street by which he had come. Down this he hurried to the corner where he had parted with—an astringent grimace tinctured the thought—his wife. Thence still back he harked, following through an unfamiliar district his stimulated recollections of the way they had come from that preposterous wedding. Many times he went abroad, and nosed his way back to the trail, furious.

At last, when he reached the dark, calamitous building in which his madness had culminated, and found the black hallway, he dashed down it, perceiving no light or sound. But he raised his voice, hailing loudly; reckless of everything but that he should find the old mischief-maker with the eyes that looked too far away to see the disaster he had wrought. The door opened, and in the stream of light Father Rogan stood, his book in hand, with his finger marking the place.

"Ah!" cried Lorison. "You are the man I want. I had a wife of you a few hours ago. I would not trouble you, but I neglected to note how it was done. Will you oblige me with the information whether the business is beyond remedy?"

"Come inside," said the priest; "there are other lodgers in the house, who might prefer sleep to even a gratified curiosity."

Lorison entered the room and took the chair offered him. The priest's eyes looked a courteous interrogation.

"I must apologize again," said the young man, "for so soon intruding upon you with my marital infelicities, but, as my wife has neglected to furnish me with her address, I am deprived of the legitimate recourse of a family row."

"I am quite a plain man," said Father Rogan pleasantly; "but I do not see how I am to ask you questions."

"Pardon my indirectness," said Lorison; "I will ask one. In this room to-night you pronounced me to be a husband. You afterward spoke of additional rites or performances that either should or could be effected. I paid little attention to your words then, but I am hungry to hear them repeated now. As matters stand, am I married past all help?"

"You are as legally and as firmly bound," said the priest, "as though it had been done in a cathedral, in the presence of thousands. The additional observances I referred to are not necessary to the strictest legality of the act, but were advised as a precaution for the future—for convenience of proof in such contingencies as wills, inheritances and the like."

Lorison laughed harshly.

"Many thanks," he said. "Then there is no mistake, and I am the happy benedict. I suppose I should go stand upon the bridal corner, and when my wife gets through walking the streets she will look me up."

Father Rogan regarded him calmly.

"My son," he said, "when a man and woman come to me to be married I always marry them. I do this for the sake of other people whom they might go away and marry if they did not marry each other. As you see, I do not seek your confidence; but your case seems to me to be one not altogether devoid of interest. Very few marriages that have come to my notice have brought such well-expressed regret within so short a time. I will hazard one question: were you not under the impression that you loved the lady you married, at the time you did so?"

"Loved her!" cried Lorison wildly. "Never so well as now, though she told me she deceived and sinned and stole. Never more than now, when, perhaps, she is laughing at the fool she cajoled and left, and scarcely a word, to return to God only knows what particular line of her former folly."

Father Rogan answered nothing. During the silence that succeeded, he sat with a quiet expectation beaming in his full, lambent eye.

"If you would listen——" began Lorison. The priest held up his hand.

"As I hoped," he said. "I thought you would trust me. Wait but a moment." He brought a long clay pipe, filled and lighted it.

"Now, my son," he said.

Lorison poured a twelve-month's accumulated confidence into Father Rogan's ear. He told all; not sparing himself or omitting the facts of his past, the events of the night, or his disturbing conjectures and fears.

"The main point," said the priest, when he had concluded, "seems to me to be this—are you reasonably sure that you love this woman whom you have married?"

"Why," exclaimed Lorison, rising impulsively to his feet—"why should I deny it? But look at me—am I fish, flesh or fowl? That is the main point to me, I assure you."

"I understand you," said the priest, also rising, and laying down his pipe. "The situation is one that has taxed the endurance of much older men than you—in fact, especially much older men than you. I will try to relieve you from it, and this night. You shall see for yourself into exactly what predicament you have fallen, and how you shall, possibly, be extricated. There is no evidence so credible as that of the eyesight."

Father Rogan moved about the room, and donned a soft black hat. Buttoning his coat to his throat, he laid his hand on the door-knob. "Let us walk," he said.

The two went out upon the street. The priest turned his face down it, and Lorison walked with him through a squalid district, where the houses loomed, awry and desolate-looking, high above them. Presently they turned into a less dismal side street, where the houses were smaller, and, though hinting of the most meagre comfort, lacked the concentrated wretchedness of the more populous by-ways.

At a segregated, two-story house Father Rogan halted, and mounted the steps with the confidence of a familiar visitor. He ushered Lorison into a narrow hallway, faintly lighted by a cobwebbed hanging lamp. Almost immediately a door to the right opened and a dingy Irishwoman protruded her head.

"Good evening to ye, Mistress Geehan," said the priest, unconsciously, it seemed, falling into a delicately flavoured brogue. "And is it yourself can tell me if Norah has gone out again, the night, maybe?"

"Oh, it's yer blissid riverence! Sure I can tell ye the same. The purty darlin' wint out, as usual, but a bit later. And she says: 'Mother Geehan,' says she, 'it's me last noight out, praise the saints, this noight is!' And, oh, yer riverence, the swate, beautiful drame of a dress she had this toime! White satin and silk and ribbons, and lace about the neck and arrums—'twas a sin, yer riverence, the gold was spint upon it."

The priest heard Lorison catch his breath painfully, and a faint smile flickered across his own clean-cut mouth.

"Well, then, Mistress Geehan," said he, "I'll just step upstairs and see the bit boy for a minute, and I'll take this gentleman up with me."

"He's awake, thin," said the woman. "I've just come down from sitting wid him the last hour, tilling him fine shtories of ould County Tyrone. 'Tis a greedy gossoon, it is, yer riverence, for me shtories."

"Small the doubt," said Father Rogan. "There's no rocking would put him to slape the quicker, I'm thinking."

Amid the woman's shrill protest against the retort, the two men ascended the steep stairway. The priest pushed open the door of a room near its top.

"Is that you already, sister?" drawled a sweet, childish voice from the darkness.

"It's only ould Father Denny come to see ye, darlin'; and a foine gintleman I've brought to make ye a gr-r-and call. And ye resaves us fast aslape in bed! Shame on yez manners!"

"Oh, Father Denny, is that you? I'm glad. And will you light the lamp, please? It's on the table by the door. And quit talking like Mother Geehan, Father Denny."

The priest lit the lamp, and Lorison saw a tiny, tousled-haired boy, with a thin, delicate face, sitting up in a small bed in a corner. Quickly, also, his rapid glance considered the room and its contents. It was furnished with more than comfort, and its adornments plainly indicated a woman's discerning taste. An open door beyond revealed the blackness of an adjoining room's interior.

The boy clutched both of Father Rogan's hands. "I'm so glad you came," he said; "but why did you come in the night? Did sister send you?"

"Off wid ye! Am I to be sint about, at me age, as was Terence McShane, of Ballymahone? I come on me own r-r-responsibility."

Lorison had also advanced to the boy's bedside. He was fond of children; and the wee fellow, laying himself down to sleep alone in that dark room, stirred his heart.

"Aren't you afraid, little man?" he asked, stooping down beside him.

"Sometimes," answered the boy, with a shy smile, "when the rats make too much noise. But nearly every night, when sister goes out, Mother Geehan stays a while with me, and tells me funny stories. I'm not often afraid, sir."

"This brave little gentleman," said Father Rogan, "is a scholar of mine. Every day from half-past six to half-past eight—when sister comes for him—he stops in my study, and we find out what's in the inside of books. He knows multiplication, division and fractions; and he's throubling me to begin wid the chronicles of Ciaran of Clonmacnoise, Corurac McCullenan and Cuan O'Lochain, the gr-r-reat Irish histhorians." The boy was evidently accustomed to the priest's Celtic pleasantries. A little, appreciative grin was all the attention the insinuation of pedantry received.

Lorison, to have saved his life, could not have put to the child one of those vital questions that were wildly beating about, unanswered, in his own brain. The little fellow was very like Norah; he had the same shining hair and candid eyes.

"Oh, Father Denny," cried the boy suddenly, "I forgot to tell you! Sister is not going away at night any more! She told me so when she kissed me good night as she was leaving. And she said she was so happy, and then she cried. Wasn't that queer? But I'm glad; aren't you?"

"Yes, lad. And now, ye omadhaun, go to sleep and say good night; we must be going."

"Which shall I do first, Father Denny?"

"Faith, he's caught me again! Wait till I get the sassenach into the annals of Tageruach, the hagiographer; I'll give him enough of the Irish idiom to make him more respectful."

The light was out, and the small, brave voice bidding them good night from the dark room. They groped downstairs, and tore away from the garrulity of Mother Geehan.

Again the priest steered them through the dim ways, but this time in another direction. His conductor was serenely silent, and Lorison followed his example to the extent of seldom speaking. Serene he could not be. His heart beat suffocatingly in his breast. The following of this blind, menacing trail was pregnant with he knew not what humiliating revelation to be delivered at its end.

They came into a more pretentious street, where trade, it could be surmised, flourished by day. And again the priest paused; this time before a lofty building, whose great doors and windows in the lowest floor were carefully shuttered and barred. Its higher apertures were dark, save in the third story, the windows of which were brilliantly lighted. Lorison's ear caught a distant, regular, pleasing thrumming, as of music above. They stood at an angle of the building. Up, along the side nearest hem, mounted an iron stairway. At its top was an upright, illuminated parallelogram. Father Rogan had stopped, and stood, musing.

"I will say this much," he remarked thoughtfully: 'I believe you to be a better man than you think yourself to be, and a better man than I thought some hours ago. But do not take this," he added, with a smile, "as much praise. I promised you a possible deliverance from an unhappy perplexity. I will have to modify that promise. I can only remove the mystery that enhanced that perplexity. Your deliverance depends upon yourself. Come."

He led his companion up the stairway. Half-way up, Lorison caught him by the sleeve. "Remember," he gasped, "I love that woman."

"You desired to know."

"I—— Go on."

The priest reached the landing at the top of the stairway. Lorison, behind him, saw that the illuminated space was the glass upper half of a door opening into the lighted room. The rhythmic music increased as they neared it; the stairs shook with the mellow vibrations.

Lorison stopped breathing when he set foot upon the highest step, for the priest stood aside, and motioned him to look through the glass of the door.

His eye, accustomed to the darkness, met first a blinding glare, and then he made out the faces and forms of many people, amid an extravagant display of splendid robings—billowy laces, brilliant-hued finery, ribbons, silks and misty drapery. And then he caught the meaning of that jarring hum, and he saw the tired, pale, happy face of his wife, bending, as were a score of others, over her sewing machine—toiling, toiling. Here was the folly she pursued, and the end of his quest.

But not his deliverance, though even then remorse struck him. His shamed soul fluttered once more before it retired to make room for the other and better one. For, to temper his thrill of joy, the shine of the satin and the glimmer of ornaments recalled the disturbing figure of the bespangled Amazon, and the base duplicate histories lit by the glare of footlights and stolen diamonds. It is past the wisdom of him who only sets the scenes, either to praise or blame the man. But this time his love overcame his scruples. He took a quick step, and reached out his hand for the door-knob. Father Rogan was quicker to arrest it and draw him back.

"You use my trust in you queerly," said the priest sternly. "What are you about to do?"

"I am going to my wife," said Lorison. "Let me pass."

"Listen," said the priest, holding him firmly by the arm. "I am about to put you in possession of a piece of knowledge of which, thus far, you have scarcely proved deserving. I do not think you ever will; but I will not dwell upon that. You see in that room the woman you married, working for a frugal living for herself and a generous comfort for an idolized brother. This building belongs to the chief costumer of the city. For months the advance orders for the coming Mardi Gras festivals have kept the work going day and night. I myself secured employment here for Norah. She toils here each night from nine o'clock until daylight, and, besides, carries home with her some of the finer costumes, requiring more delicate needlework, and works there part of the day. Somehow, you two have remained strangely ignorant of each other's lives. Are you convinced now that your wife is not walking the streets?"

"Let me go to her," cried Lorison, again struggling, "and beg her forgiveness!"

"Sir," said the priest, "do you owe me nothing? Be quiet. It seems so often that Heaven lets fall its choicest gifts into hands that must be taught to hold them. Listen again. You forgot that repentant sin must not compromise, but look up, for redemption, to the purest and best. You went to her with the fine-spun sophistry that peace could be found in a mutual guilt; and she, fearful of losing what her heart so craved, thought it worth the price to buy it with a desperate, pure, beautiful lie. I have known her since the day she was born; she is as innocent and unsullied in life and deed as a holy saint. In that lowly street where she dwells she first saw the light, and she has lived there ever since, spending her days in generous self-sacrifice for others. Och, ye spalpeen!" continued Father Rogan, raising his finger in kindly anger at Lorison. "What for, I wonder, could she be afther making a fool of hersilf, and shamin' her swate soul with lies, for the like of you!"

"Sir," said Lorison, trembling, "say what you please of me. Doubt it as you must, I will yet prove my gratitude to you, and my devotion to her. But let me speak to her once now, let me kneel for just one moment at her feet, and——"

"Tut, tut!" said the priest. "How many acts of a love drama do you think an old book-worm like me capable of witnessing? Besides, what kind of figures do we cut, spying upon the mysteries of midnight millinery? Go to meet your wife to-morrow, as she ordered you, and obey her thereafter, and maybe some time I shall get forgiveness for the part I have played in this night's work. Off wid yez down the shtairs, now! 'Tis late, and an ould man like me should be takin' his rest."

XXIV : TWO THANKSGIVING DAY GENTLEMEN

THERE is one day that is ours. There is one day when all we Americans who are not self-made go back to the old home to eat saleratus biscuits and marvel how much nearer to the porch the old pump looks than it used to. Bless the day. President Roosevelt gives it to us. We hear some talk of the Puritans, but don't just remember who they were. Bet we can lick 'em, anyhow, if they try to land again. Plymouth Rocks? Well, that sounds more familiar. Lots of us have had to come down to hens since the Turkey Trust got its work in. Bet somebody in Washington is leaking out advance information to 'em about these Thanksgiving proclamations.

The big city east of the cranberry bogs has made Thanksgiving Day an institution. The last Thursday in November is the only day in the year on which it recognizes the part of America lying across the ferries. It is the one day that is purely American. Yes, a day of celebration, exclusively American.

And now for the story which is to prove to you that we have traditions on this side of the ocean that are becoming older at a much rapider rate than those of England are—thanks to our get-up and enterprise.

Stuffy Pete took his seat on the third bench to the right as you enter Union Square from the east, at the walk opposite the fountain. Every Thanksgiving Day for nine years he had taken his seat there promptly at one o'clock. For every time he had done so things had happened to him—Charles

Dickensy things that swelled his waistcoat above his heart and equally on the other side.

But to-day Stuffy Pete's appearance at the annual trysting place seemed to have been rather the result of habit than of the yearly hunger which, as the philanthropists seem to think, afflicts the poor at such extended intervals.

Certainly Pete was not hungry. He had just come from a feast that had left him of his powers barely those of respiration and locomotion. His eyes were like two pale gooseberries firmly embedded in a swollen and gravy-smeared mask of putty. His breath came in short wheezes; a senatorial roll of adipose tissue denied a fashionable set to his upturned coat collar. Buttons that had been sewed upon his clothes by kind Salvation fingers a week before flew like popcorn, strewing the earth around him. Ragged he was, with a split shirt front open to the wishbone; but the November breeze, carrying fine snowflakes, brought him only a grateful coolness. For Stuffy Pete was overcharged with the caloric produced by a super-bountiful dinner, beginning with oysters and ending with plum pudding, and including (it seemed to him) all the roast turkey and baked potatoes and chicken salad and squash pie and ice cream in the world. Wherefore he sat, gorged, and gazed upon the world with after-dinner contempt.

The meal had been an unexpected one. He was passing a red brick mansion near the beginning of Fifth Avenue, in which lived two old ladies of ancient family and a reverence for traditions. They even denied the existence of New York, and believed that Thanksgiving Day was declared solely for

Washington Square. One of their traditional habits was to station a servant at the postern gate with orders to admit the first hungry wayfarer that came along after the hour of noon had struck, and banquet him to a finish. Stuffy Pete happened to pass by on his way to the park, and the seneschals gathered him in and upheld the custom of the castle.

After Stuffy Pete had gazed straight before him for ten minutes he was conscious of a desire for a more varied field of vision. With a tremendous effort he moved his head slowly to the left. And then his eyes bulged out fearfully, and his breath ceased, and the roughshod ends of his short legs wriggled and rustled on the gravel.

For the Old Gentleman was coming across Fourth Avenue toward his bench.

Every Thanksgiving Day for nine years the Old Gentleman had come there and found Stuffy Pete on his bench. That was a thing that the Old Gentleman was trying to make a tradition of. Every Thanksgiving Day for nine years he had found Stuffy there, and had led him to a restaurant and watched him eat a big dinner. They do those things in England unconsciously. But this is a young country, and nine years is not so bad. The Old Gentleman was a staunch American patriot, and considered himself a pioneer in American tradition. In order to become picturesque we must keep on doing one thing for a long time without ever letting it get away from us. Something like collecting the weekly dimes in industrial insurance. Or cleaning the streets.

The Old Gentleman moved, straight and stately, toward the Institution that he was rearing. Truly, the annual feeding of Stuffy Pete was nothing national in its character such as the Magna Charta or jam for breakfast was in England. But it was a step. It was almost feudal. It showed, at least, that a Custom was not impossible to New Y—ahem! —America.

The Old Gentleman was thin and tall, and sixty. He was dressed all in black, and wore the old-fashioned kind of glasses that won't stay on your nose. His hair was whiter and thinner than it had been last year, and he seemed to make more use of his big, knobby cane with the crooked handle.

As his established benefactor came up Stuffy wheezed and shuddered like some woman's overfat pug when a street dog bristles up at him. He would have flown, but all the skill of Santos-Dumont could not have separated him from his bench. Well had the myrmidons of the two old ladies done their work.

"Good morning," said the Old Gentleman. "I am glad to perceive that the vicissitudes of another year have spared you to move in health about the beautiful world. For that blessing alone this day of thanksgiving is well proclaimed to each of us. If you will come with me, my man, I will provide you with a dinner that should make your physical being accord with the mental."

That is what the Old Gentleman said every time —every Thanksgiving Day for nine years. The words themselves almost formed an Institution. Nothing could be compared with them except the Declaration of Independence. Always before they had been music in Stuffy's ears. But now he looked up at the Old Gentleman's face with tearful agony in his own. The fine snow almost sizzled when it fell upon his perspiring brow. But the Old Gentleman shivered a little and turned his back to the wind.

Stuffy had always wondered why the Old Gentleman spoke his speech rather sadly. He did not know that it was because he was wishing every time that he had a son to succeed him. A son who would come there after he was gone—a son who would stand proud and strong before some subsequent Stuffy, and say: "In memory of my father." Then it would be an Institution.

But the Old Gentleman had no relatives. He lived in rented rooms in one of the decayed old family brownstone mansions in one of the quiet streets east of the park. In the winter he raised fuchsias in a little conservatory the size of a steamer trunk. In the spring he walked in the Easter parade. In the summer he lived at a farmhouse in the New Jersey hills, and sat in a wicker armchair, speaking of a butterfly, the *ornithoptera amphrisius*, that he hoped to find some day. In the autumn he fed Stuffy a dinner. These were the Old Gentleman's occupations.

Stuffy Pete looked up at him for a half minute, stewing and helpless in his own self-pity. The Old Gentleman's eyes were bright with the giving-pleasure. His face was getting more lined each year, but his little black necktie was in as jaunty a bow as ever, and his linen was beautiful and white, and his grey moustache was curled carefully at the ends. And then Stuffy made a noise that sounded like peas bubbling in a pot. Speech was intended; and as the Old Gentleman had heard the sounds nine times before, he rightly construed them into Stuffy's old formula of acceptance.

"Thankee, sir. I'll go with ye, and much obliged. I'm very hungry, sir."

The coma of repletion had not prevented from entering Stuffy's mind the conviction that he was the basis of an Institution. His Thanksgiving appetite was not his own; it belonged by all the sacred rights of established custom, if not by the actual Statute of Limitations, to this kind old gentleman who had pre-empted it. True, America is free; but in order to establish tradition some one must be a repetend—a repeating decimal. The heroes are not all heroes of steel and gold. See one here that wielded only weapons of iron, badly silvered, and tin.

The Old Gentleman led his annual protégé southward to the restaurant, and to the table where the feast had always occurred. They were recognized.

"Here comes de old guy," said a waiter, "dat blows dat same bum to a meal Ivery Thanksgiving."

The Old Gentleman sat across the table glowing like a smoked pearl at his cornerstone of future ancient Tradition. The waiters heaped the table with holiday food—and Stuffy, with a sigh that was mistaken for hunger's expression, raised knife and fork and carved for himself a crown of imperishable bay.

No more valiant hero ever fought his way through the ranks of an enemy. Turkey, chops, soups, vegetables, pies, disappeared before him as fast as they could be served. Gorged nearly to the uttermost when he entered the restaurant, the smell of food had almost caused him to lose his honour as a gentleman, but he rallied like a true knight. He saw the look of beneficent happiness on the Old

Gentleman's face—a happier look than even the fuchsias and the *ornithoptera amphrisius* had ever brought to it—and he had not the heart to see it wane.

In an hour Stuffy leaned ack with a battle won.

"Thankee kindly, sir," he puffed like a leaky steam-pipe; "thankee kindly for a hearty meal."

Then he arose heavily with glazed eyes and started toward the kitchen. A waiter turned him about like a top, and pointed him toward the door. The Old Gentleman carefully counted out $1.30 in silver change, leaving three nickels for the waiter.

They parted as they did each year at the door, the Old Gentleman going south, Stuffy north.

Around the first corner Stuffy turned, and stood for one minute. Then he seemed to puff out his rags as an owl puffs out his feathers, and fell to the sidewalk like a sunstricken horse.

When the ambulance came the young surgeon and the driver cursed softly at his weight. There was no smell of whisky to justify a transfer to the patrol wagon, so Stuffy and his two dinners went to the hospital. There they stretched him on a bed and began to test him for strange diseases, with the hope of getting a chance at some problem with the bare steel.

And lo! an hour later another ambulance brought the Old Gentleman. And they laid him on another bed and spoke of appendicitis, for he looked good for the bill.

But pretty soon one of the young doctors met one of the young nurses whose eyes he liked, and stopped to chat with her about the cases.

"That nice old gentleman over there, now," he

said, "you wouldn't think that was a case of almost starvation. Proud old family, I guess. He told me he hadn't eaten a thing for three days."

XXV: FRIENDS IN SAN ROSARIO

THE west-bound stopped at San Rosario on time at 8.20 a.m. A man with a thick black-leather wallet under his arm left the train and walked rapidly up the main street of the town. There were other passengers who also got off at San Rosario, but they either slouched limberly over to the railroad eating-house or the Silver Dollar saloon, or joined the groups of idlers about the station.

Indecision had no part in the movements of the man with the wallet. He was short in stature, but strongly built, with very light, closely-trimmed hair, smooth, determined face, and aggressive, gold-rimmed nose glasses. He was well dressed in the prevailing Eastern style. His air denoted a quiet but conscious reserve force, if not actual authority.

After walking a distance of three squares he came to the centre of the town's business area. Here another street of importance crossed the main one, forming the hub of San Rosario's life and commerce. Upon one corner stood the post-office. Upon another Rubensky's Clothing Emporium. The other two diagonally opposing corners were occupied by the town's two banks, the First National and the Stockmen's National. Into the First National Bank of San Rosario the newcomer walked, never slowing his brisk step until he stood at the cashier's window. The bank opened for business at nine, and the working force was already assembled, each member preparing his department for the day's business. The cashier was examining the mail when he noticed the stranger standing at his window.

"Bank doesn't open 'til nine," he remarked, curtly, but without feeling. He had had to make that statement so often to early birds since San Rosario adopted city banking hours.

"I am well aware of that," said the other man, in cool, brittle tones. "Will you kindly receive my card?"

The cashier drew the small, spotless parallelogram inside the bars of his wicket, and read:

J. F. C. NETTLEWICK

National Bank Examiner

"Oh—er—will you walk around inside, Mr.—er—Nettlewick. Your first visit—didn't know your business, of course. Walk right around, please."

The examiner was quickly inside the sacred precincts of the bank, where he was ponderously introduced to each employee in turn by Mr. Edlinger, the cashier—a middle-aged gentleman of deliberation, discretion, and method.

"I was kind of expecting Sam Turner round again, pretty soon," said Mr. Edlinger. "Sam's been examining us now, for about four years. I guess you'll find us all right, though, considering the tightness in business. Not overly much money on hand, but able to stand the storms, sir, stand the storms."

"Mr. Turner and I have been ordered by the Comptroller to exchange districts," said the examiner in his decisive, formal tones. "He is covering my old territory in Southern Illinois and Indiana. I will take the cash first, please."

Perry Dorsey, the teller, was already arranging his cash on the counter for the examiner's inspection. He knew it was right to a cent and he had nothing to fear, but he was nervous and flustered. So was every man in the bank. There was something so icy and swift, so impersonal and uncompromising about this man that his very presence seemed an accusation. He looked to be a man who would never make nor overlook an error.

Mr. Nettlewick first seized the currency, and with a rapid, almost juggling motion, counted it by packages. Then he spun the sponge cup toward him and verified the count by bills. His thin, white fingers flew like some expert musician's upon the keys of a piano. He dumped the gold upon the counter with a crash, and the coins whined and sang as they skimmed across the marble slab from the tips of his nimble digits. The air was full of fractional currency when he came to the halves and quarters. He counted the last nickel and dime. He had the scales brought, and he weighed every sack of silver in the vault. He questioned Dorsey concerning each of the cash memoranda—certain checks, charge slips, etc., carried over from the previous day's work—with unimpeachable courtesy, yet with something so mysteriously momentous in his frigid manner, that the teller was reduced to pink cheeks and a stammering tongue.

This newly-imported examiner was so different from Sam Turner. It had been Sam's way to enter the bank with a shout, pass the cigars, and tell the latest stories he had picked up on his rounds. His customary greeting to Dorsey had been, "Hello, Perry! Haven't skipped out with the boodle yet, I see." Turner's way of counting the cash had been different, too. He would finger the packages of bills in a tired kind of way, and then go into the vault and kick over a few sacks of silver, and the thing was done. Halves and quarters and dimes? Not for Sam Turner. "No chicken feed for me," he would say when they were set before him. "I'm not in the agricultural department." But, then, Turner was a Texan, an old friend of the bank's president, and had known Dorsey since he was a baby.

While the examiner was counting the cash, Major Thomas B. Kingman—known to every one as "Major Tom"—the president of the First National, drove up to the side door with his old dun horse and buggy, and came inside. He saw the examiner busy with the money, and, going into the little "pony corral," as he called it, in which his desk was railed off, he began to look over his letters.

Earlier, a little incident had occurred that even the sharp eyes of the examiner had failed to notice. When he had begun his work at the cash counter, Mr. Edlinger had winked significantly at Roy Wilson, the youthful bank messenger, and nodded his head slightly toward the front door. Roy understood, got his hat, and walked leisurely out, with his collector's book under his arm. Once outside, he made a bee-line for the Stockmen's National. That bank was also getting ready to open. No customers had, as yet, presented themselves.

"Say, you people!" cried Roy, with the familiarity of youth and long acquaintance, "you want to get a move on you. There's a new bank examiner over at the First, and he's a stem-winder. He's counting nickels on Perry, and he's got the whole outfit bluffed. Mr. Edlinger gave me the tip to let you know."

Mr. Buckley, president of the Stockmen's National—a stout, elderly man, looking like a farmer dressed for Sunday—heard Roy from his private office at the rear and called him.

"Has Major Kingman come down to the bank yet?" he asked of the boy.

"Yes, sir, he was just driving up as I left," said Roy.

"I want you to take him a note. Put it into his own hands as soon as you get back."

Mr. Buckley sat down and began to write.

Roy returned and handed to Major Kingman the envelope containing the note. The major read it, folded it, and slipped it into his vest pocket. He leaned back in his chair for a few moments as if he were meditating deeply, and then rose and went into the vault. He came out with the bulky, old-fashioned leather note case stamped on the back in gilt letters, "Bills Discounted." In this were the notes due the bank with their attached securities, and the major, in his rough way, dumped the lot upon his desk and began to sort them over.

By this time Nettlewick had finished his count of the cash. His pencil fluttered like a swallow over the sheet of paper on which he had set his figures. He opened his black wallet, which seemed to be also a kind of secret memorandum book, made a few rapid figures in it, wheeled and transfixed

Dorsey with the glare of his spectacles. That look seemed to say: "You're safe this time, but——"

"Cash all correct," snapped the examiner. He made a dash for the individual bookkeeper, and for a few minutes there was a fluttering of ledger leaves and a sailing of balance sheets through the air.

"How often do you balance your pass-books?" he demanded, suddenly.

"Er—once a month," faltered the individual bookkeeper, wondering how many years they would give him.

"All right," said the examiner, turning and charging upon the general bookkeeper, who had the statements of his foreign banks and their reconcilement memoranda ready. Everything there was found to be all right. Then the stub book of the certificates of deposit. Flutter—flutter—zip—zip—check! All right. List of over-drafts, please. Thanks. H'm-m. Unsigned bills of the bank, next. All right.

Then came the cashier's turn, and easy-going Mr. Edlinger rubbed his nose and polished his glasses nervously under the quick fire of questions concerning the circulation, undivided profits, bank real estate, and stock ownership.

Presently Nettlewick was aware of a big man towering above him at his elbow—a man sixty years of age, rugged and hale, with a rough, grizzled beard, a mass of grey hair and a pair of penetrating blue eyes that confronted the formidable glasses of the examiner without a flicker.

"Er—Major Kingman, our president—er—Mr. Nettlewick," said the cashier.

Two men of very different types shook hands. One was a finished product of the world of straight lines, conventional methods, and formal affairs. The other was something freer, wider and nearer to nature. Tom Kingman had not been cut to any pattern. He had been mule-driver, cowboy, ranger, soldier, sheriff, prospector, and cattleman. Now, when he was bank president, his old comrades from the prairies, of the saddle, tent, and trail found no change in him. He had made his fortune when Texas cattle were at the high tide of value, and had organized the First National Bank of San Rosario. In spite of his largeness of heart and sometimes unwise generosity toward his old friends, the bank had prospered, for Major Tom Kingman knew men as well as he knew cattle. Of late years the cattle business had known a depression, and the major's bank was one of the few whose losses had not been great.

"And now," said the examiner, briskly, pulling out his watch, "the last thing is the loans. We will take them up now, if you please."

He had gone through the First National at almost record-breaking speed—but thoroughly, as he did everything. The running order of the bank was smooth and clean, and that had facilitated his work. There was but one other bank in the town. He received from the Government a fee of twenty-five dollars for each bank that he examined. He should be able to go over those loans and discounts in half an hour. If so, he could examine the other bank immediately afterward, and catch the 11.45, the only other train that day in the direction he was working. Otherwise, he would have to spend the night and Sunday in this uninteresting Western town. That was why Mr. Nettlewick was rushing matters.

"Come with me, sir," said Major Kingman, in his deep voice, that united the Southern drawl with the rhythmic twang of the West; "we will go over them together. Nobody in the bank knows those notes as I do. Some of 'em are a little wobbly on their legs, and some are mavericks without extra many brands on their backs, but they'll most all pay out at the round-up."

The two sat down at the president's desk. First, the examiner went through the notes at lightning speed, and added up their total, finding it to agree with the amount of loans carried on the book of daily balance. Next, he took up the larger loans, inquiring scrupulously into the condition of their endorsers or securities. The new examiner's mind seemed to course and turn and make unexpected dashes hither and thither like a bloodhound seeking a trail. Finally he pushed aside all the notes except a few, which he arranged in a neat pile before him and began a dry, formal little speech.

"I find, sir, the condition of your bank to be very good, considering the poor crops and the depression in the cattle interests of your state. The clerical work seems to be done accurately and punctually. Your past-due paper is moderate in amount, and promises only a small loss. I would recommend the calling in of your large loans, and the making of only sixty and ninety day or call loans until general business revives. And now, there is one thing more, and I will have finished with the bank. Here are six notes aggregating something like $40,000. They are secured, according to their faces, by various stocks, bonds, shares, etc., to the value of $70,000. Those securities are missing from the notes to which they should be attached.

I suppose you have them in the safe or vault. You will permit me to examine them."

Major Tom's light-blue eyes turned unflinchingly toward the examiner.

"No, sir," he said, in a low but steady tone; "those securities are neither in the safe nor the vault. I have taken them. You may hold me personally responsible for their absence."

Nettlewick felt a slight thrill. He had not expected this. He had struck a momentous trail when the hunt was drawing to a close.

"Ah!" said the examiner. He waited a moment, and then continued: "May I ask you to explain more definitely?"

"The securities were taken by me," repeated the major. "It was not for my own use, but to save an old friend in trouble. Come in here, sir, and we'll talk it over."

He led the examiner into the bank's private office at the rear, and closed the door. There was a desk, and a table, and half-a-dozen leather-covered chairs. On the wall was the mounted head of a Texas steer with horns five feet from tip to tip. Opposite hung the major's old cavalry sabre that he had carried at Shiloh and Fort Pillow.

Placing a chair for Nettlewick, the major seated himself by the window, from which he could see the post-office and the carved limestone front of the Stockmen's National. He did not speak at once, and Nettlewick felt, perhaps, that the ice should be broken by something so near its own temperature as the voice of official warning.

"Your statement," he began, "since you have failed to modify it, amounts, as you must know, to a very serious thing. You are aware, also, of what my duty must compel me to do. I shall have to go before the United States Commissioner and make——"

"I know, I know," said Major Tom, with a wave of his hand. "You don't suppose I'd run a bank without being posted on national banking laws, and the revised statutes! Do your duty. I'm not asking any favours. But, I spoke of my friend. I did want you to hear me tell you about Bob."

Nettlewick settled himself in his chair. There would be no leaving San Rosario for him that day. He would have to telegraph to the Comptroller of the Currency; he would have to swear out a warrant before the United States Commissioner for the arrest of Major Kingman; perhaps he would be ordered to close the bank on account of the loss of the securities. It was not the first crime the examiner had unearthed. Once or twice the terrible upheaval of human emotions that his investigations had loosed had almost caused a ripple in his official calm. He had seen bank men kneel and plead and cry like women for a chance—an hour's time—the overlooking of a single error. One cashier had shot himself at his desk before him. None of them had taken it with the dignity and coolness of this stern old Westerner. Nettlewick felt that he owed it to him at least to listen if he wished to talk. With his elbow on the arm of his chair, and his square chin resting upon the fingers of his right hand, the bank examiner waited to hear the confession of the president of the First National Bank of San Rosario.

"When a man's your friend," began Major Tom, somewhat didactically, "for forty years, and tried by water, fire, earth, and cyclones, when you can do him a little favour you feel like doing it."

("Embezzle for him $70,000 worth of securities," thought the examiner.)

"We were cowboys together, Bob and I," continued the major, speaking slowly, and deliberately, and musingly, as if his thoughts were rather with the past than the critical present, "and we prospected together for gold and silver over Arizona, New Mexico, and a good part of California. We were both in the war of 'sixty-one, but in different commands. We've fought Indians and horse thieves side by side; we've starved for weeks in a cabin in the Arizona mountains, buried twenty feet deep in snow; we've ridden herd together when the wind blew so hard the lightning couldn't strike—well, Bob and I have been through some rough spells since the first time we met in the branding camp of the old Anchor-Bar Ranch. And during that time we've found it necessary more than once to help each other out of tight places. In those days it was expected of a man to stick to his friend, and he didn't ask any credit for it. Probably next day you'd need him to get at your back and help stand off a band of Apaches, or put a tourniquet on your leg above a rattlesnake bite and ride for whisky. So, after all, it was give and take, and if you didn't stand square with your pardner, why, you might be shy one when you needed him. But Bob was a man who was willing to go further than that. He never played a limit.

"Twenty years ago I was sheriff of this county, and I made Bob my chief deputy. That was before the boom in cattle when we both made our stake. I was sheriff and collector, and it was a big thing for me then. I was married, and we had a boy and a girl—a four and a six year old. There was a comfortable house next to the court-house, furnished by the county, rent free, and I was saving some money. Bob did most of the office work. Both of us had seen rough times and plenty of rustling and danger, and I tell you it was great to hear the rain and the sleet dashing against the windows of nights, and be warm and safe and comfortable, and know you could get up in the morning and be shaved and have folks call you 'mister.' And then, I had the finest wife and kids that ever struck the range, and my old friend with me enjoying the first fruits of prosperity and white shirts, and I guess I was happy. Yes, I was happy about that time."

The major sighed and glanced casually out of the window. The bank examiner changed his position, and leaned his chin upon his other hand.

"One winter," continued the major, "the money for the county taxes came pouring in so fast that I didn't have time to take the stuff to the bank for a week. I just shoved the cheques into a cigar box and the money into a sack, and locked them in the big safe that belonged in the sheriff's office.

"I had been overworked that week, and was about sick, anyway. My nerves were out of order, and my sleep at night didn't seem to rest me. The doctor had some scientific name for it, and I was taking medicine. And so, added to the rest, I went to bed at night with that money on my mind. Not that there was much need of being worried, for the safe was a good one, and nobody but Bob and I knew the combination. On Friday night there was about $6,500 in cash in the bag. On Saturday morning I went to the office as usual. The safe was locked, and Bob was writing at his desk. I opened the safe, and the money was gone. I called Bob, and roused everybody in the court-house to announce the robbery. It struck me that Bob took it pretty quiet, considering how much it reflected upon both him and me.

"Two days went by and we never got a clue. It couldn't have been burglars, for the safe had been opened by the combination in the proper way. People must have begun to talk, for one afternoon in comes Alice—that's my wife—and the boy and girl, and Alice stamps her foot, and her eyes flash, and she cries out, 'The lying wretches—Tom, Tom!' and I catch her in a faint, and bring her round little by little, and she lays her head down and cries and cries for the first time since she took Tom Kingman's name and fortunes. And Jack and Zilla—the youngsters—they were always wild as tiger cubs to rush at Bob and climb all over him whenever they were allowed to come to the court-house—they stood and kicked their little shoes, and herded together like scared partridges. They were having their first trip down into the shadows of life. Bob was working at his desk, and he got up and went out without a word. The grand jury was in session then, and the next morning Bob went before them and confessed that he stole the money. He said he lost it in a poker game. In fifteen minutes they had found a true bill and sent me the warrant to arrest the man with whom I'd been closer than a thousand brothers for many a year.

"I did it, and then I said to Bob, pointing: 'There's my house, and here's my office, and up there's Maine, and out that way is California, and over there is Florida—and that's your range 'til court meets. You're in my charge, and I take the responsibility. You be here when you're wanted.'

" 'Thanks, Tom,' he said, kind of carelessly; 'I was sort of hoping you wouldn't lock me up. Court meets next Monday, so, if you don't object, I'll just loaf around the office until then. I've got one favour to ask, if it isn't too much. If you'd let the kids come out in the yard once in awhile and have a romp I'd like it.'

" 'Why not?' I answered him. 'They're welcome, and so are you. And come to my house, the same as ever.' You see, Mr. Nettlewick, you can't make a friend of a thief, but neither can you make a thief of a friend, all at once."

The examiner made no answer. At that moment was heard the shrill whistle of a locomotive pulling into the depot. That was the train on the little, narrow-gauge road that struck into San Rosario from the south. The major cocked his ear and listened for a moment, and looked at his watch. The narrow-gauge was in on time—10.35. The major continued:

"So Bob hung around the office, reading the papers and smoking. I put another deputy to work in his place, and, after awhile, the first excitement of the case wore off.

"One day when we were alone in the office Bob came over to where I was sitting. He was looking sort of grim and blue—the same look he used to get when he'd been up watching for Indians all night or herd-riding.

" 'Tom,' says he, 'it's harder than standing off redskins; it's harder than lying in the lava desert forty miles from water; but I'm going to stick it out to the end. You know that's been my style.

But if you'd tip me the smallest kind of a sign—if you'd just say, "Bob, I understand," why, it would make it lots easier.'

"I was surprised. 'I don't know what you mean, Bob,' I said. 'Of course, you know that I'd do anything under the sun to help you that I could. But you've got me guessing.'

" 'All right, Tom,' was all he said, and he went back to his newspaper and lit another cigar.

"It was the night before court met when I found out what he meant. I went to bed that night with that same old, light-headed, nervous feeling come back upon me. I dropped off to sleep about midnight. When I awoke I was standing half dressed in one of the court-house corridors. Bob was holding one of my arms, our family doctor the other, and Alice was shaking me and half crying. She had sent for the doctor without my knowing it, and when he came they had found me out of bed and missing, and had begun a search.

" 'Sleep-walking,' said the doctor.

"All of us went back to the house, and the doctor told us some remarkable stories about the strange things people had done while in that condition. I was feeling rather chilly after my trip out, and, as my wife was out of the room at the time, I pulled open the door of an old wardrobe that stood in the room and dragged out a big quilt I had seen in there. With it tumbled out the bag of money for stealing which Bob was to be tried—and convicted—in the morning.

" 'How the jumping rattlesnakes did that get there?' I yelled, and all hands must have seen how surprised I was. Bob knew in a flash.

" 'You darned old snoozer,' he said, with the

old-time look on his face. 'I saw you put it there. I watched you open the safe and take it out, and I followed you. I looked through the window and saw you hide it in that wardrobe.'

" 'Then, you blankety-blank, flop-eared, sheep-headed coyote, what did you say you took it for?'

" 'Because,' said Bob, simply, 'I didn't know you were asleep.'

"I saw him glance toward the door of the room where Jack and Zilla were, and I knew then what it meant to be a man's friend from Bob's point of view."

Major Tom paused, and again directed his glance out of the window. He saw some one in the Stockmen's National Bank reach and draw a yellow shade down the whole length of its plate-glass, big front window, although the position of the sun did not seem to warrant such a defensive movement against its rays.

Nettlewick sat up straight in his chair. He had listened patiently, but without consuming interest, to the major's story. It had impressed him as irrelevant to the situation, and it could certainly have no effect upon the consequences. Those Western people, he thought, had an exaggerated sentimentality. They were not business-like. They needed to be protected from their friends. Evidently the major had concluded. And what he had said amounted to nothing.

"May I ask," said the examiner, "if you have anything further to say that bears directly upon the question of those abstracted securities?'

"Abstracted securities, sir!" Major Tom turned suddenly in his chair, his blue eyes flashing upon the examiner. "What do you mean, sir?"

He drew from his coat pocket a batch of folded

papers held together by a rubber band, tossed them into Nettlewick's hands, and rose to his feet.

"You'll find those securities there, sir, every stock, bond, and share of 'em. I took them from the notes while you were counting the cash. Examine and compare them for yourself."

The major led the way back into the banking-room. The examiner, astounded, perplexed, nettled, at sea, followed. He felt that he had been made the victim of something that was not exactly a hoax, but that left him in the shoes of one who had been played upon, used, and then discarded, without even an inkling of the game. Perhaps, also, his official position had been irreverently juggled with. But there was nothing he could take hold of. An official report of the matter would be an absurdity. And, somehow, he felt that he would never know anything more about the matter than he did then.

Frigidly, mechanically, Nettlewick examined the securities, found them to tally with the notes, gathered his black wallet, and rose to depart.

"I will say," he protested, turning the indignant glare of his glasses upon Major Kingman, "that your statements—your misleading statements, which you have not condescended to explain—do not appear to be quite the thing, regarded either as business or humour. I do not understand such motives or actions."

Major Tom looked down at him serenely and not unkindly.

"Son," he said, "there are plenty of things in the chaparral, and on the prairies, and up the cañons that you don't understand. But I want to thank you for listening to a garrulous old man's prosy story. We old Texans love to talk about our adventures and our old comrades, and the home folks have long ago learned to run when we begin with 'Once upon a time,' so we have to spin our yarns to the stranger within our gates."

The major smiled, but the examiner only bowed coldly, and abruptly quitted the bank. They saw him travel diagonally across the street in a straight line and enter the Stockmen's National Bank.

Major Tom sat down at his desk, and drew from his vest pocket the note Roy had given him. He had read it once, but hurriedly, and now, with something like a twinkle in his eyes, he read it again. These were the words he read:

DEAR TOM,—

I hear there's one of Uncle Sam's greyhounds going through you, and that means that we'll catch him inside of a couple of hours, maybe. Now, I want you to do something for me. We've got just $2,200 in the bank, and the law requires that we have $20,000. I let Ross and Fisher have $18,000 late yesterday afternoon to buy up that Gibson bunch of cattle. They'll realize $40,000 in less than thirty days on the transaction, but that won't make my cash on hand look any prettier to that bank examiner. Now, I can't show him those notes, for they're just plain notes of hand without any security in sight, but you know very well that Pink Ross and Jim Fisher are two of the finest white men God ever made, and they'll do the square thing. You remember Jim Fisher—he was the one who shot that faro dealer in El Paso. I wired Sam Bradshaw's bank to send me $20,000, and it will get in on the narrow-gauge at 10.35. You can't let a bank examiner in to count $2,200 and close your doors. Tom, you hold that examiner. Hold him. Hold him if you have to rope him and sit on his head. Watch our front window after the narrow-gauge gets in, and when we've got the cash inside we'll pull down the shade for a signal. Don't turn him loose till then. I'm counting on you, Tom.

Your old Pard,

BOB BUCKLEY,

Prest. Stockmen's National.

The major began to tear the note into small pieces and throw them into his waste basket. He gave a satisfied little chuckle as he did so.

"Confounded old reckless cowpuncher!" he growled, contentedly, "that pays him some on account for what he tried to do for me in the sheriff's office twenty years ago."

XXVI: INNOCENTS OF BROADWAY

"I HOPE some day to retire from business," said Jeff Peters; "and when I do I don't want anybody to be able to say that I ever got a dollar of any man's money without giving him a *quid pro rata* for it. I've always managed to leave a customer some little gewgaw to paste in his scrap-book or stick between his Seth Thomas clock and the wall after we are through trading.

"There was one time I came near having to break this rule of mine and do a profligate and illaudable action, but I was saved from it by the laws and statutes of our great and profitable country.

"One summer me and Andy Tucker, my partner,

went to New York to lay in our annual assortment of clothes and gents' furnishings. We was always pompous and regardless dressers, finding that looks went further than anything else in our business, except maybe our knowledge of railroad schedules and an autograph photo of the President that Loeb sent us, probably by mistake. Andy wrote a nature letter once and sent it in about animals that he had seen caught in a trap lots of times. Loeb must have read it 'triplets,' instead of 'trap lots,' and sent the photo. Anyhow, it was useful to us to show people as a guarantee of good faith.

"Me and Andy never cared much to do business in New York. It was too much like pot-hunting. Catching suckers in that town, is like dynamiting a Texas lake for brass. All you have to do anywhere between the North and East rivers is to stand in the street with an open bag marked, 'Drop packages of money here. No cheques or loose bills taken.' You have a cop handy to club pikers who try to chip in post-office orders and Canadian money, and that's all there is to New York for a hunter who loves his profession. So me and Andy used to just nature fake the town. We'd get out our spyglasses and watch the woodcocks along the Broadway swamps putting plaster casts on their broken legs, and then we'd sneak away without firing a shot.

"One day in the papier-mâché palm-room of a chloral hydrate and hops agency in a side street about eight inches off Broadway me and Andy had thrust upon us the acquaintance of a New Yorker. We had been together until we discovered that each of us knew a man named Hellsmith, travelling for a stove factory in Duluth. This caused us to remark that the world was a very small place, and then this New Yorker busts his string and takes off his tinfoil and excelsior packing and starts in giving us his Ellen Terris, beginning with the time he used to sell shoe-laces to the Indians on the spot where Tammany Hall now stands.

"This New Yorker had made his money keeping a cigar store in Beekman Street, and he hadn't been above Fourteenth Street in ten years. Moreover, he had whiskers, and the time has gone by when a true sport will do anything to a man with whiskers. No grafter except a boy who is soliciting subscribers to an illustrated weekly to win the prize air rifle, or a widow, would have the heart to tamper with the man behind with the razor. He was a typical city Reub—I'd bet the man hadn't been out of sight of a sky-scraper in twenty-five years.

"Well, presently this metropolitan backwoodsman pulls out a roll of bills with an old blue sleeve elastic fitting tight around it and opens it up.

" 'There's $5,000, Mr. Peters,' says he, shoving it over the table to me, 'saved during my fifteen years of business. Put that in your pocket and keep it for me, Mr. Peters. I'm glad to meet you gentlemen from the West, and I may take a drop too much. I want you to take care of my money for me. Now, let's have another beer.'

" 'You'd better keep this yourself,' says I. 'We are strangers to you, and you can't trust everybody you meet. Put your roll back in your pocket,' says I. 'And you'd better run along home before some farm-hand from the Kaw River bottoms strolls in here and sells you a copper mine.'

" 'Oh, I don't know,' says Whiskers. 'I guess

Little Old New York can take care of herself. I guess I know a man that's on the square when I see him. I've always found the Western people all right. I ask you as a favour, Mr. Peters,' says he, 'to keep that roll in your pocket for me. I know a gentleman when I see him. And now let's have some more beer.'

"In about ten minutes this fall of manna leans back in his chair and snores. Andy looks at me and says: 'I reckon I'd better stay with him for five minutes or so, in case the waiter comes in.'

"I went out the side door and walked half a block up the street. And then I came back and sat down at the table.

" 'Andy,' says I, 'I can't do it. It's too much like swearing off taxes. I can't go off with this man's money without doing something to earn it, like taking advantage of the Bankrupt Act or leaving a bottle of eczema lotion in his pocket to make it look more like a square deal.'

" 'Well,' says Andy, 'it does seem kind of hard on one's professional pride to lope off with a bearded pard's competency, especially after he has nominated you custodian of his bundle in the sappy insouciance of his urban indiscrimination. Suppose we wake him up and see if we can formulate some commercial sophistry by which he will be enabled to give us both his money and a good excuse.'

"We wakes up Whiskers. He stretches himself and yawns out the hypothesis that he must have dropped off for a minute. And then he says he wouldn't mind sitting in at a little gentleman's game of poker. He used to play some when he attended high school in Brooklyn; and as he was out for a good time, why—and so forth.

"Andy brightens up a little at that, for it looks like it might be a solution to our financial troubles. So we all three go to our hotel further down Broadway and have the cards and chips brought up to Andy's room. I tried once more to make this Babe in the Horticultural Gardens take his five thousand. But no.

" 'Keep that little roll for me, Mr. Peters,' says he, 'and oblige. I'll ask you for it when I want it. I guess I know when I'm among friends. A man that's done business on Beekman Street for twenty years, right in the heart of the wisest little old village on earth, ought to know what he's about. I guess I can tell a gentleman from a con man or a flimflammer when I meet him. I've got some odd change in my clothes—enough to start the game with, I guess.'

"He goes through his pockets and rains $20 gold certificates on the table till it looked like a $10,000 'Autumn Day in a Lemon Grove' picture by Turner in the salons. Andy almost smiled.

"The first round that was dealt, this boulevardier slaps down his hand, claims low and jack and big casino and rakes in the pot.

"Andy always took a pride in his poker playing. He got up from the table and looked sadly out of the window at the street doors.

" 'Well, gentlemen,' says the cigar man, 'I don't blame you for not wanting to play. I've forgotten the fine points of the game, I guess, it's been so long since I indulged. Now, how long are you gentlemen going to be in the city?'

"I told him about a week longer. He says that'll suit him fine. His cousin is coming over from Brooklyn that evening and they are going to see the sights of New York. His cousin, he says, is in the artificial limb and lead casket business, and hasn't crossed the bridge in eight years. They expect to have the time of their lives, and he winds up by asking me to keep his roll of money for him till next day. I tried to make him take it, but it only insulted him to mention it.

" 'I'll use what I've got in loose change,' says he. 'You keep the rest for me. I'll drop in on you and Mr. Tucker to-morrow afternoon about six or seven,' says he, 'and we'll have dinner together. Be good.'

"After Whiskers had gone Andy looked at me curious and doubtful.

" 'Well, Jeff,' says he, 'it looks like the ravens are trying to feed us two Elijahs so hard that if we turned 'em down again we ought to have the Audubon Society after us. It won't do to put the crown aside too often. I know this is something like paternalism, but don't you think Opportunity has skinned its knuckles about enough knocking at our door?'

"I put my feet on the table and my hands in my pockets, which is an attitude unfavourable to frivolous thoughts.

" 'Andy,' says I, 'this man with the hirsute whiskers has got us in a predicament. We can't move hand or foot with his money. You and me have got a gentleman's agreement with Fortune that we can't break. We've done business in the West where it's more of a fair game. Out there the people we skin are trying to skin us, even the farmers and the remittance men that the magazines send out to write up Goldfields. But there's little sport in New York city for rod, reel or gun. They hunt here with either one of two things—a slung-shot or a letter of introduction. The town has been stocked so full of carp that the game fish are all gone. If you spread a net here, do you catch legitimate suckers in it, such as the Lord intended to be caught—fresh guys who know it all, sports with a little coin and the nerve to play another man's game, street crowds out for the fun of dropping a dollar or two and village smarties who know just where the little pea is? No, sir,' says I. 'What the grafters live on here is widows and orphans, and foreigners who save up a bag of money and hand it out over the first counter they see with an iron railing to it, and factory girls and little shopkeepers that never leave the block they do business on. That's what they call suckers here. They're nothing but canned sardines, and all the bait you need to catch 'em is a pocket-knife and a soda cracker.

" 'Now, this cigar man,' I went on, 'is one of the types. He's lived twenty years on one street without learning as much as you would in getting a once-over shave from a lock-jawed barber in a Kansas cross-roads town. But he's a New Yorker, and he'll brag about that all the time when he isn't picking up live wires or getting in front of street cars or paying out money to wire-tappers or standing under a safe that's being hoisted into a sky-scraper. When a New Yorker does loosen up,' says I, 'it's like the spring decomposition of the ice jam in the Allegheny River. He'll swamp you with cracked ice and backwater if you don't get out of the way.

" 'It's mighty lucky for us, Andy,' says I, 'that this cigar exponent with the parsley dressing saw fit to bedeck us with his childlike trust and altruism. For,' says I, 'this money of his is an eyesore to my sense of rectitude and ethics. We can't take it, Andy; you know we can't,' says I, 'for we haven't a shadow of a title to it—not a shadow. If there was the least bit of a way we could put in a claim to it I'd be willing to see him start in for another twenty years and make another $5,000 for himself, but we haven't sold him anything, we haven't been embroiled in a trade or anything commercial. He approached us friendly,' says I, 'and with blind and beautiful idiocy laid the stuff in our hands. We'll have to give it back to him when he wants it.'

" 'Your arguments,' says Andy, 'are past criticism or comprehension. No, we can't walk off with the money—as things now stand. I admire your conscious way of doing business, Jeff,' says Andy, 'and I wouldn't propose anything that wasn't square in line with your theories of morality and initiative.

" 'But I'll be away to-night and most of to-morrow, Jeff,' says Andy. 'I've got some business affairs that I want to attend to. When this free greenbacks party comes in to-morrow afternoon hold him here till I arrive. We've all got an engagement for dinner, you know.'

"Well, sir, about five the next afternoon in trips the cigar man, with his eyes half open.

" 'Been having a glorious time, Mr. Peters,' says he. 'Took in all the sights. I tell you New York is the onliest only. Now if you don't mind,' says he, 'I'll lie down on that couch and doze off for about nine minutes before Mr. Tucker comes. I'm not used to being up all night. And to-morrow, if you don't mind, Mr. Peters, I'll take that five thousand. I met a man last night that's got a sure winner at the race-track to-morrow. Excuse me for being so impolite as to go to sleep, Mr. Peters.'

"And so this inhabitant of the second city in the world reposes himself and begins to snore, while I sit there musing over things and wishing I was back in the West, where you could always depend on a customer fighting to keep his money hard enough to let your conscience take it from him.

"At half-past five Andy comes in and sees the sleeping form.

" 'I've been over to Trenton,' says Andy, pulling a document out of his pocket. 'I think I've got this matter fixed up all right, Jeff. Look at that.'

"I open the paper and see that it is a corporation charter issued by the State of New Jersey to 'The Peters & Tucker Consolidated and Amalgamated Aerial Franchise Development Company, Limited.'

" 'It's to buy up rights of way for airship lines,' explained Andy. 'The Legislature wasn't in session, but I found a man at a post-card stand in the lobby that kept a stock of charters on hand. There are 100,000 shares,' says Andy, 'expect to reach a par value of $1. I had one blank certificate of stock printed.'

"Andy takes out the blank and begins to fill it in with a fountain-pen.

" 'The whole bunch,' says he, 'goes to our friend in dreamland for $5,000. Did you learn his name?'

" 'Make it out to bearer,' says I.

"We put the certificate of stock in the cigar man's hand and went out to pack our suit-cases.

"On the ferry-boat Andy says to me: 'Is your conscience easy about taking the money now, Jeff?

" 'Why shouldn't it be?' says I. 'Are we any better than any other Holding Corporation?' "

XXVII: THE DEFEAT OF THE CITY

ROBERT WALMSLEY'S descent upon the city resulted in a Kilkenny struggle. He came out of the fight victor by a fortune and a reputation. On the other hand, he was swallowed up by the city. The city gave him what he demanded, and then branded him with its brand. It remodelled, cut, trimmed and stamped him to the pattern it approves. It opened its social gates to him, and shot him in on a close-cropped, formal lawn with the select herd of ruminants. In dress, habits, manners, provincialism, routine and narrowness he acquired that charming insolence, that irritating completeness, that sophisticated crassness, that overbalanced poise that makes the Manhattan gentleman so delightfully small in his greatness.

One of the up-state rural counties pointed with pride to the successful young metropolitan lawyer as a product of its soil. Six years earlier this county had removed the wheat straw from between its huckleberry-stained teeth, and emitted a derisive and bucolic laugh as old man Walmsley's freckle-faced "Bob" abandoned the certain three-per-diem meals of the one-horse farm for the discontinuous quick-lunch counters of the three-ringed metropolis. At the end of the six years no murder trial, coaching party, automobile accident or cotillion was complete in which the name of Robert Walmsley did not figure. Tailors waylaid him in the street to get a new wrinkle from the cut of his unwrinkled trousers. Hyphenated fellows in the clubs and members of the oldest subpœnaed families were glad to clap him on the back and allow him three letters of his name.

But the Matterhorn of Robert Walmsley's success was not scaled until he married Alicia Van Der Pool. I cite the Matterhorn, for just so high and cool and white and inaccessible was this daughter of the old burghers. The social Alps that ranged about her—over whose bleak passes a thousand climbers struggled—reached only to her knees. She towered in her own atmosphere, serene, chaste, prideful, wading in no fountains, dining no monkeys, breeding no dogs for bench shows. She was a Van Der Pool. Fountains were made to play for her; monkeys were made for other people's ancestors; dogs, she understood, were created to be companions of blind persons and objectionable characters who smoked pipes.

This was the Matterhorn that Robert Walmsley accomplished. If he found, with the good poet with the game foot and artificially curled hair, that he who ascends to mountain-tops will find the loftiest peaks most wrapped in clouds and snow, he concealed his chilblains beneath a brave and smiling exterior. He was a lucky man and knew it, even though he were imitating the Spartan boy with an ice-cream freezer beneath his doublet frappéeing the region of his heart.

After a brief wedding-tour abroad, the couple returned to create a decided ripple in the calm cistern (so placid and cool and sunless it is) of the best society. They entertained at their red-brick mausoleum of ancient greatness in an old square that is a cemetery of crumbled glory. And Robert Walmsley was proud of his wife; although while one of his hands shook his guests' the other held tightly to his alpenstock and thermometer.

One day Alicia found a letter written to Robert by his mother. It was an unerudite letter, full of crops and motherly love and farm notes. It chronicled the health of the pig and the recent red calf, and asked concerning Robert's in return. It was a letter direct from the soil, straight from home, full of biographies of bees, tales of turnips, pæans of new-laid eggs, neglected parents, and the slump in dried apples.

"Why have I not been shown your mother's letters?" asked Alicia. There was always something in her voice that made you think of lorgnettes, of accounts at Tiffany's, of sledges smoothly gliding on the trail from Dawson to Forty Mile, of the tinkling of pendant prisms on your grandmother's chandeliers, of snow lying on a convent roof; of a police sergeant refusing bail. "Your mother," continued Alicia, "invites us to make a visit to the farm. I have never seen a farm. We will go there for a week or two, Robert."

"We will," said Robert, with the grand air of an associate Supreme Justice concurring in an opinion. "I did not lay the invitation before you because I thought you would not care to go. I am much pleased at your decision."

"I will write to her myself," answered Alicia, with a faint foreshadowing of enthusiasm, "Félice shall pack my trunks at once. Seven, I think, will be enough. I do not suppose that your mother entertains a great deal. Does she give many house parties?"

Robert arose, and as attorney for rural places filed a demurrer against six of the seven trunks. He endeavoured to define, picture, elucidate, set forth, and describe a farm. His own words sounded strange in his ears. He had not realized how thoroughly urbsidized he had become.

A week passed, and found them landed at the little country station five hours out from the city. A grinning, stentorian, sarcastic youth driving a mule to a spring wagon hailed Robert savagely.

"Hallo, Mr. Walmsley. Found your way back at last, have you? Sorry I couldn't bring in the automobile for you, but dad's bull-tonguing the ten-acre clover patch with it to-day. Guess you'll excuse my not wearing a dress-suit over to meet you—it ain't six o'clock yet, you know."

"I'm glad to see you, Tom," said Robert, grasping his brother's hand. "Yes, I've found my way at last. You've a right to say 'at last.' It's been over two years since the last time. But it will be oftener after this, my boy."

Alicia, cool in the summer heat as an Arctic wraith, white as a Norse snow maiden in her flimsy muslin and fluttering lace parasol, came round the corner of the station; and Tom was stripped of his assurance. He became chiefly eyesight clothed in blue jeans, and on the homeward drive to the mule alone did he confide in language the inwardness of his thoughts.

They drove homeward. The low sun dropped a spendthrift flood of gold upon the fortunate fields of wheat. The cities were far away. The road lay curling around wood and dale and hill like a ribbon lost from the robe of careless summer. The wind followed like a whinnying colt in the track of Phœbus's steeds.

By and by the farmhouse peeped grey out of its faithful grove; they saw the long lane with its convoy of walnut trees running from the road to the house; they smelled the wild rose and the breath of cool, damp willows in the creek's bed. And then in unison all the voices of the soil began a chant addressed to the soul of Robert Walmsley. Out of the tilted aisles of the dim wood they came hollowly; they chirped and buzzed from the parched grass; they trilled from the ripples of the creek ford; they floated up in clear Pan's pipe notes from the dimming meadows; the whip-poor-wills joined in as they pursued midges in the upper air; slow-going cow-bells struck out a homely accompaniment —and this was what each one said: "You've found your way back at last, have you?"

The old voices of the soil spoke to him. Leaf and bud and blossom conversed with him in the old vocabulary of his careless youth—the inanimate things, the familiar stones and rails, the gates and furrows and roofs and turns of the road had an eloquence, too, and a power in the transformation. The country had smiled, and he had felt the breath of it, and his heart was drawn as if in a moment back to his old love. The city was far away.

This rural atavism, then, seized Robert Walmsley and possessed him. A queer thing he noticed in connection with it was that Alicia, sitting at his side, suddenly seemed to him a stranger. She did not belong to this recurrent phase. Never before had she seemed so remote, so colourless and high—so intangible and unreal. And yet he had never admired her more than when she sat there by him in the rickety spring wagon, chiming no more with his mood and with her environment than the Matterhorn chimes with a peasant's cabbage garden.

That night, when the greetings and the supper were over, the entire family, including Buff, the yellow dog, bestrewed itself upon the front porch. Alicia, not haughty but silent, sat in the shadow dressed in an exquisite pale-grey tea-gown. Robert's mother discoursed to her happily concerning marmalade and lumbago. Tom sat on the top step; Sisters Millie and Pam on the lowest step to catch the lightning bugs. Mother had the willow rocker. Father sat in the big arm-chair with one of its arms gone. Buff sprawled in the middle of the porch in everybody's way. The twilight pixies and pucks stole forth unseen and plunged other poignant shafts of memory into the heart of Robert. A rural madness entered his soul. The city was far away.

Father sat without his pipe, writhing in his heavy boots, a sacrifice to rigid courtesy. Robert shouted: "No, you don't!" He fetched the pipe and lit it; he seized the old gentleman's boots and tore them off. The last one slipped suddenly, and Mr. Robert Walmsley, of Washington Square, tumbled off the porch backward with Buff on top of him, howling fearfully. Tom laughed sarcastically.

Robert tore off his coat and vest and hurled them into a lilac bush.

"Come out here, you land-lubber," he cried to Tom, "and I'll put grass seed on your back. I think you called me a 'dude' a while ago. Come along and cut your capers."

Tom understood the invitation and accepted it with delight. Three times they wrestled on the grass, "side holds," even as the giants of the mat. And twice was Tom forced to bite grass at the hands of the distinguished lawyer. Dishevelled, panting, each still boasting of his own prowess, they stumbled back to the porch. Millie cast a pert reflection upon the qualities of a city brother. In an instant Robert had secured a horrid katydid in his fingers and bore down upon her. Screaming wildly, she fled up the lane, pursued by the avenging glass of form. A quarter of a mile and they returned, she full of apology to the victorious "dude." The rustic mania possessed him unabatedly.

"I can do up a cowpenful of you slow hayseeds," he proclaimed, vaingloriously. "Bring on your bulldogs, your hired men, and your log-rollers."

He turned hand-springs on the grass that prodded Tom to envious sarcasm. And then, with a whoop, he clattered to the rear and brought back Uncle Ike, a battered coloured retainer of the family, with his banjo, and strewed sand on the porch and danced "Chicken in the Bread Tray" and did buck-and-wing wonders for half an hour longer. Incredibly wild and boisterous things he did. He sang, he told stories that set all but one shrieking, he played the yokel, the humorous clodhopper; he was mad, mad with the revival of the old life in his blood.

He became so extravagant, that once his mother sought gently to reprove him. Then Alicia moved as though she were about to speak, but she did not. Through it all she sat immovable, a slim, white spirit in the dusk that no man might question or read.

By and by she asked permission to ascend to her room, saying that she was tired. On her way she passed Robert. He was standing in the door, the figure of vulgar comedy, with ruffled hair, reddened face, and unpardonable confusion of attire—no trace there of the immaculate Robert Walmsley, the courted clubman and ornament of select circles. He was doing a conjuring trick with some household utensils, and the family, now won over to him without exception, was beholding him with worshipful admiration.

As Alicia passed in Robert started suddenly. He had forgotten for the moment that she was present. Without a glance at him she went on upstairs.

After that the fun grew quiet. An hour passed in talk, and then Robert went up himself.

She was standing by the window when he entered their room. She was still clothed as when they were on the porch. Outside and crowding against the window was a giant apple tree, full-blossomed.

Robert sighed and went near the window. He was ready to meet his fate. A confessed vulgarian, he foresaw the verdict of justice in the shape of that still, white-clad form. He knew the rigid lines that a Van Der Pool would draw. He was a peasant gambolling indecorously in the valley, and the pure, cold, white, unthawed summit of the Matterhorn could not but frown on him. He had been unmasked by his own actions. All the polish, the poise, the form that the city had given him had fallen from him like an ill-fitting mantle at the first breath of a country breeze. Dully he awaited the approaching condemnation.

"Robert," said the calm, cool voice of his judge, "I thought I married a gentleman."

Yes, it was coming. And yet, in the face of it, Robert Walmsley was eagerly regarding a certain branch of the apple tree upon which he used to climb out of that very window. He believed he could do it now. He wondered how many blossoms there were on the tree—ten millions? But here was some one speaking again:

"I thought I married a gentleman," the voice went on, "but——"

Why had she come and was standing so close by his side?

"But I find that I have married"—was this Alicia talking?—"something better—a man. Bob, dear, kiss me, won't you?"

The city was far away.

XXVIII: BY COURIER

IT was neither the season nor the hour when the park had frequenters; and it is likely that the young lady, who was seated on one of the benches at the side of the walk, had merely obeyed a sudden impulse to sit for awhile and enjoy a foretaste of coming spring.

She rested there, pensive and still. A certain melancholy that touched her countenance must have been of recent birth, for it had not yet altered the fine and youthful contours of her cheek, nor subdued the arch though resolute curve of her lips.

A tall young man came striding through the park along the path near which she sat. Behind him tagged a boy carrying a suit-case. At sight of the young lady, the man's face changed to red and back to pale again. He watched her countenance as he drew nearer, with hope and anxiety mingled on his own. He passed within a few yards of her, but he saw no evidence that she was aware of his presence or existence.

Some fifty yards further on he suddenly stopped and sat on a bench at one side. The boy dropped the suit-case and stared at him with wondering, shrewd eyes. The young man took out his handkerchief, and wiped his brow. It was a good handkerchief, a good brow, and the young man was good to look at. He said to the boy:

"I want you to take a message to that young lady on that bench. Tell her I am on my way to the station, to leave for San Francisco, where I shall join that Alaska moose-hunting expedition. Tell her that, since she has commanded me neither to speak nor to write to her, I take this means of making one last appeal to her sense of justice, for the sake of what has been. Tell her that to condemn and discard one who has not deserved such treatment, without giving him her reasons or a chance to explain, is contrary to her nature as I believe it to be. Tell her that I have thus, to a certain degree disobeyed her injunctions, in the hope that she may yet be inclined to see justice done. Go, and tell her that."

The young man dropped a half-dollar into the boy's hand. The boy looked at him for a moment with bright, canny eyes out of a dirty, intelligent face, and then set off at a run. He approached the lady on the bench a little doubtfully, but unembarrassed. He touched the brim of the old plaid bicycle cap perched on the back of his head. The lady looked at him coolly, without prejudice or favour.

"Lady," he said, "dat gent on de oder bench sent yer a song and dance by me. If yer don't know de guy, and he's tryin' to do de Johnny act, say de word, and I'll call a cop in t'ree minutes. If yer does know him, and he's on de square, w'y I'll spiel yer de bunch of hot air he sent yer."

The young lady betrayed a faint interest.

"A song and dance!" she said, in a deliberate, sweet voice that seemed to clothe her words in a diaphanous garment of impalpable irony. "A new idea—in the troubadour line, I suppose. I—used to know the gentleman who sent you, so I think it will hardly be necessary to call the police. You may execute your song and dance, but do not sing too loudly. It is a little early yet for open-air vaudeville, and we might attract attention."

"Awe," said the boy, with a shrug down the length of him, "yer know what I mean, lady. 'Tain't a turn, it's wind. He told me to tell yer he's got his collars and cuffs in dat grip for a scoot clean out to 'Frisco. Den he's goin' to shoot snow-birds in de Klondike. He says yer told him not to send 'round no more pink notes nor come hangin' over de garden gate, and he takes dis means of puttin' yer wise. He says yer refereed him out like a has-been, and never gave him no chance to kick at de decision. He says yer swiped him, and never said why."

The slightly awakened interest in the young lady's eyes did not abate. Perhaps it was caused by either the originality or the audacity of the snow-bird hunter, in thus circumventing her express commands against the ordinary modes of communication. She fixed her eye on a statue standing disconsolate in the dishevelled park, and spoke into the transmitter:

"Tell the gentleman that I need not repeat to him a description of my ideals. He knows what they have been and what they still are. So far as they touch on this case, absolute loyalty and truth are the ones paramount. Tell him that I have studied my own heart as well as one can, and I know its weakness as well as I do its needs. That is why I decline to hear his pleas, whatever they may be. I did not condemn him through hearsay or doubtful evidence, and that is why I make no charge. But, since he persists in hearing what he already well knows, you may convey the matter.

"Tell him that I entered the conservatory that evening from the rear, to cut a rose for my mother. Tell him I saw him and Miss Ashburton beneath the pink oleander. The tableau was pretty, but the pose and juxtaposition were too eloquent and evident to require explanation. I left the conservatory, and, at the same time, the rose and my ideal. You may carry that song and dance to your impresario."

"I'm shy on one word, lady. Jux—jux—put me wise on dat, will yer?"

"Juxtaposition—or you may call it propinquity—or, if you like, being rather too near for one maintaining the position of an ideal."

The gravel spun from beneath the boy's feet. He stood by the other bench. The man's eyes interrogated him, hungrily. The boy's were shining with the impersonal zeal of the translator.

"De lady says dat she's on to de fact dat gals

is dead easy when a feller comes speilin' ghost stories and tryin' to make up, and dat's why she won't listen to no soft-soap. She says she caught yer dead to rights, huggin' a bunch o' calico in de hothouse. She side-stepped in to pull some posies and yer was squeezin' the oder gal to beat the band. She says it looked cute, all right all right, but it made her sick. She says yer better git busy, and make a sneak for de train."

The young man gave a low whistle and his eyes flashed with a sudden thought. His hand flew to the inside pocket of his coat, and drew out a handful of letters. Selecting one, he handed it to the boy, following it with a silver dollar from his vest pocket.

"Give that letter to the lady," he said, "and ask her to read it. Tell her that it should explain the situation. Tell her that, if she had mingled a little trust with her conception of the ideal, much heartache might have been avoided. Tell her that the loyalty she prizes so much has never wavered. Tell her I am waiting for an answer."

The messenger stood before the lady.

"De gent says he's had de ski-bunk put on him widout no cause. He says he's no bum guy; and, lady, yer read dat letter, and I'll bet yer he's a white sport, all right."

The young lady unfolded the letter, somewhat doubtfully, and read it.

"Dear Dr. Arnold: I want to thank you for your most kind and opportune aid to my daughter last Friday evening, when she was overcome by an attack of her old heart-trouble in the conservatory at Mrs. Waldron's reception. Had you not been near to catch her as she fell and to render proper attention, we might have lost her. I would be glad if you would call and undertake the treatment of her case.

"Gratefully yours,

"ROBERT ASHBURTON."

The young lady refolded the letter, and handed it to the boy.

"De gent wants an answer," said the messenger. "Wot's de word?"

The lady's eyes suddenly flashed on him, bright, smiling and wet.

"Tell that guy on the other bench," she said, with a happy, tremulous laugh, "that his girl wants him."

XXIX: BEST-SELLER

I

ONE day last summer I went to Pittsburg—well, I had to go there on business.

My chair-car was profitably well filled with people of the kind one usually sees on chair-cars. Most of them were ladies in brown silk dresses cut with square yokes, with lace insertion, and dotted veils, who refused to have the windows raised. Then there was the usual number of men who looked as if they might be in almost any business and going almost anywhere. Some students of human nature can look at a man in a Pullman and tell you where he is from, his occupation and his stations in life, both flag and social;

but I never could. The only way I can correctly judge a fellow-traveller is when the train is held up by robbers, or when he reaches at the same time as I do for the last towel in the dressing-room of the sleeper.

The porter came and brushed the collection of soot on the window-sill off to the left knee of my trousers. I removed it with an air of apology. The temperature was eighty-eight. One of the dotted-veiled ladies demanded the closing of two more ventilators, and spoke loudly of Interlaken. I leaned back idly in chair No. 7, and looked with the tepidest curiosity at the small, black, bald-spotted head just visible above the back of No. 9.

Suddenly No. 9 hurled a book to the floor between his chair and the window, and, looking, I saw that it was *The Rose Lady and Trevelyan*, one of the best-selling novels of the present day. And then the critic or Philistine, whichever he was, veered his chair toward the window, and I knew him at once for John A. Pescud, of Pittsburg, travelling salesman for a plate-glass company —an old acquaintance whom I had not seen in two years.

In two minutes we were faced, had shaken hands, and had finished with such topics as rain, prosperity, health, residence, and destination. Politics might have followed next; but I was not so ill-fated.

I wish you might know John A. Pescud. He is of the stuff that heroes are not often lucky enough to be made of. He is a small man with a wide smile, and an eye that seems to be fixed upon that little red spot on the end of your nose. I never saw him wear but one kind of necktie, and he believes in cuff-holders and button-shoes. He is as hard and true as anything ever turned out by the Cambria Steel Works; and he believes that as soon as Pittsburg makes smoke-consumers compulsory, St. Peter will come down and sit at the foot of Smithfield Street, and let somebody else attend to the gate up in the branch heaven. He believes that "our" plate-glass is the most important commodity in the world, and that when a man is in his home town he ought to be decent and law-abiding.

During my acquaintance with him in the City of Diurnal Night I had never known his views on life, romance, literature, and ethics. We had browsed, during our meetings, on local topics, and then parted, after Château Margaux, Irish stew, flannel-cakes, cottage-pudding, and coffee (hey, there!—with milk separate). Now I was to get more of his ideas. By way of facts, he told me that business had picked up since the party conventions, and that he was going to get off at Coketown.

II

"Say," said Pescud, stirring his discarded book with the toe of his right shoe, "did you ever read one of these best-sellers? I mean the kind where the hero is an American swell—sometimes even from Chicago—who falls in love with a royal princess from Europe who is travelling under an alias, and follows her to her father's kingdom or principality? I guess you have. They're all alike. Sometimes this going-away masher is a Washington newspaper correspondent and sometimes he is a Van Something from New York, or a Chicago wheat-broker worth fifty millions. But he's always ready to break into the king row of any foreign country that sends over their queens and princesses to try the new plush seats on the Big Four or the B. and O. There doesn't seem to be any other reason in the book for their being here.

"Well, this fellow chases the royal chair-warmer home, as I said, and finds out who she is. He meets her on the *corso* or the *strasse* one evening and gives us ten pages of conversation. She reminds him of the difference in their stations, and that gives him a chance to ring in three solid pages about America's uncrowned sovereigns. If you'd take his remarks and set 'em to music, and then take the music away from 'em, they'd sound exactly like one of George Cohan's songs.

"Well, you know how it runs on, if you've read any of 'em—he slaps the king's Swiss body-guards around like everything whenever they get in his way. He's a great fencer too. Now, I've known of some Chicago men who were pretty notorious fences, but I never heard of any fencers coming from there. He stands on the first landing of the royal staircase in Castle Schutzenfestenstein with a gleaming rapier in his hand, and makes a Baltimore broil of six platoons of traitors who come to massacre the said king. And then he has to fight duels with a couple of chancellors, and foil a plot by four Austrian archdukes to seize the kingdom for a gasolene-station.

"But the great scene is when his rival for the princess's hand, Count Feodor, attacks him between the portcullis and the ruined chapel, armed with a mitrailleuse, a yataghan, and a couple of Siberian bloodhounds. This scene is what runs the best-seller into the twenty-ninth edition before the publisher has had time to draw a cheque for the advance royalties.

"The American hero shucks his coat and throws it over the heads of the bloodhounds, gives the mitrailleuse a slap with his mitt, says 'Yah!' to the yataghan, and lands in Kid McCoy's best style on the count's left eye. Of course, we have a neat little prize-fight right then and there. The count —in order to make the go possible—seems to be an expert at the art of self-defence, himself; and here we have the Corbett-Sullivan fight done over into literature. The book ends with the broker and the princess doing a John Cecil Clay cover under the linden-trees on the Gorgonzola Walk. That winds up the love-story plenty good enough. But I notice that the book dodges the final issue. Even a best-seller has sense enough to shy at either leaving a Chicago grain-broker on the throne of Lobsterpotsdam or bringing over a real princess to eat fish and potato salad in an Italian chalet on Michigan Avenue. What do you think about 'em?"

"Why," said I, "I hardly know, John. There's a saying: 'Love levels all ranks,' you know."

"Yes," said Pescud, "but these kind of love-stories are rank—on the level. I know something about literature, even if I am in plate-glass. These kind of books are wrong, and yet I never go into a train but what they pile 'em up on me. No good can come out of an international clinch between the Old World aristocracy and one of us fresh Americans. When people in real life marry, they generally hunt up somebody in their own station. A fellow usually picks out a girl that went to the same high-school and belonged to the same singing-society that he did. When young millionaires fall in love, they always select the chorus-girl that likes the same kind of sauce on the lobster that he does. Washington newspaper correspondents always marry widow ladies ten years older than themselves who keep boarding-houses. No, sir, you can't make a novel sound right to me when it makes one of C. D. Gibson's bright young men go abroad and turn kingdoms upside down just because he's a Taft American and took a course at a gymnasium. And listen how they talk, too!"

Pescud picked up the best-seller and hunted his page.

"Listen at this," said he. "Trevelyan is chinning with the Princess Alwyna at the back end of the tulip-garden. This is how it goes:

" 'Say not so, dearest and sweetest of earth's flowers. Would I aspire? You are a star set high above me in a royal heaven; I am only—myself. Yet I am a man, and I have a heart to do and dare. I have no title save that of an uncrowned sovereign; but I have an arm and a sword that yet might free Schutzenfestenstein from plots of traitors.'

"Think of a Chicago man packing a sword, and talking about freeing anything that sounded as much like canned pork as that! He'd be much more likely to fight to have an import duty put on it."

"I think I understand you, John," said I. "You want fiction-writers to be consistent with their scenes and characters. They shouldn't mix Turkish pashas with Vermont farmers, or English dukes with Long Island clam-diggers, or Italian countesses with Montana cowboys, or Cincinnati brewery agents with the rajahs of India."

"Or plain business men with aristocracy high above 'em," added Pescud. "It don't jibe. People are divided into classes, whether we admit it or not, and it's everybody's impulse to stick to their own class. They do it, too. I don't see why people go to work and buy hundreds of thousands of books like that. You don't see or hear of any such didoes and capers in real life."

III

"Well, John," said I, "I haven't read a best-seller in a long time. Maybe I've had notions about them somewhat like yours. But tell me more about yourself. Getting along all right with the company?"

"Bully," said Pescud, brightening at once. "I've had my salary raised twice since I saw you, and I get a commission, too. I've bought a neat slice of real estate out in the East End, and have run up a house on it. Next year the firm is going to sell me some shares of stock. Oh, I'm in on the line of General Prosperity, no matter who's elected!"

"Met your affinity yet, John?" I asked.

"Oh, I didn't tell you about that, did I?" said Pescud with a broader grin.

"O-ho!" I said. "So you've taken time enough off from your plate-glass to have a romance?"

"No, no," said John. "No romance—nothing like that! But I'll tell you about it.

"I was on the south-bound, going to Cincinnati, about eighteen months ago, when I saw, across the aisle, the finest-looking girl I'd ever laid eyes on.

Nothing spectacular, you know, but just the sort you want for keeps. Well, I never was up to the flirtation business, either handkerchief, automobile, postage-stamp, or doorstep, and she wasn't the kind to start anything. She read a book and minded her business, which was to make the world prettier and better just by residing in it. I kept on looking out of the side doors of my eyes, and finally the proposition got out of the Pullman class into a case of a cottage with a lawn and vines running over the porch. I never thought of speaking to her, but I let the plate-glass business go to smash, for a while.

"She changed cars at Cincinnati, and took a sleeper to Louisville over the L. and N. There she bought another ticket, and went on through Shelbyville, Frankford and Lexington. Along there I began to have a hard time keeping up with her. The trains came along when they pleased, and didn't seem to be going anywhere in particular, except to keep on the track and the right of way as much as possible. Then they began to stop at junctions instead of towns, and at last they stopped altogether. I'll bet Pinkerton would outbid the plate-glass people for my services any time if they knew how I managed to shadow that young lady. I contrived to keep out of her sight as much as I could, but I never lost track of her.

"The last station she got off at was away down in Virginia, about six in the afternoon. There were about fifty houses and four hundred niggers in sight. The rest was red mud, mules, and speckled hounds.

"A tall old man, with a smooth face and white hair, looking as proud as Julius Cæsar and Roscoe

Conkling on the same post card, was there to meet her. His clothes were frazzled, but I didn't notice that till later. He took her little satchel, and they started over the plank walks and went up a road along the hill. I kept along a piece behind 'em, trying to look like I was hunting a garnet ring in the sand that my sister had lost at a picnic the previous Saturday.

"They went in a gate on top of the hill. It nearly took my breath away when I looked up. Up there in the biggest grove I ever saw was a tremendous house with round white pillars about a thousand feet high, and the yard was so full of rose-bushes and box-bushes and lilacs that you couldn't have seen the house if it hadn't been as big as the Capitol at Washington.

" 'Here's where I have to trail,' says I to myself. I thought before that she seemed to be in moderate circumstances, at least. This must be the Governor's mansion, or the Agricultural Building of a new World's Fair, anyhow. I'd better go back to the village and get posted by the postmaster, or drug the druggist for some information.

"In the village I found a pine hotel called the Bay View House. The only excuse for the name was a bay horse grazing in the front yard. I set my sample-case down, and tried to be ostensible. I told the landlord I was taking orders for plate-glass.

" 'I don't want no plates,' says he, 'but I do need another glass molasses-pitcher.'

"By and by I got him down to local gossip and answering questions.

" 'Why,' says he, 'I thought everybody knowed who lived in the big white house on the hill. It's

Colonel Allyn, the biggest man and the finest quality in Virginia, or anywhere else. They're the oldest family in the State. That was his daughter that got off the train. She's been up to Illinois to see her aunt, who is sick.'

"I registered at the hotel, and on the third day I caught the young lady walking in the front yard, down next to the paling fence. I stopped and raised my hat—there wasn't any other way.

" 'Excuse me,' says I, 'can you tell me where Mr. Hinkle lives?'

"She looks at me as cool as if I was the man come to see about the weeding of the garden, but I thought I saw just a slight twinkle of fun in her eyes.

" 'No one of that name lives in Birchton,' says she. 'That is,' she goes on, 'as far as I know. Is the gentleman you are seeking white?'

"Well, that tickled me. 'No kidding,' says I. 'I'm not looking for smoke, even if I do come from Pittsburg.'

" 'You are quite a distance from home,' says she.

" 'I'd have gone a thousand miles farther,' says I.

" 'Not if you hadn't waked up when the train started in Shelbyville,' says she; and then she turned almost as red as one of the roses on the bushes in the yard. I remembered I had dropped off to sleep on a bench in the Shelbyville station, waiting to see which train she took and only just managed to wake up in time.

"And then I told her why I had come, as respectful and earnest as I could. And I told her everything about myself, and what I was making, and how that all I asked was just to get acquainted with her and try to get her to like me.

"She smiles a little, and blushes some, but her eyes never get mixed up. They look straight at whatever she's talking to.

" 'I never had anyone talk like this to me before, Mr. Pescud,' says she. 'What did you say your name is—John?'

" 'John A.,' says I.

" 'And you came mighty near missing the train at Powhatan Junction, too,' says she, with a laugh that sounded as good as a mileage-book to me.

" 'How did you know?' I asked.

" 'Men are very clumsy,' said she. 'I knew you were on every train. I thought you were going to speak to me, and I'm glad you didn't.'

"Then we had more talk; and at last a kind of proud, serious look came on her face, and she turned and pointed a finger at the big house.

" 'The Allyns,' says she, 'have lived in Elmcroft for a hundred years. We are a proud family. Look at that mansion. It has fifty rooms. See the pillars and porches and balconies. The ceilings in the reception-rooms and the ballroom are twenty-eight feet high. My father is a lineal descendant of belted earls.'

" 'I belted one of 'em once in the Duquesne Hotel, in Pittsburg,' says I, 'and he didn't offer to resent it. He was there dividing his attentions between Monongahela whisky and heiresses, and he got fresh.'

" 'Of course,' she goes on, 'my father wouldn't allow a drummer to set his foot in Elmcroft. If he knew that I was talking to one over the fence he would lock me in my room.'

" 'Would *you* let me come there?' says I. 'Would *you* talk to me if I was to call? For,' I goes on, 'if you said I might come and see you, the earls might be belted or suspendered, or pinned up with safety-pins, as far as I am concerned.'

" 'I must not talk to you,' she says, 'because we have not been introduced. It is not exactly proper. So I will say good-bye, Mr.——'

" 'Say the name,' says I. 'You haven't forgotten it.'

" 'Pescud,' says she, a little mad.

" 'The rest of the name!' I demands, cool as could be.

" 'John,' says she.

" 'John—what?' I says.

" 'John A.,' says she, with her head high. 'Are you through, now?'

" 'I'm coming to see the belted earl to-morrow,' I says.

" 'He'll feed you to his foxhounds,' says she, laughing.

" 'If he does, it'll improve their running,' says I. 'I'm something of a hunter myself.'

" 'I must be going in now,' says she. 'I oughtn't to have spoken to you at all. I hope you'll have a pleasant trip back to Minneapolis—or Pittsburg, was it? Good-bye!'

" 'Good night,' says I, 'and it wasn't Minneapolis. What's your name, first, please?'

"She hesitated. Then she pulled a leaf off a bush, and said:

" 'My name is Jessie,' says she.

" 'Good night, Miss Allyn,' says I.

"The next morning at eleven, sharp, I rang the door-bell of that World's Fair main building.

After about three-quarters of an hour an old nigger man about eighty showed up and asked what I wanted. I gave him my business card, and said I wanted to see the colonel. He showed me in.

"Say, did you ever crack open a wormy English walnut? That's what that house was like. There wasn't enough furniture in it to fill an eight-dollar flat. Some old horsehair lounges and three-legged chairs and some framed ancestors on the walls were all that met the eye. But when Colonel Allyn comes in, the place seemed to light up. You could almost hear a band playing, and see a bunch of old-timers in wigs and white stockings dancing a quadrille. It was the style of him, although he had on the same shabby clothes I saw him wear at the station.

"For about nine seconds he had me rattled, and I came mighty near getting cold feet and trying to sell him some plate-glass. But I got my nerve back pretty quick. He asked me to sit down, and I told him everything. I told him how I followed his daughter from Cincinnati, and what I did it for, and all about my salary and prospects, and explained to him my little code of living—to be always decent and right in your home town; and when you're on the road never take more than four glasses of beer a day or play higher than a twenty-five-cent limit. At first I thought he was going to throw me out of the window, but I kept on talking. Pretty soon I got a chance to tell him that story about the Western Congressman who had lost his pocket-book and the grass widow—you remember that story. Well, that got him to laughing, and I'll bet that was the first laugh those ancestors and horsehair sofas had heard in many a day.

"We talked two hours. I told him everything I knew; and then he began to ask questions, and I told him the rest. All I asked of him was to give me a chance. If I couldn't make a hit with the little lady, I'd clear out, and not bother any more. At last he says:

" 'There was a Sir Courtenay Pescud in the time of Charles I, if I remember rightly.'

" 'If there was,' says I, 'he can't claim kin with our bunch. We've always lived in and around Pittsburg. I've got an uncle in the real-estate business, and one in trouble somewhere out in Kansas. You can inquire about any of the rest of us from anybody in old Smoky Town, and get satisfactory replies. Did you ever run across that story about the captain of the whaler who tried to make a sailor say his prayers?' says I.

" 'It occurs to me that I have never been so fortunate,' says the colonel.

"So I told it to him. Laugh! I was wishing to myself that he was a customer. What a bill of glass I'd sell him! And then he says:

" 'The relating of anecdotes and humorous occurrences has always seemed to me, Mr. Pescud, to be a particularly agreeable way of promoting and perpetuating amenities between friends. With your permission, I will relate to you a fox-hunting story with which I was personally connected, and which may furnish you some amusement.'

"So he tells it. It takes forty minutes by the watch. Did I laugh? Well, say! When I got my face straight he calls in old Pete, the superannuated darky, and sends him down to the hotel to bring up my valise. It was Elmcroft for me while I was in the town.

"Two evenings later I got a chance to speak a word with Miss Jessie alone on the porch while the colonel was thinking up another story.

" 'It's going to be a fine evening,' says I.

" 'He's coming,' says she. 'He's going to tell you, this time, the story about the old negro and the green water-melons. It always comes after the one about the Yankees and the game rooster. There was another time,' she goes on, 'that you nearly got left—it was at Pulaski City.'

" 'Yes,' says I, 'I remember. My foot slipped as I was jumping on the step, and I nearly tumbled off.'

" 'I know,' says she. 'And—and I—I *was afraid you had, John A. I was afraid you had.*'

"And then she skips into the house through one of the big windows."

IV

"Coketown!" droned the porter, making his way through the slowing car.

Pescud gathered his hat and baggage with the leisurely promptness of an old traveller.

"I married her a year ago," said John. "I told you I built a house in the East End. The belted—I mean the colonel—is there, too. I find him waiting at the gate whenever I get back from a trip to hear any new story I might have picked up on the road."

I glanced out of the window. Coketown was nothing more than a ragged hillside dotted with a score of black dismal huts propped up against dreary mounds of slag and clinkers. It rained in slanting torrents, too, and the rills foamed and splashed down through the black mud to the railroad-tracks.

"You won't sell much plate-glass here, John," said I. "Why do you get off at this end-o'-the-world?"

"Why," said Pescud, "the other day I took Jessie for a little trip to Philadelphia, and coming back she thought she saw some petunias in a pot in one of those windows over there just like some she used to raise down in the old Virginia home. So I thought I'd drop off here for the night, and see if I could dig up some of the cuttings or blossoms for her. Here we are. Good night, old man. I gave you the address. Come out and see us when you have time."

The train moved forward. One of the dotted brown ladies insisted on having windows raised now that the rain beat against them. The porter came along with his mysterious wand and began to light the car.

I glanced downward and saw the best-seller. I picked it up and set it carefully farther along on the floor of the car, where the rain-drops would not fall upon it. And then, suddenly, I smiled, and seemed to see that life has no geographical metes and bounds.

"Good luck to you, Trevelyan," I said. "And may you get the petunias for your princess!"

XXX: A FOG IN SANTONE

THE drug clerk looks sharply at the white face half concealed by the high-turned overcoat collar.

"I would rather not supply you," he said doubtfully. "I sold you a dozen morphine tablets less than an hour ago."

The customer smiles wanly. "The fault is in your crooked streets. I didn't intend to call upon you twice, but I guess I got tangled up. Excuse me."

He draws his collar higher, and moves out, slowly. He stops under an electric light at the corner, and juggles absorbedly with three or four little pasteboard boxes. "Thirty-six," he announces to himself. "More than plenty." For a grey mist had swept upon Santone that night, an opaque terror that laid a hand to the throat of each of the city's guests. It was computed that three thousand invalids were hibernating in the town. They had come from far and wide, for here, among these contracted river-sliced streets, the goddess Ozone has elected to linger.

Purest atmosphere, sir, on earth! You might think from the river winding through our town that we are malarial, but, no, sir! Repeated experiments made both by the Government and local experts show that our air contains nothing deleterious—nothing but ozone, sir, pure ozone. Litmus paper tests made all along the river show—but you can read it all in the prospectuses; or the Santonian will recite it for you, word by word.

We may achieve climate, but weather is thrust upon us. Santone, then, cannot be blamed for this cold grey fog that came and kissed the lips of the three thousand, and then delivered them to the cross. That night the tubercles, whose ravages hope holds in check, multiplied. The writhing fingers of the pale mist did not go thence bloodless. Many of the wooers of ozone capitulated with the enemy that night, turning their faces to the wall in that dumb isolated apathy that so terrifies their watchers. On the red stream of Hæmorrhagia a few souls drifted away, leaving behind pathetic heaps, white and chill as the fog itself. Two or three came to view this atmospheric wraith as the ghost of impossible joys, sent to whisper to them of the egregious folly it is to inhale breath into the lungs, only to exhale it again, and these used whatever came handy to their relief, pistols, gas or the beneficent muriate.

The purchaser of the morphia wanders into the fog, and at length finds himself upon a little iron bridge, one of the score or more in the heart of the city, under which the small tortuous river flows. He leans on the rail and gasps, for here the mist has concentrated, lying like a foot-pad to garrote such of the Three Thousand as creep that way. The iron bridge guys rattle to the strain of his cough, a mocking phthisical rattle, seeming to say to him: "Clickety-clack! just a little rusty cold, sir—but not from our river. Litmus paper all along the banks and nothing but ozone. Clacket-y-clack!"

The Memphis man at last recovers sufficiently to be aware of another overcoated man ten feet away, leaning on the rail, and just coming out of a paroxysm. There is a freemasonry among the Three Thousand that does away with formalities and introductions. A cough is your card; a hæmorrhage a letter of credit. The Memphis man, being nearer recovered, speaks first.

"Goodall. Memphis—pulmonary tuberculosis—guess last stages." The Three Thousand economize on words. Words are breath, and they need breath to write cheques for the doctors.

"Hurd," gasps the other. "Hurd; of T'leder. T'leder, Ah-hia. Catarrhal bronkeetis. Name's Dennis, too—doctor says. Says I'll live four weeks if I—take care of myself. Got your walking papers yet?"

"My doctor," says Goodall of Memphis, a little boastingly, "gives me three months."

"Oh," remarks the man from Toledo, filling up great gaps in his conversation with wheezes, "damn the difference. What's months! Expect to—cut mine down to one week—and die in a hack—a four-wheeler, not a cough. Be considerable moanin' of the bars when I put out to sea. I've patronized 'em pretty freely since I struck my—present gait. Say, Goodall of Memphis—if your doctor has set your pegs so close—why don't you—get on a big spree and go—to the devil quick and easy—like I'm doing?"

"A spree," says Goodall, as one who entertains a new idea, "I never did such a thing. I was thinking of another way, but——"

"Come on," invites the Ohioan, "and have some drinks. I've been at it—for two days, but the inf—ernal stuff won't bite like it used to. Goodall of Memphis, what's your respiration?"

"Twenty-four."

"Daily—temperature?"

"Hundred and four."

"You can do it in two days. It'll take me a—week. Tank up, friend Goodall—have all the fun you can; then—off you go, in the middle of a jag, and s-s-save trouble and expense. I'm a s-son of a gun if this ain't a health resort—for your whiskers! A Lake Erie fog'd get lost here in two minutes."

"You said something about a drink," says Goodall.

A few minutes later they line up at a glittering bar, and hang upon the arm rest. The bar-tender, blond, heavy, well-groomed, sets out their drinks, instantly perceiving that he serves two of the Three Thousand. He observes that one is a middle-aged man, well-dressed, with a lined and sunken face; the other a mere boy who is chiefly eyes and overcoat. Disguising well the tedium begotten by many repetitions, the server of drinks begins to chant the sanitary saga of Santone. "Rather a moist night, gentlemen, for our town. A little fog from our river, but nothing to hurt. Repeated Tests."

"Damn your litmus papers," gasps Toledo—"without—any personal offence intended.

"We've heard of 'em before. Let 'em turn red, white and blue. What we want is a repeated test of that—whisky. Come again. I paid for the last round, Goodall of Memphis."

The bottle oscillates from one to the other, continues to do so, and is not removed from the counter. The bar-tender sees two emaciated invalids dispose of enough Kentucky Belle to floor a dozen cowboys, without displaying any emotion save a sad and contemplative interest in the peregrinations of the bottle. So he is moved to manifest a solicitude as to the consequences.

"Not on your Uncle Mark Hanna," responds Toledo, "will we get drunk. We've been—vaccinated with whisky—and—cod-liver oil. What would send you to the police station—only gives us a thirst. S-s-set out another bottle."

It is slow work trying to meet death by that route. Some quicker way must be found. They leave the saloon and plunge again into the mist.

The sidewalks are mere flanges at the base of the houses; the street a cold ravine, the fog filling it like a freshet. Not far away is the Mexican quarter. Conducted as if by wires along the heavy air comes a guitar's tinkle, and the demoralizing voice of some señorita singing:

"En las tardes sombrillos del invierro
En el prado a Marar me reclino
Y maldigo mi fausto destino—
Una vida la mas infeliz."

The words of it they do not understand—neither Toledo nor Memphis, but words are the least important things in life. The music tears the breasts of the seekers after Nepenthe, inciting Toledo to remark:

"Those kids of mine—I wonder—by God, Mr. Goodall of Memphis, we had too little of that whisky! No slow music in mine, if you please. It makes you disremember to forget."

Hurd of Toledo here pulls out his watch, and says:

"I'm a son of a gun! Got an engagement for a hack ride out to San Pedro Springs at eleven. Forgot it. A fellow from Noo York and me, and the Castillo sisters at Rhinegelder's Garden. That Noo York chap's a lucky dog—got one whole lung—good for a year yet. Plenty of money, too. He pays for everything. I can't afford—to miss the jamboree. Sorry you ain't going along. Good-bye, Goodall of Memphis."

He rounds the corner and shuffles away, casting off thus easily the ties of acquaintanceship as the moribund do, the season of dissolution being man's supreme hour of egoism and selfishness. But he turns and calls back through the fog to the other: "I say, Goodall of Memphis! If you get there before I do, tell 'em Hurd's a-comin' too. Hurd, of T'leder, Ah-hia."

Thus Goodall's tempter deserts him. That youth, uncomplaining and uncaring, takes a spell at coughing, and, recovered, wanders desultorily on down the street, the name of which he neither knows nor recks. At a certain point he perceives swinging doors, and hears, filtering between them a noise of wind and string instruments. Two men enter from the street as he arrives, and he follows them in. There is a kind of ante-chamber, plentifully set with palms and cactuses and oleanders. At little marble-topped tables some people sit, while soft-shod attendants bring the beer. All is orderly, clean, melancholy, gay, of the German method of pleasure. At his right is the foot of a stairway. A man there holds out his hand. Goodall extends his, full of silver, the man selects therefrom a coin. Goodall goes upstairs and sees there two galleries extending along the side of a concert hall which he now perceives to lie below and beyond the ante-room he first entered. These galleries are divided into boxes or stalls, which bestow, with the aid of hanging lace curtains, a certain privacy upon their occupants.

Passing with aimless feet down the aisle contiguous to these saucy and discreet compartments, he is half checked by the sight in one of them of a young woman, alone and seated in an attitude of reflection. This young woman becomes aware of his approach. A smile from her brings him to a standstill, and her subsequent invitation draws him, though hesitating, to the other chair in the box, a little table between them.

Goodall is only nineteen. There are some whom, when the terrible god Phthisis wishes to destroy he first makes beautiful; and the boy is one of these. His face is wax, and an awful pulchritude is born of the menacing flame in his cheeks. His eyes reflect an unearthly vista engendered by the certainty of his doom. As it is forbidden man to guess accurately concerning his fate, it is inevitable that he shall tremble at the slightest lifting of the veil.

The young woman is well-dressed, and exhibits a beauty of distinctly feminine and tender sort; an Eve-like comeliness that scarcely seems predestined to fade.

It is immaterial, the steps by which the two mount to a certain plane of good understanding; they are short and few, as befits the occasion.

A button against the wall of the partition is frequently disturbed and a waiter comes, and goes at signal.

Pensive beauty would nothing of wine; two thick plaits of her blonde hair hang almost to the floor; she is a lineal descendant of the Lorelei. So the waiter brings the brew; effervescent, icy, greenish golden. The orchestra on the stage is playing "Oh, Rachel." The youngsters have exchanged a good bit of information. She calls him "Walter," and he calls her "Miss Rosa."

Goodall's tongue is loosened and he has told her everything about himself, about his home in Tennessee, the old pillared mansion under the oaks, the stables, the hunting; the friends he has; down to the chickens, and the box bushes bordering the walks. About his coming South for the climate, hoping to escape the hereditary foe of his family. All about his three months on a ranch; the deer hunts, the rattlers, and the rollicking in the cow camps. Then of his advent to Santone, where he had indirectly learned, from a great specialist, that his life's calendar probably contains but two more leaves. And then of his death-white, choking night which has come and strangled his fortitude and sent him out to seek a port amid its depressing billows.

"My weekly letter from home failed to come," he told her, "and I was pretty blue. I knew I had to go before long, and I was tired of waiting. I went out and bought morphine at every drug store where they would sell me a few tablets. I got thirty-six quarter grains and was going back to my room and take them, but I met a queer fellow on a bridge, who had a new idea."

Goodall fillips a little pasteboard box upon the table. "I put 'em all together in there."

Miss Rosa, being a woman, must raise the lid, and gave a slight shiver at the innocent looking triturates. "Horrid things! but those little white bits—they could never kill one!"

Indeed they could. Walter knew better. Nine grains of morphia! Why, half the amount might.

Miss Rosa demands to know about Mr. Hurd, of Toledo, and is told. She laughs like a delighted child. "What a funny fellow! But tell me more about your home and your sisters, Walter. I know enough about Texas and tarantulas and cowboys."

The theme is dear—just now, to his mood, and he lays before her the simple details of a true home; the little ties and endearments that so filled the exile's heart. Of his sisters, one, Alice, furnishes him a theme he loves to dwell upon.

"She is like you, Miss Rosa," he says. "Maybe not quite so pretty, but just as nice, and good and——"

"There! Walter," says Miss Rosa sharply, "now talk about something else."

But a shadow falls upon the wall outside, preceding a big, softly treading man, finely dressed, who pauses a second before the curtains and then passes on. Presently comes the waiter with a message: "Mr. Rolfe says——"

"Tell Rolfe I'm engaged."

"I don't know why it is," says Goodall of Memphis, "but I don't feel as bad as I did. An hour ago I wanted to die, but since I've met you, Miss Rosa, I'd like so much to live."

The young woman whirls around the table, lays an arm behind his neck and kisses him on the cheek.

"You must, dear boy," she says. "I know what was the matter. It was the miserable foggy weather that has lowered your spirit and mine too—a little. But look, now."

With a little spring she has drawn back the curtains. A window is in the wall opposite, and lo! the mist is cleared away. The indulgent moon is out again, re-voyaging the plumbless sky. Roof and parapet and spire are softly pearl enamelled. Twice, thrice the retrieved river flashes back, between the houses, the light of the firmament. A tonic day will dawn, sweet and prosperous.

"Talk of death when the world is so beautiful!" says Miss Rosa, laying her hand on his shoulder. "Do something to please me, Walter. Go home to your rest and say: 'I mean to get better,' and do it."

"If you ask it," says the boy, with a smile, "I will."

The waiter brings full glasses. Did they ring? No; but it is well. He may leave them. A farewell glass. Miss Rosa says: "To your better health, Walter." He says: "To our next meeting."

His eyes look no longer into the void, but gaze upon the antithesis of death. His foot is set in an undiscovered country to-night. He is obedient, ready to go. "Good night," she says.

"I never kissed a girl before," he confesses, "except my sisters."

"You didn't this time," she laughs, "I kissed you—good night."

"When shall I see you again?" he persists.

"You promised me to go home," she frowns, "and get well. Perhaps we shall meet again soon. Good night." He hesitates, his hat in hand. She smiles broadly and kisses him once more upon the forehead. She watches him far down the aisle, then sits again at the table.

The shadow falls once more against the wall. This time the big, softly stepping man parts the curtains and looks in. Miss Rosa's eyes meet his and for half a minute they remain thus, silent, fighting a battle with that king of weapons. Presently the big man drops the curtains and passes on.

The orchestra ceases playing suddenly, and an important voice can be heard loudly talking in one of the boxes farther down the aisle. No doubt some citizen entertains there some visitor to the town, and Miss Rosa leans back in her chair and smiles at some of the words she catches:

"Purest atmosphere—in the world—litmus paper

all long—nothing hurtful—our city—nothing but pure ozone."

The waiter returns for the tray and glasses. As he enters, the girl crushes a little empty pasteboard box in her hand and throws it in a corner. She is stirring something in her glass with her hatpin.

"Why, Miss Rosa," says the waiter with the civil familiarity he uses—"putting salt in your beer thus early in the night!"

XXXI: THE GIRL AND THE HABIT

HABIT—a tendency or aptitude acquired by custom or frequent repetition.

THE critics have assailed every source of inspiration save one. To that one we are driven for our moral theme. When we levied upon the masters of old they gleefully dug up the parallels to our columns. When we strove to set forth real life they reproached us for trying to imitate Henry George, George Washington, Washington Irving, and Irving Bacheller. We wrote of the West and the East, and they accused us of both Jesse and Henry James. We wrote from our heart—and they said something about a disordered liver. We took a text from Matthew or—er—yes, Deuteronomy, but the preachers were hammering away at the inspiration idea before we could get into type. So, driven to the wall, we go for our subject-matter to the reliable, old, moral, unassailable vade mecum—the unabridged dictionary.

Miss Merriam was cashier at Hinkle's. Hinkle's is one of the big downtown restaurants. It is in what the papers call the "financial district." Each day from twelve o'clock to two Kinkle's was full of hungry customers—messenger-boys, stenographers, brokers, owners of mining stock, promoters, inventors with patents pending—and also people with money.

The cashiership at Hinkle's was no sinecure. Hinkle egged and toasted and griddle-caked and coffeed a good many customers; and he lunched (as good a word as "dined") many more. It might be said that Hinkle's breakfast crowd was a contingent, but his luncheon patronage amounted to a horde.

Miss Merriam sat on a stool at a desk enclosed on three sides by a strong, high fencing of woven brass wire. Through an arched opening at the bottom you thrust your waiter's check and the money, while your heart went pit-a-pat.

For Miss Merriam was lovely and capable. She could take 45 cents out of a $2 bill and refuse an offer of marriage before you could—Next!—lost your chance—please don't shove. She could keep cool and collected while she collected your check, give you the correct change, win your heart, indicate the toothpick stand, and rate you to a quarter of a cent better than Bradstreet could to a thousand in less time than it takes to pepper an egg with one of Kinkle's casters.

There is an old and dignified allusion to the "fierce light that beats upon a throne." The light that beats upon the young lady cashier's cage is also something fierce. The other fellow is responsible for the slang.

Every male patron of Hinkle's, from the A.D.T. boys up to the kerbstone brokers, adored Miss Merriam. When they paid their checks they wooed her with every wile known to Cupid's art. Between the meshes of the brass railing went smiles, winks, compliments, tender vows, invitations to dinner, sighs, languishing looks and merry banter that was wafted pointedly back by the gifted Miss Merriam.

There is no coign of vantage more effective than the position of young lady cashier. She sits there, easily queen of the court of commerce; she is duchess of dollars and devoirs, countess of compliments and coin, leading lady of love and luncheon. You take from her a smile and a Canadian dime, and you go your way uncomplaining. You count the cheery word or two that she tosses you as misers count their treasures; and you pocket the change for a five uncomputed. Perhaps the brass-bound inaccessibility multiplies her charms—anyhow, she is a shirt-waisted angel, immaculate, trim, manicured, seductive, bright-eyed, ready, alert—Psyche, Circe and Ate in one, separating you from your circulating medium after your sirloin medium.

The young men who broke bread at Hinkle's never settled with the cashier without an exchange of badinage and open compliment. Many of them went to greater lengths and dropped promissory hints of theatre tickets and chocolates. The older men spoke plainly of orange blossoms, generally withering the tentative petals by after-allusions to Harlem flats. One broker, who had been squeezed by copper, proposed to Miss Merriam more regularly than he ate.

During a brisk luncheon hour Miss Merriam's

conversation, while she took money for checks, would run something like this:

"Good morning, Mr. Haskins—sir?—it's natural, thank you—don't be quite so fresh. . . . Hallo, Johnny—ten, fifteen, twenty—chase along now or they'll take the letters off your cap . . . Beg pardon—count it again, please—oh, don't mention it . . . Vaudeville?—thanks; not on your moving picture—I was to see Carter in Hedda Gabler on Wednesday night with Mr. Simmons . . . 'Scuse me, I thought that was a quarter . . . Twenty-five and seventy-five's a dollar—got that ham-and-cabbage habit yet? I see, Billy . . . Who are you addressing?—say—you'll get all that's coming to you in a minute . . . Oh, fudge! Mr. Bassett—you're always fooling—no——? Well, maybe I'll marry you some day—three, four and sixty-five is five . . . Kindly keep them remarks to yourself, if you please . . . Ten cents?—'scuse me; the check calls for seventy—well, maybe it is a one instead of a seven . . . Oh, do you like it that way, Mr. Saunders?—some prefer a pomp; but they say this Cleo de Merody does suit refined features . . . and ten is fifty . . . Hike along there, buddy; don't take this for a Coney Island ticket booth . . . Huh?—why, Macy's—don't it fit nice? Oh no, it isn't too cool—these light-weight fabrics is all the go this season . . . Come again, please—that's the third time you've tried to—what?—forget it—that lead quarter is an old friend of mine . . . Sixty-five?—must have had your salary raised, Mr. Wilson . . . I seen you on Sixth Avenue Tuesday afternoon, Mr. De Forest—swell?—oh, my!—who is she? . . . What's the matter with it?—why, it ain't money—what?—Colombian half?—well, this ain't South America . . . Yes, I like the mixed best—Friday?—awfully sorry, but I take my jiu-jitsu lesson on Friday—Thursday, then . . . Thanks—that's sixteen times I've been told that this morning—I guess I must be beautiful . . . Cut that out, please—who do you think I am ? . . . Why, Mr. Westbrook—do you really think so?—the idea!—one—eighty and twenty's a dollar—thank you ever so much; but I don't ever go automobile riding with gentlemen—your aunt?—well, that's different—perhaps . . . Please don't get fresh—your check was fifteen cents, I believe—kindly step aside and let . . . Hallo, Ben—coming around Thursday evening?—there's a gentleman going to send around a box of chocolates, and . . . forty and sixty is a dollar, and one is two . . ."

About the middle of one afternoon the dizzy goddess Vertigo—whose other name is Fortune—suddenly smote an old, wealthy and eccentric banker while he was walking past Hinkle's, on his way to a street car. A wealthy and eccentric banker who rides in street cars is—move up, please; there are others.

A Samaritan, a Pharisee, a man and a policeman who were first on the spot lifted Banker McRamsey and carried him into Hinkle's restaurant. When the aged but indestructible banker opened his eyes he saw a beautiful vision bending over him with a pitiful, tender smile, bathing his forehead with beef tea and chafing his hands with something *frappé* out of a chafing-dish. Mr. McRamsey sighed, lost a vest button, gazed with deep gratitude upon his fair preserveress, and then recovered consciousness.

To the Seaside Library all who are anticipating a romance! Banker McRamsey had an aged and respected wife, and his sentiments toward Miss Merriam were fatherly. He talked to her for half an hour with interest—not the kind that went with his talks during business hours. The next day he brought Mrs. McRamsey down to see her. The old couple were childless—they had only a married daughter living in Brooklyn.

To make a short story shorter, the beautiful cashier won the hearts of the good old couple. They came to Hinkle's again and again; they invited her to their old-fashioned but splendid home in one of the East Seventies. Miss Merriam's winning loveliness, her sweet frankness and impulsive heart took them by storm. They said a hundred times that Miss Merriam reminded them so much of their lost daughter. The Brooklyn matron, *née* Ramsey, had the figure of Buddha and a face like the ideal of an art photographer. Miss Merriam was a combination of curves, smiles, rose leaves, pearls, satin and hair-tonic posters. Enough of the fatuity of parents.

A month after the worthy couple became acquainted with Miss Merriam, she stood before Hinkle one afternoon and resigned her cashiership.

"They're going to adopt me," she told the bereft restaurateur. "They're funny old people, but regular dears. And the swell home they have got! Say, Hinkle, there isn't any use of talking—I'm on the *à la carte* to wear brown duds and goggles in a whiz wagon, or marry a duke at least. Still, I somehow hate to break out of the old cage. I've been cashiering so long I feel funny doing anything else. I'll miss joshing the fellows awfully when they line up to pay for the buckwheats and. But I can't let this chance slide. And they're awfully good, Hinkle; I know I'll have a swell time. You owe me nine-sixty-two and a half for the week. Cut out the half if it hurts you, Hinkle."

And they did. Miss Merriam became Miss Rosa McRamsey. And she graced the transition. Beauty is only skin-deep, but the nerves lie very near to the skin. Nerve—but just here will you oblige by perusing again the quotation with which the story begins?

The McRamseys poured out money like domestic champagne to polish their adopted one. Milliners, dancing masters and private tutors got it. Miss—er—McRamsey was grateful, loving, and tried to forget Hinkle's. To give ample credit to the adaptability of the American girl, Hinkle's did fade from her memory and speech most of the time.

Not every one will remember when the Earl of Hitesbury came to East Seventy—— Street, America. He was only a fair-to-medium earl, without debts, and he created little excitement. But you will surely remember the evening when the Daughters of Benevolence held their bazaar in the W——f-A——a Hotel. For you were there, and you wrote a note to Fannie on the hotel paper, and mailed it, just to show her that—you did not? Very well; that was the evening the baby was sick, of course.

At the Bazaar the McRamseys were prominent. Miss Mer—er—McRamsey was exquisitely beautiful. The Earl of Hitesbury had been very attentive to her since he dropped in to have a look at America. At the charity bazaar the affair was supposed to be going to be pulled off to a finish. An earl is as good as a duke. Better. His standing may be lower, but his outstanding accounts are also lower.

Our ex-young-lady-cashier was assigned to a booth. She was expected to sell worthless articles to nobs and snobs at exorbitant prices. The proceeds of the bazaar were to be used for giving to the poor children of the slums a Christmas din—— Say! did you ever wonder where they get the other 364?

Miss McRamsey—beautiful, palpitating, excited, charming, radiant—fluttered about in her booth. An imitation brass network, with a little arched opening, fenced her in.

Along came the Earl, assured, delicate, accurate, admiring—admiring greatly, and faced the open wicket.

"You look chawming, you know—'pon my word you do—my deah," he said beguilingly.

Miss McRamsey whirled around.

"Cut that joshing out," she said, coolly and briskly. "Who do you think you are talking to? Your check, please. Oh, lordy!——"

Patrons of the bazaar became aware of a commotion and pressed around a certain booth. The Earl of Hitesbury stood near by pulling a pale blond and puzzled whisker.

"Miss McRamsey has fainted," some one explained.

XXXII: SOCIOLOGY IN SERGE AND STRAW

THE season of irresponsibility is at hand. Come, let us twine round our brows wreaths of poison ivy (that is for idiocy), and wander hand in hand with sociology in the summer fields.

Likely as not the world is flat. The wise men have tried to prove that it is round, with indifferent success. They pointed out to us a ship going to sea, and bade us observe that, at length, the convexity of the earth hid from our view all but the vessel's topmast. But we picked up a telescope and looked, and saw the decks and hull again. Then the wise men said: "Oh, pshaw! anyhow, the variation of the intersection of the equator and the ecliptic proves it." We could not see this through our telescope, so we remained silent. But it stands to reason that, if the world were round, the queues of Chinamen would stand straight up from their heads instead of hanging down their backs, as travellers assure us they do.

Another hot-weather corroboration of the flat theory is the fact that all of life, as we know it, moves in little, unavailing circles. More justly than to anything else, it can be likened to the game of baseball. Crack! we hit the ball, and away we go. If we earn a run (in life we call it success), we get back to the home plate and sit upon a bench. If we are thrown out, we walk back to the home plate—and sit upon a bench.

The circumnavigators of the alleged globe may have sailed the rim of a watery circle back to the same port again. The truly great return at the high tide of their attainments to the simplicity of a child. The billionaire sits down at his mahogany to his bowl of bread and milk. When you reach the end of your career, just take down the sign "Goal" and look at the other side of it. You will find "Beginning Point" there. It has been reversed while you were going around the track.

But this is humour, and must be stopped. Let

us get back to the serious questions that arise whenever sociology turns summer boarder. You are invited to consider the scene of the story—wild, Atlantic waves, thundering against a wooded and rock-bound shore—in the Greater City of New York.

The town of Fishampton, on the south shore of Long Island, is noted for its clam fritters and the summer residence of the Van Plushvelts.

The Van Plushvelts have a hundred million dollars, and their name is a household word with tradesmen and photographers.

On the fifteenth of June the Van Plushvelts boarded up the front door of their city house, carefully deposited their cat on the sidewalk, instructed the caretaker not to allow it to eat any of the ivy on the walls, and whizzed away in a 40-horse-power to Fishampton to stray alone in the shade—Amaryllis not being in their class. If you are a subscriber to the *Toadies' Magazine*, you have often—You say you are not? Well, you buy it at a news-stand, thinking that the news-dealer is not wise to you. But he knows about it all. HE knows—HE knows! I say that you have often seen in the *Toadies' Magazine* pictures of the Van Plushvelts' summer home; so it will not be described here. Our business is with young Haywood Van Plushvelt, sixteen years old, heir to the century of millions, darling of the financial gods and great grandson of Peter Van Plushvelt, former owner of a particularly fine cabbage patch that has been ruined by an intrusive lot of down-town skyscrapers.

One afternoon young Haywood Van Plushvelt strolled out between the granite gateposts of "Dolce far Niente"—that's what they called the place; and it was an improvement on dolce Far Rockaway, I can tell you.

Haywood walked down into the village. He was human, after all, and his prospective millions weighed upon him. Wealth had wreaked upon him its direfullest. He was the product of private tutors. Even under his first hobby-horse had tan bark been strewn. He had been born with a gold spoon, lobster fork and fish-set in his mouth. For which I hope, later, to submit justification, I must ask your consideration of his haberdashery and tailoring.

Young Fortunatus was dressed in a neat suit of dark blue serge, a neat, white straw hat, neat, low-cut tan shoes, linen of the well-known "immaculate" trade mark, a neat, narrow four-in-hand tie, and carried a slender, neat bamboo cane.

Down Persimmon Street (there's never tree north of Hagerstown, Md.) came from the village "Smoky" Dodson, fifteen and a half, worst boy in Fishampton. "Smoky" was dressed in a ragged red sweater, wrecked and weather-worn golf cap, run-over shoes, and trousers of the "serviceable" brand. Dust, clinging to the moisture induced by free exercise, darkened wide areas of his face. "Smoky" carried a baseball bat, and a league ball that advertised itself in the rotundity of his trousers pocket. Haywood stopped and passed the time of day.

"Going to play ball?" he asked.

"Smoky's" eyes and countenance confronted him with a frank blue-and-freckled scrutiny.

"Me?" he said, with deadly mildness; "sure not. Can't you see I've got a divin' suit on? I'm going up in a submarine balloon to catch butterflies with a two-inch auger."

"Excuse me," said Haywood, with the insulting

politeness of his caste, "for mistaking you for a gentleman. I might have known better."

"How might you have known better if you thought I was one?" said "Smoky," unconsciously a logician.

"By your appearance," said Haywood. "No gentleman is dirty, ragged and a liar."

"Smoky" hooted once like a ferry-boat, spat on his hand, got a firm grip on his baseball bat and then dropped it against the fence.

"Say," said he, "I knows you. You're the pup that belongs in that swell private summer sanitorium for city guys over there. I seen you come out of the gate. You can't bluff nobody because you're rich. And because you got on swell clothes. Arabella! Yah!"

"Ragamuffin!" said Haywood.

"Smoky" picked up a fence-rail splinter and laid it on his shoulder.

"Dare you to knock it off," he challenged.

"I wouldn't soil my hands with you," said the aristocrat.

" 'Fraid," said "Smoky" concisely. "Youse city ducks ain't got the sand. I kin lick you with one hand."

"I don't wish to have any trouble with you," said Haywood. "I asked you a civil question; and you replied like a—like a—a cad."

"Wot's a cad?" asked "Smoky."

"A cad is a disagreeable person," answered Haywood, "who lacks manners and doesn't know his place. They sometimes play baseball."

"I can tell you what a mollycoddle is," said "Smoky." "It's a monkey dressed up by its mother and sent out to pick daisies on the lawn."

"When you have the honour to refer to the members of my family," said Haywood, with some dim ideas of a code in his mind, "you'd better leave the ladies out of your remarks."

"Ho! ladies!" mocked the rude one. "I say ladies! I know what them rich women in the city does. They drink cocktails and swear and give parties to gorillas. The papers says so."

Then Haywood knew that it must be. He took off his coat, folded it neatly and laid it on the roadside grass, placed his hat upon it and began to unknot his blue silk tie.

"Hadn't yer better ring fer yer maid, Arabella?" taunted "Smoky." "Wot yer going to do—go to bed?"

"I'm going to give you a good trouncing," said the hero. He did not hesitate, although the enemy was far beneath him socially. He remembered that his father once thrashed a cabman, and the papers gave it two columns, first page. And the *Toadies' Magazine* had a special article on Upper Cuts by the Upper Classes, and ran new pictures of the Van Plushvelt country seat, at Fishampton.

"Wot's trouncing?" asked "Smoky" suspiciously. "I don't want your old clothes. I'm no—oh, you mean to scrap! My, my! I won't do a thing to mamma's pet. Criminy! I'd hate to be a hand-laundered thing like you."

"Smoky" waited with some awkwardness for his adversary to prepare for battle. His own decks were always clear for action. When he should spit upon the palm of his terrible right it was equivalent to "You may fire now, Gridley."

The hated patrician advanced, with his shirt-sleeves neatly rolled up. "Smoky" waited, in an attitude of ease, expecting the affair to be conducted according to Fishampton's rules of war. These allowed combat to be prefaced by stigma, recrimination, epithet, abuse and insult gradually increasing in emphasis and degree. After a round of these "you're anothers" would come the chip knocked from the shoulder, or the advance across the "dare" line drawn with a toe on the ground. Next light taps given and taken, these also increasing in force until finally the blood was up and fists going at their best.

But Haywood did not know Fishampton's rules. *Noblesse oblige* kept a faint smile on his face as he walked slowly up to "Smoky" and said:

"Going to play ball?"

"Smoky" quickly understood this to be a putting of the previous question, giving him the chance to make a practical apology by answering it with civility and relevance.

"Listen this time," said he. "I'm goin' skatin' on the river. Don't you see me automobile with Chinese lanterns on it standin' and waitin' for me?"

Haywood knocked him down.

"Smoky" felt wronged. To thus deprive him of preliminary wrangle and objurgation was to send an armoured knight full tilt against a crashing lance without permitting him first to caracole around the list to the flourish of trumpets. But he scrambled up and fell upon his foe, head, feet and fists.

The fight lasted one round of an hour and ten minutes. It was lengthened until it was more like a war or a family feud than a fight. Haywood had learned some of the science of boxing and wrestling from his tutors, but these he discarded for the more instinctive methods of battle handed down by the cave-dwelling Van Plushvelts.

So, when he found himself, during the mêlée, seated upon the kicking and roaring "Smoky's" chest, he improved the opportunity by vigorously kneading handfuls of sand and soil into his adversary's ears, eyes and mouth, and when "Smoky" got the proper leg-hold and "turned" him, he fastened both hands in the Plushvelt hair and pounded the Plushvelt head against the lap of mother earth. Of course, the strife was not incessantly active. There were seasons when one sat upon the other, holding him down, while each blew like a grampus, spat out the more inconveniently large sections of gravel and earth, and strove to subdue the spirit of his opponent with a frightful and soul-paralysing glare.

At last, it seemed that, in the language of the ring, their efforts lacked steam. They broke away, and each disappeared in a cloud as he brushed away the dust of the conflict. As soon as his breath permitted, Haywood walked close to "Smoky" and said:

"Going to play ball?"

"Smoky" looked pensively at the sky, at his bat lying on the ground, and at the "leaguer" rounding his pocket.

"Sure," he said off-handedly. "The 'Yellow-jackets' plays the 'Long Islands.' I'm cap'n of the 'Long Islands.'"

"I guess I didn't mean to say you were ragged," said Haywood. "But you are dirty, you know."

"Sure," said "Smoky." "Yer get that way knockin' around. Say, I don't believe them New York papers about ladies drinkin' and havin' monkeys dinin' at the table with 'em. I guess they're lies, like they print about people eatin' out of silver plates, and ownin' dogs that cost $100."

"Certainly," said Haywood. "What do you play on your team?"

"Ketcher. Ever play any?"

"Never in my life," said Haywood. "I've never known any fellows except one or two of my cousins."

"Jer like to learn? We're goin' to have a practice game before the match. Wanter come along? I'll put yer in left-field, and yer won't be long ketchin' on."

"I'd like it bully," said Haywood. "I've always wanted to play baseball."

The ladies' maids of New York and the families of Western mine-owners with social ambitions will remember well the sensation that was created by the report that the young multi-millionaire, Haywood Van Plushvelt, was playing ball with the village youths of Fishampton. It was conceded that the millennium of democracy had come. Reporters and photographers swarmed to the island. The papers printed half-page pictures of him as short-stop stopping a hot grounder. The *Toadies' Magazine* got out a Bat and Ball number that covered the subject historically, beginning with the vampire bat and ending with the Patriarchs' ball—illustrated with interior views of the Van Plushvelt country seat. Ministers, educators and sociologists everywhere hailed the event as the tocsin call that proclaimed the universal brotherhood of man.

One afternoon I was reclining under the trees near the shore at Fishampton in the esteemed company of an eminent, bald-headed young sociologist. By way of note it may be inserted that all sociologists are more or less bald, and exactly thirty-two. Look 'em over.

The sociologist was citing the Van Plushvelt case as the most important "uplift" symptom of a generation, and as an excuse for his own existence.

Immediately before us were the village baseball grounds. And now came the sportive youth of Fishampton and distributed themselves, shouting, about the diamond.

"There," said the sociologist, pointing, "there is young Van Plushvelt."

I raised myself (so far a cosycophant with Mary Ann) and gazed.

Young Van Plushvelt sat upon the ground. He was dressed in a ragged red sweater, wrecked and weather-worn golf cap, run-over shoes, and trousers of the "serviceable" brand. Dust, clinging to the moisture induced by free exercise, darkened wide areas of his face.

"That is he," repeated the sociologist. If he had said "him" I could have been less vindictive.

On a bench, with an air, sat the young millionaire's chum.

He was dressed in a neat suit of dark blue serge, a neat, white straw hat, neat, low-cut tan shoes, linen of the well-known "immaculate" trade-mark, a neat, narrow four-in-hand tie, and carried a slender, neat bamboo cane.

I laughed loudly and vulgarly.

"What you want to do," said I to the sociologist, "is to establish a reformatory for the Logical Vicious Circle. Or else I've got wheels. It looks to me as if things are running round and round in circles instead of getting anywhere."

"What do you mean?" asked the man of progress.

"Why, look what he has done to 'Smoky,'" I replied.

"You will always be a fool," said my friend, the sociologist, getting up and walking away.

XXXIII : RUBAIYAT OF A SCOTCH HIGHBALL

THIS document is intended to strike somewhere between a temperance lecture and the *Bartender's Guide*. Relative to the latter, drink shall swell the theme and be set forth in abundance. Agreeably to the former, not an elbow shall be crooked.

Bob Babbitt was "off the stuff." Which means—as you will discover by referring to the unabridged dictionary of Bohemia—that he had "cut out the booze"; that he was "on the water wagon." The reason for Bob's sudden attitude of hostility toward the "demon rum"—as the white ribboners miscall whisky (see the *Bartender's Guide*)—should be of interest to reformers and saloon-keepers.

There is always hope for a man who, when sober, will not concede or acknowledge that he was ever drunk. But when a man will say (in the apt words of the phrase-distiller), "I had a beautiful skate on last night," you will have to put stuff in his coffee as well as pray for him.

One evening on his way home Babbitt dropped in at the Broadway bar that he liked best. Always there were three or four fellows there from the downtown offices whom he knew. And then there would be highballs and stories, and he would hurry home to dinner a little late but feeling good, and a little sorry for the poor Standard Oil Company. On this evening as he entered he heard some one say: "Babbitt was in last night as full as a boiled owl."

Babbitt walked to the bar, and saw in the mirror that his face was as white as chalk. For the first time he had looked Truth in the eyes. Others had lied to him; he had dissembled with himself. He was a drunkard, and had not known it. What he had fondly imagined was a pleasant exhilaration had been maudlin intoxication. His fancied wit had been drivel; his gay humours nothing but the noisy vagaries of a sot. But, never again!

"A glass of seltzer," he said to the bartender.

A little silence fell upon the group of his cronies, who had been expecting him to join them.

"Going off the stuff, Bob?" one of them asked politely and with more formality than the highballs ever called forth.

"Yes," said Babbitt.

Some one of the group took up the unwashed thread of a story he had been telling; the bartender shoved over a dime and a nickel change from the quarter, ungarnished with his customary smile; and Babbitt walked out.

Now, Babbitt had a home and a wife—but that is another story. And I will tell you that story, which will show you a better habit and a worse story than you could find in the man who invented the phrase.

It began away up in Sullivan County, where so many rivers and so much trouble begins—or begin; how would you say that? It was July; and Jessie was a summer boarder at the Mountain Squint Hotel, and Bob, who was just out of college, saw her one day—and they were married in September. That's the tabloid novel—one swallow of water, and it's gone.

But those July days!

Let the exclamation point expound it, for I shall not. For particulars you might read up on *Romeo and Juliet*, and Abraham Lincoln's thrilling sonnet about "You can fool some of the people," etc., and Darwin's works.

But one thing I must tell you about. Both of them were mad over Omar's *Rubaiyat*. They knew every verse of the old bluffer by heart—not consecutively, but picking 'em out here and there as you fork the mushrooms in a fifty-cent steak *à la Bordelaise*. Sullivan County is full of rocks and trees; and Jessie used to sit on them, and—please be good—used to sit on thc rocks; and Bob had a way of standing behind her with his hands over her shoulders holding her hands, and his face close to hers, and they would repeat over and over their favourite verses of the old tent-maker. They saw only the poetry and philosophy of the lines then—indeed, they agreed that the Wine was only an image, and that what was meant to be celebrated was some divinity, or maybe Love or Life. However, at that time neither of them had tasted the stuff that goes with a sixty-cent table d'hôte.

Where was I? Oh, they married and came to New York. Bob showed his college diploma, and accepted a position filling inkstands in a lawyer's office at $15 a week. At the end of two years he had worked up to $50, and gotten his first taste of Bohemia—the kind that won't stand the borax and formaldehyde tests.

They had two furnished rooms and a little kitchen. To Jess, accustomed to the mild but beautiful savour of a country town, the dreggy Bohemia was sugar and spice. She hung fish seines on the walls of her rooms, and bought a rakish-looking sideboard, and learned to play the banjo. Twice or thrice a week they dined at French or Italian tables d'hôte in a cloud of smoke, and brag and unshorn hair. Jess learned to drink a cocktail in order to get the cherry. At home she smoked a cigarette after dinner. She learned to pronounce Chianti, and leave her olive stones for the waiter to pick up. Once she essayed to say la, la, la! in a crowd; but got only as far as the second one. They met one or two couples while dining out and became friendly with them. The sideboard was stocked with Scotch and rye and a liqueur. They had their new friends in to dinner, and all were laughing at nothing by 1 a.m. Some plastering fell in the room below them, for which Bob had to pay $4.50. Thus they footed it merrily on the ragged frontiers of the country that has no boundary lines or government.

And soon Bob fell in with his cronies and learned to keep his foot on the little rail six inches above the floor for an hour or so every afternoon before he went home. Drink always rubbed him the right way, and he would reach his rooms as jolly as a sandboy. Jessie would meet him at the door, and generally they would dance some insane kind of a rigadoon about the floor by way of greeting. Once when Bob's feet became confused and he tumbled headlong over a footstool, Jessie laughed so heartily and long that he had to throw all the couch pillows at her to make her hush.

In such wise life was speeding for them on the day when Bob Babbitt first felt the power that the giftie gi'ed him.

But let us get back to our lamb and mint sauce.

When Bob got home that evening he found Jessie in a long apron cutting up a lobster for the Newburg. Usually when Bob came in mellow from his hour at the bar his welcome was hilarious, though somewhat tinctured with Scotch smoke.

By screams and snatches of song and certain audible testimonials to domestic felicity was his advent proclaimed. When she heard his foot on the stairs the old maid in the hall room always stuffed cotton into her ears. At first Jessie had shrunk from the rudeness and flavour of these spiritual greetings, but as the fog of the false Bohemia gradually encompassed her she came to accept them as love's true and proper greeting.

Bob came in without a word, smiled, kissed her neatly but noiselessly, took up a paper and sat down. In the hall room the old maid held her two plugs of cotton poised, filled with anxiety.

Jessie dropped lobster and knife and ran to him with frightened eyes.

"What's the matter, Bob, are you ill?"

"Not at all, dear."

"Then what's the matter with you?"

"Nothing."

Hearken, brethren. When She-who-has-a-right-to-ask interrogates you concerning a change she finds in your mood, answer her thus: Tell her that you, in a sudden rage, have murdered your grandmother; tell her that you have robbed orphans and that remorse has stricken you; tell her your fortune is swept away; that you are beset by enemies, by bunions, by any kind of malevolent fate; but do not, if peace and happiness are worth as much as a grain of mustard seed to you—do not answer her "Nothing."

Jessie went back to the lobster in silence. She cast looks of darkest suspicion at Bob. He had never acted that way before.

When dinner was on the table she set out the bottle of Scotch and the glasses. Bob declined.

"Tell you the truth, Jess," he said. "I've cut out the drink. Help yourself, of course. If you don't mind I'll try some of the seltzer straight."

"You've stopped drinking?" she said, looking at him steadily and unsmilingly. "What for?"

"It wasn't doing me any good," said Bob. "Don't you approve of the idea?"

Jessie raised her eyebrows and one shoulder slightly.

"Entirely," she said with a sculptured smile. "I could not conscientiously advise anyone to drink or smoke, or whistle on Sunday."

The meal was finished almost in silence. Bob tried to make talk, but his efforts lacked the stimulus of previous evenings. He felt miserable, and once or twice his eye wandered toward the bottle, but each time the scathing words of his bibulous friend sounded in his ear, and his mouth set with determination.

Jessie felt the change deeply. The essence of their lives seemed to have departed suddenly. The restless fever, the false gaiety, the unnatural excitement of the shoddy Bohemia in which they had lived had dropped away in the space of the popping of a cork. She stole curious and forlorn glances at the dejected Bob, who bore the guilty look of at least a wife-beater or a family tyrant.

After dinner the coloured maid who came in daily to perform such chores cleared away the things. Jessie, with an unreadable countenance, brought back the bottle of Scotch and the glasses and a bowl of cracked ice and set them on the table.

"May I ask," she said, with some of the ice in her tones, "whether I am to be included in your sudden spasm of goodness? If not, I'll make one for myself. It's rather chilly this evening, for some reason."

"Oh, come now, Jess," said Bob good-naturedly, "don't be too rough on me. Help yourself, by all means. There's no danger of your overdoing it. But I thought there was with me; and that's why I quit. Have yours, and then let's get out the banjo and try over that new quickstep."

"I've heard," said Jessie in the tones of the oracle, "that drinking alone is a pernicious habit. No, I don't think I feel like playing this evening. If we are going to reform we may as well abandon the evil habit of banjo-playing, too."

She took up a book and sat in her little willow rocker on the other side of the table. Neither of them spoke for half an hour.

And then Bob laid down his paper and got up with a strange, absent look on his face, and went behind her chair and reached over her shoulders, taking her hands in his, and laid his face close to hers.

In a moment to Jessie the walls of the seine-hung room vanished, and she saw the Sullivan County hills and rills. Bob felt her hands quiver in his as he began the verse from old Omar:

"Come, fill the Cup, and in the Fire of Spring
The Winter Garment of Repentance fling:
The Bird of Time has but a little way
To fly—and Lo! the Bird is on the Wing!"

And then he walked to the table and poured a stiff drink of Scotch into a glass.

But in that moment a mountain breeze had somehow found its way in and blown away the mist of the false Bohemia.

Jessie leaped and with one fierce sweep of her hand sent the bottle and glasses crashing to the floor. The same motion of her arm carried it around Bob's neck, where it met its mate and fastened tight.

"Oh, my God, Bobbie—not that verse—I see now. I wasn't always such a fool, was I? The other one, boy—the one that says: 'Remould it to the Heart's Desire.' Say that one—'to the Heart's Desire.' "

"I know that one," said Bob. "It goes:

" 'Ah! Love, could you and I with Him conspire
To grasp this sorry Scheme of Things entire
Would not we——' "

"Let me finish it," said Jessie.

" 'Would not we shatter it to bits—and then
Remould it nearer to the Heart's Desire!' "

"It's shattered all right," said Bob, crunching some glass under his heel.

In some dungeon below the accurate ear of Mrs. Pickens, the landlady, located the smash.

"It's that wild Mr. Babbitt coming home soused again," she said. "And he's got such a nice little wife, too!"

XXXIV: DRY VALLEY'S INDIAN SUMMER

DRY VALLEY JOHNSON shook the bottle. You have to shake the bottle before using; for sulphur will not dissolve. Then Dry Valley saturated a small sponge with the liquid and rubbed it carefully into the roots of his hair. Besides sulphur there was sugar of lead in it and tincture of nux vomica and bay rum. Dry Valley found the recipe in a Sunday newspaper. You must next be told why a strong man came to fall a victim to a Beauty Hint.

Dry Valley had been a sheepman. His real name was Hector, but he had been rechristened after his range to distinguish him from "Elm Creek" Johnson, who ran sheep farther down the Frio.

Many years of living face to face with sheep on their own terms wearied Dry Valley Johnson. So, he sold his ranch for eighteen thousand dollars and moved to Santa Rosa to live a life of gentlemanly ease. Being a silent and melancholy person of thirty-five—or perhaps thirty-eight—he soon became that cursed and earth-cumbering thing—an elderlyish bachelor with a hobby. Some one gave him his first strawberry to eat, and he was done for.

Dry Valley bought a four-room cottage in the village, and a library on strawberry culture. Behind the cottage was a garden of which he made a strawberry patch. In his old grey woollen shirt, his brown duck trousers, and high-heeled boots he sprawled all day on a canvas cot under a live oak tree at his back door studying the history of the seductive scarlet berry.

The school teacher, Miss De Witt, spoke of him

as "a fine, presentable man, for all his middle age." But, the focus of Dry Valley's eyes embraced no women. They were merely beings who flew skirts as a signal for him to lift awkwardly his heavy, round-crowned, broad-brimmed felt Stetson whenever he met them, and then hurry past to get back to his beloved berries.

And all this recitative by the chorus is only to bring us to the point where you may be told why Dry Valley shook up the insoluble sulphur in the bottle. So long-drawn and inconsequential a thing is history—the anamorphous shadow of a milestone reaching down the road between us and the setting sun.

When his strawberries were beginning to ripen Dry Valley bought the heaviest buggy whip in the Santa Rosa store. He sat for many hours under the live oak tree plaiting and weaving in an extension to its lash. When it was done he could snip a leaf from a bush twenty feet away with the cracker. For the bright, predatory eyes of Santa Rosa youth were watching the ripening berries, and Dry Valley was arming himself against their expected raids. No greater care had he taken of his tender lambs during his ranching days than he did of his cherished fruit, warding it from the hungry wolves that whistled and howled and shot their marbles and peered through the fence that surrounded his property.

In the house next to Dry Valley's lived a widow with a pack of children that gave the husbandman frequent anxious misgivings. In the woman there was a strain of the Spanish. She had wedded one of the name of O'Brien. Dry Valley was a connoisseur in crossed strains; and he foresaw trouble in the offspring of this union.

Between the two homesteads ran a crazy picket fence overgrown with morning glory and wild gourd vines. Often he could see little heads with mops of black hair and flashing dark eyes dodging in and out between the pickets, keeping tabs on the reddening berries.

Late one afternoon Dry Valley went to the post office. When he came back, like Mother Hubbard he found the deuce to pay. The descendants of Iberian bandits and Hibernian cattle raiders had swooped down upon his strawberry patch. To the outraged vision of Dry Valley there seemed to be a sheep corral full of them; perhaps they numbered five or six. Between the rows of green plants they were stooped, hopping about like toads, gobbling silently and voraciously his finest fruit.

Dry Valley slipped into the house, got his whip, and charged the marauders. The lash curled about the legs of the nearest—a greedy ten-year-old—before they knew they were discovered. His screech gave warning; and the flock scampered for the fence like a drove of *javelis* flushed in the chaparral. Dry Valley's whip drew a toll of two more elfin shrieks before they dived through the vine-clad fence and disappeared.

Dry Valley, less fleet, followed them nearly to the pickets. Checking his useless pursuit, he rounded a bush, dropped his whip and stood, voiceless, motionless, the capacity of his powers consumed by the act of breathing and preserving the perpendicular.

Behind the bush stood Panchita O'Brien, scorning to fly. She was nineteen, the oldest of the raiders. Her night-black hair was gathered back in a wild mass and tied with a scarlet ribbon. She stood, with reluctant feet, yet nearer the brook than to the river; for childhood had environed and detained her.

She looked at Dry Valley Johnson for a moment with magnificent insolence, and before his eyes slowly crunched a luscious berry between her white teeth. Then she turned and walked slowly to the fence with a swaying, conscious motion, such as a duchess might make use of in leading a promenade. There she turned again and grilled Dry Valley Jonhson once more in the dark flame of her audacious eyes, laughed a trifle school-girlishly, and twisted herself with pantherish quickness between the pickets to the O'Brien side of the wild gourd vine.

Dry Valley picked up his whip and went into his house. He stumbled as he went up the two wooden steps. The old Mexican woman who cooked his meals and swept his house called him to supper as he went through the rooms. Dry Valley went on, stumbled down the front steps, out the gate and down the road into a mesquite thicket at the edge of town. He sat down in the grass and laboriously plucked the spines from a prickly pear, one by one. This was his attitude of thought, acquired in the days when his problems were only those of wind and wool and water.

A thing had happened to the man—a thing that, if you are eligible, you must pray may pass you by. He had become enveloped in the Indian Summer of the Soul.

Dry Valley had had no youth. Even his childhood had been one of dignity and seriousness. At six he had viewed the frivolous gambols of the lambs on his father's ranch with silent disapproval. His life as a young man had been wasted. The divine fires and impulses, the glorious exaltations and despairs, the glow and enchantment of youth had passed above his head. Never a thrill of Romeo had he known; he was but a melancholy Jacques of the forest with a ruder philosophy, lacking the bitter-sweet flavour of experience that tempered the veteran years of the rugged ranger of Arden. And now in his sere and yellow leaf one scornful look from the eyes of Panchita O'Brien had flooded the autumnal landscape with a tardy and delusive summer heat.

But a sheepman is a hardy animal. Dry Valley Johnson had weathered too many northers to turn his back on a late summer, spiritual or real. Old? He would show them.

By the next mail went an order to San Antonio for an outfit of the latest clothes, colours and styles and prices no object. The next day went the recipe for the hair restorer clipped from a newspaper; for Dry Valley's sunburned auburn hair was beginning to turn silvery above his ears.

Dry Valley kept indoors closely for a week except for frequent sallies after youthful strawberry snatchers. Then, a few days later, he suddenly emerged brilliantly radiant in the hectic glow of his belated midsummer madness.

A jay-bird-blue tennis suit covered him outwardly, almost as far as his wrists and ankles. His shirt was ox-blood; his collar winged and tall; his necktie a floating oriflamme; his shoes a venomous bright tan, pointed and shaped on penitential lasts. A little flat straw hat with a striped band desecrated his weather-beaten head. Lemon-coloured kid gloves protected his oak-tough hands from the benignant May sunshine. This sad and optic-smiting creature teetered out of its den, smiling foolishly and smoothing its gloves for men and angels to see. To such a pass had Dry Valley Johnson been brought by Cupid, who always shoots game that is out of season with an arrow from the quiver of Momus. Reconstructing mythology, he had risen, a prismatic macaw, from the ashes of the grey-brown phœnix that had folded its tired wings to roost under the trees of Santa Rosa.

Dry Valley paused in the street to allow Santa Rosans within sight of him to be stunned; and then deliberately and slowly, as his shoes required, entered Mrs. O'Brien's gate.

Not until the eleven months' drought did Santa Rosa cease talking about Dry Valley Johnson's courtship of Panchita O'Brien. It was an unclassifiable procedure; something like a combination of cake-walking, deaf-and-dumb oratory, postage-stamp flirtation and parlour charades. It lasted two weeks and then came to a sudden end.

Of course Mrs. O'Brien favoured the match as soon as Dry Valley's intentions were disclosed. Being the mother of a woman child, and therefore a charter member of the Ancient Order of the Rat-trap, she joyfully decked out Panchita for the sacrifice. The girl was temporarily dazzled by having her dresses lengthened and her hair piled up on her head, and came near forgetting that she was only a slice of cheese. It was nice, too, to have as good a match as Mr. Johnson paying you attentions and to see the other girls fluttering the curtains at their windows to see you go by with him.

Dry Valley bought a buggy with yellow wheels and a fine trotter in San Antonio. Every day he drove out with Panchita. He was never seen to speak to her when they were walking or driving.

The consciousness of his clothes kept his mind busy; the knowledge that he could say nothing of interest kept him dumb; the feeling that Panchita was there kept him happy.

He took her to parties and dances, and to church. He tried—oh, no man ever tried so hard to be young as Dry Valley did. He could not dance; but he invented a smile which he wore on these joyous occasions, a smile that, in him, was as great a concession to mirth and gaiety as turning handsprings would be in another. He began to seek the company of the young men in the town—even of the boys. They accepted him as a decided damper, for his attempts at sportiveness were so forced that they might as well have essayed their games in a cathedral. Neither he nor any other could estimate what progress he had made with Panchita.

The end came suddenly in one day, as often disappears the false afterglow before a November sky and wind.

Dry Valley was to call for the girl one afternoon at six for a walk. An afternoon walk in Santa Rosa was a feature of social life that called for the pick of one's wardrobe. So Dry Valley began gorgeously to array himself; and so early that he finished early, and went over to the O'Brien cottage. As he neared the porch on the crooked walk from the gate he heard sounds of revelry within. He stopped and looked through the honeysuckle vines in the open door.

Panchita was amusing her younger brothers and sisters. She wore a man's clothes—no doubt those of the late Mr. O'Brien. On her head was the smallest brother's straw hat decorated with an ink-striped paper band. On her hands were flapping yellow cloth gloves, roughly cut out and sewn for the masquerade. The same material covered her shoes, giving them the semblance of tan leather. High collar and flowing necktie were not omitted.

Panchita was an actress. Dry Valley saw his affectedly youthful gait, his limp where the right shoe hurt him, his forced smile, his awkward simulation of a gallant air, all reproduced with startling fidelity. For the first time a mirror had been held up to him. The corroboration of one of the youngsters calling, "Mamma, come and see Pancha do like Mr. Johnson," was not needed.

As softly as the caricatured tans would permit, Dry Valley tiptoed back to the gate and home again.

Twenty minutes after the time appointed for the walk Panchita tripped demurely out her gate in a thin, trim white lawn and sailor hat. She strolled up the sidewalk and slowed her steps at Dry Valley's gate, her manner expressing wonder at his unusual delinquency.

Then out of his door and down the walk strode—not the polychromatic victim of a lost summertime, but the sheepman, rehabilitated. He wore his old grey woollen shirt, open at the throat, his brown duck trousers stuffed into his run-over boots, and his white felt sombrero on the back of his head. Twenty years or fifty he might look; Dry Valley cared not. His light blue eyes met Panchita's dark ones with a cold flash in them. He came as far as the gate. He pointed with his long arm to her house.

"Go home," said Dry Valley. "Go home to your mother. I wonder lightnin' don't strike a fool like me. Go home and play in the sand. What business have you got cavartin' around with grown men? I reckon I was locoed to be makin' a he poll-parrot out of myself for a kid like you. Go home and don't let me see you no more. Why I done it, will somebody tell me? Go home, and let me try and forget it."

Panchita obeyed and walked slowly toward her home, saying nothing. For some distance she kept her head turned and her large eyes fixed intrepidly upon Dry Valley's. At her gate she stood for a moment looking back at him, then ran suddenly and swiftly into the house.

Old Antonia was building a fire in the kitchen stove. Dry Valley stopped at the door and laughed harshly.

"I'm a pretty looking old rhinoceros to be gettin' stuck on a kid, ain't I, 'Tonia?" said he.

"Not verrec good thing," agreed Antonia sagely, "for too much old man to likee *muchacha*."

"You bet it ain't," said Dry Valley grimly. "It's dum foolishness; and, besides, it hurts."

He brought at one armful the regalia of his aberration—the blue tennis suit, shoes, hat, gloves and all, and threw them in a pile at Antonia's feet.

"Give them to your old man," said he, "to hunt antelope in."

Just as the first star presided palely over the twilight Dry Valley got his biggest strawberry book and sat on the back steps to catch the last of the reading light. He thought he saw the figure of some one in his strawberry patch. He laid aside the book, got his whip and hurried forth to see.

It was Panchita. She had slipped through the picket fence and was half-way across the patch. She stopped when she saw him and looked at him without wavering.

A sudden rage—a humiliating flush of unreasoning wrath—came over Dry Valley. For this child he had made himself a motley to the view. He had tried to bribe Time to turn backward for himself; he had—been made a fool of. At last he had seen his folly. There was a gulf between him and youth over which he could not build a bridge even with yellow gloves to protect his hands. And the sight of his torment coming to pester him with her elfin pranks—coming to plunder his strawberry vines like a mischievous schoolboy—roused all his anger.

"I told you to keep away from here," said Dry Valley. "Go back to your home."

Panchita moved slowly toward him.

Dry Valley cracked his whip.

"Go back home," said Dry Valley savagely, "and play theatricals some more. You'd make a fine man. You've made a fine one of me."

She came a step nearer, silent, and with that strange, defiant, steady shine in her eyes that had always puzzled him. Now it stirred his wrath.

His whiplash whistled through the air. He saw a red streak suddenly come out through her white dress above her knee where it had struck.

Without flinching and with the same unchanging dark glow in her eyes, Panchita came steadily toward him through the strawberry vines. Dry Valley's trembling hand released his whip handle. When within a yard of him Panchita stretched out her arms.

"God, kid!" stammered Dry Valley, "do you mean——?"

But the seasons are versatile; and it may have been springtime after all, instead of Indian Summer, that struck Dry Valley Johnson

XXXV: THE CHAMPION OF THE WEATHER

IF you should speak of the Kiowa Reservation to the average New Yorker he probably wouldn't know whether you were referring to a new political dodge at Albany or a leitmotif from *Parsifal*. But out in the Kiowa Reservation advices have been received concerning the existence of New York.

A party of us were on a hunting trip in the Reservation. Bud Kingsbury, our guide, philosopher, and friend, was broiling antelope steaks in camp one night. One of the party, a pinkish-haired young man in a correct hunting costume, sauntered over to the fire to light a cigarette, and remarked carelessly to Bud:

"Nice night!"

"Why, yes," said Bud, "as nice as any night could be that ain't received the Broadway stamp of approval."

Now, the young man was from New York, but the rest of us wondered how Bud guessed it. So, when the steaks were done, we besought him to lay bare his system of ratiocination. And as Bud was something of a Territorial talking machine he made oration as follows:

"How did I know he was from New York? Well, I figured it out as soon as he sprung them two words on me. I was in New York myself a couple of years ago, and I noticed some of the earmarks and hoof tracks of the Rancho Manhattan."

"Found New York rather different from the Panhandle, didn't you, Bud?" asked one of the hunters.

"Can't say that I did," answered Bud; "anyways,

not more than some. The main trail in that town which they call Broadway is plenty travelled, but they're about the same brand of bipeds that tramp around in Cheyenne and Amarillo. At first I was sort of rattled by the crowds, but I soon says to myself, 'Here, now, Bud; they're just plain folks like you and Geronimo and Grover Cleveland and the Watson boys, so don't get all flustered up with consternation under your saddle blanket,' and then I feels calm and peaceful, like I was back in the Nation again at a ghost dance or a green corn pow-wow.

"I'd been saving up for a year to give this New York a whirl. I knew a man named Summers that lived there, but I couldn't find him; so I played a lone hand at enjoying the intoxicating pleasures of the corn-fed metropolis.

"For awhile I was so frivolous and locoed by the electric lights and the noises of the phonographs and the second-story railroads that I forgot one of the crying needs of my Western system of natural requirements. I never was no hand to deny myself the pleasures of sociable vocal intercourse with friends and strangers. Out in the Territories when I meet a man I never saw before, inside of nine minutes I know his income, religion, size of collar, and his wife's temper and how much he pays for clothes, alimony, and chewing tobacco. It's a gift with me not to be penurious with my conversation.

"But this here New York was inaugurated on the idea of abstemiousness in regard to the parts of speech. At the end of three weeks nobody in the city had fired even a blank syllable in my direction except the waiter in the grub emporium where I fed. And as his outpourings of syntax wasn't nothing but plagiarisms from the bill of fare, he never satisfied my yearnings, which was to have somebody hit. If I stood next to a man at a bar he'd edge off and give a Baldwin-Ziegler look as if he suspected me of having the North Pole concealed on my person. I began to wish that I'd gone to Abilene or Waco for my *paseado*; for the mayor of them places will drink with you, and the first citizen you meet will tell you his middle name and ask you to take a chance in a raffle for a music-box.

"Well, one day when I was particular hankering for to be gregarious with something more loquacious than a lamp-post, a fellow in a caffy says to me, says he:

" 'Nice day!'

"He was a kind of a manager of the place, and I reckon he'd seen me in there a good many times. He had a face like a fish and an eye like Judas, but I got up and put one arm around his neck.

" 'Pardner,' I says, 'sure it's a nice day. You're the first gentleman in all New York to observe that the intricacies of human speech might not be altogether wasted on William Kingsbury. But don't you think,' says I, 'that 'twas a little cool early in the morning; and ain't there a feeling of rain in the air to-night? But along about noon it sure was gallupsious weather. How's all up to the house? You doing right well with the caffy, now?'

"Well, sir, that galoot just turns his back and walks off stiff, without a word, after all my trying to be agreeable! I don't know what to make of it. That night I finds a note from Summers, who'd been away from town, giving the address of his camp. I goes up to his house and has a good, old-time talk with his folks. And I tells Summers about the actions of this coyote in the caffy, and desires interpretation.

" 'Oh,' says Summers, 'he wasn't intending to strike up a conversation with you. That's just the New York style. He'd seen you was a regular customer and he spoke a word or two just to show you he appreciated your custom. You oughtn't to have followed it up. That's about as far as we care to go with a stranger. A word or so about the weather may be ventured, but we don't generally make it the basis of an acquaintance.'

" 'Billy,' says I, 'the weather and its ramifications is a solemn subject with me. Meteorology is one of my sore points. No man can open up the question of temperature or humidity or the glad sunshine with me, and then turn tail on it without its leading to a falling barometer. I'm going down to see that man again and give him a lesson in the art of continuous conversation. You say New York etiquette allows him two words and no answer. Well, he's going to turn himself into a weather bureau and finish what he begun with me, besides indulging in neighbourly remarks on other subjects.'

"Summers talked agin it, but I was irritated some and I went on the street car back to that caffy.

"The same fellow was there yet, walking round in a sort of black corral where there was tables and chairs. A few people was sitting around having drinks and sneering at one another.

"I called that man to one side and herded him

into a corner. I unbuttoned enough to show him a thirty-eight I carried stuck under my vest.

" 'Pardner,' I says, 'a brief space ago I was in here and you seized the opportunity to say it was a nice day. When I attempted to corroborate your weather signal, you turned your back and walked off. Now,' says I, 'you frog-hearted, language-shy, stiff-necked cross between a Spitzbergen sea cook and a muzzled oyster, you resume where you left off in your discourse on the weather.'

"The fellow looks at me and tries to grin, but he sees I don't and he comes around serious.

" 'Well,' says he, eyeing the handle of my gun, 'it was rather a nice day; some warmish, though.'

" 'Particulars, you mealy-mouthed snoozer,' I says—'let's have the specifications—expatiate—fill in the outlines. Whcn you start anything with me in shorthand it's bound to turn out a storm signal.'

" 'Looked like rain yesterday,' says the man, 'but it cleared off fine in the forenoon. I hear the farmers are needing rain right badly up-State.'

" 'That's the kind of a canter,' says I. 'Shake the New York dust off your hoofs and be a real agreeable kind of a centaur. You broke the ice, you know, and we're getting better acquainted every minute. Seems to me I asked you about your family?'

" 'They're all well, thanks,' says he. 'We—we have a new piano.'

" 'Now you're coming it,' I says. 'This cold reserve is breaking up at last. That little touch about the piano almost makes us brothers. What's the youngest kid's name?' I asks him.

" 'Thomas,' says he. 'He's just getting well from the measles.'

" 'I feel like I'd known you always,' says I. 'Now there was just one more—are you doing right well with the caffy, now?'

" 'Pretty well,' he says. 'I'm putting away a little money.'

" 'Glad to hear it,' say I. 'Now go back to your work and get civilized. Keep your hands off the weather unless you're ready to follow it up in a personal manner. It's a subject that naturally belongs to sociability and the forming of new ties, and I hate to see it handed out in small change in a town like this.'

"So the next day I rolls up my blankets and hits the trail away from New York City."

For many minutes after Bud ceased talking we lingered around the fire, and then all hands began to disperse for bed.

As I was unrolling my bedding I heard the pinkish-haired young man saying to Bud, with something like anxiety in his voice:

"As I say, Mr. Kingsbury, there is something really beautiful about this night. The delightful breeze and the bright stars and the clear air unite in making it wonderfully attractive."

"Yes," said Bud, "it's a nice night."

XXXVI: SHEARING THE WOLF

JEFF PETERS was always eloquent when the ethics of his profession was under discussion.

"The only times," said he, "that me and Andy Tucker ever had any hiatuses in our cordial intents was when we differed on the moral aspects of grafting. Andy had his standards and I had mine. I didn't approve of all of Andy's schemes for levying contributions from the public, and he thought I allowed my conscience to interfere too often for the financial good of the firm. We had high arguments sometimes. Once one word led on to another till he said I reminded him of Rockefeller.

" 'I know how you mean that, Andy,' says I, 'but we have been friends too long for me to take offence at a taunt that you will regret when you cool off. I have yet,' says I, 'to shake hands with a subpœna server.'

"One summer me and Andy decided to rest up a spell in a fine little town in the mountains of Kentucky called Grassdale. We was supposed to be horse drovers, and good decent citizens besides, taking a summer vacation. The Grassdale people liked us, and me and Andy declared a secession of hostilities, never so much as floating the fly-leaf of a rubber concession prospectus or flashing a Brazilian diamond while we was there.

"One day the leading hardware merchant of Grassdale drops around to the hotel where me and Andy stopped, and smokes with us, sociable, on the side porch. We knew him pretty well from pitching quoits in the afternoons in the court-house yard. He was a loud, red man, breathing hard, but fat and respectable beyond all reason.

"After we talk on all the notorious themes of the day, this Murkison—for such was his entitlements—takes a letter out of his coat pocket in a careful, careless way and hands it to us to read.

" 'Now, what do you think of that?' says he, laughing—'a letter like that to ME!'

"Me and Andy sees at a glance what it is; but we

pretend to read it through. It was one of them old-time typewritten green goods letters explaining how for $1,000 you could get $5,000 in bills that an expert couldn't tell from the genuine; and going on to tell how they were made from plates stolen by an employee of the Treasury at Washington.

" 'Think of 'em sending a letter like that to ME!' says Murkison again.

" 'Lots of good men get 'em,' says Andy. 'If you don't answer the first letter they let you drop. If you answer it they write again asking you to come on with your money and do business.'

" 'But think of 'em writing to ME!' says Murkison.

"A few days later he drops around again.

" 'Boys,' says he, 'I know you are all right or I wouldn't confide in you. I wrote to them rascals again just for fun. They answered and told me to come on to Chicago. They said telegraph to J. Smith when I would start. When I get there I'm to wait on a certain street corner till a man in a grey suit comes along and drops a newspaper in front of me. Then I am to ask him how the water is, and he knows it's me and I know it's him.'

" 'Ah, yes,' says Andy, gaping, 'it's the same old game. I've often read about it in the papers. Then he conducts you to the private abattoir in the hotel, where Mr. Jones is already waiting. They show you brand-new real money and sell you all you want at five for one. You see 'em put it in a satchel for you and know it's there. Of course it's brown paper when you come to look at it afterward.'

" 'Oh, they couldn't switch it on me,' says Murkison. 'I haven't built up the best paying business in Grassdale without having witticisms about me. You say it's real money they show you, Mr. Tucker?'

" 'I've always—I see by the papers that it always is,' says Andy.

" 'Boys,' says Murkison, 'I've got it in my mind that them fellows can't fool me. I think I'll put a couple of thousand in my jeans and go up there and put it all over 'em. If Bill Murkison gets his eyes once on them bills they show him he'll never take 'em off of 'em. They offer $5 for $1, and they'll have to stick to the bargain if I tackle 'em. That's the kind of trader Bill Murkison is. Yes, I jist believe I'll drop up Chicago way and take a 5 to 1 shot on J. Smith, I guess the water'll be fine enough.'

"Me and Andy tries to get this financial misquotation out of Murkison's head, but we might as well have tried to keep the man who rolls peanuts with a toothpick from betting on Bryan's election. No, sir; he was going to perform a public duty by catching these green goods swindlers at their own game. Maybe it would teach 'em a lesson.

"After Murkison left us me and Andy sat a while prepondering over our silent meditations and heresies of reason. In our idle hours we always improved our higher selves by ratiocination and mental thought.

" 'Jeff,' says Andy after a long time, 'quite unseldom I have seen fit to impugn your molars when you have been chewing the rag with me about your conscientious way of doing business. I may have been often wrong. But here is a case where I think we can agree. I feel that it would be wrong for us to allow Mr. Murkison to go alone to meet those Chicago green goods men. There is but one way it can end. Don't you think we would both feel better if we was to intervene in some way and prevent the doing of this deed?'

"I got up and shook Andy Tucker's hand hard and long.

" 'Andy,' says I, 'I may have had one or two hard thoughts about the heartlessness of your corporation, but I retract 'em now. You have a kind nucleus at the interior of your exterior after all. It does you credit. I was just thinking the same thing that you have expressed. It would not be honourable or praiseworthy,' says I, 'for us to let Murkison go on with this project he has taken up. If he is determined to go, let us go with him and prevent this swindle from coming off.'

"Andy agreed with me; and I was glad to see that he was in earnest about breaking up this green goods scheme.

" 'I don't call myself a religious man,' says I, 'or a fanatic in moral bigotry, but I can't stand still and see a man who has built up a business by his own efforts and brains and risk be robbed by an unscrupulous trickster who is a menace to the public good.'

" 'Right, Jeff,' says Andy. 'We'll stick right along with Murkison if he insists on going and block this funny business. I'd hate to see any money dropped in it as bad as you would.'

"Well, we went to see Murkison.

" 'No, boys,' says he. 'I can't consent to let the song of this Chicago siren waft by me on the summer breeze. I'll fry some fat out of this ignis fatuus or burn a hole in the skillet. But I'd be plumb diverted to death to have you all go along with me. Maybe you could help some when it comes to cashing in the ticket to that 5 to 1 shot. Yes, I'd really take it as a pastime and regalement if you boys would go along too.'

"Murkison gives it out in Grassdale that he is going for a few days with Mr. Peters and Mr. Tucker to look over some iron ore property in West Virginia. He wires J. Smith that he will set foot in the spider web on a given date; and the three of us lights out for Chicago.

"On the way Murkison amuses himself with premonitions and advance pleasant recollections.

" 'In a grey suit,' says he, 'on the south-west corner of Wabash Avenue and Lake Street. He drops the paper, and I ask how the water is. Oh, my, my, my!' And then he laughs all over for five minutes.

"Sometimes Murkison was serious and tried to talk himself out of his cogitations, whatever they was.

" 'Boys,' says he, 'I wouldn't have this to get out in Grassdale for ten times a thousand dollars. It would ruin me there. But I know you all are all right. I think it's the duty of every citizen,' says he, 'to try to do up these robbers that prey upon the public. I'll show 'em whether the water's fine. Five dollars for one—that's what J. Smith offers, and he'll have to keep his contract if he does business with Bill Murkison.'

"We got into Chicago about 7 p.m. Murkison was to meet the grey man at half-past nine. We had dinner at a hotel and then went up to Murkison's room to wait for the time to come.

" 'Now, boys,' says Murkison, 'let's get our gumption together and inoculate a plan for defeating the enemy. Suppose while I'm exchanging airy bandage with the grey capper you gents come along, by accident, you know, and holler, "Hello, Murk!" and shake hands with symptoms of surprise and familiarity. Then I take the capper aside and tell him you all are Jenkins and Brown of Grassdale, groceries and feed, good men and maybe willing to take a chance while away from home.'

" ' "Bring 'em along," he'll say, of course, "if they care to invest." Now, how does that scheme strike you?'

" 'What do you say, Jeff?' says Andy, looking at me.

" 'Why, I'll tell you what I say,' says I. 'I say let's settle this thing right here now. I don't see any use of wasting any more time.' I took a nickel-plated ·38 out of my pocket and clicked the cylinder around a few times.

" 'You undevout, sinful, insidious hog,' says I to Murkison, 'get out that two thousand and lay it on the table. Obey with velocity,' says I, 'for otherwise alternatives are impending. I am preferably a man of mildness, but now and then I find myself in the middle of extremities. Such men as you,' I went on after he had laid the money out, 'is what keeps the jails and court-houses going. You come up here to rob these men of their money. Does it excuse you,' I asks, 'that they were trying to skin you? No, sir; you was going to rob Peter to stand off Paul. You are ten times worse,' says I, 'than that green goods man. You go to church at home and pretend to be a decent citizen, but you'll come to Chicago and commit larceny from men that have built up a sound and profitable business by dealing with such contemptible scoundrels as you have tried to be to-day. How do you know,' says I, 'that that green goods man hasn't a large family dependent upon his extortions? It's you supposedly respectable citizens who are always on the look-out to get something for nothing,' says I, 'that support the lotteries and wild-cat mines and stock exchanges and wire-tappers of this country. If it wasn't for you they'd go out of business. The green goods man you was going to rob,' says I, 'studied maybe for years to learn his trade. Every turn he makes he risks his money and liberty and maybe his life. You come up here all sanctified and panoplied with repectability and a pleasing post-office address to swindle him. If he gets the money you can squeal to the police. If you get it he hocks the grey suit to buy supper and says nothing. Mr. Tucker and me sized you up,' says I, 'and came along to see that you got what you deserved. Hand over the money,' says I, 'you grass-fed hypocrite.'

"I put the two thousand, which was all in $20 bills, in my inside pocket.

" 'Now get out your watch,' says I to Murkison. 'No, I don't want it,' says I. 'Lay it on the table and you sit in that chair till it ticks off an hour. Then you can go. If you make any noise or leave any sooner we'll handbill you all over Grassdale. I guess your high position there is worth more than $2,000 to you.'

"Then me and Andy left.

"On the train Andy was a long time silent. Then he says: 'Jeff, do you mind my asking you a question?'

" 'Two,' says I, 'or forty.'

" 'Was that the idea you had,' says he, 'when we started out with Murkison?'

" 'Why, certainly,' says I. 'What else could it have been? Wasn't it yours too?'

"In about half an hour Andy spoke again. I think there are times when Andy don't exactly understand my system of ethics and moral hygiene.

" 'Jeff,' says he, 'some time when you have the leisure I wish you'd draw off a diagram and footnotes of that conscience of yours. I'd like to have it to refer to occasionally.' "

XXXVII: THE CLARION CALL

HALF of this story can be found in the records of the Police Department; the other half belongs behind the business counter of a newspaper office.

One afternoon two weeks after Millionaire Norcross was found in his apartment murdered by a burglar, the murderer, while strolling serenely down Broadway, ran plump against Detective Barney Woods.

"Is that you, Johnny Kernan?" asked Woods, who had been near-sighted in public for five years.

"No less," cried Kernan, heartily. "If it isn't Barney Woods, late and early of old Saint Jo! You'll have to show me! What are you doing East? Do the green-goods circulars get out that far?"

"I've been in New York some years," said Woods. "I'm on the city detective force."

"Well, well!" said Kernan, breathing smiling joy and patting the detective's arm.

"Come into Muller's," said Woods, "and let's hunt a quiet table. I'd like to talk to you awhile."

It lacked a few minutes to the hour of four. The tides of trade were not yet loosed, and they found a quiet corner of the café. Kernan, well dressed, slightly swaggering, self-confident, seated himself opposite the little detective, with his pale, sandy moustache, squinting eyes, and ready-made cheviot suit.

"What business are you in now?" asked Woods. "You know you left Saint Jo a year before I did."

"I'm selling shares in a copper mine," said Kernan. "I may establish an office here. Well, well! and so old Barney is a New York detective. You always had a turn that way. You were on the police in Saint Jo after I left there, weren't you?"

"Six months," said Woods. "And now there's one more question, Johnny. I've followed your record pretty close ever since you did that hotel job in Saratoga, and I never knew you to use your gun before. Why did you kill Norcross?"

Kernan stared for a few moments with concentrated attention at the slice of lemon in his highball; and then he looked at the detective with a sudden, crooked, brilliant smile.

"How did you guess it, Barney?" he asked, admiringly. "I swear I thought the job was as clean and as smooth as a peeled onion. Did I leave a string hanging out anywhere?"

Woods laid upon the table a small gold pencil intended for a watch-charm.

"It's the one I gave you the last Christmas we were in Saint Jo. I've got your shaving mug yet. I found this under a corner of the rug in Norcross's room. I warn you to be careful what you say. I've got it put on to you, Johnny. We were old friends once, but I must do my duty. You'll have to go to the chair for Norcross."

Kernan laughed.

"My luck stays with me," said he. "Who'd have thought old Barney was on my trail!" He slipped one hand inside his coat. In an instant Woods had a revolver against his side.

"Put it away," said Kernan, wrinkling his nose. "I'm only investigating. Aha! It takes nine tailors to make a man, but one can do a man up. There's a hole in that vest pocket. I took that pencil off my chain and slipped it in there in case of a scrap. Put up your gun Barney, and I'll tell you why I had to shoot Norcross. The old fool started down the hall after me, popping at the buttons on the back of my coat with a peevish little ·22, and I had to stop him. The old lady was a darling. She just lay in bed and saw her $12,000 diamond necklace go without a chirp, while she begged like a panhandler to have back a little thin gold ring with a garnet worth about $3. I guess she married old Norcross for his money, all right. Don't they hang on to the little trinkets from the Man Who Lost Out, though? There were six rings, two brooches, and a chatelaine watch. Fifteen thousand would cover the lot."

"I warned you not to talk," said Woods.

"Oh, that's all right," said Kernan. "The stuff is in my suit-case at the hotel. And now I'll tell you why I'm talking. Because it's safe. I'm talking to a man I know. You owe me a thousand dollars, Barney Woods, and even if you wanted to arrest me your hand wouldn't make the move."

"I haven't forgotten," said Woods. "You

counted out twenty fifties without a word. I'll pay it back some day. That thousand saved me, and—well, they were piling my furniture out on the sidewalk when I got back to the house."

"And so," continued Kernan, "you being Barney Woods, born as true as steel, and bound to play a white man's game, can't lift a finger to arrest the man you're indebted to. Oh, I have to study men as well as Yale locks and window fastenings in my business. Now, keep quiet while I ring for the waiter. I've had a thirst for a year or two that worries me a little. If I'm ever caught, the lucky sleuth will have to divide honours with old boy Booze. But I never drink during business hours. After a job I can crook elbows with my old friend Barney with a clear conscience. What are you taking?"

The waiter came with the little decanters and the siphon and left them alone again.

"You've called the turn," said Woods, as he rolled the little gold pencil about with a thoughtful forefinger. "I've got to pass you up. I can't lay a hand on you. If I'd a-paid that money back—but I didn't, and that settles it. It's a bad break I'm making, Johnny, but I can't dodge it. You helped me once, and it calls for the same."

"I knew it," said Kernan, raising his glass, with a flushed smile of self-appreciation. "I can judge men. Here's to Barney, for—'he's a jolly good fellow.'"

"I don't believe," went on Woods quietly, as if he were thinking aloud, "that if accounts had been square between you and me, all the money in all the banks in New York could have bought you out of my hands to-night."

"I know it couldn't," said Kernan. "That's why I knew I was safe with you."

"Most people," continued the detective, "look sideways at my business. They don't class it among the fine arts and the professions. But I've always taken a kind of fool pride in it. And here is where I go 'busted.' I guess I'm a man first and a detective afterward. I've got to let you go, and then I've got to resign from the force. I guess I can drive an express wagon. Your thousand dollars is farther off than ever, Johnny."

"Oh, you're welcome to it," said Kernan, with a lordly air. "I'd be willing to call the debt off, but I know you wouldn't have it. It was a lucky day for me when you borrowed it. And now, let's drop the subject. I'm off to the West on a morning train. I know a place out there where I can negotiate the Norcross sparks. Drink up, Barney, and forget your troubles. We'll have a jolly time while the police are knocking their heads together over the case. I've got one of my Sahara thirsts on to-night. But I'm in the hands—the unofficial hands—of my old friend Barney, and I won't even dream of a cop."

And then, as Kernan's ready finger kept the button and the waiter working, his weak point—a tremendous vanity and arrogant egotism—began to show itself. He recounted story after story of his successful plunderings, ingenious plots and infamous transgressions until Woods, with all his familiarity with evildoers, felt growing within him a cold abhorrence toward the utterly vicious man who had once been his benefactor.

"I'm disposed of, of course," said Woods, at length. "But I advise you to keep under cover for a spell. The newspapers may take up this Norcross affair. There has been an epidemic of burglaries and manslaughter in town this summer."

The word sent Kernan into a high glow of sullen and vindictive rage.

"To h——l with the newspapers," he growled. "What do they spell but brag and blow and boodle in box-car letters? Suppose they do take up a case—what does it amount to? The police are easy enough to fool; but what do the newspapers do? They send a lot of pin-head reporters around to the scene; and they make for the nearest saloon and have beer, while they take photos of the bartender's oldest daughter in evening dress, to print as the fiancée of the young man in the tenth storey, who thought he heard a noise below on the night of the murder. That's about as near as the newspapers ever come to running down Mr. Burglar."

"Well, I don't know," said Woods, reflecting. "Some of the papers have done good work in that line. There's the *Morning Mars*, for instance. It warmed up two or three trails, and got the man after the police had let 'em get cold."

"I'll show you," said Kernan, rising, and expanding his chest. "I'll show you what I think of newspapers in general, and your *Morning Mars* in particular."

Three feet from their table was the telephone booth. Kernan went inside and sat at the instrument, leaving the door open. He found a number in the book, took down the receiver, and made his demand upon Central. Woods sat still, looking at the sneering, cold, vigilant face waiting close to the transmitter, and listened to the words that came from the thin, truculent lips curved into a contemptuous smile.

"That the *Morning Mars*? . . . I want to speak to the managing editor. . . . Why, tell him it's some one who wants to talk to him about the Norcross murder.

"You the editor? . . . All right. . . . I am the man who killed old Norcross. . . . Wait! Hold the wire; I'm not the usual crank. . . . Oh, there isn't the slightest danger. I've just been discussing it with a detective friend of mine. I killed the old man at 2.30 a.m. two weeks ago to-morrow. . . . Have a drink with you? Now, hadn't you better leave that kind of talk to your funny man? Can't you tell whether a man's guying you or whether you're being offered the biggest scoop your dull dish-rag of a paper ever had? . . . Well, that's so; it's a bobtail scoop—but you can hardly expect me to 'phone in my name and address. . . . Why? Oh, because I heard you make a speciality of solving mysterious crimes that stump the police. . . . No, that's not all. I want to tell you that your rotten, lying, penny sheet is of no more use in tracking an intelligent murderer or highwayman than a blind poodle would be. . . . What? . . . Oh, no, this isn't a rival newspaper office; you're getting it straight. I did the Norcross job, and I've got the jewels in my suit-case at—'the name of the hotel could not be learned' —you recognize that phrase, don't you? I thought so. You've used it often enough. Kind of rattles you, doesn't it, to have the mysterious villain call up your great, big, all-powerful organ of right and justice and good government and tell you what a helpless old gas-bag you are? . . . Cut that out;

you're not that big a fool—no, you don't think I'm a fraud. I can tell it by your voice. . . . Now, listen, and I'll give you a pointer that will prove it to you. Of course, you've had this murder case worked over by your staff of bright young blockheads. Half of the second button on old Mrs. Norcross's nightgown is broken off. I saw it when I took the garnet ring off her finger. I thought it was a ruby. . . . Stop that! it won't work."

Kernan turned to Woods with a diabolic smile.

"I've got him going. He believes me now. He didn't quite cover the transmitter with his hand when he told somebody to call up Central on another 'phone and get our number. I'll give him just one more dig, and then we'll make a 'get-away.'

"Hello! . . . Yes. I'm here yet. You didn't think I'd run from such a little subsidized turn-coat rag of a newspaper, did you? . . . Have me inside of forty-eight hours? Say, will you quit being funny? Now, you let grown men alone, and attend to your business of hunting up divorce cases and street-car accidents, and printing the filth and scandal that you make your living by. Good-bye, old boy—sorry I haven't time to call on you. I'd feel perfectly safe in your sanctum asinorum. Tra-la!"

"He's as mad as a cat that's lost a mouse," said Kernan, hanging up the receiver and coming out. "And now, Barney, my boy, we'll go to a show and enjoy ourselves until a reasonable bedtime. Four hours' sleep for me, and then the west-bound."

The two dined in a Broadway restaurant. Kernan was pleased with himself. He spent money like a prince of fiction. And then a weird and gorgeous musical comedy engaged their attention.

Afterward there was a late supper in a grillroom, with champagne, and Kernan at the height of his complacency.

Half-past three in the morning found them in a corner of an all-night café, Kernan still boasting in a vapid and rambling way, Woods thinking moodily over the end that had come to his usefulness as an upholder of the law.

But, as he pondered, his eye brightened with a speculative light.

"I wonder if it's possible," he said to himself, "I won-der if it's pos-si-ble!"

And then outside the café the comparative stillness of the early morning was punctured by faint, uncertain cries that seemed mere fireflies of sound, some growing louder, some fainter, waxing and waning amid the rumble of milk-wagons and infrequent cars. Shrill cries they were when near—well-known cries that conveyed many meanings to the ears of those of the slumbering millions of the great city who waked to hear them. Cries that bore upon their significant, small volume the weight of a world's woe and laughter and delight and stress. To some, cowering beneath the protection of a night's ephemeral cover, they brought news of the hideous, bright day; to others, wrapped in happy sleep, they announced a morning that would dawn blacker than sable night. To many of the rich they brought a besom to sweep away what had been theirs while the stars shone; to the poor they brought—another day.

All over the city the cries were starting up, keen and sonorous, heralding the chances that the slipping of one cogwheel in the machinery of time had made; apportioning to the sleepers while they lay at the mercy of fate the vengeance, profit, grief, reward, and doom that the new figure in the calendar had brought them. Shrill and yet plaintive were the cries, as if the young voices grieved that so much evil and so little good was in their irresponsible hands. Thus echoed in the streets of the helpless city the transmission of the latest decrees of the gods, the cries of the newsboys—the Clarion Call of the Press.

Woods flipped a dime to the waiter, and said:

"Get me a *Morning Mars.*"

When the paper came he glanced at its first page, and then tore a leaf out of his memorandum book and began to write on it with the little gold pencil.

"What's the news?" yawned Kernan.

Woods flipped over to him the piece of writing:

"The New York *Morning Mars*:

"Please pay to the order of John Kernan the one thousand dollars reward coming to me for his arrest and conviction.

"Barnard Woods."

"I kind of thought they would do that," said Woods, "when you were jollying 'em so hard. Now, Johnny, you'll come to the police station with me."

XXXVIII: THE HIDING OF BLACK BILL

A LANK, strong, red-faced man with a Wellington beak and small, fiery eyes tempered by flaxen lashes, sat on the station platform at Los Pinos swinging his legs to and fro. At his side sat another man, fat, melancholy, and seedy, who seemed to be his friend. They had the appearance of men to whom life had appeared as a reversible coat—seamy on both sides.

"Ain't seen you in about four years, Ham," said the seedy man. "Which way you been travelling?"

"Texas," said the red-faced man. "It was too cold in Alaska for me. And I found it warm in Texas. I'll tell you about one hot spell I went through there.

"One morning I steps off the International at a water-tank and lets it go on without me. 'Twas a ranch country, and fuller of spite-houses than New York City. Only out there they build 'em twenty miles away so you can't smell what they've got for dinner, instead of running 'em up two inches from their neighbours' windows.

"There wasn't any roads in sight, so I footed it 'cross country. The grass was shoe-top deep, and the mesquite timber looked just like a peach orchard. It was so much like a gentleman's private estate that every minute you expected a kennelful of bulldogs to run out and bite you. But I must have walked twenty miles before I came in sight of a ranch-house. It was a little one, about as big as an elevated railroad station.

"There was a little man in a white shirt and brown overalls and a pink handkerchief around his neck rolling cigarettes under a tree in front of the door.

" 'Greetings,' says I. 'Any refreshment, welcome, emoluments, or even work for a comparative stranger?'

" 'Oh, come in,' says he, in a refined tone. 'Sit down on that stool, please. I didn't hear your horse coming.'

" 'He isn't near enough yet,' says I. 'I walked. I don't want to be a burden, but I wonder if you have three or four gallons of water handy.'

" 'You do look pretty dusty,' says he; 'but our bathing arrangements——'

" 'It's a drink I want,' says I. 'Never mind the dust that's on the outside.'

"He gets me a dipper of water out of a red jar hanging up, and then goes on:

" 'Do you want work?'

" 'For a time,' says I. 'This is a rather quiet section of the country, isn't it?'

" 'It is,' says he. 'Sometimes—so I have been told—one sees no human being pass for weeks at a time. I've been here only a month. I bought the ranch from an old settler who wanted to move farther west.'

" 'It suits me,' says I. 'Quiet and retirement are good for a man sometimes. And I need a job. I can tend bar, salt mines, lecture, float stock, do a little middle-weight slugging, and play the piano.'

" 'Can you herd sheep?' asks the little ranchman.

" 'Do you mean *have* I heard sheep?' says I.

" 'Can you herd 'em—take charge of a flock of 'em?' says he.

" 'Oh,' says I, 'now I understand. You mean chase 'em around and bark at 'em like collie dogs. Well, I might,' says I. 'I've never exactly done any sheep-herding, but I've often seen 'em from car windows masticating daisies, and they don't look dangerous.'

" 'I'm short a herder,' says the ranchman. 'You never can depend on the Mexicans. I've only got two flocks. You may take out my bunch of muttons—there are only eight hundred of 'em—in the morning, if you like. The pay is twelve dollars a month and your rations furnished. You camp in a tent on the prairie with your sheep. You do your own cooking, but wood and water are brought to your camp. It's an easy job.'

"'I'm on,' says I. 'I'll take the job even if I have to garland my brow and hold on to a crook and wear a loose effect and play on a pipe like the shepherds do in pictures.'

"So the next morning the little ranchman helps me drive the flock of muttons from the corral to about two miles out and let 'em graze on a little hillside on the prairie. He gives me a lot of instructions about not letting bunches of them stray off from the herd, and driving 'em down to a water-hole to drink at noon.

"'I'll bring out your tent and camping outfit and rations in the buckboard before night,' says he.

"'Fine,' says I. 'And don't forget the rations. Nor the camping outfit. And be sure to bring the tent. Your name's Zollicoffer, ain't it?'

"'My name,' says he, 'is Henry Ogden.'

"'All right, Mr. Ogden,' says I. 'Mine is Mr. Percival Saint Clair.'

"I herded sheep for five days on the Rancho Chiquito; and then the wool entered my soul. That getting next to Nature certainly got next to me. I was lonesomer than Crusoe's goat. I've seen a lot of persons more entertaining as companions than those sheep were. I'd drive 'em to the corral and pen 'em every evening, and then cook my corn-bread and mutton and coffee, and lie down in a tent the size of a tablecloth, and listen to the coyotes and whip-poor-wills singing around the camp.

"The fifth evening, after I had corralled my costly but uncongenial muttons, I walked over to the ranch-house and stepped in the door.

" 'Mr. Ogden,' says I, 'you and me have got to get sociable. Sheep are all very well to dot the landscape and furnish eight-dollar cotton suitings for man, but for table-talk and fireside companions they rank along with five-o'clock teazers. If you've got a deck of cards, or a parcheesi outfit, or a game of authors, get 'em out, and let's get on a mental basis. I've got to do something in an intellectual line, if it's only to knock somebody's brains out.'

"This Henry Ogden was a peculiar kind of ranchman. He wore finger-rings and a big gold watch and careful neckties. And his face was calm, and his nose-spectacles was kept very shiny. I saw once, in Muscogee, an outlaw hung for murdering six men, who was a dead ringer for him. But I knew a preacher in Arkansas that you would have taken to be his brother. I didn't care much for him either way; what I wanted was some fellowship and communion with holy saints or lost sinners—anything sheepless would do.

" 'Well, Saint Clair,' says he, laying down the book he was reading, 'I guess it must be pretty lonesome for you at first. And I don't deny that it's monotonous for me. Are you sure you corralled your sheep so they won't stray out?'

" 'They're shut up as tight as the jury of a millionaire murderer,' says I. 'And I'll be back with them long before they'll need their trained nurse.'

"So Ogden digs up a deck of cards, and we play casino. After five days and nights of my sheep-camp it was like a toot on Broadway. When I caught big casino I felt as excited as if I had made a million in Trinity. And when H. O. loosened up a little and told the story about the lady in the Pullman car I laughed for five minutes.

"That showed what a comparative thing life is. A man may see so much that he'd be bored to turn his head to look at a $3,000,000 fire or Joe Weber or the Adriatic Sea. But let him herd sheep for a spell, and you'll see him splitting his ribs laughing at 'Curfew Shall Not Ring To-night,' or really enjoying himself playing cards with ladies.

"By and by Ogden gets out a decanter of Bourbon, and then there is a total eclipse of sheep.

"'Do you remember reading in the papers, about a month ago,' says he, 'about a train hold-up on the M.K. & T.? The express agent was shot through the shoulder and about $15,000 in currency taken. And it's said that only one man did the job.'

"'Seems to me I do,' says I. 'But such things happen so often they don't linger long in the human Texas mind. Did they overtake, overhaul, seize, or lay hands upon the despoiler?'

"'He escaped,' says Ogden. 'And I was just reading in a paper to-day that the officers have tracked him down into this part of the country. It seems the bills the robber got were all the first issue of currency to the Second National Bank of Espinosa City. And so they've followed the trail where they've been spent, and it leads this way.'

"Ogden pours out some more Bourbon, and shoves me the bottle.

" 'I imagine,' says I, after ingurgitating another modicum of the royal booze, 'that it wouldn't be at all a disingenuous idea for a train-robber to run down into this part of the country to hide for a spell. A sheep-ranch, now,' says I, 'would be the finest kind of a place. Who'd ever expect to find such a desperate character among these song-birds and muttons and wild flowers? And, by the way,' says I, kind of looking H. Ogden over, 'was there any description mentioned of this single-handed terror? Was his lineaments or height and thickness or teeth fillings or style of habiliments set forth in print?'

" 'Why no,' says Ogden; 'they say nobody got a good sight of him because he wore a mask. But they know it was a train-robber called Black Bill, because he always works alone and because he dropped a handkerchief in the express-car that had his name on it.'

" 'All right,' says I. 'I approve of Black Bill's retreat to the sheep-ranges. I guess they won't find him.'

" 'There's one thousand dollars reward for his capture,' says Ogden.

" 'I don't need that kind of money,' says I, looking Mr. Sheepman straight in the eye. 'The twelve dollars a month you pay me is enough. I need a rest, and I can save up until I get enough to pay my fare to Texarkana, where my widowed mother lives. If Black Bill,' I goes on, looking significantly at Ogden, 'was to have come down this way—say, a month ago—and bought a little sheep-ranch and——'

" 'Stop,' says Ogden, getting out of his chair and looking pretty vicious. 'Do you mean to insinuate——'

" 'Nothing,' says I; 'no insinuations. I'm stating a hypodermical case. I say, if Black Bill had come down here and bought a sheep-ranch, and hired me to Little-Boy-Blue 'em and treated me square and friendly, as you've done, he'd never have anything to fear from me. A man is a man, regardless of any complications he may have with sheep or railroad trains. Now we know where I stand.'

"Ogden looks black as camp-coffee for nine seconds, and then he laughs, amused.

" 'You'll do, Saint Clair,' says he. 'If I *was* Black Bill I wouldn't be afraid to trust you. Let's have a game or two of seven-up to-night. That is, if you don't mind playing with a train-robber.'

" 'I've told you,' says I, 'my oral sentiments, and there's no strings to 'em.'

"While I was shuffling after the first hand, I asks Ogden, as if the idea was a kind of casualty, where he was from.

" 'Oh,' says he, 'from the Mississippi Valley.'

" 'That's a nice little place,' says I. 'I've often stopped over there. But didn't you find the sheets a little damp and the food poor? Now, I hail,' says I, 'from the Pacific Slope. Ever put up there?'

" 'Too draughty,' says Ogden. 'But if you're ever in the Middle West just mention my name, and you'll get footwarmers and dripped coffee.'

" 'Well,' says I, 'I wasn't exactly fishing for your private telephone number and the middle name of your aunt that carried off the Cumberland

Presbyterian minister. It don't matter. I just want you to know you are safe in the hands of your shepherd. Now, don't play hearts on spades, and don't get nervous.'

"'Still harping,' says Ogden, laughing again. 'Don't you suppose that if I was Black Bill and thought you suspected me, I'd put a Winchester bullet into you and stop my nervousness if I had any?'

"'Not any,' says I. 'A man who's got the nerve to hold up a train single-handed wouldn't do a trick like that. I've knocked about enough to know that them are the kind of men who put a value on a friend. Not that I can claim being a friend of yours, Mr. Ogden,' says I, 'being only your sheep-herder; but under more expeditious circumstances we might have been.'

"'Forget the sheep temporarily, I beg,' says Ogden, 'and cut for deal.'

"About four days afterward, while my muttons was nooning on the water-hole and I deep in the interstices of making a pot of coffee, up rides softly on the grass a mysterious person in the garb of the being he wished to represent. He was dressed somewhere between a Kansas City detective, Buffalo Bill, and the town dog-catcher of Baton Rouge. His chin and eye wasn't moulded on fighting lines so I knew he was only a scout.

"'Herdin' sheep?' he asks me.

"'Well,' says I, 'to a man of your evident gumptional endowments, I wouldn't have the nerve to state that I am engaged in decorating old bronzes or oiling bicycle sprockets.'

"You don't talk or look like a sheep-herder to me,' says he.

" 'But you talk like what you look like to me,' says I.

"And then he asks me who I was working for, and I shows him Rancho Chiquito, two miles away, in the shadow of a low hill, and he tells me he's a deputy sheriff.

" 'There's a train-robber called Black Bill supposed to be somewhere in these parts,' says the scout. 'He's been traced as far as San Antonio, and may be farther. Have you seen or heard of any strangers around here during the past month?'

" 'I have not,' says I, 'except a report of one over at the Mexican quarters of Loomis' ranch, on the Frio.'

" 'What do you know about him?' asks the deputy.

" 'He's three days old,' says I.

" 'What kind of a looking man is the man you work for?' he asks. 'Does old George Ramey own this place yet? He's run sheep here for the last ten years, but never had no success.'

" 'The old man has sold out and gone West,' I tells him. 'Another sheep-fancier bought him out about a month ago.'

" 'What kind of a looking man is he?' asks the deputy again.

" 'Oh,' says I, 'a big, fat kind of a Dutchman with long whiskers and blue specs. I don't think he knows a sheep from a ground-squirrel. I guess old George soaked him pretty well on the deal,' says I.

"After indulging himself in a lot more non-communicative information and two-thirds of my dinner, the deputy rides away.

"That night I mentions the matter to Ogden.

" 'They're drawing the tendrils of the octopus

around Black Bill,' says I. And then I told him about the deputy sheriff, and how I'd described him to the deputy, and what the deputy said about the matter.

" 'Oh, well,' says Ogden, 'let's don't borrow any of Black Bill's troubles. We've a few of our own. Get the Bourbon out of the cupboard and we'll drink to his health—unless,' says he, with his little cackling laugh, 'you're prejudiced against train-robbers.'

" 'I'll drink,' says I, 'to any man who's a friend to a friend. And I believe that Black Bill,' I goes on, 'would be that. So here's to Black Bill, and may he have good luck.'

"And both of us drank.

"About two weeks later comes shearing-time. The sheep had to be driven up to the ranch, and a lot of frowzy-headed Mexicans would snip the fur off of them with back-action scissors. So the afternoon before the barbers were to come I hustled my underdone muttons over the hill, across the dell, down by the winding brook, and up to the ranch-house, where I penned 'em in a corral and bade 'em my nightly adieus.

"I went from there to the ranch-house. I find H. Ogden, Esquire, lying asleep on his little cot bed. I guess he had been overcome by anti-insomnia or diswakefulness or some of the diseases peculiar to the sheep business. His mouth and vest were open, and he breathed like a second-hand bicycle pump. I looked at him and gave vent to just a few musings. 'Imperial Cæsar,' says I, 'asleep in such a way, might shut his mouth and keep the wind away.'

"A man asleep is certainly a sight to make angels weep. What good is all his brain, muscle, backing, nerve, influence, and family connections? He's at the mercy of his enemies, and more so of his friends. And he's about as beautiful as a cab-horse leaning against the Metropolitan Opera House at 12.30 a.m. dreaming of the plains of Arabia. Now, a woman asleep you regard as different. No matter how she looks, you know it's better for all hands for her to be that way.

"Well, I took a drink of Bourbon and one for Ogden, and started in to be comfortable while he was taking his nap. He had some books on his table on indigenous subjects, such as Japan and drainage and physical culture—and some tobacco, which seemed more to the point.

"After I'd smoked a few, and listened to the sartorial breathing of H. O., I happened to look out of the window towards the shearing-pens, where there was a kind of a road coming up from a kind of a road across a kind of a creek farther away.

"I saw five men riding up to the house. All of 'em carried guns across their saddles, and among 'em was the deputy that had talked to me at my camp.

"They rode up careful, in open formation, with their guns ready. I set apart with my eye the one I opinionated to be the boss muckraker of this law-and-order cavalry.

" 'Good evening, gents,' says I. 'Won't you 'light and tie your horses?'

"The boss rides up close, and swings his gun over till the opening in it seems to cover my whole front elevation.

" 'Don't you move your hands none,' says he, 'till you and me indulge in a adequate amount of necessary conversation.'

" 'I will not,' says I. 'I am no deaf-mute, and

therefore will not have to disobey your injunctions in replying.'

" 'We are on the look out,' says he, 'for Black Bill, the man that held up the Katy for $15,000 in May. We are searching the ranches and everybody on 'em. What is your name, and what do you do on this ranch?'

" 'Captain,' says I, 'Percival Saint Clair is my occupation, and my name is sheep-herder. I've got my flock of veals—no, muttons—penned here to-night. The searchers are coming to-morrow to give them a hair-cut—with baa-a-rum, I suppose.'

" 'Where's the boss of this ranch?' the captain of the gang asked me.

" 'Wait just a minute, cap'n,' says I. 'Wasn't there a kind of a reward offered for the capture of this desperate character you have referred to in your preamble?'

" 'There's a thousand dollars reward offered,' says the captain, 'but it's for his capture and conviction. There don't seem to be no provision made for an informer.'

" 'It looks like it might rain in a day or so,' says I, in a tired way, looking up at the cerulean blue sky.

" 'If you know anything about the locality, disposition, or secretiveness of this here Black Bill,' says he, in a severe dialect, 'you are amiable to the law in not reporting it.'

" 'I heard a fence-rider say,' says I, in a desultory kind of voice, 'that a Mexican told a cowboy named Jake over at Pidgin's store on the Nueces that he heard that Black Bill had been seen in Matamoras by a sheepman's cousin two weeks ago.'

" 'Tell you what I'll do, Tight Mouth,' says the captain, after looking me over for bargains. 'If you put us on so we can scoop Black Bill, I'll pay you a hundred dollars out of my own—out of our own—pockets. That's liberal,' says he. 'You ain't entitled to anything. Now, what do you say?'

" 'Cash down now?' I asked.

"The captain has a sort of discussion with his helpmates, and they all produce the contents of their pockets for analysis. Out of the general results they figured up $102.30 in cash and $31 worth of plug tobacco.

" 'Come nearer, capitan meeo,' says I, 'and listen.' He so did.

" 'I am mighty poor and low down in the world,' says I. 'I am working for twelve dollars a month trying to keep a lot of animals together whose only thought seems to be to get asunder. Although,' says I, 'I regard myself as some better than the State of South Dakota, it's a come-down to a man who has heretofore regarded sheep only in the form of chops. I'm pretty far reduced in the world on account of foiled ambitions and rum and a kind of cocktail they make along the P.R.R. all the way from Scranton to Cincinnati—dry gin, French vermouth, one squeeze of a lime, and a good dash of orange bitters. If you're ever up that way, don't fail to let one try you. And, again,' says I, 'I have never yet went back on a friend. I've stayed by 'em when they had plenty, and when adversity's overtaken me I've never forsook 'em.

" 'But,' I goes on, 'this is not exactly the case of a friend. Twelve dollars a month is only bowing-acquaintance money. And I do not consider brown beans and cornbread the food of friendship. I am a poor man,' says I, 'and I have a widowed mother in Texarkana. You will find Black Bill,' says I, 'lying asleep in this house on a cot in the room to your right. He's the man you want, as I know from his words and conversation. He was in a way a friend,' I explains, 'and if I was the man I once was the entire product of the mines of Gondola would not have tempted me to betray him. But,' says I, 'every week half of the beans was wormy, and not nigh enough wood in camp.

" 'Better go in careful, gentlemen,' says I. 'He seems impatient at times, and when you think of his late professional pursuits one would look for abrupt actions if he was come upon sudden.'

"So the whole posse unmounts and ties their horses, and unlimbers their ammunition and equipments, and tiptoes into the house. And I follows, like Delilah when she set the Philip Steins on to Samson.

"The leader of the posse shakes Ogden and wakes him up. And then he jumps up, and two more of the reward-hunters grab him. Ogden was mighty tough with all his slimness, and he gives 'em as neat a single-footed tussle against odds as I ever see.

" 'What does this mean?' he says, after they had him down.

" 'You're scooped in, Mr. Black Bill,' says the captain. 'That's all.'

" 'It's an outrage,' says H. Ogden, madder yet.

" 'It was,' says the peace-and-good-will man. 'The Katy wasn't bothering you, and there's a law against monkeying with express packages.'

"And he sits on H. Ogden's stomach and goes through his pockets symptomatically and careful.

" 'I'll make you perspire for this,' says Ogden, perspiring some himself. 'I can prove who I am.'

" 'So can I,' says the captain, as he draws from H. Ogden's inside coat-pocket a handful of new bills of the Second National Bank of Espinosa City. 'Your regular engraved Tuesdays-and-Fridays visiting-card wouldn't have a louder voice in proclaiming your indemnity than this here currency. You can get up now and prepare to go with us and expatriate your sins.'

"H. Ogden gets up and fixes his necktie. He says no more after they have taken the money off of him.

" 'A well-greased idea,' says the sheriff captain, admiring, 'to slip off down here and buy a little sheep-ranch where the hand of man is seldom heard. It was the slickest hide-out I ever see,' says the captain.

"So one of the men goes to the shearing-pen and hunts up the other herder, a Mexican they call John Sallies, and he saddles Ogden's horse, and the sheriffs all ride up close around him with their guns in hand, ready to take their prisoner to town.

"Before starting, Ogden puts the ranch in John Sallies' hands and gives him orders about the shearing and where to graze the sheep, just as if he intended to be back in a few days. And a couple of hours afterward one Percival Saint Clair, an ex-sheep-herder of the Rancho Chiquito, might have been seen, with a hundred and nine dollars—wages and blood-money—in his pocket, riding south on another horse belonging to said ranch.'

The red-faced man paused and listened. The whistle of a coming freight-train sounded far away among the low hills.

The fat, seedy man at his side sniffed, and shook his frowzy head slowly and disparagingly.

"What is it, Snipy?" asked the other. "Got the blues again?"

"No, I ain't," said the seedy one, sniffing again. "But I don't like your talk. You and me have been friends, off and on, for fifteen year; and I never yet knew or heard of you giving anybody up to the law—not no one. And here was a man whose saleratus you had et and at whose table you had played games of cards—if casino can be so called. And yet you inform him to the law and take money for it. It never was like you, I say."

"This H. Ogden," resumed the red-faced man, "through a lawyer, proved himself free by alibis, and other legal terminalities, as I so heard afterward. He never suffered no harm. He did me favours, and I hated to hand him over."

"How about the bills they found in his pocket?" asked the seedy man.

"I put 'em there," said the red-faced man, "while he was asleep, when I saw the posse riding up. I was Black Bill. Look out, Snipy, here she comes! We'll board her on the bumpers when she takes water."

XXXIX: AFTER TWENTY YEARS

THE policeman on the beat moved up the avenue impressively. The impressiveness was habitual and not for show, for spectators were few. The time was barely ten o'clock at night, but chilly gusts of wind with a taste of rain in them had well-nigh depeopled the streets.

Trying doors as he went, twirling his club with

many intricate and artful movements, turning now and then to cast his watchful eye adown the pacific thoroughfare, the officer, with his stalwart form and slight swagger, made a fine picture of a guardian of the peace. The vicinity was one that kept early hours. Now and then you might see the lights of a cigar store or of an all-night lunch counter; but the majority of the doors belonged to business places that had long since been closed.

When about midway of a certain block the policeman suddenly slowed his walk. In the doorway of a darkened hardware store a man leaned, with an unlighted cigar in his mouth. As the policeman walked up to him the man spoke up quickly.

"It's all right, officer," he said reassuringly. "I'm just waiting for a friend. It's an appointment made twenty years ago. Sounds a little funny to you, doesn't it? Well, I'll explain if you'd like to make certain it's all straight. About that long ago there used to be a restaurant where this store stands—'Big Joe' Brady's restaurant."

"Until five years ago," said the policeman. "It was torn down then."

The man in the doorway struck a match and lit his cigar. The light showed a pale, square-jawed face with keen eyes, and a little white scar near his right eyebrow. His scarf-pin was a large diamond, oddly set.

"Twenty years ago to-night," said the man, "I dined here at 'Big Joe' Brady's with Jimmy Wells, my best chum, and the finest chap in the world. He and I were raised here in New York, just like two brothers, together. I was eighteen and Jimmy was twenty. The next morning I was to start for the West to make my fortune. You couldn't have dragged Jimmy out of New York; he thought it was the only place on earth. Well, we agreed that night that we would meet here again exactly twenty years from that date and time, no matter what our conditions might be or from what distance we might have to come. We figured that in twenty years each of us ought to have our destiny worked out and our fortunes made, whatever they were going to be."

"It sounds pretty interesting," said the policeman. "Rather a long time between meets, though, it seems to me. Haven't you heard from your friend since you left?"

"Well, yes, for a time we corresponded," said the other. "But after a year or two we lost track of each other. You see, the West is a pretty big proposition, and I kept hustling around over it pretty lively. But I know Jimmy will meet me here if he's alive, for he always was the truest, stanchest old chap in the world. He'll never forget. I came a thousand miles to stand in this door to-night, and it's worth it if my old partner turns up."

The waiting man pulled out a handsome watch, the lids of it set with small diamonds.

"Three minutes to ten," he announced. "It was exactly ten o'clock when we parted here at the restaurant door."

"Did pretty well out West, didn't you?" asked the policeman.

"You bet! I hope Jimmy has done half as well. He was a kind of plodder, though, good fellow as he was. I've had to compete with some of the sharpest wits going to get my pile. A man gets in a groove in New York. It takes the West to put a razor-edge on him."

The policeman twirled his club and took a step or two.

"I'll be on my way. Hope your friend comes around all right. Going to call time on him sharp?"

"I should say not!" said the other. "I'll give him half an hour at least. If Jimmy is alive on earth he'll be here by that time. So long, officer."

"Good night, sir," said the policeman, passing on along his beat, trying doors as he went.

There was a fine, cold drizzle now falling, and the wind had risen from its uncertain puffs into a steady blow. The few foot-passengers astir in that quarter hurried dismally and silently along with coat collars turned high and pocketed hands. And in the door of the hardware store the man who had come a thousand miles to fill an appointment, uncertain almost to absurdity, with the friend of his youth, smoked his cigar and waited.

About twenty minutes he waited, and then a tall man in a long overcoat, with collar turned up to his ears, hurried across from the opposite side of the street. He went directly to the waiting man.

"Is that you, Bob?" he asked doubtfully.

"Is that you, Jimmy Wells?" cried the man in the door.

"Bless my heart!" exclaimed the new arrival, grasping both the other's hands with his own. "It's Bob, sure as fate. I was certain I'd find you here if you were still in existence. Well, well, well!—twenty years is a long time. The old restaurant's gone, Bob; I wish it had lasted, so we could have had another dinner there. How has the West treated you, old man?"

"Bully; it has given me everything I asked it for. You've changed lots, Jimmy. I never thought you were so tall by two or three inches."

"Oh, I grew a bit after I was twenty."

"Doing well in New York, Jimmy?"

"Moderately. I have a position in one of the city departments. Come on, Bob; we'll go around to a place I know of, and have a good long talk about old times."

The two men started up the street, arm in arm. The man from the West, his egotism enlarged by success, was beginning to outline the history of his career. The other, submerged in his overcoat, listened with interest.

At the corner stood a drug store, brilliant with electric lights. When they came into this glare each of them turned simultaneously to gaze upon the other's face.

The man from the West stopped suddenly and released his arm.

"You're not Jimmy Wells," he snapped. "Twenty years is a long time, but not long enough to change a man's nose from a Roman to a pug."

"It sometimes changes a good man into a bad one," said the tall man. "You've been under arrest for ten minutes, 'Silky' Bob. Chicago thinks you may have dropped over our way and wires us she wants to have a chat with you. Going quietly, are you? That's sensible. Now, before we go on to the station here's a note I was asked to hand you. You may read it here at the window. It's from Patrolman Wells."

The man from the West unfolded the little piece of paper handed him. His hand was steady when he began to read, but it trembled a little by the time he had finished. The note was rather short.

"*Bob: I was at the appointed place on time. When you struck the match to light your cigar I saw it was the face of the man wanted in Chicago. Somehow I couldn't do it myself, so I went around and got a plain-clothes man to do the job.*

"*JIMMY.*"

XL: PHŒBE

"YOU are a man of many novel adventures and varied enterprises," I said to Captain Patricio Maloné. "Do you believe that the possible element of good luck or bad luck—if there is such a thing as luck—has influenced your career or persisted for or against you to such an extent that you were forced to attribute results to the operation of the aforesaid good luck or bad luck?"

This question (of almost the dull insolence of legal phraseology) was put while we sat in Rousselin's little red-tiled café near Congo Square in New Orleans.

Brown-faced, white-hatted, finger-ringed captains of adventure came often to Rousselin's for the cognac. They came from sea and land, and were chary of relating the things they had seen—not because they were more wonderful than the fantasies of the Ananiases of print, but because they were so different. And I was a perpetual wedding-guest, always striving to cast my buttonhole over the finger of one of these mariners of fortune. This Captain Maloné was a Hiberno-Iberian Creole who had gone to and fro in the earth and walked up and down in it. He looked like any other well-dressed man of thirty-five whom you might meet, except that he was hopelessly weather-tanned, and wore on his chain an ancient ivory-and-gold Peruvian charm against evil, which has nothing at all to do with his story.

"My answer to your question," said the Captain, smiling, "will be to tell you the story of Bad-Luck Kearny. That is, if you don't mind hearing it."

My reply was to pound on the table for Rousselin.

"Strolling along Tchoupitoulas Street one night," began Captain Maloné, "I noticed, without especially taxing my interest, a small man walking rapidly toward me. He stepped upon a wooden cellar door, crashed through it and disappeared. I rescued him from a heap of soft coal below. He dusted himself briskly, swearing fluently in a mechanical tone, as an underpaid actor recites the gipsy's curse. Gratitude and the dust in his throat seemed to call for fluids to clear them away. His desire for liquidation was expressed so heartily that I went with him to a café down the street where we had some vile vermouth and bitters.

"Looking across that little table I had my first clear sight of Francis Kearny. He was about five feet seven, but as tough as a cypress knee. His hair was darkest red, his mouth such a mere slit that you wondered how the flood of his words came rushing from it. His eyes were the brightest and lightest blue and the hopefulest that I ever saw. He gave the double impression that he was at bay and that you had better not crowd him further.

" 'Just in from a gold-hunting expedition on the coast of Costa Rica,' he explained. 'Second mate of a banana steamer told me the natives were panning out enough from the beach sands to buy all the rum, red calico, and parlour melodeons in the world. The day I got there a syndicate named Incorporated Jones gets a government concession to all minerals from a given point. For a next choice I take coast fever and count green and blue lizards for six weeks in a grass hut. I had to be notified when I was well, for the reptiles were actually there. Then I shipped back as third cook on a Norwegian tramp that blew up her boiler two miles below Quarantine. I was due to bust through that cellar door here to-night, so I hurried the rest of the way up the river, roustabouting on a lower coast packet that made a landing for every fisherman that wanted a plug of tobacco. And now I'm here for what comes next. And it'll be along, it'll be along,' said this queer Mr. Kearny; 'it'll be along on the beams of my bright but not very particular star.'

"From the first the personality of Kearny charmed me. I saw in him the bold heart, the restless nature, and the valiant front against the buffets of fate that make his countrymen such valuable comrades in risk and adventure. And just then I was wanting such men. Moored at a fruit company's pier I had a 500-ton steamer ready to sail the next day with a cargo of sugar, lumber, and corrugated iron for a port in—well, let us call the country Esperando—it has not been long ago, and the name of Patricio Maloné is still spoken there when its unsettled politics are discussed. Beneath the sugar and iron were packed a thousand Winchester rifles. In Aguas Frias, the capital, Don Rafael Valdevia, Minister of War, Esperando's greatest-hearted and most able patriot, awaited my coming. No doubt you have heard, with a smile, of the insignificant wars and uprisings in those little tropic republics. They make but a faint clamour against the din of great nations' battles; but down there, under all the ridiculous uniforms and petty diplomacy and senseless countermarchings and intrigue, are to be found statesmen and patriots. Don Rafael Valdevia was one. His great ambition was to raise Esperando into peace and honest prosperity and the respect of the serious nations. So he waited for my rifles in Aguas Frias. But one would think I am trying to win a recruit in you! No; it was Francis Kearny I wanted. And so I told him, speaking long over our execrable vermouth, breathing the stifling odour from garlic and tarpaulins, which, as you know, is the distinctive flavour of cafés in the lower slant of our city. I spoke of the tyrant President Cruz and the burdens that his greed and insolent cruelty laid upon the people. And at that Kearny's tears flowed. And then I dried them with a picture of the fat rewards that would be ours when the oppressor should be overthrown and the wise and generous Valdevia in his seat. Then Kearny leaped to his feet and wrung my hand with the strength of a roustabout. He was mine, he said, till the last minion of the hated despot was hurled from the highest peaks of the Cordilleras into the sea.

"I paid the score and we went out. Near the door Kearny's elbow overturned an upright glass showcase, smashing it into little bits. I paid the storekeeper the price he asked.

"'Come to my hotel for the night,' I said to Kearny. 'We sail to-morrow at noon.'

"He agreed; but on the sidewalk he fell to cursing again in the dull, monotonous, glib way that he had done when I pulled him out of the coal cellar.

"'Captain,' said he, 'before we go any further, it's no more than fair to tell you that I'm known from Baffin's Bay to Terra del Fuego as "Bad-Luck" Kearny. And I'm It. Everything I get into goes up in the air except a balloon. Every bet I ever made I lost except when I coppered it. Every boat I ever sailed on sank except the submarines. Everything I was ever interested in went to pieces except a patent bombshell that I invented. Everything I ever took hold of and tried to run I ran into the ground except when I tried to plough. And that's why they call me Bad-Luck Kearny. I thought I'd tell you.'

"'Bad luck,' said I, 'or what goes by the name, may now and then tangle the affairs of any man. But if it persist beyond the estimate of what we may call the "averages" there must be a cause for it.'

"'There is,' said Kearny emphatically, 'and when we walk another square I will show it to you.'

"Surprised, I kept by his side until we came to Canal Street and out into the middle of its great width.

"Kearny seized me by the arm and pointed a tragic forefinger at a rather brilliant star that shone steadily about thirty degrees above the horizon.

"'That's Saturn,' said he, 'the star that presides over bad luck and evil and disappointment and nothing doing and trouble. I was born under that star. Every move I make, up bobs Saturn and blocks it. He's the hoodoo planet of the heavens. They say he's 73,000 miles in diameter and no solider of body than split-pea soup, and he's got as many disreputable and malignant rings as Chicago. Now, what kind of a star is that to be born under?'

"I asked Kearny where he had obtained all this astonishing knowledge.

" 'From Azrath, the great astrologer of Cleveland, Ohio,' said he. 'That man looked at a glass ball and told me my name before I'd taken a chair. He prophesied the date of my birth and death before I'd said a word. And then he cast my horoscope, and the sidereal system socked me in the solar plexus. It was bad luck for Francis Kearny from A to Izard and for his friends that were implicated with him. For that I gave up ten dollars. This Azrath was sorry, but he respected his profession too much to read the heavens wrong for any man. It was night time, and he took me out on a balcony and gave me a free view of the sky. And he showed me which Saturn was, and how to find it in different balconies and longitudes.

" 'But Saturn wasn't all. He was only the man higher up. He furnishes so much bad luck that they allow him a gang of deputy sparklers to help hand it out. They're circulating and revolving and hanging around the main supply all the time, each one throwing the hoodoo on his own particular district.

" 'You see that ugly little red star about eight inches above and to the right of Saturn?' Kearny asked me. 'Well, that's her. That's Phœbe.

She's got me in charge. "By the day of your birth," said Azrath to me, "your life is subjected to the influence of Saturn. By the hour and minute of it you must dwell under the sway and direct authority of Phœbe, the ninth satellite." So said this Azrath.' Kearny shook his fist viciously skyward. 'Curse her, she's done her work well,' said he. 'Ever since I was astrologized, bad luck has followed me like my shadow, as I told you. And for many years before. Now, Captain, I've told you my handicap as a man should. If you're afraid this evil star of mine might cripple your scheme, leave me out of it.'

"I reassured Kearny as well as I could. I told him that for the time we would banish astrology and astronomy from our heads. The manifest valour and enthusiasm of the man drew me. 'Let us see what a little courage and diligence will do against bad luck,' I said. 'We will sail to-morrow for Esperando.'

"Fifty miles down the Mississippi our steamer broke her rudder. We sent for a tug to tow us back and lost three days. When we struck the blue waters of the Gulf, all the storm clouds of the Atlantic seemed to have concentrated above us. We thought surely to sweeten those leaping waves with our sugar, and to stack our arms and lumber on the floor of the Mexican Gulf.

"Kearny did not seek to cast off one iota of the burden of our danger from the shoulders of his fatal horoscope. He weathered every storm on deck, smoking a black pipe, to keep which alight rain and sea-water seemed but as oil. And he shook his fist at the black clouds behind which his baleful star winked its unseen eye. When the skies cleared one evening, he reviled his malignant guardian with grim humour.

"'On watch, aren't you, you red-headed vixen? Out making it hot for little Francis Kearny and his friends, according to Hoyle. Twinkle, twinkle, little devil! You're a lady, aren't you?—dogging a man with bad luck just because he happened to be born while your boss was floorwalker. Get busy and sink the ship, you one-eyed banshee. Phœbe! H'm! Sounds as mild as a milkmaid. You can't judge a woman by her name. Why couldn't I have had a man star? I can't make the remarks to Phœbe that I could to a man. Oh, Phœbe, you be—blasted!'

"For eight days gales and squalls and water-spouts beat us from our course. Five days only should have landed us in Esperando. Our Jonah swallowed the bad credit of it with appealing frankness; but that scarcely lessened the hardships our cause was made to suffer.

"At last one afternoon we steamed into the calm estuary of the little Rio Escondido. Three miles up this we crept, feeling for the shallow channel between the low banks that were crowded to the edge with gigantic trees and riotous vegetation. Then our whistle gave a little toot, and in five minutes we heard a shout, and Carlos—my brave Carlos Quintana—crashed through the tangled vines waving his cap madly for joy.

"A hundred yards away was his camp, where three hundred chosen patriots of Esperando were awaiting our coming. For a month Carlos had been drilling them there in the tactics of war, and filling them with the spirit of revolution and liberty.

"'My Captain—*compadre mio!*' shouted Carlos,

while yet my boat was being lowered. 'You should see them in the drill by *companias*—in the column wheel—in the march by fours—they are superb! Also in the manual of arms—but, alas! performed only with sticks of bamboo. The guns, *capitan*—say that you have brought the guns!'

" 'A thousand Winchesters, Carlos,' I called to him. 'And two Gatlings.'

" '*Valgame Dios!*' he cried, throwing his cap in the air. 'We shall sweep the world!'

"At that moment Kearny tumbled from the steamer's side into the river. He could not swim, so the crew threw him a rope and drew him back aboard. I caught his eye and his look of pathetic but still bright and undaunted consciousness of his guilty luck. I told myself that although he might be a man to shun, he was also one to be admired.

"I gave orders to the sailing-master that the arms, ammunition, and provisions were to be landed at once. That was easy in the steamer's boats, except for the two Gatling guns. For their transportation ashore we carried a stout flatboat, brought for the purpose in the steamer's hold.

"In the meantime I walked with Carlos to the camp and made the soldiers a little speech in Spanish, which they received with enthusiasm; and then I had some wine and a cigarette in Carlos's tent. Later we walked back to the river to see how the unloading was being conducted.

"The small arms and provisions were already ashore, and the petty officers and squads of men conveying them to camp. One Gatling had been safely landed; the other was just being hoisted over the side of the vessel as we arrived. I noticed

Kearny darting about on board, seeming to have the ambition of ten men, and to be doing the work of five. I think his zeal bubbled over when he saw Carlos and me. A rope's end was swinging loose from some part of the tackle. Kearny leaped impetuously and caught it. There was a crackle and a hiss and a smoke of scorching hemp, and the Gatling dropped straight as a plummet through the bottom of the flatboat and buried itself in twenty feet of water and five feet of river mud.

"I turned my back on the scene. I heard Carlos's loud cries as if from some extreme grief too poignant for words. I heard the complaining murmur of the crew and the maledictions of Torres, the sailing-master—I could not bear to look.

"By night some degree of order had been restored in camp. Military rules were not drawn strictly, and the men were grouped about the fires of their several messes, playing games of chance, singing their native songs, or discussing with voluble animation the contingencies of our march upon the capital.

"To my tent, which had been pitched for me close to that of my chief lieutenant, came Kearny, indomitable, smiling, bright-eyed, bearing no traces of the buffets of his evil star. Rather was his aspect that of a heroic martyr whose tribulations were so high-sourced and glorious that he even took a splendour and a prestige from them.

" 'Well, Captain,' he said, 'I guess you realize that Bad-Luck Kearny is still on deck. It was a shame, now, about that gun. She only needed to be slewed two inches to clear the rail; and that's why I grapped that rope's end. Who'd have thought that a sailor—even a Sicilian lubber on a banana coaster—would have fastened a line in a bow-knot? Don't think I'm trying to dodge the responsibility, Captain. It's my luck.'

" 'There are men, Kearny,' said I gravely, 'who pass through life blaming upon luck and chance the mistakes that result from their own faults and incompetency. I do not say that you are such a man. But if all your mishaps are traceable to that tiny star, the sooner we endow our colleges with chairs of moral astronomy, the better.'

" 'It isn't the size of the star that counts,' said Kearny; 'it's the quality. Just the way it is with women. That's why they gave the biggest planets masculine names, and the little stars feminine ones —to even things up when it comes to getting their work in. Suppose they had called my star Agamemnon or Bill McCarty or something like that instead of Phœbe. Every time one of those old boys touched their calamity button and sent me down one of their wireless pieces of bad luck, I could talk back and tell 'em what I thought of 'em in suitable terms. But you can't address such remarks to a Phœbe.'

" 'It pleases you to make a joke of it, Kearny,' said I, without smiling. 'But it is no joke to me to think of my Gatling mired in the river ooze.'

" 'As to that,' said Kearny, abandoning his light mood at once, 'I have already done what I could. I have had some experience in hoisting stone in quarries. Torres and I have already spliced three hawsers and stretched them from the steamer's stern to a tree on shore. We will rig a tackle and have the gun on terra firma before noon to-morrow.'

"One could not remain long at outs with Bad-Luck Kearny.

" 'Once more,' said I to him, 'we will waive this question of luck. Have you ever had experience in drilling raw troops?'

" 'I was first sergeant and drill-master,' said Kearny, 'in the Chilean army for one year. And captain of artillery for another.'

" 'What became of your command?' I asked.

" 'Shot down to a man,' said Kearny, 'during the revolutions against Balmaceda.'

"Somehow the misfortunes of the evil-starred one seemed to turn to me their comedy side, I lay back upon my goat's-hide cot and laughed until the woods echoed. Kearny grinned. 'I told you how it was,' he said.

" 'To-morrow,' I said, 'I shall detail one hundred men under your command for manual-of-arms drill and company evolutions. You will rank as lieutenant. Now, for God's sake, Kearny,' I urged him, 'try to combat this superstition, if it is one. Bad luck may be like any other visitor—preferring to stop where it is expected. Get your mind off stars. Look upon Esperando as your planet of good fortune.'

" 'I thank you, Captain,' said Kearny quietly. 'I will try to make it the best handicap I ever ran.'

"By noon the next day the submerged Gatling was rescued, as Kearny had promised. Then Carlos and Manuel Ortiz and Kearny (my lieutenants) distributed Winchesters among the troops and put them through an incessant rifle drill. We fired no shots, blank or solid, for of all coasts Esperando is the stillest; and we had no desire to sound any warnings in the ear of that corrupt government until they should carry with them the message of Liberty and the downfall of Oppression.

"In the afternoon came a mule-rider bearing a written message to me from Don Rafael Valdevia in the capital, Aguas Frias.

"Whenever that man's name comes to my lips, words of tribute to his greatness, his noble simplicity, and his conspicuous genius follow irrepressibly. He was a traveller, a student of peoples and governments, a master of sciences, a poet, an orator, a leader, a soldier, a critic of the world's campaigns and the idol of the people of Esperando. I had been honoured by his friendship for years. It was I who first turned his mind to the thought that he should leave for his monument a new Esperando—a country freed from the rule of unscrupulous tyrants, and a people made happy and prosperous by wise and impartial legislation. When he had consented he threw himself into the cause with the undivided zeal with which he endowed all of his acts. The coffers of his great fortune were opened to those of us to whom were entrusted the secret moves of the game. His popularity was already so great that he had practically forced President Cruz to offer him the portfolio of Minister of War.

"The time, Don Rafael said in his letter, was ripe. Success, he prophesied, was certain. The people were beginning to clamour publicly against Cruz's misrule. Bands of citizens in the capital were even going about of nights hurling stones at public buildings and expressing their dissatisfaction. A bronze statue of President Cruz in the Botanical Gardens had been lassoed about the neck and overthrown. It only remained for me to arrive with my force and my thousand rifles, and for himself to come forward and proclaim himself the people's saviour, to overthrow Cruz in a single day. There would be but a half-hearted resistance from the six hundred Government troops stationed in the capital. The country was ours. He presumed that by this time my steamer had arrived at Quintana's camp. He proposed the eighteenth of July for the attack. That would give us six days in which to strike camp and march to Aguas Frias. In the meantime Don Rafael remained my good friend and *compadre en la causa de la libertad*.

"On the morning of the fourteenth we began our march toward the sea-following range of mountains, over the sixty-mile trail to the capital. Our small arms and provisions were laden on pack mules. Twenty men harnessed to each Gatling gun rolled them smoothly along the flat, alluvial lowlands. Our troops, well-shod and well-fed, moved with alacrity and heartiness. I and my three lieutenants were mounted on the tough mountain ponies of the country.

"A mile out of camp one of the pack mules, becoming stubborn, broke away from the train, and plunged from the path into the thicket. The alert Kearny spurred quickly after it and intercepted its flight. Rising in his stirrups, he released one foot and bestowed upon the mutinous animal a hearty kick. The mule tottered and fell with a crash broadside upon the ground. As we gathered around it, it walled its great eyes almost humanly toward Kearny and expired. That was bad; but worse, to our minds, was the concomitant disaster. Part of the mule's burden had been one hundred pounds of the finest coffee to be had in the tropics. The bag burst and spilled the priceless brown mass of the ground berries among the dense vines and weeds of the swampy land. *Mala suerte!* When you take away from an Esperandan his coffee, you abstract his patriotism and 50 per cent. of his value as a soldier. The men began to rake up the precious stuff; but I beckoned Kearny back along the trail where they would not hear. The limit had been reached.

"I took from my pocket a wallet of money and drew out some bills.

" 'Mr. Kearny,' said I, 'here are some funds belonging to Don Rafael Valdevia, which I am expending in his cause. I know of no better service it can buy for him than this. Here is one hundred dollars. Luck or no luck, we part company here. Star or no star, calamity seems to travel by your side. You will return to the steamer. She touches at Amotapa to discharge her lumber and iron, and then puts back to New Orleans. Hand this note to the sailing-master, who will give you passage.' I wrote on a leaf torn from my book, and placed it and the money in Kearny's hand.

" 'Good-bye,' I said, extending my own. 'It is not that I am displeased with you; but there is no place in this expedition for—let us say, the Señorita Phœbe.' I said this with a smile, trying to smooth the thing for him. 'May you have better luck, *companero*.'

"Kearny took the money and the paper.

" 'It was just a little touch,' said he, 'just a little lift with the toe of my boot—but what's the odds? —that blamed mule would have died if I had only dusted his ribs with a powder puff. It was my luck. Well, Captain, I would have liked to be in that little fight with you over in Aguas Frias. Success to the cause. *Adios!*'

"He turned around and set off down the trail without looking back. The unfortunate mule's pack-saddle was transferred to Kearny's pony, and we again took up the march.

"Four days we journeyed over the foot-hills and mountains, fording icy torrents, winding around the crumbling brows of ragged peaks, creeping along rocky flanges that overlooked awful precipices, crawling breathlessly over tottering bridges that crossed bottomless chasms.

"On the evening of the seventeenth we camped by a little stream on the bare hills five miles from Aguas Frias. At daybreak we were to take up the march again.

"At midnight I was standing outside my tent inhaling the fresh cold air. The stars were shining bright in the cloudless sky, giving the heavens their proper aspect of illimitable depth and distance when viewed from the vague darkness of the blotted earth. Almost at its zenith was the planet Saturn; and with a half-smile I observed the sinister red sparkle of his malignant attendant—the demon star of Kearny's ill luck. And then my thoughts strayed across the hills to the scene of our coming triumph, where the heroic and noble Don Rafael awaited our coming to set a new and shining star in the firmament of nations.

"I heard a slight rustling in the deep grass to my right. I turned and saw Kearny coming toward me. He was ragged and dew-drenched and limping. His hat and one boot were gone. About one foot he had tied some makeshift of cloth and grass. But his manner as he approached was that of a man who knows his own virtues well enough to be superior to rebuffs.

" 'Well, sir,' I said, staring at him coldly, 'if there is anything in persistence, I see no reason why you should not succeed in wrecking and ruining us yet.'

" 'I kept half a day's journey behind,' said Kearny, fishing out a stone from the covering of his lame foot, 'so the bad luck wouldn't touch you. I couldn't help it, Captain; I wanted to be in on this game. It was a pretty tough trip, especially in the department of the commissary. In the low grounds there were always bananas and oranges. Higher up it was worse; but your men left a good deal of goat meat hanging on the bushes in the camps. Here's your hundred dollars. You're nearly there now, Captain. Let me in on the scrapping to-morrow.'

" 'Not for a hundred times a hundred would I have the tiniest thing go wrong with my plans now,' I said, 'whether caused by evil planets or the blunders of mere man. But yonder is Aguas Frias, five miles away, and a clear road. I am of the mind to defy Saturn and all his satellites to spoil our success now. At any rate, I will not turn away to-night as weary a traveller and as good a soldier as you are, Lieutenant Kearny. Manuel Ortiz's tent is there by the brightest fire. Rout him out and tell him to supply you with food and blankets and clothes. We march again at daybreak.'

"Kearny thanked me briefly but feelingly and moved away.

"He had gone scarcely a dozen steps when a sudden flash of bright light illumined the surrounding hills; a sinister, growling, hissing sound like escaping steam filled my ears. Then followed a roar as of distant thunder, which grew louder every instant. This terrifying noise culminated in a tremendous explosion, which seemed to rock the hills as an earthquake would; the illumination waxed to a glare so fierce that I clapped my hands to my eyes to save them. I thought the end of the world had come. I could think of no natural phenomenon that would explain it. My wits were staggering. The deafening explosion trailed off into the rumbling roar that had preceded it; and through this I heard the frightened shouts of my troops as they stumbled from their resting-places and rushed wildly about. Also I heard the harsh tones of Kearny's voice crying: 'They'll blame it on me, of course, and what the devil it is, it's not Francis Kearny that can give you an answer.'

"I opened my eyes. The hills were still there, dark and solid. It had not been, then, a volcano or an earthquake. I looked up at the sky and saw a comet-like trail crossing the zenith and extending westward—a fiery trail waning fainter and narrower each moment.

" 'A meteor!' I called aloud. 'A meteor has fallen. There is no danger.'

"And then all other sounds were drowned by a great shout from Kearny's throat. He had raised both hands above his head and was standing tiptoe.

" 'PHŒBE'S GONE!' he cried, with all his lungs. 'She's busted and gone to hell. Look, Captain, the little red-headed hoodoo has blown herself to smithereens. She found Kearny too tough to handle, and she puffed up with spite and meanness till her boiler blew up. It'll be Bad-Luck Kearny no more. Oh, let us be joyful!

" 'Humpty Dumpty sat on a wall;
Humpty busted, and that'll be all!'

"I looked up, wondering, and picked out Saturn in his place. But the small red twinkling luminary in his vicinity, which Kearny had pointed out to me as his evil star, had vanished. I had seen it there but half an hour before; there was no doubt that one of those awful and mysterious spasms of nature had hurled it from the heavens.

"I clapped Kearny on the shoulder.

"'Little man,' said I, 'let this clear the way for you. It appears that astrology has failed to subdue you. Your horoscope must be cast anew with pluck and loyalty for controlling stars. I play you to win. Now, get to your tent, and sleep. Daybreak is the word.'

"At nine o'clock on the morning of the eighteenth of July I rode into Aguas Frias with Kearny at my side. In his clean linen suit and with his military poise and keen eye he was a model of a fighting adventurer. I had visions of him riding as commander of President Valdevia's body-guard when the plums of the new republic should begin to fall.

"Carlos followed with the troops and supplies. He was to halt in a wood outside the town and remain concealed there until he received the word to advance.

"Kearny and I rode down the Calle Ancha toward the *residencia* of Don Rafael at the other side of the town. As we passed the superb white buildings of the University of Esperando, I saw at an open window the gleaming spectacles and bald head of Herr Bergowitz, professor of the natural sciences and friend of Don Rafael and of me and of the cause. He waved his hand to me, with his broad, bland smile.

"There was no excitement apparent in Aguas Frias. The people went about leisurely as at all times; the market was thronged with bare-headed women buying fruit and *carne*; we heard the twang and tinkle of string bands in the patios of the *cantinas*. We could see that it was a waiting game that Don Rafael was playing.

"His *residencia* was a large but low building around a great courtyard in grounds crowded with ornamental trees and tropic shrubs. At his door an old woman who came informed us that Don Rafael had not yet arisen.

" 'Tell him,' said I, 'that Captain Maloné and a friend wish to see him at once. Perhaps he has overslept.'

"She came back looking frightened.

" 'I have called,' she said, 'and rung his bell many times, but he does not answer.'

"I knew where his sleeping-room was. Kearny and I pushed by her and went to it. I put my shoulder against the thin door and forced it open.

"In an arm-chair by a great table covered with maps and books sat Don Rafael with his eyes closed. I touched his hand. He had been dead many hours. On his head above one ear was a wound caused by a heavy blow. It had ceased to bleed long before.

"I made the old woman call a *mozo*, and dispatched him in haste to fetch Herr Bergowitz.

"He came, and we stood about as if we were half stunned by the awful shock. Thus can the letting of a few drops of blood from one man's veins drain the life of a nation.

"Presently Herr Bergowitz stooped and picked up a darkish stone the size of an orange which he saw under the table. He examined it closely through his great glasses with the eye of science.

" 'A fragment,' said he, 'of a detonating meteor. The most remarkable one in twenty years exploded above this city a little after midnight this morning.'

"The professor looked quickly up at the ceiling. We saw the blue sky through a hole the size of an orange nearly above Don Rafael's chair.

"I heard a familiar sound, and turned. Kearny had thrown himself on the floor and was babbling his compendium of bitter, blood-freezing curses against the star of his evil luck.

"Undoubtedly Phœbe had been feminine. Even when hurtling on her way to fiery dissolution and everlasting doom, the last word had been hers."

Captain Maloné was not unskilled in narrative. He knew the point where a story should end. I sat revelling in his effective conclusion, when he aroused me by continuing:

"Of course," said he, "our schemes were at an end. There was no one to take Don Rafael's place. Our little army melted away like dew before the sun.

"One day after I had returned to New Orleans I related this story to a friend who holds a professorship in Tulane University.

"When I had finished he laughed and asked whether I had any knowledge of Kearny's luck afterwards. I told him no, that I had seen him no more; but that when he left me, he had expressed confidence that his future would be successful now that his unlucky star had been overthrown.

" 'No doubt,' said the professor, 'he is happier not to know one fact. If he derived his bad luck from Phœbe, the ninth satellite of Saturn, that malicious lady is still engaged in overlooking his career. The star close to Saturn that he imagined to be her was near that planet simply by the chance of its orbit—probably at different times he has regarded many other stars that happened to be in Saturn's neighbourhood as his evil one. The real Phœbe is visible only through a very good telescope.'

"About a year afterward," continued Captain Maloné, "I was walking down a street that crossed the Poydras Market. An immensely stout, pink-faced lady in black satin crowded me from the narrow sidewalk with a frown. Behind her trailed a little man laden to the gunwales with bundles and bags of goods and vegetables.

"It was Kearny—but changed. I stopped and shook one of his hands, which still clung to a bag of garlic and red peppers.

" 'How is the luck, old *companero*?' I asked him. I had not the heart to tell him the truth about his star.

" 'Well,' said he, 'I am married, as you may guess.'

" 'Francis!' called the big lady, in deep tones, 'are you going to stop in the street talking all day?'

" 'I am coming, Phœbe dear,' said Kearny, hastening after her."

Captain Maloné ceased again.

"After all, do you believe in luck?" I asked.

"Do you?" answered the Captain, with his ambiguous smile shaded by the brim of his soft straw hat.

XLI: THE DUEL

THE gods, lying beside their nectar on 'Lympus and peeping over the edge of the cliff, perceive a difference in cities. Although it would seem that to their vision towns must appear as large or small ant-hills without special characteristics, yet it is not so. Studying the habits of ants from so great a height should be but a mild diversion when coupled with the soft drink that mythology tells us is their only solace. But doubtless they have amused themselves by the comparison of villages and towns; and it will be no news to them (nor, perhaps, to many mortals), that in one particularity New York stands unique among the cities of the world. This shall be the theme of a little story addressed to the man who sits smoking with his Sabbath-slippered feet on another chair, and to the woman who snatches the paper for a moment while boiling greens or a narcotized baby leaves her free. With these I love to sit upon the ground and tell sad stories of the death of Kings.

New York City is inhabited by 4,000,000 mysterious strangers; thus beating Bird Centre by three millions and half a dozen nine's. They came here in various ways and for many reasons —Hendrik Hudson, the art schools, green goods, the stork, the annual dressmakers' convention, the Pennsylvania Railroad, love of money, the stage, cheap excursion rates, brains, personal column ads., heavy walking shoes, ambition, freight trains—all these have had a hand in making up the population.

But every man Jack when he first sets foot on the stones of Manhattan has got to fight. He has got to fight at once until either he or his adversary wins. There is no resting between rounds. It is slugging from the first. It is a fight to a finish.

Your opponent is the City. You must do battle with it from the time the ferry-boat lands you on the island until either it is yours or it has conquered you. It is the same whether you have a million in your pocket or only the price of a week's lodging.

The battle is to decide whether you shall become a New Yorker or turn the rankest outlander and Philistine. You must be one or the other. You cannot remain neutral. You must be for or against —lover or enemy—bosom friend or outcast. And, oh, the city is a general in the ring. Not only by blows does it seek to subdue you. It woos you to its heart with the subtlety of a siren. It is a combination of Delilah, green Chartreuse, Beethoven, chloral and John L. in his best days.

In other cities you may wander and abide as a stranger man as long as you please. You may live in Chicago until your hair whitens, and be a citizen and still prate of beans if Boston mothered you, and without rebuke. You may become a civic pillar in any other town but Knickerbocker's, and all the time publicly sneering at its buildings, comparing them with the architecture of Colonel Telfair's residence in Jackson, Miss., whence you hail, and you will not be set upon. But in New York you must be either a New Yorker or an invader of a modern Troy, concealed in the wooden horse of your conceited provincialism. And this dreary preamble is only to introduce to you the unimportant figures of William and Jack.

They came out of the West together, where

they had been friends. They came to dig their fortunes out of the big city.

Father Knickerbocker met them at the ferry, giving one a right-hander on the nose and the other an uppercut with his left, just to let them know that the fight was on.

William was for business; Jack was for art. Both were young and ambitious; so they countered and clinched. I think they were from Nebraska or possibly Missouri or Minnesota. Anyhow, they were out for success and scraps and scads, and they tackled the city like two Lochinvars with brass knucks and a pull at the City Hall.

Four years afterward William and Jack met at luncheon. The business man blew in like a March wind, hurled his silk hat at a waiter, dropped into the chair that was pushed under him, seized the bill of fare, and had ordered as far as cheese before the artist had time to do more than nod. After the nod a humorous smile came into his eyes.

"Billy," he said, "you're done for. The city has gobbled you up. It has taken you and cut you to its pattern and stamped you with its brand. You are so nearly like ten thousand men I have seen to-day that you couldn't be picked out from them if it weren't for your laundry marks."

"Camembert," finished William. "What's that? Oh, you've still got your hammer out for New York, have you? Well, little old Noisyville-on-the-Subway is good enough for me. It's giving me mine. And, say, I used to think the West was the whole round world—only slightly flattened at the poles whenever Bryan ran. I used to yell myself hoarse about the free expense, and hang my hat on the horizon, and say cutting things in the grocery to little soap drummers from the East. But I'd never seen New York, then, Jack. Me for it from the rathskellers up. Sixth Avenue is the West to me now. Have you heard this fellow Crusoe sing? The desert isle for him, I say, but my wife made me go. Give me May Irwin or E. S. Willard any time."

"Poor Billy," said the artist, delicately fingering a cigarette. "You remember, when we were on our way to the East, how we talked about this great, wonderful city, and how we meant to conquer it and never let it get the best of us? We were going to be just the same fellows we had always been, and never let it master us. It has downed you, old man. You have changed from a maverick into a butterick."

"Don't see exactly what you are driving at," said William. "I don't wear an alpaca coat with blue trousers and a seersucker vest on dress occasions, like I used to do at home. You talk about being cut to a pattern—well, ain't the pattern all right? When you're in Rome you've got to do as the Dagoes do. This town seems to me to have other alleged metropolises skinned to flag stations. According to the railroad schedule I've got in my mind, Chicago and Saint Jo and Paris, France, are asterisk stops—which means you wave a red flag and get on every other Tuesday. I like this little suburb of Tarrytown-on-the-Hudson. There's something or somebody doing all the time. I'm clearing $8,000 a year selling automatic pumps, and I'm living like kings-up. Why, yesterday, I was introduced to John W. Gates. I took an auto ride with a wine agent's sister. I saw two men run over by a street car, and I seen Edna May play in the evening. Talk about the West, why, the other night I woke everybody up in the hotel hollering. I dreamed I was walking on a board sidewalk in Oshkosh. What have you got against this town, Jack? There's only one thing in it that I don't care for, and that's a ferry-boat."

The artist gazed dreamily at the cartridge paper on the wall. "This town," said he, "is a leech. It drains the blood of the country. Whoever comes to it accepts a challenge to a duel. Abandoning the figure of the leech, it is a juggernaut, a Moloch, a monster to which the innocence, the genius, and the beauty of the land must pay tribute. Hand to hand every newcomer must struggle with the leviathan. You've lost, Billy. It shall never conquer me. I hate it as one hates sin or pestilence or—the colour work in a ten-cent magazine. I despise its very vastness and power. It has the poorest millionaires, the littlest great men, the haughtiest beggars, the plainest beauties, the lowest skyscrapers, the dolefullest pleasures of any town I ever saw. It has caught you, old man, but I will never run beside its chariot wheels. It glosses itself as the Chinamen glosses his collars. Give me the domestic finish. I could stand a town ruled by wealth or one ruled by an aristocracy; but this is one controlled by its lowest ingredients. Claiming culture, it is the crudest; asseverating its pre-eminence, it is the basest; denying all outside values and virtue, it is the narrowest. Give me the pure air and the open heart of the West country. I would go back there to-morrow if I could."

"Don't you like this *filet mignon*?" said William. "Shucks, now, what's the use to knock the town! It's the greatest ever. I couldn't sell one automatic pump between Harrisburg and Tommy

O'Keefe's saloon, in Sacramento, where I sell twenty here. And have you seen Sara Bernhardt in 'Andrew Mack' yet?"

"The town's got you, Billy," said Jack.

"All right," said William. "I'm going to buy a cottage on Lake Ronkonkoma next summer."

At midnight Jack raised his window and sat close to it. He caught his breath at what he saw, though he had seen and felt it a hundred times.

Far below and around lay the city like a ragged purple dream. The irregular houses were like the broken exteriors of cliffs lining deep gulches and winding streams. Some were mountainous; some lay in long, monotonous rows like the basalt precipices hanging over desert cañons. Such was the background of the wonderful, cruel, enchanting, bewildering, fatal, great city. But into this background were cut myriads of brilliant parallelograms and circles and squares through which glowed many coloured lights. And out of the violet and purple depths ascended like the city's soul sounds and odours and thrills that make up the civic body. There arose the breath of gaiety unrestrained, of love, of hate, of all the passions that man can know. There below him lay all things, good or bad, that can be brought from the four corners of the earth to instruct, please, thrill, enrich, despoil, elevate, cast down, nurture or kill. Thus the flavour of it came up to him and went into his blood.

There was a knock on his door. A telegram had come for him. It came from the West, and these were its words:

"Come back home and the answer will be yes.

"Dolly."

He kept the boy waiting ten minutes, and then wrote the reply: "Impossible to leave here at present." Then he sat at the window again and let the city put its cup of mandragora to his lips again.

After all it isn't a story; but I wanted to know which one of the heroes won the battle against the city. So I went to a very learned friend and laid the case before him. What he said was: "Please don't bother me; I have Christmas presents to buy."

So there it rests; and you will have to decide for yourself.

XLII: THE SONG AND THE SERGEANT

HALF a dozen people supping at a table in one of the Upper Broadway all-night restaurants were making too much noise. Three times the manager walked past them with a politely warning glance; but their argument had waxed too warm to be quelled by a manager's gaze. It was midnight, and the restaurant was filled with patrons from the theatres of that district. Some among the dispersed audiences must have recognized among the quarrelsome sextet the faces of the players belonging to the Carroll Comedy Company.

Four of the six made up the company. Another was the author of the comedietta, "A Gay Coquette," which the quartette of players had been presenting with fair success at several vaudeville houses in the city. The sixth at the table was a person inconsequent in the realm of art, but one at whose bidding many lobsters had perished.

Loudly the six maintained their clamorous debate. No: one of the party was silent except when answers were stormed from him by the excited ones. That was the comedian of "A Gay Coquette." He was a young man with a face even too melancholy for his profession.

The oral warfare of four immoderate tongues was directed at Miss Clarice Carroll, the twinkling star of the small aggregation. Excepting the downcast comedian, all members of the party united in casting upon her with vehemence the blame of some momentous misfortune. Fifty times they told her: "It is your fault, Clarice—it is you alone who spoilt the scene. It is only of late that you have acted this way. At this rate the sketch will have to be taken off."

Miss Carroll was a match for any four. Gallic ancestry gave her a vivacity that could easily mount to fury. Her large eyes flashed a scorching denial at her accusers. Her slender, eloquent arms constantly menaced the table-ware. Her high, clear soprano voice rose to what would have been a scream had it not possessed so pure a musical quality. She hurled back at the attacking four their denunciations in tones sweet, but of too great carrying power for a Broadway restaurant.

Finally they exhausted her patience both as a woman and an artist. She sprang up like a panther, managed to smash half a dozen plates and glasses with one royal sweep of her arm, and defied her critics. They rose and wrangled more loudly. The comedian sighed and looked a trifle sadder and disinterested. The manager came tripping and suggested peace. He was told to go to the popular synonym for war so promptly that the affair might have happened at The Hague.

Thus was the manager angered. He made a sign with his hand and a waiter slipped out of the door. In twenty minutes the party of six was in a police station facing a grizzled and philosophical desk sergeant.

"Disorderly conduct in a restaurant," said the policeman who had brought the party in.

The author of "A Gay Coquette" stepped to the front. He wore nose-glasses and evening clothes, even if his shoes had been tans before they met the patent-leather-polish bottle.

"Mr. Sergeant," said he, out of his throat, like Actor Irving, "I would like to protest against this arrest. The company of actors who are performing in a little play that I have written, in company with a friend and myself, were having a little supper. We became deeply interested in the discussion as to which one of thc cast is responsible for a scene in the sketch that lately has fallen so flat that the piece is about to become a failure. We may have been rather noisy and intolerant of interruption by the restaurant people; but the matter was of considerable importance to all of us. You see that we are sober and are not the kind of people who desire to raise disturbances. I hope that the case will not be pressed and that we may be allowed to go."

"Who makes the charge?" asked the sergeant.

"Me," said a white-aproned voice in the rear. "De restaurant sent me to. De gang was raisin' a rough-house and breakin' dishes."

"The dishes were paid for," said the playwright. "They were not broken purposely. In her anger because we remonstrated with her for spoiling the scene, Miss——"

"It's not true, sergeant," cried the clear voice of

Miss Clarice Carroll. In a long coat of tan silk and a red-plumed hat, she bounded before the desk.

"It's not my fault," she cried indignantly. "How dare they say such a thing! I've played the title rôle ever since it was staged, and if you want to know who made it a success, ask the public—that's all."

"What Miss Carroll says is true in part," said the author. "For five months the comedietta was a drawing card in the best houses. But during the last two weeks it has lost favour. There is one scene in it in which Miss Carroll made a big hit. Now she hardly gets a hand out of it. She spoils it by acting it entirely different from her old way."

"It is not my fault," reiterated the actress.

"There are only two of you on in the scene," argued the playwright hotly, "you and Delmars, here——"

"Then it's his fault," declared Miss Carroll, with a lightning glance of scorn from her dark eyes. The comedian caught it, and gazed with increased melancholy at the panels of the sergeant's desk.

The night was a dull one in that particular police station.

The sergeant's long-blunted curiosity awoke a little.

"I've heard you," he said to the author. And then he addressed the thin-faced and ascetic-looking lady of the company who played "Aunt Turnip-top" in the little comedy.

"Who do you think spoils the scene you are fussing about?" he asked.

"I'm no knocker," said that lady, "and everybody knows it. So, when I say that Clarice falls down every time in that scene, I'm judging her art and not herself. She was great in it once. She does it something fierce now. It'll dope the show if she keeps it up."

The sergeant looked at the comedian.

"You and the lady have this scene together, I understand. I suppose there's no use asking you which one of you queers it?"

The comedian avoided the direct rays from the two fixed stars of Miss Carroll's eyes.

"I don't know," he said, looking down at his patent-leather toes.

"Are you one of the actors?" asked the sergeant of a dwarfish youth with a middle-aged face.

"Why, say!" replied the last Thespian witness, "you don't notice any tin spear in my hands, do you? You haven't heard me shout: 'See, the Emperor comes!' since I've been in here, have you? I guess I'm on the stage long enough for 'em not to start a panic by mistaking me for a thin curl of smoke rising above the footlights."

"In your opinion, if you've got one," said the sergeant, "is the frost that gathers on the scene in question the work of the lady or the gentleman who takes part in it?"

The middle-aged youth looked pained.

"I regret to say," he answered, "that Miss Carroll seems to have lost her grip on that scene. She's all right in the rest of the play, but—but I tell you, sergeant, she can do it—she has done it equal to any of 'em—and she can do it again."

Miss Carroll ran forward glowing and palpitating.

"Thank you, Jimmy, for the first good word I've had in many a day," she cried. And then she turned her eager face toward the desk.

"I'll show you, sergeant, whether I am to blame.

I'll show them whether I can do that same. Come, Mr. Delmars, let us begin. You will let us, won't you, sergeant?"

"How long will it take?" asked the sergeant dubiously.

"Eight minutes," said the playwright. "The entire play consumes but thirty."

"You may go ahead," said the sergeant. "Most of you seem to side against the little lady. Maybe she had a right to crack up a saucer or two in that restaurant. We'll see how she does the turn before we take that up."

The matron of the police station had been standing near, listening to the singular argument. She came nigher and stood near the sergeant's chair. Two or three of the reserves strolled in, big and yawning.

"Before beginning the scene," said the playwright, "and assuming that you have not seen a production of 'A Gay Coquette,' I will make a brief but necessary explanation. It is a musical-farce-comedy—burlesque-comedietta. As the title implies, Miss Carroll's rôle is that of a gay, rollicking, mischievous, heartless coquette. She sustains that character throughout the entire comedy part of the production. And I have designed the extravaganza features so that she may preserve and present the same coquettish idea.

"Now, the scene in which we take exception to Miss Carroll's acting is called the 'gorilla dance.' She is costumed to represent a wood nymph, and there is a great song-and-dance scene with a gorilla —played by Mr. Delmars, the comedian. A tropical-forest stage is set.

"That used to get four and five recalls. The main

thing was the acting and the dance—it was the funniest thing in New York for five months. Delmars's song, 'I'll Woo Thee to My Sylvan Home,' while he and Miss Carroll were cutting hide-and-seek capers among the tropical plants, was a winner."

"What's the trouble with the scene now?" asked the sergeant.

"Miss Carroll spoils it right in the middle of it," said the playwright wrathfully.

With a wide gesture of her ever-moving arms the actress waved back the little group of spectators, leaving a space in front of the desk for the scene of her vindication or fall. Then she whipped off her long tan cloak and tossed it across the arm of the policeman who still stood officially among them.

Miss Carroll had gone to supper well cloaked, but in the costume of the tropic wood nymph. A skirt of fern leaves touched her knee; she was like a humming bird—green and golden and purple.

And then she danced a fluttering, fantastic dance, so agile and light and mazy in her steps that the other three members of the Carroll Comedy Company broke into applause at the art of it.

And at the proper time Delmars leaped out at her side, mimicking the uncouth, hideous bounds of the gorilla so funnily that the grizzled sergeant himself gave a short laugh like the closing of a padlock. They danced together the gorilla dance, and won a hand from all.

Then began the most fantastic part of the scene—the wooing of the nymph by the gorilla. It was a kind of dance itself—eccentric and prankish, with the nymph in coquettish and seductive retreat, followed by the gorilla as he sang "I'll Woo Thee to My Sylvan Home."

The song was a lyric of merit. The words were nonsense, as befitted the play, but the music was worthy of something better. Delmars struck into it in a rich tenor that owned a quality that shamed the flippant words.

During one verse of the song the wood nymph performed the grotesque evolutions designed for the scene. At the middle of the second verse she stood still, with a strange look on her face, seeming to gaze dreamily into the depths of the scenic forest. The gorilla's last leap had brought him to her feet, and there he knelt, holding her hand, until he had finished the haunting lyric that was set in the absurd comedy like a diamond in a piece of putty.

When Delmars ceased Miss Carroll started, and covered a sudden flow of tears with both hands.

"There!" cried the playwright, gesticulating with violence; "there you have it, sergeant. For two weeks she has spoiled that scene in just that manner at every performance. I have begged her to consider that it is not Ophelia or Juliet that she is playing. Do you wonder now at our impatience? Tears for the gorilla song! The play is lost!"

Out of her bewitchment, whatever it was, the wood nymph flared suddenly, and pointed a desperate finger at Delmars.

"It is you—you who have done this," she cried wildly. "You never sang that song that way until lately. It is your doing."

"I give it up," said the sergeant.

And then the grey-haired matron of the police station came forward from behind the sergeant's chair.

"Must an old woman teach you all?" she said. She went up to Miss Carroll and took her hand.

"The man's wearing his heart out for you, my dear. Couldn't you tell it the first note you heard him sing? All of his monkey flip-flops wouldn't have kept it from me. Must you be deaf as well as blind? That's why you couldn't act your part, child. Do you love him or must he be a gorilla for the rest of his days?"

Miss Carroll whirled around and caught Delmars with a lightning glance of her eye. He came toward her, melancholy.

"Did you hear, Mr. Delmars?" she asked with a catching breath.

"I did," said the comedian. "It is true. I didn't think there was any use. I tried to let you know with the song."

"Silly!" said the matron; "why didn't you speak?"

"No, no," cried the wood nymph, "his way was the best. I didn't know, but—it was just what I wanted, Bobby."

She sprang like a green grasshopper; and the comedian opened his arms, and—smiled.

"Get out of this," roared the desk sergeant to the waiting waiter from the restaurant. "There's nothing doing here for you."

XLIII: REFORMATION OF CALLIOPE

CALLIOPE CATESBY was in his humours again. Ennui was upon him. This goodly promontory the earth—particularly that portion of it known as Quicksand—was to him no more than a pestilent congregation of vapours. Overtaken by the megrims, the philosopher may seek relief in soliloquy; my lady find solace in tears; the flaccid Easterner scold at the millinery bills of his women folk. Such recourse was insufficient to the denizens of Quicksand. Calliope, especially, was wont to express his ennui according to his lights.

Over night Calliope had hung out signals of approaching low spirits. He had kicked his own dog on the porch of the *Occidental Hotel*, and refused to apologize. He had become capricious and fault-finding in conversation. While strolling about he reached often for twigs of mesquite and chewed the leaves fiercely. That was always an ominous act. Another symptom alarming to those who were familiar with the different stages of his doldrums was his increasing politeness and a tendency to use formal phrases. A husky softness succeeded the usual penetrating drawl in his tones. A dangerous courtesy marked his manners. Later, his smile became crooked, the left side of his mouth slanting upward, and Quicksand got ready to stand from under.

At this stage Calliope generally began to drink. Finally, about midnight, he was seen going homeward, saluting those whom he met with exaggerated but inoffensive courtesy. Not yet was Calliope's melancholy at the danger point. He would seat himself at the window of the room he occupied over Silvester's tonsorial parlours and there chant lugubrious and tuneless ballads until morning, accompanying the noises by appropriate maltreatment of a jingling guitar. More magnanimous than Nero, he would thus give musical warning of the forthcoming municipal upheaval that Quicksand was scheduled to endure.

A quiet, amiable man was Calliope Catesby at

other times—quiet to indolence, and amiable to worthlessness. At best he was a loafer and a nuisance; at worst he was the Terror of Quicksand. His ostensible occupation was something subordinate in the real estate line; he drove the beguiled Easterner in buckboards out to look over lots and ranch property. Originally he came from one of the Gulf States, his lank six feet, slurring rhythm of speech, and sectional idioms giving evidence of his birthplace.

And yet, after taking on Western adjustments, this languid pine-box whittler, cracker barrel hugger, shady corner lounger of the cotton field and sumac hills of the South became famed as a bad man among men who had made a life-long study of the art of truculence.

At nine the next morning Calliope was fit. Inspired by his own barbarous melodies and the contents of his jug, he was ready primed to gather fresh laurels from the diffident brow of Quicksand. Encircled and criss-crossed with cartridge belts, abundantly garnished with revolvers, and copiously drunk, he poured forth into Quicksand's main street. Too chivalrous to surprise and capture a town by silent sortie, he paused at the nearest corner and emitted his slogan—that fearful, brassy yell, so reminiscent of the steam piano, that had gained for him the classic appellation that had superseded his own baptismal name. Following close upon his vociferation came three shots from his forty-five by way of limbering up the guns and testing his aim. A yellow dog, the personal property of Colonel Swazey, the proprietor of the *Occidental*, fell feet upward in the dust with one farewell yelp. A Mexican who was crossing the street from the Blue

Front grocery carrying in his hand a bottle of kerosene, was stimulated to a sudden and admirable burst of speed, still grasping the neck of the shattered bottle. The new gilt weathercock on Judge Riley's lemon and ultramarine two-story residence shivered, flapped, and hung by a splinter, the sport of the wanton breezes.

The artillery was in trim. Calliope's hand was steady. The high, calm ecstasy of habitual battle was upon him, though slightly embittered by the sadness of Alexander in that his conquests were limited to the small world of Quicksand.

Down the street went Calliope, shooting right and left. Glass fell like hail; dogs vamoosed; chickens flew, squawking; feminine voices shrieked concernedly to youngsters at large. The din was perforated at intervals by the *staccato* of the Terror's guns, and was drowned periodically by the brazen screech that Quicksand knew so well. The occasions of Calliope's low spirits were legal holidays in Quicksand. All along the main street in advance of his coming clerks were putting up shutters and closing doors. Business would languish for a space. The right of way was Calliope's, and as he advanced, observing the dearth of opposition and the few opportunities for distraction, his ennui perceptibly increased.

But some four squares farther down lively preparations were being made to minister to Mr. Catesby's love for interchange of compliments and repartee. On the previous night numerous messengers had hastened to advise Buck Patterson, the city marshal, of Calliope's impending eruption. The patience of that official, often strained in extending leniency toward the disturber's misdeeds, had been overtaxed. In Quicksand some indulgence was accorded the natural ebullition of human nature. Providing that the lives of the more useful citizens were not recklessly squandered, or too much property needlessly laid waste, the community sentiment was against a too strict enforcement of the law. But Calliope had raised the limit. His outbursts had been too frequent and too violent to come within the classification of a normal and sanitary relaxation of spirit.

Buck Patterson had been expecting and awaiting in his little ten-by-twelve frame office that preliminary yell announcing that Calliope was feeling blue. When the signal came the city marshal rose to his feet and buckled on his guns. Two deputy sheriffs and three citizens who had proven the edible qualities of fire also stood up, ready to bandy with Calliope's leaden jocularities.

"Gather that fellow in," said Buck Patterson, setting forth the lines of the campaign. "Don't have no talk, but shoot as soon as you can get a show. Keep behind cover and bring him down. He's a nogood 'un. It's up to Calliope to turn up his toes this time, I reckon. Go to him all spraddled out, boys. And don't git too reckless, for what Calliope shoots at he hits."

Buck Patterson, tall, muscular, and solemn-faced, with his bright "City Marshal" badge shining on the breast of his blue flannel shirt, gave his posse directions for the onslaught upon Calliope. The plan was to accomplish the downfall of the Quicksand Terror without loss to the attacking party, if possible.

The splenetic Calliope, unconscious of retributive plots, was steaming down the channel, cannonading on either side, when he suddenly became aware of breakers ahead. The city marshal and one of the deputies rose up behind some dry-goods boxes half a square to the front and opened fire. At the same time the rest of the posse, divided, shelled him from two side streets up which they were cautiously manœuvring from a well-executed detour.

The first volley broke the lock of one of Calliope's guns, cut a neat underbit in his right ear, and exploded a cartridge in his cross-belt, scorching his ribs as it burst. Feeling braced up by this unexpected tonic to his spiritual depression, Calliope executed a fortissimo note from his upper register and returned the fire like an echo. The upholders of the law dodged at his flash, but a trifle too late to save one of the deputies a bullet just above the elbow, and the marshal a bleeding cheek from a splinter that a ball tore from the box he had ducked behind.

And now Calliope met the enemy's tactics in kind. Choosing with a rapid eye the street from which the weakest and least accurate fire had come, he invaded it at a double-quick, abandoning the unprotected middle of the street. With rare cunning the opposing force in that direction—one of the deputies and two of the valorous volunteers—waited, concealed by beer barrels, until Calliope had passed their retreat, and then peppered him from the rear. In another moment they were reinforced by the marshal and his other men, and then Calliope felt that in order to successfully prolong the delights of the controversy he must find some means of reducing the great odds against him. His eye fell upon a structure that seemed to hold out this promise, providing he could reach it.

Not far away was the little railroad station, its

building a strong box house, ten by twenty feet, resting upon a platform four feet above ground. Windows were in each of its walls. Something like a fort it might become to a man thus sorely pressed by superior numbers.

Calliope made a bold and rapid spurt for it, the marshal's crowd "smoking" him as he ran. He reached the haven in safety, the station agent leaving the building by a window, like a flying squirrel, as the garrison entered the door.

Patterson and his supporters halted under protection of a pile of lumber and held consultations. In the station was an unterrified desperado who was an excellent shot and carried an abundance of ammunition. For thirty yards on each side of the besieged was a stretch of bare, open ground. It was a sure thing that the man who attempted to enter that unprotected area would be stopped by one of Calliope's bullets.

The city marshal was resolved. He had decided that Calliope Catesby should no more wake the echoes of Quicksand with his strident whoop. He had so announced. Officially and personally he felt imperatively bound to put the soft pedal on that instrument of discord. It played bad tunes.

Standing near was a hand truck used in the manipulation of small freight. It stood by a shed full of sacked wool, a consignment from one of the sheep ranches. On this truck the marshal and his men piled three heavy sacks of wool. Stooping low, Buck Patterson started for Calliope's fort, slowly pushing this loaded truck before him for protection. The posse, scattering broadly, stood ready to nip the besieged in case he should show himself in an effort to repel the juggernaut of justice that was creeping upon him. Only once did Calliope make demonstrations. He fired from a window, and some tufts of wool spurted from the marshal's trustworthy bulwark. The return shots from the posse pattered against the window frame of the fort. No loss resulted on either side.

The marshal was too deeply engrossed in steering his protected battleship to be aware of the approach of the morning train until he was within a few feet of the platform. The train was coming up on the other side of it. It stopped only one minute at Quicksand. What an opportunity it would offer to Calliope! He had only to step out the other door, mount the train, and away.

Abandoning his breastworks, Buck, with his gun ready, dashed up the steps and into the room, driving open the closed door with one heave of his weighty shoulder. The members of the posse heard one shot fired inside, and then there was silence.

At length the wounded man opened his eyes. After a blank space he again could see and hear and feel and think. Turning his eyes about, he found himself lying on a wooden bench. A tall man with a perplexed countenance, wearing a big badge with "City Marshal" engraved upon it, stood over him. A little old woman in black, with a wrinkled face and sparkling black eyes, was holding a wet handkerchief against one of his temples. He was trying to get these facts fixed in his mind and connected with past events, when the old woman began to talk.

"There now, great, big, strong man! That bullet never tetched ye! Jest skeeted along the side of your head and sort of paralysed ye for a spell. I've heerd of sech things afore; cun-cussion is what they names it. Abel Wadkins used to kill squirrels that way—barkin' 'em, Abe called it. You jest been barked, sir, and you'll be all right in a little bit. Feel lots better already, don't ye! You just lay still a while longer and let me bathe your head. You don't know me, I reckon, and 'tain't surprisin' that you shouldn't. I come in on that train from Alabama to see my son. Big son, ain't he? Lands! you wouldn't hardly think he'd ever been a baby, would ye? This is my son, sir."

Half turning, the old woman looked up at the standing man, her worn face lighting with a proud and wonderful smile. She reached out one veined and calloused hand and took one of her son's. Then smiling cheerily down at the prostrate man, she continued to dip the handkerchief in the waiting-room tin wash-basin and gently apply it to his temple. She had the benevolent garrulity of old age.

"I ain't seen my son before," she continued, "in eight years. One of my nephews, Elkanah Price, he's a conductor on one of them railroads and he got me a pass to come out here. I can stay a whole week on it, and then it'll take me back again. Jest think, now that little boy of mine has got to be a officer—a city marshal of a whole town! That's somethin' like a constable, ain't it? I never knowed he was a officer; he didn't say nothin' about it in his letters. I reckon he thought his old mother'd be skeered about the danger he was in. But, laws! I never was much of a hand to git skeered. 'Tain't no use. I heard them guns a-shootin' while I was gittin' off them cars, and I see smoke a-comin' out of the depot, but I jest walked right along. Then I see son's face lookin' out through the window. I knowed him at oncet. He met me at the door, and squeezed me 'most to death. And there you was, sir, a-lyin' there jest like you was dead, and I 'lowed we'd see what might be done to help sot you up."

"I think I'll sit up now," said the concussion patient. "I'm feeling pretty fair by this time."

He sat, somewhat weakly yet, leaning against the wall. He was a rugged man, big-boned and straight. His eyes, steady and keen, seemed to linger upon the face of the man standing so still above him. His look wandered often from the face he studied to the marshal's badge upon the other's breast.

"Yes, yes, you'll be all right," said the old woman, patting his arm, "if you don't get to cuttin' up agin, and havin' folks shootin' at you. Son told me about you, sir, while you was layin' senseless on the floor. Don't you take it as meddlesome fer an old woman with a son as big as you to talk about it. And you mustn't hold no grudge ag'in' my son for havin' to shoot at ye. A officer has got to take up for the law—it's his duty—and them that acts bad and lives wrong has to suffer. Don't blame my son any, sir—'tain't his fault. He's always been a good boy—good when he was growin' up, and kind and 'bedient and well-behaved. Won't you let me advise you, sir, not to do so no more? Be a good man, and leave liquor alone and live peaceably and godly. Keep away from bad company and work honest and sleep sweet."

The black-mittened hand of the old pleader gently touched the breast of the man she addressed. Very earnest and candid her old, worn face looked. In her rusty black dress and antique bonnet she sat, near the close of a long life, and epitomized the experience of the world. Still the man to whom she spoke gazed above her head, contemplating the silent son of the old mother.

"What does the marshal say?" he asked. "Does he believe the advice is good? Suppose the marshal speaks up and says if the talk's all right?"

The tall man moved uneasily. He fingered the badge on his breast for a moment, and then he put an arm around the old woman and drew her close to him. She smiled the unchanging mother smile of three-score years, and patted his big brown hand with her crooked mittened fingers while her son spake.

"I says this," he said, looking squarely into the eyes of the other man, "that if I was in your place I'd follow it. If I was a drunken, desp'rate character, without shame or hope, I'd follow it. If I was in your place and you was in mine I'd say: 'Marshal, I'm willin' to swear if you'll give me the chance I'll quit the racket. I'll drop the tanglefoot and the gun play, and won't play hoss no more. I'll be a good citizen and go to work and quit my foolishness. So help me God!' That's what I'd say to you if you was marshal and I was in your place."

"Hear my son talkin'," said the old woman softly. "Hear him, sir. You promise to be good and he won't do you no harm. Forty-one year ago his heart first beat ag'in' mine, and it's beat true ever since."

The other man rose to his feet, trying his limbs and stretching his muscles.

"Then," said he, "if you was in my place and said that, and I was marshal, I'd say: 'Go free, and do your best to keep your promise.' "

"Lawsy!" exclaimed the old woman, in a sudden

flutter, "ef I didn't clean forget that trunk of mine! I see a man settin' it on the platform jest as I seen son's face in the window, and it went plum out of my head. There's eight jars of home-made quince jam in that trunk that I made myself. I wouldn't have nothin' happen to them jars for a red apple."

Away to the door she trotted, spry and anxious, and then Calliope Catesby spoke out to Buck Patterson—

"I just couldn't help it, Buck. I seen her through the window a-comin' in. She never had heard a word 'bout my tough ways. I didn't have the nerve to let her know I was a worthless cuss bein' hunted down by the community. There you was lyin' where my shot laid you, like you was dead. The idea struck me sudden, and I just took your badge off and fastened it on to myself, and I fastened my reputation on to you. I told her I was the marshal and you was a holy terror. You can take your badge back now, Buck."

With shaking fingers Calliope began to unfasten the disc of metal from his shirt.

"Easy there!" said Buck Patterson. "You keep that badge right where it is, Calliope Catesby. Don't you dare to take it off till the day your mother leaves this town. You'll be city marshal of Quicksand as long as she's here to know it. After I stir around town a bit and put 'em on I'll guarantee that nobody won't give the thing away to her. And say, you leather-headed, rip-roarin', low-down son of a locoed cyclone, you follow that advice she give me! I'm goin' to take some of it myself, too."

"Buck," said Calliope feelingly, "ef I don't I hope I may——"

"Shut up," said Buck. "She's a-comin' back."

XLIV: ELSIE IN NEW YORK

NO, bumptious reader, this story is not a continuation of the Elsie series. But if your Elsie had lived over here in our big city there might have been a chapter in her books not very different from this.

Especially for the vagrant feet of youth are the roads of Manhattan beset "with pitfall and with gin." But the civic guardians of the young have made themselves acquainted with the snares of the wicked, and most of the dangerous paths are patrolled by their agents, who seek to turn straying ones away from the peril that menaces them. And this will tell you how they guided my Elsie safely through all peril to the goal that she was seeking.

Elsie's father had been a cutter for Fox & Otter, cloaks and furs, on lower Broadway. He was an old man, with a slow and limping gait, so a pothunter of a newly licensed chauffeur ran him down one day when livelier game was scarce. They took the old man home, where he lay on his bed for a year and then died, leaving $2.50 in cash and a letter from Mr. Otter offering to do anything he could to help his faithful old employee. The old cutter regarded this letter as a valuable legacy to his daughter, and he put it into her hands with pride as the shears of the dread Cleaner and Repairer snipped off his thread of life.

That was the landlord's cue; and forth he came and did his part in the great eviction scene. There was no snowstorm ready for Elsie to steal out into, drawing her little red woollen shawl about her shoulders, but she went out, regardless of the unities. And as for the red shawl—back to Blaney with it! Elsie's fall tan coat was cheap, but it had the style and fit of the best at Fox & Otter's. And her lucky stars had given her good looks, and eyes as blue and innocent as the new shade of notepaper, and she had $1 left of the $2.50. And the letter from Mr. Otter. Keep your eye on the letter from Mr. Otter. That is the clue. I desire that everything be made plain as we go. Detective stories are so plentiful now that they do not sell.

And so we find Elsie, thus equipped, starting out in the world to seek her fortune. One trouble about the letter from Mr. Otter was that it did not bear the new address of the firm, which had moved about a month before. But Elsie thought she could find it. She had heard that policemen, when politely addressed, or thumbscrewed by an investigation committee, will give up information and addresses. So she boarded a downtown car at One Hundred and Seventy-seventh Street and rode south to Forty-second, which she thought must surely be the end of the island. There she stood against the wall undecided, for the city's roar and dash was new to her. Up where she had lived was rural New York, so far out that the milkmen awaken you in the morning by the squeaking of pumps instead of the rattling of cans.

A kind-faced, sunburned young man in a soft-brimmed hat went past Elsie into the Grand Central Depot. That was Hank Ross, of the Sunflower Ranch, in Idaho, on his way home from a visit to the East. Hank's heart was heavy, for the Sunflower Ranch was a lonesome place, lacking the presence of a woman. He had hoped to find one during his visit who would congenially share his prosperity and home, but the girls of Gotham had not pleased his fancy. But, as he passed in, he noted, with a jumping of his pulses, the sweet ingenuous face of Elsie and her pose of doubt and loneliness. With true and honest Western impulse he said to himself that here was his mate. He could love her, he knew; and he would surround her with so much comfort, and cherish her so carefully that she would be happy, and make two sunflowers grow on the ranch where there grew but one before.

Hank turned and went back to her. Backed by his never before questioned honesty of purpose, he approached the girl and removed his soft-brimmed hat. Elsie had but time to sum up his handsome frank face with one shy look of modest admiration when a burly cop hurled himself upon the ranchman, seized him by the collar and backed him against the wall. Two blocks away a burglar was coming out of an apartment-house with a bag of silverware on his shoulder; but that is neither here nor there.

"Carry on yez mashin' tricks right before me eyes, will yez?" shouted the cop. "I'll teach yez to speak to ladies on me beat that ye're not acquainted with. Come along."

Elsie turned away with a sigh as the ranchman was dragged away. She had liked the effect of his light blue eyes against his tanned complexion. She walked southward, thinking herself already in the district where her father used to work, and hoping to find some one who could direct her to the firm of Fox & Otter.

But did she want to find Mr. Otter? She had inherited much of the old cutter's independence.

How much better it would be if she could find work and support herself without calling on him for aid!

Elsie saw a sign "Employment Agency" and went in. Many girls were sitting against the wall on chairs. Several well-dressed ladies were looking them over. One white-haired, kind-faced old lady in rustling black silk hurried up to Elsie.

"My dear," she said in a sweet, gentle voice, "are you looking for a position? I like your face and appearance so much. I want a young woman who will be half maid and half companion to me. You will have a good home and I will pay you $30 a month."

Before Elsie could stammer forth her gratified accceptance, a young woman with gold glasses on her bony nose and her hands in her jacket pockets seized her arm and drew her aside.

"I am Miss Ticklebaum," said she, "of the Association for the Prevention of Jobs Being Put Up on Working Girls Looking for Jobs. We prevented forty-seven girls from securing positions last week. I am here to protect you. Beware of anyone who offers you a job. How do you know that this woman does not want to make you work as a breaker-boy in a coal-mine or murder you to get your teeth? If you accept work of any kind without permission of our association you will be arrested by one of our agents."

"But what am I to do?" asked Elsie. "I have no home or money. I must do something. Why am I not allowed to accept this kind lady's offer?"

"I do not know," said Miss Ticklebaum. "That is the affair of our Committee on the Abolishment of Employers. It is my duty simply to see that you do not get work. You will give me your name and address and report to our secretary every Thursday. We have 600 girls on the waiting list who will in time be allowed to accept positions as vacancies occur on our roll of Qualified Employers, which now comprises twenty-seven names. There is prayer, music and lemonade in our chapel the third Sunday of every month."

Elsie hurried away after thanking Miss Ticklebaum for her timely warning and advice. After all, it seemed that she must try to find Mr. Otter.

But after walking a few blocks she saw a sign, "Cashier wanted," in the window of a confectionery store. In she went and applied for the place, after casting a quick glance over her shoulder to assure herself that the job-preventer was not on her trail.

The proprietor of the confectionery was a benevolent old man with a peppermint flavour, who decided, after questioning Elsie pretty closely, that she was the very girl he wanted. Her services were needed at once, so Elsie, with a thankful heart, drew off her tan coat and prepared to mount the cashier's stool.

But before she could do so a gaunt lady wearing steel spectacles and black mittens stood before her, with a long finger pointing, and exclaimed: "Young woman, hesitate!"

Elsie hesitated.

"Do you know," said the black-and-steel lady, "that in accepting this position you may this day cause the loss of a hundred lives in agonizing physical torture and the sending as many souls to perdition?"

"Why, no," said Elsie, in frightened tones. "How could I do that?"

"Rum," said the lady—"the demon rum. Do you know why so many lives are lost when a theatre catches fire? Brandy balls. The demon rum lurking in brandy balls. Our society women while in theatres sit grossly intoxicated from eating these candies filled with brandy. When the fire fiend sweeps down upon them they are unable to escape. The candy stores are the devil's distilleries. If you assist in the distribution of these insidious confections you assist in the destruction of the bodies and souls of your fellow-beings, and in the filling of our jails, asylums and almshouses. Think, girl, ere you touch the money for which brandy balls are sold."

"Dear me," said Elsie, bewildered. "I didn't know there was rum in brandy balls. But I must live by some means. What shall I do?"

"Decline the position," said the lady, "and come with me. I will tell you what to do."

After Elsie had told the confectioner that she had changed her mind about the cashiership she put on her coat and followed the lady to the sidewalk, where awaited an elegant victoria.

"Seek some other work," said the black-and-steel lady, "and assist in crushing the hydra-headed demon rum." And she got into the victoria and drove away.

"I guess that puts it up to Mr. Otter again," said Elsie ruefully, turning down the street. "And I'm sorry, too, for I'd much rather make my way without help."

Near Fourteenth Street Elsie saw a placard tacked on the side of a doorway that read: "Fifty girls, neat sewers, wanted immediately on theatrical costumes. Good pay."

She was about to enter, when a solemn man, dressed all in black, laid his hand on her arm.

"My dear girl," he said, "I entreat you not to enter that dressing-room of the devil."

"Goodness me!" exclaimed Elsie, with some impatience. "The devil seems to have a cinch on all the business in New York. What's wrong about the place?"

"It is here," said the solemn man, "that the regalia of Satan—in other words, the costumes worn on the stage—are manufactured. The stage is the road to ruin and destruction. Would you imperil your soul by lending the work of your hands to its support? Do you know, my dear girl, what the theatre leads to? Do you know where actors and actresses go after the curtain of the playhouse has fallen upon them for the last time?"

"Sure," said Elsie. "Into vaudeville. But do you think it would be wicked for me to make a little money to live on by sewing? I must get something to do pretty soon."

"The flesh-pots of Egypt," exclaimed the reverend gentleman, uplifting his hands. "I beseech you, my child, to turn away from this place of sin and iniquity."

"But what will I do for a living?" asked Elsie. "I don't care to sew for this musical comedy, if it's as rank as you say it is; but I've got to have a job."

"The Lord will provide," said the solemn man. "There is a free Bible class every Sunday afternoon in the basement of the cigar store next to the church. Peace be with you. Amen. Farewell."

Elsie went on her way. She was soon in the downtown district where factories abound. On a large brick building was a gilt sign, "Posey & Trimmer, Artificial Flowers." Below it was hung a newly stretched canvas bearing the words, "Five hundred girls wanted to learn trade. Good wages from the start. Apply one flight up."

Elsie started toward the door, near which were gathered in groups some twenty or thirty girls. One big girl with a black straw hat tipped down over her eyes stepped in front of her.

"Say, you'se," said the girl, "are you'se goin' in there after a job?"

"Yes," said Elsie; "I must have work."

"Now don't do it," said the girl. "I'm chairman of our Scab Committee. There's 400 of us girls locked out just because we demanded 50 cents a week raise in wages and ice water, and for the foreman to shave off his moustache. You're too nice a looking girl to be a scab. Wouldn't you please help us along by trying to find a job somewhere else, or would you'se rather have your face pushed in?"

"I'll try somewhere else," said Elsie.

She walked aimlessly eastward on Broadway, and there her heart leaped to see the sign, "Fox & Otter," stretching entirely across the front of a tall building. It was as though an unseen guide had led her to it through the by-ways of her fruitless search for work.

She hurried into the store and sent in to Mr. Otter, by a clerk, her name and the letter he had written her father. She was shown directly into his private office.

Mr. Otter arose from his desk as Elsie entered

and took both hands with a hearty smile of welcome. He was a slightly corpulent man of nearly middle age, a little bald, gold spectacled, polite, well dressed, radiating.

"Well, well, and so this is Beatty's little daughter! Your father was one of our most efficient and valued employees. He left nothing? Well, well. I hope we have not forgotten his faithful services. I am sure there is a vacancy now among our models. Oh, it is easy work—nothing easier."

Mr. Otter struck a bell. A long-nosed clerk thrust a portion of himself inside the door.

"Send Miss Hawkins in," said Mr. Otter. Miss Hawkins came.

"Miss Hawkins," said Mr. Otter, "bring for Miss Beatty to try on one of those Russian sable coats, and—let's see—one of those latest model black tulle hats with white tips."

Elsie stood before the full-length mirror with pink cheeks and quick breath. Her eyes shone like faint stars. She was beautiful. Alas! she was beautiful.

I wish I could stop this story here. Confound it! I will. No; it's got to run it out. I didn't make it up. I'm just repeating it.

I'd like to throw bouquets at the wise cop, and the lady who rescues Girls from Jobs, and the prohibitionist who is trying to crush brandy balls, and the sky pilot who objects to costumes for stage people (there are others), and all the thousands of good people who are at work protecting young people from the pitfalls of a great city; and then wind up by pointing out how they were the means of Elsie reaching her father's benefactor and her kind friend and rescuer from poverty.

This would make a fine Elsie story of the old sort. I'd like to do this: but there's just a word or two to follow.

While Elsie was admiring herself in the mirror, Mr. Otter went to the telephone booth and called up some number. Don't ask me what it was.

"Oscar," said he, "I want you to reserve the same table for me this evening. . . . What? Why, the one in the Moorish room to the left of the shrubbery. . . . Yes; two. . . . Yes, the usual brand; and the '85 Johannisburger with the roast. If it isn't the right temperature I'll break your neck. . . . No; not her . . . No, indeed . . . A new one—a peacherino, Oscar, a peacherino!"

Tired and tiresome reader, I will conclude, if you please, with a paraphrase of a few words that you will remember were written by him—by him of Gad's Hill, before whom, if you doff not your hat, you shall stand with a covered pumpkin—aye, sir, a pumpkin.

Lost, Your Excellency. Lost, Associations and Societies. Lost, Right Reverends and Wrong Reverends of every order. Lost, Reformers and Lawmakers, born with heavenly compassion in your hearts, but with the reverence of money in your souls. And lost thus around us every day.

XLV: THE GOLD THAT GLITTERED

A STORY with a moral appended is like the bill of a mosquito. It bores you, and then injects a stinging drop to irritate your conscience. Therefore let us have the moral first and be done with it. All is not gold that glitters, but it is a wise child that keeps the stopper in his bottle of testing acid.

Where Broadway skirts the corner of the square presided over by George the Veracious is the Little Rialto. Here stand the actors of that quarter, and this is their shibboleth: "'Nit,' says I to Frohman, 'you can't touch me for a kopeck less than two-fifty per,' and out I walks."

Westward and southward from the Thespian glare are one or two streets where a Spanish-American colony has huddled for a little tropical warmth in the nipping North. The centre of life in this precinct is "El Refugio," a café and restaurant that caters to the volatile exiles from the South. Up from Chili, Bolivia, Colombia, the rolling republics of Central America and the ireful islands of the Western Indies flit the cloaked and sombreroed señores, who are scattered like burning lava by the political eruptions of their several countries. Hither they come to lay counterplots, to bide their time, to solicit funds, to enlist filibusterers, to smuggle out arms and ammunitions, to play the game at long taw. In El Refugio they find the atmosphere in which they thrive.

In the restaurant of El Refugio are served compounds delightful to the palate of the man from Capricorn or Cancer. Altruism must halt the story thus long. On, diner, weary of the culinary subterfuges of the Gallic chef, hie thee to El Refugio! There only will you find a fish—bluefish, shad or pompano from the Gulf—baked after the Spanish method. Tomatoes give it colour, individuality and soul; chili colorado bestows upon it zest, originality and fervour; unknown herbs furnish piquancy and mystery, and—but its crowning glory deserves a new sentence. Around it, above it, beneath it, in its vicinity—but never in it—hovers an ethereal aura, an effluvium so rarefied and delicate that only the Society for Psychical Research could note its origin. Do not say that garlic is in the fish at El Refugio. It is not otherwise than as if the spirit of Garlic, flitting past, has wafted one kiss that lingers in the parsley crowned dish as haunting as those kisses in life, "by hopeless fancy feigned on lips that are for others." And then, when Conchito, the waiter, brings you a plate of brown frijoles and a carafe of wine that has never stood still between Oporto and El Refugio—ah, Dios!

One day a Hamburg-American liner deposited upon Pier No. 55 Gen. Perrico Ximenes Villablanca Falcon, a passenger from Cartagena. The General was between a claybank and a bay in complexion, had a 42-inch waist and stood 5 feet 4 with his Du Barry heels. He had the moustache of a shooting-gallery proprietor, he wore the full dress of a Texas congressman and had the important aspect of an uninstructed delegate.

Gen. Falcon had enough English under his hat to enable him to inquire his way to the street in which El Refugio stood. When he reached that neighbourhood he saw a sign before a respectable red-brick house that read, "Hotel Español." In the window was a card in Spanish, "Aqui se habla Español." The General entered, sure of a congenial port.

In the cosy office was Mrs. O'Brien, the proprietress. She had blond—oh, unimpeachably blond hair. For the rest she was amiability, and ran largely to inches around. Gen. Falcon brushed the floor with his broad-brimmed hat, and emitted a quantity of Spanish, the syllables sounding like firecrackers gently popping their way down the string of a bunch.

"Spanish or Dago?" asked Mrs. O'Brien pleasantly.

"I am a Colombian, madam," said the General proudly. "I speak the Spanish. The advisement in your window say the Spanish he is spoken here. How is that?"

"Well, you've been speaking it, ain't you?" said the madam. "I'm sure I can't."

At the Hotel Español General Falcon engaged rooms and established himself. At dusk he sauntered out upon the streets to view the wonders of this roaring city of the North. As he walked he thought of the wonderful golden hair of Mme. O'Brien. "It is here," said the General to himself, no doubt in his own language, "that one shall find the most beautiful señoras in the world. I have not in my Colombia viewed among our beauties one so fair. But no! It is not for the General Falcon to think of beauty. It is my country that claims my devotion."

At the corner of Broadway and the Little Rialto the General became involved. The street cars bewildered him, and the fender of one upset him against a pushcart laden with oranges. A cab-driver missed him an inch with a hub, and poured barbarous execrations upon his head. He scrambled to the sidewalk and skipped again in terror when the whistle of a peanut-roaster puffed a hot scream into his ear. "Válgame Dios! What devil's city is this?"

As the General fluttered out of the streamers of

passers like a wounded snipe he was marked simultaneously as game by two hunters. One was "Bully" McGuire, whose system of sport required the use of a strong arm and the misuse of an eight-inch piece of lead pipe. The other Nimrod of the asphalt was "Spider" Kelley, a sportsman with more refined methods.

In pouncing upon their self-evident prey, Mr. Kelley was a shade the quicker. His elbow fended accurately the onslaught of Mr. McGuire.

"G'wan!" he commanded harshly. "I saw it first." McGuire slunk away, awed by superior intelligence.

"Pardon me," said Mr. Kelley to the General, "but you got balled up in the shuffle, didn't you? Let me assist you." He picked up the General's hat and brushed the dust from it.

The ways of Mr. Kelley could not but succeed. The General, bewildered and dismayed by the resounding streets, welcomed his deliverer as a caballero with a most disinterested heart.

"I have a desire," said the General, "to return to the hotel of O'Brien, in which I am stop. Caramba! señor, there is a loudness and rapidness of going and coming in the city of this Nueva York."

Mr. Kelley's politeness would not suffer the distinguished Colombian to brave the dangers of the return unaccompanied. At the door of the Hotel Español they paused. A little lower down on the opposite side of the street shone the modest illuminated sign of El Refugio. Mr. Kelley, to whom few streets were unfamiliar, knew the place exteriorly as a "Dago joint." All foreigners Mr. Kelley classed under the two heads of "Dagoes" and Frenchmen. He proposed to the General that they repair thither and substantiate their acquaintance with a liquid foundation.

An hour later found General Falcon and Mr. Kelley seated at a table in the conspirators' corner of El Refugio. Bottles and glasses were between them. For the tenth time the General confided the secret of his mission to the Estados Unidos. He was here, he declared, to purchase arms—2,000 stands of Winchester rifles—for the Colombian revolutionists. He had drafts in his pocket drawn by the Cartagena Bank on its New York correspondent for $25,000. At other tables other revolutionists were shouting their political secrets to their fellow-plotters; but none was as loud as the General. He pounded the table; he hallooed for some wine; he roared to his friend that his errand was a secret one, and not to be hinted at to a living soul. Mr. Kelley himself was stirred to sympathetic enthusiasm. He grasped the General's hand across the table.

"Monseer," he said earnestly, "I don't know where this country of yours is, but I'm for it. I guess it must be a branch of the United States, though, for the poetry guys and the schoolmarms call us Columbia, too, sometimes. It's a lucky thing for you that you butted into me to-night. I'm the only man in New York that can get this gun deal through for you. The Secretary of War of the United States is me best friend. He's in the city now, and I'll see him for you to-morrow. In the meantime, monseer, you keep them drafts tight in your inside pocket. I'll call for you to-morrow, and take you to see him. Say! that ain't the District of Columbia you're talking about, is it?" concluded Mr. Kelley, with a sudden qualm. "You can't capture that with no 2,000 guns—it's been tried with more."

"No, no, no!" exclaimed the General. "It is the Republic of Colombia—it is a g-r-reat republic on the top side of America of the South. Yes. Yes."

"All right," said Mr. Kelley, reassured. "Now suppose we trek along home and go by-by. I'll write to the Secretary to-night and make a date with him. It's a ticklish job to get guns out of New York. McClusky himself can't do it."

They parted at the door of the Hotel Español. The General rolled his eyes at the moon and sighed.

"It is a great country, your Nueva York," he said. "Truly the cars in the streets devastate one, and the engine that cooks the nuts terribly makes a squeak in the ear. But, ah, Señor Kelley—the señoras with hair of much goldness, and admirable fatness—they are magnificas! Muy magnificas!"

Kelley went to the nearest telephone booth and called up McCrary's café, far up on Broadway. He asked for Jimmy Dunn.

"Is that Jimmy Dunn?" asked Kelley.

"Yes," came the answer.

"You're a liar," sang back Kelley joyfully. "You're the Secretary of War. Wait there till I come up. I've got the finest thing down here in the way of a fish you ever baited for. It's a Colorado-maduro, with a gold band around it and free coupons enough to buy a red hall lamp and a statuette of Psyche rubbering in the brook. I'll be up on the next car."

Jimmy Dunn was a A.M. of Crookdom. He was an artist in the confidence line. He never saw a bludgeon in his life; and he scorned knockout drops. In fact, he would have set nothing before an intended victim but the purest of drinks, if it had been possible to procure such a thing in New York. It was the ambition of "Spider" Kelley to elevate himself into Jimmy's class.

These two gentlemen held a conference that night at McCrary's. Kelley explained.

"He's as easy as a gum shoe. He's from the Island of Colombia, where there's a strike, or a feud, or something going on, and they've sent him up here to buy 2,000 Winchesters to arbitrate the thing with. He showed me two drafts for $10,000 each, and one for $5,000 on a bank here. 'S truth, Jimmy, I felt real mad with him because he didn't have it in thousand-dollar bills, and hand it to me on a silver waiter. Now, we've got to wait till he goes to the bank and gets the money for us."

They talked it over for two hours, and then Dunn said: "Bring him to No. — Broadway, at four o'clock to-morrow afternoon."

In due time Kelley called at the Hotel Español for the General. He found that wily warrior engaged in delectable conversation with Mrs. O'Brien.

"The Secretary of War is waitin' for us," said Kelley.

The General tore himself away with an effort.

"Ay, señor," he said, with a sigh, "duty makes a call. But, señor, the señoras of your Estados Unidos—how beauties! For exemplification, take you la Madame O'Brien—que magnifica! She is one goddess—one Juno—what you call one ox-eyed Juno."

Now Mr. Kelley was a wit; and better men have been shrivelled by the fire of their own imagination.

"Sure!" he said with a grin; "but you mean a peroxide Juno, don't you?"

Mrs. O'Brien heard, and lifted an auriferous head. Her businesslike eye rested for an instant upon the disappearing form of Mr. Kelley. Except in street cars one should never be unnecessarily rude to a lady.

When the gallant Colombian and his escort arrived at the Broadway address, they were held in an ante-room for half an hour, and then admitted into a well-equipped office where a distinguished-looking man, with a smooth face, wrote at a desk. General Falcon was presented to the Secretary of War of the United States, and his mission made known by his old friend, Mr. Kelley.

"Ah—Colombia!" said the Secretary significantly, when he was made to understand; "I'm afraid there will be a little difficulty in that case. The President and I differ in our sympathies there. He prefers the established government, while I——" the Secretary gave the General a mysterious but encouraging smile. "You, of course, know, General Falcon, that since the Tammany war, an act of Congress has been passed requiring all manufactured arms and ammunition exported from this country to pass through the War Department. Now, if I can do anything for you, I will be glad to do so to oblige my old friend, Mr. Kelley. But it must be in absolute secrecy, as the President, as I have said, does not regard favourably the efforts of your revolutionary party in Colombia. I will have my orderly bring a list of the available arms now in the warehouse."

The Secretary struck a bell, and an orderly with the letters A.D.T. on his cap stepped promptly into the room.

"Bring me Schedule B of the small arms inventory," said the Secretary.

The orderly quickly returned with a printed paper. The Secretary studied it closely.

"I find," he said, "that in Warehouse 9, of Government stores, there is a shipment of 2,000 stands of Winchester rifles that were ordered by the Sultan of Morocco, who forgot to send the cash with his order. Our rule is that legal-tender money must be paid down at the time of purchase. My dear Kelley, your friend, General Falcon, shall have this lot of arms, if he desires it, at the manufacturer's price. And you will forgive me, I am sure, if I curtail our interview. I am expecting the Japanese Minister and Charles Murphy every moment!"

As one result of this interview, the General was deeply grateful to his esteemed friend, Mr. Kelley. As another, the nimble Secretary of War was extremely busy during the next two days buying empty rifle cases and filling them with bricks, which were then stored in a warehouse rented for that purpose. As still another, when the General returned to the Hotel Español, Mrs. O'Brien went up to him, plucked a thread from his lapel, and said:

"Say, señor, I don't want to 'butt in,' but what does that monkey-faced, cat-eyed, rubber-necked tin horn tough want with you?"

"Sangre de mi vida!" exclaimed the General. "Impossible it is that you speak of my good friend, Señor Kelley."

"Come into the summer garden," said Mrs. O'Brien. "I want to have a talk to you."

Let us suppose that an hour has elapsed.

"And you say," said the General, "that for the sum of $18,000 can be purchased the furnishment of the house and the lease of one year with this garden so lovely—so resembling unto the patios of my care Colombia?"

"And dirt-cheap at that," sighed the lady.

"Ah, Dios!" breathed General Falcon. "What to me is war and politics? This spot is one paradise. My country it have other brave heroes to continue the fighting. What to me should be glory and the shooting of mans? Ah! no. It is here I have found one angel. Let us buy the Hotel Español and you shall be mine, and the money shall not be waste on guns."

Mrs. O'Brien rested her blond pompadour against the shoulder of the Colombian patriot.

"Oh, señor," she sighed happily, "ain't you terrible!"

Two days later was the time appointed for the delivery of the arms to the General. The boxes of supposed rifles were stacked in the rented warehouse, and the Secretary of War sat upon them, waiting for his friend Kelley to fetch the victim.

Mr. Kelley hurried, at the hour, to the Hotel Español. He found the General behind the desk adding up accounts.

"I have decide," said the General, "to buy not guns. I have to-day buy the insides of this hotel, and there shall be marrying of the General Perrico Ximenes Villablanca Falcon with la Madame O'Brien."

Mr. Kelley almost strangled.

"Say, you old bald-headed bottle of shoe-polish," he spluttered, "you're a swindler—that's what you are! You've bought a boarding-house with money belonging to your infernal country, wherever it is."

"Ah," said the General, footing up a column, "that is what you call politics. War and revolution they are not nice. Yes. It is not best that one shall always follow Minerva. No. It is of quite desirable to keep hotels and be with that Juno—that ox-eyed Juno. Ah! what hair of the gold it is that she have!"

Mr. Kelley choked again.

"Ah, Señor Kelley!" said the General, feelingly and finally, "is it that you have never eaten of the corned-beef hash that Madame O'Brien she make?"

XLVI: THE DISCOUNTERS OF MONEY

THE spectacle of the money-caliphs of the present day going about Bagdad-on-the-Subway trying to relieve the wants of the people is enough to make the great Al Raschid turn Haroun in his grave. If not so, then the assertion should do so, the real caliph having been a wit and a scholar and therefore a hater of puns.

How properly to alleviate the troubles of the poor is one of the greatest troubles of the rich. But one thing agreed upon by all professional philanthropists is that you must never hand over any cash to your subject. The poor are notoriously temperamental; and when they get money they exhibit a strong tendency to spend it for stuffed olives and enlarged crayon portraits instead of giving it to the instalment man.

And still, old Haroun had some advantages as an eleemosynarian. He took around with him on his rambles his vizier, Giafar (a vizier is a composite of a chauffeur, a secretary of state, and a night-and-day bank), and old Uncle Mesrour, his executioner, who toted a snickersnee. With this entourage a caliphing tour could hardly fail to be successful. Have you noticed lately any newspaper articles headed, "What Shall We Do With Our Ex-Presidents?" Well, now, suppose that Mr. Carnegie should engage *him* and Joe Gans to go about assisting in the distribution of free libraries? Do you suppose any town would have the hardihood to refuse one? That caliphalous combination would cause two libraries to grow where there had been only one set of E. P. Roe's works before.

But, as I said, the money-caliphs are handicapped. They have the idea that earth has no sorrow that dough cannot heal; and they rely upon it solely. Al Raschid administered justice, rewarded the deserving, and punished whomsoever he disliked on the spot. He was the originator of the short-story contest. Whenever he succoured any chance pick-up in the bazaars he always made the succouree tell the sad story of his life. If the narrative lacked construction, style, and *esprit* he commanded his vizier to dole him out a couple of thousand ten-dollar notes of the First National Bank of the Bosphorus, or else give him a soft job as Keeper of the Bird Seed for the Bulbuls in the Imperial Gardens. If the story was a crackerjack, he had Mesrour, the executioner, whack off his head. The report that Haroun Al Raschid is yet alive and is editing the magazine that your grandmother used to subscribe for lacks confirmation.

And now follows the Story of the Millionaire, the Inefficacious Increment, and the Babes Drawn from the Wood.

Young Howard Pilkins, the millionaire, got his money ornithologically. He was a shrewd judge of storks, and got in on the ground floor at the residence of his immediate ancestors, the Pilkins Brewing Company. For his mother was a partner in the business. Finally old man Pilkins died from a torpid liver, and then Mrs. Pilkins died from worry on account of torpid delivery-waggons—and there you have young Howard Pilkins with $4,000,000, and a good fellow at that. He was an agreeable, modestly arrogant young man, who implicitly believed that money could buy anything that the world had to offer. And Bagdad-on-the-Subway for a long time did everything possible to encourage his belief.

But the Rat-trap caught him at last; he heard the spring snap, and found his heart in a wire cage regarding a piece of cheese whose other name was Alice von der Ruysling.

The Von der Ruyslings still live in that little square about which so much has been said, and in which so little has been done. To-day you hear of Mr. Tilden's underground passage, and you hear Mr. Gould's elevated passage, and that about ends the noise in the world made by Gramercy Square. But once it was different. The Von der Ruyslings live there yet, and they received *the first key ever made to Gramercy Park*.

You shall have no description of Alice v. d. R. Just call up in your mind the picture of your own Maggie or Vera or Beatrice, straighten her nose, soften her voice, tone her down and then tone her up, make her beautiful and unattainable—and you have a faint, dry-point etching of Alice. The family owned a crumbly brick house and a coachman named Joseph in a coat of many colours, and a horse so old that he claimed to belong to the order of the Perissodactyla, and had toes instead of hoofs. In the year 1898 the family had to buy a new set of harness for the Perissodactyl. Before using it they made Joseph smear it over with a mixture of ashes and soot. It was the Von der Ruysling family that bought the territory between the Bowery and East River and Rivington Street and the Statue of Liberty, in the year 1649, from an Indian chief for a quart of passementerie and a pair of Turkey-red portières designed for a Harlem flat. I have always admired that Indian's perspicacity and good taste. All this is merely to convince you that the Von der Ruyslings were exactly the kind of poor aristocrats that turn down their noses at people who have money. Oh, well, I don't mean that; I mean people who have *just* money.

One evening Pilkins went down to the red brick house in Gramercy Square, and made what he thought was a proposal to Alice v. d. R. Alice, with her nose turned down, and thinking of his money, considered it a proposition, and refused it and him. Pilkins, summoning all his resources as any good general would have done, made an indiscreet reference to the advantages that his money would provide. That settled it. The lady turned so cold that Walter Wellman himself would have waited until spring to make a dash for her in a dog-sled.

But Pilkins was something of a sport himself. You can't fool all the millionaires every time the ball drops on the Western Union Building.

"If, at any time," he said to A. v. d. R., "you feel that you would like to reconsider your answer, send me a rose like that."

Pilkins audaciously touched a Jacque rose that she wore loosely in her hair.

"Very well," said she. "And when I do, you will understand by it that either you or I have learned something new about the purchasing power of money. You've been spoiled, my friend. No, I don't think I could marry you. To-morrow I will send you back the presents you have given me."

"Presents!" said Pilkins in surprise. "I never gave you a present in my life. I would like to see a full-length portrait of the man that you would take a present from. Why, you never would let me send you flowers or candy or even art calendars."

"You've forgotten," said Alice v. d. R., with a little smile. "It was a long time ago when our families were neighbours. You were seven, and I was trundling my doll on the sidewalk. You gave me a little grey, hairy kitten, with shoe-buttony eyes. Its head came off and it was full of candy. You paid five cents for it—you told me so. I haven't the candy to return to you—I hadn't developed a conscience at three, so I ate it. But I have the kitten yet, and I will wrap it up neatly to-night and send it to you to-morrow."

Beneath the lightness of Alice v. d. R.'s talk the steadfastness of her rejection showed firm and plain. So there was nothing left for him but to leave the crumbly red brick house, and be off with his abhorred millions.

On his way back Pilkins walked through Madison Square. The hour hand of the clock hung about eight; the air was stingingly cool, but not at the freezing-point. The dim little square seemed like a great, cold, unroofed room, with its four walls of houses spangled with thousands of insufficient lights. Only a few loiterers were huddled here and there on the benches.

But suddenly Pilkins came upon a youth sitting brave, and, as if conflicting with summer sultriness, coatless, his white shirt-sleeves conspicuous in the light from the globe of an electric. Close at his side was a girl, smiling, dreamy, happy. Around her shoulders was, palpably, the missing coat of the cold-defying youth. It appeared to be a modern panorama of the Babes in the Wood, revised and brought up to date, with the exception that the robins hadn't turned up yet with the protecting leaves.

With delight the money-caliphs view a situation that they think is relievable while you wait.

Pilkins sat on the bench, one seat removed from the youth. He glanced cautiously and saw (as men do see; and women—oh! never can) that they were of the same order.

Pilkins leaned over after a short time and spoke to the youth, who answered smilingly and courteously. From general topics the conversation concentrated to the bed-rock of grim personalities. But Pilkins did it as delicately and heartily as any caliph could have done. And when it came to the point, the youth turned to him, soft-voiced and with his undiminished smile.

"I don't want to seem unappreciative, old man," he said, with a youth's somewhat too-early spontaneity of address, "but, you see, I can't accept anything from a stranger. I know you're all right, and I'm tremendously obliged, but I couldn't think of borrowing from anybody. You see, I'm Marcus Clayton—the Claytons of Roanoke County, Virginia, you know. The young lady is Miss Eva Bedford—I reckon you've heard of the Bedfords.

She's seventeen, and one of the Bedfords of Bedford County. We've eloped from home to get married, and we wanted to see New York. We got in this afternoon. Somebody got my pocket-book on the ferryboat, and I had only three cents in change outside of it. I'll get some work somewhere to-morrow, and we'll get married."

"But, I say, old man," said Pilkins, in confidential low tones, "you can't keep the lady out here in the cold all night. Now, as for hotels——"

"I told you," said the youth, with a broader smile, "that I didn't have but three cents. Besides, if I had a thousand, we'd have to wait here until morning. You can understand that, of course. I'm much obliged, but I can't take any of your money. Miss Bedford and I have lived an out-door life, and we don't mind a little cold. I'll get work of some kind to-morrow. We've got a paper bag of cakes and chocolates, and we'll get along all right."

"Listen," said the millionaire, impressively. "My name is Pilkins, and I'm worth several million dollars. I happen to have in my pockets about $800 or $900 in cash. Don't you think you are drawing it rather fine when you decline to accept as much of it as will make you and the young lady comfortable at least for the night?"

"I can't say, sir, that I do think so," said Clayton of Roanoke County. "I've been raised to look at such things differently. But I'm mightily obliged to you, just the same."

"Then you force me to say good night," said the millionaire.

Twice that day had his money been scorned by simple ones to whom his dollars had appeared as but tin tobacco-tags. He was no worshipper of the actual minted coin or stamped paper, but he had always believed in its almost unlimited power to purchase.

Pilkins walked away rapidly, and then turned abruptly and returned to the bench where the young couple sat. He took off his hat and began to speak. The girl looked at him with the same sprightly, glowing interest that she had been giving to the lights and statuary and sky-reaching buildings that made the old square seem so far away from Bedford County.

"Mr.—er—Roanoke," said Pilkins, "I admire your—your indepen—your idiocy so much that I'm going to appeal to your chivalry. I believe that's what you Southerners call it when you keep a lady sitting outdoors on a bench on a cold night just to keep your old, out-of-date pride going. Now, I've a friend—a lady—whom I have known all my life—who lives a few blocks from here—with her parents and sisters and aunts, and all that kind of endorsement, of course. I am sure this lady would be happy and pleased to put up —that is, to have Miss—er—Bedford give her the pleasure of having her as a guest for the night. Don't you think, Mr. Roanoke, of—er—Virginia, that you could unbend your prejudices that far?"

Clayton of Roanoke rose and held out his hand.

"Old man," he said, "Miss Bedford will be much pleased to accept the hospitality of the lady you refer to."

He formally introduced Mr. Pilkins to Miss Bedford. The girl looked at him sweetly and comfortably. "It's a lovely evening, Mr. Pilkins —don't you think so?" she said slowly.

Pilkins conducted them to the crumbly red brick

house of the Von der Ruyslings. His card brought Alice downstairs wondering. The runaways were sent into the drawing-room, while Pilkins told Alice all about it in the hall.

"Of course I will take her in," said Alice. "Haven't those Southern girls a thoroughbred air? Of course, she will stay here. You will look after Mr. Clayton, of course."

"Will I?" said Pilkins, delightedly. "Oh, yes, I'll look after him! As a citizen of New York, and therefore a part owner of its public parks, I'm going to extend to him the hospitality of Madison Square to-night. He's going to sit there on a bench till morning. There's no use arguing with him. Isn't he wonderful? I'm glad you'll look after the little lady, Alice. I tell you those Babes in the Wood made my—that is, er—made Wall Street and the Bank of England look like penny arcades."

Miss von der Ruysling whisked Miss Bedford of Bedford County up to restful regions upstairs. When she came down she put an oblong small pasteboard box into Pilkins's hands.

"Your present," she said, "that I am returning to you."

"Oh, yes, I remember," said Pilkins, with a sigh, "the woolly kitten."

He left Clayton on a park bench, and shook hands with him heartily.

"After I get work," said the youth, "I'll look you up. Your address is on your card, isn't it? Thanks. Well, good night. I'm awfully obliged to you for your kindness. No, thanks, I don't smoke. Good night."

In his room, Pilkins opened the box and took

out the staring, funny kitten, long ago ravaged of his candy and minus one shoe-button eye. Pilkins looked at it sorrowfully.

"After all," he said, "I don't believe that just money alone will———"

And then he gave a shout and dug into the bottom of the box for something else that had been the kitten's resting-place—a crushed but red, red, fragrant, glorious, promising Jacqueminot rose.

XLVII: ONE DOLLAR'S WORTH

THE judge of the United States court of the district lying along the Rio Grande border found the following letter one morning in his mail:

JUDGE:

When you sent me up for four years you made a talk. Among other hard things, you called me a rattlesnake. Maybe I am one—anyhow, you hear me rattling now. One year after I got to the pen, my daughter died of—well, they said it was poverty and the disgrace together. You've got a daughter, Judge, and I'm going to make you know how it feels to lose one. And I'm going to bite that district attorney that spoke against me. I'm free now, and I guess I've turned to rattlesnake all right. I feel like one. I don't say much, but this is my rattle. Look out when I strike.

Yours respectfully,

RATTLESNAKE.

Judge Derwent threw the letter carelessly aside. It was nothing new to receive such epistles from desperate men whom he had been called upon to judge. He felt no alarm. Later on he showed the letter to Littlefield, the young district attorney, for Littlefield's name was included in the threat, and the judge was punctilious in matters between himself and his fellow-men.

Littlefield honoured the rattle of the writer, as far as it concerned himself, with a smile of contempt; but he frowned a little over the reference to the Judge's daughter, for he and Nancy Derwent were to be married in the fall.

Littlefield went to the clerk of the court and looked over the records with him. They decided that the letter might have been sent by Mexico Sam, a half-breed border desperado who had been imprisoned for manslaughter four years before. Then official duties crowded the matter from his mind, and the rattle of the revengeful serpent was forgotten.

Court was in session at Brownsville. Most of the cases to be tried were charges of smuggling, counterfeiting, post-office robberies, and violations of Federal laws along the border. One case was that of a young Mexican, Rafael Ortiz, who had been rounded up by a clever deputy marshal in the act of passing a counterfeit silver dollar. He had been suspected of many such deviations from rectitude, but this was the first time that anything provable had been fixed upon him. Ortiz languished cosily in jail, smoking brown cigarettes and waiting for trial. Kilpatrick, the deputy, brought the counterfeit dollar and handed it to the district attorney in his office in the court-house. The deputy and a reputable druggist were prepared to swear that Ortiz paid for a bottle of medicine with it. The coin was a poor counterfeit, soft, dull-looking, and made principally of lead. It was the day before the morning on which the docket would reach the case of Ortiz, and the district attorney was preparing himself for trial.

"Not much need of having in high-priced experts to prove the coin's queer, is there, Kil?" smiled Littlefield, as he thumped the dollar down upon the table, where it fell with no more ring than would have come from a lump of putty.

"I guess the Greaser's as good as behind the bars," said the deputy, easing up his holsters. "You've got him dead. If it had been just one time, these Mexicans can't tell good money from bad; but this little yaller rascal belongs to a gang of counterfeiters, I know. This is the first time I've been able to catch him doing the trick. He's got a girl down there in them Mexican jacals on the river bank. I seen her one day when I was watching him. She's as pretty as a red heifer in a flower-bed."

Littlefield shoved the counterfeit dollar into his pocket, and slipped his memoranda of the case into an envelope. Just then a bright, winsome face, as frank and jolly as a boy's, appeared in the doorway, and in walked Nancy Derwent.

"Oh, Bob, didn't court adjourn at twelve to-day until to-morrow?" she asked of Littlefield.

"It did," said the district attorney, "and I'm very glad of it. I've got a lot of rulings to look up, and——"

"Now, that's just like you. I wonder you and father don't turn to law books or rulings or something! I want you to take me out plover-shooting this afternoon. Long Prairie is just alive with them. Don't say no, please! I want to try my new twelve-bore hammerless. I've sent to the livery stable to engage Fly and Bess for the buckboard; they stand fire so nicely. I was sure you would go."

They were to be married in the fall. The glamour was at its height. The plovers won the day—or, rather, the afternoon—over the calf-bound authorities. Littlefield began to put his papers away.

There was a knock at the door. Kilpatrick answered it. A beautiful, dark-eyed girl with a skin tinged with the faintest lemon colour walked into the room. A black shawl was thrown over her head and wound once around her neck.

She began to talk in Spanish, a voluble, mournful stream of melancholy music. Littlefield did not understand Spanish. The deputy did, and he translated her talk by portions, at intervals holding up his hand to check the flow of her words.

"She came to see you, Mr. Littlefield. Her name's Joya Treviñas. She wants to see you about —well, she's mixed up with that Rafael Ortiz. She's his—she's his girl. She says he's innocent. She says she made the money and got him to pass it. Don't you believe her, Mr. Littlefield. That's the way with these Mexican girls; they'll lie, steal, or kill for a fellow when they get stuck on him. Never trust a woman that's in love!"

"Mr. Kilpatrick!"

Nancy Derwent's indignant exclamation caused the deputy to flounder for a moment in attempting to explain that he had misquoted his own sentiments, and then he went on with the translation:

"She says she's willing to take his place in the jail if you'll let him out. She says she was down sick with the fever, and the doctor said she'd die if she didn't have medicine. That's why he passed the lead dollar on the drug store. She says it saved her life. This Rafael seems to be her honey, all right; there's a lot of stuff in her talk about love and such things that you don't want to hear."

It was an old story to the district attorney.

"Tell her," said he, "that I can do nothing. The case comes up in the morning, and he will have to make his fight before the court."

Nancy Derwent was not so hardened. She was looking with sympathetic interest at Joya Treviñas and at Littlefield alternately. The deputy repeated the district attorney's words to the girl. She spoke a sentence or two in a low voice, pulled her shawl closely about her face, and left the room.

"What did she say then?" asked the district attorney.

"Nothing special," said the deputy. "She said: 'If the life of the one'—let's see how it went—'*Si la vida de ella á quien tu amas*—if the life of the girl you love is ever in danger, remember Rafael Ortiz.'"

Kilpatrick strolled out through the corridor in the direction of the marshal's office.

"Can't you do anything for them, Bob?" asked Nancy. "It's such a little thing—just one counterfeit dollar—to ruin the happiness of two lives! She was in danger of death, and he did it to save her. Doesn't the law know the feeling of pity?"

"It hasn't a place in jurisprudence, Nan," said Littlefield, "especially *in re* the district attorney's duty. I'll promise you that the prosecution will not be vindictive; but the man is as good as convicted when the case is called. Witnesses will swear to his passing the bad dollar which I have in my pocket at this moment as 'Exhibit A.' There are no Mexicans on the jury, and it will vote Mr. Greaser guilty without leaving the box."

The plover-shooting was fine that afternoon, and in the excitement of the sport the case of Rafael and the grief of Joya Treviñas was forgotten. The district attorney and Nancy Derwent drove out from the town three miles along a smooth, grassy road, and then struck across a rolling prairie toward a heavy line of timber on Piedra Creek. Beyond this creek lay Long Prairie, the favourite haunt of the plover. As they were nearing the creek they heard the galloping of a horse to their right, and saw a man with black hair and a swarthy face riding toward the woods at a tangent, as if he had come up behind them.

"I've seen that fellow somewhere," said Littlefield, who had a memory for faces, "but I can't exactly place him. Some ranchman, I suppose, taking a short cut home."

They spent an hour on Long Prairie, shooting from the buckboard. Nancy Derwent, an active, outdoor Western girl, was pleased with her twelve-bore. She had bagged within two brace of her companion's score.

They started homeward at a gentle trot. When within a hundred yards of Piedra Creek a man rode out of the timber directly toward them.

"It looks like the man we saw coming over," remarked Miss Derwent.

As the distance between them lessened, the district attorney suddenly pulled up his team sharply, with his eyes fixed upon the advancing horseman. That individual had drawn a Winchester from its scabbard on his saddle and thrown it over his arm.

"Now I know you, Mexico Sam!" muttered Littlefield to himself. "It *was* you who shook your rattles in that gentle epistle."

Mexico Sam did not leave things long in doubt. He had a nice eye in all matters relating to firearms, so when he was within good rifle range, but outside of danger from No. 8 shot, he threw up his Winchester and opened fire upon the occupants of the buckboard.

The first shot cracked the back of the seat within the two-inch space between the shoulders of Littlefield and Miss Derwent. The next went through the dashboard and Littlefield's trouser leg.

The district attorney hustled Nancy out of the buckboard to the ground. She was a little pale, but asked no questions. She had the frontier instinct that accepts conditions in an emergency without superfluous argument. They kept their guns in hand, and Littlefield hastily gathered some handfuls of cartridges from the pasteboard box on the seat and crowded them into his pockets.

"Keep behind the horses, Nan," he commanded. "That fellow is a ruffian I sent to prison once. He's trying to get even. He knows our shot won't hurt him at that distance."

"All right, Bob," said Nancy steadily. "I'm not afraid. But you come close too. Whoa, Bess; stand still now!"

She stroked Bess's mane. Littlefield stood with his gun ready, praying that the desperado would come within range.

But Mexico Sam was playing his vendetta along safe lines. He was a bird of different feather from the plover. His accurate eye drew an imaginary line of circumference around the area of danger from bird-shot, and upon this line he rode. His horse wheeled to the right, and as his victims rounded to the safe side of their equine breastwork he sent a ball through the district attorney's hat. Once he miscalculated in making a détour, and overstepped his margin. Littlefield's gun flashed, and Mexico Sam ducked his head to the harmless patter of the shot. A few of them stung his horse, which pranced promptly back to the safety line.

The desperado fired again. A little cry came from Nancy Derwent. Littlefield whirled, with blazing eyes, and saw the blood trickling down her cheek. "I'm not hurt, Bob—only a splinter struck me. I think he hit one of the wheel-spokes."

"Lord!" groaned Littlefield. "If I only had a charge of buckshot!"

The ruffian got his horse still, and took careful aim. Fly gave a snort and fell in the harness, struck in the neck. Bess, now disabused of the idea that plover were being fired at, broke her traces and galloped wildly away. Mexico Sam sent a ball neatly through the fullness of Nancy Derwent's shooting-jacket.

"Lie down—lie down!" snapped Littlefield. "Close to the horse—flat on the ground—so." He almost threw her upon the grass against the back of the recumbent Fly. Oddly enough, at that moment the words of the Mexican girl returned to his mind:

"If the life of the girl you love is ever in danger, remember Rafael Ortiz."

Littlefield uttered an exclamation.

"Open fire on him, Nan, across the horse's back! Fire as fast as you can! You can't hurt him, but keep him dodging shot for one minute while I try to work a little scheme."

Nancy gave a quick glance at Littlefield, and saw him take out his pocket-knife and open it. Then she turned her face to obey orders, keeping up a rapid fire at the enemy.

Mexico Sam waited patiently until this innocuous fusillade ceased. He had plenty of time, and he did not care to risk the chance of a bird-shot in his eye when it could be avoided by a little caution. He pulled his heavy Stetson low down over his face until the shots ceased. Then he drew a little nearer, and fired with careful aim at what he could see of his victims above the fallen horse.

Neither of them moved. He urged his horse a few steps nearer. He saw the district attorney rise to one knee and deliberately level his shot-gun. He pulled his hat down and awaited the harmless rattle of the tiny pellets.

The shot-gun blazed with a heavy report. Mexico Sam sighed, turned limp all over, and slowly fell from his horse—a dead rattlesnake.

At ten o'clock the next morning court opened, and the case of the United States *versus* Rafael Ortiz was called. The district attorney, with his arm in a sling, rose and addressed the court.

"May it please your honour," he said, "I desire to enter a *nolle pros.* in this case. Even though the defendant should be guilty, there is not sufficient evidence in the hands of the government to secure a conviction. The piece of counterfeit coin upon the identity of which the case was built is not now available as evidence. I ask, therefore, that the case be stricken off."

At the noon recess Kilpatrick strolled into the district attorney's office.

"I've just been down to take a squint at old Mexico Sam," said the deputy. "They've got him laid out. Old Mexico was a tough outfit, I reckon. The boys was wonderin' down there what you shot him with. Some said it must have been nails. I never see a gun carry anything to make holes like he had."

"I shot him," said the district attorney, "with Exhibit A of your counterfeiting case. Lucky thing for me—and somebody else—that it was as bad money as it was! It sliced up into slugs very nicely. Say, Kil, can't you go down to the jacals and find where that Mexican girl lives? Miss Derwent wants to know."

XLVIII: THE PIMIENTA PANCAKES

WHILE we were rounding up a bunch of the Triangle-O cattle in the Frio bottoms a projecting branch of a dead mesquite caught my wooden stirrup and gave my ankle a wrench that laid me up in camp for a week.

On the third day of my compulsory idleness I crawled out near the grub wagon, and reclined helpless under the conversational fire of Judson Odom, the camp cook. Jud was a monologist by nature, whom Destiny, with customary blundering, had set in a profession wherein he was bereaved, for the greater portion of his time, of an audience.

Therefore, I was manna in the desert of Jud's obmutescence.

Betimes I was stirred by invalid longings for something to eat that did not come under the caption of "grub." I had visions of the maternal pantry "deep as first love, and wild with all regret," and then I asked—

"Jud, can you make pancakes?"

Jud laid down his six-shooter, with which he was preparing to pound an antelope steak, and stood over me in what I felt to be a menacing attitude. He further endorsed my impression that his pose was resentful by fixing upon me with his light blue eyes a look of cold suspicion.

"Say, you," he said, with candid, though not excessive, choler, "did you mean that straight, or was you trying to throw the gaff into me? Some of the boys been telling you about me and that pancake racket?"

"No, Jud," I said sincerely, "I meant it. It seems to me I'd swap my pony and saddle for a stack of buttered brown pancakes with some first crop, open kettle, New Orleans sweetening. Was there a story about pancakes?"

Jud was mollified at once when he saw that I had not been dealing in allusions. He brought some mysterious bags and tin boxes from the grub wagon and set them in the shade of the hackberry where I lay reclined. I watched him as he began to arrange them leisurely and untie their many strings.

"No, not a story," said Jud, as he worked, "but just the logical disclosures in the case of me and that pink-eyed snoozer from Mired Mule Cañada and Miss Willella Learight. I don't mind telling you.

"I was punching then for old Bill Toomey, on the San Miguel. One day I gets all ensnared up in aspirations for to eat some canned grub that hasn't ever mooed or baaed or grunted or been in peck measures. So, I gets on my bronc and pushes the wind for Uncle Emsley Telfair's store at the Pimienta Crossing on the Nueces.

"About three in the afternoon I throwed my bridle rein over a mesquite limb and walked the last twenty yards into Uncle Emsley's store. I got up on the counter and told Uncle Emsley that the signs pointed to the devastation of the fruit crop of the world. In a minute I had a bag of crackers and a long-handled spoon, with an open can each of apricots and pineapples and cherries and greengages beside of me with Uncle Emsley busy chopping away with the hatchet at the yellow clings. I was feeling like Adam before the apple stampede, and was digging my spurs into the side of the counter and working with my twenty-four-inch spoon when I happened to look out of the window into the yard of Uncle Emsley's house, which was next to the store.

"There was a girl standing there—an imported girl with fixings on—philandering with a croquet maul and amusing herself by watching my style of encouraging the fruit-canning industry.

"I slid off the counter and delivered up my shovel to Uncle Emsley.

" 'That's my niece,' says he; 'Miss Willella Learight, down from Palestine on a visit. Do you want that I should make you acquainted?'

" 'The Holy Land,' I says to myself, my thoughts milling some as I tried to run 'em into the corral. 'Why not? There was sure angels in Pales——Why yes, Uncle Emsley,' I says out loud, 'I'd be awful edified to meet Miss Learight.'

"So Uncle Emsley took me out in the yard and gave us each other's entitlements.

"I never was shy about women. I never could

understand why some men who can break a mustang before breakfast and shave in the dark, get all left-handed and full of perspiration and excuses when they see a bolt of calico draped around what belongs in it. Inside of eight minutes me and Miss Willella was aggravating the croquet balls around as amiable as second cousins. She gave me a dig about the quantity of canned fruit I had eaten, and I got back at her, flat-footed, about how a certain lady named Eve started the fruit trouble in the first free-grass pasture—'Over in Palestine, wasn't it?' says I, as easy and pat as roping a one-year-old.

"That was how I acquired cordiality for the proximities of Miss Willella Learight; and the disposition grew larger as time passed. She was stopping at Pimienta Crossing for her health, which was very good, and for the climate, which was forty per cent. hotter than Palestine. I rode over to see her once every week for a while, and then I figured it out that if I doubled the number of trips I would see her twice as often.

"One week I slipped in a third trip, and that's where the pancakes and the pink-eyed snoozer busted into the game.

"That evening, while I set on the counter with a peach and two damsons in my mouth, I asked Uncle Emsley how Miss Willella was.

" 'Why,' says Uncle Emsley, 'she's gone riding with Jackson Bird, the sheep man from over at Mired Mule Cañada.'

"I swallowed the peach seed and the two damson seeds. I guess somebody held the counter by the bridle while I got off; and then I walked out straight ahead till I butted against the mesquite where my roan was tied.

" 'She's gone riding,' I whispered in my bronc's ear, 'with Birdstone Jack, the hired mule from Sheep Man's Cañada. Did you get that, old Leather-and-Gallops?'

"That bronc of mine wept, in his way. He'd been raised a cow pony and he didn't care for snoozers.

"I went back and said to Uncle Emsley: 'Did you say a sheep man?'

" 'I said a sheep man,' says Uncle again. 'You must have heard tell of Jackson Bird. He's got eight sections of grazing and four thousand head of the finest Merinos south of the Arctic Circle.'

"I went out and sat on the ground in the shade of the store and leaned against a prickly pear. I sifted sand into my boots with unthinking hands while I soliloquized a quantity about this bird with the Jackson plumage to his name.

"I never had believed in harming sheep men. I see one, one day, reading a Latin grammar on hoss-back, and I never touched him! They never irritated me like they do most cowmen. You wouldn't go to work now, and impair and disfigure snoozers, would you, that eat on tables and wear little shoes and speak to you on subjects? I had always let 'em pass, just as you would a jack-rabbit; with a polite word and a guess about the weather, but no stopping to swap canteens. I never thought it was worth while to be hostile with a snoozer. And because I'd been lenient, and let 'em live, here was one going around riding with Miss Willella Learight!

"An hour by sun they came loping back and stopped at Uncle Emsley's gate. The sheep person helped her off; and they stood throwing each other sentences all sprightful and sagacious for a while. And then this feathered Jackson flies up in his saddle and raises his little stewpot of a hat, and trots off in the direction of his mutton ranch. By this time I had turned the sand out of my boots and unpinned myself from the prickly pear; and by the time he gets half a mile out of Pimienta, I singlefoots up beside him on my bronc.

"I said that snoozer was pink-eyed, but he wasn't. His seeing arrangement was grey enough, but his eyelashes was pink and his hair was sandy, and that gave you the idea. Sheep man?—he wasn't more than a lamb man, anyhow—a little thing with his neck involved in a yellow silk handkerchief, and shoes tied up in bowknots.

" 'Afternoon!' says I to him. 'You now ride with a equestrian who is commonly called Dead-Moral-Certainty Judson, on account of the way I shoot. When I want a stranger to know me I always introduce myself before the draw, for I never did like to shake hands with ghosts.'

" 'Ah,' says he, just like that—'Ah, I'm glad to know you, Mr. Judson. I'm Jackson Bird, from over at Mired Mule Ranch.'

"Just then one of my eyes saw a roadrunner skipping down the hill with a young tarantula in his bill, and the other eye noticed a rabbit-hawk sitting on a dead limb in a water-elm. I popped over one after the other with my forty-five, just to show him. 'Two out of three,' says I. 'Birds just naturally seem to draw my fire wherever I go.'

" 'Nice shooting,' says the sheep man, without a flutter. 'But don't you sometimes ever miss the third shot? Elegant fine rain that was last week for the young grass, Mr. Judson?' says he.

" 'Willie,' says I, riding over close to his palfrey,

'your infatuated parents may have denounced you by the name of Jackson, but you sure moulted into a twittering Willie—let us slough off this here analysis of rain and the elements, and get down to talk that is outside the vocabulary of parrots. That is a bad habit you have got of riding with young ladies over at Pimienta. I've known birds,' says I, 'to be served on toast for less than that. Miss Willella,' says I, 'don't ever want any nest made out of sheep's wool by a tomtit of the Jacksonian branch of ornithology. Now, are you going to quit, or do you wish for to gallop up against this Dead-Moral-Certainty attachment to my name, which is good for two hyphens and at least one set of funeral obsequies?'

"Jackson Bird flushed up some, and then he laughed.

" 'Why, Mr. Judson,' says he, 'you've got the wrong idea. I've called on Miss Learight a few times; but not for the purpose you imagine. My object is purely a gastronomical one.'

"I reached for my gun.

" 'Any coyote,' says I, 'that would boast of dishonourable——'

" 'Wait a minute,' says this Bird, 'till I explain. What would I do with a wife? If you ever saw that ranch of mine! I do my own cooking and mending. Eating—that's all the pleasure I get out of sheep-raising. Mr. Judson, did you ever taste the pancakes that Miss Learight makes?'

" 'Me? No,' I told him. 'I never was advised that she was up to any culinary manœuvres.'

" 'They're golden sunshine,' says he; 'honey-browned by the ambrosial fires of Epicurus. I'd give two years of my life to get the recipe for making them pancakes. That's what I went to see Miss Learight for,' says Jackson Bird, 'but I haven't been able to get it from her. It's an old recipe that's been in the family for seventy-five years. They hand it down from one generation to another, but they don't give it away to outsiders. If I could get that recipe, so I could make them pancakes for myself on my ranch, I'd be a happy man,' says Bird.

" 'Are you sure,' I says to him, 'that it ain't the hand that mixes the pancakes that you're after?'

" 'Sure,' says Jackson. 'Miss Learight is a mighty nice girl, but I can assure you my intentions go no further than the gastro——' but he seen my hand going down to my holster and he changed his similitude—'than the desire to procure a copy of the pancake recipe,' he finishes.

" 'You ain't such a bad little man,' says I, trying to be fair. 'I was thinking some of making orphans of your sheep, but I'll let you fly away this time. But you stick to pancakes,' says I, 'as close as the middle one of a stack; and don't go and mistake sentiments for syrup, or there'll be singing at your ranch, and you won't hear it.'

" 'To convince you that I am sincere,' says the sheep man, 'I'll ask you to help me. Miss Learight and you being closer friends, maybe she would do for you what she wouldn't for me. If you will get me a copy of that pancake recipe, I give you my word that I'll never call upon her again.'

" 'That's fair,' I says, and I shook hands with Jackson Bird. 'I'll get it for you if I can, and glad to oblige.' And he turned off down the big pear flat on the Piedra, in the direction of Mired Mule; and I steered north-west for old Bill Toomey's ranch.

"It was five days afterward when I got another chance to ride over to Pimienta. Miss Willella and me passed a gratifying evening at Uncle Emsley's. She sang some, and exasperated the piano quite a lot with quotations from the operas. I gave imitations of a rattlesnake, and told her about Snaky McFee's new way of skinning cows, and described the trip I made to Saint Louis once. We was getting along in one another's estimations fine. Thinks I, if Jackson Bird can now be persuaded to migrate, I win. I recollect his promise about the pancake recipe, and I thinks I will persuade it from Miss Willella and give it to him; and then if I catches Birdie off of Mired Mule again, I'll make him hop the twig.

"So, along about ten o'clock, I put on a wheedling smile and says to Miss Willella: 'Now, if there's anything I do like better than the sight of a red steer on green grass it's the taste of a nice hot pancake smothered in sugar-house molasses.'

"Miss Willella gives a little jump on the piano stool, and looked at me curious.

" 'Yes,' says she, 'they're real nice. What did you say was the name of that street in Saint Louis, Mr. Odom, where you lost your hat?"

" 'Pancake Avenue,' says I, with a wink, to show her that I was on about the family recipe, and couldn't be side-corralled off of the subject. 'Come, now Miss Willella,' I says; 'let's hear how you make 'em. Pancakes is just whirling in my head like wagon wheels. Start her off, now—pound of flour, eight dozen eggs, and so on. How does the catalogue of constituents run?'

" 'Excuse me for a moment, please,' says Miss Willella, and she gives me a quick kind of sideways look, and slides off the stool. She ambled out into the other room, and directly Uncle Emsley comes in in his shirt sleeves, with a pitcher of water. He turns around to get a glass on the table, and I see a forty-five in his hip pocket. 'Great post-holes!' thinks I, 'but here's a family thinks a heap of cooking recipes, protecting it with fire-arms. I've known outfits that wouldn't do that much by a family feud.'

" 'Drink this here down,' says Uncle Emsley, handing me the glass of water. 'You've rid too far to-day, Jud, and got yourself over-excited. Try to think about something else now.'

" 'Do you know how to make them pancakes, Uncle Emsley?' I asked.

" 'Well, I'm not as apprised in the anatomy of them as some,' says Uncle Emsley, 'but I reckon you take a sifter of plaster of paris and a little dough and saleratus and corn meal, and mix 'em with eggs and buttermilk as usual. Is old Bill going to ship beeves to Kansas City again this spring, Jud?'

"That was all the pancake specifications I could get that night. I didn't wonder that Jackson Bird found it uphill work. So I dropped the subject and talked with Uncle Emsley a while about hollow-horn and cyclones. And then Miss Willella came and said 'Good night,' and I hit the breeze for the ranch.

"About a week afterward I met Jackson Bird riding out of Pimienta as I rode in, and we stopped in the road for a few frivolous remarks.

" 'Got the bill of particulars for them flapjacks yet?' I asked him.

" 'Well, no,' says Jackson. 'I don't seem to have any success in getting hold of it. Did you try?'

" 'I did,' says I, 'and 'twas like trying to dig a prairie dog out of his hole with a peanut hull. That pancake recipe must be a jookalorum, the way they hold on to it.'

" 'I'm most ready to give it up,' says Jackson, so discouraged in his pronunciations that I felt sorry for him; 'but I did want to know how to make them pancakes to eat on my lonely ranch,' says he. 'I lie awake of nights thinking how good they are.'

" 'You keep on trying for it,' I tells him, 'and I'll do the same. One of us is bound to get a rope over its horns before long. Well, so-long, Jacksy.'

"You see, by this time we was on the peacefullest of terms. When I saw that he wasn't after Miss Willella I had more endurable contemplations of that sandy-haired snoozer. In order to help out the ambitions of his appetite I kept on trying to get that recipe from Miss Willella. But every time I would say 'pancakes,' she would get sort of remote and fidgety about the eye, and try to change the subject. If I held her to it she would slide out and round up Uncle Emsley with his pitcher of water and hip-pocket howitzer.

"One day I galloped over to the store with a fine bunch of blue verbenas that I cut out of a herd of wild flowers over on Poisoned Dog Prairie. Uncle Emsley looked at 'em with one eye shut and says—

" 'Haven't ye heard the news?'

" 'Cattle up?' I asks.

" 'Willella and Jackson Bird was married in Palestine yesterday,' says he. 'Just got a letter this morning.'

"I dropped them flowers in a cracker-barrel, and let the news trickle in my ears and down towards my upper left-hand shirt pocket until I got to my feet.

" 'Would you mind saying that over again once more, Uncle Emsley?' says I. 'Maybe my hearing has got wrong, and you only said that prime heifers was 4.80 on the hoof, or something like that.'

" 'Married yesterday,' says Uncle Emsley, 'and gone to Waco and Niagara Falls on a wedding tour. Why, didn't you see none of the signs all along? Jackson Bird has been courting Willella ever since that day he took her out riding.'

" 'Then,' says I, in a kind of yell, 'what was all this zizzaparoola he gives me about pancakes? Tell me *that*.'

"When I said 'pancakes,' Uncle Emsley sort of dodged and stepped back.

" 'Somebody's been dealing me pancakes from the bottom of the deck,' I says, 'and I'll find out. I believe you know. Talk up,' says I, 'or we'll mix a panful of batter right here.'

"I slid over the counter after Uncle Emsley. He grabbed at his gun, but it was in a drawer, and he missed it two inches. I got him by the front of his shirt and shoved him in a corner.

" 'Talk pancakes,' says I, 'or be made into one. Does Miss Willella make 'em?'

" 'She never made one in her life and I never saw one,' says Uncle Emsley, soothing. 'Calm down now, Jud—calm down. You've got excited, and that wound in your head is contaminating your sense of intelligence. Try not to think about pancakes.'

" 'Uncle Emsley,' says I, 'I'm not wounded in the head except so far as my natural cogitative instincts run to runts. Jackson Bird told me he was calling on Miss Willella for the purpose of finding out her system of producing pancakes, and he asked me to help him get the bill of lading of the ingredients. I done so, with the result as you see. Have I been sodded down with Johnson grass by a pink-eyed snoozer, or what?'

" 'Slack up your grip on my dress shirt,' says Uncle Emsley, 'and I'll tell you. Yes, it looks like Jackson Bird has gone and humbugged you some. The day after he went riding with Willella he came back and told me and her to watch out for you whenever you got to talking about pancakes. He said you was in camp once where they was cooking flapjacks, and one of the fellows cut you over the head with a frying-pan. Jackson said that whenever you got overhot or excited that wound hurt you and made you kind of crazy, and you went raving about pancakes. He told us to just get you worked off of the subject and soothed down, and you wouldn't be dangerous. So, me and Willella done the best by you we know how. Well, well,' says Uncle Emsley, 'that Jackson Bird is sure a seldom kind of a snoozer.' "

During the progress of Jud's story he had been slowly but deftly combining certain portions of the contents of his sacks and cans. Toward the close of it he set before me the finished product—a pair of red-hot, rich-hued pancakes on a tin plate. From some secret hoarding place he also brought a lump of excellent butter and a bottle of golden syrup.

"How long ago did these things happen?" I asked him.

"Three years," said Jud. "They're living on the Mired Mule Ranch now. But I haven't seen either of 'em since. They say Jackson Bird was fixing his ranch up fine with rocking-chairs and window curtains all the time he was putting me up the pancake tree. Oh, I got over it after a while. But the boys kept the racket up."

"Did you make these cakes by the famous recipe?" I asked.

"Didn't I tell you there wasn't no recipe?" said Jud. "The boys hollered pancakes till they got pancake hungry, and I cut this recipe out of a newspaper. How does the truck taste?"

"They're delicious," I answered. "Why don't you have some, too, Jud?"

I was sure I heard a sigh.

"Me?" said Jud. "I don't never eat 'em."

XLIX: MIDSUMMER KNIGHT'S DREAM

"The knights are dead;
Their swords are rust.
Except a few who have to hust-
Le all the time
To raise the dust."

DEAR READER: It was summer-time. The sun glared down upon the city with pitiless ferocity. It is difficult for the sun to be ferocious and exhibit compunction simultaneously. The heat was—oh, bother thermometers!—who cares for standard measures, anyhow? It was so hot that——

The roof gardens put on so many extra waiters that you could hope to get your gin fizz now—as soon as all the other people got theirs. The hospitals were putting in extra cots for bystanders.

For when little woolly dogs loll their tongues out and say "woof, woof!" at the fleas that bite 'em, and nervous old back bombazine ladies screech "Mad dog!" and policemen begin to shoot, somebody is going to get hurt. The man from Pompton, N.J., who always wears an overcoat in July, had turned up in a Broadway hotel drinking hot Scotches and enjoying his annual ray from the calcium. Philanthropists were petitioning the Legislature to pass a bill requiring builders to make tenement fire-escapes more commodious, so that families might die all together of the heat instead of one or two at a time. So many men were telling you about the number of baths they took each day that you wondered how they got along after the real lessee of the apartment came back to town and thanked 'em for taking such good care of it. The young man who called loudly for cold beef and beer in the restaurant, protesting that roast pullet and Burgundy was really too heavy for such weather, blushed when he met your eye, for you had heard him all winter calling, in modest tones, for the same ascetic viands. Soup, pocketbooks, shirt waists, actors and baseball excuses grew thinner. Yes, it was summer-time.

A man stood at Thirty-fourth street waiting for a downtown car. A man of forty, grey-haired, pink-faced, keen, nervous, plainly dressed, with a harassed look around the eyes. He wiped his forehead and laughed loudly when a fat man with an outing look stopped and spoke with him.

"No, siree," he shouted with defiance and scorn. "None of your old mosquito-haunted swamps and skyscraper mountains without elevators for me. When I want to get away from hot weather I know how to do it. New York, sir, is the finest summer resort in the country. Keep in the shade and watch your diet, and don't get too far away from an electric fan. Talk about your Adirondacks and your Catskills! There's more solid comfort in the borough of Manhattan than in all the rest of the country together. No, siree! No tramping up perpendicular cliffs and being waked up at four in the morning by a million flies, and eating canned goods straight from the city, for me. Little old New York will take a few select summer boarders; comforts and conveniences of homes—that's the ad. that I answer every time."

"You need a vacation," said the fat man, looking closely at the other. "You haven't been away from town in years. Better come with me for two weeks, anyhow. The trout in the Beaverkill are jumping at anything now that looks like a fly. Harding writes me that he landed a three-pound brown last week."

"Nonsense!" cried the other man. "Go ahead, if you like, and boggle around in rubber boots wearing yourself out trying to catch fish. When I want one I go to a cool restaurant and order it. I laugh at you fellows whenever I think of you bustling around in the heat in the country thinking you are having a good time. For me Father Knickerbocker's little improved farm with the big shady lane running through the middle of it."

The fat man sighed over his friend and went his way. The man who thought New York was the greatest summer resort in the country boarded a car and went buzzing down to his office. On the way he threw away his newspaper and looked up at a ragged patch of sky above the housetops.

"Three pounds!" he muttered absently. "And Harding isn't a liar. I believe, if I could—but it's impossible—they've got to have another month—another month at least."

In his office the upholder of urban midsummer joys dived, headforemost, into the swimming pool of business. Adkins, his clerk, came and added a spray of letters, memoranda and telegrams.

At five o'clock in the afternoon the busy man leaned back in his office chair, put his feet on the desk and mused aloud:

"I wonder what kind of bait Harding used."

* * * * *

She was all in white that day; and thereby Compton lost a bet to Gaines. Compton had wagered she would wear light blue, for she knew that was his favourite colour, and Compton was a millionaire's son, and that almost laid him open to the charge of betting on a sure thing. But white was her choice, and Gaines held up his head with twenty-five's lordly air.

The little summer hotel in the mountains had a lively crowd that year. There were two or three young college men and a couple of artists and a young naval officer on one side. On the other there were enough beauties among the young ladies for the correspondent of a society paper to refer to them as a "bevy." But the moon among the stars was Mary Sewell. Each one of the young men greatly desired to arrange matters so that he could pay her millinery bills, and fix the furnace, and have her do away with the "Sewell" part of her name for ever. Those who could stay only a week or two went away hinting at pistols and blighted hearts. But Compton stayed like the mountains themselves, for he could afford it. And Gaines stayed because he was a fighter and wasn't afraid of millionaire's sons, and —well, he adored the country.

"What do you think, Miss Mary?" he said once. "I knew a duffer in New York who claimed to like it in the summer-time. Said you could keep cooler there than you could in the woods. Wasn't he an awful silly? I don't think I could breathe on Broadway after the 1st of June."

"Mamma was thinking of going back week after next," said Miss Mary with a lovely frown.

"But when you think of it," said Gaines, "there are lots of jolly places in town in the summer. The roof gardens, you know, and the—er—the roof gardens."

Deepest blue was the lake that day—the day when they had the mock tournament, and the men rode clumsy farm horses around in a glade in the woods and caught curtain rings on the end of a lance. Such fun!

Cool and dry as the finest wine came the breath of the shadowed forest. The valley below was a vision seen through an opal haze. A white mist from hidden falls blurred the green of a hand's breadth of tree tops half-way down the gorge. Youth made merry hand-in-hand with young summer. Nothing on Broadway like that.

The villagers gathered to see the city folks pursue their mad drollery. The woods rang with the laughter of pixies and naiads and sprites. Gaines caught most of the rings. His was the privilege to crown the queen of the tournament. He was the conquering knight—as far as the rings went. On his arm he wore a white scarf. Compton wore light blue. She had declared her preference for blue, but she wore white that day.

Gaines looked about for the queen to crown her. He heard her merry laugh, as if from the clouds. She had slipped away and climbed Chimney Rock, a little granite bluff, and stood there, a white fairy among the laurels, fifty feet above their heads.

Instantly he and Compton accepted the implied challenge. The bluff was easily mounted at the rear, but the front offered small hold to hand or foot. Each man quickly selected his route and began to climb. A crevice, a bush, a slight projection, a vine or tree branch—all of these were aids that counted in the race. It was all foolery—there was no stake; but there was youth in it, cross reader, and light hearts, and something else that Miss Clay writes so charmingly about.

Gaines gave a great tug at the root of a laurel and pulled himself to Miss Mary's feet. On his arm he carried the wreath of roses; and while the villagers and summer boarders screamed and applauded below he placed it on the queen's brow.

"You are a gallant knight," said Miss Mary.

"If I could be your true knight always," began Gaines, but Miss Mary laughed him dumb, for Compton scrambled over the edge of the rock one minute behind time.

What a twilight that was when they drove back to the hotel! The opal of the valley turned slowly to purple, the dark woods framed the lake as a mirror, the tonic air stirred the very soul in one. The first pale stars came out over the mountain tops where yet a faint glow of——

* * * * *

"I beg your pardon, Mr. Gaines," said Adkins.

The man who believed New York to be the finest

summer resort in the world opened his eyes and kicked over the mucilage bottle on his desk.

"I—I believe I was asleep," he said.

"It's the heat," said Adkins. "It's something awful in the city these——"

"Nonsense!" said the other. "The city beats the country ten to one in summer. Fools go out tramping in muddy brooks and wear themselves out trying to catch little fish as long as your finger. Stay in town and keep comfortable—that's my idea."

"Some letters just came," said Adkins. "I thought you might like to glance at them before you go."

Let us look over his shoulder and read just a few lines of one of them:

MY DEAR, DEAR HUSBAND: Just received your letter ordering us to stay another month. . . . Rita's cough is almost gone. . . . Johnny has simply gone wild like a little Indian. . . . Will be the making of both children . . . work so hard, and I know that your business can hardly afford to keep us here so long . . . best man that ever . . . you always pretend that you like the city in summer . . . trout fishing that you used to be so fond of . . . and all to keep us well and happy . . . come to you if it were not doing the babies so much good. . . . I stood last evening on Chimney Rock in exactly the same spot where I was when you put the wreath of roses on my head . . . through all the world . . . when you said you would be my true knight . . . fifteen years ago, dear, just think! . . . have always been that to me . . . ever and ever.

MARY.

The man who said he thought New York the finest summer resort in the country dropped into a café on his way home and had a glass of beer under an electric fan.

"Wonder what kind of a fly old Harding used," he said to himself.

L: MAKES THE WHOLE WORLD KIN

THE burglar stepped inside the window quickly, and then he took his time. A burglar who respects his art always takes his time before taking anything else.

The house was a private residence. By its boarded front door and untrimmed Boston ivy the burglar knew that the mistress of it was sitting on some ocean-side piazza telling a sympathetic man in a yachting cap that no one had ever understood her sensitive, lonely heart. He knew by the light in the third-story front windows, and by the lateness of the season, that the master of the house had come home, and would soon extinguish his light and retire. For it was September of the year and of the soul, in which season the house's good man comes to consider roof-gardens and stenographers as vanities, and to desire the return of his mate and the more durable blessings of decorum and the moral excellences.

The burglar lighted a cigarette. The guarded glow of the match illuminated his salient points for a moment. He belonged to the third type of burglars.

This third type has not yet been recognized and accepted. The police have made us familiar with the first and second. Their classification is simple. The collar is the distinguishing mark.

When a burglar is caught who does not wear a collar, he is described as a degenerate of the lowest type, singularly vicious and depraved, and is suspected of being the desperate criminal who stole the handcuffs out of Patrolman Hennessy's pocket in 1878 and walked away to escape arrest.

The other well-known type is the burglar who wears a collar. He is always referred to as a Raffles in real life. He is invariably a gentleman by daylight, breakfasting in a dress suit, and posing as a paperhanger, while after dark he plies his nefarious occupation of burglary. His mother is an extremely wealthy and respected resident of Ocean Grove, and when he is conducted to his cell he asks at once for a nail file and the *Police Gazette*. He always has a wife in every State in the Union and fiancées in all the Territories, and the newspapers print his matrimonial gallery out of their stock of cuts of the ladies who were cured by only one bottle after having been given up by five doctors, experiencing great relief after the first dose.

The burglar wore a blue sweater. He was neither a Raffles nor one of the chiefs from Hell's Kitchen. The police would have been baffled had they attempted to classify him. They have not yet heard of the respectable, unassuming burglar who is neither above nor below his station.

This burglar of the third class began to prowl. He wore no masks, dark lanterns, or gum shoes. He carried a 38-calibre revolver in his pocket, and he chewed peppermint gum thoughtfully.

The furniture of the house was swathed in its summer dust-protectors. The silver was far away in safe-deposit vaults. The burglar expected no remarkable "haul." His objective point was that dimly lighted room where the master of the house should be sleeping heavily after whatever solace he had sought to lighten the burden of his loneliness. A "touch" might be made there to the extent of legitimate, fair professional profits—loose money, a watch, a jewelled stick-pin—nothing exorbitant or beyond reason. He had seen the window left open and had taken the chance.

The burglar softly opened the door of the lighted room. The gas was turned low. A man lay in the bed asleep. On the dresser lay many things in confusion—a crumpled roll of bills, a watch, keys, three poker chips, crushed cigars, a pink silk hair bow, and an unopened bottle of bromo-seltzer for a bulwark in the morning.

The burglar took three steps toward the dresser. The man in the bed suddenly uttered a squeaky groan and opened his eyes. His right hand slid under his pillow, but remained there.

"Lay still," said the burglar in conversational tone. Burglars of the third type do not hiss. The citizen in the bed looked at the round end of the burglar's pistol and lay still.

"Now hold up both your hands," commanded the burglar.

The citizen had a little, pointed, brown-and-grey beard, like that of a painless dentist. He looked solid, esteemed, irritable, and disgusted. He sat up in bed and raised his right hand above his head.

"Up with the other one," ordered the burglar. "You might be amphibious and shoot with your left. You can count two, can't you? Hurry up, now."

"Can't raise the other one," said the citizen, with a contortion of his lineaments.

"What's the matter with it?"

"Rheumatism in the shoulder."

"Inflammatory?"

"Was. The inflammation has gone down."

The burglar stood for a moment or two, holding his gun on the afflicted one. He glanced at the plunder on the dresser and then, with a half-embarrassed air, back at the man in the bed. Then he, too, made a sudden grimace.

"Don't stand there making faces," snapped the citizen, bad-humouredly. "If you've come to burgle, why don't you do it? There's some stuff lying around."

"'Scuse me," said the burglar, with a grin; "but it just socked me one, too. It's good for you that rheumatism and me happens to be old pals. I got it in my left arm too. Most anybody but me would have popped you when you wouldn't hoist that left claw of yours."

"How long have you had it?" inquired the citizen.

"Four years. I guess that ain't all. Once you've got it, it's you for a rheumatic life—that's my judgment."

"Ever try rattlesnake oil?" asked the citizen, interestedly.

"Gallons," said the burglar. "If all the snakes I've used the oil of was strung out in a row they'd reach eight times as far as Saturn, and the rattles could be heard at Valparaiso, Indiana, and back."

"Some use Chiselum's Pills," remarked the citizen.

"Fudge!" said the burglar. "Took 'em five months. No good. I had some relief the year I tried Finkelham's Extract, Balm of Gilead poultices and Pott's Pain Pulverizer; but I think it was the buckeye I carried in my pocket what done the trick."

"Is yours worse in the morning or at night?" asked the citizen.

"Night," said the burglar; "just when I'm busiest. Say, take down that arm of yours—I guess you won't—— Say! did you ever try Blickerstaff's Blood Builder?"

"I never did. Does yours come in paroxysms or is it a steady pain?"

The burglar sat down on the foot of the bed and rested his gun on his crossed knee.

"It jumps," said he. "It strikes me when I ain't looking for it. I had to give up second-story work because I got stuck sometimes half-way up. Tell you what—I don't believe the bloomin' doctors know what is good for it."

"Same here. I've spent a thousand dollars without getting any relief. Yours swell any?"

"Of mornings. And when it's goin' to rain—great Christopher!"

"Me, too," said the citizen. "I can tell when a streak of humidity the size of a tablecloth starts from Florida on its way to New York. And if I pass a theatre where there's an *East Lynne* matinée going on, the moisture starts my left arm jumping like a toothache."

"It's undiluted—hades!" said the burglar.

"You're dead right," said the citizen.

The burglar looked down at his pistol and thrust it into his pocket with an awkward attempt at ease.

"Say, old man," he said constrainedly, "ever try opodeldoc?"

"Slop!" said the citizen angrily. "Might as well rub on restaurant butter."

"Sure," concurred the burglar. "It's a salve suitable for little Minnie when the kitty scratches her finger. I'll tell you what! We're up against it. I only find one thing that eases her up. Hey? Little old sanitary, ameliorating, lest-we-forget Booze. Say—this job's off—'scuse me—get on your clothes and let's go out and have some. 'Scuse the liberty, but—ouch! There she goes again!"

"For a week," said the citizen. "I haven't been able to dress myself without help. I'm afraid Thomas is in bed, and——"

"Climb out," said the burglar. "I'll help you get into your duds."

The conventional returned as a tidal wave and flooded the citizen. He stroked his brown-and-grey beard.

"It's very unusual——" he began.

"Here's your shirt," said the burglar, "fall out. I knew a man who said Omberry's Ointment fixed him in two weeks so he could use both hands in tying his four-in-hand."

As they were going out the door the citizen turned and started back.

" 'Liked to forget my money," he explained; "laid it on the dresser last night."

The burglar caught him by the right sleeve.

"Come on," he said bluffly. "I ask you. Leave it alone. I've got the price. Ever try witch hazel and oil of wintergreen?"

LI: THE OCTOPUS MAROONED

"A TRUST is its weakest point," said Jeff Peters.

"That," said I, "sounds like one of those unintelligible remarks such as, 'Why is a policeman?' "

"It is not," said Jeff. "There are no relations between a trust and a policeman. My remark was an epitogram—an axis—a kind of mulct'em in parvo. What it means is that a trust is like an egg, and it is not like an egg. If you want to break an egg you have to do it from the outside. The only way to break up a trust is from the inside. Keep sitting on it until it hatches. Look at the brood of young colleges and libraries that's chirping and peeping all over the country. Yes, sir, every trust bears in its own bosom the seeds of its destruction like a rooster that crows near a Georgia coloured Methodist camp meeting, or a Republican announcing himself a candidate for governor of Texas."

I asked Jeff, jestingly, if he had ever, during his checkered, plaided, mottled, pied and dappled career, conducted an enterprise of the class to which the word "trust" had been applied. Somewhat to my surprise he acknowledged the corner.

"Once," said he. "And the state seal of New Jersey never bit into a charter that opened up a solider and safer piece of legitimate octopusing. We had everything in our favour—wind, water, police, nerve, and a clean monopoly of an article indispensable to the public. There wasn't a trust buster on the globe that could have found a weak spot in our scheme. It made Rockefeller's little kerosene speculation look like a bucket-shop. But we lost out."

"Some unforeseen opposition came up, I suppose," I said.

"No, sir, it was just as I said. We were self-curbed. It was a case of auto-suppression. There was a rift within the loot, as Albert Tennyson says.

"You remember I told you that me and Andy Tucker was partners for some years. That man was the most talented conniver at stratagems I ever saw. Whenever he saw a dollar in another man's hands he took it as a personal grudge, if he couldn't take it any other way. Andy was educated, too, besides having a lot of useful information. He had acquired a big amount of experience out of books, and could talk for hours on any subject connected with ideas and discourse. He had been in every line of graft from lecturing on Palestine with a lot of magic-lantern pictures of the annual Custom-made Clothiers' Association Convention at Atlantic City to flooding Connecticut with bogus wood alcohol distilled from nutmegs.

"One Spring me and Andy had been over in Mexico on a flying trip during which a Philadelphia capitalist had paid us $2,500 for a half interest in a silver mine in Chihuahua. Oh, yes, the mine was all right. The other half interest must have been worth two or three hundred thousand. I often wondered who owned that mine.

"In coming back to the United States me and Andy stubbed our toes against a little town in Texas on the bank of the Rio Grande. The name of it was Bird City; but it wasn't. The town had about 2,000 inhabitants, mostly men. I figured out that their principal means of existence was in living close to tall chaparral. Some of 'em were stockmen and some gamblers and some horse peculators and plenty were in the smuggling line. Me and Andy put up at a hotel that was built like something between a roof-garden and a sectional bookcase. It began to rain the day we got there. As the saying is, Juniper Aquarius was sure turning on the water-plugs on Mount Amphibious.

"Now, there were three saloons in Bird City, though neither Andy nor me drank. But we could see the townspeople making a triangular procession from one to another all day and half the night. Everybody seemed to know what to do with as much money as they had.

"The third day of the rain it slacked up awhile in the afternoon, so me and Andy walked out to the edge of town to view the mudscape. Bird City was built between the Rio Grande and a deep wide arroyo that used to be the old bed of the river. The bank between the stream and its old bed was cracking and giving away, when we saw it, on account of the high water caused by the rain. Andy looks at it a long time. That man's intellects was never idle. And then he unfolds to me a instantaneous idea that has occurred to him. Right there was organized a trust; and we walked back into town and put it on the market.

"First we went to the main saloon in Bird City, called the Blue Snake, and bought it. It cost us $1,200. And then we dropped in, casual, at Mexican Joe's place, referred to the rain, and bought him out for $500. The other one came easy at $400.

"The next morning Bird City woke up and found itself an island. The river had busted through its old channel, and the town was surrounded by roaring torrents. The rain was still raining, and there was heavy clouds in the north-west that presaged about six more mean annual rainfalls during the next two weeks. But the worst was yet to come.

"Bird City hopped out of its nest, waggled its pin feathers and strolled out for its matutinal toot. Lo! Mexican Joe's place was closed and likewise the other little 'dobe life-saving station. So, naturally, the body politic emits thirsty ejaculations of surprise and ports hellum for the Blue Snake. And what does it find there?

"Behind one end of the bar sits Jefferson Peters, octopus, with a sixshooter on each side of him, ready to make change or corpses as the case may be. There are three bartenders; and on the wall is a ten-foot sign reading: 'All Drinks One Dollar.' Andy sits on the safe in his neat blue suit and gold-banded cigar, on the look-out for emergencies. The town marshal is there with two deputies to keep order, having been promised free drinks by the trust.

"Well, sir, it took Bird City just ten minutes to realize that it was in a cage. We expected trouble; but there wasn't any. The citizens saw that we had 'em. The nearest railroad was thirty miles away; and it would be two weeks at least before the river would be fordable. So they began to cuss, amiable, and throw down dollars on the bar till it sounded like a selection on the xylophone.

"There was about 1,500 grown-up adults in Bird City that had arrived at years of indiscretion; and the majority of 'em required from three to twenty drinks a day to make life endurable. The Blue Snake was the only place where they could get 'em till the flood subsided. It was beautiful and simple as all truly great swindles are.

"About ten o'clock the silver dollars dropping on the bar slowed down to playing two-steps and marches instead of jigs. But I looked out the windows and saw a hundred or two of our customers standing in line at the Bird City Savings and Loan Co., and I knew they were borrowing more money to be sucked in by the clammy tendrils of the octopus.

"At the fashionable hour of noon everybody went home to dinner. We told the bartenders to take advantage of the lull, and do the same. Then me and Andy counted the receipts. We had taken in $1,300. We calculated that if Bird City would only remain an island for two weeks the trust would be able to endow the Chicago University with a new dormitory of padded cells for the faculty, and present every worthy poor man in Texas with a farm, provided he furnished the site for it.

"Andy was especial inroaded by self-esteem at our success, the rudiments of the scheme having originated in his own surmises and premonitions. He got off the safe and lit the biggest cigar in the house.

" 'Jeff,' says he, 'I don't suppose that anywhere in the world you could find three cormorants with brighter ideas about down-treading the proletariat than the firm of Peters, Satan and Tucker, incorporated. We have sure handed the small consumer a giant blow in the sole apoplectic region. No?'

" 'Well,' says I, 'it does look as if we would have to take up gastritis and golf or be measured for kilts in spite of ourselves. This little turn in bug juice is, verily, all to the Skibo. And I can stand it,' says I. 'I'd rather batten than bant any day.'

"Andy pours himself out four fingers of our best rye and does with it as was so intended. It was the first drink I had ever known him to take.

" 'By way of liberation,' says he, 'to the gods.'

"And then after thus doing umbrage to the heathen diabetes he drinks another to our success. And then he begins to toast the trade, beginning with Raisuli and the Northern Pacific, and on down the line to the little ones like the school book combine and the oleomargarine outrages and the Lehigh Valley and Great Scott Coal Federation.

" 'It's all right, Andy,' says I, 'to drink the health of our brother monopolists, but don't overdo the wassail. You know our most eminent and loathed multi-corruptionists live on weak tea and dog biscuits.'

"Andy went in the back room awhile and came out dressed in his best clothes. There was a kind of murderous and soulful look of gentle riotousness in his eye that I didn't like. I watched him to see what turn the whisky was going to take in him. There are two times when you never can tell what is going to happen. One is when a man takes his first drink; and the other is when a woman takes her latest.

"In less than an hour Andy's skate had turned to an ice yacht. He was outwardly decent and managed to preserve his aquarium, but inside he was impromptu and full of unexpectedness.

" 'Jeff,' says he, 'do you know that I'm a crater —a living crater?'

" 'That's a self-evident hypothesis,' says I. 'But you're not Irish. Why don't you say "creature," according to the rules and syntax of America?'

" 'I'm the crater of a volcano,' says he. 'I'm all

aflame and crammed inside with an assortment of words and phrases that have got to have an exodus. I can feel millions of synonyms and parts of speech rising in me,' says he, 'and I've got to make a speech of some sort. Drink,' says Andy, 'always drives me to oratory.'

" 'It could do no worse,' says I.

" 'From my earliest recollections,' says he, 'alcohol seemed to stimulate my sense of recitation and rhetoric. Why, in Bryan's second campaign,' says Andy, 'they used to give me three gin rickeys and I'd speak two hours longer than Billy himself could on the silver question. Finally they persuaded me to take the gold cure.'

" 'If you've got to get rid of your excess verbiage,' says I, 'why not go out on the river bank and speak a piece? It seems to me there was an old spellbinder named Cantharides that used to go and disincorporate himself of his windy numbers along the seashore.'

" 'No,' says Andy, 'I must have an audience. I feel like if I once turned loose people would begin to call Senator Beveridge the Grand Young Sphinx of the Wabash. I've got to get an audience together, Jeff, and get this oral distension assuaged or it may turn in on me and I'd go about feeling like a deckle-edge edition de luxe of Mrs. E. D. E. N. Southworth.'

" 'On what special subject of the theorems and topics does your desire for vocality seem to be connected with?' I asks.

" 'I ain't particular,' says Andy. 'I am equally good and varicose on all subjects. I can take up the matter of Russian immigration, or the poetry of John W. Keats, or the tariff, or Kabyle literature, or drainage, and make my audience weep, cry, sob and shed tears by turns.'

"'Well, Andy,' says I, 'if you are bound to get rid of this accumulation of vernacular, suppose you go out in town and work it on some indulgent citizen. Me and the boys will take care of the business. Everybody will be through dinner pretty soon, and salt pork and beans makes a man pretty thirsty. We ought to take in $1,500 more by midnight.'

"So Andy goes out of the Blue Snake, and I see him stopping men on the street and talking to 'em. By and by he has half a dozen in a bunch listening to him; and pretty soon I see him waving his arms and elocuting at a good-sized crowd on a corner. When he walks away they string out after him, talking all the time; and he leads 'em down the main street of Bird City with more men joining the procession as they go. It reminded me of the old lergerdemain that I'd read in books about the Pied Piper of Heidsieck charming the children away from the town.

"One o'clock came; and then two; and three got under the wire for place; and not a Bird citizen came in for a drink. The streets were deserted except for some ducks and ladies going to the stores. There was only a light drizzle falling then.

"A lonesome man came along and stopped in front of the Blue Snake to scrape the mud off his boots.

"'Pardner,' says I, 'what has happened? This morning there was hectic gaiety afoot; and now it seems more like one of them ruined cities of Tyre and Siphon where the lone lizard crawls on the walls of the main portcullis.'

"'The whole town,' says the muddy man, 'is up

in Sperry's wool warehouse listening to your side-kicker make a speech. He is some gravy on delivering himself of audible sounds relating to matters and conclusions,' says the man.

" 'Well, I hope he'll adjourn, *sine qua non*, pretty soon,' says I, 'for trade languishes.'

"Not a customer did we have that afternoon. At six o'clock two Mexicans brought Andy to the saloon lying across the back of a burro. We put him to bed while he still muttered and gesticulated with his hands and feet.

"Then I locked up the cash and went out to see what had happened. I met a man who told me all about it. Andy had made the finest two-hour speech that had ever been heard in Texas, he said, or anywhere else in the world.

" 'What was it about?' I asked.

" 'Temperance,' says he. 'And when he got through, every man in Bird City signed the pledge for a year.' "

LII: A PHILISTINE IN BOHEMIA

GEORGE WASHINGTON, with his right arm upraised, sits his iron horse at the lower corner of Union Square, for ever signalling the Broadway cars to stop as they round the curve into Fourteenth Street. But the cars buzz on, heedless, as they do at the beck of a private citizen, and the great General must feel, unless his nerves are iron, that rapid transit gloria mundi.

Should the General raise his left hand as he has raised his right, it would point to a quarter of the city that forms a haven for the oppressed and suppressed of foreign lands. In the cause of national or personal freedom they have found a refuge here, and the patriot who made it for them sits his steed, overlooking their district, while he listens through his left ear to vaudeville that caricatures the posterity of his protégés. Italy, Poland, the former Spanish possessions and the polyglot tribes of Austria-Hungary have spilled here a thick lather of their effervescent sons. In the eccentric cafés and lodging-houses of the vicinity they hover over their native wines and political secrets. The colony changes with much frequency. Faces disappear from the haunts, to be replaced by others. Whither do these uneasy birds flit? For half of the answer observe carefully the suave foreign air and foreign courtesy of the next waiter who serves your table d'hôte. For the other half, perhaps if the barber shops had tongues (and who will dispute it?) they could tell their share.

Titles are as plentiful as finger-rings among these transitory exiles. For lack of proper exploitation, a stock of titled goods large enough to supply the trade of upper Fifth Avenue is here condemned to a mere pushcart traffic. The new-world landlords who entertain these offshoots of nobility are not dazzled by coronets and crests. They have dough-nuts to sell instead of daughters. With them it is a serious matter of trading in flour and sugar instead of pearl powder and bonbons.

These assertions are deemed fitting as an introduction to the tale, which is of plebeians, and contains no one with even the ghost of a title.

Katy Dempsey's mother kept a furnished-room

house in this oasis of the aliens. The business was not profitable. If the two scraped together enough to meet the landlord's agent on rent day and negotiate for the ingredients of a daily Irish stew they called it success. Often the stew lacked both meat and potatoes. Sometimes it became as bad as consommé with music.

In this mouldy old house Katy waxed plump and pert and wholesome, and as beautiful and freckled as a tiger lily. She was the good fairy who was guilty of placing the damp clean towels and cracked pitchers of freshly-laundered Croton in the lodgers' rooms.

You are informed (by virtue of the privileges of astronomical discovery) that the star lodger's name was Mr. Brunelli. His wearing a yellow tie and paying his rent promptly distinguished him from the other lodgers. His raiment was splendid, his complexion olive, his moustache fierce, his manners a prince's, his rings and pins as magnificent as those of a travelling dentist.

He had breakfast served in his room, and he ate it in a red dressing-gown with green tassels. He left the house at noon and returned at midnight. Those were mysterious hours, but there was nothing mysterious about Mrs. Dempsey's lodgers except the things that were not mysterious. One of Mr. Kipling's poems is addressed to "Ye who hold the unwritten clue to all save all unwritten things." The same "readers" are invited to tackle the foregoing assertion.

Mr. Brunelli, being impressionable and a Latin, fell to conjugating the verb "amare," with Katy in the objective case, though not because of antipathy. She talked it over with her mother.

"Sure, I like him," said Katy. "He's more politeness than twinty candidates for Alderman, and he makes me feel like a queen whin he walks at me side. But what is he, I dinno? I've me suspicions. The marnin'll coom whin he'll throt out the picture av his baronial halls and ax to have the week's rint hung up in the ice chist along wid all the rist of 'em."

"'Tis thrue," admitted Mrs. Dempsey, "that he seems to be a sort iv a Dago, and too coolchured in his spache for a rale gintleman. But ye may be misjudgin' him. Ye should niver suspect any wan of bein' of noble descint that pays cash and pathronizes the laundry rig'lar."

"He's the same thricks of spakin' and blarneyin' wid his hands," sighed Katy, "as the Frinch nobleman at Mrs. Toole's that ran away wid Mr. Toole's Sunday pants and left the photograph of the Bastille, his grandfather's chat-taw, as security for tin weeks' rint."

Mr. Brunelli continued his calorific wooing. Katy continued to hesitate. One day he asked her out to dine, and she felt that a dénouement was in the air. While they are on their way, with Katy in her best muslin, you must take as an entr'acte a brief peep at New York's Bohemia.

'Tonio's restaurant is in Bohemia. The very location of it is secret. If you wish to know where it is ask the first person you meet. He will tell you in a whisper. 'Tonio discountenances custom; he keeps his house-front black and forbidding; he gives you a pretty bad dinner; he locks his door at the dining hour; but he knows spaghetti as the boarding-house knows cold veal; and—he has deposited many dollars in a certain Banco di ——

something with many gold vowels in the name on its windows.

To this restaurant Mr. Brunelli conducted Katy. The house was dark and the shades were lowered; but Mr. Brunelli touched an electric button by the basement door, and they were admitted.

Along a long, dark, narrow hallway they went, and then through a shining and spotless kitchen that opened directly upon a back yard.

The walls of houses hemmed three sides of the yard; a high, board fence, surrounded by cats, the other. A wash of clothes was suspended high upon a line stretched from diagonal corners. Those were property clothes, and were never taken in by 'Tonio. They were there that wits with defective pronunciation might make puns in connection with the ragout.

A dozen and a half little tables set upon the bare ground were crowded with Bohemia-hunters, who flocked there because 'Tonio pretended not to want them and pretended to give them a good dinner. There was a sprinkling of real Bohemians present who came for a change because they were tired of the real Bohemia, and a smart shower of the men who originate the bright sayings of Congressmen and the little nephew of the well-known general passenger agent of the Evansville and Terre Haute Railroad Company.

Here is a bon mot that was manufactured at 'Tonio's:

"A dinner at 'Tonio's," said a Bohemian, "always amounts to twice the price that is asked for it."

Let us assume that an accommodating voice inquires:

"How so?"

"The dinner costs you 40 cents; you give 10 cents to the waiter, and it makes you feel like 30 cents."

Most of the diners were confirmed table d'hôters—gastronomic adventurers, for ever seeking the El Dorado of a good claret, and consistently coming to grief in California.

Mr. Brunelli escorted Katy to a little table embowered with shrubbery in tubs, and asked her to excuse him for a while.

Katy sat, enchanted by a scene so brilliant to her. The grand ladies, in splendid dresses and plumes and sparkling rings; the fine gentlemen who laughed so loudly, the cries of "Garsong!" and "We, monseer," and "Hello, Mame!" that distinguish Bohemia; the lively chatter, the cigarette smoke, the interchange of bright smiles and eye-glances—all this display and magnificence overpowered the daughter of Mrs. Dempsey and held her motionless.

Mr. Brunelli stepped into the yard, and seemed to spread his smile and bow over the entire company. And everywhere there was a great clapping of hands and a few cries of "Bravo!" and "'Tonio! 'Tonio!" whatever those words might mean. Ladies waved their napkins at him, gentlemen almost twisted their necks off, trying to catch his nod.

When the ovation was concluded Mr. Brunelli, with a final bow, stepped nimbly into the kitchen and flung off his coat and waistcoat.

Flaherty, the nimblest "garsong" among the waiters, had been assigned to the special service of Katy. She was a little faint from hunger, for the Irish stew on the Dempsey table had been particularly weak that day. Delicious odours from unknown dishes tantalized her. And Flaherty began to bring to her table course after course of ambrosial food that the gods might have pronounced excellent.

But even in the midst of her Lucullian repast Katy laid down her knife and fork. Her heart sank as lead, and a tear fell upon her filet mignon. Her haunting suspicions of the star lodger arose again, fourfold. Thus courted and admired and smiled upon by that fashionable and gracious assembly, what else could Mr. Brunelli be but one of those dazzling titled patricians, glorious of name but shy of rent money, concerning whom experience had made her wise? With a sense of his ineligibility growing within her, there was mingled a torturing conviction that his personality was becoming more pleasing to her day by day. And why had he left her to dine alone?

But here he was coming again, now coatless, his snowy shirt-sleeves rolled high above his Jeffriesonian elbows, a white yachting cap perched upon his jetty curls.

"'Tonio! 'Tonio!" shouted many, and "The spaghetti! The spaghetti!" shouted the rest.

Never at 'Tonio's did a waiter dare to serve a dish of spaghetti until 'Tonio came to test it, to prove the sauce, and add the needful dash of seasoning that gave it perfection.

From table to table moved 'Tonio, like a prince in his palace, greeting his guests. White, jewelled hands signalled him from every side.

A glass of wine with this one and that, smiles for all, a jest and repartee for any that might challenge—truly few princes could be so agreeable a host! And what artist could ask for further appreciation of his handiwork? Katy did not know that the proudest consummation of a New Yorker's ambition is to shake hands with a spaghetti chef or to receive a nod from a Broadway head waiter.

At last the company thinned, leaving but a few couples and quartet lingering over new wine and old stories. And then came Mr. Brunelli to Katy's secluded table, and drew a chair close to hers.

Katy smiled at him dreamily. She was eating the last spoonful of a raspberry roll with Burgundy sauce.

"You have seen!" said Mr. Brunelli, laying one hand upon his collar-bone. "I am Antonio Brunelli! Yes; I am the great 'Tonio! You have not suspect that! I loave you, Katy, and you shall marry with me. Is it not so? Call me 'Antonio,' and say that you will be mine."

Katy's head drooped to the shoulder that was now freed from all suspicion of having received the knightly accolade.

"Oh, Andy," she sighed, "this is great! Sure, I'll marry wid ye. But why didn't ye tell me ye was the cook? I was near turnin' ye down for bein' one of thim foreign counts!"

LIII: THE GREEN DOOR

SUPPOSE you should be walking down Broadway after dinner with the ten minutes allotted to the consummation of your cigar while you are choosing between a diverting tragedy and something serious in the way of vaudeville. Suddenly a hand is laid upon your arm. You turn to look into the thrilling eyes of a beautiful woman, wonderful in diamonds and Russian sables. She thrusts hurriedly into your hand an extremely hot buttered roll, flashes out a tiny pair of scissors, snips off the second button of your overcoat, meaningly ejaculates the one word "parallelogram!" and swiftly flies down a cross-street, looking back fearfully over her shoulder.

That would be pure adventure. Would you accept it? Not you. You would flush with embarrassment; you would sheepishly drop the roll and continue down Broadway, fumbling feebly for the missing button. This you would do unless you are one of the blessed few in whom the pure spirit of adventure is not dead.

True adventurers have never been plentiful. They who are set down in print as such have been mostly business men with newly invented methods. They have been out after the things they wanted—golden fleeces, holy grails, lady-loves, treasure, crowns and fame. The true adventurer goes forth aimless and uncalculating to meet and greet unknown fate. A fine example was the Prodigal Son—when he started back home.

Half-adventurers—brave and splendid figures—have been numerous. From the Crusades to the Palisades they have enriched the arts of history and fiction and the trade of historical fiction. But each of them had a prize to win, a goal to kick, an axe to grind, a race to run, a new thrust in tierce to deliver, a name to carve, a crow to pick—so they were not followers of true adventure.

In the big city the twin spirits Romance and Adventure are always abroad seeking worthy wooers. As we roam the streets they slyly peep at us and challenge us in twenty different guises. Without knowing why, we look up suddenly to see in a window a face that seems to belong to our gallery of intimate portraits; in a sleeping thoroughfare we hear a cry of agony and fear coming from an empty and shuttered house; instead of at our familiar curb a cab-driver deposits us before a strange door, which one, with a smile, opens for us and bids us enter; a slip of paper, written upon, flutters down to our feet from the high lattices of Chance; we exchange glances of instantaneous hate, affection and fear with hurrying strangers in the passing crowds; a sudden souse of rain—and our umbrella may be sheltering the daughter of the Full Moon and first cousin of the Sidereal System; at every corner handkerchiefs drop, fingers beckon, eyes besiege, and the lost, the lonely, the rapturous, the mysterious, the perilous, changing clues of adventure are slipped into our fingers. But few of us are willing to hold and follow them. We are grown stiff with the ramrod of convention down our backs. We pass on; and some day we come, at the end of a very dull life, to reflect that our romance has been a pallid thing of a marriage or two, a satin rosette kept in a safe-deposit drawer, and a lifelong feud with a steam radiator.

Rudolf Steiner was a true adventurer. Few are the evenings on which he did not go forth from his hall bedchamber in search of the unexpected and the egregious. The most interesting thing in life seemed to him to be what might lie just around the next corner. Sometimes his willingness to tempt fate led him into strange paths. Twice he had spent the night in a station-house; again and again he had found himself the dupe of ingenious and mercenary tricksters; his watch and money had been the price of one flattering allurement. But with undiminished ardour he picked up every glove cast before him into the merry lists of adventure.

One evening Rudolf was strolling along a cross-town street in the older central part of the city. Two streams of people filled the sidewalks—the home-hurrying, and that restless contingent that abandons home for the specious welcome of the thousand-candle-power table d'hôte.

The young adventurer was of pleasing presence, and moved serenely and watchfully. By daylight he was a salesman in a piano store. He wore his tie drawn through a topaz ring instead of fastened with a stick pin; and once he had written to the editor of a magazine that *Junie's Love Test*, by Miss Libbey, had been the book that had most influenced his life.

During his walk a violent chattering of teeth in a glass case on the sidewalk seemed at first to draw his attention (with a qualm) to a restaurant before which it was set; but a second glance revealed the electric letters of a dentist's sign high above the next door. A giant negro, fantastically dressed in a red embroidered coat, yellow trousers and a military cap, discreetly distributed cards to those of the passing crowd who consented to take them.

This mode of dentistic advertising was a common sight to Rudolf. Usually he passed the dispenser of the dentist's cards without reducing his store; but to-night the African slipped one into his hands so deftly that he retained it there, smiling a little at the successful feat.

When he had travelled a few yards further he

glanced at the card indifferently. Surprised, he turned it over and looked again with interest. One side of the card was blank; on the other was written in ink three words, "The Green Door." And then Rudolf saw, three steps in front of him, a man throw down the card the negro had given him as he passed. Rudolf picked it up. It was printed with the dentist's name and address and the usual schedule of "plate work" and "bridge work" and "crowns," and specious promises of "painless" operations.

The adventurous piano salesman halted at the corner and considered. Then he crossed the street, walked down a block, recrossed and joined the upward current of people again. Without seeming to notice the negro as he passed the second time, he carelessly took the card that was handed him. Ten steps away he inspected it. In the same handwriting that appeared on the first card "The Green Door" was inscribed upon it. Three or four cards were tossed to the pavement by pedestrians both following and leading him. These fell blank side up. Rudolf turned them over. Every one bore the printed legend of the dental "parlours."

Rarely did the arch-sprite Adventure need to beckon twice to Rudolf Steiner, his true follower. But twice it had been done, and the quest was on.

Rudolf walked slowly back to where the giant negro stood by the case of rattling teeth. This time as he passed he received no card. In spite of his gaudy and ridiculous garb, the Ethiopian displayed a natural barbaric dignity as he stood, offering the cards suavely to some, allowing others to pass unmolested. Every half-minute he chanted a harsh, unintelligible phrase akin to the jabber of car conductors and grand opera. And not only did he withhold a card this time, but it seemed to Rudolf that he received from the shining and massive black countenance a look of cold, almost contemptuous disdain.

The look stung the adventurer. He read in it a silent accusation that he had been found wanting. Whatever the mysterious written words on the cards might mean, the black had selected him twice from the throng for their recipient; and now seemed to have condemned him as deficient in the wit and spirit to engage the enigma.

Standing aside from the rush, the young man made a rapid estimate of the building in which he conceived that his adventure must lie. Five stories high it rose. A small restaurant occupied the basement.

The first floor, now closed, seemed to house millinery or furs. The second floor, by the winking electric letters, was the dentist's. Above this a polyglot babel of signs struggled to indicate the abodes of palmists, dressmakers, musicians and doctors. Still higher up draped curtains and milk bottles white on the window-sills proclaimed the regions of domesticity.

After concluding his survey Rudolf walked briskly up the high flight of stone steps into the house. Up two flights of the carpeted stairway he continued; and at its top paused. The hallway there was dimly lighted by two pale jets of gas—one far to his right, the other nearer, to his left. He looked toward the nearer light and saw, within its wan halo, a green door. For one moment he hesitated; then he seemed to see the contumelious sneer of the African juggler of cards; and then he walked straight to the green door and knocked against it.

Moments like those that passed before his knock was answered measure the quick breath of true adventure. What might not be behind those green panels! Gamesters at play; cunning rogues baiting their traps with subtle skill; beauty in love with courage, and thus planning to be sought by it; danger, death, love, disappointment, ridicule—any of these might respond to that temerarious rap.

A faint rustle was heard inside, and the door slowly opened. A girl not yet twenty stood there, white-faced and tottering. She loosed the knob and swayed weakly, groping with one hand. Rudolf caught her and laid her on a faded couch that stood against the wall. He closed the door and took a swift glance around the room by the light of a flickering gas-jet. Neat but extreme poverty was the story that he read.

The girl lay still, as if in a faint. Rudolf looked around the room excitedly for a barrel. People must be rolled upon a barrel who—no, no; that was for drowned persons. He began to fan her with his hat. That was successful, for he struck her nose with the brim of his derby and she opened her eyes. And then the young man saw that hers, indeed, was the one missing face from his heart's gallery of intimate portraits. The frank grey eyes, the little nose, turning pertly outward; the chestnut hair, curling like the tendrils of a pea vine, seemed the right end and reward of all his wonderful adventures. But the face was woefully thin and pale.

The girl looked at him calmly, and then smiled.

"Fainted, didn't I?" she asked weakly. "Well,

who wouldn't? You try going without anything to eat for three days and see!"

"Himmel!" exclaimed Rudolf, jumping up. "Wait till I come back."

He dashed out the green door and down the stairs. In twenty minutes he was back again, kicking at the door with his toe for her to open it. With both arms he hugged an array of wares from the grocery and the restaurant. On the table he laid them—bread and butter, cold meats, cakes, pies, pickles, oysters, a roasted chicken, a bottle of milk and one of red-hot tea.

"This is ridiculous," said Rudolf blusteringly, "to go without eating. You must quit making election bets of this kind. Supper is ready." He helped her to a chair at the table and asked: "Is there a cup for the tea?" "On the shelf by the window," she answered. When he turned again with the cup he saw her, with eyes shining rapturously, beginning upon a huge Dill pickle that she had rooted out from the paper bags with a woman's unerring instinct. He took it from her, laughingly, and poured the cup full of milk. "Drink that first," he ordered, "and then you shall have some tea, and then a chicken wing. If you are very good you shall have a pickle to-morrow. And, now, if you'll allow me to be your guest we'll have supper."

He drew up the other chair. The tea brightened the girl and brought back some of her colour. She began to eat with a sort of dainty ferocity like some starved wild animal. She seemed to regard the young man's presence and the aid he had rendered her as a natural thing—not as though she undervalued the conventions; but as one whose great stress gave her the right to put aside the artificial for the human. But gradually, with the return of strength and comfort, came also a sense of the little conventions that belong; and she began to tell him her little story. It was one of a thousand such as the city yawns at every day—the shop-girl's story of insufficient wages, further reduced by "fines" that go to swell the store's profits; of time lost through illness; and then of lost positions, lost hope, and—the knock of the adventurer upon the green door.

But to Rudolf the history sounded as big as the Iliad or the crisis in *Junie's Love Test*.

"To think of you going through all that," he exclaimed.

"It was something fierce," said the girl solemnly.

"And you have no relatives or friends in the city?"

"None whatever."

"I am all alone in the world, too," said Rudolf, after a pause.

"I am glad of that," said the girl promptly; and somehow it pleased the young man to hear that she approved of his bereft condition.

Very suddenly her eyelids dropped and she sighed deeply.

"I'm awfully sleepy," she said, "and I feel so good."

Rudolf rose and took his hat.

"Then I'll say good night. A long night's sleep will be fine for you."

He held out his hand, and she took it and said "good night." But her eyes asked a question so eloquently, so frankly and pathetically, that he answered it with words.

"Oh, I'm coming back to-morrow to see how you are getting along. You can't get rid of me so easily."

Then, at the door, as though the way of his coming had been so much less important than the fact that he had come, she asked: "How did you come to knock at my door?"

He looked at her for a moment, remembering the cards, and felt a sudden jealous pain. What if they had fallen into other hands as adventurous as his? Quickly he decided that she must never know the truth. He would never let her know that he was aware of the strange expedient to which she had been driven by her great distress.

"One of our piano tuners lives in this house," he said. "I knocked at your door by mistake."

The last thing he saw in the room before the green door closed was her smile.

At the head of the stairway he paused and looked curiously about him. And then he went along the hallway to its other end; and, coming back, ascended to the floor above and continued his puzzled explorations. Every door that he found in the house was painted green.

Wondering, he descended to the sidewalk. The fantastic African was still there. Rudolf confronted him with his two cards in his hand.

"Will you tell me why you gave me these cards and what they mean?" he asked.

In a broad, good-natured grin the negro exhibited a splendid advertisement of his master's profession.

"Dar it is, boss," he said, pointing down the street. "But I 'spect you is a little late for de fust act."

Looking the way he pointed, Rudolf saw above the entrance to a theatre the blazing electric sign of its new play, "The Green Door."

"I'm informed dat it's a fust-rate show, sah," said the negro. "De agent what represents it pussented me with a dollar, sah, to distribute a few of his cards along with de doctah's. May I offer you one of de doctah's cards, sah?"

At the corner of the block in which he lived Rudolf stopped for a glass of beer and a cigar. When he had come out with his lighted weed he buttoned his coat, pushed back his hat, and said, stoutly, to the lamp-post on the corner:

"All the same, I believe it was the hand of Fate that doped out the way for me to find her."

Which conclusion, under the circumstances, certainly admits Rudolf Steiner to the ranks of the true followers of Romance and Adventure.

LIV: HE ALSO SERVES

IF I could have a thousand years—just one little thousand years—more of life, I might, in that time, draw near enough to true Romance to touch the hem of her robe.

Up from ships men come, and from waste places and forest and road and garret and cellar to maunder to me in strangely distributed words of the things they have seen and considered. The recording of their tales is no more than a matter of ears and fingers. There are only two fates I dread—deafness and writer's cramp. The hand is yet steady; let the ear bear the blame if these printed words be not in the order they were delivered to me by Hunky Magee, true camp-follower of fortune.

Biography shall claim you but an instant—I first knew Hunky when he was head-waiter at Chubb's little beefsteak restaurant and café on Third Avenue. There was only one waiter besides.

Then, successively, I caromed against him in the little streets of the Big City after his trip to Alaska, his voyage as cook with a treasure-seeking expedition to the Caribbean, and his failure as a pearl-fisher in the Arkansas River. Between these dashes into the land of adventure he usually came back to Chubb's for awhile. Chubb's was a port for him when gales blew too high; but when you dined there and Hunky went for your steak you never knew whether he would come to anchor in the kitchen or in the Malayan Archipelago. You wouldn't care for his description—he was soft of voice and hard of face, and rarely had to use more than one eye to quell any approach to a disturbance among Chubb's customers.

One night I found Hunky standing at a corner of Twenty-third Street and Third Avenue after an absence of several months. In ten minutes we had a little round table between us in a quiet corner, and my ears began to get busy. I leave out my sly ruses and feints to draw Hunky's word-of-mouth blows—it all came to something like this:

"Speaking of the next election," said Hunky, "did you ever know much about Indians? No? I don't mean the Cooper, Beadle, cigar-store, or Laughing Water kind—I mean the modern Indian—the kind that takes Greek prizes in colleges and scalps the half-back on the other side in football games. The kind that eats macaroons and tea in the afternoons with the daughter of the professor of biology, and fills up on grasshoppers and fried rattlesnake when they get back to the ancestral wickiup.

"Well, they ain't so bad. I like 'em better than most foreigners that have come over in the last few hundred years. One thing about the Indian is this: when he mixes with the white race he swaps all his own vices for them of the pale-faces—and he retains all his own virtues. Well, his virtues are enough to call out the reserves whenever he lets 'em loose. But the imported foreigners adopt our virtues and keep their own vices—and it's going to take our whole standing army some day to police that gang.

"But let me tell you about the trip I took to Mexico with High Jack Snakefeeder, a Cherokee twice removed, a graduate of a Pennsylvania college and the latest thing in pointed-toed, rubber-heeled, patent kid moccasins and Madras hunting-shirt with turned-back cuffs. He was a friend of mine. I met him in Tahlequah when I was out there during the land boom, and we got thick. He had got all there was out of colleges and had come back to lead his people out of Egypt. He was a man of first-class style and wrote essays, and had been invited to visit rich guys' houses in Boston and such places.

"There was a Cherokee girl in Muscogee that High Jack was foolish about. He took me to see her a few times. Her name was Florence Blue Feather—but you want to clear your mind of all ideas of squaws with nose-rings and army-blankets. This young lady was whiter than you are, and better educated than I ever was. You couldn't have told her from any of the girls shopping in the swell

Third Avenue stores. I liked her so well that I got to calling on her now and then when High Jack wasn't along, which is the way of friends in such matters. She was educated at the Muscogee College, and was making a speciality of—let's see —eth—yes, ethnology. That's the art that goes back and traces the descent of different races of people, leading up from jellyfish through monkeys and to the O'Briens. High Jack had took up that line too, and had read papers about it before all kinds of riotous assemblies—Chautauquas and Choctaws and chowder-parties, and such. Having a mutual taste for musty information like that was what made 'em like each other, I suppose. But I don't know! What they call congeniality of tastes ain't always it. Now, when Miss Blue Feather and me was talking together, I listened to her affidavits about the first families of the Land of Nod being cousins german (well, if the Germans don't nod, who does?) to the mound-builders of Ohio with incomprehension and respect. And when I'd tell her about the Bowery and Coney Island, and sing her a few songs that I'd heard the Jamaica niggers sing at their church lawn-parties, she didn't look much less interested than she did when High Jack would tell her that he had a pipe that the first inhabitants of America originally arrived here on stilts after a freshet at Tenafly, New Jersey.

"But I was going to tell you more about High Jack.

"About six months ago I get a letter from him, saying he'd been commissioned by the Minority Report Bureau of Ethnology at Washington to go down to Mexico and translate some excavations or dig up the meaning of some shorthand notes on some ruins—or something of that sort. And if I'd go along he could squeeze the price into the expense account.

"Well, I'd been holding a napkin over my arm at Chubb's about long enough then, so I wired High Jack 'Yes'; and he sent me a ticket, and I met him in Washington, and he had a lot of news to tell me. First of all was that Florence Blue Feather had suddenly disappeared from her home and environments.

" 'Run away?' I asked.

" 'Vanished,' says High Jack. 'Disappeared like your shadow when the sun goes under a cloud. She was seen on the street, and then she turned a corner and nobody ever seen her afterward. The whole community turned out to look for her, but we never found a clue.'

" 'That's bad—that's bad,' says I. 'She was a mighty nice girl, and as smart as you find 'em.'

"High Jack seemed to take it hard. I guess he must have esteemed Miss Blue Feather quite highly. I could see that he referred the matter to the whisky-jug. That was his weak point—and many another man's. I've noticed that when a man loses a girl he generally takes to drink either just before or just after it happens.

"From Washington we railroaded it to New Orleans, and there took a tramp steamer bound for Belize. And a gale pounded us all down the Caribbean, and nearly wrecked us on the Yucatan coast opposite a little town without a harbour called Boca de Coacoyula. Suppose the ship had run against that name in the dark!

" 'Better fifty years of Europe than a cyclone

in the bay,' says High Jack Snakefeeder. So we get the captain to send us ashore in a dory when the squall seemed to cease from squalling.

"'We will find ruins here or make 'em,' says High. 'The Government doesn't care which we do. An appropriation is an appropriation.'

"Boca de Coacoyula was a dead town. Them biblical towns we read about—Tired and Siphon—after they was destroyed they must have looked like Forty-second Street and Broadway compared to this Boca place. It still claimed 1,300 inhabitants as estimated and engraved on the stone courthouse by the census-taker in 1597. The citizens were a mixture of Indians and other Indians; but some of 'em was light-coloured, which I was surprised to see. The town was huddled up on the shore, with woods so thick around it that a subpœna-server couldn't have reached a monkey ten yards away with the papers. We wondered what kept it from being annexed to Kansas; but we soon found out that it was Major Bing.

"Major Bing was the ointment around the fly. He had the cochineal, sarsaparilla, log-wood, annatto, hemp, and all other dye-woods and pure food adulteration concessions cornered. He had five-sixths of the Boca de Thingamajiggers working for him on shares. It was a beautiful graft. We used to brag about Morgan and E. H. and others of our wisest when I was in the provinces—but now no more. That peninsula has got our little country turned into a submarine without even the observation tower showing.

"Major Bing's idea was this: He had the population go forth into the forest and gather these products. When they brought 'em in he gave 'em one-fifth for their trouble. Sometimes they'd strike and demand a sixth. The Major always gave in to 'em.

"The Major had a bungalow so close on the sea that the nine-inch tide seeped through the cracks in the kitchen floor. Me and him and High Jack Snakefeeder sat on the porch and drank rum from noon till midnight. He said he had piled up $300,000 in New Orleans banks, and High and me could stay with him for ever if we would. But High Jack happened to think of the United States, and began to talk ethnology.

" 'Ruins!' says Major Bing. 'The woods are full of 'em. I don't know how far they date back, but they was here before I came.'

"High Jack asks what form of worship the citizens of that locality are addicted to.

" 'Why,' says the Major, rubbing his nose, 'I can't hardly say. I imagine it's infidel or Aztec or Nonconformist or something like that. There's a church here—a Methodist or some other kind—with a parson named Skidder. He claims to have converted the people to Christianity. He and me don't assimilate except on state occasions. I imagine they worship some kind of gods or idols yet. But Skidder says he has 'em in the fold.'

"A few days later High Jack and me, prowling around, strikes a plain path into the forest, and follows it a good four miles. Then a branch turns to the left. We go a mile, maybe, down that, and run up against the finest ruin you ever saw—solid stone with trees and vines and underbrush all growing up against it and in it and through it. All over it was chiselled carvings of funny beasts and people that would have been arrested if they'd ever come out in vaudeville that way. We approached it from the rear.

"High Jack had been drinking too much rum ever since we landed in Boca. You know how an Indian is—the palefaces fixed his clock when they introduced him to firewater. He'd brought a quart along with him.

" 'Hunky,' says he, 'we'll explore the ancient temple. It may be that the storm that landed us here was propitious. The Minority Report Bureau of Ethnology,' says he, 'may yet profit by the vagaries of wind and tide.'

"We went in the rear door of the bum edifice. We struck a kind of alcove without bath. There was a granite davenport, and a stone wash-stand without any soap or exit for the water, and some hardwood pegs drove into holes in the wall, and that was all. To go out of that furnished apartment into a Harlem hall bedroom would make you feel like getting back home from an amateur violoncello solo at an East Side Settlement house.

" While High was examining some hieroglyphics on the wall that the stone-masons must have made when their tools slipped, I stepped into the front room. That was at least thirty by fifty feet, stone floor, six little windows like square port-holes that didn't let much light in.

"I looked back over my shoulder, and sees High Jack's face three feet away.

" 'High,' says I, 'of all the——'

"And then I noticed he looked funny, and I turned around.

"He'd taken off his clothes to the waist, and he didn't seem to hear me. I touched him, and came near beating it. High Jack had turned to stone. I had been drinking some rum myself.

"'Ossified!' I says to him, loudly. 'I knew what would happen if you kept it up.'

"And then High Jack come in from the alcove when he hears me conversing with nobody, and we have a look at Mr. Snakefeeder No. 2. It's a stone idol, or god, or revised statute or something, and it looks as much like High Jack as one green pea looks like itself. It's got exactly his face and size and colour, but it's steadier on its pins. It stands on a kind of rostrum or pedestal, and you can see it's been there ten million years.

"'He's a cousin of mine,' sings High, and then he turns solemn.

"'Hunky,' he says, putting one hand on my shoulder and one on the statue's, 'I'm in the holy temple of my ancestors.'

"'Well, if looks goes for anything,' says I, 'you've struck a twin. Stand side by side with buddy, and let's see if there's any difference.'

"There wasn't. You know an Indian can keep his face as still as an iron dog's when he wants to, so when High Jack froze his features you couldn't have told him from the other one.

"'There's some letters,' says I, 'on his nob's pedestal, but I can't make 'em out. The alphabet of this country seems to be composed of sometimes *a*, *e*, *i*, *o*, and *u*, generally, *z's*, *l's*, and *t's*.'

"High Jack's ethnology gets the upper hand of his rum for a minute, and he investigates the inscription.

"'Hunky,' says he, 'this is a statue of Tlotopaxl, one of the most powerful gods of the ancient Aztecs.'

" 'Glad to know him,' says I, 'but in his present condition he reminds me of the joke Shakespeare got off on Julius Cæsar. We might say about your friend:

" 'Imperious What's his-name, dead and turned to stone—
No use to write or call him on the 'phone.'

" 'Hunky,' says High Jack Snakefeeder, looking at me funny, 'do you believe in reincarnation?'

" 'It sounds to me,' says I, 'like either a clean-up of the slaughter-houses or a new kind of Boston pink. I don't know.'

" 'I believe,' says he, 'that I am the reincarnation of Tlotopaxl. My researches have convinced me that the Cherokees, of all the North American tribes, can boast of the straightest descent from the proud Aztec race. That,' says he, 'was a favourite theory of mine and Florence Blue Feather's. And she—what if she——'

"High Jack grabs my arm and walls his eyes at me. Just then he looked more like his eminent co-Indian murderer, Crazy Horse.

" 'Well,' says I, 'what if she, what if she, what if she? You're drunk,' says I. 'Impersonating idols and believing in—what was it?—recarnalization? Let's have a drink,' says I. 'It's as spooky here as a Brooklyn artificial-limb factory at midnight with the gas turned down.'

"Just then I heard somebody coming, and I dragged High Jack into the bedless bed-chamber. There was peepholes bored through the wall, so we could see the whole front part of the temple. Major Bing told me afterward that the ancient priests in charge used to rubber through them at the congregation.

"In a few minutes an old Indian woman came in with a big oval earthen dish full of grub. She set it on a square block of stone in front of the graven image, and laid down and walloped her face on the floor a few times, and then took a walk for herself.

"High Jack and me was hungry, so we came out and looked it over. There was goat steaks and fried rice-cakes, and plantains and cassava, and broiled land-crabs and mangoes—nothing like what you get at Chubb's.

"We ate hearty—and had another round of rum.

" 'It must be old Tecumseh's—or whatever you call him—birthday,' says I. 'Or do they feed him every day? I thought gods only drank vanilla on Mount Catawampus.'

"Then some more native parties in short kimonos that showed their aboriginees punctured the near-horizon, and me and High had to skip back into Father Axletree's private boudoir. They came by ones, twos, and threes, and left all sorts of offerings—there was enough grub for Binham's nine gods of war, with plenty left over for the Peace Conference at The Hague. They brought jars of honey, and bunches of bananas, and bottles of wine, and stacks of tortillas, and beautiful shawls worth one hundred dollars apiece that the Indian women weave of a kind of vegetable fibre like silk. All of 'em got down and wriggled on the floor in front of that hard-finish god, and then sneaked off through the woods again.

" 'I wonder who gets this rake-off?' remarks High Jack.

" 'Oh,' says I, 'there's priests or deputy idols or a committee of disarrangements somewhere in the woods on the job. Wherever you find a god you'll find somebody waiting to take charge of the burnt offerings.'

"And then we took another swig of rum and walked out to the parlour front door to cool off, for it was as hot inside as a summer camp on the Palisades.

"And while we stood there in the breeze we looks down the path and sees a young lady approaching the blasted ruin. She was bare-footed and had on a white robe, and carried a wreath of white flowers in her hand. When she got nearer we saw she had a long blue feather stuck through her black hair. And when she got nearer still me and High Jack Snakefeeder grabbed each other to keep from tumbling down on the floor; for the girl's face was as much like Florence Blue Feather's as his was like old King Toxicology's.

"And then was when High Jack's booze drowned his system of ethnology. He dragged me inside back of the statue, and says:

" 'Lay hold of it, Hunky. We'll pack it into the other room. I felt it all the time,' says he. 'I'm the reconsideration of the god Locomotor-ataxia, and Florence Blue Feather was my bride a thousand years ago. She has come to seek me in the temple where I used to reign.'

" 'All right,' says I. 'There's no use arguing against the rum question. You take his feet.'

"We lifted the three-hundred-pound stone god, and carried him into the back room of the café—the temple, I mean—and leaned him against the wall. It was more work than bouncing three live ones from an all-night Broadway joint on New-Year's Eve.

"Then High Jack ran out and brought in a couple of them Indian silk shawls and began to undress himself.

" 'Oh, figs!' says I. 'Is it thus? Strong drink is an adder and subtractor, too. Is it the heat or the call of the wild that's got you?'

"But High Jack is too full of exaltation and cane-juice to reply. He stops the disrobing business just short of the Manhattan Beach rules, and then winds them red-and-white shawls around him, and goes out and stands on the pedestal as steady as any platinum deity you ever saw. And I looks through a peek-hole to see what he is up to.

"In a few minutes in comes the girl with the flower wreath. Danged if I wasn't knocked a little silly when she got close, she looked so exactly much like Florence Blue Feather. 'I wonder,' says I to myself, 'if she has been reincarcerated, too? If I could see,' says I to myself, 'whether she has a mole on her left——' But the next minute I thought she looked one-eighth of a shade darker than Florence; but she looked good at that. And High Jack hadn't drunk all the rum that had been drank.

"The girl went up within ten feet of the bum idol, and got down and massaged her nose with the floor, like the rest did. Then she went nearer and laid the flower wreath on the block of stone at High Jack's feet. Rummy as I was, I thought it was kind of nice of her to think of offering flowers instead of household and kitchen provisions. Even a stone god ought to appreciate a little sentiment like that on top of the fancy groceries they had piled up in front of him.

"And then High Jack steps down from his

pedestal, quiet, and mentions a few words that sounded just like the hieroglyphics carved on the walls of the ruin. The girl gives a little jump backward, and her eyes fly open as big as doughnuts; but she don't beat it.

"Why didn't she? I'll tell you why I think why. It don't seem to a girl so supernatural, unlikely, strange, and startling that a stone god should come to life for *her*. If he was to do it for one of them snub-nosed brown girls on the other side of the woods, now, it would be different—but *her*! I'll bet she said to herself: 'Well, goodness me! you've been a long time getting on your job. I've half a mind not to speak to you.'

"But she and High Jack holds hands and walks away out of the temple together. By the time I'd had time to take another drink and enter upon the scene they was twenty yards away, going up the path in the woods that the girl had come down. With the natural scenery already in place, it was just like a play to watch 'em—she looking up at him, and him giving her back the best that an Indian can hand out in the way of a goo-goo eye. But there wasn't anything in that recarnification and revulsion to tintype for me.

" 'Hey! Injun!' I yells out to High Jack. 'We've got a board-bill due in town, and you're leaving me without a cent. Brace up and cut out the Neapolitan fisher-maiden, and let's go back home.'

"But on the two goes without looking once back until, as you might say, the forest swallowed 'em up. And I never saw or heard of High Jack Snakefeeder from that day to this. I don't know if the Cherokees came from the Aspics; but if they did, one of 'em went back.

"All I could do was to hustle back to that Boca place and panhandle Major Bing. He detached himself from enough of his winnings to buy me a ticket home. And I'm back again on the job at Chubb's, sir, and I'm going to hold it steady. Come round, and you'll find the steaks as good as ever."

I wondered what Hunky Magee thought about his own story; so I asked him if he had any theories about reincarnation and transmogrification and such mysteries as he had touched upon.

"Nothing like that," said Hunky, positively. "What ailed High Jack was too much booze and education. They'll do an Indian up every time."

"But what about Miss Blue Feather?" I persisted.

"Say," said Hunky, with a grin, "that little lady that stole High Jack certainly did give mc a jar when I first took a look at her, but it was only for a minute. You remember I told you High Jack said that Miss Florence Blue Feather disappeared from home about a year ago? Well, where she landed four days later was in as neat a five-room flat on East Twenty-third Street as you ever walked sideways through—and she's been Mrs. Magee ever since."

LV: HYGEIA AT THE SOLITO

IF you are knowing in the chronicles of the ring, you will recall to mind an event in the early 'nineties when, for a minute and sundry odd seconds, a champion and a "would-be" faced each other on the alien side of an international river. So brief a conflict had rarely imposed upon the fair promise of true sport. The reporters made what they could of it, but, divested of padding, the action was sadly fugacious. The champion merely smote his victim, turned his back upon him, remarking, "I know what I done to dat stiff," and extended an arm like a ship's mast for his glove to be removed.

Which accounts for a trainload of extremely disgusted gentlemen in an uproar of fancy vests and neckwear being spilled from their Pullmans in San Antonio in the early morning following the fight. Which also partly accounts for the unhappy predicament in which "Cricket" McGuire found himself as he tumbled from his car and sat upon the depôt platform, torn by a spasm of that hollow, racking cough so familiar to San Antonian ears. At that time, in the uncertain light of dawn, that way passed Curtis Raidler, the Nueces County cattleman—may his shadow never measure under six feet two.

The cattleman, out thus early to catch the southbound for his ranch station, stopped at the side of the distressed patron of sport, and spoke in the kindly drawl of his ilk and region, "Got it pretty bad, bud?"

"Cricket" McGuire, ex-feather-weight prizefighter, tout, jockey, follower of the "ponies," allround sport, and manipulator of the gum balls and walnut shells, looked up pugnaciously at the imputation cast by "bud."

"G'wan," he rasped, "telegraph pole. I didn't ring for yer."

Another paroxysm wrung him, and he leaned limply against a convenient baggage truck. Raidler waited patiently, glancing around at the white hats, short overcoats, and big cigars thronging the platform. "You're from the No'th, ain't you, bud?" he asked when the other was partially recovered. "Come down to see the fight?"

"Fight!" snapped McGuire. "Puss-in-the corner! 'Twas a hypodermic injection. Handed him just one like a squirt of dope, and he's asleep, and no tan-bark needed in front of his residence. Fight!" He rattled a bit, coughed, and went on, hardly addressing the cattleman, but rather for the relief of voicing his troubles. "No more dead sure t'ings for me. But Rus Sage himself would have snatched at it. Five to one dat de boy from Cork wouldn't stay t'ree rounds is what I invested in. Put my last cent on, and could already smell the sawdust in dat all-night joint of Jimmy Delaney's on T'irty-seventh Street I was goin' to buy. And den—say, telegraph pole, what a gazaboo a guy is to put his whole roll on one turn of the gaboozlum!"

"You're plenty right," said the big cattleman; "more 'specially when you lose. Son, you get up and light out for a hotel. You got a mighty bad cough. Had it long?"

"Lungs," said McGuire comprehensively. "I got it. The croaker says I'll come to time for six months longer—maybe a year if I hold my gait. I wanted to settle down and take care of myself. Dat's why I speculated on dat five to one perhaps. I had a t'ousand iron dollars saved up. If I winned I was goin' to buy Delaney's café. Who'd a t'ought dat stiff would take a nap in de foist round —say?"

"It's a hard deal," commented Raidler, looking down at the diminutive form of McGuire crumpled against the truck. "But you go to a hotel and rest. There's the Menger and the Maverick, and——"

"And the Fi'th Av'noo, and the Waldorf-Astoria," mimicked McGuire. "Told you I went broke. I've got one dime left. Maybe a trip to Europe or a sail in me private yacht would fix me up—pa-per!"

He flung his dime at a newsboy, got his *Express*, propped his back against the truck, and was at once rapt in the account of his Waterloo, as expanded by the ingenious press.

Curtis Raidler interrogated an enormous gold watch, and laid his hand on McGuire's shoulder.

"Come on, bud," he said. "We got three minutes to catch the train."

Sarcasm seemed to be McGuire's vein.

"You ain't seen me cash in any chips or call a turn since I told you I was broke, a minute ago, have you? Friend, chase yourself away."

"You're going down to my ranch," said the cattle-man, "and stay till you get well. Six months'll fix you good as new." He lifted McGuire with one hand, and half dragged him in the direction of the train.

"What about the money?" said McGuire, struggling weakly to escape.

"Money for what?" asked Raidler, puzzled. They eyed each other, not understanding, for they touched only as at the gear of bevelled cog-wheels—at right angles, and moving upon different axles.

Passengers on the south-bound saw them seated together, and wondered at the conflux of two such antipodes. McGuire was five feet one, with a countenance belonging to either Yokohama or Dublin. Bright-beady of eye, bony of cheek and jaw, scarred, toughened, broken and reknit, indestructible, grisly, gladiatorial as a hornet, he was a type neither new nor unfamiliar. Raidler was the product of a different soil. Six feet two in height, miles broad, and no deeper than a crystal brook, he represented the union of the West and South. Few accurate pictures of his kind have been made, for art galleries are so small and the mutoscope is as yet unknown in Texas. After all, the only possible medium of portrayal of Raidler's kind would be the fresco—something high and simple and cool and unframed.

They were rolling southward on the International. The timber was huddling into little, dense green motts at rare distances before the inundation of the downright, vert prairies. This was the land of the ranchers; the domain of the kings of the kine.

McGuire sat, collapsed into his corner of the seat, receiving with acid suspicion the conversation of the cattleman. What was the "game" of this big "geezer" who was carrying him off? Altruism would have been McGuire's last guess. "He ain't no farmer," thought the captive, "and he ain't no con man, for sure. W'at's his lay? You trail in, Cricket, and see how many cards he draws. You're up against it, anyhow. You got a nickel and gallopin' consumption, and you better lay low. Lay low and see w'at's his game."

At Rincon, a hundred miles from San Antonio, they left the train for a buckboard which was waiting there for Raidler. In this they travelled the thirty miles between the station and their destination. If anything could, this drive should have stirred the acrimonious McGuire to a sense of his ransom. They sped upon velvety wheels across an exhilarant savanna. The pair of Spanish ponies struck a nimble, tireless trot, which gait they occasionally relieved by a wild, untrammelled gallop. The air was wine and seltzer, perfumed, as they absorbed it, with the delicate redolence of prairie flowers. The road perished, and the buckboard swam the uncharted billows of the grass itself, steered by the practised hand of Raidler, to whom each tiny distant mott of trees was a signboard, each convolution of the low hills a voucher of course and distance. But McGuire reclined upon his spine, seeing nothing but a desert, and receiving the cattleman's advances with sullen distrust. "W'at's he up to?" was the burden of his thoughts; "w'at kind of a gold brick has the big guy got to sell?" McGuire was only applying the measure of the streets he had walked to a range bounded by the horizon and the fourth dimension.

A week before, while riding the prairies, Raidler had come upon a sick and weakling calf deserted and bawling. Without dismounting he had reached and slung the distressed bossy across his saddle and dropped it at the ranch for the boys to attend to. It was impossible for McGuire to know or comprehend that, in the eyes of the cattleman, his case and that of the calf were identical in interest and demand upon his assistance. A creature was ill and helpless; he had the power to render aid—these were the only postulates required for the cattleman to act. They formed his system of logic and the most of his creed. McGuire was the seventh invalid whom Raidler had picked up thus casually in San Antonio, where so many thousands go for the ozone that is said to linger about its contracted streets. Five of them had been guests of Solito Ranch until they had been able to leave, cured or better, and exhausting the vocabulary of tearful gratitude. One came too late, but rested very comfortably, at last, under a ratama tree in the garden.

So, then, it was no surprise to the ranchhold when the buckboard spun to the door, and Raidler took up his debile *protégé* like a handful of rags and set him down upon the gallery.

McGuire looked upon things strange to him. The ranch-house was the best in the county. It was built of brick hauled one hundred miles by wagon, but it was of but one story, and its four rooms were completely encircled by a mud floor "gallery." The miscellaneous setting of horses, dogs, saddles, wagons, guns, and cowpunchers' paraphernalia oppressed the metropolitan eye of the wrecked sportsman.

"Well, here we are at home," said Raidler cheeringly.

"It's a h——l of a looking place," said McGuire promptly, as he rolled upon the gallery floor in a fit of coughing.

"We'll try to make it comfortable for you, buddy," said the cattleman gently. "It ain't fine inside; but it's the outdoors, anyway, that'll do you the most good. This'll be your room, in here. Anything we got, you ask for it."

He led McGuire into the east room. The floor was bare and clean. White curtains waved in the gulf breeze through the open windows. A big willow rocker, two straight chairs, a long table covered with newspapers, pipes, tobacco, spurs, and cartridges stood in the centre. Some well-mounted heads of deer and one of an enormous black javeli projected from the walls. A wide, cool cot-bed stood in a corner. Nueces County people regarded this guest chamber as fit for a prince. McGuire showed his eyeteeth at it. He took out his nickel and spun it up to the ceiling.

"T'ought I was lyin' about the money, did ye? Well, you can frisk me if you wanter. Dat's the last simoleon in the treasury. Who's goin' to pay?"

The cattleman's clear grey eyes looked steadily from under his grizzly brows into the huckleberry optics of his guest. After a little he said simply, and not ungraciously, "I'll be much obliged to you, son, if you won't mention money any more. Once was quite a plenty. Folks I ask to my ranch don't have to pay anything, and they very scarcely ever offers it. Supper'll be ready in half an hour. There's water in the pitcher, and some, cooler, to drink, in that red jar hanging on the gallery."

"Where's the bell?" asked McGuire, looking about.

"Bell for what?"

"Bell to ring for things. I can't—see here," he exploded in a sudden, weak fury, "I never asked you to bring me here. I never held you up for a cent. I never give you a hard-luck story till you asked me. Here I am fifty miles from a bell-boy or a cocktail. I'm sick. I can't hustle. Gee! but I'm up against it!" McGuire fell upon the cot and sobbed shiveringly.

Raidler went to the door and called. A slender, bright-complexioned Mexican youth about twenty came quickly. Raidler spoke to him in Spanish—

"Ylario, it is in my mind that I promised you the position of *vaquero* on the San Carlos range at the fall *rodea*."

"*Si*, *señor*, such was your goodness."

"Listen. This *señorito* is my friend. He is very sick. Place yourself at his side. Attend to his wants at all times. Have much patience and care with him. And when he is well, or—and when he is well, instead of *vaquero* I will make you *mayordomo* of the Rancho de las Piedras. *Esta bueno?*"

"*Si, si—mil gracias, señor.*" Ylario tried to kneel upon the floor in his gratitude, but the cattleman kicked at him benevolently, growling, "None of your opery-house antics, now."

Ten minutes later Ylario came from McGuire's room and stood before Raidler.

"The little *señor*," he announced, "presents his compliments" (Raidler credited Ylario with the preliminary) "and desires some pounded ice, one hot bath, one gin feez-z, that the windows be all closed, toast, one shave, one Newyorkheral', cigarettes, and to send one telegram."

Raidler took a quart bottle of whisky from his medicine cabinet. "Here, take him this," he said.

Thus was instituted the reign of terror at the Solito Ranch. For a few weeks McGuire blustered and boasted and swaggered before the cowpunchers who rode in for miles around to see this latest importation of Raidler's. He was an absolutely new experience to them. He explained to them all the intricate points of sparring and the tricks of training and defence. He opened to their minds' view all the indecorous life of a tagger after professional sports. His jargon of slang was a continuous joy and surprise to them. His gestures, his strange poses, his frank ribaldry of tongue and principle fascinated them. He was like a being from a new world.

Strange to say, this new world he had entered

did not exist to him. He was an utter egoist of bricks and mortar. He had dropped out, he felt, into open space for a time, and all it contained was an audience for his reminiscences. Neither the limitless freedom of the prairie days nor the grand hush of the close-drawn, spangled nights touched him. All the hues of Aurora could not win him from the pink pages of a sporting journal. "Get something for nothing," was his mission in life; "T'irty-seventh" Street was his goal.

Nearly two months after his arrival he began to complain that he felt worse. It was then that he became the ranch's incubus, its harpy, its Old Man of the Sea. He shut himself in his room like some venomous kobold or flibbertigibbet, whining, complaining, cursing, accusing. The keynote of his plaint was that he had been inveigled into a gehenna against his will; that he was dying of neglect and lack of comforts. With all his dire protestations of increasing illness, to the eyes of others he remained unchanged. His currant-like eyes were as bright and diabolic as ever; his voice was as rasping; his callous face, with the skin drawn tense as a drum-head, had no flesh to lose. A flush on his prominent cheek-bones each afternoon hinted that a clinical thermometer might have revealed a symptom, and percussion might have established the fact that McGuire was breathing with only one lung, but his appearance remained the same.

In constant attendance upon him was Ylario, whom the coming reward of the *mayordomo*ship must have greatly stimulated, for McGuire chained him to a bitter existence. The air—the man's only chance for life—he commanded to be kept out by closed windows and drawn curtains. The room was always blue and foul with cigarette smoke; whosoever entered it must sit, suffocating, and listen to the imp's interminable gasconade concerning his scandalous career.

The oddest thing of all was the relation existing between McGuire and his benefactor. The attitude of the invalid toward the cattleman was something like that of a peevish, perverse child toward an indulgent parent. When Raidler would leave the ranch McGuire would fall into a fit of malevolent, silent sullenness. When he returned, he would be met by a string of violent and stinging reproaches. Raidler's attitude towards his charge was quite inexplicable in its way. The cattleman seemed actually to assume and feel the character assigned him by McGuire's intemperate accusations—the character of tyrant and guilty oppressor. He seemed to have adopted the responsibility of the fellow's condition, and he always met his tirades with a pacific, patient, and even remorseful kindness that never altered.

One day Raidler said to him, "Try more air, son. You can have the buckboard and a driver every day if you'll go. Try a week or two in one of the cow camps. I'll fix you up plum comfortable. The ground, and the air next to it—them's the things to cure you. I knowed a man from Philadelphy, sicker than you are, got lost on the Guadalupe, and slept on the bare grass in sheep camps for two weeks. Well, sir, it started him getting well, which he done. Close to the ground—that's where the medicine in the air stays. Try a little hossback riding now. There's a gentle pony——"

"What've I done to yer?" screamed McGuire. "Did I ever doublecross yer? Did I ask you to bring me here? Drive me out to yer camps if you wanter; or stick a knife in me and save trouble. Ride! I can't lift my feet. I couldn't sidestep a jab from a five-year-old kid. That's what your d——d ranch has done for me. There's nothing to eat, nothing to see, and nobody to talk to but a lot of Ruebens who don't know a punching bag from a lobster salad."

"It's a lonesome place, for certain," apologized Raidler abashedly. "We got plenty, but it's rough enough. Anything you think of you want, the boys'll ride up and fetch it down for you."

It was Chad Murchison, a cowpuncher from the Circle Bar outfit, who first suggested that McGuire's illness was fraudulent. Chad had brought a basket of grapes for him thirty miles, and four out of his way, tied to his saddle-horn. After remaining in the smoke-tainted room for a while, he emerged and bluntly confided his suspicions to Raidler.

"His arm," said Chad, "is harder'n a diamond. He interduced me to what he called a shore-per-plexus punch, and 'twas like being kicked twice by a mustang. He's playin' it low down on you, Curt. He ain't no sicker'n I am. I hate to say it, but the runt's workin' you for range and shelter."

The cattleman's ingenuous mind refused to entertain Chad's view of the case, and when, later, he came to apply the test, doubt entered not into his motives.

One day, about noon, two men drove up to the ranch, alighted, hitched, and came in to dinner; standing and general invitations being the custom of the country. One of them was a great San Antonio doctor, whose costly services had been engaged by a wealthy cowman who had been laid low by an accidental bullet. He was now being driven to the station to take the train back to town. After dinner Raidler took him aside, pushed a twenty-dollar bill against his hand, and said—

"Doc., there's a young chap in that room I guess has got a bad case of consumption. I'd like for you to look him over and see just how bad he is, and if we can do anything for him."

"How much was that dinner I just ate, Mr. Raidler?" said the doctor bluffly, looking over his spectacles. Raidler returned the money to his pocket. The doctor immediately entered McGuire's room, and the cattleman seated himself upon a heap of saddles on the gallery, ready to reproach himself in the event the verdict should be unfavourable.

In ten minutes the doctor came briskly out. "Your man," he said promptly, "is as sound as a new dollar. His lungs are better than mine. Respiration, temperature, and pulse normal. Chest expansion four inches. Not a sign of weakness anywhere. Of course I didn't examine for the bacillus, but it isn't there. You can put my name to the diagnosis. Even cigarettes and a vilely close room haven't hurt him. Coughs, does he? Well, you tell him it isn't necessary. You asked if there is anything we could do for him. Well, I advise you to set him digging postholes or breaking mustangs. There's our team ready. Good day, sir." And like a puff of wholesome, blustery wind the doctor was off.

Raidler reached out and plucked a leaf from a mesquite bush by the railing, and began chewing it thoughtfully.

The branding season was at hand, and the next

morning Ross Hargis, foreman of the outfit, was mustering his force of some twenty-five men at the ranch, ready to start for the San Carlos range, where the work was to begin. By six o'clock the horses were all saddled, the grub wagon ready, and the cowpunchers were swinging themselves upon their mounts, when Raidler bade them wait. A boy was bringing up an extra pony, bridled and saddled, to the gate. Raidler walked to McGuire's room, and threw open the door. McGuire was lying on his cot, not yet dressed, smoking.

"Get up," said the cattleman, and his voice was clear and brassy, like a bugle.

"How's that?" asked McGuire, a little startled.

"Get up and dress. I can stand a rattlesnake, but I hate a liar. Do I have to tell you again?" He caught McGuire by the neck and stood him on the floor.

"Say, friend," cried McGuire wildly, "are you mad? I'm sick—see? I'll croak if I got to hustle. What've I done to yer?"—he began his chronic whine—"I never asked yer to——"

"Put on your clothes," called Raidler in a rising tone.

Swearing, stumbling, shivering, keeping his amazed, shiny eyes upon the now menacing form of the aroused cattleman, McGuire managed to tumble into his clothes. Then Raidler took him by the collar and shoved him out and across the yard to the extra pony hitched at the gate. The cowpunchers lolled in their saddles, open-mouthed.

"Take this man," said Raidler to Ross Hargis, "and put him to work. Make him work hard, sleep hard, and eat hard. You boys know I done what I could for him, and he was welcome. Yesterday the best doctor in San Antone examined him, and says he's got the lungs of a burro and the constitution of a steer. You know what to do with him, Ross."

Ross Hargis only smiled grimly.

"Aw," said McGuire, looking intently at Raidler, with a peculiar expression upon his face, "the croaker said I was all right, did he? Said I was fakin', did he? You put him on to me. You t'ought I wasn't sick. You said I was a liar. Say, friend, I talked rough, I know, but I didn't mean most of it. If you felt like I did—aw! I forgot—I ain't sick, the croaker says. Well, friend, now I'll go work for yer. Here's where you play even."

He sprang into the saddle easily as a bird, got the quirt from the horn, and gave his pony a slash with it. "Cricket," who once brought in Good Boy by a neck at Hawthorne—and a 10 to 1 shot—had his foot in the stirrups again.

McGuire led the cavalcade as they dashed away for San Carlos, and the cowpunchers gave a yell of applause as they closed in behind his dust.

But in less than a mile he had lagged to the rear, and was last man when they struck the patch of high chaparral below the horse pens. Behind a clump of this he drew rein, and held a handkerchief to his mouth. He took it away drenched with bright, arterial blood, and threw it carefully into a clump of prickly pear. Then he slashed with his quirt again, gasped "G'wan" to his astonished pony, and galloped after the gang.

That night Raidler received a message from his old home in Alabama. There had been a death in the family; an estate was to divide, and they called for him to come. Daylight found him in the buckboard, skimming the prairies for the station. It was two months before he returned. When he arrived at the ranch-house he found it well-nigh deserted save for Ylario, who acted as a kind of steward during his absence. Little by little the youth made him acquainted with the work done while he was away. The branding camp, he was informed, was still doing business. On account of many severe storms the cattle had been badly scattered, and the branding had been accomplished but slowly. The camp was now in the valley of the Guadalupe, twenty miles away.

"By the way," said Raidler, suddenly remembering, "that fellow I sent along with them—McGuire—is he working yet?"

"I do not know," said Ylario. "Mans from the camp come verree few times to the ranch. So plentee work with the leetle calves. They no say. Oh, I think that fellow McGuire he dead much time ago."

"Dead!" said Raidler. "What you talking about?"

"Verree sick fellow, McGuire," replied Ylario, with a shrug of his shoulder. "I theenk he no live one, two month when he go away."

"Shucks!" said Raidler. "He humbugged you, too, did he? The doctor examined him and said he was sound as a mesquite knot."

"That doctor," said Ylario, smiling, "he tell you so? That doctor no see McGuire."

"Talk up," ordered Raidler. "What the devil do you mean?"

"McGuire," continued the boy tranquilly, "he getting drink water outside when that doctor come in room. That doctor take me and pound me all over here with his fingers"—putting his hand to his chest—"I not know for what. He put his ear here and here and here, and listen—I not know for what. He put little glass stick in my mouth. He feel my arm here. He make me count like whisper—so—twenty, *treinta*, *cuarenta*. Who knows," concluded Ylario, with a deprecating spread of his hands, "for what that doctor do those verree droll and such-like things?"

"What horses are up?" asked Raidler shortly.

"Paisano is grazing but behind the little corral, *señor*."

"Saddle him for me at once."

Within a very few minutes the cattleman was mounted and away. Paisano, well named after that ungainly but swift-running bird, struck into his long lope that ate up the road like a strip of macaroni. In two hours and a quarter Raidler, from a gentle swell, saw the branding camp by a water-hole in the Guadalupe. Sick with expectancy of the news he feared, he rode up, dismounted, and dropped Paisano's reins. So gentle was his heart that at that moment he would have pleaded guilty to the murder of McGuire.

The only being in the camp was the cook, who was just arranging the hunks of barbecued beef, and distributing the tin coffee cups for supper. Raidler evaded a direct question concerning the one subject in his mind.

"Everything all right in camp, Pete?" he managed to inquire.

"So, so," said Pete conservatively. "Grub give out twice. Wind scattered the cattle, and we've had to rake the brush for forty mile. I need a new coffee-pot. And the mosquitoes is some more hellish than common."

"The boys—all well?"

Pete was no optimist. Besides, inquiries concerning the health of cow-punchers were not only superfluous, but bordered on flaccidity. It was not like the boss to make them.

"What's left of 'em don't miss no calls to grub," the cook conceded.

"What's left of 'em?" repeated Raidler in a husky voice. Mechanically he began to look around for McGuire's grave. He had in his mind a white slab such as he had seen in the Alabama churchyard. But immediately he knew that was foolish.

"Sure," said Pete; "what's left. Cow camps change in two months. Some's gone."

Raidler nerved himself.

"That—chap—I sent along—McGuire—did—he——"

"Say," interrupted Pete, rising with a chunk of corn bread in each hand, "that was a dirty shame, sending that poor, sick kid to a cow camp. A doctor that couldn't tell he was graveyard meat ought to be skinned with a cinch buckle. Game as he was, too—it's a scandal among snakes—lemme tell you what he done. First night in camp the boys started to initiate him in the leather breeches degree. Ross Hargis busted him one swipe with his chaparreras, and what do you reckon the poor child did? Got up, the little skeeter, and licked Ross. Licked Ross Hargis. Licked him good. Hit him plenty and everywhere and hard. Ross'd just get up and pick out a fresh place to lay down on agin.

"Then that McGuire goes off there and lays down

with his head in the grass and bleeds. A hem'ridge they calls it. He lays there eighteen hours by the watch, and they can't budge him. Then Ross Hargis, who loves any man who can lick him, goes to work and damns the doctors from Greenland to Poland Chiny; and him and Green Branch Johnson they gets McGuire in a tent, and spells each other feedin' him chopped raw meat and whisky.

"But it looks like the kid ain't got no appetite to git well, for they misses him from the tent in the night and finds him rootin' in the grass, and likewise a drizzle fallin'. 'Gwan,' he says, 'lemme go and die like I wanter. He said I was a liar and a fake and I was playin' sick. Lemme alone.'

"Two weeks," went on the cook, "he laid around, not noticin' nobody, and then——"

A sudden thunder filled the air, and a score of galloping centaurs crashed through the brush into camp.

"Illustrious rattlesnakes!" exclaimed Pete, springing all ways at once; "here's the boys come, and I'm an assassinated man if supper ain't ready in three minutes."

But Raidler saw only one thing. A little, brown-faced, grinning chap, springing from his saddle in the full light of the fire. McGuire was not like that, and yet——

In another instant the cattleman was holding him by the hand and shoulder.

"Son, son, how goes it?" was all he found to say.

"Close to the ground, says you," shouted McGuire, crunching Raidler's fingers in a grip of steel; "and dat's where I found it—healt' and strengt', and tumbled to what a cheap skate I been actin'. T'anks fer kickin' me out, old man. And—say!

de joke's on dat croaker, ain't it? I looked t'rough the window and see him playin' tag on dat Dago kid's solar plexus."

"You son of a tinker," growled the cattleman, "whyn't you talk up and say the doctor never examined you?"

"Aw—gwan!" said McGuire, with a flash of his old asperity, "nobody can't bluff me. You never ast me. You made your spiel, and you t'rowed me out, and I let it go at dat. And, say, friend, dis chasin' cows is outer sight. Dis is de whitest bunch of sports I ever travelled with. You'll let me stay, won't yer, old man?"

Raidler looked wonderingly toward Ross Hargis.

"That cussed little runt," remarked Ross tenderly, "is the Jo-dartin'est hustler—and the hardest hitter in anybody's cow camp."

LVI: THE PLUTONIAN FIRE

THERE are a few editor men with whom I am privileged to come in contact. It has not been long since it was their habit to come in contact with me. There is a difference.

They tell me that with a large number of the manuscripts that are submitted to them come advices (in the way of a boost) from the author asseverating that the incidents in the story are true. The destination of such contributions depends wholly upon the question of the enclosure of stamps. Some are returned, the rest are thrown on the floor in a corner on top of a pair of gum shoes, an overturned statuette of the Winged Victory, and a pile of old magazines containing a picture of the editor in the act of reading the latest copy of *Le Petit Journal*, right side up—you can tell by the illustrations. It is only a legend that there are waste baskets in editors' offices.

Thus is truth held in disrepute. But in time truth and science and nature will adapt themselves to art. Things will happen logically, and the villain be discomfited instead of being elected to the board of directors. But in the meantime fiction must not only be divorced from fact, but must pay alimony and be awarded custody of the press dispatches.

This preamble is to warn you off the grade crossing of a true story. Being that, it shall be told simply, with conjunctions substituted for adjectives wherever possible, and whatever evidences of style may appear in it shall be due to the linotype man. It is a story of the literary life in a great city, and it should be of interest to every author within a 20-mile radius of Gosport, Ind., whose desk holds a MS. story beginning thus: "While the cheers following his nomination were still ringing through the old court-house, Harwood broke away from the congratulating handclasps of his henchmen, and hurried to Judge Creswell's house to find Ida."

Pettit came up out of Alabama to write fiction. The Southern papers had printed eight of his stories under an editorial caption identifying the author as the son of "the gallant Major Pettingill Pettit, our former County Attorney, and hero of the Battle of Look-out Mountain."

Pettit was a rugged fellow, with a kind of shamefaced culture, and my good friend. His father kept a general store in a little town called Hosea. Pettit had been raised in the pine-woods and broom-sedge fields adjacent thereto. He had in his gripsack two manuscript novels of the adventures in Picardy of one Gaston Laboulaye, Vicompte de Montrepos, in the year 1329. That's nothing. We all do that. And some day, when we make a hit with the little sketch about a newsy and his lame dog, the editor prints the other one for us—or "on us," as the saying is—and then—and then we have to get a big valise and peddle those patent air-draft gas-burners. At $1.25 everybody should have 'em.

I took Pettit to the red-brick house which was to appear in an article entitled "Literary Landmarks of Old New York," some day when we got through with it. He engaged a room there, drawing on the general store for his expenses. I showed New York to him, and he did not mention how much narrower Broadway is than Lee Avenue in Hosea. This seemed a good sign, so I put the final test.

"Suppose you try your hand at a descriptive article," I suggested, "giving your impressions of New York as seen from the Brooklyn Bridge. The fresh point of view, the——"

"Don't be a fool," said Pettit. "Let's go have some beer. On the whole, I rather like the city."

We discovered and enjoyed the only true Bohemia. Every day and night we repaired to one of those palaces of marble and glass and tilework, where goes on a tremendous and sounding epic of life. Valhalla itself could not be more glorious and sonorous. The classic marble on which we ate, the great, light-flooded vitreous front, adorned with snow-white scrolls; the grand Wagnerian din of clanking cups and bowls, the flashing staccato of brandishing cutlery, the piercing recitative of the white-aproned grub-maidens at the morgue-like banquet tables; the recurrent lied-motif of the cash-register—it was a gigantic, triumphant welding of art and sound, a deafening, soul-uplifting pageant of heroic and emblematic life. And the beans were only ten cents. We wondered why our fellow-artists cared to dine at sad little tables in their so-called Bohemian restaurants; and we shuddered lest they should seek out our resorts and make them conspicuous with their presence.

Pettit wrote many stories, which the editors returned to him. He wrote love stories, a thing I have always kept free from, holding the belief that the well-known and popular sentiment is not properly a matter for publication, but something to be privately handled by the alienists and florists. But the editors had told him that they wanted love stories, because they said the women read them.

Now, the editors are wrong about that, of course. Women do not read the love stories in the magazines. They read the poker-game stories and the recipes for cucumber lotion. The love stories are read by fat cigar drummers and little ten-year-old girls. I am not criticizing the judgment of editors. They are mostly very fine men, but a man can be but one man, with individual opinions and tastes. I knew two associate editors of a magazine who were wonderfully alike in almost everything. And yet one of them was very fond of Flaubert, while the other preferred gin.

Pettit brought me his returned manuscripts, and we looked them over together to find out why they were not accepted. They seemed to me pretty fair stories, written in a good style, and ended, as they should, at the bottom of the last page.

They were well constructed, and the events were

marshalled in orderly and logical sequence. But I thought I detected a lack of living substance—it was much as if I gazed at a symmetrical array of presentable clamshells from which the succulent and vital inhabitants had been removed. I intimated that the author might do well to get better acquainted with his theme.

"You sold a story last week," said Pettit, "about a gun fight in an Arizona mining town in which the hero drew his Colt's ·45 and shot seven bandits as fast as they came in the door. Now, if a six-shooter could——"

"Oh, well," said I, "that's different. Arizona is a long way from New York. I could have a man stabbed with a lariat or chased by a pair of chaparreras if I wanted to, and it wouldn't be noticed until the usual error-sharp from around McAdams Junction isolates the erratum and writes in to the papers about it. But you are up against another proposition. This thing they call love is as common around New York as it is in Sheboygan during the young onion season. It may be mixed here with a little commercialism—they read Byron, but they look up Bradstreet's, too, while they're among the B's, and Brigham also if they have time—but it's pretty much the same old internal disturbance everywhere. You can fool an editor with a fake picture of a cowboy mounting a pony with his left hand on the saddle-horn, but you can't put him up a tree with a love story. So you've got to fall in love and then write the real thing."

Pettit did. I never knew whether he was taking my advice or whether he fell an accidental victim.

There was a girl he had met at one of these studio contrivances—a glorious, impudent, lucid, open-minded girl with hair the colour of Culmbacher, and a good-natured way of despising you. She was a New York girl.

Well (as the narrative style permits us to say infrequently), Pettit went to pieces. All those pains, those lover's doubts, those heart-burnings and tremors of which he had written so unconvincingly were his. Talk about Shylock's pound of flesh! Twenty-five pounds Cupid got from Pettit. Which is the usurer?

One night Pettit came to my room exalted. Pale and haggard, but exalted. She had given him a jonquil.

"Old Hoss," said he, with a new smile flickering around his mouth, "I believe I could write that story to-night—the one, you know, that is to win out. I can feel it. I don't know whether it will come out or not, but I can feel it."

I pushed him out of my door. "Go to your room and write it," I ordered. "Else I can see your finish. I told you this must come first. Write it to-night, and put it under my door when it is done. Put it under my door to-night when it is finished—don't keep it until to-morrow."

I was reading my bully old pal Montaigne at two o'clock, when I heard the sheets rustle under my door. I gathered them up and read the story.

The hissing of geese, the languishing cooing of doves, the braying of donkeys, the chatter of irresponsible sparrows—these were in my mind's ear as I read. "Suffering Sappho!" I exclaimed to myself. "Is this the divine fire that is supposed to ignite genius, and make it practicable and wage-earning?"

The story was sentimental drivel, full of whimpering soft-heartedness and gushing egoism. All the art that Pettit had acquired was gone. A perusal of its buttery phrases would have made a cynic of a sighing chamber-maid.

In the morning Pettit came to my room. I read him his doom mercilessly. He laughed idiotically.

"All right, Old Hoss," he said, cheerily, "make cigar-lighters of it. What's the difference? I'm going to take her to lunch at Claremont to-day."

There was about a month of it. And then Pettit came to me bearing an invisible mitten, with the fortitude of a dish-rag. He talked of the grave and South America and prussic acid; and I lost an afternoon getting him straight. I took him out, and saw that large and curative doses of whisky were administered to him. I warned you this was a true story—'ware your white ribbons if you follow this tale. For two weeks I fed him whisky and Omar, and read to him regularly every evening the column in the evening paper that reveals the secrets of female beauty. I recommend the treatment.

After Pettit was cured he wrote more stories. He recovered his old-time facility, and did work just short of good enough. Then the curtain rose on the third act.

A little, dark-eyed, silent girl from New Hampshire, who was studying applied design, fell deeply in love with him. She was the intense sort, but externally *glacé*, such as New England sometimes fools us with. Pettit liked her mildly, and took her about a good deal. She worshipped him, and now and then bored him.

There came a climax when she tried to jump out of a window, and he had to save her by some perfunctory, unmeant wooing. Even I was shaken by the depths of the absorbing affection she showed.

Home, friends, traditions, creeds went up like thistle-down in the scale against her love. It was really discomposing.

One night again Pettit sauntered in, yawning. As he had told me before, he said he felt that he could do a great story, and as before I hunted him to his room and saw him open his inkstand. At one o'clock the sheets of paper slid under my door.

I read that story, and I jumped up, late as it was, with a whoop of joy. Old Pettit had done it. Just as though it lay there, red and bleeding, a woman's heart was written into the lines. You couldn't see the joining, but art, exquisite art, and pulsing nature had been combined into a love story that took you by the throat like the quinsy. I broke into Pettit's room and beat him on the back and called him names —names high up in the galaxy of the immortals that we admired. And Pettit yawned and begged to be allowed to sleep.

On the morrow I dragged him to an editor. The great man read, and, rising, gave Pettit his hand. That was a decoration, a wreath of bay, and a guarantee of rent.

And then old Pettit smiled slowly. I call him Gentleman Pettit now to myself. It's a miserable name to give a man, but it sounds better than it looks in print.

"I see," said old Pettit, as he took up his story and began tearing it into small strips, "I see the game now. You can't write with ink, and you can't write with your own heart's blood, but you can write with the heart's blood of some one else. You have to be a cad before you can be an artist. Well, I am for old Alabam and the Major's store. Have you got a light, Old Hoss?"

I went with Pettit to the depot and died hard.

"Shakespeare's sonnets?" I blurted, making a last stand. "How about him?"

"A cad," said Pettit. "They give it to you, and you sell it—love, you know. I'd rather sell ploughs for father."

"But," I protested, "you are reversing the decision of the world's greatest——"

"Good-bye, Old Hoss," said Pettit.

"Critics," I continued. "But — say — if the Major can use a fairly good salesman and book-keeper down there in the store, let me know, will you?"

LVII: THE LONESOME ROAD

BROWN as a coffee-berry, rugged, pistolled, spurred, wary, indefeasible, I saw my old friend, Deputy-Marshal Buck Caperton, stumble, with jingling rowels, into a chair in the marshal's outer office.

And because the court-house was almost deserted at that hour, and because Buck would sometimes relate to me things that were out of print, I followed him in and tricked him into talk through knowledge of a weakness he had. For, cigarettes rolled with sweet corn husk were as honey to Buck's palate; and though he could finger the trigger of a ·45 with skill and suddenness, he never could learn to roll a cigarette.

It was through no fault of mine (for I rolled the cigarettes tight and smooth), but the upshot of some whim of his own, that instead of to an Odyssey of the chaparral, I listened to—a dissertation upon matrimony! This from Buck Caperton! But I maintain that the cigarettes were impeccable, and crave absolution for myself.

"We just brought in Jim and Bud Granberry," said Buck. "Train robbing, you know. Held up the Aransas Pass last month. We caught 'em in the Twenty-Mile pear flat, south of the Nueces."

"Have much trouble corralling them?" I asked, for here was the meat that my hunger for epics craved.

"Some," said Buck; and then, during a little pause, his thoughts stampeded off the trail. "It's kind of queer about women," he went on, "and the place they're supposed to occupy in botany. If I was asked to classify them I'd say they was a human loco weed. Ever see a bronc that had been chewing loco? Ride him up to a puddle of water two feet wide, and he'll give a snort and fall back on you. It looks as big as the Mississippi River to him. Next trip he'd walk into a cañon a thousand feet deep thinking it was a prairie-dog hole. Same way with a married man.

"I was thinking of Perry Rountree, that used to be my side-kicker before he committed matrimony. In them days me and Perry hated disturbances of any kind. We roamed around considerable, stirring up the echoes and making 'em attend to business. Why, when me and Perry wanted to have some fun in a town it was a picnic for the census takers. They just counted the marshal's posse that it took to subdue us, and there was your population. But then there came along this Mariana Good-night girl and looked at Perry sideways, and he was all bridle-wise and saddle-broke before you could skin a yearling.

"I wasn't even asked to the wedding. I reckon

the bride had my pedigree and the front elevation of my habits all mapped out, and she decided that Perry would trot better in double harness without any unconverted mustang like Buck Caperton whickering around on the matrimonial range. So it was six months before I saw Perry again.

"One day I was passing on the edge of town, and I see something like a man in a little yard by a little house with a sprinkling-pot squirting water on a rose-bush. Seemed to me, I'd seen something like it before, and I stopped at the gate, trying to figure out its brands. 'Twas not Perry Rountree, but 'twas the kind of a curdled jelly-fish matrimony had made out of him.

"Homicide was what that Mariana had perpetrated. He was looking well enough, but he had on a white collar and shoes, and you could tell in a minute that he'd speak polite and pay taxes and stick his little finger out while drinking just like a sheep man or a citizen. Great skyrockets! but I hated to see Perry all corrupted and Willie-ized like that.

"He came out to the gate, and shook hands; and I says, with scorn, and speaking like a paroquet with the pip: 'Beg pardon—Mr. Rountree, I believe. Seems to me I sagatiated in your associations once, if I am not mistaken.'

" 'Oh, go to the devil, Buck,' says Perry, polite, as I was afraid he'd be.

" 'Well, then,' says I, 'you poor, contaminated adjunct of a sprinkling-pot and degraded household pet, what did you go and do it for? Look at you, all decent and unriotous, and only fit to sit on juries and mend the wood-house door. You was a man once. I have hostility for all such acts. Why don't you go in the house and count the tidies or set the clock, and not stand out here in the atmosphere? A jack-rabbit might come along and bite you.'

" 'Now, Buck,' says Perry, speaking mild, and some sorrowful, 'you don't understand. A married man has got to be different. He feels different from a tough old cloudburst like you. It's sinful to waste time pulling up towns just to look at their roots, and playing faro and looking upon red liquor, and such restless policies as them.'

" 'There was a time,' I says, and I expect I sighed when I mentioned it, 'when a certain domesticated little Mary's lamb I could name was some instructed himself in the line of pernicious sprightliness. I never expected, Perry, to see you reduced down from a full-grown pestilence to such a frivolous fraction of a man. Why,' says I, 'you've got a necktie on; and you speak a senseless kind of indoor drivel that reminds me of a storekeeper or a lady. You look to me like you might tote an umbrella and wear suspenders, and go home of nights.'

" 'The little woman,' says Perry, 'has made some improvements, I believe. You can't understand, Buck. I haven't been away from the house at night since we was married.'

"We talked on awhile, me and Perry, and, as sure as I live, that man interrupted me in the middle of my talk to tell me about six tomato plants he had growing in his garden. Shoved his agricultural degradation right up under my nose while I was telling him about the fun we had tarring and feathering that faro dealer at California Pete's layout! But by and by Perry shows a flicker of sense.

" 'Buck,' says he, 'I'll have to admit that it is a little dull at times. Not that I'm not perfectly happy with the little woman, but a man seems to require some excitement now and then. Now, I'll tell you: Mariana's gone visiting this afternoon, and she won't be home till seven o'clock. That's the limit for both of us—seven o'clock. Neither of us ever stays out a minute after that time unless we are together. Now, I'm glad you came along, Buck,' says Perry, 'for I'm feeling just like having one more rip-roaring razoo with you for the sake of old times. What you say to us putting in the afternoon having fun—I'd like it fine,' says Perry.

"I slapped that old captive range-rider half across his little garden.

" 'Get your hat, you old dried-up alligator,' I shouts, 'you ain't dead yet. You're part human, anyhow, if you did get all bogged up in matrimony. We'll take this town to pieces and see what makes it tick. We'll make all kinds of profligate demands upon the science of cork pulling. You'll grow horns yet, old muley cow,' says I, punching Perry in the ribs, 'if you trot around on the trail of vice with your Uncle Buck.'

" 'I'll have to be home by seven, you know,' says Perry again.

" 'Oh, yes,' says I, winking to myself, for I knew the kind of seven o'clocks Perry Rountree got back by after he once got to passing repartee with the bar-tenders.

"We goes down to the Grey Mule saloon—that old 'dobe building by the depot.

" 'Give it a name,' says I, as soon as we got one hoof on the foot-rest.

" 'Sarsaparilla,' says Perry.

"You could have knocked me down with a lemon peeling.

" 'Insult me as much as you want to,' I says to

Perry, 'but don't startle the bar-tender. He may have heart-disease. Come on, now; your tongue got twisted. The tall glasses,' I orders, 'and the bottle in the left-hand corner of the ice-chest.'

" 'Sarsaparilla,' repeats Perry, and then his eyes get animated, and I see he's got some great scheme in his mind he wants to emit.

" 'Buck,' he says, all interested, 'I'll tell you what! I want to make this a red-letter day. I've been keeping close at home, and I want to turn myself a-loose. We'll have the highest old time you ever saw. We'll go in the back room here and play checkers till half-past six.'

"I leaned against the bar, and I says to Gotch-eared Mike, who was on watch:

" 'For God's sake don't mention this. You know what Perry used to be. He's had the fever, and the doctor says we must humour him.'

" 'Give us the checker-board and the men, Mike,' says Perry. 'Come on, Buck, I'm just wild to have some excitement.'

"I went in the back room with Perry. Before we closed the door, I says to Mike :

" 'Don't ever let it straggle out from under your hat that you seen Buck Caperton fraternal with sarsaparilla or *persona grata* with a checker-board, or I'll make a swallow-fork in your other ear.'

"I locked the door, and me and Perry played checkers. To see that poor old humiliated piece of household bric-à-brac sitting there and sniggering out loud whenever he jumped a man, and all obnoxious with animation when he got into my king row, would have made a sheep-dog sick with mortification. Him that was once satisfied only when he was pegging six boards at keno or giving the faro dealers nervous prostration—to see him pushing them checkers about like Sally Louisa at a school-children's party—why, I was all smothered up with mortification.

"And I sits there playing the black men, all sweating for fear somebody I knew would find it out. And I thinks to myself some about this marrying business, and how it seems to be the same kind of a game as that Mrs. Delilah played. She give her old man a hair cut, and everybody knows what a man's head looks like after a woman cuts his hair. And then when the Pharisees came around to guy him he was so 'shamed he went to work and kicked the whole house down on top of the whole outfit. 'Them married men,' thinks I, 'lose all their spirit and instinct for riot and foolishness. They won't drink, they won't buck the tiger, they won't even fight. What do they want to go and stay married for?' I asks myself.

"But Perry seems to be having hilarity in considerable quantities.

" 'Buck, old hoss,' says he, 'isn't this just the hell-roaringest time we ever had in our lives? I don't know when I've been stirred up so. You see, I've been sticking pretty close to home since I married, and I haven't been on a spree in a long time.'

" 'Spree!' Yes, that's what he called it. Playing checkers in the back room of the Grey Mule! I suppose it did seem to him a little more immoral and nearer to a prolonged debauch than standing over six tomato plants with a sprinkling-pot.

"Every little bit Perry looks at his watch and says:

" 'I got to be home, you know, Buck, at seven.'

" 'All right,' I'd say. 'Romp along and move. This here excitement's killing me. If I don't reform some, and loosen up the strain of this checkered dissipation I won't have a nerve left.'

"It might have been half-past six when commotions began to go on outside in the street. We heard a yelling and a six-shootering, and a lot of galloping and manœuvres.

" 'What's that?' I wonders.

" 'Oh, some nonsense outside,' says Perry. 'It's your move. We just got time to play this game.'

" 'I'll just take a peep through the window,' says I, 'and see. You can't expect a mere mortal to stand the excitement of having a king jumped and listen to an unidentified conflict going on at the same time.'

"The Grey Mule saloon was one of them old Spanish 'dobe buildings, and the back room only had two little windows a foot wide, with iron bars in 'em. I looked out one, and I see the cause of the rucus.

"There was the Trimble gang—ten of 'em—the worst outfit of desperadoes and horse-thieves in Texas coming up the street shooting right and left. They was coming right straight for the Grey Mule. Then they got past the range of my sight, but we heard 'em ride up to the front door, and then they socked the place full of lead. We heard the big looking-glass behind the bar knocked all to pieces and the bottles crashing. We could see Gotch-eared Mike in his apron running across the plaza like a coyote, with the bullets puffing up the dust all around him. Then the gang went to work in the saloon, drinking what they wanted and smashing what they didn't.

"Me and Perry both knew that gang, and they knew us. The year before Perry married, him and me was in the same ranger company—and we fought that outfit down on the San Miguel, and brought back Ben Trimble and two others for murder.

" 'We can't get out,' says I. 'We'll have to stay in here till they leave.'

Perry looked at his watch.

" 'Twenty-five to seven,' says he. 'We can finish that game. I got two men on you. It's your move, Buck. I got to be home at seven, you know.'

"We sat down and went on playing. The Trimble gang had a rough house for sure. They were getting good and drunk. They'd drink awhile and holler awhile, and then they'd shoot up a few bottles and glasses. Two or three times they came and tried to open our door. Then there was some more shooting outside and I looked out the window again. Ham Gossett, the town marshal, had a posse in the houses and stores across the street, and was trying to bag a Trimble or two through the windows.

"I lost that game of checkers. I'm free in saying that I lost three kings that I might have saved if I had been corralled in a more peaceful pasture. But that drivelling married man sat there and cackled when he won a man like an unintelligent hen picking up a grain of corn.

"When the game was over Perry gets up and looks at his watch.

" 'I've had a glorious time, Buck,' says he, 'but I'll have to be going now. It's a quarter to seven, and I got to be home by seven, you know.'

"I thought he was joking.

" 'They'll clear out or be dead drunk in half an hour or an hour,' says I. 'You ain't that tired of being married that you want to commit any more sudden suicide, are you?' says I, giving him the laugh.

" 'One time,' says Perry, 'I was half an hour late getting home. I met Mariana on the street looking for me. If you could have seen her, Buck—but you don't understand. She knows what a wild kind of a snoozer I've been, and she's afraid something will happen. I'll never be late getting home again. I'll say good-bye to you, now, Buck.'

"I got between him and the door.

" 'Married man,' says I, 'I know you was christened a fool the minute the preacher tangled you up, but don't you never sometimes think one little think on a human basis? There's ten of that gang in there, and they're pizen with whisky and desire for murder. They'll drink you up like a bottle of booze before you get half-way to the door. Be intelligent, now, and use at least wild-hog sense. Sit down and wait till we have some chance to get out without being carried in baskets.'

" 'I got to be home by seven, Buck,' repeats this hen-pecked thing of little wisdom, like an unthinking poll-parrot. 'Mariana,' says he, ' 'll be looking out for me.' And he reaches down and pulls a leg out of the checker table. 'I'll go through this Trimble outfit,' says he, 'like a cottontail through a brush corral. I'm not pestered any more with a desire to engage in rucuses, but I got to be home by seven. You lock the door after me, Buck. And don't you forget—I won three out of them five games. I'd play longer, but Mariana——'

" 'Hush up, you old locoed road-runner,' I interrupts. 'Did you ever notice your Uncle Buck locking doors against trouble? I'm not married,' says I, 'but I'm as big a d——n fool as any Mormon. One from four leaves three,' says I, and I gathers out another leg of the table. 'We'll get home by seven,' says I, 'whether it's the heavenly one or the other. May I see you home?' says I, 'you sarsaparilla-drinking, checker-playing glutton for death and destruction.'

"We opened the door easy, and then stampeded for the front. Part of the gang was lined up at the bar; part of 'em was passing over the drinks, and two or three was peeping out the door and window taking shots at the marshal's crowd. The room was so full of smoke we got half-way to the front door before they noticed us. Then I heard Berry Trimble's voice somewhere yell out:

" 'How'd that Buck Caperton get in here?' and he skinned the side of my neck with a bullet. I reckon he felt bad over that miss, for Berry's the best shot south of the Southern Pacific Railroad. But the smoke in the saloon was some too thick for good shooting.

"Me and Perry smashed over two of the gang with our table-legs, which didn't miss like the guns did, and as we run out the door I grabbed a Winchester from a fellow who was watching the outside, and I turned and regulated the account of Mr. Berry.

"Me and Perry got out and around the corner all right. I never much expected to get out, but I wasn't going to be intimidated by that married man. According to Perry's idea, checkers was the event of the day, but if I am any judge of gentle recreations that little table-leg parade through the Grey Mule saloon deserved the headlines in the bill of particulars.

" 'Walk fast,' says Perry, 'it's two minutes to seven, and I got to be home by——'

" 'Oh, shut up,' says I. 'I had an appointment as chief performer at an inquest at seven, and I'm not kicking about not keeping it.'

"I had to pass by Perry's little house. His Mariana was standing at the gate. We got there at five minutes past seven. She had on a blue wrapper, and her hair was pulled back smooth like little girls do when they want to look grown-folksy. She didn't see us till we got close, for she was gazing up the other way. Then she backed around, and saw Perry, and a kind of a look scooted around over her face—danged if I can describe it. I heard her breathe long, just like a cow when you turn her calf in the lot, and she says: 'You're late, Perry.'

" 'Five minutes,' says Perry, cheerful. 'Me and old Buck was having a game of checkers.'

"Perry introduces me to Mariana, and they ask me to come in. No, sir-ee. I'd had enough truck with married folks for that day. I says I'll be going along and that I've spent a very pleasant afternoon with my old partner—'especially,' says I, just to jostle Perry, 'during that game when the table-legs came all loose.' But I'd promised him not to let her know anything.

"I've been worrying over that business ever since it happened," continued Buck. "There's one thing about it that's got me all twisted up, and I can't figure it out."

"What was that?" I asked, as I rolled and handed Buck the last cigarette.

"Why, I'll tell you. When I saw the look that little woman give Perry when she turned round and saw him coming back to the ranch safe—why was it I got the idea all in a minute that that look of hers was worth more than the whole caboodle of us—sarsaparilla, checkers, and all, and that the d——n fool in the game wasn't named Perry Rountree at all?"

LVIII: BABES IN THE JUNGLE

MONTAGUE SILVER, the finest street man and art grafter in the West, says to me once in Little Rock: "If you ever lose your mind, Billy, and get too old to do honest swindling among grown men, go to New York. In the West a sucker is born ever minute; but in New York they appear in chunks of roe—you can't count 'em!"

Two years afterward I found that I couldn't remember the names of the Russian admirals, and I noticed some grey hairs over my left ear; so I knew the time had arrived for me to take Silver's advice.

I struck New York about noon one day, and took a walk up Broadway. And I run against Silver himself, all encompassed up in a spacious kind of haberdashery, leaning against a hotel and rubbing the half-moons on his nails with a silk handkerchief.

"Paresis or superannuated?" I asks him.

"Hello, Billy," says Silver; "I'm glad to see you. Yes, it seemed to me that the West was accumulating a little too much wiseness. I've been saving New York for dessert. I know it's a low-down trick to take things from these people. They only know this and that and pass to and fro and think ever and anon. I'd hate for my mother to know I was skinning these weak-minded ones. She raised me better."

"Is there a crush already in the waiting-rooms of the old doctor that does skin grafting?" I asks.

"Well, no," says Silver; "you needn't back Epidermis to win to-day. I've only been here a month. But I'm ready to begin; and the members of Willie Manhattan's Sunday-school class, each of whom has volunteered to contribute a portion of cuticle toward this rehabilitation, may as well send their photos to the *Evening Daily*.

"I've been studying the town," says Silver; "and reading the papers every day, and I know it as well as the cat in the City Hall knows an O'Sullivan. People here lie down on the floor and scream and kick when you are the least bit slow about taking money from them. Come up in my room and I'll tell you. We'll work the town together, Billy, for the sake of old times."

Silver takes me up in a hotel. He has a quantity of irrelevant objects lying about.

"There's more ways of getting money from these metropolitan hayseeds," says Silver, "than there is of cooking rice in Charleston, S.C. They'll bite at anything. The brains of most of 'em commute. The wiser they are in intelligence the less perception of cognizance they have. Why, didn't a man the other day sell J. P. Morgan an oil portrait of Rockefeller, Jr., for Andrea del Sarto's celebrated painting of the young Saint John?

"You see that bundle of printed stuff in the corner, Billy? That's gold-mining stock. I started out one day to sell that, but I quit it in two hours. Why? Got arrested for blocking the street. People fought to buy it. I sold the policeman a block of it on the way to the station-house, and then I took it off the market. I don't want people to give me their money. I want some little consideration connected with the transaction to keep my pride from being hurt. I want 'em to guess the missing letter in Chic—go, or draw to a pair of nines before they pay me a cent of money.

"Now there's another little scheme that worked so easy I had to quit it. You see that bottle of blue ink on the table? I tattooed an anchor on the back of my hand and went to a bank and told 'em I was Admiral Dewey's nephew. They offered to cash my draft on him for a thousand, but I didn't know my uncle's first name. It shows, though, what an easy town it is. As for burglars, they won't go in a house now unless there's a hot supper ready and a few college students to wait on 'em. They're slugging citizens all over the upper part of the city, and I guess, taking the town from end to end, it's a plain case of assault and battery."

"Monty," says I, when Silver had slacked up, "you may have Manhattan correctly discriminated in your perorative, but I doubt it. I've only been in town two hours, but it don't dawn upon me that it's ours with a cherry in it. There ain't enough rus in urbe about it to suit me. I'd be a good deal much better satisfied if the citizens had a straw or more in their hair, and run more to velveteen vests and buckeye watch charm. They don't look easy to me."

"You've got it, Billy," says Silver. "All emigrants have it. New York's bigger than Little Rock or Europe, and it frightens a foreigner. You'll be all right. I tell you I feel like slapping the people here because they don't send me all their money in laundry baskets, with germicide sprinkled over it. I hate to go down on the street to get it. Who wears the diamonds in this town? Why, Winnie, the Wiretapper's wife, and Bella, the Buncosteerer's bride. New Yorkers can be worked easier than a blue rose on a tidy. The only thing that bothers me is I know I'll break the cigars in my vest pocket when I get my clothes all full of twenties."

"I hope you are right, Monty," says I; "but I wish all the same I had been satisfied with a small business in Little Rock. The crop of farmers is never so short out there but what you can get a few of 'em to sign a petition for a new post office that you can discount for $200 at the county bank. The people here appear to possess instincts of self-preservation and illiberality. I fear me that we are not cultured enough to tackle this game."

"Don't worry," says Silver, "I've got this Jayville-near-Tarrytown correctly estimated as sure as North River is the Hudson and East River ain't a river. Why, there are people living in four blocks of Broadway who never saw any kind of a building except a skyscraper in their lives! A good, live hustling Western man ought to get conspicuous enough here inside of three months to incur either Jerome's clemency or Lawson's displeasure."

"Hyperbole aside," says I, "do you know of any immediate system of buncoing the community out of a dollar or two except by applying to the Salvation Army or having a fit on Miss Helen Gould's doorsteps?"

"Dozens of 'em," says Silver. "How much capital have you got, Billy?"

"A thousand," I told him.

"I've got $1,200," says he. "We'll pool and do a big piece of business. There's so many ways we can make a million that I don't know how to begin."

The next morning Silver meets me at the hotel and he is all sonorous and stirred with a kind of silent joy.

"We're to meet J. P. Morgan this afternoon," says he. "A man I know in the hotel wants to introduce us. He's a friend of his. He says he likes to meet people from the West."

"That sounds nice and plausible," says I. "I'd like to know Mr. Morgan."

"It won't hurt us a bit," says Silver, "to get acquainted with a few finance kings. I kind of like the social way New York has with strangers."

The man Silver knew was named Klein. At three o'clock Klein brought his Wall Street friend to see us in Silver's room. "Mr. Morgan" looked some like his pictures, and he had a Turkish towel wrapped around his left foot, and he walked with a cane.

"Mr. Silver and Mr. Pescud," says Klein. "It sounds superfluous," says he, "to mention the name of the greatest financial——"

"Cut it out, Klein," says Mr. Morgan. "I'm glad to know you gents; I take great interest in the West. Klein tells me you're from Little Rock. I think I've a railroad or two out there somewhere. If either of you guys would like to deal a hand or two of stud poker I——"

"Now, Pierpont," cuts in Klein, "you forget!"

"Excuse me, gents!" says Morgan; "since I've had the gout so bad I sometimes play a social game of cards at my house. Neither of you never knew One-eyed Peters, did you, while you was around Little Rock? He lived in Seattle, New Mexico."

Before we could answer, Mr. Morgan hammers on the floor with his cane and begins to walk up and down, swearing in a loud tone of voice.

"They have been pounding your stocks to-day on the Street, Pierpont?" asks Klein, smiling.

"Stocks! No!" roars Mr. Morgan. "It's that picture I sent an agent to Europe to buy. I just thought about it. He cabled me to-day that it ain't to be found in all Italy. I'd pay $50,000 to-morrow for that picture—yes, $75,000. I give the agent *à la carte* in purchasing it. I cannot understand why the art galleries will allow a De Vinchy to——"

"Why, Mr. Morgan," says Klein, "I thought you owned all of the De Vinchy paintings."

"What is the picture like, Mr. Morgan?" asks Silver. "It must be as big as the side of the Flatiron Building."

"I'm afraid your art education is on the bum, Mr. Silver," says Morgan. "The picture is 27 inches by 42; and it is called 'Love's Idle Hour.' It represents a number of cloak models doing the two-step on the bank of a purple river. The cablegram said it might have been brought to this country. My collection will never be complete without that picture. Well, so long, gents; us financiers must keep early hours."

Mr. Morgan and Klein went away together in a cab. Me and Silver talked about how simple and unsuspecting great people was; and Silver said what a shame it would be to try to rob a man like Mr. Morgan; and I said I thought it would be rather imprudent, myself. Klein proposes a stroll after dinner; and me and him and Silver walks down toward Seventh Avenue to see the sights. Klein sees a pair of cuff-links that instigate his admiration in a pawnshop window, and we all go in while he buys 'em.

After we got back to the hotel and Klein had gone, Silver jumps at me and waves his hands.

"Did you see it?" says he. "Did you see it, Billy?"

"What?" I asks.

"Why, that picture that Morgan wants. It's hanging in that pawnshop, behind the desk. I didn't say anything because Klein was there. It's the article sure as you live. The girls are as natural as paint can make them, all measuring 36 and 25 and 42 skirts, if they had any skirts, and they're doing a buck-and-wing on the bank of a river with the blues. What did Mr. Morgan say he'd give for it? Oh, don't make me tell you. They can't know it is in that pawnshop."

When the pawnshop opened the next morning me and Silver was standing there as anxious as if we wanted to soak our Sunday suit to buy a drink. We sauntered inside, and began to look at watch-chains.

"That's a violent specimen of a chromo you've got up there," remarked Silver, casual, to the pawnbroker. "But I kind of enthuse over the girl with the shoulder-blades and red bunting. Would an offer of $2.25 for it cause you to knock over any fragile articles of your stock in hurrying it off the nail?"

The pawnbroker smiles and goes on showing us plate watch-chains.

"That picture," says he, "was pledged a year ago by an Italian gentleman. I loaned him $500 on it. It is called 'Love's Idle Hour,' and it is by Leonardo de Vinchy. Two days ago the legal time expired, and it became an unredeemed pledge. Here is a style of chain that is worn a great deal now."

At the end of half an hour me and Silver paid the pawnbroker $2,000 and walked out with the picture. Silver got into a cab with it and started for Morgan's office. I goes to the hotel and waits for him. In two hours Silver comes back.

"Did you see Mr. Morgan?" I asks. "How much did he pay you for it?"

Silver sits down and fools with a tassel on the table-cover.

"I never exactly saw Mr. Morgan," he says, "because Mr. Morgan's been in Europe for a month. But what's worrying me, Billy, is this: The department stores have all got that same picture on sale, framed, for $3.48. And they charge $3.50 for the frame alone—that's what I can't understand."

LIX: THE RANSOM OF RED CHIEF

IT looked like a good thing: but wait till I tell you. We were down South, in Alabama—Bill Driscoll and myself—when this kidnapping idea struck us. It was, as Bill afterward expressed it, "during a moment of temporary mental apparition"; but we didn't find that out till later.

There was a town down there, as flat as a flannel-cake, and called Summit, of course. It contained inhabitants of as undeleterious and self-satisfied a class of peasantry as ever clustered around a Maypole.

Bill and me had a joint capital of about six hundred dollars, and we needed just two thousand dollars more to pull off a fraudulent town-lot scheme in Western Illinois with. We talked it over on the front steps of the hotel. Philo-progenitiveness, says we, is strong in semi-rural communities; therefore, and for other reasons, a kidnapping project ought to do better there than in the radius of newspapers that send reporters out in plain clothes to stir up talk about such things. We knew that Summit couldn't get after us with anything stronger than constables and, maybe, some lackadaisical bloodhounds and a diatribe or two in the *Weekly Farmers' Budget*. So, it looked good.

We selected for our victim the only child of a prominent citizen named Ebenezer Dorset. The father was respectable and tight, a mortgage fancier and a stern, upright collection-plate passer and forecloser. The kid was a boy of ten, with bas-relief freckles, and hair the colour of the cover of the magazine you buy at the news-stand when you want to catch a train. Bill and me figured that Ebenezer would melt down for a ransom of two thousand dollars to a cent. But wait till I tell you.

About two miles from Summit was a little mountain, covered with a dense cedar brake. On the rear elevation of this mountain was a cave. There we stored provisions.

One evening after sundown, we drove in a buggy past old Dorset's house. The kid was in the street, throwing rocks at a kitten on the opposite fence.

"Hey, little boy!" says Bill, "would you like to have a bag of candy and a nice ride?"

The boy catches Bill neatly in the eye with a piece of brick.

"That will cost the old man an extra five hundred dollars," says Bill, climbing over the wheel.

That boy put up a fight like a welter-weight cinnamon bear; but, at last, we got him down in the bottom of the buggy and drove away. We took him up to the cave, and I hitched the horse in the cedar break. After dark I drove the buggy to the little village, three miles away, where we had hired it, and walked back to the mountain.

Bill was pasting court-plaster over the scratches and bruises on his features. There was a fire burning behind the big rock at the entrance of the cave, and the boy was watching a pot of boiling coffee, with two buzzard tailfeathers stuck in his red hair. He points a stick at me when I come up, and says:

"Ha! cursed paleface, do you dare to enter the camp of Red Chief, the terror of the plains?"

"He's all right now," says Bill, rolling up his trousers and examining some bruises on his shins. "We're playing Indian. We're making Buffalo Bill's show look like magic-lantern views of Palestine in the town hall. I'm Old Hank, the Trapper, Red Chief's captive, and I'm to be scalped at daybreak. By Geronimo! that kid can kick hard."

Yes, sir, that boy seemed to be having the time of his life. The fun of camping out in a cave had made him forget that he was a captive himself. He immediately christened me Snake-eye, the Spy, and announced that, when his braves returned from the warpath, I was to be broiled at the stake at the rising of the sun.

Then we had supper; and he filled his mouth full of bacon and bread and gravy, and began to talk. He made a during-dinner speech something like this:

"I like this fine. I never camped out before; but I had a pet 'possum once, and I was nine last birthday. I hate to go to school. Rats ate up sixteen of Jimmy Talbot's aunt's speckled hen's eggs. Are there any real Indians in these woods? I want some more gravy. Does the trees moving make the wind blow? We had five puppies. What makes your nose so red, Hank? My father has lots of money. Are the stars hot? I whipped Ed Walker twice, Saturday. I don't like girls. You dassent catch toads unless with a string. Do oxen make any noise? Why are oranges round? Have you got beds to sleep on in this cave? Amos Murray has got six toes. A parrot can talk, but a monkey or a fish can't. How many does it take to make twelve?"

Every few minutes he would remember that he was a pesky redskin, and pick up his stick rifle and tiptoe to the mouth of the cave to rubber for the scouts of the hated paleface. Now and then he would let out a war-whoop that made Old Hank the Trapper shiver. That boy had Bill terrorized from the start.

"Red Chief," says I to the kid, "would you like to go home?"

"Aw, what for?" says he. "I don't have any fun at home. I hate to go to school. I like to camp out. You won't take me back home again, Snake-eye, will you?"

"Not right away," says I. "We'll stay here in the cave a while."

"All right!" says he. "That'll be fine. I never had such fun in all my life."

We went to bed about eleven o'clock. We spread down some wide blankets and quilts and put Red Chief between us. We weren't afraid he'd run away. He kept us awake for three hours, jumping up and reaching for his rifle and screeching, "Hist! pard," in mine and Bill's ears, as the fancied crackle of a twig or the rustle of a leaf revealed to his young imagination the stealthy approach of the outlaw band. At last, I fell into a troubled sleep, and dreamed that I had been kidnapped and chained to a tree by a ferocious pirate with red hair.

Just at daybreak, I was awakened by a series of awful screams from Bill. They weren't yells, or howls, or shouts, or whoops, or yawps, such as you'd expect from a manly set of vocal organs—they were simply indecent, terrifying, humiliating screams, such as women emit when they see ghosts or caterpillars. It's an awful thing to hear a strong, desperate, fat man scream incontinently in a cave at daybreak.

I jumped up to see what the matter was. Red Chief was sitting on Bill's chest, with one hand twined in Bill's hair. In the other he had the sharp case-knife we used for slicing bacon; and he was industriously and realistically trying to take Bill's scalp, according to the sentence that had been pronounced upon him the evening before.

I got the knife away from the kid and made him lie down again. But, from that moment, Bill's spirit was broken. He laid down on his side of the bed, but he never closed an eye again in sleep as long as that boy was with us. I dozed off for a while, but along toward sun-up I remembered that Red Chief had said I was to be burned at the stake at the rising of the sun. I wasn't nervous or afraid; but I sat up and lit my pipe and leaned against a rock.

"What you getting up so soon for, Sam?" asked Bill.

"Me?" says I. "Oh, I got a kind of a pain in my shoulder. I thought sitting up would rest it."

"You're a liar!" says Bill. "You're afraid. You

was to be burned at sunrise, and you was afraid he'd do it. And he would, too, if he could find a match. Ain't it awful, Sam? Do you think anybody will pay out money to get a little imp like that back home?"

"Sure," said I. "A rowdy kid like that is just the kind that parents dote on. Now, you and the Chief get up and cook breakfast, while I go up on the top of this mountain and reconnoitre."

I went up on the peak of the little mountain and ran my eye over the contiguous vicinity. Over toward Summit I expected to see the sturdy yeomanry of the village armed with scythes and pitchforks beating the country-side for the dastardly kidnappers. But what I saw was a peaceful landscape dotted with one man ploughing with a dun mule. Nobody was dragging the creek; no couriers dashed hither and yon, bringing tidings of no news to the distracted parents. There was a sylvan attitude of somnolent sleepiness pervading that section of the external outward surface of Alabama that lay exposed to my view. "Perhaps," says I to myself, "it has not yet been discovered that the wolves have borne away the tender lambkin from the fold. Heaven help the wolves!" says I, and I went down the mountain to breakfast.

When I got to the cave I found Bill backed up against the side of it, breathing hard, and the boy threatening to smash him with a rock half as big as a coco-nut.

"He put a red-hot boiled potato down my back," explained Bill, "and then mashed it with his foot; and I boxed his ears. Have you got a gun about you, Sam?"

I took the rock away from the boy and kind of

patched up the argument. "I'll fix you," says the kid to Bill. "No man ever yet struck the Red Chief but what he got paid for it. You better beware!"

After breakfast the kid takes a piece of leather with strings wrapped around it out of his pocket and goes outside the cave unwinding it.

"What's he up to now?" says Bill anxiously. "You don't think he'll run away, do you, Sam?"

"No fear of it," says I. "He don't seem to be much of a home body. But we've got to fix up some plan about the ransom. There don't seem to be much excitement around Summit on account of his disappearance; but maybe they haven't realized yet that he's gone. His folks may think he's spending the night with Aunt Jane or one of the neighbours. Anyhow, he'll be missed to-day. To-night we must get a message to his father demanding the two thousand dollars for his return."

Just then we heard a kind of war-whoop, such as David might have emitted when he knocked out the champion Goliath. It was a sling that Red Chief had pulled out of his pocket, and he was whirling it around his head.

I dodged, and heard a heavy thud and a kind of a sigh from Bill, like a horse gives out when you take his saddle off. A niggerhead rock the size of an egg had caught Bill just behind his left ear. He loosened himself all over and fell in the fire across the frying-pan of hot water for washing the dishes. I dragged him out and poured cold water on his head for half an hour.

By and by, Bill sits up and feels behind his ear and says: "Sam, do you know who my favourite Biblical character is?"

"I'll be back some time this afternoon," says I. "You must keep the boy amused and quiet till I return. And now we'll write the letter to old Dorset."

Bill and I got paper and pencil and worked on the letter while Red Chief, with a blanket wrapped around him, strutted up and down, guarding the mouth of the cave. Bill begged me tearfully [illegible] make the ransom fifteen hundred dollars [illegible] two thousand. "I ain't attempting," [illegible] decry the celebrated moral aspect of parental affection, but we're dealing with humans, and it ain't human for anybody to give up two thousand dollars for that forty-pound chunk of freckled wildcat. I'm willing to take a chance at fifteen hundred dollars. You can charge the difference up to me."

So, to relieve Bill, I acceded, and we collaborated a letter that ran this way:

Ebenezer Dorset, Esq.:

We have your boy concealed in a place far from Summit. It is useless for you or the most skilful detectives to attempt to find him. Absolutely the only terms on which you can have him restored to you are these: We demand fifteen hundred dollars in large bills for his return; the money to be left at midnight to-night at the same spot and in the same box as your reply—as hereinafter described. If you agree to these terms, send your answer in writing by a solitary messenger to-night at half-past eight o'clock. After crossing Owl Creek, on the road to Poplar Cove, there are three large trees about a hundred yards apart, close to the fence of the wheat-field on the right-hand side.

with a red handkerchief. The kid stopped about eight feet behind him.

"Sam," says Bill, "I suppose you'll think I'm a renegade, but I couldn't help it. I'm a grown person with masculine proclivities and habits of self-defence, but there is a time when all systems of egotism and predominance fail. The boy is gone. I have sent him home. All is off. There was martyrs in old times," goes on Bill, "that suffered death rather than give up the particular graft they enjoyed. None of 'em ever was subjugated to such supernatural tortures as I have been. I tried to be faithful to our articles of depredation; but there came a limit."

"What's the trouble, Bill?" I asks him.

"I was rode," says Bill, "the ninety miles to the stockade, not barring an inch. Then, when the settler was rescued, I was given oats. Sand ain't a palatable substitute. And then, for an hour I had to try to explain to him why there was nothin' in holes, how a road can run both ways and what makes the grass green. I tell you, Sam, a human can only stand so much. I takes him by the neck of his clothes and drags him down the mountain. On the way he kicks my legs black-and-blue from the knees down; and I've got to have two or three bites on my thumb and hand cauterized.

"But he's gone"—continues Bill—"gone home. I showed him the road to Summit and kicked him about eight feet nearer there at one kick. I'm sorry we lose the ransom; but it was either that or Bill Driscoll to the madhouse."

Bill is puffing and blowing, but there is a look of ineffable peace and growing content on his rose-pink features.

"Bill," says I, "there isn't any heart disease in your family, is there?"

"No," says Bill, "nothing chronic except malaria and accidents. Why?"

"Then you might turn around," says I, "and have a look behind you."

Bill turns and sees the boy, and loses his complexion and sits down plump on the ground and begins to pluck aimlessly at grass and little sticks. For an hour I was afraid of his mind. And then I told him that my scheme was to put the whole job through immediately and that we would get the ransom and be off with it by midnight if old Dorset fell in with our proposition. So Bill braced up enough to give the kid a weak sort of a smile and a promise to play the Russian in a Japanese war with him as soon as he felt a little better.

I had a scheme for collecting that ransom without danger of being caught by counterplots that ought to commend itself to professional kidnappers. The tree under which the answer was to be left—and the money later on—was close to the road fence with big, bare fields on all sides. If a gang of constables should be watching for anyone to come for the note they could see him a long way off crossing the fields or in the road. But no, sirree! At half-past eight I was up in that tree as well hidden as a tree toad, waiting for the messenger to arrive.

Exactly on time, a half-grown boy rides up the road on a bicycle, locates the pasteboard box at the foot of the fence-post, slips a folded piece of paper into it and pedals away again back toward Summit.

I waited an hour and then concluded the thing was square. I slid down the tree, got the note, slipped along the fence till I struck the woods, and was back at the cave in another half an hour. I opened the note, got near the lantern and read it to Bill. It was written with a pen in a crabbed hand, and the sum and substance of it was this:

TWO DESPERATE MEN.

GENTLEMEN,—I received your letter to-day by post, in regard to the ransom you ask for the return of my son. I think you are a little high in your demands, and I hereby make you a counter-proposition, which I am inclined to believe you will accept. You bring Johnny home and pay me two hundred and fifty dollars in cash, and I agree to take him off your hands. You had better come at night, for the neighbours believe he is lost, and I couldn't be responsible for what they would do to anybody they saw bringing him back.

Very respectfully,
EBENEZER DORSET.

"Great pirates of Penzance!" says I; "of all the impudent——"

But I glanced at Bill, and hesitated. He had the most appealing look in his eyes I ever saw on the face of a dumb or a talking brute.

"Sam," says he, "what's two hundred and fifty dollars, after all? We've got the money. One more night of this kid will send me to a bed in Bedlam. Besides being a thorough gentleman, I think Mr. Dorset is a spendthrift for making us such a liberal offer. You ain't going to let the chance go, are you?"

"Tell you the truth, Bill," says I, "this little he ewe lamb has somewhat got on my nerves too.

We'll take him home, pay the ransom and make our get-away."

We took him home that night. We got him to go by telling him that his father had bought a silver-mounted rifle and a pair of moccasins for him, and we were going to hunt bears the next day.

It was just twelve o'clock when we knocked at Ebenezer's front door. Just at the moment when I should have been abstracting the fifteen hundred dollars from the box under the tree, according to the original proposition, Bill was counting out two hundred and fifty dollars into Dorset's hand.

When the kid found out we were going to leave him at home he started up a howl like a calliope and fastened himself as tight as a leech to Bill's leg. His father peeled him away gradually, like a porous plaster.

"How long can you hold him?" asks Bill.

"I'm not as strong as I used to be," says old Dorset, "but I think I can promise you ten minutes."

"Enough," says Bill. "In ten minutes I shall cross the Central, Southern and Middle Western States, and be legging it trippingly for the Canadian border."

And, as dark as it was, and as fat as Bill was, and as good a runner as I am, he was a good mile and a half out of Summit before I could catch up with him.

LX: THE PRINCESS AND THE PUMA

THERE had to be a king and queen, of course. The king was a terrible old man who wore six-shooters and spurs, and shouted in such a tremendous voice that the rattlers on the prairie would run into their holes under the prickly pear. Before there was a royal family they called the man "Whispering Ben." When he came to own 50,000 acres of land and more cattle than he could count, they called him O'Donnell "the Cattle King."

The queen had been a Mexican girl from Laredo. She made a good, mild, Colorado-claro wife, and even succeeded in teaching Ben to modify his voice sufficiently in the house to keep the dishes from being broken. When Ben got to be king she would sit on the gallery of Espinosa Ranch and weave rush mats. When wealth became so irresistible and oppressive that upholstered chairs and a centre table were brought down from San Antone in the wagons, she bowed her smooth, dark head, and shared the fate of the Danaë.

To avoid *lèse-majesté* you have been presented first to the king and queen. They do not enter the story, which might be called "The Chronicle of the Princess, the Happy Thought, and the Lion that Bungled his Job."

Josefa O'Donnell was the surviving daughter, the princess. From her mother she inherited warmth of nature and a dusky, semi-tropic beauty. From Ben O'Donnell the royal she acquired a store of intrepidity, common sense, and the faculty of ruling. The combination was one worth going miles to see. Josefa while riding her pony at a gallop could put five out of six bullets through a tomato-can swinging at the end of a string. She could play for hours with a white kitten she owned, dressing it in all manner of absurd clothes. Scorning a pencil, she could tell you out of her head what 1,545 two-year-olds would bring on the hoof, at $8.50 per head. Roughly speaking, the Espinosa Ranch is forty miles long and thirty broad—but mostly leased land. Josefa, on her pony, had prospected over every mile of it. Every cow-puncher on the range knew her by sight and was a loyal vassal. Ripley Givens, foreman of one of the Espinosa outfits, saw her one day, and made up his mind to form a royal matrimonial alliance. Presumptuous? No. In those days in the Nueces country a man was a man. And, after all, the title of cattle king does not presuppose blood royal. Often it only signifies that its owner wears the crown in token of his magnificent qualities in the art of cattle stealing.

One day Ripley Givens rode over to the Double-Elm Ranch to inquire about a bunch of strayed yearlings. He was late in setting out on his return trip, and it was sundown when he struck the White Horse Crossing of the Nueces. From there to his own camp it was sixteen miles. To the Espinosa ranch-house it was twelve. Givens was tired. He decided to pass the night at the Crossing.

There was a fine water-hole in the river-bed. The banks were thickly covered with great trees, undergrown with brush. Back from the water-hole fifty yards was a stretch of curly mesquite grass—supper for his horse and bed for himself. Givens staked his horse, and spread out his saddle blankets to dry. He sat down with his back against a tree and rolled a cigarette. From somewhere in the dense timber along the river came a sudden, rageful, shivering wail. The pony danced at the end of his rope and blew a whistling snort of comprehending fear. Givens puffed at his cigarette, but he reached leisurely for his pistol-belt, which lay on the grass, and twirled the cylinder of his weapon tentatively. A great gar plunged with a loud splash into the water-hole. A little brown rabbit skipped around a bunch of cat-claw and sat twitching his whiskers and looking humorously at Givens. The pony went on eating grass.

It is well to be reasonably watchful when a Mexican lion sings soprano along the arroyos at sundown. The burden of his song may be that young calves and fat lambs are scarce, and that he has a carnivorous desire for your acquaintance.

In the grass lay an empty fruit can, cast there by some former sojourner. Givens caught sight of it with a grunt of satisfaction. In his coat pocket tied behind his saddle was a handful or two of ground coffee. Black coffee and cigarettes! What ranchero could desire more?

In two minutes he had a little fire going clearly. He started, with his can, for the water-hole. When within fifteen yards of its edge he saw, between the bushes, a side-saddled pony with down-dropped reins cropping grass a little distance to his left. Just rising from her hands and knees on the brink of the water-hole was Josefa O'Donnell. She had been drinking water, and she brushed the sand from the palms of her hands. Ten yards away, to her right, half concealed by a clump of sacuista, Givens saw the crouching form of the Mexican lion. His amber eyeballs glared hungrily; six feet from them was the tip of the tail stretched straight, like a pointer's.

His hind-quarters rocked with the motion of the cat tribe preliminary to leaping.

Givens did what he could. His six-shooter was thirty-five yards away lying on the grass. He gave a loud yell, and dashed between the lion and the princess.

The "rucus," as Givens called it afterward, was brief and somewhat confused. When he arrived on the line of attack he saw a dim streak in the air, and heard a couple of faint cracks. Then a hundred pounds of Mexican lion plumped down upon his head and flattened him, with a heavy jar, to the ground. He remembered calling out: "Let up, now—no fair gouging!" and then he crawled from under the lion like a worm, with his mouth full of grass and dirt, and a big lump on the back of his head where it had struck the root of a water-elm. The lion lay motionless. Givens, feeling aggrieved, and suspicious of fouls, shook his fist at the lion, and shouted: "I'll rastle you again for twenty——" and then he got back to himself.

Josefa was standing in her tracks, quietly reloading her silver-mounted ·38. It had not been a difficult shot. The lion's head made an easier mark than a tomato-can swinging at the end of a string. There was a provoking, teasing, maddening smile upon her mouth and in her dark eyes. The would-be rescuing knight felt the fire of his fiasco burn down to his soul. Here had been his chance, the chance that he had dreamed of; and Momus, and not Cupid, had presided over it. The satyrs in the wood were, no doubt, holding their sides in hilarious, silent laughter. There had been something like vaudeville—say Signor Givens and his funny knockabout act with the stuffed lion.

"Is that you, Mr. Givens?" said Josefa, in her deliberate, saccharine contralto. "You nearly spoiled my shot when you yelled. Did you hurt your head when you fell?"

"Oh, no," said Givens quietly; "that didn't hurt." He stooped ignominiously and dragged his best Stetson hat from under the beast. It was crushed and wrinkled to a fine comedy effect. Then he knelt down and softly stroked the fierce, open-jawed head of the dead lion.

"Poor old Bill!" he exclaimed mournfully.

"What's that?" asked Josefa sharply.

"Of course you didn't know, Miss Josefa," said Givens, with an air of one allowing magnanimity to triumph over grief. "Nobody can blame you. I tried to save him, but I couldn't let you know in time."

"Save who?"

"Why, Bill. I've been looking for him all day. You see, he's been our camp pet for two years. Poor old fellow, he wouldn't have hurt a cotton-tail rabbit. It'll break the boys all up when they hear about it. But you couldn't tell, of course, that Bill was just trying to play with you."

Josefa's black eyes burned steadily upon him. Ripley Givens met the test successfully. He stood rumpling the yellow-brown curls on his head pensively. In his eyes was regret, not unmingled with a gentle reproach. His smooth features were set to a pattern of indisputable sorrow. Josefa wavered.

"What was your pet doing here?" she asked, making a last stand. "There's no camp near the White Horse Crossing."

"The old rascal ran away from camp yesterday,"

answered Givens readily. "It's a wonder the coyotes didn't scare him to death. You see, Jim Webster, our horse wrangler, brought a little terrier pup into camp last week. The pup made life miserable for Bill—he used to chase him around and chew his hind legs for hours at a time. Every night when bedtime came Bill would sneak under one of the boys' blankets and sleep to keep the pup from finding him. I reckon he must have been worried pretty desperate or he wouldn't have run away. He was always afraid to get out of sight of camp."

Josefa looked at the body of the fierce animal. Givens gently patted one of the formidable paws that could have killed a yearling calf with one blow. Slowly a red flush widened upon the dark olive face of the girl. Was it the signal of shame of the true sportsman who has brought down ignoble quarry? Her eyes grew softer, and the lowered lids drove away all their bright mockery.

"I'm very sorry," she said humbly; "but he looked so big, and jumped so high that——"

"Poor old Bill was hungry," interrupted Givens, in quick defence of the deceased. "We always made him jump for his supper in camp. He would lie down and roll over for a piece of meat. When he saw you he thought he was going to get something to eat from you."

Suddenly Josefa's eyes opened wide.

"I might have shot you!" she exclaimed. "You ran right in between. You risked your life to save your pet! That was fine, Mr. Givens. I like a man who is kind to animals."

Yes; there was even admiration in her gaze now. After all, there was a hero rising out of the ruins of the anti-climax. The look on Givens's face would have secured him a high position in the S.P.C.A.

"I always loved 'em," said he; "horses, dogs, Mexican lions, cows, alligators——"

"I hate alligators," instantly demurred Josefa; "crawly, muddy things!"

"Did I say alligators?" said Givens. "I meant antelopes, of course."

Josefa's conscience drove her to make further amends. She held out her hand penitently. There was a bright, unshed drop in each of her eyes.

"Please forgive me, Mr. Givens, won't you? I'm only a girl, you know, and I was frightened at first. I'm very, very sorry I shot Bill. You don't know how ashamed I feel. I wouldn't have done it for anything."

Givens took the proffered hand. He held it for a time while he allowed the generosity of his nature to overcome his grief at the loss of Bill. At last it was clear that he had forgiven her.

"Please don't speak of it any more, Miss Josefa. 'Twas enough to frighten any young lady the way Bill looked. I'll explain it all right to the boys."

"Are you really sure you don't hate me?" Josefa came closer to him impulsively. Her eyes were sweet—oh, sweet and pleading with gracious penitence. "I would hate any one who would kill my kitten. And how daring and kind of you to risk being shot when you tried to save him! How very few men would have done that!" Victory wrested from defeat! Vaudeville turned into drama! Bravo, Ripley Givens!

It was now twilight. Of course Miss Josefa could not be allowed to ride on to the ranch-house alone. Givens resaddled his pony in spite of that animal's reproachful glances, and rode with her. Side by side they galloped across the smooth grass, the princess and the man who was kind to animals. The prairie odours of fruitful earth and delicate bloom were thick and sweet around them. Coyotes yelping over there on the hill! No fear. And yet——

Josefa rode closer. A little hand seemed to grope. Givens found it with his own. The ponies kept an even gait. The hands lingered together, and the owner of one explained—

"I never was frightened before, but just think! How terrible it would be to meet a really wild lion! Poor Bill! I'm so glad you came with me!"

O'Donnell was sitting on the ranch gallery.

"Hallo, Rip!" he shouted—"that you?"

"He rode in with me," said Josefa. "I lost my way and was late."

"Much obliged," called the cattle king. "Stop over, Rip, and ride to camp in the morning."

But Givens would not. He would push on to camp. There was a bunch of steers to start off on the trail at daybreak. He said good night, and trotted away.

An hour later, when the lights were out, Josefa, in her night-robe, came to her door and called to the king in his own room across the brick-paved hallway—

"Say, pop, you know that old Mexican lion they call the 'Gotch-eared Devil'—the one that killed Gonzales, Mr. Martin's sheep herder, and about fifty calves on the Salado range? Well, I settled his hash this afternoon over at the White Horse Crossing. Put two balls in his head with my ·38 while he was on the jump. I knew him by the slice gone from his left ear that old Gonzales cut off with his machete. You couldn't have made a better shot yourself, daddy."

"Bully for you!" thundered Whispering Ben from the darkness of the royal chamber.

LXI: THE HARBINGER

LONG before the springtide is felt in the dull bosom of the yokel does the city man know that the grass-green goddess is upon her throne. He sits at his breakfast eggs and toast, begirt by stone walls, opens his morning paper and sees journalism leave vernalism at the post.

For whereas spring's couriers were once the evidence of our finer senses, now the Associated Press does the trick.

The warble of the first robin in Hackensack, the stirring of the maple sap in Bennington, the budding of the pussy willows along Main Street in Syracuse, the first chirp of the bluebird, the swan song of the Blue Point, the annual tornado in St. Louis, the plaint of the peach pessimist from Pompton, N.J., the regular visit of the tame wild goose with a broken leg to the pond near Bilgewater Junction, the base attempt of the Drug Trust to boost the price of quinine foiled in the House by Congressman Jinks, the first tall poplar struck by lightning and the usual stunned picknickers who had taken refuge, the first crack of the ice jam in the Allegheny River, the finding of a violet in its mossy bed by the correspondent at Round Corners—these are the advanced signs of the burgeoning season that are wired into the wise city, while the farmer sees nothing but winter upon his dreary fields.

But these be mere externals. The true harbinger is the heart. When Strephon seeks his Chloe and Mike his Maggie, then only is spring arrived and the newspaper report of the five-foot rattler killed in Squire Pettigrew's pasture confirmed.

Ere the first violet blew, Mr. Peters, Mr. Ragsdale and Mr. Kidd sat together on a bench in Union Square and conspired. Mr. Peters was the D'Artagnan of the loafers there. He was the dingiest, the laziest, the sorriest brown blot against the green background of any bench in the park. But just then he was the most important of the trio.

Mr. Peters had a wife. This had not heretofore affected his standing with Ragsy and Kidd. But to-day it invested him with a peculiar interest. His friends, having escaped matrimony, had shown a disposition to deride Mr. Peters for his venture on that troubled sea. But at last they had been forced to acknowledge that either he had been gifted with a large foresight or that he was one of Fortune's lucky sons.

For, Mrs. Peters had a dollar. A whole dollar bill, good and receivable by the Government for customs, taxes, and all public dues. How to get possession of that dollar was the question up for discussion by the three musty musketeers.

"How do you know it was a dollar?" asked Ragsy, the immensity of the sum inclining him to scepticism.

"The coalman seen her have it," said Mr. Peters. "She went out and done some washing yesterday.

And look what she give me for breakfast—the heel of a loaf and a cup of coffee, and her with a dollar!"

"It's fierce," said Ragsy.

"Say we go up and punch 'er and stick a towel in 'er mouth and cop the coin," suggested Kidd, viciously. "Y' ain't afraid of a woman, are you?"

"She might holler and have us pinched," demurred Ragsy. "I don't believe in slugging no woman in a houseful of people."

"Gent'men," said Mr. Peters severely, through his russet stubble, "remember that you are speaking of my wife. A man who would lift his hand to a lady except in the way of——"

"Maguire," said Ragsy, pointedly, "has got his bock beer sign out. If we had a dollar we could——"

"Hush up!" said Mr. Peters, licking his lips. "We got to get that case note somehow, boys. Ain't what's a man's wife's his? Leave it to me. I'll go over to the house and get it. Wait here for me."

"I've seen 'em give up quick, and tell you where it's hid if you kick 'em in the ribs," said Kidd.

"No man would kick a woman," said Peters, virtuously. "A little choking—just a touch on the windpipe—that gets away with 'em—and no marks left. Wait for me. I'll bring back that dollar, boys."

High up in a tenement-house between Second Avenue and the river lived the Peterses in a back room so gloomy that the landlord blushed to take the rent for it. Mrs. Peters worked at sundry times, doing odd jobs of scrubbing and washing. Mr. Peters had a pure, unbroken record of five years without having earned a penny. And yet they clung together, sharing each other's hatred and misery, being creatures of habit. Of habit, the power that keeps the earth from flying to pieces; though there is some silly theory of gravitation.

Mrs. Peters reposed her 200 pounds on the safer of the two chairs and gazed stolidly out the one window at the brick wall opposite. Her eyes were red and damp. The furniture could have been carried away on a pushcart, but no pushcart man would have removed it as a gift.

The door opened to admit Mr. Peters. His fox-terrier eyes expressed a wish. His wife's diagnosis located correctly the seat of it, but misread it hunger instead of thirst.

"You'll get nothing more to eat till night," she said, looking out of the window again. "Take your hound-dog's face out of the room."

Mr. Peters's eye calculated the distance between them. By taking her by surprise it might be possible to spring upon her, overthrow her, and apply the throttling tactics of which he had boasted to his waiting comrades. True, it had been only a boast; never yet had he dared to lay violent hands upon her; but with the thoughts of the delicious, cool bock or Culmbacher bracing his nerves, he was near to upsetting his own theories of the treatment due by a gentleman to a lady. But, with his loafer's love for the more artistic and less strenuous way, he chose diplomacy first, the high card in the game—the assumed attitude of success already attained.

"You have a dollar," he said, loftily, but significantly in the tone that goes with the lighting of a cigar—when the properties are at hand.

"I have," said Mrs. Peters, producing the bill from her bosom and crackling it, teasingly.

"I am offered a position in a—in a tea store," said Mr. Peters. "I am to begin work to-morrow. But it will be necessary for me to buy a pair of——"

"You are a liar," said Mrs. Peters, reinterring the note. "No tea store, nor no A B C store, nor no junk shop would have you. I rubbed the skin off both me hands washin' jumpers and overalls to make that dollar. Do you think it come out of them suds to buy the kind you put into you? Skiddoo! Get your mind off of money."

Evidently the poses of Talleyrand were not worth one hundred cents on that dollar. But diplomacy is dexterous. The artistic temperament of Mr. Peters lifted him by the straps of his congress gaiters and set him on new ground. He called up a look of desperate melancholy to his eyes.

"Clara," he said, hollowly, "to struggle further is useless. You have always misunderstood me. Heaven knows I have striven with all my might to keep my head above the waves of misfortune, but——"

"Cut out the rainbow of hope and that stuff about walkin' one by one through the narrow isles of Spain," said Mrs. Peters, with a sigh. "I've heard it so often. There's an ounce bottle of carbolic on the shelf behind the empty coffee can. Drink hearty."

Mr. Peters reflected. What next! The old expedients had failed. The two musty musketeers were awaiting him hard by the ruined château—that is to say, on a park bench with rickety cast-iron legs. His honour was at stake. He had engaged to storm the castle single-handed and bring back the treasure that was to furnish them wassail and solace. And all that stood between them and the coveted dollar was his wife, once a little girl whom he could—aha!—why not again? Once with soft words he could, as they say, twist her around his little finger. Why not again? Not for years had he tried it. Grim poverty and mutual hatred had killed all that. But Ragsy and Kidd were waiting for him to bring the dollar!

Mr. Peters took a surreptitiously keen look at his wife. Her formless bulk overflowed the chair. She kept her eyes fixed out the window in a strange kind of trance. Her eyes showed that she had been recently weeping.

"I wonder," said Mr. Peters to himself, "if there'd be anything in it."

The window was open upon its outlook of brick walls and drab, barren back yards. Except for the mildness of the air that entered, it might have been midwinter yet in the city that turns such a frowning face to besieging spring. But spring doesn't come with the thunder of cannon. She is a sapper and a miner, and you must capitulate.

"I'll try it," said Mr. Peters to himself, making a wry face.

He went up to his wife and put his arm across her shoulders.

"Clara, darling," he said in tones that shouldn't have fooled a baby seal, "why should we have hard words? Ain't you my own tootsum wootsums?"

A black mark against you, Mr. Peters, in the sacred ledger of Cupid. Charges of attempted graft are filed against you, and of forgery and utterance of two of Love's holiest of appellations.

But the miracle of spring was wrought. Into the back room over the back alley between the black walls had crept the Harbinger. It was ridiculous, and yet—— Well, it is a rat-trap, and you, madam and sir and all of us, are in it.

Red and fat and crying like Niobe or Niagara, Mrs. Peters threw her arms around her lord and dissolved upon him. Mr. Peters would have striven to extricate the dollar bill from its deposit vault, but his arms were bound to his sides.

"Do you love me, James?" asked Mrs. Peters.

"Madly," said James, "but——"

"You are ill!" exclaimed Mrs. Peters. "Why are you so pale and tired-looking?"

"I feel weak," said Mr. Peters. "I——"

"Oh, wait; I know what it is. Wait, James. I'll be back in a minute."

With a parting hug that revived in Mr. Peters recollections of the Terrible Turk, his wife hurried out of the room and down the stairs.

Mr. Peters hitched his thumbs under his suspenders.

"All right," he confided to the ceiling. "I've got her going. I hadn't any idea the old girl was soft any more under the foolish rib. Well, sir; ain't I the Claude Melnotte of the lower East Side? What? It's a 100 to 1 shot that I get the dollar. I wonder what she went out for. I guess she's gone to tell Mrs. Muldoon on the second floor that we're reconciled. I'll remember this. Soft soap! And Ragsy was talking about slugging her!"

Mrs. Peters came back with a bottle of sarsaparilla.

"I'm glad I happened to have that dollar," she said. "You're all run down, honey."

Mr. Peters had a tablespoonful of the stuff inserted into him. Then Mrs. Peters sat on his lap and murmured:

"Call me tootsum wootsums again, James."

He sat still, held there by his materialized goddess of spring.

Spring had come.

On the bench in Union Square Mr. Ragsdale and Mr. Kidd squirmed, tongue-parched, awaiting D'Artagnan and his dollar.

"I wish I had choked her at first," said Mr. Peters to himself.

LXII: THE GREATER CONEY

"NEXT Sunday," said Dennis Carnahan, "I'll be after going down to see the new Coney Island that's risen like a phœnix bird from the ashes of the old resort. I'm going with Norah Flynn, and we'll fall victims to all the dry goods deceptions, from the red-flannel eruption of Mount Vesuvius to the pink silk ribbons on the race-suicide problems in the incubator kiosk.

"Was I there before? I was. I was there last Tuesday. Did I see the sights? I did not.

"Last Monday I amalgamated myself with the Bricklayers' Union, and in accordance with the rules I was ordered to quit work the same day on account of a sympathy strike with the Lady Salmon Canners' Lodge No. 2, of Tacoma, Washington.

"'Twas disturbed I was in mind and proclivities by losing me job, bein' already harassed in me soul on account of havin' quarrelled with Norah

Flynn a week before by reason of hard words spoken at the Dairymen and Street-Sprinkler Drivers' semi-annual ball, caused by jealousy and prickly heat and that divil, Andy Coghlin.

"So, I says, it will be Coney for Tuesday; and if the chutes and the short change and the green-corn silk between the teeth don't create diversions and get me feeling better, then I don't know at all.

"Ye will have heard that Coney had received moral reconstruction. The old Bowery, where they used to take your tintype by force and give ye knockout drops before having your palm read, is now called the Wall Street of the island. The wienerwurst stands are required by law to keep a news ticker in 'em; and the doughnuts are examined every four years by a retired steamboat inspector. The nigger man's head that was used by the old patrons to throw baseballs at is now illegal; and by the order of the Police Commissioner the image of a man drivin' an automobile has been substituted. I hear that the old immoral amusements have been suppressed. People who used to go down from New York to sit in the sand and dabble in the surf now give up their quarters to squeeze through turnstiles and see imitations of city fires and floods painted on canvas. The reprehensible and degradin' resorts that disgraced old Coney are said to be wiped out. The wipin'-out process consists of raisin' the price from ten cents to twenty-five cents, and hirin' a blonde named Maudie to sell tickets instead of Micky, the Bowery Bite. That's what they say—I don't know.

"But to Coney I goes a-Tuesday. I gets off the 'L' and starts for the glitterin' show. 'Twas a fine sight. The Babylonian towers and the Hindoo roof-gardens was blazin' with thousands of electric lights, and the streets was thick with people. 'Tis a true thing they say that Coney levels all rank. I see millionaires eatin' popcorn and trampin' along with the crowd; and I see eight-dollar-a-week clothin'-store clerks in red automobiles fightin' one another for who'd squeeze the horn when they come to a corner.

" 'I made a mistake,' I says to myself. 'Twas not Coney I needed. When a man's sad 'tis not scenes of hilarity he wants. 'Twould be far better for him to meditate in a graveyard or to attend services at the Paradise Roof Gardens. 'Tis no consolation when a man's lost his sweetheart to order hot corn and have the waiter bring him the powdered sugar cruet instead of salt and then conceal himself, or to have Zozookum, the gipsy palmist, tell him that he has three children and to look out for another serious calamity; price twenty-five cents.

"I walked far away down on the beach, to the ruins of an old pavilion near one corner of this new private park, Dreamland. A year ago that old pavilion was standin' straight and the old-style waiters was slammin' a week's supply of clam chowder down in front of you for a nickel and callin' you 'cully' friendly, and vice was rampant, and you got back to New York with enough change to take a car at the bridge. Now they tell me that they serve Welsh rabbits on Surf Avenue, and you get the right change back in the movin'-picture joints.

"I sat down at one side of the old pavilion and looked at the surf spreadin' itself on the beach and thought about the time me and Norah Flynn sat on that spot last summer. 'Twas before reform struck the island; and we was happy. We had tintypes and chowder in the ribald dives, and the Egyptian Sorceress of the Nile told Norah out of her hand, while I was waitin' in the door, that 'twould be the luck of her to marry a red-headed gossoon with two crooked legs, and was overrunnin' with joy on account of the allusion. And 'twas there that Norah Flynn put her two hands in mine a year before and talked of flats and the things she could cook and the love business that goes with such episodes. And that was Coney as we loved it, and as the hand of Satan was upon it, friendly and noisy and your money's worth, with no fence around the ocean and not too many electric lights to show the sleeve of a black serge coat against a white shirtwaist.

"I sat with my back to the parks where they had the moon and the dreams and the steeples corralled, and longed for the old Coney. There wasn't many people on the beach. Lots of them was feedin' pennies into the slot machines to see the 'Interrupted Courtship' in the movin' pictures; and a good many was takin' the sea air in the Canals of Venice and some was breathin' the smoke of the sea battle by actual warships in a tank filled with real water. A few was down on the sands enjoyin' the moonlight and the water. And the heart of me was heavy for the new morals of the old island, while the bands behind me played and the sea pounded on the bass drum in front.

"And directly I got up and walked along the old pavilion, and there on the other side of it, half in the dark, was a slip of a girl sittin' on the tumble-down timbers, and unless I'm a liar she was cryin' by herself there, all alone.

" 'Is it trouble you are in, now, Miss?' says I; 'and what's to be done about it?'

" ''Tis none of your business at all, Denny Carnahan,' says she, sittin' up straight. And it was the voice of no other than Norah Flynn.

" 'Then it's not,' says I, 'and we're after having a pleasant evening, Miss Flynn. Have ye seen the sights of this new Coney Island, then? I presume ye have come here for that purpose,' says I.

" 'I have,' says she. 'Me mother and Uncle Tim they are waiting beyond. 'Tis an elegant evening I've had. I've seen all the attractions that be.'

" 'Right ye are,' says I to Norah; and I don't know when I've been that amused. After disportin' meself among the most laughable moral improvements of the revised shell games I took meself to the shore for the benefit of the cool air. 'And did ye observe the Durbar, Miss Flynn?'

" 'I did,' says she, reflectin'; 'but 'tis not safe, I'm thinkin', to ride down them slantin' things into the water.'

" 'How did ye fancy the shoot the chutes?' I asks.

" 'True, then, I'm afraid of guns,' says Norah. 'They make such noise in my ears. But Uncle Tim, he shot them, he did, and won cigars. 'Tis a fine time we had this day, Mr. Carnahan.'

" 'I'm glad you've enjoyed yerself,' I says. 'I suppose you've had a roarin' fine time seein' the sights. And how did the incubators and the helter-skelter and the midgets suit the taste of ye?'

" 'I—I wasn't hungry,' says Norah, faint. 'But mother ate a quantity of all of 'em. I'm that pleased with the fine things in the new Coney

Island,' says she, 'that it's the happiest day I've seen in a long time, at all.'

" 'Did you see Venice?' says I.

" 'We did,' says she. 'She was a beauty. She was dressed in red, she was, with——'

"I listened no more to Norah Flynn. I stepped up and gathered her in my arms.

" ' 'Tis a story-teller ye are, Norah Flynn,' says I. 'Ye've seen no more of the greater Coney Island that I have meself. Come, now, tell the truth—ye came to sit by the old pavilion by the waves where you sat last summer and made Dennis Carnahan a happy man. Speak up, and tell the truth.'

"Norah stuck her nose against me vest.

" 'I despise it, Denny,' she says, half cryin'. 'Mother and Uncle Tim went to see the shows, but I came down here to think of you. I couldn't bear the lights and the crowd. Are you forgivin' me, Denny, for the words we had?'

" ' 'Twas me fault,' says I. 'I came here for the same reason meself. Look at the lights, Norah,' I says, turning my back to the sea—'ain't they pretty?'

" 'They are,' says Norah, with her eyes shinin'; 'and do ye hear the bands playin'? Oh, Denny, I think I'd like to see it all.'

" 'The old Coney is gone, darlin',' I says to her. 'Everything moves. When a man's glad it's not scenes of sadness he wants. 'Tis a greater Coney we have here, but we couldn't see it till we got in the humour for it. Next Sunday, Norah darlin', we'll see the new place from end to end.' "

LXIII: A CHAPARRAL PRINCE

NINE o'clock at last, and the drudging toil of the day was ended. Lena climbed to her room in the third half-story of the *Quarrymen's Hotel.* Since daylight she had slaved, doing the work of a full-grown woman, scrubbing the floors, washing the heavy ironstone plates and cups, making the beds, and supplying the insatiate demands for wood and water in that turbulent and depressing hostelry.

The din of the day's quarrying was over—the blasting and drilling, the creaking of the great cranes, the shouts of the foremen, the backing and shifting of the flat-cars hauling the heavy blocks of limestone. Down in the hotel office three or four of the labourers were growling and swearing over a belated game of checkers. Heavy odours of stewed meat, hot grease, and cheap coffee hung like a depressing fog about the house.

Lena lit the stump of a candle and sat limply upon her wooden chair. She was eleven years old, thin and ill-nourished. Her back and limbs were sore and aching. But the ache in her heart made the biggest trouble. The last straw had been added to the burden upon her small shoulders. They had taken away Grimm. Always at night, however tired she might be, she had turned to Grimm for comfort and hope. Each time had Grimm whispered to her that the prince or the fairy would come and deliver her out of the wicked enchantment. Every night she had taken fresh courage and strength from Grimm.

To whatever tale she read she found an analogy in her own condition. The woodcutter's lost child, the unhappy goose girl, the persecuted stepdaughter, the little maiden imprisoned in the witch's hut—all these were but transparent disguises for Lena, the overworked kitchenmaid in the *Quarrymen's Hotel*. And always when the extremity was direst came the good fairy or the gallant prince to the rescue.

So, here in the ogre's castle, enslaved by a wicked spell, Lena had leaned upon Grimm and waited, longing for the powers of goodness to prevail. But on the day before Mrs. Maloney had found the book in her room and had carried it away, declaring sharply that it would not do for servants to read at night; they lost sleep and did not work briskly the next day. Can one only eleven years old, living away from one's mamma, and never having any time to play, live entirely deprived of Grimm? Just try it once and you will see what a difficult thing it is.

Lena's home was in Texas, away up among the little mountains on the Pedernales River, in a little town called Fredericksburg. They are all German people who live in Fredericksburg. Of evenings they sit at little tables along the sidewalk and drink beer and play pinochle and scat. They are very thrifty people.

Thriftiest among them was Peter Hildesmuller, Lena's father. And that is why Lena was sent to work to the hotel at the quarries, thirty miles away. She earned three dollars every week there, and Peter added her wages to his well-guarded store. Peter had an ambition to become as rich as his neighbour, Hugo Heffelbauer, who smoked a meerschaum pipe three feet long and had wiener schnitzel and hassenpfeffer for dinner every day in the week. And now Lena was quite old enough to work and assist in the accumulation of riches. But conjecture, if you can, what it means to be sentenced at eleven years of age from a home in the pleasant little Rhine village to hard labour in the ogre's castle, where you must fly to serve the ogres, while they devour cattle and sheep, growling fiercely as they stamp white limestone dust from their great shoes for you to sweep and scour with your weak, aching fingers. And then—to have Grimm taken away from you!

Lena raised the lid of an old empty case that had once contained canned corn and got out a sheet of paper and a piece of pencil. She was going to write a letter to her mamma. Tommy Ryan was going to post it for her at Ballinger's. Tommy was seventeen, worked in the quarries, went home to Ballinger's every night, and was now waiting in the shadows under Lena's window for her to throw the letter out to him. That was the only way she could send a letter to Fredericksburg. Mrs. Maloney did not like for her to write letters.

The stump of candle was burning low, so Lena hastily bit the wood from around the lead of her pencil and began. This is the letter she wrote—

DEAREST MAMMA:—I want so much to see you. And Gretel and Claus and Heinrich and little Adolf. I am so tired. I want to see you. To-day I was slapped by Mrs. Maloney and had no supper. I could not bring in enough wood, for my hand hurt. She took my book yesterday. I mean *Grimms's Fairy Tales*, which Uncle Leo gave me. It did not hurt anyone for me to read the book. I try to work as well as I can, but there is so much to do. I read only a little bit every night. Dear mamma, I shall tell you what I am going to do. Unless you send for me to-morrow to bring me home I shall go to a deep place I know in the river and drown. It is wicked to drown, I suppose, but I wanted to see you, and there is no one else. I am very tired, and Tommy is waiting for the letter. You will excuse me, mamma, if I do it.

Your respectful and loving daughter,

LENA.

Tommy was still waiting faithfully when the letter was concluded, and when Lena dropped it out she saw him pick it up and start up the steep hill-side. Without undressing she blew out the candle and curled herself upon the mattress on the floor.

At 10.30 o'clock old man Ballinger came out of his house in his stocking feet and leaned over the gate, smoking his pipe. He looked down the big road, white in the moonshine, and rubbed one ankle with the toe of his other foot. It was time for the Fredericksburg mail to come pattering up the road.

Old man Ballinger had waited only a few minutes when he heard the lively hoofbeats of Fritz's team of little black mules, and very soon afterward his covered spring wagon stood in front of the gate. Fritz's big spectacles flashed in the moonlight and his tremendous voice shouted a greeting to the postmaster of Ballinger's. The mail-carrier jumped out and took the bridles from the mules, for he always fed them oats at Ballinger's.

While the mules were eating from their feed bags old man Ballinger brought out the mail sack and threw it into the wagon.

Fritz Bergmann was a man of three sentiments—or to be more accurate—four, the pair of mules deserving to be reckoned individually. Those mules were the chief interest and joy of his existence.

Next came the Emperor of Germany and Lena Hildesmuller.

"Tell me," said Fritz, when he was ready to start, "contains the sack a letter to Frau Hildesmuller from the little Lena at the quarries? One came in the last mail to say that she is a little sick, already. Her mamma is very anxious to hear again."

"Yes," said old man Ballinger, "thar's a letter for Mrs. Helterskelter, or some sich name. Tommy Ryan brung it over when he come. Her little gal workin' over thar, you say?"

"In the hotel," shouted Fritz, as he gathered up the lines; "eleven years old and not bigger as a frankfurter. The close-fist of a Peter Hildesmuller!—some day shall I with a big club pound that man's dummkopf—all in and out the town. Perhaps in this letter Lena will say that she is yet feeling better. So, her mamma will be glad. *Auf wiedersehen*, Herr Ballinger—your feets will take cold out in the night air."

"So long, Fritzy," said old man Ballinger. "You got a nice cool night for your drive."

Up the road went the little black mules at their steady trot, while Fritz thundered at them occasional words of endearment and cheer.

These fancies occupied the mind of the mail-carrier until he reached the big post oak forest, eight miles from Ballinger's. Here his ruminations were scattered by the sudden flash and report of pistols and a whooping as if from a whole tribe of Indians. A band of galloping centaurs closed in around the mail wagon. One of them leaned over the front wheel, covered the driver with his revolver, and ordered him to stop. Others caught at the bridles of Doder and Blitzen.

"Donnerwetter!" shouted Fritz, with all his tremendous voice—"wass ist? Release your hands from dose mules. Ve vas der United States mail!"

"Hurry up, Dutch!" drawled a melancholy voice. "Don't you know when you're in a stick-up? Reverse your mules and climb out of the cart."

It is due to the breadth of Hondo Bill's demerit and the largeness of his achievements to state that the holding up of the Fredericksburg mail was not perpetrated by way of an exploit. As the lion while in the pursuit of prey commensurate to his prowess might set a frivolous foot upon a casual rabbit in his path, so Hondo Bill and his gang had swooped sportively upon the pacific transport of Meinherr Fritz.

The real work of their sinister night ride was over. Fritz and his mail bag and his mules came as a gentle relaxation, graceful after the arduous duties of their profession. Twenty miles to the south-east stood a train with a killed engine, hysterical passengers and a looted express and mail car. That represented the serious occupation of Hondo Bill and his gang. With a fairly rich prize of currency and silver the robbers were making a wide détour to the west through the less populous country, intending to seek safety in Mexico by means of some fordable spot on the Rio Grande. The booty from the train had melted the desperate bushrangers to jovial and happy skylarkers.

Trembling with outraged dignity and no little personal apprehension, Fritz climbed out to the road after replacing his suddenly removed spectacles. The band had dismounted and were singing, capering, and whooping, thus expressing their satisfied delight in the life of a jolly outlaw. Rattlesnake

Rogers, who stood at the heads of the mules, jerked a little too vigorously at the rein of the tender-mouthed Donder, who reared and emitted a loud, protesting snort of pain. Instantly Fritz, with a scream of anger, flew at the bulky Rogers and began to assiduously pommel that surprised freebooter with his fists.

"Villain!" shouted Fritz, "dog, bigstiff! Dot mule he has a soreness by his mouth. I vill knock off your shoulders mit your head—robbermans!"

"Yi-yi!" howled Rattlesnake, roaring with laughter and ducking his head, "somebody git this here sourkrout off'n me!"

One of the band yanked Fritz back by the coat-tail and the woods rang with Rattlesnake's vociferous comments.

"The dog-goned little wienerwurst," he yelled amiably. "He's not so much of a skunk, for a Dutchman. Took up for his animile plum quick, didn't he? I like to see a man like his hoss, even if it is a mule. The dad-blamed little Limburger he went for me, didn't he! Whoa, now, muley—I ain't a-goin' to hurt your mouth agin any more."

Perhaps the mail would not have been tampered with had not Ben Moody, the lieutenant, possessed certain wisdom that seemed to promise more spoils.

"Say, Cap," he said, addressing Hondo Bill, "there's liable to be good pickings in these mail sacks. I've done some hoss tradin' with these Dutchmen around Fredericksburg, and I know the style of the varmints. There's big money goes through the mails to that town. Them Dutch risk a thousand dollars sent wrapped in a piece of paper before they'd pay the banks to handle the money."

Hondo Bill, six feet two, gentle of voice and

impulsive in action, was dragging the sacks from the rear of the wagon before Moody had finished his speech. A knife shone in his hand, and they heard the ripping sound as it bit through the tough canvas. The outlaws crowded around and began tearing open letters and packages, enlivening their labours by swearing affably at the writers, who seemed to have conspired to confute the prediction of Ben Moody. Not a dollar was found in the Fredericksburg mail.

"You ought to be ashamed of yourself," said Hondo Bill to the mail-carrier in solemn tones, "to be packing around such a lot of old, trashy paper as this. What d'you mean by it, anyhow? Where do you Dutchers keep your money at?"

The Ballinger mail sack opened like a cocoon under Hondo's knife. It contained but a handful of mail. Fritz had been fuming with terror and excitement until this sack was reached. He now remembered Lena's letter. He addressed the leader of the band, asking that that particular missive be spared.

"Much obliged, Dutch," he said to the disturbed carrier. "I guess that's the letter we want. Got spondulicks in it, ain't it? Here she is. Make a light, boys."

Hondo found and tore open the letter to Mrs. Hildesmuller. The others stood about, lighting twisted-up letters one from another. Hondo gazed with mute disapproval at the single sheet of paper covered with the angular German script.

"Whatever is this you've humbugged us with, Dutchy? You call this here a valuable letter? That's a mighty low-down trick to play on your friends what come along to help you distribute your mail."

"That's Chiny writin'," said Sandy Grundy, peering over Hondo's shoulder.

"You're off your kazip," declared another of the gang, an effective youth, covered with silk handkerchiefs and nickel plating. "That's shorthand. I seen 'em do it once in court."

"Ach, no, no, no—dot is German," said Fritz. "It is no more as a little girl writing a letter to her mamma. One poor little girl, sick and vorking hard avay from home. Ach! it is a shame. Good Mr. Robberman, you vill please let me have dot letter?"

"What the devil do you take us for, old Pretzels?" said Hondo with sudden and surprising severity. "You ain't presumin' to insinuate that we gents ain't possessed of sufficient politeness for to take an interest in the miss's health, are you? Now, you go on, and you read that scratchin' out loud and in plain United States language to this here company of educated society."

Hondo twirled his six-shooter by its trigger guard and stood towering above the little German, who at once began to read the letter, translating the simple words into English. The gang of rovers stood in absolute silence, listening intently.

"How old is that kid?" asked Hondo when the letter was done.

"Eleven," said Fritz.

"And where is she at?"

"At dose rock quarries—working. Ach, mein Gott—little Lena, she speak of drowning. I do not know if she vill do it, but if she shall I schwear I vill dot Peter Hildesmuller shoot mit a gun."

"You Dutchers," said Hondo Bill, his voice swelling with fine contempt, "make me plenty tired. Hirin' out your kids to work when they ought to be playin' dolls in the sand. You're a hell of a sect of a people. I reckon we'll fix your clock for a while just to show what we think of your old cheesy nation. Here, boys!"

Hondo Bill parleyed aside briefly with his band, and then they seized Fritz and conveyed him off the road to one side. Here they bound him fast to a tree with a couple of lariats. His team they tied to another tree near by.

"We ain't going to hurt you bad," said Hondo reassuringly. "'Twon't hurt you to be tied up for a while. We will now pass you the time of day, as it is up to us to depart. Ausgespielt.—nixcumrous, Dutchy. Don't get any more impatience."

Fritz heard a great squeaking of saddles as the men mounted their horses. Then a loud yell and a great clatter of hoofs as they galloped pell-mell back along the Fredericksburg road.

For more than two hours Fritz sat against his tree, tightly but not painfully bound. Then from the reaction after his exciting adventure he sank into slumber. How long he slept he knew not, but he was at last awakened by a rough shake. Hands were untying his ropes. He was lifted to his feet, dazed, confused in mind, and weary of body. Rubbing his eyes, he looked and saw that he was again in the midst of the same band of terrible bandits. They shoved him up to the seat of his wagon and placed the lines in his hands.

"Hit it out for home, Dutch," said Hondo Bill's voice commandingly. "You've given us lots of trouble and we're pleased to see the back of your neck. Spiel! Zwei bier! Vamoose!"

Hondo reached out and gave Blitzen a smart cut with his quirt.

The little mules sprang ahead, glad to be moving again. Fritz urged them along, himself dizzy and muddled over his fearful adventure.

According to schedule time, he should have reached Fredericksburg at daylight. As it was, he drove down the long street of the town at eleven o'clock a.m. He had to pass Peter Hildesmuller's house on his way to the post office. He stopped his team at the gate and called. But Frau Hildesmuller was watching for him. Out rushed the whole family of Hildesmullers.

Frau Hildesmuller, fat and flushed, inquired if he had a letter from Lena, and then Fritz raised his voice and told the tale of his adventure. He told the contents of the letter that the robber had made him read, and then Frau Hildesmuller broke into wild weeping. Her little Lena drown herself! Why had they sent her from home? What could be done? Perhaps it would be too late by the time they could send for her now. Peter Hildesmuller dropped his meerschaum on the walk and it shivered into pieces.

"Woman!" he roared at his wife, "why did you let that child go away? It is your fault if she comes home to us no more."

Every one knew that it was Peter Hildesmuller's fault, so they paid no attention to his words.

A moment afterward a strange faint voice was heard to call: "Mamma!" Frau Hildesmuller at first thought it was Lena's spirit calling, and then she rushed to the rear of Fritz's covered wagon, and, with a loud shriek of joy, caught up Lena herself, covering her pale little face with kisses and smothering her with hugs. Lena's eyes were heavy with the deep slumber of exhaustion, but she smiled and lay close to the one she had longed to see. There among the mail sacks, covered in a nest of strange blankets and comforters, she had lain asleep until wakened by the voices around her.

Fritz stared at her with eyes that bulged behind his spectacles.

"Gott in Himmel!" he shouted. "How did you get in that wagon? Am I going crazy as well as to be murdered and hanged by robbers this day?"

"You brought her to us, Fritz," cried Frau Hildesmuller. "How can we ever thank you enough?"

"Tell mamma how you came in Fritz's wagon," said Frau Hildesmuller.

"I don't know," said Lena. "But I know how I got away from the hotel. The Prince brought me."

"By the Emperor's crown!" shouted Fritz, "we are all going crazy."

"I always knew he would come," said Lena, sitting down on her bundle of bedclothes on the sidewalk. "Last night he came with his armed knights and captured the ogre's castle. They broke the dishes and kicked down the doors. They pitched Mr. Maloney into a barrel of rain-water and threw flour all over Mrs. Maloney. The workmen in the hotel jumped out of the windows and ran into the woods when the knights began firing their guns. They wakened me up and I peeped down the stair. And then the Prince came up and wrapped me in the bedclothes and carried me out. He was so tall and strong and fine. His face was as rough as a scrubbing brush, and he talked soft and kind and smelled of schnapps. He took me on his horse before him and we rode away among the knights.

He held me close and I went to sleep that way, and didn't wake up till I got home."

"Rubbish!" cried Fritz Bergmann. "Fairy tales! How did you come from the quarries to my wagon?"

"The Prince brought me," said Lena confidently.

And to this day the good people of Fredericksburg haven't been able to make her give any other explanation.

LXIV: FOREIGN POLICY OF COMPANY 99

JOHN BYRNES, hose-cart driver of Engine Company No. 99, was afflicted with what his comrades called Japanitis.

Byrnes had a war map spread permanently upon a table in the second story of the engine-house, and he could explain to you at any hour of the day or night the exact positions, conditions and intentions of both the Russian and Japanese armies. He had little clusters of pins stuck in the map which represented the opposing forces, and these he moved about from day to day in conformity with the war news in the daily papers.

Whenever the Japs won a victory John Byrnes would shift his pins, and then he would execute a war dance of delight, and the other firemen would hear him yell: "Go it, you blamed little, sawed-off, huckleberry-eyed, monkey-faced hot tamales! Eat 'em up, you little sleight-o'-hand, bow-legged bull terriers—give 'em another of them Yalu looloos, and you'll eat rice in St. Petersburg. Talk about your Russians—say, wouldn't they give you a painsky when it comes to a scrapovitch?"

Not even on the fair island of Nippon was there a more enthusiastic champion of the Mikado's men. Supporters of the Russian cause did well to keep clear of Engine-House No. 99.

Sometimes all thoughts of the Japs left John Byrnes's head. That was when the alarm of fire had sounded and he was strapped in his driver's seat on the swaying cart, guiding Erebus and Joe, the finest team in the whole department—according to the crew of 99.

Of all the codes adopted by man for regulating his actions toward his fellow-mortals, the greatest are these—the code of King Arthur's Knights of the Round Table, the Constitution of the United States, and the unwritten rules of the New York Fire Department. The Round Table methods are no longer practicable since the invention of street cars and breach-of-promise suits, and our Constitution is being found more and more unconstitutional every day, so the code of our firemen must be considered in the lead, with the Golden Rule and Jeffries's new punch trying for place and show.

The Constitution says that one man is as good as another; but the Fire Department says he is better. This is a too generous theory, but the law will not allow itself to be construed otherwise. All of which comes perilously near to being a paradox, and commends itself to the attention of the S.P.C.A.

One of the transatlantic liners dumped out at Ellis Island a lump of protozoa which was expected to evolve into an American citizen. A steward kicked him down the gangway, a doctor pounced upon his eyes like a raven, seeking for trachoma or ophthalmia; he was hustled ashore and ejected into the city in the name of Liberty—perhaps, theoretically, thus inoculating against kingocracy with a drop of its own virus. This hypodermic injection of Europeanism wandered happily into the veins of the city with the broad grin of a pleased child. It was not burdened with baggage, cares or ambitions. Its body was lithely built and clothed in a sort of foreign fustian; its face was brightly vacant, with a small, flat nose, and was mostly covered by a thick, ragged, curling beard like the coat of a spaniel. In the pocket of the imported Thing were a few coins—denarii—scudi—kopecks — pfennigs — pilasters — whatever the financial nomenclature of his unknown country may have been.

Prattling to himself, always broadly grinning, pleased by the roar and movement of the barbarous city into which the steamship cutrates had shunted him, the alien strayed away from the sea, which he hated, as far as the district covered by Engine Company No. 99. Light as a cork, he was kept bobbing along by the human tide, the crudest atom in all the silt of the stream that emptied into the reservoir of Liberty.

While crossing Third Avenue he slowed his steps, enchanted by the thunder of the elevated trains above him and the soothing crash of the wheels on the cobbles. And then there was a new, delightful chord in the uproar—the musical clanging of a gong and a great shining juggernaut belching fire and smoke, that people were hurrying to see.

This beautiful thing, entrancing to the eye, dashed past, and the protoplasmic immigrant stepped into the wake of it with his broad, enraptured, uncomprehending grin. And so stepping, stepped into the path of No. 99's flying hose-cart, with John Byrnes gripping, with arms of steel, the reins over the plunging backs of Erebus and Joe.

The unwritten constitutional code of the firemen has no exceptions or amendments. It is a simple thing—as simple as the rule of three. There was the heedless unit in the right of way; there was the hose-cart and the iron pillar of the elevated railroad.

John Byrnes swung all his weight and muscle on the left rein. The team and cart swerved that way and crashed like a torpedo into the pillar. The men on the cart went flying like skittles. The driver's strap burst, the pillar rang with the shock, and John Byrnes fell on the car track with a broken shoulder twenty feet away, while Erebus—beautiful, raven-black, best-loved Erebus—lay whickering in his harness with a broken leg.

In consideration for the feelings of Engine Company No. 99 the details will be lightly touched. The company does not like to be reminded of that day. There was a great crowd, and hurry calls were sent in; and while the ambulance gong was clearing the way the men of No. 99 heard the crack of the S.P.C.A. agent's pistol, and turned their heads away, not daring to look toward Erebus again.

When the firemen got back to the engine-house they found that one of them was dragging by the collar the cause of their desolation and grief. They set it in the middle of the floor and gathered grimly about it. Through its whiskers the calamitous object chattered effervescently and waved its hands.

"Sounds like a seidlitz powder," said Mike

Dowling, disgustedly, "and it makes me sicker than one. Call that a man!—that hoss was worth a steamer full of such two-legged animals. It's a immigrant—that's what it is."

"Look at the doctor's chalk mark on its coat," said Reilly, the desk man. "It's just landed. It must be a kind of a Dago or a Hun or one of them Finns, I guess. That's the kind of truck that Europe unloads on to us."

"Think of a thing like that getting in the way and laying John up in hospital and spoiling the best fire team in the city," groaned another fireman. "It ought to be taken down to the dock and drowned."

"Somebody go around and get Sloviski," suggested the engine driver, "and let's see what nation is responsible for this conglomeration of hair and head noises."

Sloviski kept a delicatessen store around the corner on Third Avenue, and was reputed to be a linguist.

One of the men fetched him—a fat, cringing man, with a discursive eye and the odours of many kinds of meats upon him.

"Take a whirl at this importation with your jaw-breakers, Sloviski," requested Mike Dowling. "We can't quite figure out whether he's from the Hackensack bottoms or Hongkong-on-the-Ganges."

Sloviski addressed the stranger in several dialects, that ranged in rhythm and cadence from the sounds produced by a tonsillitis gargle to the opening of a can of tomatoes with a pair of scissors. The immigrant replied in accents resembling the uncorking of a bottle of ginger ale.

"I have you his name," reported Sloviski. "You

shall not pronounce it. Writing of it in paper is better." They gave him paper, and he wrote. "Demetre Svangvsk."

"Looks like short-hand," said the desk man.

"He speaks some language," continued the interpreter, wiping his forehead, "of Austria and mixed with a little Turkish. And, den, he have some Magyar words and a Polish or two, and many like the Roumanian, but not without talk of one tribe in Bessarabia. I do not him quite understand."

"Would you call him a Dago or a Polocker, or what?" asked Mike, frowning at the polyglot description.

"He is a"—answered Sloviski—"he is a—I dink he come from—I dink he is a fool," he concluded, impatient at his linguistic failure, "and if you pleases I will go back at mine delicatessen."

"Whatever he is, he's a bird," said Mike Dowling; "and you want to watch him fly."

Taking by the wing the alien fowl that had fluttered into the nest of Liberty, Mike led him to the door of the engine-house and bestowed upon him a kick hearty enough to convey the entire animus of Company 99. Demetre Svangvsk hustled away down the sidewalk, turning once to show his ineradicable grin to the aggrieved firemen.

In three weeks John Byrnes was back at his post from the hospital. With great gusto he proceeded to bring his war map up to date. "My money on the Japs every time," he declared. "Why, look at them Russians—they're nothing but wolves. Wipe 'em out, I say—and the little old jiu-jitsu gang are just the cherry blossoms to do the trick, and don't you forget it!"

The second day after Byrnes's reappearance came Demetre Svangvsk, the unidentified, to the engine-house, with a broader grin than ever. He managed to convey the idea that he wished to congratulate the hose-cart driver on his recovery and to apologise for having caused the accident. This he accomplished by so many extravagant gestures and explosive noises that the company was diverted for half an hour. Then they kicked him out again, and on the next day he came back grinning. How or where he lived no one knew. And then John Byrnes's nine-year-old son, Chris, who brought him convalescent delicacies from home to eat, took a fancy to Svangvsk, and they allowed him to loaf about the door of the engine-house occasionally.

One afternoon the big drab automobile of the Deputy Fire Commissioner buzzed up to the door of No. 99, and the Deputy stepped inside for an informal inspection. The men kicked Svangvsk out a little harder than usual and proudly escorted the Deputy around 99, in which everything shone like my lady's mirror.

The Deputy respected the sorrow of the company concerning the loss of Erebus, and he had come to promise it another mate for Joe that would do him credit. So they let Joe out of his stall and showed the Deputy how deserving he was of the finest mate that could be in horsedom.

While they were circling around Joe confabbing, Chris climbed into the Deputy's auto and threw the power full on. The men heard a monster puffing and a shriek from the lad, and sprang out too late. The big auto shot away, luckily taking a straight course down the street. The boy knew nothing of its machinery; he sat clutching the cushions and howling. With the power on, nothing could have stopped that auto except a brick house, and there was nothing for Chris to gain by such a stoppage.

Demetre Svangvsk was just coming in again with a grin for another kick when Chris played his merry little prank. While the others sprang for the door Demetre sprang for Joe. He glided upon the horse's bare back like a snake and shouted something at him like the crack of a dozen whips. One of the firemen afterwards swore that Joe answered him back in the same language. Ten seconds after the auto started the big horse was eating up the asphalt behind it like a strip of macaroni.

Some people two blocks and a half away saw the rescue. They said that the auto was nothing but a drab noise with a black speck in the middle of it for Chris, when a big bay horse with a lizard lying on its back cantered up alongside of it, and the lizard reached over and picked the black speck out of the noise.

Only fifteen minutes after Svangvsk's last kicking at the hands—or rather the feet—of Engine Company No. 99 he rode Joe back through the door with the boy safe, but acutely conscious of the licking he was going to receive.

Svangvsk slipped to the floor, leaned his head against Joe's and made a noise like a clucking hen. Joe nodded and whistled loudly through his nostrils, putting to shame the knowledge of Sloviski, of the delicatessen.

John Byrnes walked up to Svangvsk, who grinned, expecting to be kicked. Byrnes gripped the outlander so strongly by the hand that Demetre grinned anyhow, conceiving it to be a new form of punishment.

"The heathen rides like a Cossack," remarked a fireman who had seen a Wild West show, "they're the greatest riders in the world."

The word seemed to electrify Svangvsk. He grinned wider than ever.

"Yas—yas—me Cossack," he spluttered, striking his chest.

"Cossack!" repeated John Byrnes, thoughtfully, "ain't that a kind of a Russian?"

"They're one of the Russian tribes, sure," said the desk man, who read books between fire alarms.

Just then Alderman Foley, who was on his way home and did not know of the runaway, stopped at the door of the engine-house and called to Byrnes:

"Hello there, Jimmy, me boy—how's the war coming along? Japs still got the bear on the trot, have they?"

"Oh, I don't know," said John Byrnes, argumentatively, "them Japs haven't got any walkover. You wait till Kuropatkin gets a good whack at 'em and they won't be knee-high to a puddle-ducksky."

LXV: TOBIN'S PALM

TOBIN and me, the two of us, went down to Coney one day, for there was four dollars between us, and Tobin had need of distractions. For there was Katie Mahorner, his sweetheart, of County Sligo, lost since she started for America three months before with two hundred dollars, her own savings, and one hundred dollars from the sale of Tobin's inherited estate, a fine cottage and pig on the Bog Shannaugh. And since the letter that Tobin got saying that she had started to come to him not a bit of news had he heard or seen of Katie Mahorner. Tobin advertised in the papers, but nothing could be found of the colleen.

So, to Coney me and Tobin went, thinking that a turn at the chutes and the smell of the popcorn might raise the heart in his bosom. But Tobin was a hard-headed man, and the sadness stuck in his skin. He ground his teeth at the crying balloons; he cursed the moving pictures; and, though he would drink whenever asked, he scorned Punch and Judy, and was for licking the tintype men as they came.

So I gets him down a side way on a board walk where the attractions were some less violent. At a little six by eight stall Tobin halts, with a more human look in his eye.

"'Tis here," says he, "I will be diverted. I'll have the palm of me hand investigated by the wonderful palmist of the Nile, and see if what is to be will be."

Tobin was a believer in signs and the unnatural in nature. He possessed illegal convictions in his mind along the subject of black cats, lucky numbers, and the weather predictions in the papers.

We went into the enchanted chicken coop, which was fixed mysterious with red cloth and pictures of hands with lines crossing 'em like a railroad centre. The sign over the door says it is Madame Zozo the Egyptian Palmist. There was a fat woman inside in a red jumper with pothooks and beasties embroidered upon it. Tobin gives her ten cents and extends one of his hands. She lifts Tobin's hand, which is own brother to the hoof of a dray-horse, and examines it to see whether 'tis a stone in the frog or a cast shoe he has come for.

"Man," says this Madame Zozo, "the line of your fate shows——"

"'Tis not me foot at all," says Tobin, interrupting. "Sure, 'tis no beauty, but ye hold the palm of me hand."

"The line shows," says the Madame, "that ye've not arrived at your time of life without bad luck. And there's more to come. The mount of Venus—or is that a stone bruise?—shows that ye've been in love. There's been trouble in your life on account of your sweetheart."

"'Tis Katie Mahorner she has references with," whispers Tobin to me in a loud voice to one side.

"I see," says the palmist, "a great deal of sorrow and tribulation with one whom ye cannot forget. I see the lines of designation point to the letter K and the letter M in her name."

"Whist!" says Tobin to me; "do ye hear that?"

"Look out," goes on the palmist, "for a dark man and a light woman; for they'll both bring ye trouble. Ye'll make a voyage upon the water very soon, and have a financial loss. I see one line that brings good luck. There's a man coming into your life who will fetch ye good fortune. Ye'll know him when ye see him by his crooked nose."

"Is his name set down?" asks Tobin. "'Twill be convenient in the way of greeting when he backs up to dump off the good luck."

"His name," says the palmist, thoughtful-looking, "is not spelled out by the lines, but they indicate 'tis a long one, and the letter 'o' should be in it. There's no more to tell. Good evening. Don't block up the door."

" 'Tis wonderful how she knows," says Tobin as we walk to the pier.

As we squeezed through the gates a nigger man sticks his lighted segar against Tobin's ear, and there is trouble. Tobin hammers his neck, and the women squeal, and by presence of mind I drag the little man out of the way before the police comes. Tobin is always in an ugly mood when enjoying himself.

On the boat going back, when the man calls "Who wants the good-looking waiter?" Tobin tried to plead guilty, feeling the desire to blow the foam off a crock of suds, but when he felt in his pocket he found himself discharged for lack of evidence. Somebody had disturbed his change during the commotion. So we sat, dry, upon the stools, listening to the Dagoes fiddling on deck. If anything, Tobin was lower in spirits and less congenial with his misfortunes than when we started.

On a seat against the railing was a young woman dressed suitable for red automobiles, with hair the colour of an unsmoked meerschaum. In passing by, Tobin kicks her foot without intentions, and, being polite to ladies when in drink, he tries to give his hat a twist while apologizing. But he knocks it off, and the wind carries it overboard.

Tobin came back and sat down, and I began to look out for him, for the man's adversities were becoming frequent. He was apt, when pushed so close by hard luck, to kick the best-dressed man he could see, and try to take command of the boat.

Presently Tobin grabs my arm and says, excited:

"Jawn," says he, "do ye know what we're doing? We're taking a voyage upon the water."

"There now," says I; "subdue yeself. The boat'll land in ten minutes more."

"Look," says he, "at the light lady upon the bench. And have ye forgotten the nigger man that burned me ear? And isn't the money I had gone —a dollar sixty-five it was?"

I thought he was no more than summing up his catastrophes so as to get violent with good excuse, as men will do, and I tried to make him understand such things was trifles.

"Listen," says Tobin. "Ye've no ear for the gift of prophecy or the miracles of the inspired. What did the palmist lady tell ye out of me hand? 'Tis coming true before your eyes. 'Look out,' says she, 'for a dark man and a light woman; they'll bring ye trouble.' Have ye forgot the nigger man, though he got some of it back from me fist? Can ye show me a lighter woman than the blonde lady that was the cause of me hat falling in the water? And where's the dollar sixty-five I had in me vest when we left the shooting gallery?"

The way Tobin put it, it did seem to corroborate the art of prediction, though it looked to me that these accidents could happen to anyone at Coney without the implication of palmistry.

Tobin got up and walked around on deck, looking close at the passengers out of his little red eyes. I asked him the interpretation of his movements. Ye never know what Tobin has in his mind until he begins to carry it out.

"Ye should know," says he, "I'm working out the salvation promised by the lines in me palm. I'm looking for the crooked-nose man that's to bring the good luck. 'Tis all that will save us. Jawn, did ye ever see a straighter-nosed gang of hellions in the days of your life?"

'Twas the nine-thirty boat, and we landed and walked up-town, through Twenty-second Street, Tobin being without his hat.

On a street corner, standing under a gaslight and looking over the elevated road at the moon, was a man. A long man he was, dressed decent, with a segar between his teeth, and I saw that his nose made two twists from bridge to end, like the wriggle of a snake. Tobin saw it at the same time, and I heard him breathe hard like a horse when you take the saddle off. He went straight up to the man, and I went with him.

"Good night to ye," Tobin says to the man. The man takes out his segar and passes the compliments, sociable.

"Would ye hand us your name," asks Tobin, "and let us look at the size of it? It may be our duty to become acquainted with ye."

"My name," says the man, polite, "is Friedenhausman—Maximus G. Friedenhausman."

"'Tis the right length," says Tobin. "Do you spell it with an 'o' anywhere down the stretch of it?"

"I do not," says the man.

"*Can* ye spell it with an 'o'?" inquires Tobin, turning anxious.

"If your conscience," says the man with the nose, "is indisposed toward foreign idioms ye might, to please yourself, smuggle the letter into the penultimate syllable."

"'Tis well," says Tobin. "Ye're in the presence of Jawn Malone and Daniel Tobin."

"'Tis highly appreciated," says the man, with a bow. "And now since I cannot conceive that ye would hold a spelling bee upon the street corner, will ye name some reasonable excuse for being at large?"

"By the two signs," answers Tobin, trying to explain, "which ye display according to the reading of the Egyptian palmist from the sole of me hand, ye've been nominated to offset with good luck the lines of trouble leading to the nigger man and the blonde lady with her feet crossed in the boat, besides the financial loss of a dollar sixty-five, all so far fulfilled according to Hoyle."

The man stopped smoking and looked at me.

"Have ye any amendments," he asks, "to offer to that statement, or are ye one too? I thought by the looks of ye ye might have him in charge."

"None," says I to him, "except that as one horseshoe resembles another so are ye the picture of good luck as predicted by the hand of me friend. If not, then the lines of Danny's hand may have been crossed, I don't know."

"There's two of ye," says the man with the nose, looking up and down for the sight of a policeman. "I've enjoyed your company immense. Good night."

With that he shoves his segar in his mouth and moves across the street, stepping fast. But Tobin sticks close to one side of him and me at the other.

"What!" says he, stopping on the opposite sidewalk and pushing back his hat; "do ye follow me? I tell ye," he says, very loud, "I'm proud to have met ye. But it is my desire to be rid of ye. I am off to me home."

"Do," says Tobin, leaning against his sleeve.

"Do be off to your home. And I will sit at the door of it till ye come out in the morning. For the dependence is upon ye to obviate the curse of the nigger man and the blonde lady and the financial loss of the one-sixty-five."

"'Tis a strange hallucination," says the man, turning to me as a more reasonable lunatic. "Hadn't ye better get him home?"

"Listen, man," says I to him. "Daniel Tobin is as sensible as he ever was. Maybe he is a bit deranged on account of having drink enough to disturb but not enough to settle his wits, but he is no more than following out the legitimate path of his superstitions and predicaments, which I will explain to you." With that I relates the facts about the palmist lady and how the finger of suspicion points to him as an instrument of good fortune. "Now, understand," I concludes, "my position in this riot. I am the friend of me friend Tobin, according to me interpretations. 'Tis easy to be a friend to the prosperous, for it pays; 'tis not hard to be a friend to the poor, for ye get puffed up by gratitude and have your picture printed standing in front of a tenement with a scuttle of coal and an orphan in each hand. But it strains the art of friendship to be true friend to a born fool. And that's what I'm doing," says I, "for, in my opinion, there's no fortune to be read from the palm of me hand that wasn't printed there with the handle of a pick. And, though ye've got the crookedest nose in New York City, I misdoubt that all the fortune-tellers doing business could milk good luck from ye. But the lines of Danny's hand pointed to ye fair, and I'll assist him to experiment with ye until he's convinced ye're dry."

After that the man turns, sudden, to laughing. He leans against a corner and laughs considerable. Then he claps me and Tobin on the backs of us and takes us by an arm apiece.

"'Tis my mistake," says he. "How could I be expecting anything so fine and wonderful to be turning the corner upon me? I came near being found unworthy. Hard by," says he, "is a café, snug and suitable for the entertainment of idiosyncrasies. Let us go there and have drink while we discuss the unavailability of the categorical."

So saying, he marched me and Tobin to the back room of a saloon, and ordered the drinks, and laid the money on the table. He looks at me and Tobin like brothers of his, and we have the segars.

"Ye must know," says the man of destiny, "that me walk in life is one that is called the literary. I wander abroad be night seeking idiosyncrasies in the masses and truth in the heavens above. When ye came upon me I was in contemplation of the elevated road in conjunction with the chief luminary of night. The rapid transit is poetry and art: the moon but a tedious, dry body, moving by rote. But these are private opinions, for, in the business of literature, the conditions are reversed. 'Tis me hope to be writing a book to explain the strange things I have discovered in life."

"Ye will put me in a book," says Tobin, disgusted; "will ye put me in a book?"

"I will not," says the man, "for the covers will not hold ye. Not yet. The best I can do is to enjoy ye meself, for the time is not ripe for destroying the limitations of print. Ye would look fantastic in type. All alone by meself must I drink this cup of joy. But, I thank ye, boys; I am truly grateful."

"The talk of ye," says Tobin, blowing through his moustache and pounding the table with his fist, "is an eyesore to me patience. There was good luck promised out of the crook of your nose, but ye bear fruit like the bang of a drum. Ye resemble, with your noise of books, the wind blowing through a crack. Sure, now, I would be thinking the palm of me hand lied but for the coming true of the nigger man and the blonde lady and——"

"Whist!" says the long man; "would ye be led astray by physiognomy? Me nose will do what it can within bounds. Let us have these glasses filled again, for 'tis good to keep idiosyncrasies well moistened, they being subject to deterioration in a dry moral atmosphere."

So, the man of literature makes good, to my notion, for he pays, cheerful, for everything, the capital of me and Tobin being exhausted by prediction. But Tobin is sore, and drinks quiet, with the red showing in his eye.

By and by we moved out, for 'twas eleven o'clock, and stands a bit upon the sidewalk. And then the man says he must be going home, and invites me and Tobin to walk that way. We arrives on a side street two blocks away where there is a stretch of brick houses with high stoops and iron fences. The man stops at one of them and looks up at the top windows which he finds dark.

"'Tis me humble dwelling," says he, "and I begin to perceive by the signs that me wife has retired to slumber. Therefore I will venture a bit in the way of hospitality. 'Tis me wish that ye enter the basement-room, where we dine, and partake of a reasonable refreshment. There will be some fine cold fowl and cheese and a bottle or two of ale. Ye will be welcome to enter and eat, for I am indebted to ye for diversions."

The appetite and conscience of me and Tobin was congenial to the proposition, though 'twas sticking hard in Danny's superstitions to think that a few drinks and a cold lunch should represent the good fortune promised by the palm of his hand.

"Step down the steps," says the man with the crooked nose, "and I will enter by the door above and let ye in. I will ask the new girl we have in the kitchen," says he, "to make ye a pot of coffee to drink before ye go. 'Tis fine coffee Katie Mahorner makes for a green girl just landed three months. Step in," says the man, "and I'll send her down to ye."

LXVI: THE HIGHER PRAGMATISM

I

WHERE to go for wisdom has become a question of serious import. The ancients are discredited; Plato is boiler-plate; Aristotle is tottering; Marcus Aurelius is reeling; Æsop has been copyrighted by Indiana; Solomon is too solemn; you couldn't get anything out of Epictetus with a pick.

The ant, which for many years served as a model of intelligence and industry in the school-readers, has been proven to be a doddering idiot and a waster of time and effort. The owl to-day is hooted at. Chautauqua conventions have abandoned culture and adopted diabolo. Greybeards give glowing testimonials to the vendors of patent hair-restorers. There are typographical errors in the almanacs published by the daily newspapers. College professors have become——

But there shall be no personalities.

To sit in classes, to delve into the encyclopedia or the past-performances page, will not make us wise. As the poet says, "Knowledge comes, but wisdom lingers." Wisdom is dew, which, while we know it not, soaks into us, refreshes us, and makes us grow. Knowledge is a strong stream of water turned on us through a hose. It disturbs our roots.

Then, let us rather gather wisdom. But how to do so requires knowledge. If we know a thing, we know it; but very often we are not wise to it that we are wise, and——

But let's go on with the story.

II

Once upon a time I found a ten-cent magazine lying on a bench in a little city park. Anyhow, that was the amount he asked me for when I sat on the bench next to him. He was a musty, dingy, and tattered magazine, with some queer stories bound in him, I was sure. He turned out to be a scrap-book.

"I am a newspaper reporter," I said to him, to try him. "I have been detailed to write up some of the experiences of the unfortunate ones who spend their evenings in this park. May I ask you to what you attribute your downfall in——"

I was interrupted by a laugh from my purchase —a laugh so rusty and unpractised that I was sure it had been his first for many a day.

"Oh, no, no," said he. "You ain't a reporter.

Reporters don't talk that way. They pretend to be one of us, and say they've just got in on the blind baggage from St. Louis. I can tell a reporter on sight. Us park bums get to be fine judges of human nature. We sit here all day and watch the people go by. I can size up anybody who walks past my bench in a way that would surprise you."

"Well," I said, "go on and tell me. How do you size me up?"

"I should say," said the student of human nature with unpardonable hesitation, "that you was, say, in the contracting business—or maybe worked in a store—or was a sign-painter. You stopped in the park to finish your cigar, and thought you'd get a little free monologue out of me. Still, you might be a plasterer or a lawyer—it's getting kind of dark, you see. And your wife won't let you smoke at home."

I frowned gloomily.

"But, judging again," went on the reader of men, "I'd say you ain't got a wife."

"No," said I, rising restlessly. "No, no, no, I ain't. But I *will* have, by the arrows of Cupid! That is, if——"

My voice must have trailed away and muffled itself in uncertainty and despair.

"I see you have a story yourself," said the dusty vagrant—impudently, it seemed to me. "Suppose you take your dime back and spin your yarn for me. I'm interested myself in the ups and downs of unfortunate ones who spend their evenings in the park."

Somehow, that amused me. I looked at the frowsy derelict with more interest. I did have a story. Why not tell it to him? I had told none of my friends. I had always been a reserved and bottled-up man. It was psychical timidity or sensitiveness—perhaps both. And I smiled to myself in wonder when I felt an impulse to confide in this stranger and vagabond.

"Jack," said I.

"Mack," said he.

"Mack," said I, "I'll tell you."

"Do you want the dime back in advance?" said he.

I handed him a dollar.

"The dime," said I, "was the price of listening to *your* story."

"Right on the point of the jaw," said he. "Go on."

And then, incredible as it may seem to the lovers in the world who confide their sorrows only to the night wind and the gibbous moon, I laid bare my secret to that wreck of all things that you would have supposed to be in sympathy with love.

I told him of the days and weeks and months that I had spent in adoring Mildred Telfair. I spoke of my despair, my grievous days and wakeful nights, my dwindling hopes and distress of mind. I even pictured to this night-prowler her beauty and dignity, the great sway she had in society, and the magnificence of her life as the elder daughter of an ancient race whose pride overbalanced the dollars of the city's millionaires.

"Why don't you cop the lady out?" asked Mack, bringing me down to earth and dialect again.

I explained to him that my worth was so small, my income so minute, and my fears so large that I hadn't the courage to speak to her of my worship. I told him that in her presence I could only blush and stammer, and that she looked upon me with a wonderful, maddening smile of amusement.

"She kind of moves in the professional class, don't she?" asked Mack.

"The Telfair family——" I began, haughtily.

"I mean professional beauty," said my hearer.

"She is greatly and widely admired," I answered, cautiously.

"Any sisters?"

"One."

"You know any more girls?"

"Why, several," I answered. "And a few others."

"Say," said Mack, "tell me one thing—can you hand out the dope to other girls? Can you chin 'em and make matinée eyes at 'em and squeeze 'em? You know what I mean. You're just shy when it comes to this particular dame—the professional beauty—ain't that right?"

"In a way you have outlined the situation with approximate truth," I admitted.

"I thought so," said Mack, grimly. "Now that reminds me of my own case. I'll tell you about it."

I was indignant, but concealed it. What was this loafer's case or anybody's case compared with mine? Besides, I had given him a dollar and ten cents.

"Feel my muscle," said my companion, suddenly flexing his biceps. I did so mechanically. The fellows in gyms are always asking you to do that. His arm was as hard as cast-iron.

"Four years ago," said Mack. "I could lick any man in New York outside the professional ring. Your case and mine is just the same. I come from the West Side—between Thirtieth and Fourteenth—and I won't give the number on the door. I was a scrapper when I was ten, and when I was twenty no amateur in the city could stand up four rounds with me. 'S a fact. You know Bill McCarty? No? He managed the smokers for some of them swell clubs. Well, I knocked out everything Bill brought up before me. I was a middle-weight, but could train down to a welter when necessary. I boxed all over the West Side at bouts and benefits and private entertainments, and was never put out once.

"But, say, the first time I put my foot in the ring with a professional I was no more than a canned lobster. I dunno how it was—I seemed to lose heart. I guess I got too much imagination. There was a formality and publicness about it that kind of weakened my nerve. I never won a fight in the ring. Light-weights and all kinds of scrubs used to sign up with my manager and then walk up and tap me on the wrist and see me fall. The minute I seen the crowd and a lot of gents in evening clothes down in front, and seen a professional come inside the ropes, I got weak as ginger-ale.

"Of course, it wasn't long till I couldn't get no backers, and I didn't have any more chances to fight a professional—or many amateurs, either. But lemme tell you—I was as good as most men inside the ring or out. It was just that dumb, dead feeling I had when I was up against a regular that always done me up.

"Well, sir, after I had got out of the business, I got a mighty grouch on. I used to go round town licking private citizens and all kinds of unprofessionals just to please myself. I'd lick cops in dark streets and car-conductors and cab-drivers and draymen whenever I could start a row with 'em. It didn't make any difference how big they were, or how much science they had, I got away with 'em. If I'd only just have had the confidence in the ring that I had beating up the best men outside of it, I'd be wearing black pearls and heliotrope silk socks to-day.

"One evening I was walking along near the Bowery, thinking about things, when along comes a slumming-party. About six or seven they was, all in swallowtails, and these silk hats that don't shine. One of the gang kind of shoves me off the sidewalk. I hadn't had a scrap in three days, and I just says, 'Delight-ed!' and hits him back of the ear.

"Well, we had it. That Johnnie put up as decent a little fight as you'd want to see in the moving pictures. It was on a side street, and no cops around. The other guy had a lot of science, but it only took me about six minutes to lay him out.

"Some of the swallowtails dragged him up against some steps and began to fan him. Another one of 'em comes over to me and says:

" 'Young man, do you know what you've done?'

" 'Oh, beat it,' says I. 'I've done nothing but a little punching-bag work. Take Freddy back to Yale and tell him to quit studying sociology on the wrong side of the sidewalk.'

" 'My good fellow,' says he, 'I don't know who you are, but I'd like to. You've knocked out Reddy Burns, the champion middle-weight of the world! He came to New York yesterday, to try to get a match on with Jim Jeffries. If you——'

"But when I come out of my faint I was laying on the floor in a drug-store saturated with aromatic spirits of ammonia. If I'd known that was Reddy Burns, I'd have got down in the gutter and crawled past him instead of handing him one like I did. Why, if I'd ever been in a ring and seen him climbing over the ropes I'd have been all to the sal-volatile.

"So that's what imagination does," concluded Mack. "And as I said, your case and mine is simultaneous. You'll never win out. You can't go up against the professionals. I tell you, it's a park bench for yours in this romance business."

Mack, the pessimist, laughed harshly.

"I'm afraid I don't see the parallel," I said coldly. "I have only a very slight acquaintance with the prize ring."

The derelict touched my sleeve with his forefinger, for emphasis, as he explained his parable.

"Every man," said he, with some dignity, "has got his lamps on something that looks good to him. With you, it's this dame that you're afraid to say your say to. With me, it was to win out in the ring. Well, you'll lose just like I did."

"Why do you think I shall lose?" I asked warmly.

" 'Cause," said he, "you're afraid to go in the ring. You dassen't stand up before a professional. Your case and mine is just the same. You're a amateur! and that means that you'd better keep outside of the ropes."

"Well, I must be going," I said, rising and looking with elaborate care at my watch.

When I was twenty feet away the park-bencher called to me.

"Much obliged for the dollar," he said. "And

for the dime. But you'll never get 'er. You're in the amateur class."

"Serves you right," I said to myself, "for hob-nobbing with a tramp. His impudence!"

But, as I walked, his words seemed to repeat themselves over and over again in my brain. I think I even grew angry at the man.

"I'll show him!" I finally said, aloud. "I'll show him that I can fight Reddy Burns, too—even knowing who he is."

I hurried to a telephone-booth and rang up the Telfair residence.

A soft, sweet voice answered. Didn't I know that voice? My hand holding the receiver shook.

"Is that *you*?" said I, employing the foolish words that form the vocabulary of every talker through the telephone.

"Yes, this is I," came back the answer in the low, clear-cut tones that are an inheritance of the Telfairs. "Who is it, please?"

"It's me," said I, less ungrammatically than egotistically. "It's me, and I've got a few things that I want to say to you right now and immediately and straight to the point."

"*Dear* me," said the voice. "Oh, it's you, Mr. Arden!"

I wondered if any accent on the first word was intended. Mildred was fine at saying things that you had to study out afterwards.

"Yes," said I, "I hope so. And now to come down to brass tacks." I thought that rather a vernacularism, if there is such a word, as soon as I had said it; but I didn't stop to apologize. "You know, of course, that I love you, and that I have been in that idiotic state for a long time. I don't want any more foolishness about it—that is, I mean I want an answer from you right now. Will you marry me or not? Hold the wire, please. Keep out, Central. Hello, hello! Will you, or will you *not*?"

That was just the uppercut for Reddy Burns' chin. The answer came back:

"Why, Phil, dear, of course I will! I didn't know that you—that is, you never said—oh, come up to the house, please—I can't say what I want to over the 'phone. You are so importunate. But please come up to the house, won't you?"

Would I?

I rang the bell of the Telfair house violently. Some sort of a human came to the door and shooed me into the drawing-room.

"Oh, well," said I to myself, looking at the ceiling, "anyone can learn from anyone. That was a pretty good philosophy of Mack's, anyhow. He didn't take advantage of his experience, but I get the benefit of it. If you want to get into the professional class, you've got to——"

I stopped thinking then. Some one was coming down the stairs. My knees began to shake. I knew then how Mack had felt when a professional began to climb over the ropes. I looked around foolishly for a door or a window by which I might escape. If it had been any other girl approaching, I mightn't have——

But just then the door opened, and Bess, Mildred's younger sister, came in. I'd never seen her look so much like a glorified angel. She walked straight up to me, and—and——

I'd never noticed before what perfectly wonderful eyes and hair Elizabeth Telfair had.

"Phil," she said, in the Telfair, sweet, thrilling tones, "why didn't you tell me about it before? I thought it was sister you wanted all the time, until you telephoned to me a few minutes ago!"

I suppose Mack and I always will be hopeless amateurs. But, as the thing has turned out in my case, I'm mighty glad of it.

LXVII: THE CALL OF THE TAME

WHEN the inauguration was accomplished—the proceedings were made smooth by the presence of the Rough Riders—it is well known that a herd of those competent and loyal ex-warriors paid a visit to the big city. The newspaper reporters dug out of their trunks the old broad-brimmed hats and leather belts that they wear to North Beach fish-fries, and mixed with the visitors. No damage was done beyond the employment of the wonderful plural "tenderfeet" in each of the scribe's stories. The Westerners mildly contemplated the skyscrapers as high as the third story, yawned at Broadway, hunched down in the big chairs in hotel corridors, and altogether looked as bored and dejected as a member of Ye Ancient and Honourable Artillery separated during a sham battle from his valet.

Out of this sightseeing delegation of good King Teddy's Gentlemen of the Royal Bearhounds dropped one Greenbrier Nye, of Pin Feather, Ariz.

The daily cyclone of Sixth Avenue's rush hour swept him away from the company of his pardners true. The dust from a thousand rustling skirts filled his eyes. The mighty roar of trains rushing across the sky deafened him. The lightning-flash of twice ten hundred beaming eyes confused his vision.

The storm was so sudden and tremendous that Greenbrier's first impulse was to lie down and grab a root. And then he remembered that the disturbance was human, and not elemental; and he backed out of it with a grin into a doorway.

The reporters had written that but for the wide-brimmed hats the West was not visible upon these gauchos of the North. Heaven sharpen their eyes! The suit of black diagonal, wrinkled in impossible places; the bright blue four-in-hand, factory tied; the low, turned-down collar pattern of the days of Seymour and Blair, white glazed as the letters on the window of the open-day-and-night-except-Sunday restaurants; the outcurve of the knees from the saddle grip; the peculiar spread of the half-closed right thumb and fingers from the stiff hold upon the circling lasso; the deeply absorbed weather tan that the hottest sun of Cape May can never equal; the seldom-winking blue eyes that unconsciously divided the rushing crowds into fours, as though they were being counted out of a corral; the segregated loneliness and solemnity of expression, as of an Emperor or of one whose horizons have not intruded upon him nearer than a day's ride—these brands of the West were set upon Greenbrier Nye. Oh yes; he wore a broad-brimmed hat, gentle reader—just like those the Madison Square Post Office mail carriers wear when they go up to Bronx Park on Sunday afternoons.

Suddenly Greenbrier Nye jumped into the drifting herd of metropolitan cattle, seized upon a man, dragged him out of the stream and gave him a buffet upon his collar-bone that sent him reeling against a wall.

The victim recovered his hat, with the angry look of a New Yorker who has suffered an outrage and intends to write to the Trib. about it. But he looked at his assailant, and knew that the blow was in consideration of love and affection after the manner of the West, which greets its friends with contumely and uproar and pounding fists, and receives its enemies in decorum and order, such as the judicious placing of the welcoming bullet demands.

"God in the mountains!" cried Greenbrier, holding fast to the foreleg of his cull. "Can this be Longhorn Merritt?"

The other man was—oh, look on Broadway any day for the pattern—business man—latest rolled-brim derby—good barber, business, digestion and tailor.

"Greenbrier Nye!" he exclaimed, grasping the hand that had smitten him. "My dear fellow! So glad to see you! How did you come to—oh, to be sure—the inaugural ceremonies—I remember you joined the Rough Riders. You must come and have luncheon with me, of course."

Greenbrier pinned him sadly but firmly to the wall with a hand the size, shape and colour of a McClellan saddle.

"Longy," he said, in a melancholy voice that disturbed traffic, "what have they been doing to you? You act just like a citizen. They done made you into a inmate of the city directory. You never made no such Johnny Branch execration of yourself as that out on the Gila. 'Come and have lunching with me!' You never defined grub by any such terms of reproach in them days."

"I've been living in New York seven years," said Merritt. "It's been eight since we punched cows together in Old Man Garcia's outfit. Well, let's go to a café, anyhow. It sounds good to hear it called 'grub' again."

They picked their way through the crowd to a hotel, and drifted, as by a natural law, to the bar.

"Speak up," invited Greenbrier.

"A dry Martini," said Merritt.

"Oh, Lord!" cried Greenbrier; "and yet me and you once saw the same pink Gila monsters crawling up the walls of the same hotel in Cañon Diablo! A dry—but let that pass. Whisky straight—and they're on you."

Merritt smiled, and paid.

They lunched in a small extension of the dining-room that connected with the café. Merritt dexterously diverted his friend's choice, that hovered over ham and eggs, to a purée of celery, a salmon cutlet, a partridge pie and a desirable salad.

"On the day," said Greenbrier, grieved and thunderous, "when I can't hold but one drink before eating when I meet a friend I ain't seen in eight years at a 2-by-4 table in a thirty-cent town at 1 o'clock on the third day of the week, I want nine broncos to kick me forty times over a 640-acre section of land. Get them statistics?"

"Right, old man," laughed Merritt. "Waiter, bring an *absinthe frappé* and—what's yours, Greenbrier?"

"Whisky straight," mourned Nye. "Out of the neck of a bottle you used to take it, Longy—straight out of the neck of a bottle on a galloping pony—Arizona redeye, not this ab—oh, what's the use? They're on you."

Merritt slipped the wine card under his glass.

"All right. I suppose you think I'm spoiled by the city. I'm as good a Westerner as you are, Greenbrier; but, somehow, I can't make up my mind to go back out there. New York is comfortable—comfortable. I make a good living, and I live it. No more wet blankets and riding herd in snowstorms, and bacon and cold coffee and blowouts once in six months for me. I reckon I'll hang out here in the future. We'll take in the theatre to-night, Greenbrier, and after that we'll dine at——"

"I'll tell you what you are, Merritt," said Greenbrier, laying one elbow in his salad and the other in his butter. "You are a concentrated, effete, unconditional, short-sleeved, gotch-eared Miss Sally Walker. God made you perpendicular and suitable to ride straddle and use cuss words in the original. Wherefore you have suffered His handiwork to elapse by removing yourself to New York and putting on little shoes tied with strings, and making faces when you talk. I've seen you rope and tie a steer in 42½. If you was to see one now you'd write to the Police Commissioner about it. And these flapdoodle drinks that you inoculate your system with—these little essences of cowslip with acorns in 'em, and paregoric flip—they ain't anyways in assent with the cordiality of manhood. I hate to see you this way."

"Well, Greenbrier," said Merritt, with apology in his tone, "in a way you are right. Sometimes I do feel like I was being raised on the bottle. But, I tell you, New York is comfortable—comfortable. There's something about it—the sights and the crowds, and the way it changes every day, and the very air of it that seems to tie a one-mile-long stake rope around a man's neck, with the other end fastened somewhere about Thirty-fourth Street. I don't know what it is."

"God knows," said Greenbrier sadly, "and I know. The East has gobbled you up. You was venison, and now you're veal. You put me in mind of a japonica in a window. You've been signed, sealed and diskivered. Requiescat in hoc signo. You make me thirsty."

"A green Chartreuse here," said Merritt to the waiter.

"Whisky straight," sighed Greenbrier, "and they're on you, you renegade of the round-ups."

"Guilty, with an application for mercy," said Merritt. "You don't know how it is, Greenbrier. It's so comfortable here that——"

"Please loan me your smelling salts," pleaded Greenbrier. "If I hadn't seen you once bluff three bluffers from Mazatzal City with an empty gun in Phœnix——"

Greenbrier's voice died away in pure grief.

"Cigars!" he called harshly to the waiter, to hide his emotion.

"A pack of Turkish cigarettes for mine," said Merritt.

"They're on you," chanted Greenbrier, struggling to conceal his contempt.

At seven they dined in the Where-to-Dine-Well column.

That evening a galaxy had assembled there. Bright shone the lights o'er fair women and br—let it go, anyhow—brave men. The orchestra played charmingly. Hardly had a tip from a diner been placed in its hands by a waiter when it would burst forth into soniferousness. The more beer you contributed to it the more Meyerbeer it gave you. Which is reciprocity.

Merritt put forth exertions on the dinner. Greenbrier was his old friend, and he liked him. He persuaded him to drink a cocktail.

"I take the horehound tea," said Greenbrier, "for old times' sake. But I'd prefer whisky straight. They're on you."

"Right!" said Merritt. "Now, run your eye down that bill of fare and see if it seems to hitch on any of the items."

"Lay me on my lava bed!" said Greenbrier, with bulging eyes. "All these specimens of nutriment in the grub wagon! What's this? Horse with the heaves? I pass. But look along! Here's truck for twenty round-ups all spelled out in different sections. Wait till I see."

The viands ordered, Merritt turned to the wine list.

"This Medoc isn't bad," he suggested.

"You're the doc," said Greenbrier. "I'd rather have whisky straight. It's on you."

Greenbrier looked around the room. The waiter brought things and took dishes away. He was observing. He saw a New York restaurant crowd enjoying itself.

"How was the range when you left the Gila?" asked Merritt.

"Fine," said Greenbrier. "You see that lady in the red speckled silk at that table? Well, she could warm over her beans at my camp-fire. Yes, the range was good. She looks as nice as a white mustang I see once on Black River."

When the coffee came, Greenbrier put one foot on the seat of the chair next to him.

"You said it was a comfortable town, Longy," he said meditatively. "Yes, it's a comfortable town. It's different from the plains in a blue norther. What did you call that mess in the crock with the handle, Longy? Oh yes, squabs in a cash roll. They're worth the roll. That white mustang had just such a way of turning his head and shaking his mane—look at her, Longy. If I thought I could sell out my ranch at a fair price, I believe I'd——

"Gyar—song!" he suddenly cried, in a voice that paralysed every knife and fork in the restaurant.

The waiter dived toward the table.

"Two more of them cocktail drinks," ordered Greenbrier.

Merritt looked at him and smiled significantly.

"They're on me," said Greenbrier, blowing a puff of smoke to the ceiling.

LXVIII: THE ROADS WE TAKE

TWENTY miles west of Tucson the "Sunset Express" stopped at a tank to take on water. Besides the aqueous addition the engine of that famous flyer acquired some other things that were not good for it.

While the fireman was lowering the feeding hose, Bob Tidball, "Shark" Dodson and a quarter-bred Creek Indian called John Big Dog climbed on the engine and showed the engineer three round orifices in pieces of ordnance that they carried. These orifices so impressed the engineer with their possibilities that he raised both hands in a gesture such as accompanies the ejaculation "Do tell!"

At the crisp command of Shark Dodson, who was leader of the attacking force, the engineer descended to the ground and uncoupled the engine and tender. Then John Big Dog, perched upon the coal, sportively held two guns upon the engine driver and the fireman, and suggested that they run the engine fifty yards away and there await further orders.

Shark Dodson and Bob Tidball, scorning to put such low-grade ore as the passengers through the mill, struck out for the rich pocket of the express car. They found the messenger serene in the belief that the "Sunset Express" was taking on nothing more stimulating and dangerous than aqua pura. While Bob was knocking this idea out of his head with the butt-end of his six-shooter Shark Dodson was already dosing the express-car safe with dynamite.

The safe exploded to the tune of $30,000, all gold and currency. The passengers thrust their heads casually out of the windows to look for the thunder-cloud. The conductor jerked at the bell-rope, which sagged down loose and unresisting at his tug. Shark Dodson and Bob Tidball, with their booty in a stout canvas bag, tumbled out of the express car and ran awkwardly in their high-heeled boots to the engine.

The engineer, sullenly angry but wise, ran the engine, according to orders, rapidly away from the inert train. But before this was accomplished the express messenger, recovered from Bob Tidball's persuader to neutrality, jumped out of his car with a Winchester rifle and took a trick in the game. Mr. John Big Dog, sitting on the coal tender, unwittingly made a wrong lead by giving an imitation of a target, and the messenger trumped him.

With a ball exactly between his shoulder-blades the Creek chevalier of industry rolled off to the ground, thus increasing the share of his comrades in the loot by one-sixth each.

Two miles from the tank the engineer was ordered to stop.

The robbers waved a defiant adieu and plunged down the steep slope into the thick woods that lined the track. Five minutes of crashing through a thicket of chaparral brought them to open woods, where three horses were tied to low-hanging branches. One was waiting for John Big Dog, who would never ride by night or day again. This animal the robbers divested of saddle and bridle and set free. They mounted the other two with the bag across one pommel, and rode fast and with discretion through the forest and up a primeval lonely gorge. Here the animal that bore Bob Tidball slipped on a mossy boulder and broke a foreleg. They shot him through the head at once and sat down to hold a council of flight. Made secure for the present by the tortuous trail they had travelled, the question of time was no longer so big. Many miles and hours lay between them and the spriest posse that could follow. Shark Dodson's horse, with trailing rope and dropped bridle, panted and cropped thankfully of the grass along the stream in the gorge. Bob Tidball opened the sack, drew out double handfuls of the neat packages of currency and the one sack of gold and chuckled with the glee of a child.

"Say, you old double-decked pirate," he called joyfully to Dodson, "you said we could do it—you got a head for financing that knocks the horns off of anything in Arizona."

"What are we going to do about a hoss for you, Bob? We ain't got long to wait here. They'll be on our trail before daylight in the mornin'."

"Oh, I guess that cayuse of yourn'll carry double for a while," answered the sanguine Bob. "We'll annex the first animal we come across. By jingoes, we made a haul, didn't we? Accordin' to the marks on this money there's $30,000—$15,000 apiece!"

"It's short of what I expected," said Shark Dodson, kicking softly at the packages with the toe of his boot. And then he looked pensively at the wet sides of his tired horse.

"Old Bolivar's mighty nigh played out," he said slowly. "I wish that sorrel of yours hadn't got hurt."

"So do I," said Bob heartily, "but it can't be helped. Bolivar's got plenty of bottom—he'll get us both far enough to get fresh mounts. Dang it, Shark, I can't help thinkin' how funny it is that an Easterner like you can come out here and give us Western fellows cards and spades in the desperado business. What part of the East was you from, anyway?"

"New York State," said Shark Dodson, sitting down on a boulder and chewing a twig. "I was born on a farm in Ulster County. I ran away from home when I was seventeen. It was an accident my comin' West. I was walkin' along the road with my clothes in a bundle, makin' for New York City. I had an idea of goin' there and makin' lots of money. I always felt like I could do it. I came to a place one evenin' where the road forked and I didn't know which fork to take. I studied about it for half an hour, and then I took the left hand. That night I run into the camp of a Wild West show that was travellin' among the little towns, and I went West with it. I've often wondered if I wouldn't have turned out different if I'd took the other road."

"Oh, I reckon you'd have ended up about the same," said Bob Tidball, cheerfully philosophical. "It ain't the roads we take; it's what's inside of us that makes us turn out the way we do."

Shark Dodson got up and leaned against a tree.

"I'd a good deal rather that sorrel of yourn hadn't hurt himself, Bob," he said again, almost pathetically.

"Same here," agreed Bob; "he was sure a first-rate kind of a crowbait. But Bolivar, he'll pull us through all right. Reckon we'd better be movin' on, hadn't we, Shark? I'll bag this boodle ag'in and we'll hit the trail for higher timber."

Bob Tidball replaced the spoil in the bag and tied the mouth of it tightly with a cord. When he looked up the most prominent object that he saw was the muzzle of Shark Dodson's ·45 held upon him without a waver.

"Stop your funnin'," said Bob, with a grin. "We got to be hittin' the breeze."

"Set still," said Shark. "You ain't goin' to hit no breeze, Bob. I hate to tell you, but there ain't any chance for but one of us. Bolivar, he's plenty tired, and he can't carry double."

"We been pards, me and you, Shark Dodson, for three year," Bob said quietly. "We've risked our lives together time and again. I've always give you a square deal, and I thought you was a man. I've heard some queer stories about you shootin' one or two men in a peculiar way, but I never believed 'em. Now if you're just havin' a little fun with me, Shark, put your gun up, and we'll get on Bolivar and vamose. If you mean to shoot—shoot, you blackhearted son of a tarantula!"

Shark Dodson's face bore a deeply sorrowful look.

"You don't know how bad I feel," he sighed, "about that sorrel of yourn breakin' his leg, Bob."

The expression on Dodson's face changed in an instant to one of cold ferocity mingled with inexorable cupidity. The soul of the man showed itself for a moment like an evil face in the window of a reputable house.

Truly Bob Tidball was never to "hit the breeze" again. The deadly ·45 of the false friend cracked and filled the gorge with a roar that the walls hurled back with indignant echoes. And Bolivar, unconscious accomplice, swiftly bore away the last of the holders-up of the "Sunset Express," not put to the stress of "carrying double."

But as "Shark" Dodson galloped away the woods seemed to fade from his view; the revolver in his right hand turned to the curved arm of a mahogany chair; his saddle was strangely upholstered, and he opened his eyes and saw his feet, not in stirrups, but resting quietly on the edge of a quartered-oak desk.

I am telling you that Dodson, of the firm of Dodson & Decker, Wall Street brokers, opened his eyes. Peabody, the confidential clerk, was standing by his chair, hesitating to speak. There was a confused hum of wheels below, and the sedative buzz of an electric fan.

"Ahem! Peabody," said Dodson, blinking. "I must have fallen asleep. I had a most remarkable dream. What is it, Peabody?"

"Mr. Williams, sir, of Tracy & Williams, is outside. He has come to settle his deal in X. Y. Z. The market caught him short, sir, if you remember."

"Yes, I remember. What is X. Y. Z. quoted at to-day, Peabody?"

"One eighty-five, sir."

"Then that's his price."

"Excuse me," said Peabody, rather nervously, "for speaking of it, but I've been talking to Williams. He's an old friend of yours, Mr. Dodson, and you practically have a corner in X. Y. Z. I thought you might—that is, I thought you might not remember that he sold you the stock at 98. If he settles at the market price it will take every cent he has in the world and his home too to deliver the shares."

The expression on Dodson's face changed in an instant to one of cold ferocity mingled with inexorable cupidity. The soul of the man showed itself for a moment like an evil face in the window of a reputable house.

"He will settle at one eighty-five," said Dodson. "Bolivar cannot carry double."

LXIX: SEATS OF THE HAUGHTY

GOLDEN by day and silver by night, a new trail now leads to us across the Indian Ocean. Dusky kings and princes have found out our Bombay of the West; and few be their trails that do not lead down Broadway on their journey for to admire and for to see.

If chance should ever lead you near a hotel that

transiently shelters some one of these splendid touring grandees, I counsel you to seek Lucullus Polk among the republican tuft-hunters that besiege its entrances. He will be there. You will know him by his red, alert, Wellington-nosed face, by his manner of nervous caution mingled with determination, by his assumed promoter's or broker's air of busy impatience, and by his bright-red necktie, gallantly redressing the wrongs of his maltreated blue serge suit, like a battle standard still waving above a lost cause. I found him profitable; and so may you. When you do look for him, look among the light-horse troop of Bedouins that besiege the picket-line of the travelling potentate's guards and secretaries—among the wild-eyed genii of Arabian Afternoons that gather to make astounding and egregious demands upon the prince's coffers.

I first saw Mr. Polk coming down the steps of the hotel at which sojourned His Highness the Gaekwar of Baroda, most enlightened of the Mahratta Princes, who, of late, ate bread and salt in our Metropolis of the Occident.

Lucullus moved rapidly, as though propelled by some potent moral force that imminently threatened to become physical. Behind him closely followed the impetus—a hotel detective, if ever white Alpine hat, hawk's nose, implacable watch-chain, and loud refinement of manner spoke the truth. A brace of uniformed porters at his heels preserved the smooth decorum of the hotel, repudiating by their air of disengagement any suspicion that they formed a reserve squad of ejectment.

Safe on the sidewalk, Lucullus Polk turned and shook a freckled fist at the caravansary. And, to my joy, he began to breathe deep invective in strange words—

"Rides in howdahs, does he?" he cried loudly and sneeringly. "Rides on elephants in howdahs and calls himself a prince! Kings—yah! Comes over here and talks horse till you would think he was a president; and then goes home and rides in a private dining-room strapped on to an elephant. Well, well, well!"

The ejecting committee quietly retired. The scorner of princes turned to me and snapped his fingers.

"What do you think of that?" he shouted derisively. "The Gaekwar of Baroda rides on an elephant in a howdah! And there's old Bikram Shamsher Jang scorching up and down the pig-paths of Khatmandu on a motor-cycle. Wouldn't that maharajah you? And the Shah of Persia, that ought to have been Muley-on-the-spot for at least three, he's got the palanquin habit. And that funny-hat prince from Korea—wouldn't you think he could afford to amble around on a milk-white palfrey once in a dynasty or two? Nothing doing! His idea of a Balaklava charge is to tuck his skirts under him and do his mile in six days over the hoe-wallows of Seoul in a bull-cart. That's the kind of visiting potentates that come to this country now. It's a hard deal, friend."

I murmured a few words of sympathy. But it was uncomprehending, for I did not know his grievance against the rulers who flash, meteor-like, now and then upon our shores.

"The last one I sold," continued the displeased one, "was to that three-horse-tailed Turkish pasha that came over a year ago. Five hundred dollars he paid for it, easy. I says to his executioner or secretary—he was a kind of a Jew or a Chinaman —'His Turkey Giblets is found of horses, then?'

" 'Him?' says the secretary. 'Well, no. He's got a big, fat wife in the harem named Bad Dora that he don't like. I believe he intends to saddle her up and ride her up and down the board-walk in the Bulbul Gardens a few times every day. You haven't got a pair of extra long spurs you could throw in on the deal, have you?' Yes, sir; there's mighty few real rough-riders among the royal sports these days."

As soon as Lucullus Polk got cool enough I picked him up, and with no greater effort than you would employ in persuading a drowning man to clutch a straw, I inveigled him into accompanying me to a cool corner in a dim café.

And it came to pass that men-servants set before us brewage; and Lucullus Polk spake unto me, relating the wherefores of his beleaguering the ante-chambers of the princes of the earth.

"Did you ever hear of the S.A. & A.P. Railroad in Texas? Well, that don't stand for Samaritan Actor's Aid Philanthropy. I was down that way managing a summer bunch of the gum and syntax-chewers that play the Idlewild Parks in the Western hamlets. Of course, we went to pieces when the soubrette ran away with a prominent barber of Bee-ville. I don't know what became of the rest of the company. I believe there were some salaries due; and the last I saw of the troupe was when I told them that forty-three cents was all the treasury contained. I say I never saw any of them after that; but I heard them for about twenty minutes. I didn't have time to look back. But after dark I came out of the woods and struck the S.A. & A.P. agent for means of transportation. He at once extended to me the courtesies of the entire railroad, kindly warning me, however, not to get aboard any of the rolling-stock.

"About ten the next morning I steps off the ties into a village that calls itself Atascosa City. I bought a thirty-cent breakfast and a ten-cent cigar, and stood on Main Street jingling the three pennies in my pocket—dead broke. A man in Texas with only three cents in his pocket is no better off than a man that has no money and owes two cents.

"One of luck's favourite tricks is to soak a man for his last dollar so quick that he don't have time to look it. There I was in a swell St. Louis tailor-made, blue and green plaid suit, and an eighteen-carat sulphate of copper scarf-pin, with no hope in sight except the two great Texas industries, the cotton fields and grading new railroads. I never picked cotton, and I never cottoned to a pick, so the outlook had ultramarine edges.

"All of a sudden, while I was standing on the edge of the wooden sidewalk, down out of the sky falls two fine gold watches into the middle of the street. One hits a chunk of mud and sticks. The other falls hard and flies open, making a fine drizzle of little springs and screws and wheels. I looks up for a balloon or an air-ship; but not seeing any, I steps off the sidewalk to investigate.

"But I hear a couple of yells and see two men running up the street in leather overalls and high-heeled boots and cart-wheel hats. One man is six or eight feet high, with open-plumbed joints and a heartbroken cast of countenance. He picks up the watch that has stuck in the mud. The other man, who is little, with pink hair and white eyes, goes for the empty case, and says, 'I win.' Then the elevated pessimist goes down under his leather leg-holsters and hands a handful of twenty-dollar gold pieces to his albino friend. I don't know how much money it was; it looked as big as an earthquake relief fund to me.

" 'I'll have this here case filled up with works,' says Shorty, 'and throw you again for five hundred.'

" 'I'm your company,' says the high man. 'I'll meet you at the *Smoked Dog Saloon* an hour from now.'

"The little man hustles away with a kind of Swiss movement towards a jewellery store. The heart-broken person stoops over and takes a telescopic view of my haberdashery.

" 'Them's a mighty slick outfit of habiliments you have got on, Mr. Man,' says he. 'I'll bet a hoss you never acquired the right, title, and interest in and to them clothes in Atascosa City.'

" 'Why, no,' says I, being ready enough to exchange personalities with this money monument of melancholy. 'I had this suit tailored from a special line of coatericks, vestures, and paintings in St. Louis. Would you mind putting me sane,' says I, 'on this watch-throwing contest? I've been used to seeing timepieces treated with more politeness and esteem—except women's watches, of course, which by nature they abuse by cracking walnuts with 'em and having 'em taken showing in tintype pictures.'

" 'Me and George,' he explains, 'are up from the ranch, having a spell of fun. Up to last month we owned four sections of watered grazing down on the San Miguel. But along come one of these oil prospectors and begins to bore. He strikes a gusher that flows out twenty thousand—or maybe it was twenty million—barrels of oil a day. And me and George gets one hundred and fifty thousand dollars—seventy-five thousand dollars apiece—for the land. So now and then we saddles up and hits the breeze for Atascosa City for a few days of excitement and damage. Here's a little bunch of the *dinera* that I drawed out of the bank this morning,' says he, and shows a roll of twenties and fifties as big around as a sleeping-car pillow. The yellow-backs glowed like a sunset on the gable end of Rockefeller's barn. My knees got weak, and I sat down on the edge of the board sidewalk.

" 'You must have knocked around a right smart,' goes on this oil Grease-us. 'I shouldn't be surprised if you have saw towns more livelier than what Atascosa City is. Sometimes it seems to me that there ought to be some more ways of having a good time than there is here, 'specially when you've got plenty of money and don't mind spending it.'

"Then this Mother Cary's chick of the desert sits down by me and we hold a conversationfest. It seems that he was money-poor. He'd lived in ranch camps all his life; and he confessed to me that his supreme idea of luxury was to ride into camp, tired out from a round-up, eat a peck of Mexican beans, hobble his brains with a pint of raw whisky, and go to sleep with his boots for a pillow. When this bargeload of unexpected money came to him and his pink but perky partner, George, and they hied themselves to this clump of outhouses called Atascosa City, you know what happened to them. They had money to buy anything they wanted; but they didn't know what to want. Their ideas of spendthriftiness were limited to three—whisky, saddles, and gold watches. If there was anything else in the world to throw away fortunes on, they had never heard about it. So, when they wanted to have a hot time, they'd ride into town and get a city directory and stand in front of the principal saloon and call up the population alphabetically for free drinks. Then they would order three or four new California saddles from the storekeeper, and play crack-loo on the sidewalk with twenty-dollar gold pieces. Betting who could throw his gold watch the farthest was an inspiration of George's; but even that was getting to be monotonous.

"Was I on to the opportunity? Listen.

"In thirty minutes I had dashed off a word picture of metropolitan joys that made life in Atascosa City look as dull as a trip to Coney Island with your own wife. In ten minutes more we shook hands on an agreement that I was to act as his guide, interpreter, and friend in and to the aforesaid wassail and amenity. And Solomon Mills, which was his name, was to pay all expenses for a month. At the end of that time, if I had made good as director-general of the rowdy life, he was to pay me one thousand dollars. And then, to clinch the bargain, we called the roll of Atascosa City and put all of its citizens except the ladies and minors under the table, except one man named Horace Westervelt St. Clair. Just for that we bought a couple of hatfuls of cheap silver watches and egged him out of town with 'em. We wound up by dragging the harness-maker out of bed and setting him to work on three new saddles; and then we went to sleep across the railroad track at the depôt, just to annoy the S.A. & A.P. Think of having seventy-five thousand dollars and trying to avoid the disgrace of dying rich in a town like that!

"The next day George, who was married or something, started back to the ranch. Me and Solly, as I now called him, prepared to shake off our mothballs and wing our way against the arc-lights of the joyous and tuneful East.

" 'No way-stops,' says I to Solly, 'except long enough to get you barbered and haberdashed. This is no Texas feet shampetter,' says I, 'where you eat chili-concarne-con-huevos and then holler "Whoopee!" across the plaza. We're now going against the real high life. We're going to mingle with the set that carries a Spitz, wears spats, and hits the ground in high spots.'

"Solly puts six thousand dollars in century bills in one pocket of his brown ducks, and bills of lading for ten thousand dollars on Eastern banks in another. Then I resume diplomatic relations with the S.A. & A.P., and we hike in a north-westerly direction on our circuitous route to the spice gardens of the Yankee Orient.

"We stopped in San Antonio long enough for Solly to buy some clothes, and eight rounds of drinks for the guests and employees of the *Menger Hotel*, and order four Mexican saddles with silver trimmings and white Angora *suaderos* to be shipped down to the ranch. From there we made a big jump to St. Louis. We got there in time for dinner; and I put our thumb-prints on the register of the most expensive hotel in the city.

" 'Now,' says I to Solly, with a wink at myself, 'here's the first dinner-station we've struck where we can get a real good plate of beans.' And while he was up in his room trying to draw water out of the gaspipe, I got one finger in the buttonhole of the head waiter's Tuxedo, drew him apart, inserted a two-dollar bill, and closed him up again.

" 'Frankoyse,' says I, 'I have a pal here for dinner that's been subsisting for years on cereals and short stogies. You see the *chef* and order a dinner for us such as you serve to Dave Francis and the general passenger agent of the Iron Mountain when they eat here. We've got more than Bernhardt's tent full of money; and we want the nose-bags crammed with all the Chief Deveries *de cuisine*. Object is no expense. Now, show us.'

"At six o'clock me and Solly sat down to dinner. Spread! There's nothing been seen like it since the Cambon snack. It was all served at once. The *chef* called it *dinnay à la poker*. It's a famous thing among the gormands of the West. The dinner comes in threes of a kind. There was guinea-fowls, guinea-pigs, and Guinness's stout; roast veal, mock turtle soup, and chicken pâté; shad-roe, caviar, and tapioca; canvas-back duck, canvas-back ham, and cotton-tail rabbit; Philadelphia capon, fried snails, and sloe gin—and so on, in threes. The idea was that you eat nearly all you can of them, and then the waiter takes away the discard and gives you pears to fill on.

"I was sure Solly would be tickled to death with these hands, after the bobtail flushes he'd been eating on the ranch; and I was a little anxious that he should, for I didn't remember his having honoured my efforts with a smile since we left Atascosa City.

"We were in the main dining-room, and there was a fine-dressed crowd there, all talking loud and enjoyable about the two St. Louis topics, the water supply and the colour line. They mix the two subjects so fast that strangers often think they are discussing water-colours; and that has given the old town something of a rep as an art centre. And over in the corner was a fine brass band playing; and now, thinks I, Solly will become conscious of the spiritual oats of life nourishing and exhilarating his system. But, *nong*, *mong frang*.

"He gazed across the table at me. There was four square yards of it, looking like the path of a cyclone that has wandered through a stock-yard, a poultry farm, a vegetable garden, and an Irish linen mill. Solly gets up and comes around to me.

" 'Luke,' says he, 'I'm pretty hungry after our ride. I thought you said they had some beans here. I'm going out and get something I can eat. You can stay and monkey with this artificial layout of grub if you want to.'

" 'Wait a minute,' says I.

"I called the waiter, and slapped 'S. Mills' on the back of the cheque for thirteen dollars and fifty cents.

" 'What do you mean,' says I, 'by serving gentlemen with a lot of truck only suitable for deck-hands on a Mississippi steamboat? We're going out to get something decent to eat.'

"I walked up the street with the unhappy plainsman. He saw a saddle-shop open, and some of the sadness faded from his eyes. We went in, and he ordered and paid for two more saddles—one with a solid silver horn and nails and ornaments and a six-inch border of rhinestones and imitation rubies around the flaps. The other one had to have a gold-mounted horn, quadruple-plated stirrups, and the leather inlaid with silver beadwork wherever it would stand it. Eleven hundred dollars the two cost him.

"Then he goes out and heads towards the river, following his nose. In a little side street, where there was no street and no sidewalks and no houses, he finds what he is looking for. We go into a shanty and sit on high stools among stevedores and boatmen, and eat beans with tin spoons. Yes, sir, beans—beans boiled with salt pork.

" 'I kind of thought we'd strike some over this way,' says Solly.

" 'Delightful,' says I. 'That stylish hotel grub may appeal to some; but for me, give me the husky *table d'goat.*'

"When we had succumbed to the beans I leads him out of the tarpaulin steam under a lamp-post and pulls out a daily paper with the amusement column folded out.

" 'But now, what ho for a merry round of pleasure,' says I. 'Here's one of Hall Caine's shows, and a stockyard company in *Hamlet*, and skating at the Hollowhorn Rink, and Sarah Bernhardt, and the Shapely Syrens Burlesque Company. I should think, now, that the Shapely——'

"But what does this healthy, wealthy, and wise man do but reach his arms up to the second-story windows and gape noisily.

" 'Reckon I'll be going to bed,' says he; 'it's about my time. St. Louis is a kind of quiet place, ain't it?'

" 'Oh, yes,' says I; 'ever since the railroads ran in here the town's been practically ruined. And the building-and-loan associations and the fair have about killed it. Guess we might as well go to bed.

Wait till you see Chicago, though. Shall we get tickets for the Big Breeze to-morrow?'

"'Mought as well,' says Solly. 'I reckon all these towns are about alike.'

"Well, maybe the wise cicerone and personal conductor didn't fall hard in Chicago! Loolooville-on-the-Lake is supposed to have one or two things in it calculated to keep the rural visitor awake after the curfew rings. But not for the grass-fed man of the pampas! I tried him with theatres, rides in automobiles, sails on the lake, champagne suppers, and all those little inventions that hold the simple life in check; but in vain. Solly grew sadder day by day. And I got fearful about my salary, and knew I must play my trump card. So I mentioned New York to him, and informed him that these Western towns were no more than gateways to the great walled city of the whirling dervishes.

"After I bought the tickets I missed Solly. I knew his habits by then; so in a couple of hours I found him in a saddle-shop. They had some new ideas there in the way of trees and girths that had strayed down from the Canadian mounted police; and Solly was so interested that he almost looked reconciled to live. He invested about nine hundred dollars in there.

"At the depôt I telegraphed a cigar-store man I knew in New York to meet me at the Twenty-third Street ferry with a list of all the saddle-stores in the city. I wanted to know where to look for Solly when he got lost.

"Now I'll tell you what happened in New York. I says to myself: 'Friend Heherezade, you want to get busy and make Bagdad look pretty to the sad sultan of the sour countenance, or it'll be the bow-string for yours.' But I never had any doubt I could do it.

"I began with him like you'd feed a starving man. I showed him the horse-cars on Broadway and the Staten Island ferry-boats. And then I piled up the sensations on him, but always keeping a lot of warmer ones up my sleeve.

"At the end of the third day he looked like a composite picture of five thousand orphans too late to catch a picnic steamboat, and I was wilting down a collar every two hours wondering how I could please him and whether I was going to get my thou. He went to sleep looking at the Brooklyn Bridge; he disregarded the sky-scrapers above the third story; it took three ushers to wake him up at the liveliest vaudeville in town.

"Once I thought I had him. I nailed a pair of cuffs on him one morning before he was awake; and I dragged him that evening to the palm-cage of one of the biggest hotels in the city—to see the Johnnies and the Alice-sit-by-the-hours. They were out in numerous quantities, with the fat of the land showing in their clothes. While we were looking them over, Solly divested himself of a fearful, rusty kind of laugh—like moving a folding bed with one roller broken. It was his first in two weeks, and it gave me hope.

" 'Right you are,' says I. 'They're a funny lot of post-cards, aren't they?'

" 'Oh, I wasn't thinking of them dudes and culls on the hoof,' says he. 'I was thinking of the time me and George put sheep-dip in Horsehead Johnson's whisky. I wish I was back in Atascosa City,' says he.

"I felt a cold chill run down my back. 'Me to play and mate in one move,' says I to myself.

"I made Solly promise to stay in the café for half an hour and I hiked out in a cab to Lolabelle Delatour's flat on Forty-third Street. I knew her well. She was a chorus-girl in a Broadway musical comedy.

" 'Jane,' says I when I found her, 'I've got a friend from Texas here. He's all right, but—well, he carries weight. I'd like to give him a little whirl after the show this evening—bubbles, you know, and a buzz out to a casino for the whitebait and pickled walnuts. Is it a go?'

" 'Can he sing?' asks Lolabelle.

" 'You know,' says I, 'that I wouldn't take him away from home unless his notes were good. He's got pots of money—bean-pots full of it.'

" 'Bring him around after the second act,' says Lolabelle, 'and I'll examine his credentials and securities.'

"So about ten o'clock that evening I led Solly to Miss Delatour's dressing-room, and her maid let us in. In ten minutes in comes Lolabelle, fresh from the stage, looking stunning in the costume she wears when she steps from the ranks of the lady grenadiers and says to the king, 'Welcome to our May-day revels.' And you can bet it wasn't the way she spoke the lines that got her the part.

"As soon as Solly saw her he got up and walked straight out through the stage entrance into the street. I followed him. Lolabelle wasn't paying my salary. I wondered whether anybody was.

" 'Luke,' says Solly, outside, 'that was an awful mistake. We must have got into the lady's private room. I hope I'm gentleman enough to do anything possible in the way of apologies. Do you reckon she'd ever forgive us?'

"'She may forget it,' says I. 'Of course it was a mistake. Let's go find some beans.'

"That's the way it went. But pretty soon afterward Solly failed to show up at dinner-time for several days. I cornered him. He confessed that he had found a restaurant on Third Avenue where they cooked beans in Texas style. I made him take me there. The minute I set foot inside the door I threw up my hands.

"There was a young woman at the desk, and Solly introduced me to her. And then we sat down and had beans.

"Yes, sir, sitting at the desk was the kind of a young woman that can catch any man in the world as easy as lifting a finger. There's a way of doing it. She knew. I saw her working it. She was healthy looking and plain dressed. She had her hair drawn back from her forehead and face—no curls or frizzes; that's the way she looked. Now I'll tell you the way they work the game; it's simple. When she wants a man, she manages it so that every time he looks at her he finds her looking at him. That's all.

"The next evening Solly was to go to Coney Island with me at seven. At eight o'clock he hadn't showed up. I went out and found a cab. I felt sure there was something wrong.

"'Drive to the Back Home Restaurant on Third Avenue,' says I. 'And if I don't find what I want there, take in these saddle-shops.' I handed him the list.

"'Boss,' says the cabby, 'I et a steak in that

restaurant once. If you're real hungry, I advise you to try the saddle-shops first.'

"'I'm a detective,' says I, 'and I don't eat. Hurry up!'

"As soon as I got to the restaurant I felt in the lines of my palms that I should beware of a tall, red, damfool man, and I was going to lose a sum of money.

"Solly wasn't there. Neither was the smooth-haired lady.

"I waited; and in an hour they came in a cab and got out, hand in hand. I asked Solly to step around the corner for a few words. He was grinning clear across his face; but I had not administered the grin.

"'She's the greatest that ever sniffed the breeze,' says he.

"'Congrats,' says I. 'I'd like to have my thousand now, if you please.'

"'Well, Luke,' says he, 'I don't know that I've had such a skyhoodlin' fine time under your tutelage and dispensation. But I'll do the best I can for you—I'll do the best I can,' he repeats. 'Me and Miss Skinner was married an hour ago. We're leaving for Texas in the morning.'

"'Great!' says I. 'Consider yourself covered with rice and Congress gaiters. But don't let's tie so many satin bows on our business relations that we lose sight of 'em. How about my honorarium?'

"'Missis Mills,' says he, 'has taken possession of my money and papers except six bits. I told her what I'd agreed to give you; but she says it's an irreligious and illegal contract, and she won't pay a cent of it. But I ain't going to see you treated unfair,' says he. 'I've got eighty-seven saddles on the ranch what I've bought on this trip; and when I get back I'm going to pick out the best six in the lot and send 'em to you.' "

"And did he?" I asked, when Lucullus ceased talking.

"He did. And they are fit for kings to ride on. The six he sent me must have cost him three thousand dollars. But where is the market for 'em? Who would buy one except one of these rajahs and princes of Asia and Africa? I've got 'em all on the list. I know every tan royal dub and smoked princerino from Mindanao to the Caspian Sea."

"It's a long time between customers," I ventured.

"They're coming faster," said Polk. "Nowadays, when one of the murdering mutts gets civilized enough to abolish suttee and quit using his whiskers for a napkin, he calls himself the Roosevelt of the East, and comes over to investigate our Chautauquas and cocktails. I'll place 'em all yet. Now look here."

From an inside pocket he drew a tightly folded newspaper with much-worn edges, and indicated a paragraph.

"Read that," said the saddler to royalty. The paragraph run thus—

"His Highness Seyyid Feysal bin Turkee, Imam of Muskat, is one of the most progressive and enlightened rulers of the Old World. His stables contain more than a thousand horses of the purest Persian breeds. It is said that this powerful prince contemplates a visit to the United States at an early date."

"There!" said Mr. Polk triumphantly. "My

best saddle is as good as sold—the one with turquoises set in the rim of the cantle. Have you three dollars that you could loan me for a short time?"

It happened that I had; and I did.

If this should meet the eye of the Imam of Muskat, may it quicken his whim to visit the land of the free! Otherwise I fear that I shall be longer than a short time separated from my dollars three.

LXX: A BIRD OF BAGDAD

WITHOUT doubt much of the spirit and genius of the Caliph Harun Al Rashid descended to the Margrave August Michael von Paulsen Quigg.

Quigg's restaurant is in Fourth Avenue—that street that the city seems to have forgotten in its growth. Fourth Avenue—born and bred in the Bowery—staggers northward full of good resolutions.

Where it crosses Fourteenth Street it struts for a brief moment proudly in the glare of the museums and cheap theatres. It may yet become a fit mate for its high-born sister boulevard to the west, or its roaring, polyglot, broad-waisted cousin to the east. It passes Union Square; and here the hoofs of the dray horses seem to thunder in unison, recalling the tread of marching hosts—Hooray! But now come the silent and terrible mountains—buildings square as forts, high as the clouds, shutting out the sky, where thousands of slaves bend over desks all day. On the ground floors are only little fruit-shops and laundries and book-shops, where you see copies of *Littell's Living Age* and G. W. M. Reynolds's novels in the windows. And next—poor Fourth Avenue!—the street glides into a mediæval solitude. On each side are the shops devoted to "Antiques."

Let us say it is night. Men in rusty armour stand in the windows and menace the hurrying cars with raised, rusty iron gauntlets. Hauberks and helms, blunderbusses, Cromwellian breastplates, matchlocks, creeses, and the swords and daggers of an army of dead-and-gone gallants gleam dully in the ghostly light. Here and there from a corner saloon (lit with Jack-o'-lanterns or phosphorus) stagger forth shuddering, home-bound citizens, nerved by the tankards within to their fearsome journey adown that eldrich avenue lined with the bloodstained weapons of the fighting dead. What street could live enclosed by these mortuary relics, and trod by these spectral citizens in whose sunken hearts scarce one good whoop or tra-la-la remained?

Not Fourth Avenue. Not after the tinsel but enlivening glories of the Little Rialto—not after the echoing drum-beats of Union Square. There need be no tears, ladies and gentlemen; 'tis but the suicide of a street. With a shriek and a crash Fourth Avenue dives headlong into the tunnel at Thirty-fourth and is never seen again.

Near the sad scene of the thoroughfare's dissolution stood the modest restaurant of Quigg. It stands there yet if you care to view its crumbling red-brick front, its show window heaped with oranges, tomatoes, layer cakes, pies, canned asparagus—its papier-mâché lobster and two Maltese kittens asleep on a bunch of lettuce—if you care to sit at one of the little tables upon whose cloth has been traced in the yellowest of coffee stains the trail of the Japanese advance—to sit there with one eye on your umbrella and the other upon the bogus bottle from which you drop the counterfeit sauce foisted upon us by the cursed charlatan who assumes to be our dear old lord and friend, the "Nobleman in India."

Quigg's title came through his mother. One of her ancestors was a Margravine of Saxony. His father was a Tammany brave. On account of the dilution of his heredity he found that he could neither become a reigning potentate nor get a job in the City Hall. So he opened a restaurant. He was a man full of thought and reading. The business gave him a living, though he gave it little attention. One side of his house bequeathed to him a poetic and romantic nature. The other gave him the restless spirit that made him seek adventure. By day he was Quigg, the restaurateur. By night he was the Margrave—the Caliph—the Prince of Bohemia—going about the city in search of the odd, the mysterious, the inexplicable, the recondite.

One night at nine, at which hour the restaurant closed, Quigg set forth upon his quest. There was a mingling of the foreign, the military and the artistic in his appearance as he buttoned his coat high up under his short-trimmed brown and grey beard and turned westward toward the more central life conduits of the city. In his pocket he had stored an assortment of cards, written upon, without which he never stirred out of doors. Each of those cards was good at his own restaurant for its face value. Some called simply for a bowl of soup or sandwiches and coffee; others entitled their bearer to one, two, three or more days of full meals; a few were for single regular meals; a very few were, in effect, meal tickets good for a week.

Of riches and power Margrave Quigg had none; but he had a Caliph's heart—it may be forgiven him if his head fell short of the measure of Harun Al Rashid's. Perhaps some of the gold pieces in Bagdad had put less warmth and hope into the complainants among the bazaars than had Quigg's beef stew among the fishermen and one-eyed calenders of Manhattan.

Continuing his progress in search of romance to divert him, or of distress that he might aid, Quigg became aware of a fast-gathering crowd that whooped and fought and eddied at a corner of Broadway and the crosstown street that he was traversing. Hurrying to the spot he beheld a young man of an exceedingly melancholy and pre-occupied demeanour engaged in the pastime of casting silver money from his pockets to the middle of the street. With each motion of the generous one's hand the crowd huddled upon the falling largesse with yells of joy. Traffic was suspended. A policeman in the centre of the mob stooped often to the ground as he urged the blockaders to move on.

The Margrave saw at a glance that here was food for his hunger after knowledge concerning abnormal workings of the human heart. He made his way swiftly to the young man's side and took his arm. "Come with me at once," he said, in the low but commanding voice that his waiters had learned to fear.

"Pinched," remarked the young man, looking up at him with expressionless eyes. "Pinched by a painless dentist. Take me away, flatty, and give me gas. Some lay eggs and some lay none. When is a hen?"

Still deeply seized by some inward grief, but tractable, he allowed Quigg to lead him away and down the street to a little park.

There, seated on a bench, he upon whom a corner of the great Caliph's mantle has descended, spake with kindness and discretion, seeking to know what evil had come upon the other, disturbing his soul and driving him to such ill-considered and ruinous waste of his substance and stores.

"I was doing the Monte Cristo act as adopted by Pompton, N.J., wasn't I?" asked the young man.

"You were throwing small coins into the street for the people to scramble after," said the Margrave.

"That's it. You buy all the beer you can hold, and then you throw chicken feed to—— Oh, curse that word chicken, and hens, feathers, roosters, eggs, and everything connected with it!"

"Young sir," said the Margrave kindly, but with dignity, "though I do not ask your confidence, I invite it. I know the world and I know humanity. Man is my study, though I do not eye him as the scientist eyes a beetle or as the philanthropist gazes at the objects of his bounty—through a veil of theory and ignorance. It is my pleasure and distraction to interest myself in the peculiar and complicated misfortunes that life in a great city visits upon my fellow-men. You may be familiar with the history of that glorious and immortal ruler, the Caliph Harun Al Rashid, whose wise and beneficent excursions among his people in the city of Bagdad secured him the privilege of relieving so much of their distress. In my humble way I walk in his footsteps. I seek for romance and adventure in city streets—not in ruined castles or in crumbling palaces. To me the greatest marvels of magic are those that take place in men's hearts when acted upon by the furious and diverse forces of a crowded population. In your strange behaviour this evening I fancy a story lurks. I read in your act something deeper than the wanton wastefulness of a spendthrift. I observe in your countenance the certain traces of consuming grief or despair. I repeat—I invite your confidence. I am not without some power to alleviate and advise. Will you not trust me?"

"Gee, how you talk!" exclaimed the young man, a gleam of admiration supplanting for a moment the dull sadness of his eyes. "You've got the Astor Library skinned to a synopsis of preceding chapters. I mind that old Turk you speak of. I read *The Arabian Nights* when I was a kid. He was a kind of Bill Devery and Charlie Schwab rolled into one. But, say, you might wave enchanted dish-rags and make copper bottles smoke up coon giants all night without ever touching me. My case won't yield to that kind of treatment."

"If I could hear your story," said the Margrave, with his lofty, serious smile.

"I'll spiel it in about nine words," said the young man, with a deep sigh, "but I don't think you can help me any. Unless you're a peach at guessing it's back to the Bosphorus for you on your magic linoleum."

THE STORY OF THE YOUNG MAN AND THE HARNESS MAKER'S RIDDLE

"I work in Hildebrant's saddle and harness shop down in Grand Street. I've worked there five years. I get $18 a week. That's enough to marry on, ain't it? Well, I'm not going to get married. Old Hildebrant is one of these funny Dutchmen—you know the kind—always getting off bum jokes. He's got about a million riddles and things that he faked from Rogers Brothers' great-grandfather. Bill Watson works there, too. Me and Bill have to stand for them chestnuts day after day. Why do we do it? Well, jobs ain't to be picked off every Anheuser bush—— And then there's Laura.

"What? The old man's daughter. Comes in the shop every day. About nineteen, and the picture of the blonde that sits on the palisades of the Rhine and charms the clam-diggers into the surf. Hair the colour of straw matting, and eyes as black and shiny as the best harness blacking—think of that!

"Me? Well, it's either me or Bill Watson. She treats us both equal. Bill is all to the psychopathic about her; and me?—well, you saw my plating the road-bed of the Great Maroon Way with silver to-night. That was on account of Laura. I was spiflicated, Your Highness, and I wot not of what I wouldst.

"How? Why, old Hildebrant says to me and Bill this afternoon: 'Boys, one riddle have I for you gehabt haben. A young man who cannot riddles antworten, he is not so good by business for ein family to provide—is not that—hein?' And he hands us a riddle—a conundrum, some calls it—and he chuckles interiorly and gives both of us till to-morrow morning to work out the answer to it. And he says whichever of us guesses the repartee end of it goes to his house o' Wednesday night to his daughter's birthday party. And it means Laura for whichever of us goes, for she's naturally aching for a husband, and it's either me or Bill Watson, for old Hildebrant likes us both, and wants her to marry somebody that'll carry on the business after he's stitched his last pair of traces.

"The riddle? Why, it was this: 'What kind of a hen lays the longest?' Think of that! What kind of a hen lays the longest? Ain't it like a Dutchman to risk a man's happiness on a fool proposition like that? Now what's the use? What I don't know about hens would fill several incubators. You say you're giving imitations of the old Arab guy that gave way—libraries in Bagdad. Well, now, can you whistle up a fairy that'll solve this hen query, or not?"

When the young man ceased the Margrave arose and paced to and fro by the park bench for several minutes. Finally he sat again, and said, in grave and impressive tones:

"I must confess, sir, that during the eight years that I have spent in search of adventure and in relieving distress I have never encountered a more interesting or a more perplexing case. I fear that I have overlooked hens in my researches and observations. As to their habits, their times and manner of laying, their many varieties and cross-breedings, their span of life, their——"

"Oh, don't make an Ibsen drama of it!" interrupted the young man flippantly. "Riddles—especially old Hildebrant's riddles—don't have to be worked out seriously. They are light themes such as Sim Ford and Harry Thurston Peck like to handle. But, somehow, I can't just strike the answer. Bill Watson may, and he may not. To-morrow will tell. Well, Your Majesty, I'm glad anyhow that you butted in and whiled the time away. I guess Mr. Al Rashid himself would have bounced back if one of his constituents had conducted him up against this riddle. I'll say good night. Peace fo' yours, and what-you-may-call-its of Allah."

The Margrave, with a gloomy air, held out his hand.

"I cannot express my regret," he said sadly. "Never before have I found myself unable to assist in some way. 'What kind of a hen lays the longest?' It is a baffling problem. There is a hen, I believe, called the Plymouth Rock that——"

"Cut it out," said the young man. "The Caliph trade is a mighty serious one. I don't suppose you'd even see anything funny in a preacher's defence of John D. Rockefeller. Well, good night, Your Nibs."

From habit the Margrave began to fumble in his pockets. He drew forth a card and handed it to the young man.

"Do me the favour to accept this, anyhow," he said. "The time may come when it might be of use to you."

"Thanks!" said the young man, pocketing it carelessly. "My name is Simmons."

* * * * *

Shame to him who would hint that the reader's interest shall altogether pursue the Margrave August Michael von Paulsen Quigg. I am indeed astray if my hand fail in keeping the way where my peruser's heart would follow. Then let us, on the morrow, peep quickly in at the door of Hildebrant, harness maker.

Hildebrant's 200 pounds reposed on a bench, silver-buckling a raw leather martingale.

Bill Watson came in first.

"Vell," said Hildebrant, shaking all over with the vile conceit of the joke-maker, "haf you guessed him? 'Vat kind of a hen lays der longest?' "

"Er—why, I think so," said Bill, rubbing a servile chin. "I think so, Mr. Hildebrant—the one that lives the longest—— Is that right?"

"Nein!" said Hildebrant, shaking his head violently. "You haf not guessed der answer."

Bill passed on and donned a bed-tick apron and bachelorhood.

In came the young man of the Arabian Night's fiasco—pale, melancholy, hopeless.

"Vell," said Hildebrant, "haf you guessed him? 'Vat kind of a hen lays der longest?' "

Simmons regarded him with dull savagery in his eye. Should he curse this mountain of pernicious humour—curse him and die? Why should—— But there was Laura.

Dogged, speechless, he thrust his hands into his coat pockets and stood. His hand encountered the strange touch of the Margrave's card. He drew it out and looked at it, as men about to be hanged look at a crawling fly. There was written on it in Quigg's bold, round hand: "Good for one roast chicken to bearer."

Simmons looked up with a flashing eye.

"A dead one!" said he.

"Goot!" roared Hildebrant, rocking the table with giant glee. "Dot is right! You gome at mine house at eight o'clock to der party."

LXXI : GEORGIA'S RULING

IF you should chance to visit the General Land Office, step into the draughtsmen's room and ask to be shown the map of Salado County. A leisurely German—possibly old Kampfer himself—will bring it to you. It will be four feet square, on heavy drawing-cloth. The lettering and the figures will be beautifully clear and distinct. The title will be in splendid, undecipherable German text, ornamented with classic Teutonic designs—very likely Ceres or Pomona leaning against the initial letters with cornucopias venting grapes and wieners. You must tell him that this is not the map you wish to see; that he will kindly bring you its official predecessor. He will then say, "Ach, so!" and bring out a map half the size of the first, dim, old, tattered, and faded.

By looking carefully near its north-west corner you will presently come upon the worn contours of Chiquito River, and, maybe, if your eyes are good, discern the silent witness to this story.

The Commissioner of the Land Office was of the old style; his antique courtesy was too formal for his day. He dressed in fine black, and there was a suggestion of Roman drapery in his long coat-skirts. His collars were "undetached" (blame haberdashery for the word); his tie was a narrow, funereal strip, tied in the same knot as were his shoe-strings. His grey hair was a trifle too long behind, but he kept it smooth and orderly. His face was cleanshaven, like the old statesmen's. Most people thought it a stern face, but when its official expression was off, a few had seen altogether a different countenance. Especially tender and gentle it had appeared to those who were about him during the last illness of his only child.

The Commissioner had been a widower for years, and his life, outside his official duties, had been so devoted to little Georgia that people spoke of it as a touching and admirable thing. He was a reserved man, and dignified almost to austerity, but the child had come below it all and rested upon his very heart, so that she scarcely missed the mother's love that had been taken away. There was a wonderful companionship between them, for she had many of his own ways, being thoughtful and serious beyond her years.

One day, while she was lying with the fever burning brightly in her cheeks, she said suddenly:

"Papa, I wish I could do something good for a whole lot of children!"

"What would you like to do, dear?" asked the Commissioner. "Give them a party?"

"Oh, I don't mean those kind. I mean poor children who haven't homes, and aren't loved and cared for as I am. I tell you what, papa?"

"What, my own child?"

"If I shouldn't get well, I'll leave them you—not *give* you, but just lend you, for you must come to mamma and me when you die too. If you can find time, wouldn't you do something to help them, if I ask you, papa?"

"Hush, hush, dear, dear child," said the Commissioner, holding her hot little hand against his cheek; "you'll get well real soon, and you and I will see what we can do for them together."

But in whatsoever paths of benevolence, thus vaguely premeditated, the Commissioner might tread, he was not to have the company of his beloved. That night the little frail body grew suddenly too tired to struggle further, and Georgia's exit was made from the great stage when she had scarcely begun to speak her little piece before the footlights. But there must be a stage manager who understands. She had given the cue to the one who was to speak after her.

A week after she was laid away, the Commissioner reappeared at the office, a little more courteous, a little paler and sterner, with the black frock-coat hanging a little more loosely from his tall figure.

His desk was piled with work that had accumulated during the four heartbreaking weeks of his absence. His chief clerk had done what he could, but there were questions of law, of fine judicial decisions to be made concerning the issue of patents, the marketing and leasing of school lands, the classification into grazing, agricultural, watered, and timbered, of new tracts to be opened to settlers.

The Commissioner went to work silently and obstinately, putting back his grief as far as possible, forcing his mind to attack the complicated and important business of his office. On the second day after his return he called the porter, pointed to a leather-covered chair that stood near his own, and ordered it removed to a lumber-room at the top of the building. In that chair Georgia would always sit when she came to the office for him of afternoons.

As time passed, the Commissioner seemed to grow more silent, solitary, and reserved. A new phase of mind developed in him. He could not endure the presence of a child. Often when a clattering youngster belonging to one of the clerks would come chattering into the big business-room adjoining his little apartment, the Commissioner would steal softly and close the door. He would always cross the street to avoid meeting the school-children when they came dancing along in happy groups upon the sidewalk, and his firm mouth would close into a mere line.

It was nearly three months after the rains had washed the last dead flower-petals from the mound above little Georgia when the "land-shark" firm of Hamlin and Avery filed papers upon what they considered the "fattest" vacancy of the year.

It should not be supposed that all who were termed "land-sharks" deserved the name. Many of them were reputable men of good business character. Some of them could walk into the most august councils of the state and say: "Gentlemen, we would like to have this, and that, and matters go thus." But, next to a three years' drought and the boll-worm, the Actual Settler hated the Land-shark. The Land-shark haunted the Land Office, where all the land records were kept and hunted "vacancies"—that is, tracts of unappropriated public domain, generally invisible upon the official maps, but actually existing "upon the ground." The law entitled anyone possessing certain state scrip to file by virtue of same upon any land not previously legally appropriated. Most of the scrip was now in the hands of the land-sharks. Thus, at the cost of a few hundred dollars, they often secured lands worth as many thousands. Naturally, the search for "vacancies" was lively.

But often—very often—the land they thus secured, though legally "unappropriated," would be occupied by happy and contented settlers, who had laboured for years to build up their homes, only to discover that their titles were worthless, and to receive peremptory notice to quit. Thus came about the bitter and not unjustifiable hatred felt by the toiling settlers toward the shrewd and seldom merciful speculators who so often turned them forth destitute and homeless from their fruitless labours. The history of the state teems with their antagonism. Mr. Land-shark seldom showed his face on "locations" from which he should have to eject the unfortunate victims of a monstrously tangled land system, but let his emissaries do the work. There was lead in every cabin, moulded into balls for him; many of his brothers had enriched the grass with their blood. The fault of it all lay far back.

When the state was young, she felt the need of attracting new-comers, and of rewarding those pioneers already within her borders. Year after year she issued land scrip—Headrights, Bounties, Veteran Donations, Confederates; and to railroads, irrigation companies, colonies, and tillers of the soil galore. All required of the grantee was that he or it should have the scrip properly surveyed upon the public domain by the county or district surveyor, and the land thus appropriated became the property of him or it, or his or its heirs and assigns, for ever.

In those days—and here is where the trouble began—the state's domain was practically inexhaustible, and the old surveyors, with princely—yea, even Western American—liberality, gave good measure and overflowing. Often the jovial man of metes and bounds would dispense altogether with the tripod and chain. Mounted on a pony that could cover something near a "vara" at a step, with a pocket compass to direct his course, he would trot out a survey by counting the beat of his pony's hoofs, mark his corners, and write out his field notes with the complacency produced by an act of duty well performed. Sometimes—and who could blame the surveyor?—when the pony was "feeling his oats," he might step a little higher and farther, and in that case the beneficiary of the scrip might get a thousand or two more acres in his survey than the scrip called for. But look at the boundless leagues the state had to spare! However, no one ever had to complain of the pony under-stepping. Nearly every old survey in the state contained an excess of land.

In later years, when the state became more populous, and land values increased, this careless work entailed incalculable trouble, endless litigation, a period of riotous land-grabbing, and no little bloodshed. The land-sharks voraciously attacked these excesses in the old surveys, and filed upon such portions with new scrip as unappropriated public domain. Wherever the identifications of the old tracts were vague, and the corners were not to be clearly established, the Land Office would recognize the newer locations as valid, and issue title to the locators. Here was the greatest hardship to be found. These old surveys, taken from the pick of the land, were already nearly all occupied by unsuspecting and peaceful settlers, and thus their titles were demolished, and the choice was placed before them either to buy their land over at a double price or to vacate it, with their families and personal belongings, immediately. Land locators sprang up by hundreds. The country was held up and searched for "vacancies" at the point of a compass. Hundreds of thousands of dollars' worth of splendid acres were wrested from their innocent purchasers and holders. There began a vast hegira of evicted settlers in tattered wagons; going nowhere, cursing injustice, stunned, purposeless, homeless, hopeless. Their children began to look up to them for bread, and cry.

It was in consequence of these conditions that Hamilton and Avery had filed upon a strip of land about a mile wide and three miles long, comprising about two thousand acres, it being the excess over complement of the Elias Denny three-league survey on Chiquito River, in one of the middle-western counties. This two-thousand-acre body of land was asserted by them to be vacant land, and improperly considered a part of the Denny survey. They based this assertion and their claim upon the land upon the demonstrated facts that the beginning corner of the Denny survey was plainly identified; that its field notes called to run west 5,760 varas, and then called for Chiquito River; thence it ran south, with the meanders—and so on—and that the Chiquito River was, on the ground, fully a mile farther west from the point reached by course and distance. To sum up: there were two thousand acres of vacant land between the Denny survey proper and Chiquito River.

One sweltering day in July the Commissioner called for the papers in connection with this new location. They were brought, and heaped, a foot deep, upon his desk—field notes, statements, sketches, affidavits, connecting lines—documents of every description that shrewdness and money could call to the aid of Hamlin and Avery.

The firm was pressing the Commissioner to issue a patent upon their location. They possessed inside information concerning a new railroad that would probably pass somewhere near this land.

The General Land Office was very still while the Commissioner was delving into the heart of the mass of evidence. The pigeons could be heard on the roof of the old, castle-like building, cooing and fretting. The clerks were droning everywhere, scarcely pretending to earn their salaries. Each little sound echoed hollow and loud from the bare, stone-flagged floors, the plastered walls, and the iron-joisted ceiling. The impalpable, perpetual limestone dust, that never settled, whitened a long streamer of sunlight that pierced the tattered window-awning.

It seemed that Hamlin and Avery had builded well. The Denny survey was carelessly made, even for a careless period. Its beginning corner was identical with that of a well-defined old Spanish grant, but its other calls were sinfully vague. The field notes contained no other object that survived—no tree, no natural object save Chiquito River, and it was a mile wrong there. According to precedent, the Office would be justified in giving it its complement by course and distance, and considering the remainder vacant instead of a mere excess.

The Actual Settler was besieging the office with wild protests *in re*. Having the nose of a pointer and the eye of a hawk for the land-shark, he had observed his myrmidons running the lines upon his ground. Making inquiries, he learned that the spoiler had attacked his home, and he left the plough in the furrow and took his pen in hand.

One of the protests the Commissioner read twice. It was from a woman, a widow, the granddaughter of Elias Denny himself. She told how her grandfather had sold most of the survey years before at a trivial price—land that was now a principality in extent and value. Her mother had also sold a part, and she herself had succeeded to this western portion, along Chiquito River. Much of it she had been forced to part with in order to live, and now she owned only about three hundred acres, on which she had her home. Her letter wound up rather pathetically:

"I've got eight children, the oldest fifteen years. I work all day and half the night to till what little land I can and keep us in clothes and books. I teach my children too. My neighbours is all poor and has big families. The drought kills the crops every two or three years and then we has hard times to get enough to eat. There is ten families on this land what the land-sharks is trying to rob us of, and all of them got titles from me. I sold to them cheap, and they ain't paid out yet, but part of them is, and if their land should be took from them I would die. My grandfather was an honest man, and he helped to build up this state, and he taught his children to be honest, and how could I make it up to them who bought from me? Mr. Commissioner, if you let them land-sharks take the roof from over my children and the little from them as they has to live on, whoever again calls this state great or its government just will have a lie in their mouths."

The Commissioner laid this letter aside with a sigh. Many, many such letters he had received. He had never been hurt by them, nor had he ever felt that they appealed to him personally. He was but the state's servant, and must follow its laws. And yet, somehow, this reflection did not always eliminate a certain responsible feeling that hung upon him. Of all the state's officers he was supremest in his department, not even excepting the Governor. Broad, general land laws he followed, it was true, but he had a wide latitude in particular ramifications. Rather than law, what he followed was Rulings: Office Rulings and precedents. In the complicated and new questions that were being engendered by the state's development the Commissioner's ruling was rarely appealed from. Even the courts sustained it when its equity was apparent.

The Commissioner stepped to the door and spoke to a clerk in the other room—spoke as he always did, as if he were addressing a prince of the blood:

"Mr. Weldon, will you be kind enough to ask Mr. Ashe, the state school-land appraiser, to please come to my office as soon as convenient?"

Ashe came quickly from the big table where he was arranging his reports.

"Mr. Ashe," said the Commissioner, "you worked

along the Chiquito River, in Salado County, during your last trip, I believe. Do you remember anything of the Elias Denny three-league survey?"

"Yes, sir, I do," the blunt, breezy surveyor answered. "I crossed it on my way to Block H, on the north side of it. The road runs with the Chiquito River, along the valley. The Denny survey fronts three miles on the Chiquito."

"It is claimed," continued the Commissioner, "that it fails to reach the river by as much as a mile."

The appraiser shrugged his shoulder. He was by birth and instinct an Actual Settler, and the natural foe of the land-shark.

"It has always been considered to extend to the river," he said dryly.

"But that is not the point I desired to discuss," said the Commissioner. "What kind of country is this valley portion of (let us say, then) the Denny tract?"

The spirit of the Actual Settler beamed in Ashe's face.

"Beautiful," he said, with enthusiasm. "Valley as level as this floor, with just a little swell on, like the sea, and rich as cream. Just enough brakes to shelter the cattle in winter. Black loamy soil for six feet, and then clay. Holds water. A dozen nice little houses on it, with windmills and gardens. People pretty poor, I guess—too far from market—but comfortable. Never saw so many kids in my life."

"They raise flocks?" inquired the Commissioner.

"Ho, ho! I mean two-legged kids," laughed the surveyor; "two-legged, and bare-legged, and tow-headed."

"Children! oh, children!" mused the Commissioner, as though a new view had opened to him; "they raise children!"

"It's a lonesome country, Commissioner," said the surveyor. "Can you blame 'em?"

"I suppose," continued the Commissioner slowly, as one carefully pursues deductions from a new, stupendous theory, "not all of them are tow-headed. It would not be unreasonable, Mr. Ashe, I conjecture, to believe that a portion of them have brown, or even black, hair."

"Brown and black, sure," said Ashe; "also red."

"No doubt," said the Commissioner. "Well, I thank you for your courtesy in informing me, Mr. Ashe. I will not detain you any longer from your duties."

Later, in the afternoon, came Hamlin and Avery, big, handsome, genial, sauntering men, clothed in white duck and low-cut shoes. They permeated the whole office with an aura of debonair prosperity. They passed among the clerks and left a wake of abbreviated given names and fat brown cigars.

These were the aristocracy of the land-sharks, who went in for big things. Full of serene confidence in themselves, there was no corporation, no syndicate, no railroad company or attorney general too big for them to tackle. The peculiar smoke of their rare, fat brown cigars was to be perceived in the sanctum of every department of state, in every committee-room of the Legislature, in every bank parlour and every private caucus-room in the state Capital. Always pleasant, never in a hurry, in seeming to possess unlimited leisure, people wondered when they gave their attention to the many audacious enterprises in which they were known to be engaged.

By and by the two dropped carelessly into the Commissioner's room and reclined lazily in the big, leather upholstered arm-chairs. They drawled a good-natured complaint of the weather, and Hamlin told the Commissioner an excellent story he had amassed that morning from the Secretary of State.

But the Commissioner knew why they were there. He had half promised to render a decision that day upon their location.

The chief clerk now brought in a batch of duplicate certificates for the Commissioner to sign. As he traced his sprawling signature, "Hollis Summerfield, Comr. Genl. Land Office," on each one, the chief clerk stood, deftly removing them and applying the blotter.

"I notice," said the chief clerk, "you've been going through that Salado County location. Kampfer is making a new map of Salado, and I believe is platting in that section of the county now."

"I will see it," said the Commissioner. A few moments later he went to the draughtsmen's room.

As he entered he saw five or six of the draughtsmen grouped about Kampfer's desk, gargling away at each other in pectoral German, and gazing at something thereupon. At the Commissioner's approach they scattered to their several places. Kampfer, a wizened little German, with long, frizzled ringlets and a watery eye, began to stammer forth some sort of an apology, the Commissioner thought, for the congregation of his fellows about his desk.

"Never mind," said the Commissioner, "I wish to see the map you are making"; and passing around the old German, seated himself upon the high draughtsman's stool. Kampfer continued to break English in trying to explain.

"Herr Gommissioner, I assure you blenty sat I haf not it bremeditated—sat it wass—sat it itself make. Look you! from se field notes wass it blatted—blease to observe se calls: South, 10 degrees west 1,050 varas; south, 10 degrees east 300 varas; south, 100; south, 9 west, 200; south, 40 degrees west 400—and so on Herr Gommissioner, nefer would I have——"

The Commissioner raised one white hand, silently. Kampfer dropped his pipe and fled.

With a hand at each side of his face, and his elbows resting upon the desk, the Commissioner sat staring at the map which was spread and fastened there—staring at the sweet and living profile of little Georgia drawn thereupon—at her face, pensive, delicate, and infantile, outlined in a perfect likeness.

When his mind at length came to inquire into the reason of it, he saw that it must have been, as Kampfer had said, unpremeditated. The old draughtsman had been platting in the Elias Denny survey, and Georgia's likeness, striking though it was, was formed by nothing more than the meanders of Chiquito River. Indeed, Kampfer's blotter, whereon his preliminary work was done, showed the laborious tracings of the calls and the countless pricks of the compasses. Then, over his faint pencilling, Kampfer had drawn in India ink with a full, firm pen the similitude of Chiquito River, and forth had blossomed mysteriously the dainty, pathetic profile of the child.

The Commissioner sat for half an hour with his face in his hands, gazing downward, and none dared approach him. Then he arose and walked out. In the business office he paused long enough to ask that the Denny file be brought to his desk.

He found Hamlin and Avery still reclining in their chairs, apparently oblivious of business. They were lazily discussing summer opera, it being their habit—perhaps their pride also—to appear supernaturally indifferent whenever they stood with large interests imperilled. And they stood to win more on this stake than most people knew. They possessed inside information to the effect that a new railroad would, within a year, split this very Chiquito River valley and send land values ballooning all along its route. A dollar under thirty thousand profit on this location, if it should hold good, would be a loss to their expectations. So, while they chatted lightly and waited for the Commissioner to open the subject, there was a quick, sidelong sparkle in their eyes, evincing a desire to read their title clear to those fair acres on the Chiquito.

A clerk brought in the file. The Commissioner seated himself and wrote upon it in red ink. Then he rose to his feet and stood for a while looking straight out of the window. The Land Office capped the summit of a bold hill. The eyes of the Commissioner passed over the roofs of many houses set in a packing of deep green, the whole checkered by strips of blinding white streets. The horizon, where his gaze was focused, swelled to a fair wooded eminence flecked with faint dots of shining white. There was the cemetery, where lay many who were forgotten, and a few who had not lived in vain. And one lay there occupying very small space, whose childish heart had been large enough to desire, while near its last beats, good to others. The Commissioner's lips moved slightly as he whispered to himself: "It was her last will and testament, and I have neglected it so long!"

The big brown cigars of Hamlin and Avery were fireless, but they still gripped them between their teeth and waited, while they marvelled at the absent expression upon the Commissioner's face.

By and by he spoke suddenly and promptly.

"Gentlemen, I have just endorsed the Elias Denny survey for patenting. This office will not regard your location upon a part of it as legal." He paused a moment, and then, extending his hand as those dear old-time ones used to do in debate, he enunciated the spirit of that Ruling that subsequently drove the land-sharks to the wall, and placed the seal of peace and security over the doors of ten thousand homes.

"And, furthermore," he continued, with a clear, soft light upon his face, "it may interest you to know that from this time on this office will consider that when a survey of land made by virtue of a certificate granted by this state to the men who wrested it from the wilderness and the savage —made in good faith, settled in good faith, and left in good faith to their children or innocent purchasers—when such a survey, although overrunning its complement, shall call for any natural object visible to the eye of man, to that object it shall hold, and be good and valid. And the children of this state shall lie down to sleep at night, and rumours of disturbers of title shall not disquiet them. For," concluded the Commissioner, "of such is the Kingdom of Heaven."

In the silence that followed, a laugh floated up

from the patent-room below. The man who carried down the Denny file was exhibiting it among the clerks.

"Look here," he said delightedly, "the old man has forgotten his name. He's written 'Patent to original grantee,' and signed it 'Georgia Summerfield, Comr.' "

The speech of the Commissioner rebounded lightly from the impregnable Hamlin and Avery. They smiled, rose gracefully, spoke of the baseball team, and argued feelingly that quite a perceptible breeze had arisen from the east. They lit fresh fat brown cigars, and drifted courteously away. But later they made another tiger-spring for their quarry in the courts. But the courts, according to reports in the papers, "coolly roasted them" (a remarkable performance, suggestive of liquid-air didocs), and sustained the Commissioner's Ruling.

And this Ruling itself grew to be a Precedent, and the Actual Settler framed it, and taught his children to spell from it, and there was sound sleep o' nights from the pines to the sage-brush, and from the chaparral to the great brown river of the north.

But I think, and I am sure the Commissioner never thought otherwise, that whether Kampfer was a snuffy old instrument of destiny, or whether the meanders of the Chiquito accidentally platted themselves into that memorable sweet profile or not, that was brought about "something good for a whole lot of children," and the result ought to be called "Georgia's Ruling."

LXXII: THE UNKNOWN QUANTITY

THE poet Longfellow—or was it Confucius, the inventor of wisdom?—remarked:

> "Life is real, life is earnest;
> And things are not what they seem."

As mathematics are—or is: thanks, old subscriber! —the only just rule by which questions of life can be measured, let us, by all means, adjust our theme to the straight edge and the balanced column of the great goddess Two-and-Two-Makes-Four. Figures —unassailable sums in addition—shall be set over against whatever opposing element there may be.

A mathematician, after scanning the above two lines of poetry, would say: "Ahem! young gentlemen, if we assume that X plus—that is, that life is real—then things (all of which life includes) are real. Anything that is real is what it seems. Then if we consider the proposition that 'things are not what they seem,' why——"

But this is heresy, and not poesy. We woo the sweet nymph Algebra; we would conduct you into the presence of the elusive, seductive, pursued, satisfying, mysterious X.

Not long before the beginning of this century, Septimus Kinsolving, an old New Yorker, invented an idea. He originated the discovery that bread is made from flour and not from wheat futures. Perceiving that the flour crop was short, and that the Stock Exchange was having no perceptible effect on the growing wheat, Mr. Kinsolving cornered the flour market.

The result was that when you or my landlady

(before the war she never had to turn her hand to anything; Southerners accommodated) bought a five-cent loaf of bread you laid down an additional two cents, which went to Mr. Kinsolving as a testimonial to his perspicacity.

A second result was that Mr. Kinsolving quit the game with $2,000,000 prof—er—rake-off.

Mr. Kinsolving's son Dan was at college when the mathematical experiment in breadstuffs was made. Dan came home during vacation, and found the old gentleman in a red dressing-gown reading *Little Dorrit* on the porch of his estimable red-brick mansion in Washington Square. He had retired from business with enough extra two-cent pieces from bread buyers to reach, if laid side by side, fifteen times around the earth and lap as far as the public debt of Paraquay.

Dan shook hands with his father, and hurried over to Greenwich Village to see his old high-school friend, Kenwitz. Dan had always admired Kenwitz. Kenwitz was pale, curly-haired, intense, serious, mathematical, studious, altruistic, socialistic and the natural foe of oligarchies. Kenwitz had forgone college, and was learning watch-making in his father's jewellery store. Dan was smiling, jovial, easy-tempered and tolerant alike of kings and rag-pickers. The two forgathered joyously, being opposites. And then Dan went back to college, and Kenwitz to his mainsprings—and to his private library in the rear of the jewellery shop.

Four years later Dan came back to Washington Square with the accumulations of B.A. and two years of Europe thick upon him. He took a filial look at Septimus Kinsolving's elaborate tombstone in Greenwood, and a tedious excursion through typewritten documents with the family lawyer; and then, feeling himself a lonely and hopeless millionaire, hurried down to the old jewellery store across Sixth Avenue.

Kenwitz unscrewed a magnifying glass from his eye, routed out his parent from a dingy rear room, and abandoned the interior of watches for outdoors. He went with Dan, and they sat on a bench in Washington Square. Dan had not changed much; he was stalwart, and had a dignity that was inclined to relax into a grin. Kenwitz was more serious, more intense, more learned, philosophical and socialistic.

"I know about it now," said Dan finally. "I pumped it out of the eminent legal lights that turned over to me poor old dad's collection of bonds and boodle. It amounts to $2,000,000, Ken. And I am told that he squeezed it out of the chaps that pay their pennies for loaves of bread at the little bakeries around the corner. You've studied economics, Ken, and you know all about monopolies, and the masses, and octopuses, and the rights of labouring people. I never thought about those things before. Football and trying to be white to my fellow-man were about the extent of my college curriculum.

"But since I came back and found out how dad made his money I've been thinking. I'd like awfully well to pay back those chaps who had to give up too much money for bread. I know it would buck the line of my income for a good many yards; but I'd like to make it square with 'em. Is there any way it can be done, old Ways and Means?"

Kenwitz's big black eyes glowed fierily. His thin, intellectual face took on almost a sardonic cast. He caught Dan's arm with the grip of a friend and a judge.

"You can't do it!" he said, emphatically. "One of the chief punishments of you men of ill-gotten wealth is that when you do repent you find that you have lost the power to make reparation or restitution. I admire your good intentions, Dan, but you can't do anything. Those people were robbed of their precious pennies. It's too late to remedy the evil. You can't pay them back."

"Of course," said Dan, lighting his pipe, "we couldn't hunt up every one of the duffers and hand 'em back the right change. There's an awful lot of 'em buying bread all the time. Funny taste they have—I never cared for bread especially, except for a toasted cracker with the Roquefort. But we might find a few of 'em and chuck some of dad's cash back where it came from. I'd feel better if I could. It seems tough for people to be held up for a soggy thing like bread. Onc wouldn't mind standing a rise in broilcd lobsters or devilled crabs. Get to work and think, Ken. I want to pay back all of that money I can."

"There are plenty of charities," said Kenwitz mechanically.

"Easy enough," said Dan, in a cloud of smoke. "I suppose I could give the city a park, or endow an asparagus bed in a hospital. But I don't want Paul to get away with the proceeds of the gold brick we sold Peter. It's the bread shorts I want to cover, Ken."

The thin fingers of Kenwitz moved rapidly.

"Do you know how much money it would take to pay back the losses of consumers during that corner in flour?" he asked.

"I do not," said Dan stoutly. "My lawyer tells me that I have two millions."

"If you had a hundred millions," said Kenwitz vehemently, "you couldn't repair a thousandth part of the damage that has been done. You cannot conceive of the accumulated evils produced by misapplied wealth. Each penny that was wrung from the lean purses of the poor reacted a thousandfold to their harm. You do not understand. You do not see how hopeless is your desire to make restitution. Not in a single instance can it be done."

"Back up, philosopher!" said Dan. "The penny has no sorrow that the dollar cannot heal."

"Not in one instance," repeated Kenwitz. "I will give you one, and let us see. Thomas Boyne had a little bakery over there in Varick Street. He sold bread to the poorest people. When the price of flour went up he had to raise the price of bread. His customers were too poor to pay it, Boyne's business failed and he lost his $1,000 capital—all he had in the world."

Dan Kinsolving struck the park bench a mighty blow with his fist.

"I accept the instance," he cried. "Take me to Boyne. I will repay his thousand dollars and buy him a new bakery."

"Write your cheque," said Kenwitz, without moving, "and then begin to write cheques in payment of the train of consequences. Draw the next one for $50,000. Boyne went insane after his failure and set fire to the building from which he was about to be evicted. The loss amounted to that much. Boyne died in an asylum."

"Stick to the instance," said Dan. "I haven't noticed any insurance companies on my charity list."

"Draw you next cheque for $100,000," went on

Kenwitz. "Boyne's son fell into bad ways after the bakery closed, and was accused of murder. He was acquitted last week after a three years' legal battle, and the State draws upon taxpayers for that much expense."

"Back to the bakery!" exclaimed Dan impatiently. "The Government doesn't need to stand in the bread line."

"The last item of the instance is—come and I will show you," said Kenwitz, rising.

The socialistic watchmaker was happy. He was a millionaire-baiter by nature and a pessimist by trade. Kenwitz would assure you in one breath that money was but evil and corruption, and that your brand-new watch needed cleaning and a new ratchet-wheel.

He conducted Kinsolving southward out of the square and into ragged, poverty-haunted Varick Street. Up the narrow stairway of a squalid brick tenement he led the penitent offspring of the Octopus. He knocked on a door, and a clear voice called to them to enter.

In that almost bare room a young woman sat sewing at a machine. She nodded to Kenwitz as to a familiar acquaintance. One little stream of sunlight through the dingy window burnished her heavy hair to the colour of an ancient Tuscan's shield. She flashed a rippling smile at Kenwitz and a look of somewhat flustered inquiry.

Kinsolving stood regarding her clear and pathetic beauty in heart-throbbing silence. Thus they came into the presence of the last item of the Instance.

"How many this week, Miss Mary?" asked the watchmaker. A mountain of coarse grey shirts lay upon the floor.

"Nearly thirty dozen," said the young woman cheerfully. "I've made almost $4. I'm improving, Mr. Kenwitz. I hardly know what to do with so much money." Her eyes turned, brightly soft, in the direction of Dan. A little pink spot came out on her round, pale cheek.

Kenwitz chuckled like a diabolic raven.

"Miss Boyne," he said, "let me present Mr. Kinsolving, the son of the man who put bread up five years ago. He thinks he would like to do something to aid those who were inconvenienced by that act."

The smile left the young woman's face. She rose and pointed her forefinger toward the door. This time she looked Kinsolving straight in the eye, but it was not a look that gave delight.

The two men went down into Varick Street. Kenwitz, letting all his pessimism and rancour and hatred of the Octopus come to the surface, gibed at the moneyed side of his friend in an acrid torrent of words. Dan appeared to be listening, and then turned to Kenwitz and shook hands with him warmly.

"I'm obliged to you, Ken, old man," he said vaguely—"a thousand times obliged."

"Mein Gott! you are crazy!" cried the watchmaker, dropping his spectacles for the first time in years.

Two months afterward Kenwitz went into a large bakery on lower Broadway with a pair of gold-rimmed eyeglasses that he had mended for the proprietor.

A lady was giving an order to a clerk as Kenwitz passed her.

"These loaves are ten cents," said the clerk.

"I always get them at eight cents up-town," said the lady. "You need not fill the order. I will drive by there on my way home."

The voice was familiar. The watchmaker paused.

"Mr. Kenwitz!" cried the lady heartily. "How do you do?"

Kenwitz was trying to train his socialistic and economic comprehension on her wonderful fur boa and the carriage waiting outside.

"Why, Miss Boyne!" he began.

"Mrs. Kinsolving," she corrected. "Dan and I were married a month ago."

LXXIII: THE RANSOM OF MACK

ME and old Mack Lonsbury, we got out of that Little Hide-and-Seek gold mine affair with about $40,000 apiece. I say "old" Mack; but he wasn't old. Forty-one, I should say; but he always seemed old.

"Andy," he says to me, "I'm tired of hustling. You and me have been working hard together for three years. Say we knock off for a while, and spend some of this idle money we've coaxed our way."

"The proposition hits me just right," says I. "Let's be nabobs a while and see how it feels. What'll we do—take in the Niagara Falls, or buck at faro?"

"For a good many years," says Mack, "I've thought that if I ever had extravagant money I'd rent a two-room cabin somewhere, hire a Chinaman to cook, and sit in my stocking feet and read Buckle's *History of Civilization*."

"That sounds self-indulgent and gratifying without vulgar ostentation," says I; "and I don't see how money could be better invested. Give me a cuckoo clock and a Sep Winner's *Self-Instructor for the Banjo*, and I'll join you."

A week afterward me and Mack hits this small town of Piña, about thirty miles out from Denver, and finds an elegant two-room house that just suits us. We deposited half a peck of money in the Piña bank and shook hands with every one of the 340 citizens in the town. We brought along the Chinaman and the cuckoo clock and Buckle and the Instructor with us from Denver; and they made the cabin seem like home at once.

Never believe it when they tell you riches don't bring happiness. If you could have seen old Mack sitting in his rocking-chair with his blue-yarn sock feet up in the window and absorbing in that Buckle stuff through his specs you'd have seen a picture of content that would have made Rockefeller jealous. And I was learning to pick out "Old Zip Coon" on the banjo, and the cuckoo was on time with his remarks, and Ah Sing was messing up the atmosphere with the handsomest smell of ham and eggs that ever laid the honeysuckle in the shade. When it got too dark to make out Buckle's nonsense and the notes in the Instructor, me and Mack would light our pipes and talk about science and pearl diving and sciatica and Egypt and spelling and fish and trade winds and leather and gratitude and eagles, and a lot of subjects that we'd never had time to explain our sentiments about before.

One evening Mack spoke up and asked me if I

was much apprised in the habits and policies of women-folks.

"Why, yes," says I, in a tone of voice; "I know 'em from Alfred to Omaha. The feminine nature and similitude," says I, "is as plain to my sight as the Rocky Mountains is to a blue-eyed burro. I'm on to all their little side-steps and punctual discrepancies."

"I tell you, Andy," says Mack, with a kind of sigh, "I never had the least amount of intersection with their predispositions. Maybe I might have had a proneness in respect to their vicinity, but I never took the time. I made my own living since I was fourteen; and I never seemed to get my ratiocinations equipped with the sentiments usually depicted toward the sect. I sometimes wish I had," says old Mack.

"They'rc an adverse study," says I, "and adapted to points of view. Although they vary in rationale, I have found 'em quite often obviously differing from each other in divergences of contrast."

"It seems to me," goes on Mack, "that a man had better take 'em in and secure his inspirations of the sects when he's young and so preordained. I let my chance go by; and I guess I'm too old now to go hopping into the curriculum."

"Oh, I don't know," I tells him. "Maybe you better credit yourself with a barrel of money and a lot of emancipation from a quantity of uncontent. Still, I don't regret my knowledge of 'em," I says. "It takes a man who understands the symptoms and by-plays of women-folk to take care of himself in this world."

We stayed on in Piña because we liked the place. Some folks might enjoy their money with noise and rapture and locomotion; but me and Mack we had had plenty of turmoils and hotel towels. The people were friendly; Ah Sing got the swing of the grub we liked; Mack and Buckle were as thick as two body-snatchers, and I was hitting out a cordial resemblance to "Buffalo Gals, Can't You Come Out To-night," on the banjo.

One day I got a telegram from Speight, the man that was working a mine I had an interest in out in New Mexico. I had to go out there; and I was gone two months. I was anxious to get back to Piña and enjoy life once more.

When I struck the cabin I nearly fainted. Mack was standing in the door; and if angels ever wept, I saw no reason why they should be smiling then.

That man was a spectacle. Yes, he was worse; he was a spy-glass, he was the great telescope in the Lick Observatory. He had on a coat and shiny shoes and a white vest and a high silk hat, and a geranium as big as an order of spinach was spiked on to his front. And he was smirking and warping his face like an infernal storekeeper or a kid with colic.

"Hallo, Andy," says Mack, out of his face. "Glad to see you back. Things have happened since you went away."

"I know it," says I, "and a sacrilegious sight it is. God never made you that way, Mack Lonsbury. Why do you scarify His works with this presumptuous kind of ribaldry?"

"Why, Andy," says he, "they've elected me justice of the peace since you left."

I looked at Mack close. He was restless and inspired. A justice of the peace ought to be disconsolate and assuaged.

Just then a young woman passed on the sidewalk; and I saw Mack kind of half snicker and blush, and then he raised up his hat and smiled and bowed, and she smiled and bowed, and went on by.

"No hope for you," says I, "if you've got the Mary Jane infirmity at your age. I thought it wasn't going to take on you. And patent leather shoes! All this in two little short months!"

"I'm going to marry the young lady who just passed to-night," says Mack, in a kind of a flutter.

"I forgot something at the post office," says I, and walked away quick.

I overtook that young woman a hundred yards away. I raised my hat and told her my name. She was about nineteen, and young for her age. She blushed, and then looked at me cold, like I was the snow scene from the *Two Orphans*.

"I understand you are to be married to-night," I said.

"Correct," says she. "You got any objections?"

"Listen, sissy," I begins.

"My name is Miss Rebosa Redd," says she in a pained way.

"I know it," says I. "Now, Rebosa, I'm old enough to have owed money to your father. And that old, specious, dressed-up, garbled, sea-sick ptomaine prancing around avidiously like an irremediable turkey gobbler with patent leather shoes on is my best friend. Why did you go and get him invested in this marriage business?"

"Why, he was the only chance there was," answers Miss Rebosa.

"Nay," says I, giving a sickening look of admiration at her complexion and style of features; "with your beauty you might pick any kind of a man.

Listen, Rebosa. Old Mack ain't the man you want. He was twenty-two when you was *née* Reed, as the papers say. This bursting into bloom won't last with him. He's all ventilated with oldness and rectitude and decay. Old Mack's down with a case of Indian summer. He overlooked his bet when he was young; and now he's suing Nature for the interest on the promissory note he took from Cupid instead of the cash. Rebosa, are you bent on having this marriage occur?"

"Why, sure I am," says she, oscillating the pansies on her hat, "and so is somebody else, I reckon."

"What time is it to take place?" I asks.

"At six o'clock," says she.

I made up my mind right away what to do. I'd save old Mack if I could. To have a good, seasoned, ineligible man like that turn chicken for a girl that hadn't quit eating slate pencils and buttoning in the back was more than I could look on with easiness.

"Rebosa," says I, earnest, drawing upon my display of knowledge concerning the feminine intuitions of reason—"ain't there a young man in Piña—a nice young man that you think a heap of?"

"Yep," says Rebosa, nodding her pansies—"Sure there is! What do you think! Gracious!"

"Does he like you?" I asks. "How does he stand in the matter?"

"Crazy," says Rebosa. "Ma has to wet down the front steps to keep him from sitting there all the time. But I guess that'll be all over after to-night," she winds up with a sigh.

"Rebosa," says I, "you don't really experience any of this adoration called love for old Mack, do you?"

"Lord! no," says the girl, shaking her head. "I think he's as dry as a lava bed. The idea!"

"Who is this young man that you like, Rebosa?" I inquires.

"It's Eddie Bayles," says she. "He clerks in Crosby's grocery. But he don't make but thirty-five a month. Ella Noakes was wild about him once."

"Old Mack tells me," I says, "that he's going to marry you at six o'clock this evening."

"That's the time," says she. "It's to be at our house."

"Rebosa," says I, "listen to me. If Eddie Bayles had a thousand dollars cash—a thousand dollars, mind you, would buy him a store of his own—if you and Eddie had that much to excuse matrimony on, would you consent to marry him this evening at five o'clock?"

The girl looks at me a minute; and I can see these inaudible cogitations going on inside of her, as women will.

"A thousand dollars?" says she. "Of course I would."

"Come on," says I. "We'll go and see Eddie."

We went up to Crosby's store and called Eddie outside. He looked to be estimable and freckled; and he had chills and fever when I made my proposition.

"At five o'clock?" says he, "for a thousand dollars? Please don't wake me up! Well, you *are* the rich uncle retired from the spice business in India! I'll buy out old Crosby and run the store myself."

We went inside and got old man Crosby apart and explained it. I wrote my cheque for a thousand dollars and handed it to him. If Eddie and Rebosa married each other at five he was to turn the money over to them.

And then I gave 'em my blessing, and went to wander in the wild-wood for a season. I sat on a log and made cogitations on life and old age and the zodiac and the ways of women and all the disorder that goes with a lifetime. I passed myself congratulations that I had probably saved my old friend Mack from his attack of Indian summer. I knew when he got well of it and shed his infatuation and his patent leather shoes, he would feel grateful. "To keep old Mack disinvolved," thinks I, "from relapses like this, is worth more than a thousand dollars." And most of all I was glad that I'd made a study of women, and wasn't to be deceived any by their means of conceit and evolution.

It must have been half-past five when I got back home. I stepped in; and there sat old Mack on the back of his neck in his old clothes with his blue socks on the window and the *History of Civilization* propped up on his knees.

"This don't look like getting ready for a wedding at six," I says, to seem innocent.

"Oh," says Mack, reaching for his tobacco, "that was postponed back to five o'clock. They sent me a note saying the hour had been changed. It's all over now. What made you stay away so long, Andy?"

"You heard about the wedding?" I asks.

"I operated it," says he. "I told you I was justice of the peace. The preacher is off East to visit his folks, and I'm the only one in town that can perform the dispensations of marriage. I promised Eddie and Rebosa a month ago I'd marry 'em. He's a busy lad; and he'll have a grocery of his own some day."

"He will," says I.

"There was lots of women at the wedding," says Mack, smoking up. "But I didn't seem to get any ideas from 'em. I wish I was informed in the structure of their attainments like you said you was."

"That was two months ago," says I, reaching up for the banjo.

LXXIV: A LITTLE LOCAL COLOUR

I MENTIONED to Rivington that I was in search of characteristic New York scenes and incidents—something typical, I told him, without necessarily having to spell the first syllable with an "i."

"Oh, for your writing business," said Rivington; "you couldn't have applied to a better shop. What I don't know about little old New York wouldn't make a sonnet to a sunbonnet. I'll put you right in the middle of so much local colour that you won't know whether you are a magazine cover or in the erysipelas ward. When do you want to begin?"

Rivington is a young-man-about-town and a New Yorker by birth, preference and incommutability.

I told him that I would be glad to accept his escort and guardianship so that I might take notes of Manhattan's grand, gloomy and peculiar idiosyncrasies, and that the time of so doing would be at his own convenience.

"We'll begin this very evening," said Rivington, himself interested, like a good fellow. "Dine with me at seven, and then I'll steer you up against metropolitan phases so thick you'll have to have a kinetoscope to record 'em."

So I dined with Rivington pleasantly at his club, in Forty-eleventh street, and then we set forth in pursuit of the elusive tincture of affairs.

As we came out of the club there stood two men on the sidewalk near the steps in earnest conversation.

"And by what process of ratiocination," said one of them, "do you arrive at the conclusion that the division of society into producing and non-possessing classes predicates failure when compared with competitive systems that are monopolizing in tendency and result inimically to industrial evolution?"

"Oh, come off your perch!" said the other man, who wore glasses. "Your premises won't come out in the wash. You wind-jammers who apply bandy-legged theories to concrete categorical syllogisms send logical conclusions skally-bootin' into the infinitesimal ragbag. You can't pull my leg with an old sophism with whiskers on it. You quote Marx and Hyndman and Kautsky—what are they? —shines! Tolstoi?—his garret is full of rats. I put it to you over the home-plate that the idea of a co-operative commonwealth and an abolishment of competitive systems simply takes the rag off the bush and gives me hyperesthesia of the roopteetoop! The skookum house for yours!"

I stopped a few yards away and took out my little notebook.

"Oh, come ahead," said Rivington, somewhat nervously; "you don't want to listen to that."

"Why, man," I whispered, "this is just what I do want to hear. These slang types are among your city's most distinguishing features. Is this the Bowery variety? I really must hear more of it."

"If I follow you," said the man who had spoken first, "you do not believe it possible to reorganize society on the basis of common interest?"

"Shinny on your own side!" said the man with glasses. "You never heard any such music from my foghorn. What I said was that I did not believe it practicable just now. The guys with wads are not in the frame of mind to slack up on the mazuma, and the man with the portable tin banqueting canister isn't exactly ready to join the Bible-class. You can bet your variegated socks that the situation is all spifflicated up from the Battery to breakfast! What the country needs is for some bully old bloke like Cobden or some wise guy like old Ben Franklin to sashay up to the front and biff the nigger's head with the baseball. Do you catch my smoke? What?"

Rivington pulled me by the arm impatiently.

"Please come on," he said. "Let's go see something. This isn't what you want."

"Indeed it is," I said, resisting. "This tough talk is the very stuff that counts. There is a picturesqueness about the speech of the lower order of people that is quite unique. Did you say that this is the Bowery variety of slang?"

"Oh, well," said Rivington, giving it up, "I'll tell you straight. That's one of our college professors talking. He ran down for a day or two at the club. It's a sort of fad with him lately to use slang in his conversation. He thinks it improves language. The man he is talking to is one of New York's famous social economists. Now will you come on? You can't use that, you know."

"No," I agreed; "I can't use that. Would you call that typical of New York?"

"Of course not," said Rivington, with a sigh of relief. "I'm glad you see the difference. But if you want to hear the real old tough Bowery slang, I'll take you down where you'll get your fill of it."

"I would like it," I said; "that is, if it's the real thing. I've often read it in books, but I never heard it. Do you think it will be dangerous to go unprotected among those characters?"

"Oh, no," said Rivington; "not at this time of night. To tell the truth, I haven't been along the Bowery in a long time, but I know it as well as I do Broadway. We'll look up some of the typical Bowery boys and get them to talk. It'll be worth your while. They talk a peculiar dialect that you won't hear anywhere else on earth."

Rivington and I went east in a Forty-second street car and then south on the Third avenue line.

At Houston street we got off and walked.

"We are now on the famous Bowery," said Rivington; "the Bowery celebrated in song and story."

We passed block after block of "gents' " furnishing stores—the windows full of shirts with prices attached and cuffs inside. In other windows were neckties and no shirts. People walked up and down the sidewalks.

"In some ways," said I, "this reminds me of Kokomono, Ind., during the peach-crating season."

Rivington was nettled.

"Step into one of these saloons or vaudeville shows," said he, "with a large roll of money, and see how quickly the Bowery will sustain its reputation."

"You make impossible conditions," said I coldly.

By and by Rivington stopped and said we were in the heart of the Bowery. There was a policeman on the corner whom Rivington knew.

"Hallo, Donahue!" said my guide. "How goes it? My friend and I are down this way looking up a bit of local colour. He's anxious to meet one of the Bowery types. Can't you put us on to something genuine in that line—something that's got the colour, you know?"

Policeman Donahue turned himself about ponderously, his florid face full of good-nature. He pointed with his club down the street.

"Sure!" he said huskily. "Here comes a lad now that was born on the Bowery and knows every inch of it. If he's ever been above Bleecker street he's kept it to himself."

A man about twenty-eight or twenty-nine, with a smooth face, was sauntering toward us with his hands in his coat pockets. Policeman Donahue stopped him with a courteous wave of his club.

"Evening, Kerry," he said. "Here's a couple of gents, friends of mine, that want to hear you spiel something about the Bowery. Can you reel 'em off a few yards?"

"Certainly, Donahue," said the young man pleasantly. "Good evening, gentlemen," he said to us, with a pleasant smile. Donahue walked off on his beat.

"This is the goods," whispered Rivington, nudging me with his elbow. "Look at his jaw!"

"Say, cull," said Rivington, pushing back his hat, "wot's doin'? Me and my friend's taking a look down de old line—see? De copper tipped us off dat you was wise to de Bowery. Is dat right?"

I could not help admiring Rivington's power of adapting himself to his surroundings.

"Donahue was right," said the young man frankly; "I was brought up on the Bowery. I have been newsboy, teamster, pugilist, member of an organized band of 'toughs,' bartender, and a 'sport' in various meanings of the word. The experience certainly warrants the supposition that I have at least a passing acquaintance with a few phases of Bowery life. I will be pleased to place whatever knowledge and experience I have at the service of my friend Donahue's friends."

Rivington seemed ill at ease.

"I say," he said—somewhat entreatingly, "I thought—you're not stringing us, are you? It isn't just the kind of talk we expected. You haven't even said 'Hully gee!' once. Do you really belong on the Bowery?"

"I am afraid," said the Bowery boy smilingly, "that at some time you have been enticed into one of the dives of literature and had the counterfeit coin of the Bowery passed upon you. The 'argot' to which you doubtless refer was the invention of certain of your literary 'discoverers' who invaded the unknown wilds below Third avenue and put strange sounds into the mouths of the inhabitants. Safe in their homes far to the north and west, the credulous readers who were beguiled by this new 'dialect' perused and believed. Like Marco Polo and Mungo Park—pioneers indeed, but ambitious souls who could not draw the line of demarcation between discovery and invention—the literary bones of these explorers are dotting the trackless wastes of the subway. While it is true that after the publication of the mythical language attributed to the dwellers along the Bowery certain of its pat phrases and apt metaphors were adopted and, to a limited extent, used in this locality, it was because our people are prompt in assimilating whatever is to their commercial advantage. To the tourists who visited our newly discovered clime, and who expected a realization of their literary guide-books, they supplied the demands of the market.

"But perhaps I am wandering from the question. In what way can I assist you, gentlemen? I beg you will believe that the hospitality of the street is extended to all. There are, I regret to say, many catchpenny places of entertainment, but I cannot conceive that they would entice you."

I felt Rivington lean somewhat heavily against me.

"Say!" he remarked, with uncertain utterance; "comc and have a drink with us."

"Thank you but I never drink. I find that alcohol, even in the smallest quantities, alters the perspective. And I must preserve my perspective, for I am studying the Bowery. I have lived in it nearly thirty years, and I am just beginning to understand its heartbeats. It is like a great river fed by a hundred alien streams. Each influx brings strange seeds on its flood, strange silt and weeds, and now and then a flower of rare promise. To construe this river requires a man who can build dykes against the overflow, who is a naturalist, a geologist, a humanitarian, a diver and a strong swimmer. I love my Bowery. It was my cradle and is my inspiration. I have published one book. The critics have been kind. I put my heart in it. I am writing another, into which I hope to put both heart and brain. Consider me your guide, gentlemen. Is there anything I can take you to see, any place to which I can conduct you?"

I was afraid to look at Rivington except with one eye.

"Thanks," said Rivington. "We were looking up . . . that is . . . my friend . . . confound it; it's against all precedent, you know . . . awfully obliged . . . just the same."

"In case," said our friend, "you would like to meet some of our Bowery young men, I would be pleased to have you visit the quarters of our East Side Kappa Delta Phi Society, only two blocks east of here."

"Awfully sorry," said Rivington, "but my friend's got me on the jump to-night. He's a terror when he's out after local colour. Now, there's nothing I would like better than to drop in at the Kappa Delta Phi, but—some other time!"

We said our farewells and boarded a home-bound car. We had a rabbit on Upper Broadway, and then I parted with Rivington on a street corner.

"Well, anyhow," said he, braced and recovered, "it couldn't have happened anywhere but in little old New York."

Which, to say the least, was typical of Rivington.

LXXV: A NIGHT IN NEW ARABIA

THE great city of Bagdad-on-the-Subway is caliph-ridden. Its palaces, bazaars, khans, and by-ways are thronged with Al Rashids in divers disguises, seeking diversion and victims for their unbridled generosity. You can scarcely find a poor beggar whom they are willing to let enjoy his spoils unsuccoured, nor a wrecked unfortunate upon whom they will not reshower the means of fresh misfortune. You will hardly find anywhere a hungry one who has not had the opportunity to tighten his belt in gift libraries, nor a poor pundit who has not blushed at the holiday basket of celery-crowned turkey forced resoundingly through his door by the eleemosynary press.

So then, fearfully through the Harun-haunted streets creep the one-eyed calenders, the Little Hunchback and the Barber's Sixth Brother, hoping to escape the ministrations of the roving horde of caliphoid sultans.

Entertainment for many Arabian nights might be had from the histories of those who have escaped the largesse of the army of Commanders of the Faithful. Until dawn you might sit on the enchanted rug and listen to such stories as are told of the powerful genie Roc-Ef-El-Er, who sent the Forty Thieves to soak up the oil plant of Ali Baba; of the good Caliph Kar-Neg-Ghe, who gave away palaces; of the Seven Voyages of Sailbad, the Sinner, who frequented wooden excursion steamers among the islands; of the Fisherman and the Bottle; of the Barmecides' Boarding-house; of Aladdin's rise to wealth by means of his Wonderful Gasmeter.

But now, there being ten sultans to one Sheherazade, she is held too valuable to be in fear of the bowstring. In consequence, the art of narrative languishes. And, as the lesser caliphs are hunting the happy poor and the resigned unfortunate from cover to cover in order to heap upon them strange mercies and mysterious benefits, too often comes the report from Arabian headquarters that the captive refused "to talk."

This reticence, then, in the actors who perform the sad comedies of their philanthropy-scourged world, must, in a degree, account for the shortcomings of this painfully gleaned tale, which shall be called:

THE STORY OF THE CALIPH WHO ALLEVIATED HIS CONSCIENCE

Old Jacob Spraggins mixed for himself some Scotch and lithia water at his $1,200 oak sideboard. Inspiration must have resulted from its imbibition, for immediately afterward he struck the quartered oak soundly with his fist and shouted to the empty dining-room:

"By the coke ovens of hell, it must be that ten thousand dollars! If I can get that squared, it'll do the trick."

Thus, by the commonest artifice of the trade, having gained your interest, the action of the story will now be suspended, leaving you grumpily to consider a sort of dull biography beginning fifteen years before.

When old Jacob was young Jacob he was a breaker boy in a Pennsylvania coal mine. I don't know what a breaker boy is, but his occupation seems to be standing by a coal dump with a wan look and a dinner-pail to have his picture taken for magazine articles. Anyhow, Jacob was one. But, instead of dying of overwork at nine, and leaving his helpless parents and brothers at the mercy of the union strikers' reserve fund, he hitched up his galluses, put a dollar or two in a side proposition now and then, and at forty-five was worth $20,000,000.

There now! it's over. Hardly had time to yawn, did you? I've seen biographies that—but let us dissemble.

I want you to consider Jacob Spraggins, Esq., after he had arrived at the seventh stage of his career. The stages meant are, first, humble origin; second, deserved promotion; third, stockholder; fourth, capitalist; fifth, trust magnate; sixth, rich malefactor; seventh, caliph; eighth, *x*. The eighth stage shall be left to the higher mathematics.

At fifty-five Jacob retired from active business. The income of a czar was still rolling in on him from coal, iron, real estate, oil, railroads, manufactories, and corporations, but none of it touched Jacob's hands in a raw state. It was a sterilized increment, carefully cleaned and dusted and fumigated until it arrived at its ultimate stage of untainted, spotless cheques in the white fingers of his private secretary. Jacob built a three-million-dollar palace on a corner lot fronting on Nabob Avenue, city of New Bagdad, and began to feel the mantle of the late H. A. Rashid descending upon him. Eventually Jacob slipped the mantle under his collar, tied it in a neat four-in-hand, and became a licensed harrier of our Mesopotamian proletariat.

When a man's income becomes so large that the butcher actually sends him the kind of steak he orders, he begins to think about his soul's salvation. Now, the various stages or classes of rich men must not be forgotten. The capitalist can tell you to a dollar the amount of his wealth. The trust magnate "estimates" it. The rich malefactor hands you a cigar and denies that he has bought the P. D. & Q. The caliph merely smiles and talks about Hammerstein and the musical lasses. There is a record of tremendous altercation at breakfast in a "Where-to-Dine-Well" tavern between a magnate and his wife, the rift within the loot being that the wife calculated their fortune at a figure $3,000,000 higher than did her future *divorcé.* Oh, well, I, myself, heard a similar quarrel between a man and his wife because he found fifty cents less in his pockets than he thought he had. After all, we are all human—Count Tolstoi, R. Fitzsimmons, Peter Pan, and the rest of us.

Don't lose heart because the story seems to be degenerating into a sort of moral essay for intellectual readers.

There will be dialogue and stage business pretty soon.

When Jacob first began to compare the eyes of needles with the camels in the Zoo he decided upon organized charity. He had his secretary send a cheque for one million to the Universal Benevolent Association of the Globe. You may have looked down through a grating in front of a decayed warehouse for a nickel that you had dropped through. But that is neither here nor there. The Association acknowledged receipt of his favour of the 24th ult. with enclosure as stated. Separated by a double line, but still mighty close to the matter under the caption of "Oddities of the Day's News" in an evening paper, Jacob Spraggins read that one "Jasper Spargyous" had "donated $100,000 to the U. B. A. of G." A camel may have a stomach for each day in the week; but I dare not venture to accord him whiskers, for fear of the Great Displeasure at Washington; but if he have whiskers, surely not one of them will seem to have been inserted in the eye of a needle by that effort of that rich man to enter the K. of H. The right is reserved to reject any and all bids; signed, S. Peter, secretary and gatekeeper.

Next, Jacob selected the best endowed college he could scare up and presented it with a $200,000 laboratory. The college did not maintain a scientific course, but it accepted the money and built an elaborate lavatory instead, which was no diversion of funds so far as Jacob ever discovered.

The faculty met and invited Jacob to come over and take his A B C degree. Before sending the invitation they smiled, cut out the C, added the proper punctuation marks, and all was well.

While walking on the campus before being capped and gowned, Jacob saw two professors strolling near by. Their voices, long adapted to indoor acoustics, undesignedly reached his ear.

"There goes the latest *chevalier d'industrie*," said one of them, "to buy a sleeping powder from us. He gets his degree to-morrow."

"*In foro conscientiæ*," said the other. "Let's 'eave 'arf a brick at 'im."

Jacob ignored the Latin, but the brick pleasantry was not too hard for him. There was no mandragora in the honorary draught of learning that he had bought. That was before the passage of the Pure Food and Drugs Act.

Jacob wearied of philanthropy on a large scale.

"If I could see folks made happier," he said to himself—"if I could see 'em myself and hear 'em express their gratitude for what I done for 'em it would make me feel better. This donatin' funds to institutions and societies is about as satisfactory as dropping money into a broken slot machine."

So Jacob followed his nose, which led him through unswept streets to the homes of the poorest.

"The very thing!" said Jacob. "I will charter two river steamboats, pack them full of these unfortunate children and—say ten thousand dolls and drums and a thousand freezers of ice-cream, and give them a delightful outing up the Sound. The sea breezes on that trip ought to blow the taint off some of this money that keeps coming in faster than I can work it off my mind."

Jacob must have leaked some of his benevolent intentions, for an immense person with a bald face and a mouth that looked as if it ought to have a "Drop Letters Here" sign over it hooked a finger around him and set him in a space between a barber's pole and a stack of ash-cans. Words came out of the post-office slit—smooth, husky words with gloves on 'em, but sounding as if they might turn to bare knuckles any moment.

"Say, Sport, do you know where you are? Well, dis is Mike O'Grady's district you're buttin' into—see? Mike's got de stomach-ache privilege for every kid in dis neighbourhood—see? And if dere's any picnics or red balloons to be dealt out here, Mike's money pays for 'em—see? Don't you butt in, or something'll be handed to you. Youse d—— settlers and reformers with your social ologies and your millionaire detectives have got dis district in a hell of a fix, anyhow. With your college students and professors rough-housing de soda-water stands and dem rubberneck coaches fillin' de streets, de folks down here are 'fraid to go out of de houses. Now, you leave 'em to Mike. Dey belongs to him, and he knows how to handle 'em. Keep on your own side of de town. Are you some wiser now, uncle, or do you want to scrap wit' Mike O'Grady for de Santa Claus belt in dis district?"

Clearly, that spot in the moral vineyard was pre-empted. So Caliph Spraggins menaced no more the people in the bazaars of the East Side. To keep down his growing surplus he doubled his donations to organized charity, presented the Y.M.C.A. of his native town with a $10,000 collection of butterflies, and sent a cheque to the famine sufferers in China big enough to buy new emerald eyes and diamond-filled teeth for all their gods. But none of these charitable acts seemed to bring peace to the caliph's heart. He tried to get a personal note into his benefactions by tipping bell-boys and waiters $10 and $20 bills. He got well snickered at and derided for that by the millions who accept with respect gratuities commensurate to the service performed. He sought out an ambitious and talented but poor young woman, and bought for her the star part in a new comedy. He might have gotten rid of $50,000 more of his cumbersome money in this philanthropy if he had not neglected to write letters to her. But she lost the suit for lack of evidence, while his capital still kept piling up, and his *optikos needleorum camelibus*—or rich man's disease—was unrelieved.

In Caliph Spraggins' $3,000,000 home lived his sister Henrietta, who used to cook for the coal miners in a twenty-five-cent eating house in Coketown, Pa., and who now would have offered John Mitchell only two fingers of her hand to shake. And his daughter Celia, nineteen, back from boarding-school and from being polished off by private instructors in the restaurant languages and those études and things.

Celia is the heroine. Lest the artist's delineation of her charms on this very page humbug your fancy, take from me her authorized description. She was a nice-looking, awkward, loud, rather bashful, brown-haired girl, with a sallow complexion, bright eyes, and a perpetual smile. She had a wholesome, Spraggins-inherited love for plain food, loose clothing, and the society of the lower classes. She had too much health and youth to feel the burden of wealth. She had a wide mouth that kept the peppermint-pepsin tablets rattling like hail from the slot-machine wherever she went, and she could whistle hornpipes. Keep this picture in mind, and let the artist do his worst.

Celia looked out of her window one day and gave her heart to the grocer's young man. The receiver thereof was at that moment engaged in conceding immortality to his horse and calling down upon him the ultimate fate of the wicked; so he did not notice the transfer. A horse should stand still when you are lifting a crate of strictly new-laid eggs out of the wagon.

Young lady reader, you would have liked that grocer's young man yourself. But you wouldn't have given him your heart, because you are saving it for a riding-master, or a shoe-manufacturer with a torpid liver, or something quiet but rich in grey tweeds at Palm Beach. Oh, I know about it. So I am glad the grocer's young man was for Celia, and not for you.

The grocer's young man was slim and straight and as confident and easy in his movements as the man in the back of the magazines who wears the new frictionless roller suspenders. He wore a grey bicycle cap on the back of his head, and his hair was straw-coloured and curly, and his sun-burned face looked like one that smiled a good deal when he was not preaching the doctrine of everlasting punishment to delivery-wagon horses. He slung imported A1 fancy groceries about as though they were only the stuff he delivered at boarding-houses; and when he picked up his whip, your mind instantly recalled Mr. Tackett and his air with the buttonless foils.

Tradesmen delivered their goods at a side gate at the rear of the house. The grocer's wagon came about ten in the morning. For three days Celia watched the driver when he came, finding something new each time to admire in the lofty and almost contemptuous way he had of tossing around the choicest gifts of Pomona, Ceres, and the canning factories. Then she consulted Annette.

To be explicit, Annette McCorkle, the second housemaid, who deserves a paragraph herself. Annette Fletcherized large numbers of romantic novels which she obtained at a free public library branch (donated by one of the biggest caliphs in the business). She was Celia's side-kicker and chum, though Aunt Henrietta didn't know it, you may hazard a bean or two.

"Oh, canary-bird seed!" exclaimed Annette. "Ain't it a corkin' situation? You a heiress, and fallin' in love with him on sight! He's a sweet boy, too, and above his business. But he ain't sus-pectible like the common run of grocer's assistants. He never pays no attention to me."

"He will to me," said Celia.

"Riches——" began Annette, unsheathing the not unjustifiable feminine sting.

"Oh, you're not so beautiful," said Celia, with her wide, disarming smile. "Neither am I; but he shan't know that there's any money mixed up with my looks, such as they are. That's fair. Now, I want you to lend me one of your caps and an apron, Annette."

"Oh, marshmallows!" cried Annette. "I see. Ain't it lovely? It's just like 'Lurline the Left-handed; or, A Buttonhole Maker's Wrongs.' I bet he'll turn out to be a count."

There was a long hallway (or "passageway," as they call it in the land of the Colonels) with one side latticed, running along the rear of the house. The grocer's young man went through this to deliver his goods. One morning he passed a girl in there with shining eyes, sallow complexion, and wide, smiling mouth, wearing a maid's cap and apron. But as he was cumbered with a basket of Early Drumhead lettuce and Trophy tomatoes and three bunches of asparagus and six bottles of the most expensive Queen olives, he saw no more than that she was one of the maids.

But on his way out he came up behind her, and she was whistling "Fisher's Hornpipe" so loudly and clearly that all the piccolos in the world should have disjointed themselves and crept into their cases for shame.

The grocer's young man stopped and pushed back his cap until it hung on his collar button behind.

"That's out o' sight, Kid," said he.

"My name is Celia, if you please," said the whistler, dazzling him with a three-inch smile.

"That's all right. I'm Thomas McLeod. What part of the house do you work in?"

"I'm the—the second parlourmaid."

"Do you know the 'Falling Waters'?"

"No," said Celia, "we don't know anybody. We got rich too quick—that is, Mr. Spraggins did."

"I'll make you acquainted," said Thomas McLeod. "It's a strathspey—a first cousin to a hornpipe."

If Celia's whistling put the piccolos out of commission, Thomas McLeod's surely made the biggest flutes hunt their holes. He could actually whistle *bass*.

When he stopped Celia was ready to jump into his delivery wagon and ride with him clear to the end of the pier and on to the ferry-boat of the Charon line.

"I'll be around to-morrow at 10.15," said Thomas, "with some spinach and a case of carbonic."

"I'll practise that what-you-may-call-it," said Celia. "I can whistle a fine second."

The processes of courtship are personal, and do not belong to general literature. They should be chronicled in detail only in advertisements of iron tonics and in the secret by-laws of the Woman's Auxiliary of the Ancient Order of the Rat Trap. But genteel writing may contain a description of certain stages of its progress without intruding upon the province of the X-ray or of park policemen.

A day came when Thomas McLeod and Celia lingered at the end of the latticed "passage."

"Sixteen a week isn't much," said Thomas, letting his cap rest on his shoulder-blades.

Celia looked through the lattice-work and whistled

a dead march. Shopping with Aunt Henrietta the day before, she had paid that much for a dozen handkerchiefs.

"Maybe I'll get a raise next month," said Thomas. "I'll be around to-morrow at the same time with a bag of flour and the laundry soap."

"All right," said Celia. "Annette's married cousin pays only $20 a month for a flat in the Bronx."

Never for a moment did she count on the Spraggins money. She knew Aunt Henrietta's invincible pride of caste and pa's mightiness as a Colossus of cash, and she understood that if she chose Thomas she and her grocer's young man might go whistle for their living.

Another day came, Thomas violating the dignity of Nabob Avenue with "The Devil's Dream," whistled keenly between his teeth.

"Raised to eighteen a week yesterday," he said. "Been pricing flats around Morningside. You want to start untying those apron-strings and unpinning that cap, old girl."

"Oh, Tommy!" said Celia, with her broadest smile. "Won't that be enough? I got Betty to show me how to make a cottage pudding. I guess we could call it a flat pudding if we wanted to."

"And tell no lie," said Thomas.

"And I can sweep and polish and dust—of course, a parlourmaid learns that. And we could whistle duets of evenings."

"The old man said he'd raise me to twenty at Christmas if Bryan couldn't think of any harder name to call a Republican than a 'postponer,'" said the grocer's young man.

"I can sew," said Celia; "and I know that you must make the gas company's man show his badge when he comes to look at the meter; and I know how to put up quince jam and window curtains."

"Bully! you're all right, Cele. Yes, I believe we can pull it off on eighteen."

As he was jumping into the wagon the second parlourmaid braved discovery by running swiftly to the gate.

"And, oh, Tommy, I forgot," she called softly. "I believe I could make your neckties."

"Forget it," said Thomas decisively.

"And another thing," she continued. "Sliced cucumbers at night will drive away cockroaches."

"And sleep too, you bet," said Mr. McLeod. "Yes, I believe if I have a delivery to make on the West Side this afternoon I'll look in at a furniture store I know over there."

It was just as the wagon dashed away that old Jacob Spraggins struck the sideboard with his fist and made the mysterious remark about ten thousand dollars that you perhaps remember. Which justifies the reflection that some stories, as well as life, and puppies thrown into wells, move around in circles. Painfully but briefly we must shed light on Jacob's words.

The foundation of his fortune was made when he was twenty. A poor coal-digger (ever hear of a rich one?) had saved a dollar or two and bought a small tract of land on a hill-side on which he tried to raise corn. Not a nubbin. Jacob, whose nose was a divining-rod, told him there was a vein of coal beneath. He bought the land from the miner for $125 and sold it a month afterward for $10,000. Luckily the miner had enough left of his sale money to drink himself into a black coat opening in the back, as soon as he heard the news.

And so, forty years afterwards, we find Jacob illuminated with the sudden thought that if he could make restitution of this sum of money to the heirs or assigns of the unlucky miner, respite and Nepenthe might be his.

And now must come swift action, for we have here some four thousand words and not a tear shed and never a pistol, joke, safe, nor bottle cracked.

Old Jacob hired a dozen private detectives to find the heirs, if any existed, of the old miner, Hugh McLeod.

Get the point? Of course, I know as well as you do that Thomas is going to be the heir. I might have concealed the name; but why always hold back your mystery till the end? I say, let it come near the middle so people can stop reading there if they want to.

After the detectives had trailed false clues about three thousand dollars—I mean miles—they cornered Thomas at the grocery and got his confession that Hugh McLeod had been his grandfather, and that there were no other heirs. They arranged a meeting for him and old Jacob one morning in one of their offices.

Jacob liked the young man very much. He liked the way he looked straight at him when he talked, and the way he threw his bicycle cap over the top of a rose-coloured vase on the centre-table.

There was a slight flaw in Jacob's system of restitution. He did not consider that the act, to be perfect, should include confession. So he represented himself to be the agent of the purchaser of the land who had sent him to refund the sale price for the ease of his conscience.

"Well, sir," said Thomas, "this sounds to me

like an illustrated post card from South Boston with 'We're having a good time here' written on it. I don't know the game. Is this ten thousand dollars money, or do I have to save so many coupons to get it?"

Old Jacob counted out to him twenty five-hundred-dollar bills.

That was better, he thought, than a cheque. Thomas put them thoughtfully into his pocket.

"Grandfather's best thanks," he said, "to the party who sends it."

Jacob talked on, asking him about his work, how he spent his leisure time, and what his ambitions were. The more he saw and heard of Thomas, the better he liked him. He had not met many young men in Bagdad so frank and wholesome.

"I would like to have you visit my house," he said. "I might help you in investing or laying out your money. I am a very wealthy man. I have a daughter about grown, and I would like for you to know her. There are not many young men I would care to have call on her."

"I'm obliged," said Thomas. "I'm not much at making calls. It's generally the side entrance for mine. And, besides, I'm engaged to a girl that has the Delaware peach crop killed in the blossom. She's a parlourmaid in a house where I deliver goods. She won't be working there much longer, though. Say, don't forget to give your friend my grandfather's best regards. You'll excuse me now; my wagon's outside with a lot of green stuff that's got to be delivered. See you again, sir."

At eleven Thomas delivered some bunches of

parsley and lettuce at the Spraggins mansion. Thomas was only twenty-two; so, as he came back, he took out the handful of five-hundred-dollar bills and waved them carelessly. Annette took a pair of eyes as big as creamed onions to the cook.

"I told you he was a count," she said, after relating. "He never would carry on with me."

"But you say he showed money," said the cook.

"Hundreds of thousands," said Annette. "Carried around loose in his pockets. And he never would look at me."

"It was paid to me to-day," Thomas was explaining to Celia outside. "It came from my grandfather's estate. Say, Cele, what's the use of waiting now? I'm going to quit the job to-night. Why can't we get married next week?"

"Tommy," said Celia, "I'm no parlourmaid. I've been fooling you. I'm Miss Spraggins—Celia Spraggins. The newspapers say I'll be worth forty million dollars some day."

Thomas pulled his cap down straight on his head for the first time since we have known him.

"I suppose then," said he, "I suppose then you'll not be marrying me next week? But you *can* whistle."

"No," said Celia, "I'll not be marrying you next week. My father would never let me marry a grocer's clerk. But I'll marry you to-night, Tommy, if you say so."

Old Jacob Spraggins came home at 9.30 p.m., in his motor-car. The make of it you will have to surmise sorrowfully; I am giving you unsubsidized fiction; had it been a street car I could have told you its voltage and the number of flat wheels it had. Jacob called for his daughter; he had bought a ruby necklace for her, and wanted to hear her say what a kind, thoughtful, dear old dad he was.

There was a brief search in the house for her, and then came Annette, glowing with the pure flame of truth and loyalty well mixed with envy and histrionics.

"Oh, sir," said she, wondering if she should kneel, "Miss Celia's just this minute running away out of the side gate with a young man to be married. I couldn't stop her, sir. They went in a cab."

"What young man?" roared old Jacob.

"A millionaire, if you please, sir—a rich nobleman in disguise. He carries his money with him, and the red peppers and the onions was only to blind us, sir. He never did seem to take to me."

Jacob rushed out in time to catch his car. The chauffeur had been delayed by trying to light a cigarette in the wind.

"Here, Gaston, or Mike, or whatever you call yourself, scoot around the corner quicker than blazes and see if you can see a cab. If you do, run it down."

There was a cab in sight a block away. Gaston, or Mike, with his eyes half shut and his mind on his cigarette, picked up the trail, neatly crowded the cab to the kerb and pocketed it.

"What t'ell you doin'?" yelled the cabman.

"Pa!" shrieked Celia.

"Grandfather's remorseful friend's agent!" said Thomas. "Wonder what's on his conscience now."

"A thousand thunders!" said Gaston, or Mike. "I have no other match."

"Young man," said old Jacob severely, "how about that parlourmaid you were engaged to?"

A couple of years afterwards old Jacob went into the office of his private secretary.

"The Amalgamated Missionary Society solicits a contribution of $30,000 toward the conversion of the Koreans," said the secretary.

"Pass 'em up," said Jacob.

"The University of Plumville writes that its yearly endowment fund of $50,000 that you bestowed upon it is past due."

"Tell 'em it's been cut out."

"The Scientific Society of Clam Cove, Long Island, asks for $10,000 to buy alcohol to preserve specimens."

"Waste basket."

"The Society for Providing Healthful Recreation for Working Girls wants $20,000 from you to lay out a golf course."

"Tell 'em to see an undertaker.

"Cut 'em all out," went on Jacob. "I've quit being a good thing. I need every dollar I can scrape or save. I want you to write to the directors of every company that I'm interested in and recommend a 10-per-cent. cut in salaries. And say—I noticed half a cake of soap lying in a corner of the hall as I came in. I want you to speak to the scrubwoman about waste. I've got no money to throw away. And say—we've got vinegar pretty well in hand, haven't we?"

"The Globe Spice & Seasons Company," said the secretary, "controls the market at present."

"Raise vinegar two cents a gallon. Notify all our branches."

Suddenly Jacob Spraggins's plump red face relaxed into a pulpy grin. He walked over to the secretary's desk and showed a small red mark on his thick forefinger.

"Bit it," he said, "darned if he didn't, and he ain't had the tooth three weeks—Jaky McLeod, my Celia's kid. He'll be worth a hundred millions by the time he's twenty-one if I can pile it up for him."

As he was leaving, old Jacob turned at the door, and said:

"Better make that vinegar raise three cents instead of two. I'll be back in an hour and sign the letters."

The true history of the Caliph Harun Al Rashid relates that toward the end of his reign he wearied of philanthropy, and caused to be beheaded all his former favourites and companions of his "Arabian Nights" rambles. Happy are we in these days of enlightenment, when the only death-warrant the caliphs can serve on us is in the form of a tradesman's bill.

LXXVI: A MATTER OF ELEVATION

ONE winter the Alcazar Opera Company of New Orleans made a speculative trip along the Mexican, Central American and South American coasts. The venture proved a most successful one. The music-loving, impressionable Spanish-Americans deluged the company with dollars and "vivas." The manager waxed plump and amiable. But for the prohibitive climate he would have put forth the distinctive flower of his prosperity—the overcoat of fur, braided, frogged and opulent. Almost was he persuaded to raise the salaries of his company. But with a mighty effort he conquered the impulse toward such an unprofitable effervescence of joy.

At Macuto, on the coast of Venezuela, the company scored its greatest success. Imagine Coney Island translated into Spanish and you will comprehend Macuto. The fashionable season is from November to March. Down from La Guayra and Caracas and Valencia and other interior towns flock the people for their holiday season. There are bathing and fiestas and bullfights and scandal. And then the people have a passion for music that the bands in the plaza and on the sea beach stir but do not satisfy. The coming of the Alcazar Opera Company aroused the utmost ardour and zeal among the pleasure-seekers.

The illustrious Guzman Blanco, President and Dictator of Venezuela, sojourned in Macuto with his court for the season. That potent ruler—who himself paid a subsidy of 40,000 pesos each year to grand opera in Caracas—ordered one of the Government warehouses to be cleared for a temporary theatre. A stage was quickly constructed and rough wooden benches made for the audience. Private boxes were added for the use of the President and the notables of the army and Government.

The company remained in Macuto for two weeks. Each performance filled the house as closely as it could be packed. Then the music-mad people fought for room in the open doors and windows, and crowded about, hundreds deep, on the outside. Those audiences formed a brilliantly diversified patch of colour. The hue of their faces ranged from the clear olive of the pure-blood Spaniards down through the yellow and brown shades of the Mestizos to the coal-black Carib and the Jamaica Negro. Scattered among them were little groups of Indians with faces like stone idols, wrapped in gaudy fibre-woven blankets—Indians down from the mountain states of Zamora and Los Andes and Miranda to trade their gold dust in the coast towns.

The spell cast upon these denizens of the interior fastnesses was remarkable. They sat in petrified ecstasy, conspicuous among the excitable Macutians, who wildly strove with tongue and hand to give evidence of their delight. Only once did the sombre rapture of these aboriginals find expression. During the rendition of "Faust," Guzman Blanco, extravagantly pleased by the "Jewel Song," cast upon the stage a purse of gold pieces. Other distinguished citizens followed his lead to the extent of whatever loose coin they had convenient, while some of the fair and fashionable señoras were moved, in imitation, to fling a jewel or a ring or two at the feet of the Marguerite—who was, according to the bills, Mlle. Nina Giraud. Then, from different parts of the house rose sundry of the stolid hillmen and cast upon the stage little brown and dun bags that fell with soft "thumps" and did not rebound. It was, no doubt, pleasure at the tribute to her art that caused Mlle. Giraud's eyes to shine so brightly when she opened these little deerskin bags in her dressing-room and found them to contain pure gold dust. If so, the pleasure was rightly hers, for her voice in song, pure, strong and thrilling with the feeling of the emotional artist, deserved the tribute that it earned.

But the triumph of the Alcazar Opera Company is not the theme; it but leans upon and colours it. There happened in Macuto a tragic thing, an unsolvable mystery, that sobered for a time the gaiety of the happy season.

One evening between the short twilight and the time when she should have whirled upon the stage in the red and black of the ardent Carmen, Mlle. Nina Giraud disappeared from the sight and ken of 6,000 pairs of eyes and as many minds in Macuto. There was the usual turmoil and hurrying to seek her. Messengers flew to the little French-kept hotel where she stayed; others of the company hastened here or there where she might be lingering in some *tienda* or unduly prolonging her bath upon the beach. All search was fruitless. Mademoiselle had vanished.

Half an hour passed and she did not appear. The dictator, unused to the caprices of prime donne, became impatient. He sent an aide from his box to say to the manager that if the curtain did not at once rise he would immediately hale the entire company to the calabosa, though it would desolate his heart, indeed, to be compelled to such an act. Birds in Macuto could be made to sing.

The manager abandoned hope for the time of Mlle. Giraud. A member of the chorus, who had dreamed hopelessly for years of the blessed opportunity, quickly Carmenized herself and the opera went on.

Afterward, when the lost cantatrice appeared not, the aid of the authorities was invoked. The President at once set the army, the police and all citizens to the search. Not one clue to Mlle. Giraud's disappearance was found. The Alcazar left to fill engagements farther down the coast.

On the way back the steamer stopped at Macuto and the manager made anxious inquiry. Not a trace of the lady had been discovered. The Alcazar could do no more. The personal belongings of the missing lady were stored in the hotel against her possible later reappearance and the opera company continued upon its homeward voyage to New Orleans.

* * * * *

On the *camino real* along the beach the two saddle mules and the four pack mules of Don Señor Johnny Armstrong stood, patiently awaiting the crack of the whip of the *arriero*, Luis. That would be the signal for the start on another long journey into the mountains. The pack mules were loaded with a varied assortment of hardware and cutlery. These articles Don Johnny traded to the interior Indians for the gold dust that they washed from the Andean streams and stored in quills and bags against his coming. It was a profitable business, and Señor Armstrong expected soon to be able to purchase the coffee plantation that he coveted.

Armstrong stood on the narrow sidewalk, exchanging garbled Spanish with old Peralto, the rich native merchant who had just charged him four prices for half a gross of pot-metal hatchets, and abridged English with Rucker, the little German who was Consul for the United States.

"Take with you, señor," said Peralto, "the blessings of the saints upon your journey."

"Better try quinine," growled Rucker through his pipe. "Take two grains every night. And don't make your trip too long, Johnny, because we haf needs of you. It is ein villainous game dot

Melville play of whist, and dere is no oder substitute. *Auf wiedersehen*, und keep your eyes dot mule's ears between when you on der edge of der brecipices ride."

The bells of Luis's mule jingled and the pack train filed after the warning note. Armstrong waved a good-bye and took his place at the tail of the procession. Up the narrow street they turned, and passed the two-story wooden Hotel Ingles, where Ives and Dawson and Richards and the rest of the chaps were dawdling on the broad piazza, reading week-old newspapers. They crowded to the railing and shouted many friendly and wise and foolish farewells after him. Across the plaza they trotted slowly past the bronze statue of Guzman Blanco, within its fence of bayoneted rifles captured from revolutionists, and out of the town between the rows of thatched huts swarming with the unclothed youth of Macuto. They plunged into the damp coolness of banana groves at length to emerge upon a bright stream, where brown women in scant raiment laundered clothes destructively upon the rocks. Then the pack train, fording the stream, attacked the sudden ascent, and bade adieu to such civilization as the coast afforded.

For weeks Armstrong, guided by Luis, followed his regular route among the mountains. After he had collected an arroba of the precious metal, winning a profit of nearly $5,000, the heads of the lightened mules were turned down-trail again. Where the head of the Guarico River springs from a great gash in the mountainside, Luis halted the train.

"Half a day's journey from here, señor," said he, "is the village of Tacuzama, which we have never visited. I think many ounces of gold may be procured there. It is worth the trial."

Armstrong concurred, and they turned again upward toward Tacuzama. The trail was abrupt and precipitous, mounting through a dense forest. As night fell, dark and gloomy, Luis once more halted. Before them was a black chasm, bisecting the path as far as they could see.

Luis dismounted. "There should be a bridge," he called, and ran along the cleft a distance. "It is here," he cried, and remounting, led the way. In a few moments Armstrong heard a sound as though a thunderous drum were beating somewhere in the dark. It was the falling of the mules' hoofs upon the bridge made of strong hides lashed to poles and stretched across the chasm. Half a mile farther was Tacuzama. The village was a congregation of rock and mud huts set in the profundity of an obscure wood. As they rode in, a sound inconsistent with that brooding solitude met their ears. From a long, low mud hut that they were nearing rose the glorious voice of a woman in song. The words were English, the air familiar to Armstrong's memory, but not to his musical knowledge.

He slipped from his mule and stole to a narrow window in one end of the house. Peering cautiously inside, he saw, within three feet of him, a woman of marvellous, imposing beauty, clothed in a splendid loose robe of leopard skins. The hut was packed close to the small space in which she stood with the squatting figures of Indians.

The woman finished her song, and seated herself close to the little window, as if grateful for the unpolluted air that entered it. When she had ceased several of the audience rose and cast little softly-falling bags at her feet. A harsh murmur —no doubt a barbarous kind of applause and comment—went through the grim assembly.

Armstrong was used to seizing opportunities promptly. Taking advantage of the noise, he called to the woman in a low but distinct voice: "Do not turn your head this way, but listen. I am an American. If you need assistance, tell me how I can render it. Answer as briefly as you can."

The woman was worthy of his boldness. Only by a sudden flush of her pale cheek did she acknowledge understanding of his words. Then she spoke, scarcely moving her lips.

"I am held a prisoner by these Indians. God knows I need help. In two hours come to the little hut twenty yards toward the mountainside. There will be a light and a red curtain in the window. There is always a guard at the door whom you will have to overcome. For the love of heaven, do not fail to come."

The story seems to shrink from adventure and rescue and mystery. The theme is one too gentle for those brave and quickening tones. And yet it reaches as far back as time itself. It has been named "environment," which is as weak a word as any to express the unnamable kinship of man to nature, that queer fraternity that causes stones and trees and salt water and clouds to play upon our emotions. Why are we made serious and solemn and sublime by mountain heights, grave and contemplative by an abundance of overhanging trees, reduced to inconstancy and monkey capers by the ripples on a sandy beach? Did the protoplasm—but enough. The chemists are looking into the matter, and before long they will have all life in the table of the symbols.

Briefly, then, in order to confine the story within scientific bounds, John Armstrong went to the hut, choked the Indian guard and carried away Mlle. Giraud. With her was also conveyed a number of pounds of gold dust she had collected during her six months' forced engagement in Tacuzama. The Carabobo Indians are easily the most enthusiastic lovers of music between the equator and the French Opera House in New Orleans. They are also strong believers that the advice of Emerson was good when he said: "The thing thou wantest, O discontented man—take it, and pay the price." A number of them had attended the performance of the Alcazar Opera Company in Macuto, and found Mlle. Giraud's style and technique satisfactory. They wanted her, so they took her one evening suddenly and without any fuss. They treated her with much consideration, exacting only one song recital each day. She was quite pleased at being rescued by Mr. Armstrong. So much for mystery and adventure. Now to resume the theory of the protoplasm.

John Armstrong and Mlle. Giraud rode among the Andean peaks, enveloped in their greatness and sublimity. The mightiest cousins, farthest removed, in nature's great family become conscious of the tie. Among those huge piles of primordial upheaval, amid those gigantic silences and elongated fields of distance, the littlenesses of men are precipitated as one chemical throws down a sediment from another. They moved reverently, as in a temple. Their souls were uplifted in unison with the stately heights. They travelled in a zone of majesty and peace.

To Armstrong the woman seemed almost a holy thing. Yet bathed in the white, still dignity of her martyrdom that purified her earthly beauty and gave out, it seemed, an aura of transcendent loveliness, in those first hours of companionship she drew from him an adoration that was half human love, half the worship of a descended goddess.

Never yet since her rescue had she smiled. Over her dress she still wore the robe of leopard skins, for the mountain air was cold. She looked to be some splendid princess belonging to those wild and awesome altitudes. The spirit of the region chimed with hers. Her eyes were always turned upon the sombre cliffs, the blue gorges and the snow-clad turrets, looking a sublime melancholy equal to their own. At times on the journey she sang thrilling te deums and misereres that struck the true note of the hills, and made their route seem like a solemn march down a cathedral aisle. The rescued one spoke but seldom, her mood partaking of the hush of nature that surrounded them. Armstrong looked upon her as an angel. He could not bring himself to the sacrilege of attempting to woo her as other women may be wooed.

On the third day they had descended as far as the *tierra templada*, the zone of the tablelands and foothills. The mountains were receding in their rear, but still towered, exhibiting yet impressively their formidable heads. Here they met signs of man. They saw the white houses of coffee plantations gleam across the clearings. They struck into a road where they met travellers and pack-mules. Cattle were grazing on the slopes. They passed a little village where the round-eyed *niños* shrieked and called at sight of them.

Mlle. Giraud laid aside her leopard-skin robe. It seemed to be a trifle incongruous now. In the mountains it had appeared fitting and natural. And if Armstrong was not mistaken she laid aside with it something of the high dignity of her demeanour. As the country became more populous and significant of comfortable life he saw, with a feeling of joy, that the exalted princess and priestess of the Andean peaks was changing to a woman—an earth woman, but no less enticing. A little colour crept to the surface of her marble cheek. She arranged the conventional dress that the removal of the robe now disclosed with the solicitous touch of one who is conscious of the eyes of others. She smoothed the careless sweep of her hair. A mundane interest, long latent in the chilling atmosphere of the ascetic peaks, showed in her eyes.

This thaw in his divinity sent Armstrong's heart going faster. So might an Arctic explorer thrill at his first ken of green fields and liquescent waters. They were on a lower plane of earth and life and were succumbing to its peculiar, subtle influence. The austerity of the hills no longer thinned the air they breathed. About them was the breath of fruit and corn and builded homes, the comfortable smell of smoke and warm earth and the consolations man has placed between himself and the dust of his brother earth from which he sprung. While traversing those awful mountains, Mlle. Giraud had seemed to be wrapped in their spirit of reverent reserve. Was this that same woman—now palpitating, warm, eager, throbbing with conscious life and charm, feminine to her finger-tips? Pondering over this, Armstrong felt certain misgivings intrude upon his thoughts. He wished he could stop there with this changing creature, descending no farther. Here was the elevation and environment to which her nature seemed to respond with its best. He feared to go down upon the man-dominated levels. Would her spirit not yield still further in that artificial zone to which they were descending?

Now from a little plateau they saw the sea flash at the edge of the green lowlands. Mlle. Giraud gave a little, catching sigh.

"Oh! look, Mr. Armstrong, there is the sea! Isn't it lovely? I'm so tired of mountains." She heaved a pretty shoulder in a gesture of repugnance. "Those horrid Indians! Just think of what I suffered! Although I suppose I attained my ambition of becoming a stellar attraction, I wouldn't care to repeat the engagement. It was very nice of you to bring me away. Tell me, Mr. Armstrong —honestly, now—do I look such an awful, awful fright? I haven't looked into a mirror, you know, for months."

Armstrong made answer according to his changed moods. Also he laid his hand upon hers as it rested upon the horn of her saddle. Luis was at the head of the pack train and could not see. She allowed it to remain there, and her eyes smiled frankly into his.

Then at sundown they dropped upon the coast level under the palms and lemons among the vivid greens and scarlets and ochres of the *tierra caliente*. They rode into Macuto, and saw the line of volatile bathers frolicking in the surf. The mountains were very far away.

Mlle. Giraud's eyes were shining with a joy that could not have existed under the chaperonage of the mountain-tops. There were other spirits calling to her—nymphs of the orange groves, pixies from the chattering surf, imps, born of the music, the perfumes, colours and the insinuating presence of humanity. She laughed aloud, musically, at a sudden thought.

"Won't there be a sensation?" she called to Armstrong. "Don't I wish I had an engagement just now, though! What a picnic the press agent would have! 'Held a prisoner by a band of savage Indians subdued by the spell of her wonderful voice'—wouldn't that make great stuff? But I guess I quit the game winner, anyhow—there ought to be a couple of thousand dollars in that sack of gold dust I collected as encores, don't you think?"

He left her at the door of the little Hotel de Buen Descansar, where she had stopped before. Two hours later he returned to the hotel. He glanced in at the open door of the little combined reception-room and café.

Half a dozen of Macuto's representative social and official *caballeros* were distributed about the room. Señor Villablanca, the wealthy rubber concessionist, reposed his fat figure on two chairs, with an emollient smile beaming upon his chocolate-coloured face. Guilbert, the French mining engineer, leered through his polished nose-glasses. Colonel Mendez, of the regular army, in gold-laced uniform and fatuous grin, was busily extracting corks from champagne bottles. Other patterns of Macutian gallantry and fashion pranced and posed. The air was hazy with cigarette smoke. Wine dripped upon the floor.

Perched upon a table in the centre of the room in an attitude of easy pre-eminence was Mlle.

Giraud. A chic costume of white lawn and cherry ribbons supplanted her travelling garb. There was a suggestion of lace, and a frill or two, with a discreet, small implication of hand-embroidered pink hosiery. Upon her lap rested a guitar. In her face was the light of resurrection, the peace of elysium attained through fire and suffering. She was singing to a lively accompaniment a little song:

> "When you see de big round moon
> Comin' up like a balloon,
> Dis nigger skips fur to kiss de lips
> Ob his stylish, black-faced coon."

The singer caught sight of Armstrong.

"Hi! there, Johnny," she called; "I've been expecting you for an hour. What kept you? Gee! but these smoked guys are the slowest you ever saw. They ain't on, at all. Come along in, and I'll make this coffee-coloured old sport with the gold epaulettes open one for you right off the ice."

"Thank you," said Armstrong; "not just now, I believe. I've several things to attend to."

He walked out and down the street, and met Rucker coming up from the Consulate.

"Play you a game of billiards," said Armstrong. "I want something to take the taste of the sea level out of my mouth."

LXXVII: THE MISSING CHORD

I STOPPED overnight at the sheep-ranch of Rush Kinney, on the Sandy Fork of the Nueces. Mr. Kinney and I had been strangers up to the time when I called "Hallo!" at his hitching-rack; but from that moment until my departure on the next morning we were, according to the Texas code, undeniable friends.

After supper the ranchman and I lugged our chairs outside the two-room house, to its floorless gallery roofed with chaparral and sacuista grass. With the rear legs of our chairs sinking deep into the hard-packed loam, each of us reposed against an elm pillar of the structure and smoked El Toro tobacco, while we wrangled amicably concerning the affairs of the rest of the world.

As for conveying adequate conception of the engaging charm of that prairie evening, despair waits upon it. It is a bold chronicler who will undertake the description of a Texas night in the early spring. An inventory must suffice.

The ranch rested upon the summit of a lenient slope. The ambient prairie, diversified by arroyos and murky patches of brush and pear, lay around us like a darkened bowl at the bottom of which we reposed as dregs. Like a turquoise cover the sky pinned us there. The miraculous air, heady with ozone and made memorably sweet by leagues of wild flowerets, gave tang and savour to the breath. In the sky was a great, round, mellow searchlight which we knew to be no moon, but the dark lantern of summer, who came to hunt northward the cowering spring. In the nearest corral a flock of sheep lay silent until a groundless panic would send a squad of them huddling together with a drumming rush. For other sounds a shrill family of coyotes yapped beyond the shearing-pen, and whippoorwills twittered in the long grass. But even these dissonances hardly rippled the clear torrent of the mockingbirds' notes that fell from a dozen neighbouring shrubs and trees. It would not have been preposterous for one to tiptoe and essay to touch the stars, they hung so bright and imminent.

Mr. Kinney's wife, a young and capable woman, we had left in the house. She remained to busy herself with the domestic round of duties, in which I had observed that she seemed to take a buoyant and contented pride. In one room we had supped. Presently, from the other, as Kinney and I sat without, there burst a volume of sudden and brilliant music. If I could justly estimate the art of piano-playing, the construer of that rollicking fantasia had creditably mastered the secrets of the keyboard. A piano, and one so well played, seemed to me to be an unusual thing to find in that small and unpromising ranch-house. I must have looked my surprise at Rush Kinney, for he laughed in his soft, Southern way, and nodded at me through the moonlit haze of our cigarettes.

"You don't often hear as agreeable a noise as that on a sheep-ranch," he remarked; "but I never see any reason for not playing up to the arts and graces just because we happen to live out in the brush. It's a lonesome life for a woman; and if a little music can make it any better, why not have it? That's the way I look at it."

"A wise and generous theory," I assented. "And Mrs. Kinney plays well. I am not learned in the science of music, but I should call her an uncommonly good performer. She has technic and more than ordinary power."

The moon was very bright, you will understand, and I saw upon Kinney's face a sort of amused and pregnant expression, as though there were things behind it that might be expounded.

"You came up the trail from the Double-Elm Fork," he said promisingly. "As you crossed it you must have seen an old deserted *jacal* to your left under a comma mott."

"I did," said I. "There was a drove of *javalis* rooting around it. I could see by the broken corrals that no one lived there."

"That's where this music proposition started," said Kinney. "I don't mind telling you about it while we smoke. That's where old Cal Adams lived. He had about eight hundred graded merinos and a daughter that was solid silk and as handsome as a new stake-rope on a thirty-dollar pony. And I don't mind telling you that I was guilty in the second degree of hanging around old Cal's ranch all the time I could spare away from lambing and shearing. Miss Marilla was her name; and I had figured it out by the rule of two that she was destined to become the châtelaine and lady superior of Rancho Lomito, belonging to R. Kinney, Esq., where you are now a welcome and honoured guest.

"I will say that old Cal wasn't distinguished as a sheepman. He was a little, old, stoop-shouldered *hombre* about as big as a gun scabbard, with scraggy white whiskers, and condemned to the continuous use of language. Old Cal was so obscure in his chosen profession that he wasn't even hated by the cowmen. And when a sheepman don't get eminent enough to acquire the hostility of the cattlemen, he is mighty apt to die unwept and considerably unsung.

"But that Marilla girl was a benefit to the eye. And she was the most elegant kind of a housekeeper. I was the nearest neighbour, and I used to ride over to the Double-Elm anywhere from nine to sixteen times a week with fresh butter or a quarter of venison or a sample of new sheep-dip just as a frivolous excuse to see Marilla. Marilla and me got to be extensively inveigled with each other, and I was pretty sure I was going to get my rope around her neck and lead her over to the Lomito. Only she was so everlastingly permeated with filial sentiments toward old Cal that I never could get her to talk about serious matters.

"You never saw anybody in your life that was as full of knowledge and had less sense than old Cal. He was advised about all the branches of information contained in learning, and he was up to all the rudiments of doctrines and enlightenment. You couldn't advance him any ideas on any of the parts of speech or lines of thought. You would have thought he was a professor of the weather and politics and chemistry and natural history and the origin of derivations. Any subject you brought up old Cal could give you an abundant synopsis of it from the Greek root up to the time it was sacked and on the market.

"One day just after the fall shearing I rides over to the Double-Elm with a lady's magazine about fashions for Marilla and a scientific paper for old Cal.

"While I was tying my pony to a mesquite, out runs Marilla, 'tickled to death' with some news that couldn't wait.

" 'Oh, Rush,' she says, all flushed up with esteem and gratification, 'what do you think! Dad's going to buy me a piano. Ain't it grand! I never dreamed I'd ever have one.'

" 'It's sure joyful,' says I. 'I always admired the agreeable uproar of a piano. It'll be lots of company for you. That's mighty good of Uncle Cal to do that.'

" 'I'm all undecided,' says Marilla, 'between a piano and a organ. A parlour organ is nice.'

" 'Either of 'em,' says I, 'is first-class for mitigating the lack of noise around a sheep-ranch. For my part,' I says, 'I shouldn't like anything better than to ride home of an evening and listen to a few waltzes and jigs, with somebody about your size sitting on the piano-stool and rounding up the notes.'

" 'Oh, hush about that,' says Marilla, 'and go on in the house. Dad hasn't rode out to-day. He's not feeling well.'

"Old Cal was inside, lying on a cot. He had a pretty bad cold and a cough. I stayed to supper.

" 'Going to get Marilla a piano, I hear,' says I to him.

" 'Why, yes, something of the kind, Rush,' says he. 'She's been hankering for music for a long spell; and I allow to fix her up with something in that line right away. The sheep sheared six pounds all round this fall; and I'm going to get Marilla an instrument if it takes the price of the whole clip to do it.'

" '*Star wayno*,' says I. 'The little girl deserves it.'

" 'I'm going to San Antone on the last load of wool,' says Uncle Cal, 'and select an instrument for her myself.'

" 'Wouldn't it be better,' I suggest, 'to take Marilla along and let her pick out one that she likes?'

"I might have known that would set Uncle Cal going. Of course, a man like him, that knew everything about everything, would look at that as a reflection on his attainments.

" 'No, sir, it wouldn't,' says he, pulling at his white whiskers. 'There ain't a better judge of musical instruments in the whole world than what I am. I had an uncle,' says he, 'that was a partner in a piano factory, and I've seen thousands of 'em put together. I know all about musical instruments from a pipe-organ to a corn-stalk fiddle. There ain't a man lives, sir, that can tell me any news about any instrument that has to be pounded, blowed, scraped, grinded, picked, or wound with a key.'

" 'You get me what you like, dad,' says Marilla, who couldn't keep her feet on the floor from joy. 'Of course you know what to select. I'd just as lief it was a piano or a organ or what.'

" 'I see in St. Louis once what they call a orchestrion,' says Uncle Cal, 'that I judged was about the finest thing in the way of music ever invented. But there ain't room in this house for one. Anyway, I imagine they'd cost a thousand dollars. I reckon something in the piano line would suit Marilla the best. She took lessons in that respect for two years over at Birdstail. I wouldn't trust the buying of an instrument to anybody else but myself. I reckon if I hadn't took up sheep-raising I'd have been one of the finest composers or piano-and-organ manufacturers in the world.'

"That was Uncle Cal's style. But I never lost any patience with him, on account of his thinking so much of Marilla. And she thought just as much of him. He sent her to the academy over at Birdstail for two years when it took nearly every pound of wool to pay the expenses.

"Along about Tuesday Uncle Cal put out for San Antone on the last wagonload of wool. Marilla's uncle Ben, who lived in Birdstail, come over and stayed at the ranch while Uncle Cal was gone.

"It was ninety miles to San Antone, and forty to

the nearest railroad station, so Uncle Cal was gone about four days. I was over at the Double-Elm when he come rolling back one evening about sundown. And up there in the wagon, sure enough, was a piano or a organ—we couldn't tell which—all wrapped up in woolsacks, with a wagon-sheet tied over it in case of rain. And out skips Marilla, hollering, 'Oh, oh!' with her eyes shining and her hair a-flying. 'Dad—dad,' she sings out, 'have you brought it—have you brought it?'—and it right there before her eyes, as women will do.

" 'Finest piano in San Antone,' says Uncle Cal, waving his hand, proud. 'Genuine rosewood, and the finest, loudest tone you ever listened to. I hear the storekeeper play it, and I took it on the spot and paid cash down.'

"Me and Ben and Uncle Cal and a Mexican lifted it out of the wagon and carried it in the house and set it in a corner. It was one of them upright instruments, and not very heavy or very big.

"And then all of a sudden Uncle Cal flops over and says he's mighty sick. He's got a high fever, and he complains of his lungs. He gets into bed, while me and Ben goes out to unhitch and put the horses in the pasture, and Marilla flies around to get Uncle Cal something hot to drink. But first she puts both arms on that piano and hugs it with a soft kind of a smile, like you see kids doing with their Christmas toys.

"When I came in from the pasture, Marilla was in the room where the piano was. I could see by the strings and woolsacks on the floor that she had had it unwrapped. But now she was tying the wagon-sheet over it again, and there was a kind of solemn, whitish look on her face.

" 'Ain't wrapping up the music again, are you, Marilla?' I asks. 'What's the matter with just a couple of tunes for to see how she goes under the saddle?'

" 'Not to-night, Rush,' says she. 'I don't want to play any to-night. Dad's too sick. Just think, Rush, he paid three hundred dollars for it—nearly a third of what the wool-clip brought!'

" 'Well, it ain't anyways in the neighbourhood of a third of what you are worth,' I told her. 'And I don't think Uncle Cal is too sick to hear a little agitation of the piano-keys just to christen the machine.'

" 'Not to-night, Rush,' says Marilla, in a way that she had when she wanted to settle things.

"But it seems that Uncle Cal was plenty sick, after all. He got so bad that Ben saddled up and rode over to Birdstail for Doc Simpson. I stayed around to see if I'd be needed for anything.

"When Uncle Cal's pain let up on him a little he called Marilla and says to her: 'Did you look at your instrument, honey? And do you like it?'

" 'It's lovely, dad,' says she, leaning down by his pillow; 'I never saw one so pretty. How dear and good it was of you to buy it for me!'

" 'I haven't heard you play on it any yet,' says Uncle Cal; 'and I've been listening. My side don't hurt quite so bad now—won't you play a piece, Marilla?'

"But no; she puts Uncle Cal off and soothes him down like you've seen women do with a kid. It seems she's made up her mind not to touch that piano at present.

"When Doc Simpson comes over he tells us that Uncle Cal has pneumonia the worst kind; and as the old man was past sixty and nearly on the lift anyhow, the odds was against his walking on grass any more.

"On the fourth day of his sickness he calls for Marilla again and wants to talk piano. Doc Simpson was there, and so was Ben and Mrs. Ben, trying to do all they could.

" 'I'd have made a wonderful success in anything connected with music,' says Uncle Cal. 'I got the finest instrument for the money in San Antone. Ain't that piano all right in every respect, Marilla?'

" 'It's just perfect, dad,' says she. 'It's got the finest tone I ever heard. But don't you think you could sleep a little while now, dad?'

" 'No, I don't,' says Uncle Cal. 'I want to hear that piano. I don't believe you've even tried it yet. I went all the way to San Antone and picked it out for you myself. It took a third of the fall clip to buy it; and I don't mind that if it makes my good girl happier. Won't you play a little bit for dad, Marilla?'

"Doc Simpson beckoned Marilla to one side and recommended her to do what Uncle Cal wanted, so it would get him quieted. And her uncle Ben and his wife asked her, too.

" 'Why not hit out a tune or two with the soft pedal on?' I asks Marilla. 'Uncle Cal has begged you so often. It would please him a good deal to hear you touch up the piano he's bought for you. Don't you think you might?'

"But Marilla stands there with big tears rolling down from her eyes and says nothing. And then she runs over and slips her arm under Uncle Cal's neck and hugs him tight.

" 'Why, last night, dad,' we heard her say, 'I played ever so much. Honest—I have been playing it. And it's such a splendid instrument, you don't know how I love it. Last night I played "Bonnie Dundee" and the "Anvil Polka" and the "Blue Danube"—and lots of pieces. You must surely have heard me playing a little, didn't you, dad? I didn't like to play loud when you was so sick.'

" 'Well, well,' says Uncle Cal, 'maybe I did. Maybe I did and forgot about it. My head is a little cranky at times. I heard the man in the store play it fine. I'm mighty glad you like it, Marilla. Yes, I believe I could go to sleep a while if you'll stay right beside me till I do.'

"There was where Marilla had me guessing. Much as she thought of that old man, she wouldn't strike a note on that piano that he'd bought her. I couldn't imagine why she told him she'd been playing it, for the wagon-sheet hadn't ever been off it since she put it back on the same day it came. I knew she could play a little anyhow, for I'd once heard her snatch some pretty fair dance-music out of an old piano at the Charco Largo Ranch.

"Well, in about a week the pneumonia got the best of Uncle Cal. They had the funeral over at Birdstail, and all of us went over. I brought Marilla back home in my buckboard. Her uncle Ben and his wife were going to stay there a few days with her.

"That night Marilla takes me in the room where the piano was, while the others were out on the gallery.

" 'Come here, Rush,' says she; 'I want you to see this now.'

"She unties the rope, and drags off the wagon-sheet.

"If you ever rode a saddle without a horse, or fired off a gun that wasn't loaded, or took a drink out of an empty bottle, why, then you might have been able to scare an opera or two out of the instrument Uncle Cal had bought.

"Instead of a piano, it was one of them machines they've invented to play the piano with. By itself it was about as musical as the holes of a flute without the flute.

"And that was the piano that Uncle Cal had selected; and standing by it was the good, fine, all-wool girl that never let him know it.

"And what you heard playing a little while ago," concluded Mr. Kinney, "was that same deputy-piano machine; only just at present it's shoved up against a six-hundred-dollar piano that I bought for Marilla as soon as we was married."

LXXVIII: SCHOOLS AND SCHOOLS

I

OLD Jerome Warren lived in a hundred-thousand-dollar house at 35 East Fifty-Soforth Street. He was a down-town broker, so rich that he could afford to walk for his health a few blocks in the direction of his office every morning and then call a cab.

He had an adopted son, the son of an old friend named Gilbert—Cyril Scott could play him nicely—who was becoming a successful painter as fast as he could squeeze the paint out of his tubes. Another member of the household was Barbara Ross, a step-niece. Man is born to trouble; so, as old Jerome had no family of his own, he took up the burdens of others.

Gilbert and Barbara got along swimmingly. There was a tacit and tactical understanding all round that the two would stand up under a floral bell some high noon, and promise the minister to keep old Jerome's money in a state of high commotion. But at this point complications must be introduced.

Thirty years before, when old Jerome was young Jerome, there was a brother of his named Dick. Dick went West to seek his or somebody else's fortune. Nothing was heard of him until one day old Jerome had a letter from his brother. It was badly written on ruled paper that smelled of salt bacon and coffee-grounds. The writing was asthmatic and the spelling St. Vitusy.

It appeared that instead of Dick having forced Fortune to stand and deliver, he had been held up himself, and made to give hostages to the enemy. That is, as his letter disclosed, he was on the point of pegging out with a complication of disorders that even whisky had failed to check. All that his thirty years of prospecting had netted him was one daughter, nineteen years old, as per invoice, whom he was shipping East, charges prepaid, for Jerome to clothe, feed, educate, comfort, and cherish for the rest of her natural life or until matrimony should them part.

Old Jerome was a board-walk. Everybody knows that the world is supported by the shoulders of Atlas; and that Atlas stands on a rail-fence; and that the rail-fence is built on a turtle's back. Now, the turtle has to stand on something; and that is a board-walk made of men like old Jerome.

I do not know whether immortality should accrue to man; but if not so, I would like to know when men like old Jerome get what is due them?

They met Nevada Warren at the station. She was a little girl, deeply sunburned and wholesomely good-looking, with a manner that was frankly unsophisticated, yet one that not even a cigar-drummer would intrude upon without thinking twice. Looking at her, somehow you would expect to see her in a short skirt and leather leggings, shooting glass balls or taming mustangs. But in her plain white waist and black skirt she sent you guessing again. With an easy exhibition of strength she swung along a heavy valise, which the uniformed porters tried in vain to wrest from her.

"I am sure we shall be the best of friends," said Barbara, pecking at the firm, sunburned cheek.

"I hope so," said Nevada.

"Dear little niece," said old Jerome, "you are as welcome to my house as if it were your father's own."

"Thanks," said Nevada.

"And I am going to call you 'cousin,'" said Gilbert, with his charming smile.

"Take the valise, please," said Nevada. "It weighs a million pounds. It's got samples from six of dad's old mines in it," she explained to Barbara. "I calculate they'd assay about nine cents to the thousand tons, but I promised him to bring them along."

II

It is a common custom to refer to the usual complication between one man and two ladies, or one lady and two men, or a lady and a man and a nobleman, or—well, any of those problems—as the triangle. But they are never unqualified triangles. They are always isosceles—never equilateral. So, upon the coming of Nevada Warren, she and Gilbert and Barbara Ross lines up into such a figurative triangle; and of that triangle Barbara formed the hypotenuse.

One morning old Jerome was lingering long after breakfast over the dullest morning paper in the city before setting forth to his down-town fly-trap. He had become quite fond of Nevada, finding in her much of his dead brother's quiet independence and unsuspicious frankness.

A maid brought in a note for Miss Nevada Warren.

"A messenger-boy delivered it at the door, please," she said. "He's waiting for an answer."

Nevada, who was whistling a Spanish waltz between her teeth, and watching the carriages and autos roll by in the street, took the envelope. She knew it was from Gilbert, before she opened it, by the little gold palette in the upper left-hand corner.

After tearing it open she pored over the contents for a while, absorbedly. Then, with a serious face, she went and stood at her uncle's elbow.

"Uncle Jerome, Gilbert is a nice boy, isn't he?"

"Why, bless the child!" said old Jerome, crackling his paper loudly; "of course he is. I raised him myself."

"He wouldn't write anything to anybody that wasn't exactly—I mean that everybody couldn't know and read, would he?"

"I'd just like to see him try it," said uncle, tearing a handful from his newspaper. "Why, what——"

"Read this note he just sent me, uncle, and see if

you think it's all right and proper. You see, I don't know much about city people and their ways."

Old Jerome threw his paper down and set both his feet upon it. He took Gilbert's note and fiercely perused it twice, and then a third time.

"Why, child," said he, "you had me almost excited, although I was sure of that boy. He's a duplicate of his father, and he was a gilt-edged diamond. He only asks if you and Barbara will be ready at four o'clock this afternoon for an automobile drive over to Long Island. I don't see anything to criticize in it except the stationery. I always did hate that shade of blue."

"Would it be all right to go?" asked Nevada, eagerly.

"Yes, yes, yes, child; of course. Why not? Still, it pleases me to see you so careful and candid. Go, by all means."

"I didn't know," said Nevada demurely. "I thought I'd ask you. Couldn't you go with us, uncle?"

"I? No, no, no, no! I've ridden once in a car that boy was driving. Never again! But it's entirely proper for you and Barbara to go. Yes, yes. But I will not. No, no, no, no!"

Nevada flew to the door, and said to the maid:

"You bet we'll go. I'll answer for Miss Barbara. Tell the boy to say to Mr. Warren, 'You bet we'll go.'"

"Nevada," called old Jerome, "pardon me, my dear, but wouldn't it be as well to send him a note in reply? Just a line would do."

"No, I won't bother about that," said Nevada, gaily. "Gilbert will understand—he always does. I never rode in an automobile in my life; but I've paddled a canoe down Little Devil River through the Lost Horse Cañon, and if it's any livelier than that I'd like to know!"

III

Two months are supposed to have elapsed.

Barbara sat in the study of the hundred-thousand-dollar house. It was a good place for her. Many places are provided in the world where men and women may repair for the purpose of extricating themselves from divers difficulties. There are cloisters, wailing-places, watering-places, confessionals, hermitages, lawyers' offices, beauty-parlours, airships, and studies; and the greatest of these are studies.

It usually takes a hypotenuse a long time to discover that it is the longest side of a triangle. But it's a long line that has no turning.

Barbara was alone. Uncle Jerome and Nevada had gone to the theatre. Barbara had not cared to go. She wanted to stay at home and study in the study. If you, miss, were a stunning New York girl, and saw every day that a brown, ingenuous Western witch was getting hobbles and a lasso on the young man you wanted for yourself, you, too, would lose taste for the oxidized silver setting of a musical comedy.

Barbara sat by the quartered-oak library table. Her right arm rested upon the table, and her dextral fingers nervously manipulated a sealed letter. The letter was addressed to Nevada Warren; and in the upper left-hand corner of the envelope was Gilbert's little gold palette. It had been delivered at nine o'clock, after Nevada had left.

Barbara would have given her pearl necklace to

know what the letter contained; but she could not open and read it by the aid of steam, or a pen-handle, or a hairpin, or any of the generally approved methods because her position in society forbade such an act. She had tried to read some of the lines of the letter by holding the envelope up to a strong light and pressing it hard against the paper, but Gilbert had too good a taste in stationery to make that possible.

At eleven-thirty the theatre-goers returned. It was a delicious winter night. Even so far as from the cab to the door they were powdered thickly with the big flakes downpouring diagonally from the east. Old Jerome growled good-naturedly about villainous cab service and blockaded streets. Nevada, coloured like a rose, with sapphire eyes, babbled of the stormy nights in the mountains around dad's cabin. During all these wintry apostrophes, Barbara, cold at heart, sawed wood—the only appropriate thing she could think of to do.

Old Jerome went immediately upstairs to hot-water bottles and quinine. Nevada fluttered into the study, the only cheerful lighted room, subsided into an arm-chair, and while at the interminable task of unbuttoning her elbow gloves, gave oral testimony as to the demerits of the "show."

"Yes, I think Mr. Fields is really amusing—sometimes," said Barbara. "Here is a letter for you, dear, that came by special delivery just after you had gone."

"Who is it from?" asked Nevada, tugging at a button.

"Well, really," said Barbara, with a smile, "I can only guess. The envelope has that queer little thing in one corner that Gilbert calls a palette, but which looks to me rather like a gilt heart on a school-girl's valentine."

"I wonder what he's writing to me about," remarked Nevada listlessly.

"We're all alike," said Barbara; "all women. We try to find out what is in a letter by studying the postmark. As a last resort we use scissors, and read it from the bottom upward. Here it is."

She made a motion as if to toss the letter across the table to Nevada.

"Great catamounts!" exclaimed Nevada. "These centre-fire buttons are a nuisance. I'd rather wear buckskins. Oh, Barbara, please shuck the hide off that letter and read it. It'll be midnight before I get these gloves off!"

"Why, dear, you don't want me to open Gilbert's letter to you? It's for you, and you wouldn't wish anyone else to read it, of course!"

Nevada raised her steady, calm, sapphire eyes from her gloves.

"Nobody writes me anything that everybody mightn't read," she said. "Go on, Barbara. May-be Gilbert wants us to go out in his car again to-morrow."

Curiosity can do more things than kill a cat; and if emotions, well recognized as feminine, are inimical to feline life, then jealousy would soon leave the whole world catless. Barbara opened the letter, with an indulgent, slightly bored air.

"Well, dear," she said, "I'll read it if you want me to."

She slit the envelope, and read the missive with swift-travelling eyes; read it again, and cast a quick, shrewd glance at Nevada, who, for the time, seemed to consider gloves as the world of her interest, and letters from rising artists as no more than messages from Mars.

For a quarter of a minute Barbara looked at Nevada with a strange steadfastness; and then a smile so small that it widened her mouth only the sixteenth part of an inch, and narrowed her eyes no more than a twentieth flashed like an inspired thought across her face.

Since the beginning no woman has been a mystery to another woman. Swift as light travels, each penetrates the chart and mind of another, sifts her sister's words of their cunningest disguises, reads her most hidden desires, and plucks the sophistry from her wiliest talk like hairs from a comb, twiddling them sardonically between her thumb and fingers before letting them float away on the breezes of fundamental doubt. Long ago Eve's son rang the door-bell of the family residence in Paradise Park, bearing a strange lady on his arm, whom he introduced. Eve took her daughter-in-law aside and lifted a classic eyebrow.

"The Land of Nod," said the bride, languidly flirting the leaf of a palm. "I suppose you've been there, of course?"

"Not lately," said Eve, absolutely unstaggered. "Don't you think the apple-sauce they serve over there is execrable? I rather like that mulberry-leaf tunic effect, dear; but, of course, the real fig goods are not to be had over there. Come over behind this lilac-bush while the gentlemen split a celery tonic. I think the caterpillar-holes have made your dress open a little in the back."

So, then and there—according to the records—was the alliance formed by the only two who's-who ladies in the world. Then it was agreed that women should for ever remain as clear as a pane of glass—though glass was yet to be discovered—to other women, and that she should palm herself off on man as a mystery.

Barbara seemed to hesitate.

"Really, Nevada," she said, with a little show of embarrassment, "you shouldn't have insisted on my opening this. I—I'm sure it wasn't meant for anyone else to know."

Nevada forgot her gloves for a moment.

"Then read it aloud," she said. "Since you've already read it, what's the difference? If Mr. Warren has written to me something that anyone else oughtn't to know, that is all the more reason why everybody should know it."

"Well," said Barbara, "this is what it says: 'Dearest Nevada—Come to my studio at twelve o'clock to-night. Do not fail.' " Barbara rose and dropped the note in Nevada's lap. "I'm awfully sorry," she said, "that I knew. It isn't like Gilbert. There must be some mistake. Just consider that I am ignorant of it, will you, dear? I must go upstairs now, I have such a headache. I'm sure I don't understand the note. Perhaps Gilbert has been dining too well, and will explain. Good night!"

IV

Nevada tiptoed to the hall, and heard Barbara's door close upstairs. The bronze clock in the study told the hour of twelve was fifteen minutes away. She ran swiftly to the front door, and let herself out into the snowstorm. Gilbert Warren's studio was six squares away.

By aerial ferry the white silent forces of the storm

attacked the city from beyond the sullen East River. Already the snow lay a foot deep on the pavements, the drifts heaping themselves like scaling-ladders against the walls of the besieged town. The Avenue was as quiet as a street in Pompeii. Cabs now and then skimmed past like white-winged gulls over a moonlit ocean; and less frequent motor-cars—sustaining the comparison—hissed through the foaming waves like submarine boats on their jocund, perilous journeys.

Nevada plunged like a wind-driven storm-petrel on her way. She looked up at the ragged sierras of cloud-capped buildings that rose above the streets, shaded by the night lights and the congealed vapours to grey, drab ashen, lavender, dun, and cerulean tints. They were so like the wintry mountains of her Western home that she felt a satisfaction such as the hundred-thousand-dollar house had seldom brought her.

A policeman caused her to waver on a corner just by his eye and weight.

"Hello, Mabel!" said he. "Kind of late for you to be out, ain't it?"

"I—I am just going to the drug store," said Nevada, hurrying past him.

The excuse serves as a passport for the most sophisticated. Does it prove that woman never progresses, or that she sprang from Adam's rib, full-fledged in intellect and wiles?

Turning eastward, the direct blast cut down Nevada's speed one half. She made zigzag tracks in the snow; but she was as tough as a piñon sapling, and bowed to it as gracefully. Suddenly the studio-building loomed before her, a familiar landmark, like a cliff above some well-remembered cañon.

The haunt of business and its hostile neighbour, art, was darkened and silent. The elevator stopped at ten.

Up eight flights of Stygian stairs Nevada climbed, and rapped firmly at the door numbered "89." She had been there many times before, with Barbara and Uncle Jerome.

Gilbert opened the door. He had a crayon pencil in one hand, a green shade over his eyes, and a pipe in his mouth. The pipe dropped to the floor.

"Am I late?" asked Nevada. "I came as quick as I could. Uncle and me were at the theatre this evening. Here I am, Gilbert!"

Gilbert did a Pygmalion-and-Galatea act. He changed from a statue of stupefaction to a young man with a problem to tackle. He admitted Nevada, got a whisk-broom, and began to brush the snow from her clothes. A great lamp, with a green shade, hung over an easel, where the artist had been sketching in crayon.

"You wanted me," said Nevada simply, "and I came. You said so in your letter. What did you send for me for?"

"You read my letter?" inquired Gilbert, sparring for wind.

"Barbara read it to me. I saw it afterward. It said: 'Come to my studio at twelve to-night, and do not fail.' I thought you were sick, of course, but you don't seem to be."

"Aha!" said Gilbert irrelevantly. "I'll tell you why I asked you to come, Nevada. I want you to marry me immediately—to-night. What's a little snowstorm? Will you do it?"

"You might have noticed that I would, long ago,"

said Nevada. "And I'm rather stuck on the snowstorm idea myself. I surely would hate one of these flowery church noon-weddings. Gilbert, I didn't know you had grit enough to propose it this way. Let's shock 'em—it's our funeral, ain't it?"

"You bet!" said Gilbert. "Where did I hear that expression?" he added to himself. "Wait a minute, Nevada; I want to do a little 'phoning."

He shut himself in a little dressing-room, and called upon the lightnings of the heavens—condensed into unromantic numbers and districts.

"That you, Jack? You confounded sleepy-head! Yes, wake up; this is me—or I—oh, bother the difference in grammar! I'm going to be married right away. Yes! Wake up your sister—don't answer me back; bring her along, too—you *must*. Remind Agnes of the time I saved her from drowning in Lake Ronkonkoma—I know it's caddish to refer to it, but she *must* come with you. Yes! Nevada is here, waiting. We've been engaged quite a while. Some opposition among the relatives, you know, and we have to pull it off this way. We're waiting here for you. Don't let Agnes out-talk you—bring her! You will? Good old boy! I'll order a carriage to call for you, double-quick time. Confound you, Jack, you're all right!"

Gilbert returned to the room where Nevada waited.

"My old friend, Jack Peyton, and his sister were to have been here at a quarter to twelve," he explained; "but Jack is so confoundedly slow. I've just 'phoned them to hurry. They'll be here in a few minutes. I'm the happiest man in the world, Nevada! What did you do with the letter I sent you to-day?"

"I've got it cinched here," said Nevada, pulling it out from beneath her opera-cloak.

Gilbert drew the letter from the envelope and looked it over carefully. Then he looked at Nevada thoughtfully.

"Didn't you think it rather queer that I should ask you to come to my studio at midnight?" he asked.

"Why, no," said Nevada, rounding her eyes. "Not if you needed me. Out West, when a pal sends you a hurry call—ain't that what you say here?—we get there first and talk about it after the row is over. And it's usually snowing there, too, when things happen. So I didn't mind."

Gilbert rushed into another room, and came back burdened with overcoats warranted to turn wind, rain, or snow.

"Put this raincoat on," he said, holding it for her. "We have a quarter of a mile to go. Old Jack and his sister will be here in a few minutes." He began to struggle into a heavy coat. "Oh, Nevada," he said, "just look at the headlines on the front page of that evening paper on the table, will you? It's about your section of the West, and I know it will interest you."

He waited a full minute, pretending to find trouble in the getting on of his overcoat and then turned. Nevada had not moved. She was looking at him with strange and pensive directness. Her cheeks had a flush on them beyond the colour that had been contributed by the wind and snow; but her eyes were steady.

"I was going to tell you," she said, "anyhow, before—you—before we—before—well, before anything. Dad never gave me a day of schooling. I never learned to read or write a darned word. Now if——"

Pounding their uncertain way upstairs, the feet of Jack, the somnolent, and Agnes, the grateful, were heard.

V

When Mr. and Mrs. Gilbert Warren were spinning softly homeward in a closed carriage, after the ceremony, Gilbert said:

"Nevada, would you really like to know what I wrote you in the letter that you received to-night?"

"Fire away!" said his bride.

"Word for word," said Gilbert, "it was this: 'My dear Miss Warren—You were right about the flower. It was a hydrangea, and not a lilac.' "

"All right," said Nevada. "But let's forget it. The joke's on Barbara, anyway!"

LXXIX: THE WORLD AND THE DOOR

A FAVOURITE dodge to get your story read by the public is to assert that it is true, and then add that Truth is stranger than Fiction. I do not know if the yarn I am anxious for you to read is true; but the Spanish purser of the fruit steamer *El Carrero* swore to me by the shrine of Santa Guadalupe that he had the facts from the U.S. vice-consul at La Paz—a person who could not possibly have been cognizant of half of them.

As for the adage quoted above, I take pleasure in puncturing it by affirming that I read in a purely fictional story the other day the line: "Be it so," said the policeman. Nothing so strange has yet cropped out in Truth.

When H. Ferguson Hedges, millionaire promotor, investor and man-about-New-York, turned his thoughts upon matters convivial, and word of it went "down the line," bouncers took a precautionary turn at the Indian clubs, waiters put ironstone china on his favourite tables, cab-drivers crowded close to the curbstone in front of all-night cafés, and careful cashiers in his regular haunts charged up a few bottles to his account by way of preface and introduction.

As a money power a one-millionaire is of small account in a city where the man who cuts your slice of beef behind the free-lunch counter rides to work in his own automobile. But Hedges spent his money as lavishly, loudly and showily as though he were only a clerk squandering a week's wages. And, after all, the bar-tender takes no interest in your reserve fund. He would rather look you up on his cash register than in Bradstreet.

On the evening that the material allegation of facts begins, Hedges was bidding dull care begone on the company of five or six good fellows—acquaintances and friends who had gathered in his wake.

Among them were two younger men—Ralph Merriam, a broker, and Wade, his friend.

Two deep-sea cabmen were chartered. At Columbus Circle they hove to long enough to revile the statue of the great navigator, unpatriotically rebuking him for having voyaged in search of land instead of liquids. Midnight overtook the party marooned in the rear of a cheap café far uptown.

Hedges was arrogant, overriding and quarrelsome. He was burly and tough, iron-grey but vigorous, "good" for the rest of the night. There was a dispute—about nothing that matters—and the five-fingered words were passed—the words that represent the glove cast into the lists. Merriam played the rôle of the verbal Hotspur.

Hedges rose quickly, seized his chair, swung it once and smashed wildly down at Merriam's head. Merriam dodged, drew a small revolver and shot Hedges in the chest. The leading roysterer stumbled, fell in a wry heap, and lay still.

Wade, a commuter, had formed that habit of promptness. He juggled Merriam out a side door, walked him to the corner, ran him a block and caught a hansom. They rode five minutes and then got out on a dark corner and dismissed the cab. Across the street the lights of a small saloon betrayed its hectic hospitality.

"Go in the back room of that saloon," said Wade, "and wait. I'll go find out what's doing and let you know. You may take two drinks while I am gone—no more."

At ten minutes to one o'clock Wade returned.

"Brace up, old chap," he said. "The ambulance got there just as I did. The doctor says he's dead. You may have one more drink. You let me run this thing for you. You've got to skip. I don't believe a chair is legally a deadly weapon. You've got to make tracks, that's all there is to it."

Merriam complained of the cold querulously, and asked for another drink. "Did you notice what big veins he had on the back of his hands?" he said. "I never could stand—I never could——"

"Take one more," said Wade, "and then come on. I'll see you through."

Wade kept his promise so well that at eleven o'clock the next morning Merriam, with a new suit-case full of new clothes and hair-brushes, stepped quietly on board a little 500-ton fruit steamer at an East River pier. The vessel had brought the season's first cargo of limes from Port Limon, and was homeward bound. Merriam had his bank balance of $2,800 in his pocket in large bills, and brief instructions to pile up as much water as he could between himself and New York. There was no time for anything more.

From Port Limon Merriam worked down the coast by schooner and sloop to Colon, thence across the isthmus to Panama, where he caught a tramp bound for Callao and such intermediate ports as might tempt the discursive skipper from his course.

It was at La Paz that Merriam decided to land —La Paz the Beautiful, a little harbourless town smothered in a living green ribbon that banded the foot of a cloud-piercing mountain. Here the little steamer stopped to tread water while the captain's dory took him ashore that he might feel the pulse of the coco-nut market. Merriam went too, with his suit-case, and remained.

Kalb, the vice-consul, a Græco-Armenian citizen of the United States, born in Hessen-Darmstadt, and educated in Cincinnati ward primaries, considered all Americans his brothers and bankers. He attached himself to Merriam's elbow, introduced him to every one in La Paz who wore shoes, borrowed ten dollars and went back to his hammock.

There was a little wooden hotel in the edge of

a banana grove, facing the sea, that catered to the tastes of the few foreigners that had dropped out of the world into the *triste* Peruvian town. At Kalb's introductory, "Shake hands with——," he had obediently exchanged manuan salutations with a German doctor, one French and two Italian merchants, and three or four Americans who were spoken of as gold men, rubber men, mahogany men—anything but men of living tissue.

After dinner Merriam sat in a corner of the broad front *galeria* with Bibb, a Vermonter interested in hydraulic mining, and smoked and drank Scotch "smoke." The moonlit sea, spreading infinitely before him, seemed to separate him beyond all apprehension from his old life. The horrid tragedy in which he had played such a disastrous part now began, for the first time since he stole on board the fruiter, a wretched fugitive, to lose its sharper outlines. Distance lent assuagement to his view. Bibb had opened the flood-gates of a stream of long-dammed discourse, overjoyed to have captured an audience that had not suffered under a hundred repetitions of his views and theories.

"One year more," said Bibb, "and I'll go back to God's country. Oh, I know it's pretty here, and you get *dolce far niente* handed to you in chunks, but this country wasn't made for a white man to live in. You've got to have to plug through snow now and then, and see a game of baseball and wear a stiff collar and have a policeman cuss you. Still, La Paz is a good sort of a pipe-dreamy old hole. And Mrs. Conant is here. When any of us feels particularly like jumping into the sea we rush around to her house and propose. It's nicer to be rejected by Mrs. Conant than it is to be drowned. And they say drowning is a delightful sensation."

"Many like her here?" asked Merriam.

"Not anywhere," said Bibb, with a comfortable sigh. "She's the only white woman in La Paz. The rest range from a dappled dun to the colour of a b-flat piano key. She's been here a year. Comes from—well, you know how a woman can talk—ask 'em to say 'string' and they'll say 'crow's foot' or 'cat's cradle.' Sometimes you'd think she was from Oshkosh, and again from Jacksonville, Florida, and the next day from Cape Cod."

"Mystery?" ventured Merriam.

"M—well, she looks it; but her talk's translucent enough. But that's a woman. I suppose if the Sphinx were to begin talking she'd merely say: 'Goodness me! more visitors coming for dinner, and nothing to eat but the sand which is here.' But you won't think about that when you meet her, Merriam. You'll propose to her too."

To make a hard story soft, Merriam did meet her and propose to her. He found her to be a woman in black with hair the colour of a bronze turkey's wings, and mysterious, *remembering* eyes that—well, that looked as if she might have been a trained nurse looking on when Eve was created. Her words and manner, though, were translucent, as Bibb had said. She spoke, vaguely, of friends in California and some of the lower parishes in Louisiana. The tropical climate and indolent life suited her; she had thought of buying an orange grove later on; La Paz, all in all, charmed her!

Merriam's courtship of the Sphinx lasted three

months, although he did not know that he was courting her. He was using her as an antidote for remorse, until he found, too late, that he had acquired the habit. During that time he had received no news from home. Wade did not know where he was; and he was not sure of Wade's exact address, and was afraid to write. He thought he had better let matters rest as they were for a while.

One afternoon he and Mrs. Conant hired two ponies and rode out along the mountain trail as far as the little cold river that came tumbling down the foothills. There they stopped for a drink, and Merriam spoke his piece—he proposed, as Bibb had prophesied.

Mrs. Conant gave him one glance of brilliant tenderness, and then her face took on such a strange, haggard look that Merriam was shaken out of his intoxication and back to his senses.

"I beg your pardon, Florence," he said, releasing her hand; "but I'll have to hedge on part of what I said. I can't ask you to marry me, of course. I killed a man in New York—a man who was my friend—shot him down—in quite a cowardly manner, I understand. Of course, the drinking didn't excuse it. Well, I couldn't resist having my say; and I'll always mean it. I'm here as a fugitive from justice, and—I suppose that ends our acquaintance."

Mrs. Conant plucked little leaves assiduously from the low-hanging branch of a lime tree.

"I suppose so," she said, in low and oddly uneven tones; "but that depends upon you. I'll be as honest as you were. I poisoned my husband. I am a self-made widow. A man cannot love a murderess. So I suppose that ends our acquaintance."

She looked up at him slowly. His face turned a little pale, and he stared at her blankly, like a deaf-and-dumb man who was wondering what it was all about.

She took a swift step toward him, with stiffened arms and eyes blazing.

"Don't look at me like that!" she cried, as though she were in acute pain. "Curse me, or turn your back on me, but don't look that way. Am I a woman to be beaten? If I could show you—here on my arms, and on my back are scars—and it has been more than a year—scars that he made in his brutal rages. A holy nun would have risen and struck the fiend down. Yes, I killed him. The foul and horrible words that he hurled at me that last day are repeated in my ears every night when I sleep. And then came his blows, and the end of my endurance. I got the poison that afternoon. It was his custom to drink every night in the library before going to bed a hot punch made of rum and wine. Only from my fair hands would he receive it—because he knew the fumes of spirits always sickened me. That night when the maid brought it to me I sent her downstairs on an errand. Before taking him his drink I went to my little private cabinet and poured into it more than a teaspoonful of tincture of aconite—enough to kill three men, so I had learned. I had drawn $6,000 that I had in bank, and with that and a few things in a satchel I left the house without anyone seeing me. As I passed the library I heard him stagger up and fall heavily on a couch. I took a night train for

New Orleans, and from there I sailed to the Bermudas. I finally cast anchor in La Paz. And now what have you to say? Can you open your mouth?"

Merriam came back to life.

"Florence," he said earnestly, "I want you. I don't care what you've done. If the world——"

"Ralph," she interrupted almost with a scream, "be my world!"

Her eyes melted; she relaxed magnificently and swayed toward Merriam so suddenly that he had to jump to catch her.

Dear me! in such scenes how the talk runs into artificial prose. But it can't be helped. It's the subconscious smell of the footlights' smoke that's in all of us. Stir the depths of your cook's soul sufficiently and she will discourse in Bulwer-Lyttonese.

Merriam and Mrs. Conant were very happy. He announced their engagement at the Hotel Orilla del Mar. Eight foreigners and four native Astors pounded his back and shouted insincere congratulations at him. Pedrito, the Castilian-mannered barkeep, was goaded to extra duty until his agility would have turned a Boston cherry-phosphate clerk a pale lilac with envy.

They were both very happy. According to the strange mathematics of the god of mutual affinity, the shadows that clouded their pasts when united became only half as dense instead of darker. They shut the world out and bolted the doors. Each was the other's world. Mrs. Conant lived again. The remembering look left her eyes. Merriam was with her every moment that was possible. On a little plateau under a grove of palms and calabash trees they were going to build a fairy bungalow. They were to be married in two months. Many hours of the day they had their heads together over the house plans. Their joint capital would set up a business in fruit or woods that would yield a comfortable support. "Good night, my world," would say Mrs. Conant every evening when Merriam left her for his hotel. They were very happy. Their love had, circumstantially, that element of melancholy in it that it seems to require to attain its supremest elevation. And it seemed that their mutual great misfortune or sin was a bond that nothing could sever.

One day a steamer hove in the offing. Bare-legged and bare-shouldered La Paz scampered down to the beach, for the arrival of a steamer was their loop-the-loop, circus, Emancipation Day and four-o'clock tea.

When the steamer was near enough, wise ones proclaimed that she was the *Pajaro*, bound up-coast from Callao to Panama.

The *Pajaro* put on brakes a mile off shore. Soon a boat came bobbing shoreward. Merriam strolled down on the beach to look on. In the shallow water the Carib sailors sprang out and dragged the boat with a mighty rush to the firm shingle. Out climbed the purser, the captain and two passengers, ploughing their way through the deep sand toward the hotel. Merriam glanced toward them with the mild interest due to strangers. There was something familiar to him in the walk of one of the passengers. He looked again, and his blood seemed to turn to strawberry ice-cream in his veins. Burly, arrogant, debonair as ever, H. Ferguson Hedges, the man he had killed, was coming toward him ten feet away.

When Hedges saw Merriam his face flushed a dark red. Then he shouted in his old, bluff way: "Hello, Merriam. Glad to see you. Didn't expect to find you out here. Quinby, this is my old friend Merriam, of New York—Merriam, Mr. Quinby."

Merriam gave Hedges and then Quinby an ice-cold hand.

"Br-r-r-r!" said Hedges. "But you've got a frappéd flipper! Man, you're not well, You're as yellow as a Chinamen. Malarial here? Steer us to a bar if there is such a thing, and let's take a prophylactic."

Merriam, still half comatose, led them toward the Hotel Orilla del Mar.

"Quinby and I," explained Hedges, puffing through the slippery sand, "are looking out along the coast for some investments. We've just come up from Concepción and Valparaiso and Lima. The captain of this subsidized ferry boat told us there was some good picking around here in silver mines. So we got off. Now, where is that café, Merriam? Oh, in this portable soda-water pavilion?"

Leaving Quinby at the bar, Hedges drew Merriam aside.

"Now, what does this mean?" he said, with gruff kindness. "Are you sulking about that fool row we had?"

"I thought," stammered Merriam—"I heard—they told me you were—that I had——"

"Well, you didn't, and I'm not," said Hedges. "That fool young ambulance surgeon told Wade I was a candidate for a coffin just because I'd got tired and quit breathing. I laid up in a private hospital for a month; but here I am, kicking as hard as ever. Wade and I tried to find you, but couldn't. Now, Merriam, shake hands and forget it all. I was as much to blame as you were; and the shot really did me good—I came out of the hospital as healthy and fit as a cab-horse. Come on; that drink's waiting."

"Old man," said Merriam brokenly, "I don't know how to thank you—I—well, you know———"

"Oh, forget it," boomed Hedges, "Quinby'll die of thirst if we don't join him."

Bibb was sitting on the shady side of the gallery waiting for the eleven-o'clock breakfast. Presently Merriam came out and joined him. His eye was strangely bright.

"Bibb, my boy," said he, slowly waving his hand, "do you see those mountains and that sea and sky and sunshine?—they're mine, Bibbsy—all mine."

"You go in," said Bibb, "and take eight grains of quinine, right away. It won't do in this climate for a man to get to thinking he's Rockefeller, or James O'Neill either."

Inside, the purser was untying a great roll of newspapers, many of them weeks old, gathered in the lower ports by the *Pajaro* to be distributed at casual stopping-places. Thus do the beneficent voyagers scatter news and entertainment among the prisoners of sea and mountains.

Tio Pancho, the hotel proprietor, set his great silver-rimmed *anteojos* upon his nose and divided the papers into a number of smaller rolls. A barefooted *muchacho* dashed in, desiring the post of messenger.

"*Bien venido*," said Tio Pancho. "This to Señora Conant; that to el Doctor S-S-Sch-legel—*Dios!* what a name to say!—that to Señor Davis

—one for Don Alberto. These two for the *Casa de Huespedes*, *Numero* 6, *en la calle de las Buenas Gracias*. And say to them all, *muchacho*, that the *Pajaro* sails for Panama at three this afternoon. If any have letters to send by the post, let them come quickly, that they may first pass through the *correo*."

Mrs. Conant received her roll of newspapers at four o'clock. The boy was late in delivering them because he had been deflected from his duty by an iguana that crossed his path and to which he immediately gave chase. But it made no hardship, for she had no letters to send.

She was idling in a hammock in the *patio* of the house that she occupied, half awake, half happily dreaming of the paradise that she and Merriam had created out of the wrecks of their pasts. She was content now for the horizon of that shimmering sea to be the horizon of her life. They had shut out the world and closed the door.

Merriam was coming to her house at seven, after his dinner at the hotel. She would put on a white dress and an apricot-coloured lace mantilla, and they would walk an hour under the coconut palms by the lagoon. She smiled contentedly, and chose a paper at random from the roll the boy had brought.

At first the words of a certain headline of a Sunday newspaper meant nothing to her; they conveyed only a visualized sense of familiarity. The largest type ran thus: "Lloyd B. Conant secures divorce." And then the sub-headings: "Well-known Saint Louis paint manufacturer wins suit, pleading one year's absence of wife." "Her mysterious disappearance recalled." "Nothing has been heard of her since."

Twisting herself quickly out of the hammock, Mrs. Conant's eye soon traversed the half-column of the *Recall.* It ended thus: "It will be remembered that Mrs. Conant disappeared one evening in March of last year. It was freely rumoured that her marriage with Lloyd B. Conant resulted in much unhappiness. Stories were not wanting to the effect that his cruelty toward his wife had more than once taken the form of physical abuse. After her departure a full bottle of tincture of aconite, a deadly poison, was found in a small medicine cabinet in her bedroom. This might have been an indication that she meditated suicide. It is supposed that she abandoned such an intention if she possessed it, and left her home instead."

Mrs. Conant slowly dropped the paper, and sat on a chair, clasping her hands tightly.

"Let me think—O God!—let me think," she whispered. "I took the bottle with me . . . I threw it out of the window of the train . . . I—— . . . there was another bottle in the cabinet . . . there were two, side by side—the aconite—and the valerian that I took when I could not sleep. . . . If they found the aconite bottle full, why—but, he is alive, of course—I gave him only a harmless dose of valerian. . . . I am not a murderess in fact. . . . Ralph, I—O God, don't let this be a dream!"

She went into the part of the house that she rented from the old Peruvian man and his wife, shut the door, and walked up and down her room swiftly and feverishly for half an hour. Merriam's photograph stood in a frame on a table. She picked it up, looked at it with a smile of exquisite tenderness, and—dropped four tears on it. And Merriam only twenty rods away! Then she stood still for ten minutes, looking into space. She looked into space through a slowly opening door. On her side of the door was the building material for a castle of Romance—love, an Arcady of waving palms, a lullaby of waves on the shore of a haven of rest, respite, peace, a lotus land of dreamy ease and security—a life of poetry and heart's ease and refuge. Romanticist, will you tell me what Mrs. Conant saw on the other side of the door? You cannot?—that is, you will not? Very well; then listen,

She saw herself go into a department store and buy five spools of silk thread and three yards of gingham to make an apron for the cook. "Shall I charge it, ma'am?" asked the clerk. As she walked out a lady whom she met greeted her cordially. "Oh, where did you get the pattern for those sleeves, dear Mrs. Conant?" she said. At the corner a policeman helped her across the street and touched his helmet. "Any callers?" she asked the maid when she reached home. "Mrs. Waldron," answered the maid, "and the two Misses Jenkinson." "Very well," she said. "You may bring me a cup of tea, Maggie."

Mrs. Conant went to the door and called Angela, the old Peruvian woman. "If Mateo is there send him to me." Mateo, a half-breed, shuffling and old but efficient, came.

"Is there a steamer or a vessel of any kind leaving this coast to-night or to-morrow that I can get passage on?" she asked.

Mateo considered.

"At Punta Reina, thirty miles down the coast,

señora," he answered, "there is a small steamer loading with cinchona and dyewoods. She sails for San Francisco to-morrow at sunrise. So says my brother, who arrived in his sloop to-day, passing by Punta Reina."

"You must take me in that sloop to that steamer to-night. Will you do that?"

"Perhaps——" Mateo shrugged a suggestive shoulder. Mrs. Conant took a handful of money from a drawer and gave it to him.

"Get the sloop ready behind the little point of land below the town," she ordered. "Get sailors, and be ready to sail at six o'clock. In half an hour bring a cart partly filled with straw into the *patio* here, and take my trunk to the sloop. There is more money yet. Now, hurry."

For one time Mateo walked away without shuffling his feet.

"Angela," cried Mrs. Conant, almost fiercely, "come and help me pack. I am going away. Out with this trunk. My clothes first. Stir yourself. Those dark dresses first. Hurry."

From the first she did not waver from her decision. Her view was clear and final. Her door had opened and let the world in. Her love for Merriam was not lessened; but it now appeared a hopeless and unrealizable thing. The visions of their future that had seemed so blissful and complete had vanished. She tried to assure herself that her renunciation was rather for his sake than for her own. Now that she was cleared of her burden—at least, technically—would not his own weigh too heavily upon him? If she should cling to him, would not the difference for ever silently mar and corrode their happiness? Thus she reasoned: but there were a thousand little voices calling to her that she could feel rather than hear, like the hum of distant, powerful machinery—the little voices of the world, that, when raised in unison, can send their insistent call through the thickest door.

Once while packing, a brief shadow of the lotus dream came back to her. She held Merriam's picture to her heart with one hand, while she threw a pair of shoes into the trunk with her other.

At six o'clock Mateo returned and reported the sloop ready. He and his brother lifted the trunk into the cart, covered it with straw and conveyed it to the point of embarkation. From there they transferred it on board in the sloop's dory. Then Mateo returned for additional orders.

Mrs. Conant was ready. She had settled all business matters with Angela, and was impatiently waiting. She wore a long, loose black-silk duster that she often walked about in when the evenings were chilly. On her head was a small round hat, and over it the apricot-coloured lace mantilla.

Dusk had quickly followed the short twilight. Mateo led her by dark and grass-grown streets toward the point behind which the sloop was anchored. On turning a corner they beheld the Hotel Orilla del Mar three streets away, nebulously aglow with its array of kerosene lamps.

Mrs. Conant paused, with streaming eyes. "I must, I *must* see him once before I go," she murmured in anguish. But even then she did not falter in her decision. Quickly she invented a plan by which she might speak to him, and yet make her departure without his knowing. She would walk past the hotel, ask some one to call him out and talk a few moments on some trivial excuse, leaving him expecting to see her at her home at seven.

She unpinned her hat and gave it to Mateo. "Keep this, and wait here till I come," she ordered. Then she draped the mantilla over her head as she usually did when walking after sunset, and went straight to the Orilla del Mar.

She was glad to see the bulky, white-clad figure of Tio Pancho standing alone on the gallery.

"Tio Pancho," she said, with a charming smile, "may I trouble you to ask Mr. Merriam to come out for just a few moments that I may speak with him?"

Tio Pancho bowed as an elephant bows.

"*Buenas tardes*, Señora Conant," he said, as a cavalier talks. And then he went on, less at his ease:

"But does not the señora know that Señor Merriam sailed on the *Pajaro* for Panama at three o'clock of this afternoon?"

LXXX: THE VENTURERS

LET the story wreck itself on the spreading rails of the *Non Sequitur* Limited, if it will, first you must take your seat in the observation car "*Raison d'être*" for one moment. It is for no longer than to consider a brief essay on the subject —let us call it: "What's Around the Corner."

Omne mundus in duas partes divisum est—men who wear rubbers and pay poll-taxes, and men who discover new continents. There are no more continents to discover; but by the time overshoes are out of date and the poll has developed into an income tax, the other half will be paralleling the canals of Mars with radium railways.

Fortune, Chance, and Adventure are given as synonyms in the dictionaries. To the knowing each has a different meaning. Fortune is a prize to be won. Adventure is the road to it. Chance is what may lurk in the shadows at the roadside. The face of Fortune is radiant and alluring; that of Adventure flushed and heroic. The face of Chance is the beautiful countenance—perfect because vague and dream-born—that we see in our tea-cups at breakfast while we growl over our chops and toast.

The VENTURER is one who keeps his eye on the hedgerows and wayside groves and meadows while he travels the road to Fortune. That is the difference between him and the Adventurer. Eating the forbidden fruit was the best record ever made by a Venturer. Trying to prove that it happened is the highest work of the Adventuresome. To be either is disturbing to the cosmogony of creation. So, as bracket-sawed and city-directoried citizens, let us light our pipes, chide the children and the cat, arrange ourselves in the willow rocker under the flickering gas-jet at the coolest window and scan this little tale of two modern followers of Chance.

"Did you ever hear that story about the man from the West?" asked Billinger, in the little dark-oak room to your left as you penetrate the interior of the Powhatan Club.

"Doubtless," said John Reginald Forster, rising and leaving the room.

Forster got his straw hat (straws will be in and maybe out again long before this is printed) from the check-room boy, and walked out of the air (as Hamlet says). Billinger was used to having his stories insulted and would not mind. Forster was in his favourite mood and wanted to go away from anywhere. A man, in order to get on good terms with himself, must have his opinions corroborated and his moods matched by some one else. (I had written that "somebody"; but an A.D.T. boy who once took a telegram for me pointed out that I could save money by using the compound word. This is a vice versa case.)

Forster's favourite mood was that of greatly desiring to be a follower of Chance. He was a Venturer by nature, but convention, birth, tradition and the narrowing influences of the tribe of Manhattan had denied him full privilege. He had trodden all the main-travelled thoroughfares and many of the side roads that are supposed to relieve the tedium of life. But none had sufficed. The reason was that he knew what was to be found at the end of every street. He knew from experience and logic almost precisely to what end each digression from routine must lead. He found a depressing monotony in all the variations that the music of his sphere had grafted upon the tune of life. He had not learned that, although the world was made round, the circle had been squared, and that its true interest is to be found in "What's Around the Corner."

Forster walked abroad aimlessly from the Powhatan, trying not to tax either his judgment or his desire as to what streets he travelled. He would have been glad to lose his way if it were possible;

but he had no hope of that. Adventure and Fortune move at your beck and call in the greater city; but Chance is oriental. She is a veiled lady in a sedan chair, protected by a special traffic squad of dragomans. Cross-town, uptown, and down-town you may move without seeing her.

At the end of an hour's stroll, Forster stood on a corner of a broad, smooth avenue, looking disconsolately across it at a picturesque old hotel softly but brilliantly lit. Disconsolately, because he knew that he must dine; and dining in that hotel was no venture. It was one of his favourite caravansaries, and so silent and swift would be the service and so delicately choice the food, that he regretted the hunger that must be appeased by the "dead perfection" of the place's cuisine. Even the music there seemed to be always playing *da capo*.

Fancy came to him that he would dine at some cheap, even dubious, restaurant lower down in the city, where the erratic chefs from all countries of the world spread their national cookery for the omnivorous American. Something might happen there out of the routine—he might come upon a subject without a predicate, a road without an end, a question without an answer, a cause without an effect, a gulf stream in life's salt ocean. He had not dressed for evening; he wore a dark business suit that would not be questioned even where the waiters served the spaghetti in their shirt sleeves.

So John Reginald Forster began to search his clothes for money; because the more cheaply you dine, the more surely must you pay. All of the thirteen pockets, large and small, of his business suit he explored carefully and found not a penny. His bank-book showed a balance of five figures to his credit in the Old Ironsides Trust Company, but——

Forster became aware of a man near by at his left hand who was really regarding him with some amusement. He looked like any business man of thirty or so, neatly dressed and standing in the attitude of one waiting for a street car. But there was no car line on that avenue. So his proximity and unconcealed curiosity seemed to Forster to partake of the nature of a personal intrusion. But, as he was a consistent seeker after "What's Around the Corner," instead of manifesting resentment he only turned a half-embarrassed smile upon the other's grin of amusement.

"All in?" asked the intruder, drawing nearer.

"Seems so," said Forster. "Now, I thought there was a dollar in——"

"Oh, I know," said the other man, with a laugh. "But there wasn't. I've just been through the same process myself, as I was coming around the corner. I found in an upper vest pocket—I don't know how they got there—exactly two pennies. You know what kind of a dinner exactly two pennies will buy!"

"You haven't dined, then?" asked Forster.

"I have not. But I would like to. Now, I'll make you a proposition. You look like a man who would take up one. Your clothes look neat and respectable. Excuse personalities. I think mine will pass the scrutiny of a head waiter, also. Suppose we go over to that hotel and dine together. We will choose from the menu like millionaires—or, if you prefer, like gentlemen in moderate circumstances dining extravagantly for once. When we have finished we will match with my two pennies to see which of us will stand the brunt of the house's displeasure and vengeance. My name is Ives. I think we have lived in the same station of life—before our money took wings."

"You're on," said Forster joyfully.

Here was a venture at least within the borders of the mysterious country of Chance—anyhow, it promised something better than the stale infestivity of a table d'hôte. The two were soon seated at a corner table in the hotel dining-room. Ives chucked one of his pennies across the table to Forster.

"Match for which of us gives the order," he said.

Forster lost.

Ives laughed and began to name liquids and viands to the waiter with the absorbed but calm deliberation of one who was to the menu born. Forster, listening, gave his admiring approval of the order.

"I am a man," said Ives, during the oysters, "who has made a lifetime search after the to-be-continued-in-our-next. I am not like the ordinary adventurer who strikes for a coveted prize. Nor yet am I like a gambler who knows he is either to win or lose a certain set stake. What I want is to encounter an adventure to which I can predict no conclusion. It is the breath of existence to me to dare Fate in its blindest manifestations. The world has come to run so much by rote and gravitation that you can enter upon hardly any footpath of chance in which you do not find signboards informing you of what you may expect at its end. I am like the clerk in the Circumlocution Office who always complained bitterly when anyone came in to ask information. 'He wanted to *know*, you know!' was the kick he made to his fellow-clerks. Well, I don't want to know, I don't want to reason, I don't want to guess—I want to bet my hand without seeing it."

"I understand," said Forster delightedly. "I've often wanted the way I feel put into words. You've done it. I want to take chances on what's coming. Suppose we have a bottle of Moselle with the next course."

"Agreed," said Ives. "I'm glad you catch my idea. It will increase the animosity of the house toward the loser. If it does not weary you, we will pursue the theme. Only a few times have I met a true venturer—one who does not ask a schedule and map from Fate when he begins a journey. But, as the world becomes more civilized and wiser, the more difficult it is to come upon an adventure the end of which you cannot foresee. In the Elizabethan days you could assault the watch, wring knockers from doors and have a jolly set-to with the blades in any convenient angle of a wall and 'get away with it.' Nowadays, if you speak disrespectfully to a policeman, all that is left to the most romantic fancy is to conjecture in what particular police station he will land you."

"I know—I know," said Forster, nodding approval.

"I returned to New York to-day," continued Ives, "from a three years' ramble around the globe. Things are not much better abroad than they are at home. The whole world seems to be overrun by conclusions. The only thing that interests me greatly is a premise. I've tried shooting big game in Africa. I know what an express rifle will do at so many yards; and when an elephant or a rhinoceros falls to the bullet, I enjoy it about as much as I did when I was kept in after school to do a sum in long division on the blackboard."

"I know—I know," said Forster.

"There might be something in aeroplanes," went on Ives reflectively. "I've tried ballooning; but it seems to me merely a cut-and-dried affair of wind and ballast."

"Women," suggested Forster, with a smile.

"Three months ago," said Ives, "I was pottering around in one of the bazaars in Constantinople. I noticed a lady, veiled, of course, but with a pair of especially fine eyes visible, who was examining some amber and pearl ornaments at one of the booths. With her was an attendant—a big Nubian, as black as coal. After a while this attendant drew nearer to me by degrees and slipped a scrap of paper into my hand. I looked at it when I got a chance. On it was scrawled hastily in pencil: 'The arched gate of the Nightingale Garden at nine to-night.' Does that appear to you to be an interesting premise, Mr. Forster?"

"Go on," said Forster eagerly.

"I made inquiries and learned that the Nightingale Garden was the property of an old Turk—a grand vizier, or something of the sort. Of course I prospected for the arched gate and was there at nine. The same Nubian attendant opened the gate promptly on time, and I went inside and sat on a bench by a perfumed fountain with the veiled lady. We had quite an extended chat. She was Myrtle Thompson, a lady journalist, who was writing up the Turkish harems for a Chicago newspaper. She said she noticed the New York cut of my clothes in the bazaar and wondered if I couldn't work something into the metropolitan papers about it."

"I see," said Forster. "I see."

"I've canoed through Canada," said Ives, "down many rapids and over many falls. But I didn't seem to get what I wanted out of it because I knew there were only two possible outcomes—I would either go to the bottom or arrive at the sea level. I've played all games at cards; but the mathematicians have spoiled that sport by computing the percentages. I've made acquaintances on trains, I've answered advertisements, I've rung strange door-bells, I've taken every chance that presented itself; but there has always been the conventional ending—the logical conclusion to the premise."

"I know," repeated Forster. "I've felt it all. But I've had few chances to take my chance at chances. Is there any life so devoid of impossibilities as life in this city? There seems to be a myriad of opportunities for testing the undeterminable; but not one in a thousand fails to land you where you expected it to stop. I wish the subways and street cars disappointed one as seldom."

"The sun has risen," said Ives, "on the Arabian nights. There are no more caliphs. The fisherman's vase is turned to a vacuum bottle, warranted to keep any genie boiling or frozen for forty-eight hours. Life moves by rote. Science has killed adventure. There are no more opportunities such as Columbus and the man who ate the first oyster had. The only certain thing is that there is nothing uncertain."

"Well," said Forster, "my experience has been the limited one of a city man. I haven't seen the world as you have; but it seems that we view it with the same opinion. But, I tell you I am grateful for even this little venture of ours into the borders of the haphazard. There may be at least one breathless moment when the bill for the dinner is presented. Perhaps, after all, the pilgrims who travelled without scrip or purse found a keener taste to life than did the knights of the Round Table who rode abroad with a retinue and King Arthur's certified checks in the lining of their helmets. And now, if you've finished your coffee, suppose we match one of your insufficient coins for the impending blow of Fate. What have I up?"

"Heads," called Ives.

"Heads it is," said Forster, lifting his hand. "I lose. We forgot to agree upon a plan for the winner to escape. I suggest that when the waiter comes you make a remark about telephoning to a friend. I will hold the fort and the dinner check long enough for you to get your hat and be off. I thank you for an evening out of the ordinary, Mr. Ives, and wish we might have others."

"If my memory is not at fault," said Ives, laughing, "the nearest police station is in Macdougal Street. I have enjoyed the dinner, too, let me assure you."

Forster crooked his finger for the waiter. Victor, with a locomotive effort that seemed to owe more to pneumatics than to pedestrianism, glided to the table and laid the card, face downwards, by the loser's cup. Forster took it up and added the figures with deliberate care. Ives leaned back comfortably in his chair.

"Excuse me," said Forster; "but I thought you

were going to ring up Grimes about that theatre party for Thursday night. Had you forgotten about it?"

"Oh," said Ives, settling himself more comfortably, "I can do that later on. Get me a glass of water, waiter."

"Want to be in at the death, do you?" asked Forster.

"I hope you don't object," said Ives pleadingly. "Never in my life have I seen a gentleman arrested in a public restaurant for swindling it out of a dinner."

"All right," said Forster, calmly. "You are entitled to see a Christian die in the arena as your *pousse-café*."

Victor came with the glass of water and remained, with the disengaged air of an inexorable collector.

Forster hesitated for fifteen seconds, and then took a pencil from his pocket and scribbled his name on the dinner check. The water bowed and took it away.

"The fact is," said Forster, with a little embarrassed laugh, "I doubt whether I'm what they call a 'game sport,' which means the same as a 'soldier of Fortune.' I'll have to make a confession. I've been dining at this hotel two or three times a week for more than a year. I always sign my checks." And then, with a note of appreciation in his voice: "It was first-rate of you to stay to see me through with it when you knew I had no money, and that you might be scooped in too."

"I guess I'll confess too," said Ives, with a grin. "I own the hotel. I don't run it, of course, but

I always keep a suite on the third floor for my use when I happen to stray into town."

He called a waiter and said: "Is Mr. Gilmore still behind the desk? All right. Tell him that Mr. Ives is here, and ask him to have my rooms made ready and aired."

"Another venture cut short by the inevitable," said Forster. "Is there a conundrum without an answer in the next number? But let's hold to our subject just for a minute or two, if you will. It isn't often that I meet a man who understands the flaws I pick in existence. I am engaged to be married a month from to-day."

"I reserve comment," said Ives.

"Right; I am going to add to the assertion. I am devotedly fond of the lady; but I can't decide whether to show up at the church or make a sneak for Alaska. It's the same idea, you know, that we were discussing—it does for a fellow as far as possibilities are concerned. Everybody knows the routine—you get a kiss flavoured with Ceylon tea after breakfast; you go to the office; you come back home and dress for dinner—theatre twice a week—bills—moping around most evenings trying to make conversation—a little quarrel occasionally—maybe sometimes a big one, and a separation—or else a settling down into middle-aged contentment, which is worst of all."

"I know," said Ives, nodding wisely.

"It's the dead certainty of the thing," went on Forster, "that keeps me in doubt. There'll nevermore be anything around the corner."

"Nothing after the 'Little Church,'" said Ives. "I know."

"Understand," said Forster, "that I am in no

doubt as to my feelings towards the lady. I may say that I love her truly and deeply. But there is something in the current that runs through my veins that cries out against any form of the calculable. I do not know what I want; but I know that I want it. I'm talking like an idiot, I suppose, but I'm sure of what I mean."

"I understand you," said Ives, with a slow smile. "Well, I think I will be going up to my rooms now. If you would dine with me here one evening soon, Mr. Forster, I'd be glad."

"Thursday?" suggested Forster.

"At seven, if it's convenient," answered Ives.

"Seven goes," assented Forster.

At half-past eight Ives got into a cab and was driven to a number in one of the correct West Seventies. His card admitted him to the reception-room of an old-fashioned house into which the spirits of Fortune, Chance, and Adventure had never dared to enter. On the walls were the Whistler etchings, the steel engravings by Oh-what's-his-name?, the still-life paintings of the grapes and garden truck with the water-melon seeds spilled on the table as natural as life, and the Greuze head. It was a household. There were even brass andirons. On the table was an album, half-morocco, with oxidized-silver protections on the corners of the lids. A clock on the mantel ticked loudly, with a warning click at five minutes to nine. Ives looked at it curiously, remembering a timepiece in his grandmother's home that gave such a warning.

And then down the stairs and into the room came Mary Marsden. She was twenty-four, and I leave her to your imagination. But I must say this much—youth and health and simplicity and courage and greenish-violet eyes are beautiful, and she had all these. She gave Ives her hand with the sweet cordiality of an old friendship.

"You can't think what a pleasure it is," she said, "to have you drop in once every three years or so."

For half an hour they talked. I confess that I cannot repeat the conversation. You will find it in books in the circulating library. When that part of it was over, Mary said:

"And did you find what you wanted while you were abroad?"

"What I wanted?" said Ives.

"Yes. You know you were always queer. Even as a boy you wouldn't play with marbles or baseball or any game with rules. You wanted to dive in water where you didn't know whether it was ten inches or ten feet deep. And when you grew up you were just the same. We've often talked about your peculiar ways."

"I suppose I am an incorrigible," said Ives. "I am opposed to the doctrine of predestination, to the rule of three, gravitation, taxes and everything of the kind. Life has always seemed to me something like a serial story would be if they printed above each instalment a synopsis of *succeeding* chapters."

Mary laughed merrily.

"Bob Ames told us once," she said, "of a funny thing you did. It was when you and he were on a train in the South, and you got off at a town where you hadn't intended to stop just because the brakeman hung up a sign in the end of the car with the name of the next station on it."

"I remember," said Ives. "That 'next station'

has been the thing I've always tried to get away from."

"I know it," said Mary. "And you've been very foolish. I hope you didn't find what you wanted not to find, or get off at the station where there wasn't any, or whatever it was you expected wouldn't happen to you during the three years you've been away."

"There was something I wanted before I went away," said Ives.

Mary looked in his eyes clearly, with a slight but perfectly sweet smile.

"There was," she said. "You wanted me. And you could have had me, as you very well know."

Without replying, Ives let his gaze wander slowly about the room. There had been no change in it since last he had been in it, three years before. He vividly recalled the thoughts that had been in his mind then. The contents of that room were as fixed, in their way, as the everlasting hills. No change would ever come there except the inevitable ones wrought by time and decay. That silver-mounted album would occupy that corner of that table, those pictures would hang on the walls, those chairs be found in their same places every morn and noon and night while the household hung together. The brass andirons were monuments to order and stability. Here and there were relics of a hundred years ago which were still living mementoes and would be for many years to come. One going from and coming back to that house would never need to forecast or doubt. He would find what he left, and leave what he found. The veiled lady, Chance, would never lift her hand to the knocker on the outer door.

And before him sat the lady who belonged in the room. Cool and sweet and unchangeable she was. She offered no surprises. If one should pass his life with her, though she might grow white-haired and wrinkled, he would never perceive the change. Three years he had been away from her, and she was still waiting for him as established and constant as the house itself. He was sure that she had once cared for him. It was the knowledge that she would always do so that had driven him away. Thus his thoughts ran.

"I am going to be married soon," said Mary.

On the next Thursday afternoon Forster came hurriedly to Ives's hotel.

"Old man," said he, "we'll have to put that dinner off for a year or so; I'm going abroad. The steamer sails at four. That was a great talk we had the other night, and it decided me. I'm going to knock around the world and get rid of that incubus that has been weighing on both you and me—the terrible dread of knowing what's going to happen. I've done one thing that hurts my conscience a little; but I know it's best for both of us. I've written to the lady to whom I was engaged and explained everything—told her plainly why I was leaving—that the monotony of matrimony would never do for me. Don't you think I was right?"

"It is not for me to say," answered Ives. "Go ahead and shoot elephants if you think it will bring the element of chance into your life. We've got to decide these things for ourselves. But I tell you one thing, Forster, I've found the way. I've found out the biggest hazard in the world—a game of chance that never is concluded, a venture that may end in the highest heaven or the blackest pit. It will keep a man on edge until the clods fall on his coffin, because he will never know—not until his last day, and not then will he know. It is a voyage without a rudder or compass, and you must be captain and crew and keep watch, every day and night, yourself, with no one to relieve you. I have found the VENTURE. Don't bother yourself about leaving Mary Marsden, Forster. I married her yesterday at noon."

LXXXI: THE ROBE OF PEACE

MYSTERIES follow one another so closely in a great city that the reading public and the friends of Johnny Bellchambers have ceased to marvel at his sudden and unexplained disappearance nearly a year ago. This particular mystery has now been cleared up, but the solution is so strange and incredible to the mind of the average man that only a select few who were in close touch with Bellchambers will give it full credence.

Johnny Bellchambers, as is well known, belonged to the intrinsically inner circle of the élite. Without any of the ostentation of the fashionable ones, who endeavour to attract notice by eccentric display of wealth and show, he still was *au fait* in everything that gave deserved lustre to his high position in the ranks of society.

Especially did he shine in the matter of dress. In this he was the despair of imitators. Always correct, exquisitely groomed, and possessed of an unlimited wardrobe, he was conceded to be the best-dressed man in New York, and, therefore, in America. There was not a tailor in Gotham who would not have deemed it a precious boon to have been granted the privilege of making Bellchambers' clothes without a cent of pay. As he wore them, they would have been a priceless advertisement. Trousers were his especial passion. Here nothing but perfection would he notice. He would have worn a patch as quickly as he would have overlooked a wrinkle. He kept a man in his apartments always busy pressing his ample supply. His friends said that three hours was the limit of time that he would wear these garments without exchanging.

Bellchambers disappeared very suddenly. For three days his absence brought no alarm to his friends, and then they began to operate the usual methods of inquiry. All of them failed. He had left absolutely no trace behind. Then the search for a motive was instituted, but none was found. He had no enemies, he had no debts, there was no woman. There were several thousand dollars in his bank to his credit. He had never showed any tendency toward mental eccentricity; in fact, he was of a particularly calm and well-balanced temperament. Every means of tracing the vanished man was made use of, but without avail. It was one of those cases—more numerous in late years—where men seemed to have gone out like the flame of a candle, leaving not even a trail of smoke as a witness.

In May, Tom Eyres and Lancelot Gilliam, two of Bellchambers' old friends, went for a little run on the other side. While pottering around in

Italy and Switzerland, they happened one day to hear of a monastery in the Swiss Alps that promised something outside of the ordinary tourist-beguiling attractions. The monastery was almost inaccessible to the average sightseer, being on an extremely rugged and precipitous spur of the mountains. The attractions it possessed but did not advertise were, first, an exclusive and divine cordial made by the monks that was said to far surpass Benedictine and Chartreuse. Next a huge brass bell so purely and accurately cast that it had not ceased sounding since it was first rung three hundred years ago. Finally, it was asserted that no Englishman had ever set foot within its walls. Eyres and Gilliam decided that these three reports called for investigation.

It took them two days with the aid of two guides to reach the monastery of St. Gondrau. It stood upon a frozen, wind-swept crag with the snow piled about it in treacherous, drifting masses. They were hospitably received by the brothers whose duty it was to entertain the infrequent guest. They drank of the precious cordial, finding it rarely potent and reviving. They listened to the great, ever-echoing bell, and learned that they were pioneer travellers, in those grey stone walls, over the Englishman whose restless feet have trodden nearly every corner of the earth.

At three o'clock on the afternoon they arrived, the two young Gothamites stood with good Brother Cristofer in the great, cold hallway of the monastery to watch the monks march past on their way to the refectory. They came slowly, pacing by twos, with their heads bowed, treading noiselessly with sandalled feet upon the rough stone flags. As the procession slowly filed past, Eyres suddenly gripped Gilliam by the arm. "Look," he whispered eagerly, "at the one just opposite you now—the one on this side, with his hand at his waist—if that isn't Johnny Bellchambers, then I never saw him!"

Gilliam saw and recognized the lost glass of fashion.

"What the deuce," said he wonderingly, "is old Bell doing here? Tommy, it surely can't be he! Never heard of Bell having a turn for the religious. Fact is, I've heard him say things when a four-in-hand didn't seem to tie up just right that would bring him up for court-martial before any church."

"It's Bell, without a doubt," said Eyres firmly, "or I'm pretty badly in need of an oculist. But think of Johnny Bellchambers, the Royal High Chancellor of swell togs and the Mahatma of pink teas, up here in cold storage doing penance in a snuff-coloured bathrobe! I can't get it straight in my mind. Let's ask the jolly old boy that's doing the honours."

Brother Cristofer was appealed to for information. By that time the monks had passed into the refectory. He could not tell to which one they referred. Bellchambers? Ah, the brothers of St. Gondrau abandoned their worldly names when they took the vows. Did the gentlemen wish to speak with one of the brothers? If they would come to the refectory and indicate the one they wished to see, the reverend abbot in authority would, doubtless, permit it.

Eyres and Gilliam went into the dining-hall and pointed out to Brother Cristofer the man they had seen. Yes, it was Johnny Bellchambers. They saw his face plainly now, as he sat among the dingy brothers, never looking up, eating broth from a coarse, brown bowl.

Permission to speak to one of the brothers was granted to the two travellers by the abbot, and they waited in a reception-room for him to come. When he did come, treading softly in his sandals, both Eyres and Gilliam looked at him in perplexity and astonishment. It was Johnny Bellchambers, but he had a different look. Upon his smooth-shaven face was an expression of ineffable peace, of rapturous attainment, of perfect and complete happiness. His form was proudly erect, his eyes shone with a serene and gracious light. He was as neat and well-groomed as in the old New York days, but how differently was he clad! Now he seemed clothed in but a single garment—a long robe of rough brown cloth, gathered by a cord at the waist, and falling in straight, loose folds nearly to his feet. He shook hands with his visitors with his old ease and grace of manner. If there was any embarrassment in that meeting it was not manifested by Johnny Bellchambers. The room had no seats; they stood to converse.

"Glad to see you, old man," said Eyres, somewhat awkwardly. "Wasn't expecting to find you up here. Not a bad idea, though, after all. Society's an awful sham. Must be a relief to shake the giddy whirl and retire to—er—contemplation and —er—prayer and hymns, and those things."

"Oh, cut that, Tommy," said Bellchambers cheerfully. "Don't be afraid that I'll pass around the plate. I go through those thing-um-bobs with the rest of these old boys because they are the rules. I'm Brother Ambrose here, you know. I'm given just ten minutes to talk to you fellows. That's rather a new design in waistcoats you have on, isn't it, Gilliam? Are they wearing those things on Broadway now?"

"It's the same old Johnny," said Gilliam joyfully. "What the devil—I mean why—— Oh, confound it! What did you do it for, old man?"

"Peel the bathrobe," pleaded Eyres, almost tearfully, "and go back with us. The old crowd'll go wild to see you. This isn't in your line, Bell. I know half a dozen girls that wore the willow on the quiet when you shook us in that unaccountable way. Hand in your resignation, or get a dispensation, or whatever you have to do to get a release from this ice factory. You'll get catarrh here, Johnny—and—— My God! you haven't got any socks on!"

Bellchambers looked down at his sandalled feet and smiled.

"You fellows don't understand," he said soothingly. "It's nice of you to want me to go back, but the old life will never know me again. I have reached here the goal of all my ambitions. I am entirely happy and contented. Here I shall remain for the remainder of my days. You see this robe that I wear?" Bellchambers caressingly touched the straight-hanging garment: "At last I have found something that will not bag at the knees. I have attained——"

At that moment the deep boom of the great brass bell reverberated through the monastery. It must have been a summons to immediate devotions, for Brother Ambrose bowed his head, turned and left the chamber without another word. A slight wave of his hand as he passed through the stone doorway seemed to say farewell to his old friends. They left the monastery without seeing him again.

And this is the story that Tommy Eyres and Lancelot Gilliam brought back with them from their latest European tour.

CABBAGES AND KINGS

THE PROEM: BY THE CARPENTER

THEY will tell you in Anchuria, that President Miraflores, of that volatile republic, died by his own hand in the coast town of Coralio; that he had reached thus far in flight from the inconveniences of an imminent revolution; and that one hundred thousand dollars, government funds, which he carried with him in an American leather valise as a souvenir of his tempestuous administration, was never afterward recovered.

For a real, *a boy will show you his grave. It is back of the town near a little bridge that spans a mangrove swamp. A plain slab of wood stands at its head. Some one has burned upon the headstone with a hot iron this inscription:*

RAMON ANGEL DE LAS CRUZES
Y MIRAFLORES
PRESIDENTE DE LA REPUBLICA
DE ANCHURIA
QUE SEA SU JUEZ DIOS

It is characteristic of this buoyant people that they pursue no man beyond the grave. "Let God be his judge!"—Even with the hundred thousand unfound, though greatly coveted, the hue and cry went no further than that.

To the stranger or the guest the people of Coralio will relate the story of the tragic end of their former president: how he strove to escape from the country with the public funds and also with Doña Isabel Guilbert, the young American opera singer; and how, being apprehended by members of the opposing political party in Coralio, he shot himself through the head rather than give up the funds, and, in consequence, the Señorita *Guilbert. They will relate further that Doña Isabel, her adventurous bark of fortune shoaled by the simultaneous loss of her distinguished admirer and the souvenir hundred thousand, dropped anchor on this stagnant coast, awaiting a rising tide.*

They say in Coralio, that she found a prompt and prosperous tide in the form of Frank Goodwin, an American resident of the town, an investor who had grown wealthy by dealing in the products of the country—a banana king, a rubber prince, a sarsaparilla, indigo, and mahogany baron. The Señorita *Guilbert, you will be told, married* Señor *Goodwin one month after the president's death, thus, in the very moment when Fortune had ceased to smile, wresting from her a gift greater than the prize withdrawn.*

Of the American, Don Frank Goodwin, and of his wife the natives have nothing but good to say. Don Frank has lived among them for years, and has compelled their respect. His lady is easily queen of what social life the sober coast affords. The wife of the governor of the district, herself, who was of the proud Castilian family of Monteleon y Dolorosa de los Santos y Mendez, feels honoured to unfold her napkin with olive-hued, ringed hands at the table of Señora *Goodwin. Were you to refer (with your northern prejudices) to the vivacious past of Mrs. Goodwin, when her audacious and gleeful abandon in light opera captured the mature president's fancy, or to her share in that statesman's downfall and malfeasance, the Latin shrug of the shoulder would be your only answer and rebuttal. What prejudices there were in Coralio concerning* Señora *Goodwin seemed now to be in her favour, whatever they had been in the past.*

It would seem that the story is ended, instead of begun; that the close of a tragedy and the climax of a romance have covered the ground of interest; but, to the more curious reader, it shall be some slight instruction to trace the close threads that underlie the ingenuous web of circumstances.

The headpiece, bearing the name of President Miraflores, is daily scrubbed with soap-bark and sand. An old half-breed Indian tends the grave with fidelity and the dawdling minuteness of inherited sloth. He chops down the weeds and ever-springing grass with his machete, he plucks ants and scorpions and beetles from it with his horny fingers, and sprinkles its turf with water from the plaza fountain. There is no grave anywhere so well kept and ordered.

Only by following out the underlying threads will it be made clear why the old Indian, Galvez, is secretly paid to keep green the grave of President Miraflores by one who never saw the unfortunate statesman in life or in death, and why that one was wont to walk in the twilight, casting from a distance looks of gentle sadness upon that unhonoured mound.

Elsewhere than at Coralio one learns of the impetuous career of Isabel Guilbert. New Orleans gave her birth and the mingled French and Spanish creole nature that tinctured her life with such turbulence and warmth. She had little education, but a knowledge of men and motives that seemed to have come by instinct. Far beyond the common woman was she endowed with intrepid rashness, with a love for the pursuit of adventure to the brink of danger, and with desire for the pleasures of life. Her spirit was one to chafe under any curb; she was Eve after the fall, but before the bitterness of it was felt. She wore life as a rose in her bosom.

Of the legion of men who had been at her feet it was said that but one was so fortunate as to engage her fancy. To President Miraflores, the brilliant but unstable ruler of Anchuria, she yielded the key to her resolute heart. How, then, do we find her (as the Coralians would have told you) the wife of Frank Goodwin, and happily living a life of dull and dreamy inaction?

The underlying threads reach far, stretching across the sea. Following them out it will be made plain why "Shorty" O'Day, of the Columbia Detective Agency, resigned his position. And, for a lighter pastime, it shall be a duty and a pleasing sport to wander with Momus beneath the tropic stars where Melpomene once stalked austere. Now to cause laughter to echo from those lavish jungles and frowning crags, where formerly rang the cries of pirates' victims; to lay aside pike and cutlass and attack with quip and jollity; to draw one saving titter of mirth from the rusty casque of Romance —this were pleasant to do in the shade of the lemon-trees on that coast that is curved like lips set for smiling.

For there are yet tales of the Spanish Main. That segment of continent washed by the tempestuous Caribbean, and presenting to the sea a formidable border of tropical jungle topped by the overweening Cordilleras, is still begirt by mystery and romance. In past times buccaneers and revolutionists roused the echoes of its cliffs, and the condor wheeled perpetually above where, in the green groves, they made food for him with their match-locks and toledos. Taken and retaken by sea rovers, by adverse powers, and by sudden uprising of rebellious factions, the historic 300 miles of adventurous coast has scarcely known for hundreds of years whom rightly to call its master. Pizarro, Balboa, Sir Francis Drake, and Bolivar did what they could to make it a part of Christendom. Sir John Morgan, Lafitte and other eminent swashbucklers bombarded and pounded it in the name of Abaddon.

The game still goes on. The guns of the rovers are silenced, but the tintype man, the enlarged photograph brigand, the kodaking tourist and the scouts of the gentle brigade of fakirs have found it out, and carry on the work. The hucksters of Germany, France, and Sicily now bag its small change across their counters. Gentle-man adventurers throng the waiting-rooms of its rulers with proposals for railways and concessions. The little opéra-bouffe *nations play at government and intrigue until some day a big, silent gunboat glides into the offing and warns them not to break their toys. And with these changes comes also the small adventurer, with empty pockets to fill, light of heart, busy-brained—the modern fairy prince, bearing an alarm clock with which, more surely than by the sentimental kiss, to awaken the beautiful tropics from their centuries' sleep. Generally he wears a shamrock, which he matches pridefully against the extravagant palms; and it is he who has driven Melpomene to the wings, and set Comedy to dancing before the footlights of the Southern Cross.*

So, there is a little tale to tell of many things. Perhaps to the promiscuous ear of the Walrus it shall come with most avail; for in it there are indeed shoes and ships and sealing-wax and cabbage-palms and presidents instead of kings.

Add to these a little love and counterplotting, and scatter everywhere throughout the maze a trail of tropical dollars—dollars warmed no more by the torrid sun than by the hot palms of the scouts of Fortune—and, after all, here seems to be Life itself, with talk enough to weary the most garrulous of Walruses.

LXXXII: "FOX-IN-THE-MORNING"

CORALIO reclined, in the midday heat, like some vacuous beauty lounging in a guarded harem. The town lay at the sea's edge on a strip of alluvial coast. It was set like a little pearl in an emerald band. Behind it, and seeming almost to topple, imminent, above it, rose the sea-following range of the Cordilleras. In front the sea was spread, a smiling jailer, but even more incorruptible than the frowning mountains. The waves swished along the smooth beach; the parrots screamed in the orange and ceiba-trees; the palms waved their limber fronds foolishly, like an awkward chorus at the prima donna's cue to enter.

Suddenly the town was full of excitement. A native boy dashed down a grass-grown street, shrieking: "*Busca el Señor Goodwin. Ha venido un telégrafo por el!*"

The word passed quickly. Telegrams do not often come to anyone in Coralio. The cry for *Señor* Goodwin was taken up by a dozen officious voices. The main street running parallel to the beach became populated with those who desired to expedite the delivery of the dispatch. Knots of women with complexions varying from palest olive to deepest brown gathered at street corners and plaintively caroled: "*Un telégrafo por Señor Goodwin!*" The *comandante*, Don Señor el Coronel Encarnación Rios, who was loyal to the Ins and suspected Goodwin's devotion to the Outs, hissed "Aha!" and wrote in his secret memorandum book the accusive fact that *Señor* Goodwin had on that momentous date received a telegram.

In the midst of the hullabaloo a man stepped to the door of a small wooden building and looked out. Above the door was a sign that read "Keogh and Clancy"—a nomenclature that seemed not to be indigenous to that tropical soil. The man in the door was Billy Keogh, scout of fortune and progress, and latter-day rover of the Spanish Main. Tintypes and photographs were the weapons with which Keogh and Clancy were at that time assailing the hopeless shores. Outside the shop were set two large frames filled with specimens of their art and skill.

Keogh leaned in the doorway, his bold and humorous countenance wearing a look of interest at the unusual influx of life and sound into the street. When the meaning of the disturbance became clear to him he placed a hand beside his mouth and shouted: "Hey! Frank!" in such a robustious voice that the feeble clamour of the natives was drowned and silenced.

Fifty yards away, on the seaward side of the street, stood the abode of the consul for the United States. Out from the door of this building tumbled Goodwin at the call. He had been smoking with Willard Geddie, the consul, on the back porch of the consulate, which was conceded to bet he coolest spot in Coralio.

"Hurry up," shouted Keogh. "There's a riot in town on account of a telegram that's come for you. You want to be careful about these things, my boy. It won't do to trifle with the feelings of the public this way. You'll be getting a pink note some day with violet scent on it; and then the country'll be steeped in the throes of a revolution."

Goodwin had strolled up the street and met the boy with the message. The ox-eyed women gazed at him with shy admiration, for his type drew them. He was big, blond, and jauntily dressed in white linen, with buckskin *zapatos*. His manner was courtly, with a sort of kindly truculence in it, tempered by a merciful eye. When the telegram had been delivered, and the bearer of it dismissed with a gratuity, the relieved populace returned to the contiguities of shade from which curiosity had drawn it—the women to their baking in the mud ovens under the orange-trees, or to the interminable combing of their long, straight hair; the men to their cigarettes and gossip in the cantinas.

Goodwin sat on Keogh's doorstep, and read his telegram. It was from Bob Englehart, an American, who lived in San Mateo, the capital city of Anchuria, eighty miles in the interior. Englehart was a gold miner, an ardent revolutionist and "good people." That he was a man of resource and imagination was proven by the telegram he had sent. It had been his task to send a confidential message to his friend in Coralio. This could not have been accomplished in either Spanish or English, for the eye politic in Anchuria was an active one. The Ins and the Outs were perpetually on their guard. But Englehart was a diplomatist. There existed but one code upon which he might make requisition with promise of safety—the great and potent code of Slang. So here is the message that slipped, unconstrued, through the fingers of curious officials, and came to the eye of Goodwin:

"His Nibs skedaddled yesterday per jack-rabbit line with all the coin in the kitty and the bundle of muslin he's spoony about. The boodle is six figures short. Our crowd in good shape, but we need the spondulicks. You collar it. The main guy and the dry goods are headed for the briny. You know what to do.

"Bob."

This screed, remarkable as it was, had no mystery for Goodwin. He was the most successful of the small advance-guard of speculative Americans that had invaded Anchuria, and he had not reached that enviable pinnacle without having well exercised the arts of foresight and deduction. He had taken up political intrigue as a matter of business. He was acute enough to wield a certain influence among the leading schemers, and he was prosperous enough to be able to purchase the respect of the petty office-holders. There was always a revolutionary party; and to it he had always allied himself; for the adherents of a new administration received the rewards of their labours. There was now a Liberal party seeking to overturn President Miraflores. If the wheel successfully revolved, Goodwin stood to win a concession to 30,000 manzanas of the finest coffee lands in the interior. Certain incidents in the recent career of President Miraflores had excited a shrewd suspicion in Goodwin's mind that the government was near a dissolution from another cause than that of a revolution, and now Englehart's telegram had come as a corroboration of his wisdom.

The telegram, which had remained unintelligible to the Anchurian linguists, who had applied to it in vain their knowledge of Spanish and elemental English, conveyed a stimulating piece of news to Goodwin's understanding. It informed him that the president of the republic had decamped from the capital city with the contents of the treasury. Furthermore, that he was accompanied in his flight by that winning adventuress, Isabel Guilbert, the opera singer, whose troupe of performers had been entertained by the president at San Mateo during the past month on a scale less modest than that with which royal visitors are often content. The reference to the "jack-rabbit line" could mean nothing else than the mule-back system of transport that prevailed between Coralio and the capital. The hint that the "boodle" was "six figures short" made the condition of the national treasury lamentably clear. Also it was convincingly true that the ingoing party—its way now made a pacific one—would need the "spondulicks." Unless its pledges should be fulfilled, and the spoils held for the delectation of the victors, precarious indeed would be the position of the new government. Therefore it was exceeding necessary to "collar the main guy," and recapture the sinews of war and government.

Goodwin handed the message to Keogh.

"Read that, Billy," he said. "It's from Bob Englehart. Can you manage the cipher?"

Keogh sat in the other half of the doorway, and carefully perused the telegram.

"'Tis not a cipher," he said, finally. "'Tis what they call literature, and that's a system of language put in the mouths of people that they've never been introduced to by writers of imagination. The magazines invented it, but I never knew before that President Norvin Green had stamped it with the seal of his approval. 'Tis now no longer literature, but language. The dictionaries tried, but they couldn't make it go for anything but dialect. Sure, now that the Western Union indorses it, it won't be long till a race of people will spring up that speaks it."

"You're running too much to philology, Billy," said Goodwin. "Do you make out the meaning of it?"

"Sure," replied the philosopher of Fortune. "All languages come easy to the man who must know 'em. I've even failed to misunderstand an order to evacuate in classical Chinese when it was backed up by the muzzle of a breech-loader. This little literary essay I hold in my hands means a game of 'Fox-in-the-Morning.' Ever play that, Frank, when you was a kid?"

"I think so," said Goodwin, laughing. "You join hands all 'round, and——"

"You do not," interrupted Keogh. "You've got a fine sporting game mixed up in your head with 'All Around the Rose-bush.' The spirit of 'Fox-in-the-Morning' is opposed to the holding of hands. I'll tell you how it's played. This president man and his companion in play, they stand up over in San Mateo, ready for the run, and shout: 'Fox-in-the-Morning!' Me and you, standing here, we say: 'Goose and the Gander!' They say: 'How many miles is it to London town?' We say: 'Only a few, if your legs are long enough. How many comes out?' They say: 'More than you're able to catch.' And then the game commences."

"I catch the idea," said Goodwin. "It won't do to let the goose and gander slip through our fingers, Billy; their feathers are too valuable. Our crowd is prepared and able to step into the shoes of the government at once; but with the treasury empty we'd stay in power about as long as a tenderfoot would stick on an untamed bronco. We must play the fox on every foot of the coast to prevent their getting out of the country."

"By the mule-back schedule," said Keogh, "it's five days down from San Mateo. We've got plenty of time to set our outposts. There's only three places on the coast where they can hope to sail from—here and Solitas and Alazan. They're the only points we'll have to guard. It's as easy as a chess problem—fox to play, and mate in three moves. Oh, goosey, goosey, gander, whither do you wander? By the blessing of the literary telegraph the boodle of this benighted fatherland shall be preserved to the honest political party that is seeking to overthrow it."

The situation had been justly outlined by Keogh. The down trail from the capital was at all times a weary road to travel. A jiggety-joggety journey it was; ice-cold and hot, wet and dry. The trail climbed appalling mountains, wound like a rotten string about the brows of breathless precipices, plunged through chilling snow-fed streams, and wriggled like a snake through sunless forests teeming with menacing insect and animal life. After descending to the foothills it turned to a trident, the central prong ending at Alazan. Another branched off to Coralio; the third penetrated to

Solitas. Between the sea and the foothills stretched the five miles' breadth of alluvial coast. Here was the flora of the tropics in its rankest and most prodigal growth. Spaces here and there had been wrested from the jungle and planted with bananas and cane and orange groves. The rest was a riot of wild vegetation, the home of monkeys, tapirs, jaguars, alligators and prodigious reptiles and insects. Where no road was cut a serpent could scarcely make its way through the tangle of vines and creepers. Across the treacherous mangrove swamps few things without wings could safely pass. Therefore the fugitives could hope to reach the coast only by one of the routes named.

"Keep the matter quiet, Billy," advised Goodwin. "We don't want the Ins to know that the president is in flight. I suppose Bob's information is something of a scoop in the capital as yet. Otherwise he would not have tried to make his message a confidential one; and, besides, everybody would have heard the news. I'm going around now to see Dr. Zavalla, and start a man up the trail to cut the telegraph wire."

As Goodwin rose, Keogh threw his hat upon the grass by the door and expelled a tremendous sigh.

"What's the trouble, Billy?" asked Goodwin, pausing. "That's the first time I ever heard you sigh."

" 'Tis the last," said Keogh. "With that sorrowful puff of wind I resign myself to a life of praiseworthy but harassing honesty. What are tintypes, if you please, to the opportunities of the great and hilarious class of ganders and geese? Not that I would be a president, Frank—and the boodle he's got is too big for me to handle—but in some ways

I feel my conscience hurting me for addicting myself to photographing a nation instead of running away with it. Frank, did you ever see the 'bundle of muslin' that His Excellency has wrapped up and carried off?"

"Isabel Guilbert?" said Goodwin, laughing. "No, I never did. From what I've heard of her, though, I imagine that she wouldn't stick at anything to carry her point. Don't get romantic, Billy. Sometimes I begin to fear that there's Irish blood in your ancestry."

"I never saw her either," went on Keogh; "but they say she's got all the ladies of mythology, sculpture, and fiction reduced to chromos. They say she can look at a man once, and he'll turn monkey and climb trees to pick coconuts for her. Think of that president man with Lord knows how many hundreds of thousands of dollars in one hand, and this muslin siren in the other, galloping downhill on a sympathetic mule amid songbirds and flowers! And here is Billy Keogh, because he is virtuous, condemned to the unprofitable swindle of slandering the faces of missing links on tin for an honest living! 'Tis an injustice of nature."

"Cheer up," said Goodwin. "You are a pretty poor fox to be envying a gander. Maybe the enchanting Guilbert will take a fancy to you and your tintypes after we impoverish her royal escort."

"She could do worse," reflected Keogh; "but she won't. 'Tis not a tintype gallery, but the gallery of the gods that she's fitted to adorn. She's a very wicked lady, and the president man is in luck. But I hear Clancy swearing in the back room for having to do all the work." And Keogh plunged for the rear of the "gallery," whistling gaily in a spontaneous way that belied his recent sigh over the questionable good luck of the flying president.

Goodwin turned from the main street into a much narrower one that intersected it at a right angle.

These side streets were covered by a growth of thick, rank grass, which was kept to a navigable shortness by the machetes of the police. Stone sidewalks, little more than a ledge in width, ran along the base of the mean and monotonous adobe houses. At the outskirts of the village these streets dwindled to nothing, and here were set the palm-thatched huts of the Caribs and the poorer natives, and the shabby cabins of negroes from Jamaica and the West India islands. A few structures raised their heads above the red-tiled roofs of the one-story houses—the bell-tower of the *Calaboza*, the Hotel de los Estranjeros, the residence of the Vesuvius Fruit Company's agent, the store and residence of Bernard Brannigan, a ruined cathedral in which Columbus had once set foot, and, most imposing of all, the Casa Morena—the summer "White House" of the President of Anchuria. On the principal street running along the beach—the Broadway of Coralio—were the larger stores, the government *bodega* and post office, the *cuartel*, the rum-shops and the market-place.

On his way Goodwin passed the house of Bernard Brannigan. It was a modern wooden building, two stories in height. The ground floor was occupied by Brannigan's store, the upper one contained the living apartments. A wide cool porch ran around the house half-way up its outer walls. A handsome, vivacious girl neatly dressed in flowing white leaned over the railing and smiled down upon Goodwin.

She was no darker than many an Andalusian of high descent; and she sparkled and glowed like a tropical moonlight.

"Good evening, Miss Paula," said Goodwin, taking off his hat, with his ready smile. There was little difference in his manner whether he addressed women or men. Everybody in Coralio liked to receive the salutation of the big American.

"Is there any news, Mr. Goodwin? Please don't say no. Isn't it warm? I feel just like Mariana in her moated grange—or was it a range?—it's hot enough."

"No, there's no news to tell, I believe," said Goodwin, with a mischievous look in his eye, "except that old Geddie is getting grumpier and crosser every day. If something doesn't happen to relieve his mind I'll have to quit smoking on his back porch—and there's no other place available that is cool enough."

"He isn't grumpy," said Paula Brannigan, impulsively, "when he——"

But she ceased suddenly, and drew back with a deepening colour; for her mother had been a *mestizo* lady, and the Spanish blood had brought to Paula a certain shyness that was an adornment to the other half of her demonstrative nature.

LXXXIII: THE LOTUS AND THE BOTTLE

WILLARD GEDDIE, consul for the United States in Coralio, was working leisurely on his yearly report. Goodwin, who had strolled in as he did daily for a smoke on the much-coveted porch, had found him so absorbed in his work that he departed after roundly abusing the consul for his lack of hospitality.

"I shall complain to the civil service department," said Goodwin—"or is it a department?—perhaps it's only a theory. One gets neither civility nor service from you. You won't talk; and you won't set out anything to drink. What kind of a way is that of representing your government?"

Goodwin strolled out and across to the hotel to see if he could bully the quarantine doctor into a game on Coralio's solitary billiard-table. His plans were completed for the interception of the fugitives from the capital; and now it was but a waiting game that he had to play.

The consul was interested in his report. He was only twenty-four; and he had not been in Coralio long enough for his enthusiasm to cool in the heat of the tropics—a paradox that may be allowed between Cancer and Capricorn.

So many thousand bunches of bananas, so many thousand oranges and coconuts, so many ounces of gold dust, pounds of rubber, coffee, indigo and sarsaparilla—actually, exports were twenty per cent. greater than for the previous year!

A little thrill of satisfaction ran through the consul. Perhaps, he thought, the State Department, upon reading his introduction, would notice—and then he leaned back in his chair and laughed. He was getting as bad as the others. For the moment he had forgotten that Coralio was an insignificant town in an insignificant republic lying along the by-ways of a second-rate sea. He thought of Gregg, the quarantine doctor, who subscribed for the London *Lancet*, expecting to find it quoting his reports to the home Board of Health concerning the yellow fever germ. The consul knew that not one in fifty of his acquaintances in the States had ever heard of Coralio. He knew that two men, at any rate, would have to read his report—some underling in the State Department and a compositor in the Public Printing Office. Perhaps the typesticker would note the increase of commerce in Coralio, and speak of it, over the cheese and beer, to a friend.

He had just written: "Most unaccountable is the supineness of the large exporters in the United States in permitting the French and German houses to practically control all trade interests of this rich and productive country"—when he heard the hoarse notes of a steamer's siren.

Geddie laid down his pen and gathered his Panama hat and umbrella. By the sound he knew it to be the *Valhalla*, one of the line of fruit vessels plying for the Vesuvius Company. Down to the *niños* of five years, every one in Coralio could name you each incoming steamer by the note of her siren.

The consul sauntered by a roundabout, shaded way to the beach. By reason of long practice he gauged his stroll so accurately that by the time he arrived on the sandy shore the boat of the customs officials was rowing back from the steamer, which had been boarded and inspected according to the laws of Anchuria.

There is no harbour at Coralio. Vessels of the draught of the *Valhalla* must ride at anchor a mile from shore. When they take on fruit it is conveyed on lighters and freighter sloops. At Solitas, where there was a fine harbour, ships of many kinds were to be seen, but in the roadstead off Coralio scarcely any save the fruiters paused. Now and then a tramp coaster, or a mysterious brig from Spain, or a saucy French barque would hang innocently for a few days in the offing. Then the custom-house crew would become doubly vigilant and wary. At night a sloop or two would be making strange trips in and out along the shore; and in the morning the stock of Three-Star Hennessey, wines and drygoods in Coralio would be found vastly increased. It has also been said that the customs officials jingled more silver in the pockets of their red-striped trousers, and that the record books showed no increase in import duties received.

The customs boat and the *Valhalla* gig reached the shore at the same time. When they grounded in the shallow water there was still five yards of rolling surf between them and dry sand. Then half-clothed Caribs dashed into the water, and brought in on their backs the *Valhalla's* purser, and the little native officials in their cotton undershirts, blue trousers with red stripes, and flapping straw hats.

At college Geddie had been a treasure as a first-baseman. He now closed his umbrella, stuck it upright in the sand, and stooped, with his hands resting upon his knees. The purser, burlesquing the pitcher's contortions, hurled at the consul the heavy roll of newspaper, tied with a string, that the steamer always brought for him. Geddie leaped high and caught the roll with a sounding "thwack." The loungers on the beach—about a third of the population of the town—laughed and applauded delightedly. Every week they expected to see that roll of papers delivered and received in that same manner, and they were never disappointed. Innovations did not flourish in Coralio.

The consul re-hoisted his umbrella and walked back to the consulate.

This home of a great nation's representative was a wooden structure of two rooms, with a native-built gallery of poles, bamboo and nipa palm running on three sides of it. One room was the official apartment, furnished chastely with a flat-top desk, a hammock, and three uncomfortable cane-seated chairs. Engravings of the first and latest president of the country represented hung against the wall. The other room was the consul's living apartment.

It was eleven o'clock when he returned from the beach, and therefore breakfast-time. Chanca, the Carib woman who cooked for him, was just serving the meal on the side of the gallery facing the sea —a spot famous as the coolest in Coralio. The breakfast consisted of shark's fin soup, stew of land crabs, breadfruit, a boiled iguana steak, aguacates, a freshly cut pineapple, claret and coffee.

Geddie took his seat, and unrolled with luxurious laziness his bundle of newspapers. Here in Coralio for two days or longer he would read of goings-on in the world very much as we of the world read those whimsical contributions to inexact science that assume to portray the doings of the Martians. After he had finished with the papers they would be sent on the rounds of the other English-speaking residents of the town.

The paper that came first to his hand was one of those bulky mattresses of printed stuff upon which the readers of certain New York journals are supposed to take their Sabbath literary nap. Opening this the consul rested it upon the table, supporting its weight with the aid of the back of a chair. Then he partook of his meal deliberately, turning the leaves from time to time and glancing half idly at the contents.

Presently he was struck by something familiar to him in a picture—a half-page, badly printed reproduction of a photograph of a vessel. Languidly interested, he leaned for a nearer scrutiny and a view of the florid headlines of the column next to the picture.

Yes; he was not mistaken. The engraving was of the eight-hundred-ton yacht *Idalia*, belonging to "that prince of good fellows, Midas of the money market, and society's pink of perfection, J. Ward Tolliver."

Slowly sipping his black coffee, Geddie read the column of print. Following a listed statement of Mr. Tolliver's real estate and bonds, came a description of the yacht's furnishings, and then the grain of news no bigger than a mustard seed. Mr. Tolliver, with a party of favoured guests, would sail the next day on a six weeks' cruise along the Central American and South American coasts and among the Bahama Islands. Among the guests were Mrs. Cumberland Payne and Miss Ida Payne, of Norfolk.

The writer, with the fatuous presumption that was demanded of him by his readers, had concocted a romance suited to their palates. He bracketed the names of Miss Payne and Mr. Tolliver until he had well-nigh read the marriage ceremony over them. He played coyly and insinuatingly with the strings of "*on dit*" and "Madame Rumour" and "a little bird" and "no one would be surprised," and ended with congratulations.

Geddie, having finished his breakfast, took his papers to the edge of the gallery, and sat there in his favourite steamer chair with his feet on the bamboo railing. He lighted a cigar, and looked out upon the sea. He felt a glow of satisfaction at finding he was so little disturbed by what he had read. He told himself that he had conquered the distress that had sent him, a voluntary exile, to this far land of the lotus. He could never forget Ida, of course; but there was no longer any pain in thinking about her. When they had had that misunderstanding and quarrel he had impulsively sought this consulship, with the desire to retaliate upon her by detaching himself from her world and presence. He had succeeded thoroughly in that. During the twelve months of his life in Coralio no word had passed between them, though he had sometimes heard of her through the dilatory correspondence with the few friends to whom he still wrote. Still he could not repress a little thrill of satisfaction at knowing that she had not yet married Tolliver or anyone else. But evidently Tolliver had not yet abandoned hope.

Well, it made no difference to him now. He had eaten of the lotus. He was happy and content in this land of perpetual afternoon. Those old days of life in the States seemed like an irritating dream. He hoped Ida would be as happy as he was. The climate as balmy as that of distant Avalon; the fetterless, idyllic round of enchanted days; the life among this indolent, romantic people—a life full of music, flowers, and low laughter; the influence of the imminent sea and mountains, and the many shapes of love and magic and beauty that bloomed in the white tropic nights—with all he was more than content. Also, there was Paula Brannigan.

Geddie intended to marry Paula—if, of course,

she would consent; but he felt rather sure that she would do that. Somehow, he kept postponing his proposal. Several times he had been quite near to it; but a mysterious something always held him back. Perhaps it was only the unconscious, instinctive conviction that the act would sever the last tie that bound him to his old world.

He could be very happy with Paula. Few of the native girls could be compared with her. She had attended a convent school in New Orleans for two years; and when she chose to display her accomplishments no one could detect any difference between her and the girls of Norfolk and Manhattan. But it was delicious to see her at home dressed, as she sometimes was, in the native costume, with bare shoulders and flowing sleeves.

Bernard Brannigan was the great merchant of Coralio. Besides his store, he maintained a train of pack mules, and carried on a lively trade with the interior towns and villages. He had married a native lady of high Castilian descent, but with a tinge of Indian brown showing through her olive cheek. The union of the Irish and the Spanish had produced, as it so often has, an offshoot of rare beauty and variety. They were very excellent people indeed, and the upper story of their house was ready to be placed at the service of Geddie and Paula as soon as he should make up his mind to speak about it.

By the time two hours were whiled away the consul tired of reading. The papers lay scattered about him on the gallery. Reclining there, he gazed dreamily out upon an Eden. A clump of banana plants interposed their broad shields between him and the sun. The gentle slope from the consulate to the sea was covered with the dark-green foliage of lemon-trees and orange-trees just bursting into bloom. A lagoon pierced the land like a dark, jagged crystal, and above it a pale ceiba-tree rose almost to the clouds. The waving coco-nut palms on the beach flared their decorative green leaves against the slate of an almost quiescent sea. His senses were cognisant of brilliant scarlet and ochres amid the vert of the coppice, of odours of fruit and bloom and the smoke from Chanca's clay oven under the calabash-tree; of the treble laughter of the native women in their huts, the song of the robin, the salt taste of the breeze, the diminuendo of the faint surf running along the shore—and, gradually, of a white speck, growing to a blur, that intruded itself upon the drab prospect of the sea.

Lazily interested, he watched this blur increase until it became the *Idalia* steaming at full speed, coming down the coast. Without changing his position he kept his eyes upon the beautiful white yacht as she drew slowly near, and came opposite to Coralio. Then, sitting upright, he saw her float steadily past and on. Scarcely a mile of sea had separated her from the shore. He had seen the frequent flash of her polished brass work and the stripes of her deck awnings—so much, and no more. Like a ship on a magic-lantern slide the *Idalia* had crossed the illuminated circle of the consul's little world, and was gone. Save for the tiny cloud of smoke that was left hanging over the brim of the sea, she might have been an immaterial thing, a chimera of his idle brain.

Geddie went into his office and sat down to dawdle over his report. If the reading of the article in the paper had left him unshaken, this silent passing of the *Idalia* had done for him still more: It had brought the calm and peace of a situation from which all uncertainty had been erased. He knew that men sometimes hope without being aware of it. Now, since she had come two thousand miles and had passed without a sign, not even his unconscious self need cling to the past any longer.

After dinner, when the sun was low behind the mountains, Geddie walked on the little strip of beach under the coconuts. The wind was blowing mildly landward, and the surface of the sea was rippled by tiny wavelets.

A miniature breaker, spreading with a soft "swish" upon the sand, brought with it something round and shiny that rolled back again as the wave receded. The next influx beached it clear, and Geddie picked it up. The thing was a long-necked wine bottle of colourless glass. The cork had been driven in tightly to the level of the mouth, and the end covered with dark-red sealing-wax. The bottle contained only what seemed to be a sheet of paper, much curled from the manipulation it had undergone while being inserted. In the sealing-wax was the impression of a seal—probably of a signet-ring, bearing the initials of a monogram; but the impression had been hastily made, and the letters were past anything more certain than a shrewd conjecture. Ida Payne had always worn a signet-ring in preference to any other finger decoration. Geddie thought he could make out the familiar "I.P.," and a queer sensation of disquietude went over him. More personal and intimate was this reminder of her than had been the sight of the vessel she was doubtless on. He walked back to his house, and set the bottle on his desk.

Throwing off his hat and coat, and lighting a lamp—for the night had crowded precipitately upon the brief twilight—he began to examine his piece of sea salvage.

By holding the bottle near the light and turning it judiciously, he made out that it contained a double sheet of note-paper filled with close writing; further, that the paper was of the same size and shade as that always used by Ida; and that, to the best of his belief, the handwriting was hers. The imperfect glass of the bottle so distorted the rays of light that he could read no word of the writing; but certain capital letters, of which he caught comprehensive glimpses, were Ida's, he felt sure.

There was a little smile both of perplexity and amusement in Geddie's eyes as he set the bottle down, and laid three cigars side by side on his desk. He fetched his steamer chair from the gallery, and stretched himself comfortably. He would smoke those three cigars while considering the problem.

For it amounted to a problem. He almost wished that he had not found the bottle; but the bottle was there. Why should it have drifted in from the sea, whence come so many disquieting things, to disturb his peace?

In this dreamy land, where time seemed so redundant, he had fallen into the habit of bestowing much thought upon trifling matters.

He began to speculate upon many fanciful theories concerning the story of the bottle, rejecting each in turn.

Ships in danger of wreck or disablement sometimes cast forth such precarious messengers calling for aid. But he had seen the *Idalia* not three hours before, safe and speeding. Suppose the crew had mutinied and imprisoned the passengers below, and the message was one begging for succour! But, premising such an improbable outrage, would the agitated captives have taken the pains to fill four pages of note-paper with carefully penned arguments to their rescue?

Thus by elimination he soon rid the matter of the more unlikely theories, and was reduced—though aversely—to the less assailable one that the bottle contained a message to himself. Ida knew he was in Coralio; she must have launched the bottle while the yacht was passing and the wind blowing fairly toward the shore.

As soon as Geddie reached this conclusion a wrinkle came between his brows and a stubborn look settled around his mouth. He sat looking out through the doorway at the gigantic fireflies traversing the quiet streets.

If this was a message to him from Ida, what could it mean save an overture toward a reconciliation? And if that, why had she not used the sane methods of the post instead of this uncertain and even flippant means of communication? A note in an empty bottle, cast into the sea! There was something light and frivolous about it, if not actually contemptuous.

The thought stirred his pride and subdued whatever emotions had been resurrected by the finding of the bottle.

Geddie put on his coat and hat and walked out. He followed a street that led him along the border of the little plaza, where a band was playing and people were rambling, care-free and indolent. Some timorous *señoritas*, scurrying past with fireflies tangled in the jetty braids of their hair, glanced at him with shy, flattering eyes. The air was languorous with the scent of jasmine and orange-blossoms.

The consul stayed his steps at the house of Bernard Brannigan. Paula was swinging in a hammock on the gallery. She rose from it like a bird from its nest. The colour came to her cheek at the sound of Geddie's voice.

He was charmed at the sight of her costume—a flounced muslin dress, with a little jacket of white flannel, all made with neatness and style. He suggested a stroll, and they walked out to the old Indian well on the hill road. They sat on the curb, and there Geddie made the expected but long-deferred speech. Certain though he had been that she would not say him nay, he was thrilled with joy at the completeness and sweetness of her surrender. Here was surely a heart made for love and steadfastness. Here was no caprice or questionings or captious standards of convention.

When Geddie kissed Paula at the door that night he was happier than he had ever been before. "Here in this hollow lotus land, ever to live and lie reclined," seemed to him, as it has seemed to many mariners, the best as well as the easiest. His future would be an ideal one. He had attained a Paradise without a serpent. His Eve would be indeed a part of him, unbeguiled, and therefore more beguiling. He had made his decision to-night, and his heart was full of serene, assured content.

Geddie went back to his house whistling that finest and saddest love song, "La Golondrina." At the door his tame monkey leaped down from his shelf, chattering briskly. The consul turned to his desk to get him some nuts he usually kept there. Reaching in the half-darkness, his hand struck against the bottle. He started as if he had touched the cold rotundity of a serpent.

He had forgotten that the bottle was there.

He lighted the lamp and fed the monkey. Then, very deliberately, he lighted a cigar, and took the bottle in his hand, and walked down the path to the beach.

There was a moon, and the sea was glorious. The breeze had shifted, as it did each evening, and was now rushing steadily seaward.

Stepping to the water's edge, Geddie hurled the unopened bottle far out into the sea. It disappeared for a moment, and then shot upward twice its length. Geddie stood still, watching it. The moonlight was so bright that he could see it bobbing up and down with the little waves. Slowly it receded from the shore, flashing and turning as it went. The wind was carrying it out to sea. Soon it became a mere speck, doubtfully discerned at irregular intervals; and then the mystery of it was swallowed up by the greater mystery of the ocean. Geddie stood still upon the beach, smoking and looking out upon the water.

"Simon!—Oh, Simon!—wake up there, Simon!" bawled a sonorous voice at the edge of the water.

Old Simon Cruz was a half-breed fisherman and smuggler who lived in a hut on the beach. Out of his earliest nap Simon was thus awakened.

He slipped on his shoes and went outside. Just landing from one of the *Valhalla's* boats was the third mate of that vessel, who was an acquaintance of Simon's, and three sailors from the fruiter.

"Go up, Simon," called the mate, "and find Dr. Gregg or Mr. Goodwin or anybody that's a friend to Mr. Geddie, and bring 'em here at once."

"Saints of the skies!" said Simon sleepily, "nothing has happened to Mr. Geddie?"

"He's under that tarpauling," said the mate, pointing to the boat, "and he's rather more than half drownded. We seen him from the steamer nearly a mile out from shore, swimmin' like mad after a bottle that was floatin' in the water, outward bound. We lowered the gig and started for him. He nearly had his hand on the bottle, when he gave out and went under. We pulled him out in time to save him, maybe; but the doctor is the one to decide that."

"A bottle?" said the old man, rubbing his eyes. He was not yet fully awake. "Where is the bottle?"

"Driftin' along out there some'eres," said the mate, jerking his thumb toward the sea. "Get on with you, Simon."

LXXXIV: SMITH

GOODWIN and the ardent patriot, Zavalla, took all the precautions that their foresight could contrive to prevent the escape of President Miraflores and his companion. They sent trusted messengers up the coast to Solitas and Alazan to warn the local leaders of the flight, and to instruct them to patrol the water-line and arrest the fugitives at all hazards should they reveal themselves in that territory. After this was done there remained only to cover the district about Coralio and await the coming of the quarry. The nets were well spread. The roads were so few, the opportunities for embarkation so limited, and the two or three probable points of exit so well guarded that it would be strange indeed if there should slip through the meshes so much of the country's dignity, romance, and collateral. The president would, without doubt, move as secretly as possible, and endeavour to board a vessel by stealth from some secluded point along the shore.

On the fourth day after the receipt of Englehart's telegram, the *Karlsefin*, a Norwegian steamer chartered by the New Orleans fruit trade, anchored off Coralio with three hoarse toots of her siren. The *Karlsefin* was not one of the line operated by the Vesuvius Fruit Company. She was something of a dilettante, doing odd jobs for a company that was scarcely important enough to figure as a rival to the Vesuvius. The movements of the *Karlsefin* were dependent upon the state of the market. Sometimes she would ply steadily between the Spanish Main and New Orleans in the regular transport of fruit; next she would be making erratic trips to Mobile or Charleston, or even as far north as New York, according to the distribution of the fruit supply.

Goodwin lounged upon the beach with the usual crowd of idlers that had gathered to view the steamer. Now that President Miraflores might be expected to reach the borders of his abjured country at any time, the orders were to keep a strict and unrelenting watch. Every vessel that approached the shores might now be considered a possible means of escape for the fugitives; and an eye was kept even on the sloops and dories that belonged to the sea-going contingent of Coralio. Goodwin and Zavalla moved everywhere, but without ostentation, watching the loopholes of escape.

The customs officials crowded importantly into their boat and rowed out to the *Karlsefin*. A boat from the steamer landed her purser with his papers, and took out the quarantine doctor with his green umbrella and clinical thermometer. Next a swarm of Caribs began to load upon lighters the thousands of bunches of bananas heaped upon the shore and row them out to the steamer. The *Karlsefin* had no passenger list, and was soon done with the attention of the authorities. The purser declared that the steamer would remain at anchor until morning, taking on her fruit during the night. The *Karlsefin* had come, he said, from New York, to which port her latest cargo of oranges and coconuts had been conveyed. Two or three of the freighter sloops were engaged to assist in the work, for the captain was anxious to make a quick return in order to reap the advantage offered by a certain dearth of fruit in the States.

About four o'clock in the afternoon another of those marine monsters, not very familiar in those waters, hove in sight, following the fateful *Idalia* —a graceful steam yacht, painted a light buff, clean-cut as a steel engraving. The beautiful vessel hovered off-shore, see-sawing the waves as lightly as a duck in a rain barrel. A swift boat manned by a crew in uniform came ashore, and a stocky-built man leaped to the sands.

The new-comer seemed to turn a disapproving eye upon the rather motley congregation of native Anchurians, and made his way at once toward

Goodwin, who was the most conspicuously Anglo-Saxon figure present. Goodwin greeted him with courtesy.

Conversation developed that the newly landed one was named Smith, and that he had come in a yacht. A meagre biography, truly; for the yacht was most apparent; and the "Smith" not beyond a reasonable guess before the revelation. Yet to the eye of Goodwin, who had seen several things, there was a discrepancy between Smith and his yacht. A bullet-headed man Smith was, with an oblique, dead eye and the moustache of a cocktail-mixer. And unless he had shifted costumes before putting off for shore he had affronted the deck of his correct vessel clad in a pearl-grey derby, a gay plaid suit and vaudeville neckwear. Men owning pleasure yachts generally harmonize better with them.

Smith looked business, but he was no advertiser. He commented upon the scenery, remarking upon its fidelity to the pictures in the geography; and then inquired for the United States consul. Goodwin pointed out the starred-and-striped bunting hanging above the little consulate, which was concealed behind the orange-trees.

"Mr. Geddie, the consul, will be sure to be there," said Goodwin. "He was very nearly drowned a few days ago while taking a swim in the sea, and the doctor has ordered him to remain indoors for some time."

Smith ploughed his way through the sand to the consulate, his haberdashery creating violent discord against the smooth tropical blues and greens.

Geddie was lounging in his hammock, somewhat pale of face and languid in pose. On that night when the *Valhalla's* boat had brought him ashore, apparently drenched to death by the sea, Doctor Gregg and his other friends had toiled for hours to preserve the little spark of life that remained to him. The bottle, with its impotent message, was gone out to sea, and the problem that it had provoked was reduced to a simple sum in addition—one and one make two, by the rule of arithmetic; one by the rule of romance.

There is a quaint old theory that man may have two souls—a peripheral one which serves ordinarily, and a central one which is stirred only at certain times, but then with activity and vigour. While under the domination of the former a man will shave, vote, pay taxes, give money to his family, buy subscription books and comport himself on the average plan. But let the central soul suddenly become dominant, and he may, in the twinkling of an eye, turn upon the partner of his joys with furious execration; he may change his politics while you could snap your fingers; he may deal out deadly insult to his dearest friend; he may get him, instanter, to a monastery or a dance hall; he may elope, or hang himself—or he may write a song or poem, or kiss his wife unasked, or give his funds to the search of a microbe. Then the peripheral soul will return; and we have our safe, sane citizen again. It is but the revolt of the Ego against Order; and its effect is to shake up the atoms only that they may settle where they belong.

Geddie's revulsion had been a mild one—no more than a swim in a summer sea after so inglorious an object as a drifting bottle. And now he was himself again. Upon his desk, ready for the post, was a letter to his government tendering his resignation as consul, to be effective as soon as another could be appointed in his place. For Bernard Brannigan, who never did things in a half-way manner, was to take Geddie at once for a partner in his very profitable and various enterprises; and Paula was happily engaged in plans for refurnishing and decorating the upper story of the Brannigan house.

The consul rose from his hammock when he saw the conspicuous stranger in his door.

"Keep your seat, old man," said the visitor, with an airy wave of his large hand. "My name's Smith; and I've come in a yacht. You are the consul—is that right? A big, cool guy on the beach directed me here. Thought I'd pay my respects to the flag."

"Sit down," said Geddie. "I've been admiring your craft ever since it came in sight. Looks like a fast sailer. What's her tonnage?"

"Search me!" said Smith. "I don't know what she weighs in at. But she's got a tidy gait. The *Rambler*—that's her name—don't take the dust of anything afloat. This is my first trip on her. I'm taking a squint along this coast just to get an idea of the countries where the rubber and red pepper and revolutions come from. I had no idea there was so much scenery down here. Why, Central Park ain't in it with this neck of the woods. I'm from New York. They get monkeys, and cocoanuts, and parrots down here—is that right?"

"We have them all," said Geddie. "I'm quite sure that our fauna and flora would take a prize over Central Park."

"Maybe they would," admitted Smith cheerfully. "I haven't seen them yet. But I guess you've got us skinned on the animal and vegetation question. You don't have much travel here, do you?"

"Travel?" queried the consul. "I suppose you

mean passengers on the steamers. No; very few people land in Coralio. An investor now and then—tourists and sightseers generally go farther down the coast to one of the larger towns where there is a harbour."

"I see a ship out there loading up with bananas," said Smith. "Any passengers on her?"

"That's the *Karlsefin*," said the consul. "She's a tramp fruiter—made her last trip to New York, I believe. No; she brought no passengers. I saw her boat come ashore, and there was no one. About the only exciting recreation we have here is watching steamers when they arrive; and a passenger on one of them generally causes the whole town to turn out. If you are going to remain in Coralio a while, Mr. Smith, I'll be glad to take you around to meet some people. There are four or five American chaps that are good to know, besides the native high-fliers."

"Thanks," said the yachtsman, "but I wouldn't put you to the trouble. I'd like to meet the guys you speak of, but I won't be here long enough to do much knocking around. That cool gent on the beach spoke of a doctor; can you tell me where I could find him? The *Rambler* ain't quite as steady on her feet as a Broadway hotel; and a fellow gets a touch of sea-sickness now and then. Thought I'd strike the croaker for a handful of the little sugar pills, in case I need 'em."

"You will be apt to find Dr. Gregg at the hotel," said the consul. "You can see it from the door—it's that two-story building with the balcony, where the orange-trees are."

The Hotel de los Estranjeros was a dreary hostelry, in great disuse both by strangers and friends. It stood at a corner of the Street of the Holy Sepulchre. A grove of small orange-trees crowded against one side of it, enclosed by a low, rock wall over which a tall man might easily step. The house was of plastered adobe, stained a hundred shades of colour by the salt breeze and the sun. Upon its upper balcony opened a central door and two windows containing broad jalousies instead of sashes.

The lower floor communicated by two doorways with the narrow, rock-paved sidewalk. The *pulperia*—or drinking shop—of the proprietress, Madama Timotea Ortiz, occupied the ground floor. On the bottles of brandy, *anisada*, Scotch "smoke," and inexpensive wines behind the little counter, the dust lay thick, save where the fingers of infrequent customers had left irregular prints. The upper story contained four or five guest-rooms which were rarely put to their destined use. Sometimes a fruit-grower, riding in from his plantation to confer with his agent, would pass a melancholy night in the dismal upper story; sometimes a minor native official on some trifling government quest would have his pomp and majesty awed by Madama's sepulchral hospitality. But Madama sat behind her bar content, not desiring to quarrel with Fate. If anyone required meat, drink or lodging at the Hotel de los Estranjeros they had but to come, and be served. *Está bueno.* If they came not, why, then, they came not. *Está bueno.*

As the exceptional yachtsman was making his way down the precarious sidewalk of the Street of the Holy Sepulchre, the solitary permanent guest of that decaying hotel sat at its door, enjoying the breeze from the sea.

Dr. Gregg, the quarantine physician, was a man

of fifty or sixty, with a florid face and the longest beard between Topeka and Terra del Fuego. He held his position by virtue of an appointment by the Board of Health of a seaport city in one of the Southern states. That city feared the ancient enemy of every Southern seaport—the yellow fever—and it was the duty of Dr. Gregg to examine crew and passengers of every vessel leaving Coralio for preliminary symptoms. The duties were light, and the salary, for one who lived in Coralio, ample. Surplus time there was in plenty; and the good doctor added to his gains by a large private practice among the residents of the coast. The fact that he did not know ten words of Spanish was no obstacle; a pulse could be felt and a fee collected without one being a linguist. Add to the description the facts that the doctor had a story to tell concerning the operation of trepanning which no listener had ever allowed him to conclude, and that he believed in brandy as a prophylactic; and the special points of interest possessed by Dr. Gregg will have become exhausted.

The doctor had dragged a chair to the sidewalk. He was coatless, and he leaned back against the wall and smoked, while he stroked his beard. Surprise came into his pale blue eyes when he caught sight of Smith in his unusual and prismatic clothes.

"You're Dr. Gregg—is that right?" said Smith, feeling the dog's-head pin in his tie. "The constable—I mean the consul, told me you hung out at this caravansary. My name's Smith; and I came in a yacht. Taking a cruise around, looking at the monkeys and pineapple trees. Come inside and have a drink, Doc. This café looks on the blink, but I guess it can set out something wet."

"I will join you, sir, in just a taste of brandy," said Dr. Gregg, rising quickly. "I find that as a prophylactic a little brandy is almost a necessity in this climate."

As they turned to enter the *pulperia* a native man, barefoot, glided noiselessly up and addressed the doctor in Spanish. He was yellowish-brown, like an over-ripe lemon; he wore a cotton shirt and ragged linen trousers girded by a leather belt. His face was like an animal's, live and wary, but without promise of much intelligence. This man jabbered with animation and so much seriousness that it seemed a pity that his words were to be wasted.

Dr. Gregg felt his pulse.

"You sick?" he inquired.

"*Mi mujer está enferma en la casa*," said the man, thus endeavouring to convey the news in the only language open to him, that his wife lay ill in her palm-thatched hut.

The doctor drew a handful of capsules filled with a white powder from his trousers pocket. He counted out ten of them into the native's hand, and held up his forefinger impressively.

"Take one," said the doctor, "every two hours." He then held up two fingers, shaking them emphatically before the native's face. Next he pulled out his watch and ran his finger round its dial twice. Again the two fingers confronted the patient's nose. "Two—two—two hours," repeated the doctor.

"*Si, Señor*," said the native, sadly.

He pulled a cheap silver watch from his own pocket and laid it in the doctor's hand. "Me bring," said he, struggling painfully with his scant English, "other watchy to-morrow." Then he departed down-heartedly with his capsules.

"A very ignorant race of people, sir," said the doctor, as he slipped the watch into his pocket. "He seems to have mistaken my directions for taking the physic for the fee. However, it is all right. He owes me an account, anyway. The chances are that he won't bring the other watch. You can't depend on anything they promise you. About that drink, now? How did you come to Coralio, Mr. Smith? I was not aware that any boats except the *Karlsefin* had arrived for some days."

The two leaned against the deserted bar; and Madama set out a bottle without waiting for the doctor's order. There was no dust on it.

After they had drank twice, Smith said:

"You say there were no passengers on the *Karlsefin*, Doc? Are you sure about that? It seems to me I heard somebody down on the beach say that there was one or two aboard."

"They were mistaken, sir. I myself went out and put all hands through a medical examination, as usual. The *Karlsefin* sails as soon as she gets her bananas loaded, which will be about daylight in the morning, and she got everything ready this afternoon. No, sir, there was no passenger list. Like that Three-Star? A French schooner landed two sloopsloads of it a month ago. If any customs duties on it went to the distinguished republic of Anchuria you may have my hat. If you won't have another, come out and let's sit in the cool a while. It isn't often we exiles get a chance to talk with somebody from the outside world."

The doctor brought out another chair to the sidewalk for his new acquaintance. The two seated themselves.

"You are a man of the world," said Dr. Gregg; "a man of travel and experience. Your decision in a matter of ethics and, no doubt, on the point of equity, ability and professional probity should be of value. I would be glad if you will listen to the history of a case that I think stands unique in medical annals.

"About nine years ago, while I was engaged in the practice of medicine in my native city, I was called to treat a case of contusion of the skull. I made the diagnosis that a splinter of bone was pressing upon the brain, and that the surgical operation known as trepanning was required. However, as the patient was a gentleman of wealth and position, I called in for consultation Dr.——"

Smith rose from his chair, and laid a hand, soft with apology, upon the doctor's shirt sleeve.

"Say, Doc," he said, solemnly, "I want to hear that story. You've got me interested; and I don't want to miss the rest of it. I know it's a loola by the way it begins; and I want to tell it at the next meeting of the Barney O'Flynn Association, if you don't mind. But I've got one or two matters to attend to first. If I get 'em attended to in time I'll come right back and hear you spiel the rest before bedtime—is that right?"

"By all means," said the doctor, "get your business attended to, and then return. I shall wait up for you. You see, one of the most prominent physicians at the consultation diagnosed the trouble as a blood clot; another said it was an abscess, but I——"

"Don't tell me now, Doc. Don't spoil the story. Wait till I come back. I want to hear it as it runs off the reel—is that right?"

The mountains reached up their bulky shoulders to receive the level gallop of Apollo's homing steeds, the day died in the lagoons and in the shadowed banana groves and in the mangrove swamps, where the great blue crabs were beginning to crawl to land for the nightly ramble. And it died, at last, upon the highest peaks. Then the brief twilight, ephemeral as the flight of a moth, came and went; the Southern Cross peeped with its topmost eye above a row of palms, and the fire-flies heralded with their torches the approach of soft-footed night.

In the offing the *Karlsefin* swayed at anchor, her lights seeming to penetrate the water to countless fathoms with their shimmering, lanceolate reflections. The Caribs were busy loading her by means of the great lighters heaped full from the piles of fruit ranged upon the shore.

On the sandy beach, with his back against a coconut tree and the stubs of many cigars lying around him, Smith sat waiting, never relaxing his sharp gaze in the direction of the steamer.

The incongruous yachtsman had concentrated his interest upon the innocent fruiter. Twice had he been assured that no passengers had come to Coralio on board of her. And yet, with a persistence not to be attributed to an idling voyager, he had appealed the case to the higher court of his own eyesight. Surprisingly like some gay-coated lizard, he crouched at the foot of the coconut palm, and with the beady, shifting eyes of the selfsame reptile, sustained his espionage on the *Karlsefin*.

On the white sands a whiter gig belonging to the yacht was drawn up, guarded by one of the white-ducked crew. Not far away in a *pulperia* on the shore-following Calle Grande three other sailors swaggered with their cues around Coralio's solitary billiard-table. The boat lay there as if under orders to be ready for use at any moment. There was in the atmosphere a hint of expectation, of waiting for something to occur, which was foreign to the air of Coralio.

Like some passing bird of brilliant plumage, Smith alights on this palmy shore but to preen his wings for an instant and then to fly away upon silent pinions. When morning dawned there was no Smith, no waiting gig, no yacht in the offing. Smith left no intimation of his mission there, no footprints to show where he had followed the trail of his mystery on the sands of Coralio that night. He came; he spake his strange jargon of the asphalt and the cafés; he sat under the coconut tree, and vanished. The next morning Coralio, Smithless, ate its fried plantain and said: "The man of pictured clothing went himself away." With the *siesta* the incident passed, yawning, into history.

So, for a time, must Smith pass behind the scenes of the play. He comes no more to Coralio nor to Doctor Gregg, who sits in vain, wagging his redundant beard, waiting to enrich his derelict audience with his moving tale of trepanning and jealousy.

But prosperously to the lucidity of these loose pages, Smith shall flutter among them again. In the nick of time he shall come to tell us why he strewed so many anxious cigar stumps around the coconut palm that night. This he must do; for, when he sailed away before the dawn in his yacht *Rambler*, he carried with him the answer to a riddle so big and preposterous that few in Anchuria had ventured even to propound it.

LXXXV: CAUGHT

THE plans for the detention of the flying President Miraflores and his companion at the coast line seemed hardly likely to fail. Dr. Zavalla himself had gone to the port of Alazan to establish a guard at that point. At Coralio the Liberal patriot Varras could be depended upon to keep close watch. Goodwin held himself responsible for the district about Coralio.

The news of the president's flight had been disclosed to no one in the coast towns save trusted members of the ambitious political party that was desirous of succeeding to power. The telegraph wire running from San Mateo to the coast had been cut far up on the mountain trail by an emissary of Zavalla's. Long before this could be repaired and word received along it from the capital the fugitives would have reached the coast and the question of escape or capture been solved.

Goodwin had stationed armed sentinels at frequent intervals along the shore for a mile in each direction from Coralio. They were instructed to keep a vigilant lookout during the night to prevent Miraflores from attempting to embark stealthily by means of some boat or sloop found by chance at the water's edge. A dozen patrols walked the streets of Coralio unsuspected, ready to intercept the truant official should he show himself there.

Goodwin was very well convinced that no precautions had been overlooked. He strolled about the streets that bore such high-sounding names and were but narrow, grass-covered lanes, lending his own aid to the vigil that had been entrusted to him by Bob Englehart.

The town had begun the tepid round of its nightly diversions. A few leisurely dandies, clad in white duck, with flowing neckties, and swinging slim bamboo canes, threaded the grassy by-ways toward the houses of their favoured *señoritas*. Those who wooed the art of music dragged tirelessly at whining concertinas, or fingered lugubrious guitars at doors and windows. An occasional soldier from the *cuartel*, with flapping straw hat, without coat or shoes, hurried by, balancing his long gun like a lance in one hand. From every density of the foliage the giant tree frogs sounded their loud and irritating clatter. Further out, where the by-ways perished at the brink of the jungle, the gutteral cries of marauding baboons and the coughing of the alligators in the black estuaries fractured the vain silence of the wood.

By ten o'clock the streets were deserted. The oil lamps that had burned, a sickly yellow, at random corners, had been extinguished by some economical civic agent. Coralio lay sleeping calmly between toppling mountains and encroaching sea like a stolen babe in the arms of its abductors. Somewhere over in that tropical darkness—perhaps already threading the profundities of the alluvial lowlands—the high adventurer and his mate were moving toward land's end. The game of Fox-in-the-Morning should be soon coming to its close.

Goodwin, at his deliberate gait, passed the long, low *cuartel* where Coralio's contingent of Anchuria's military force slumbered, with its bare toes pointed heavenward. There was a law that no civilian might come so near the headquarters of that citadel of war after nine o'clock, but Goodwin was always forgetting the minor statutes.

"*Quién vive?*" shrieked the sentinel, wrestling prodigiously with his lengthy musket.

"*Americano*," growled Goodwin, without turning his head, and passed on, unhalted.

To the right he turned, and to the left up the street that ultimately reached the Plaza Nacional. When within the toss of a cigar stump from the intersecting Street of the Holy Sepulchre, he stopped suddenly in the pathway.

He saw the form of a tall man, clothed in black and carrying a large valise, hurry down the cross-street in the direction of the beach. And Goodwin's second glance made him aware of a woman at the man's elbow on the farther side, who seemed to urge forward, if not even to assist, her companion in their swift but silent progress. They were no Coralians, those two.

Goodwin followed at increased speed, but without any of the artful tactics that are so dear to the heart of the sleuth. The American was too broad to feel the instinct of the detective. He stood as an agent for the people of Anchuria, and but for political reasons he would have demanded then and there the money. It was the design of his party to secure the imperilled fund, to restore it to the treasury of the country, and to declare itself in power without bloodshed or resistance.

The couple halted at the door of the Hotel de los Estranjeros, and the man struck upon the wood with the impatience of one unused to his entry being stayed. Madama was long in response; but after a time her light showed, the door was opened, and the guests housed.

Goodwin stood in the quiet street, lighting another cigar. In two minutes a faint gleam began to show between the slats of the jalousies in the upper story of the hotel. "They have engaged rooms," said Goodwin to himself. "So, then, their arrangements for sailing have yet to be made."

At that moment there came along one Estebán Delgado, a barber, an enemy to existing government, a jovial plotter against stagnation in any form. This barber was one of Coralio's saddest dogs, often remaining out of doors as late as eleven, post meridian. He was a partisan Liberal; and he greeted Goodwin with flatulent importance as a brother in the cause. But he had something important to tell.

"What think you, Don Frank!" he cried, in the universal tone of the conspirator. "I have to-night shaved *la barba*—what you call the 'weeskers' of the *Presidente* himself, of this countree! Consider! He sent for me to come. In the poor *casita* of an old woman he awaited me—in a verree leetle house in a dark place. *Carramba!—el Señor Presidente* to make himself thus secret and obscured! I think he desired not to be known—but, *carajo!* can you shave a man and not see his face? This gold piece he gave me, and said it was to be all quite still. I think, Don Frank, there is what you call a chip over the bug."

"Have you ever seen President Miraflores before?" asked Goodwin.

"But once," answered Estebán. "He is tall; and he had weeskers, verree black and sufficient."

"Was anyone else present when you shaved him?"

"An old Indian woman, *Señor*, that belonged with the *casa*, and one *señorita*—a ladee of so much beautee!—*ah, Dios!*"

"All right, Estebán," said Goodwin. "It's very lucky that you happened along with your tonsorial information. The new administration will be likely to remember you for this."

Then in a few words he made the barber acquainted with the crisis into which the affairs of the nation had culminated, and instructed him to remain outside, keeping watch upon the two sides of the hotel that looked upon the street, and observing whether anyone should attempt to leave the house by any door or window. Goodwin himself went to the door through which the guests had entered, opened it and stepped inside.

Madama had returned downstairs from her journey above to see after the comfort of her lodgers. Her candle stood upon the bar. She was about to take a thimbleful of rum as a solace for having her rest disturbed. She looked up without surprise or alarm as her third caller entered.

"Ah! it is the *Señor* Goodwin. Not often does he honour my poor house by his presence."

"I must come oftener," said Goodwin, with the Goodwin smile. "I hear that your cognac is the best between Belize to the north and Rio to the south. Set out the bottle, Madama, and let us have the proof in *un vasito* for each of us."

"My *aguardiente*," said Madama, with pride, "is the best. It grows, in beautiful bottles, in the dark places among the banana-trees. *Si*, *Señor*. Only at midnight can they be picked by sailor-men who bring them, before daylight comes, to your back door. Good *aguardiente* is a verree difficult fruit to handle, *Señor* Goodwin."

Smuggling, in Coralio, was much nearer than competition to being the life of trade. One spoke of it slyly, yet with a certain conceit, when it had been well accomplished.

"You have guests in the house to-night," said Goodwin, laying a silver dollar upon the counter.

"Why not?" said Madama, counting the change. "Two; but the smallest while finished to arrive. One *señor*, not quite old, and one *señorita*, of sufficient handsomeness. To their rooms they have ascended, not desiring the to-eat nor the to-drink. Two rooms—*Numero* 9 and *Numero* 10."

"I was expecting that gentleman and that lady," said Goodwin. "I have important *negocios* that must be transacted. Will you allow me to see them?"

"Why not?" sighed Madama, placidly. "Why should not *Señor* Goodwin ascend and speak to his friends? *Está bueno*. Room *Numero* 9 and room *Numero* 10."

Goodwin loosened in his coat pocket the American revolver that he carried, and ascended the steep, dark stairway.

In the hallway above, the saffron light from a hanging lamp allowed him to select the gaudy numbers on the doors. He turned the knob of Number 9, entered and closed the door behind him.

If that was Isabel Guilbert seated by the table in that poorly furnished room, report had failed to do her charms justice. She rested her head upon one hand. Extreme fatigue was signified in every line of her figure; and upon her countenance a deep perplexity was written. Her eyes were grey-irised, and of that mould that seems to have belonged to the orbs of all the famous queens of hearts. Their whites were singularly clear and brilliant, concealed above the irises by heavy horizontal lids, and showing a snowy line below them. Such eyes denote great nobility, vigour, and, if you can conceive of it, a most generous selfishness. She looked up when the American entered, with an expression of surprised inquiry, but without alarm.

Goodwin took off his hat and seated himself, with his characteristic deliberate ease, upon a corner of the table. He held a lighted cigar between his fingers. He took this familiar course because he was sure that preliminaries would be wasted upon Miss Guilbert. He knew her history, and the small part that the conventions had played in it.

"Good evening," he said. "Now, madame, let us come to business at once. You will observe that I mention no names, but I know who is in the next room, and what he carries in that valise. That is the point which brings me here. I have come to dictate terms of surrender."

The lady neither moved nor replied, but steadily regarded the cigar in Goodwin's hand.

"We," continued the dictator, thoughtfully regarding the neat buckskin shoe on his gently-swinging foot—"I speak for a considerable majority of the people—demand the return of the stolen funds belonging to them. Our terms go very little further than that. They are very simple. As an accredited spokesman, I promise that our interference will cease if they are accepted. Give up the money, and you and your companion will be permitted to proceed wherever you will. In fact, assistance will be given you in the matter of securing a passage by any outgoing vessel you may choose. It is on my personal responsibility that I add congratulations to the gentleman in Number 10 upon his taste in feminine charms."

Returning his cigar to his mouth, Goodwin

observed her, and saw that her eyes followed it and rested upon it with icy and significant concentration. Apparently she had not heard a word he had said. He understood, tossed the cigar out the window, and, with an amused laugh, slid from the table to his feet.

"That is better," said the lady. "It makes it possible for me to listen to you. For a second lesson in good manners, you might now tell me by whom I am being insulted."

"I am sorry," said Goodwin, leaning one hand on the table, "that my time is too brief for devoting much of it to a course of etiquette. Come, now; I appeal to your good sense. You have shown yourself, in more than one instance, to be well aware of what is to your advantage. This is an occasion that demands the exercise of your undoubted intelligence. There is no mystery here. I am Frank Goodwin; and I have come for the money. I entered this room at a venture. Had I entered the other I would have had it before now. Do you want it in words? The gentleman in Number 10 has betrayed a great trust. He has robbed his people of a large sum, and it is I who will prevent their losing it. I do not say who that gentleman is; but if I should be forced to see him and he should prove to be a certain high official of the republic, it will be my duty to arrest him. The house is guarded. I am offering you liberal terms. It is not absolutely necessary that I confer personally with the gentleman in the next room. Bring me the valise containing the money, and we will call the affair ended."

The lady arose from her chair and stood for a moment, thinking deeply.

"Do you live here, Mr. Goodwin?" she asked, presently.

"Yes."

"What is your authority for this intrusion?"

"I am an instrument of the republic. I was advised by wire of the movements of the—gentleman in Number 10."

"May I ask you two or three questions? I believe you to be a man more apt to be truthful than —timid. What sort of a town is this—Coralio, I think they call it?"

"Not much of a town," said Goodwin, smiling. "A banana town, as they run. Grass huts, 'dobes, five or six two-story houses, accommodations limited, population half-breed Spanish and Indian, Caribs and blackamoors. No sidewalks to speak of, no amusements. Rather unmoral. That's an offhand sketch, of course."

"Are there any inducements, say in a social or in a business way, for people to reside here?"

"Oh, yes," answered Goodwin, smiling broadly. "There are no afternoon teas, no hand-organs, no department stores—and there is no extradition treaty."

"He told me," went on the lady, speaking as if to herself, and with a slight frown, "that there were towns on this coast of beauty and importance; that there was a pleasing social order—especially an American colony of cultured residents."

"There is an American colony," said Goodwin, gazing at her in some wonder. "Some of the members are all right. Some are fugitives from justice from the States. I recall two exiled bank presidents, an army paymaster under a cloud, a couple of manslayers, and a widow—arsenic, I believe, was the suspicion in her case. I myself complete the colony, but, as yet, I have not distinguished myself by any particular crime."

"Do not lose hope," said the lady, dryly; "I see nothing in your actions to-night to guarantee you further obscurity. Some mistake has been made; I do not know just where. But *him* you shall not disturb to-night. The journey has fatigued him so that he has fallen asleep, I think, in his clothes. You talk of stolen money! I do not understand you. Some mistake has been made. I will convince you. Remain where you are and I will bring you the valise that you seem to covet so, and show it to you."

She moved toward the closed door that connected the two rooms, but stopped, and half turned and bestowed on Goodwin a grave, searching look that ended in a quizzical smile.

"You force my door," she said, "and you follow your ruffianly behaviour with the basest accusations; and yet"—she hesitated, as if to reconsider what she was about to say—"and yet—it is a puzzling thing—I am sure there has been some mistake."

She took a step toward the door, but Goodwin stayed her by a light touch upon her arm. I have said before that women turned to look at him in the streets. He was the viking sort of man, big, good-looking, and with an air of kindly truculence. She was dark and proud, glowing or pale as her mood moved her. I do not know if Eve were light or dark, but if such a woman had stood in the Garden I know that the apple would have been eaten. This woman was to be Goodwin's fate, and he did not know it; but he must have felt the first throes of destiny, for, as he faced her, the knowledge of what report named her turned bitter in his throat.

"If there has been any mistake," he said hotly, "it was yours. I do not blame the man who has lost his country, his honour, and is about to lose the poor consolation of his stolen riches, as much as I blame you, for, by heaven! I can very well see how he was brought to it. I can understand, and pity him. It is such women as you that strew this degraded coast with wretched exiles, that make men forget their trusts, that drag——"

The lady interrupted him with a weary gesture.

"There is no need to continue your insults," she said coldly. "I do not understand what you are saying, nor do I know what mad blunder you are making; but if the inspection of the contents of a gentleman's portmanteau will rid me of you, let us delay it no longer."

She passed quickly and noiselessly into the other room, and returned with the heavy leather valise, which she handed to the American with an air of patient contempt.

Goodwin set the valise quickly upon the table and began to unfasten the straps. The lady stood by, with an expression of infinite scorn and weariness upon her face.

The valise opened wide to a powerful, sidelong wrench. Goodwin dragged out two or three articles of clothing, exposing the bulk of its contents—package after package of tightly packed United States bank and treasury notes of large denomination. Reckoning from the high figures written upon the paper bands that bound them, the total must have come closely upon the hundred thousand mark.

Goodwin glanced swiftly at the woman, and saw, with surprise and a thrill of pleasure that he wondered at, that she had experienced an unmistakable shock. Her eyes grew wide, she gasped, and leaned heavily against the table. She had been ignorant, then, he inferred, that her companion had looted the government treasury. But why, he angrily asked himself, should he be so well pleased to think this wandering and unscrupulous singer not so black as report had painted her?

A noise in the other room startled them both. The door swung open, and a tall, elderly, dark-complexioned man, recently shaven, hurried into the room.

All the pictures of President Miraflores represent him as the possessor of a luxuriant supply of dark and carefully tended whiskers; but the story of the barber, Estebán, had prepared Goodwin for the change.

The man stumbled in from the dark room, his eyes blinking at the lamplight, and heavy from sleep.

"What does this mean?" he demanded in excellent English, with a keen and perturbed look at the American—"robbery?"

"Very near it," answered Goodwin. "But I rather think I'm in time to prevent it. I represent the people to whom this money belongs, and I have come to convey it back to them." He thrust his hand into a pocket of his loose, linen coat.

The other man's hand went quickly behind him.

"Don't draw," called Goodwin sharply; "I've got you covered from my pocket."

The lady stepped forward, and laid one hand upon the shoulder of her hesitating companion.

She pointed to the table. "Tell me the truth—the truth," she said, in a low voice. "Whose money is that?"

The man did not answer. He gave a deep, long-drawn sigh, leaned and kissed her on the forehead, stepped back into the other room and closed the door.

Goodwin foresaw his purpose, and jumped for the door, but the report of the pistol echoed as his hand touched the knob. A heavy fall followed, and some one swept him aside and struggled into the room of the fallen man.

A desolation, thought Goodwin, greater than that derived from the loss of cavalier and gold must have been in the heart of the enchantress to have wrung from her, in that moment, the cry of one turning to the all-forgiving, all-comforting earthly consoler—to have made her call out from that bloody and dishonoured room—"Oh, mother, mother, mother!"

But there was an alarm outside. The barber, Estebán, at the sound of the shot, had raised his voice; and the shot itself had aroused half the town. A pattering of feet came up the street, and official orders rang out on the still air. Goodwin had a duty to perform. Circumstances had made him the custodian of his adopted country's treasure. Swiftly cramming the money into the valise, he closed it, leaned far out of the window and dropped it into a thick orange-tree in the little enclosure below.

They will tell you in Coralio, as they delight in telling the stranger, of the conclusion of that tragic fight. They will tell you how the upholders of the law came apace when the alarm was sounded

—the *comandante* in red slippers and a jacket like a head waiter's, and girded sword, the soldiers with their interminable guns, followed by outnumbering officers struggling into their gold lace and epaulettes; the barefooted policemen (the only capables in the lot), and ruffled citizens of every hue and description.

They say that the countenance of the dead man was marred sadly by the effects of the shot; but he was identified as the fallen president by both Goodwin and the barber Estebán. On the next morning messages began to come over the mended telegraph wire; and the story of the flight from the capital was given out to the public. In San Mateo the revolutionary party had seized the sceptre of government without opposition, and the *vivas* of the mercurial populace quickly effaced the interest belonging to the unfortunate Miraflores.

They will relate to you how the new government sifted the towns and raked the roads to find the valise containing Anchuria's surplus capital, which the president was known to have carried with him, but all in vain. In Coralio *Señor* Goodwin himself led the searching party which combed that town as carefully as a woman combs her hair; but the money was not found.

So they buried the dead man, without honours, back of the town near the little bridge that spans the mangrove swamp; and for a *real* a boy will show you his grave. They say that the old woman, in whose hut the barber shaved the president, placed the wooden slab at his head, and burned the inscription upon it with a hot iron.

You will hear also that *Señor* Goodwin, like a tower of strength, shielded Doña Isabel Guilbert through those subsequent distressful days; and that his scruples as to her past career (if he had any) vanished; and her adventuresome waywardness (if she had any) left her, and they were wedded and were happy.

The American built a home on a little foothill near the town. It is a conglomerate structure of native woods that, exported, would be worth a fortune, and of brick, palm, glass, bamboo and adobe. There is a paradise of nature about it; and something of the same sort within. The natives speak of its interior with hands uplifted in admiration. There are floors polished like mirrors and covered with hand-woven Indian rugs of silk fibre, tall ornaments and pictures, musical instruments and papered walls—"figure-it-to-yourself!" they exclaim.

But they cannot tell you in Coralio (as you shall learn) what became of the money that Frank Goodwin dropped into the orange-tree. But that shall come later; for the palms are fluttering in the breeze, bidding us to sport and gaiety.

LXXXVI: CUPID'S EXILE NUMBER TWO

THE United States of America, after looking over its stock of consular timber, selected Mr. John De Graffenreid Atwood, of Dalesburg, Alabama, for a successor to Willard Geddie, resigned.

Without prejudice to Mr. Atwood, it will have to be acknowledged that, in this instance, it was the man who sought the office. As with the self-banished Geddie, it was nothing less than the artful smiles of lovely woman that had driven Johnny Atwood to the desperate expedient of accepting office under a despised Federal Government so that he might go far, far away and never see again the false, fair face that had wrecked his young life. The consulship at Coralio seemed to offer a retreat sufficiently removed and romantic enough to inject the necessary drama into the pastoral scenes of Dalesburg life.

It was while playing the part of Cupid's exile that Johnny added his handiwork to the long list of casualties along the Spanish Main by his famous manipulation of the shoe market, and his unparalleled feat of elevating the most despised and useless weed in his own country from obscurity to be a valuable product in international commerce.

The trouble began, as trouble often begins instead of ending, with a romance. In Dalesburg there was a man named Elijah Hemstetter, who kept a general store. His family consisted of one daughter called Rosine, a name that atoned much for "Hemstetter." This young woman was possessed of plentiful attractions, so that the young men of the community were agitated in their bosoms. Among the more agitated was Johnny, the son of Judge Atwood, who lived in the big colonial mansion on the edge of Dalesburg.

It would seem that the desirable Rosine should have been pleased to return the affection of an Atwood, a name honoured all over the state long before and since the war. It does seem that she should have gladly consented to have been led into that stately but rather empty colonial mansion. But not so. There was a cloud on the horizon, a threatening, cumulous cloud, in the shape of a lively and shrewd young farmer in the neighbourhood who dared to enter the lists as a rival to the high-born Atwood.

One night Johnny propounded to Rosine a question that is considered of much importance by the young of the human species. The accessories were all there—moonlight, oleanders, magnolias, the mock-bird's song. Whether or no the shadow of Pinkney Dawson, the prosperous young farmer, came between them on that occasion is not known; but Rosine's answer was unfavourable. Mr. John De Graffenreid Atwood bowed till his hat touched the lawn grass, and went away with his head high, but with a sore wound in his pedigree and heart. A Hemstetter refuse an Atwood! Zounds!

Among other accidents of that year was a Democratic president. Judge Atwood was a warhorse of Democracy. Johnny persuaded him to set the wheels moving for some foreign appointment. He would go away—away. Perhaps in years to come Rosine would think how true, how faithful his love had been, and would drop a tear—maybe in the cream she would be skimming for Pink Dawson's breakfast.

The wheels of politics revolved; and Johnny was appointed consul to Coralio. Just before leaving he dropped in at Hemstetter's to say good-bye. There was a queer, pinkish look about Rosine's eyes; and had the two been alone, the United States might have had to cast about for another consul. But Pink Dawson was there, of course, talking about his 400-acre orchard, and the three-mile alfalfa tract, and the 200-acre pasture. So Johnny shook hands with Rosine as coolly as if he were only going to run up to Montgomery for a couple of days. They had the royal manner when they chose, those Atwoods.

"If you happen to strike anything in the way of a good investment down there, Johnny," said Pink Dawson, "just let me know, will you? I reckon I could lay my hands on a few extra thousands 'most any time for a profitable deal."

"Certainly, Pink," said Johnny pleasantly. "If I strike anything of the sort I'll let you in with pleasure."

So Johnny went down to Mobile and took a fruit steamer for the coast of Anchuria.

When the new consul arrived in Coralio the strangeness of the scenes diverted him much. He was only twenty-two; and the grief of youth is not worn like a garment as it is by older men. It has its seasons when it reigns; and then it is unseated for a time by the assertion of the keen senses.

Billy Keogh and Johnny seemed to conceive a mutual friendship at once. Keogh took the new consul about town and presented him to the handful of Americans and the smaller number of French and Germans who made up the "foreign" contingent. And then, of course, he had to be more formally introduced to the native officials, and have his credentials transmitted through an interpreter.

There was something about the young Southerner that the sophisticated Keogh liked. His manner was simple almost to boyishness; but he possessed the cool carelessness of a man of far greater age and experience. Neither uniforms nor titles, red tape nor foreign languages, mountains nor sea weighed upon his spirits. He was heir to all the ages, an Atwood, of Dalesburg; and you might know every thought conceived in his bosom.

Geddie came down to the consulate to explain the duties and workings of the office. He and Keogh tried to interest the new consul in their description of the work that his government expected him to perform.

"It's all right," said Johnny from the hammock that he had set up as the official reclining place. "If anything turns up that has to be done I'll let you fellows do it. You can't expect a Democrat to work during his first term of holding office."

"You might look over these headings," suggested Geddie, "of the different lines of exports you will have to keep account of. The fruit is classified; and there are the valuable woods, coffee, rubber ——"

"That last account sounds all right," interrupted Mr. Atwood. "Sounds as if it could be stretched. I want to buy a new flag, a monkey, a guitar and a barrel of pineapples. Will that rubber account stretch over 'em?"

"That's merely statistics," said Geddie, smiling. "The expense account is what you want. It is supposed to have a slight elasticity. The 'stationery' items are sometimes carelessly audited by the State Department."

"We're wasting our time," said Keogh. "This man was born to hold office. He penetrates to the root of the art at one step of his eagle eye. The true genius of government shows its hand in every word of his speech."

"I didn't take this job with any intention of working," explained Johnny, lazily. "I wanted to go somewhere in the world where they didn't talk about farms. There are none here, are there?"

"Not the kind you are acquainted with," answered the ex-consul. "There is no such art here as agriculture. There never was a plough or a reaper within the boundaries of Anchuria."

"This is the country for me," murmured the consul, and immediately he fell asleep.

The cheerful tintypist pursued his intimacy with Johnny in spite of open charges that he did so to obtain a pre-emption on a seat in that coveted spot, the rear gallery of the consulate. But whether his designs were selfish or purely friendly, Keogh achieved that desirable privilege. Few were the nights on which the two could not be found reposing there in the sea-breeze, with their heels on the railing, and the cigars and brandy conveniently near.

One evening they sat thus, mainly silent, for their talk had dwindled before the stilling influence of an unusual night.

There was a great, full moon; and the sea was mother-of-pearl. Almost every sound was hushed, for the air was but faintly stirring; and the town lay panting, waiting for the night to cool. Offshore lay the fruit steamer *Andador*, of the Vesuvius line, full-laden and scheduled to sail at six in the morning. There were no loiterers on the beach. So bright was the moonlight that the two men could see the small pebbles shining on the beach where the gentle surf wetted them.

Then down the coast, tacking close to shore, slowly swam a little sloop, white-winged like some snowy sea-fowl. Its course lay within twenty points of the wind's eye; so it veered in and out again in long, slow strokes like the movements of a graceful skater.

Again the tactics of its crew brought it close inshore, this time nearly opposite the consulate;

and then there blew from the sloop clear and surprising notes as if from a horn of elfland. A fairy bugle it might have been, sweet and silvery and unexpected, playing with spirit the familiar air of "Home, Sweet Home."

It was a scene set for the land of the lotus. The authority of the sea and the tropics, the mystery that attends unknown sails, and the prestige of drifting music on moonlit waters gave it an anodynous charm. Johnny Atwood felt it, and thought of Dalesburg; but as soon as Keogh's mind had arrived at a theory concerning the peripatetic solo he sprang to the railing, and his ear-rending yawp fractured the silence of Coralio like a cannon shot.

"Mel-lin-ger a-hoy!"

The sloop was now on its outward tack; but from it came a clear, answering hail:

"Good-bye, Billy . . . go-ing home—bye!"

The *Andador* was the sloop's destination. No doubt some passenger with a sailing permit from some up-the-coast point had come down in this sloop to catch the regular fruit steamer on its return trip. Like a coquettish pigeon the little boat tacked on its eccentric way until at last its white sail was lost to sight against the larger bulk of the fruiter's side.

"That's old H. P. Mellinger," explained Keogh, dropping back into his chair. "He's going back to New York. He was private secretary of the late hot-foot president of this grocery and fruit stand that they call a country. His job's over now; and I guess old Mellinger is glad."

"Why does he disappear to music, like Zozo, the magic queen?" asked Johnny. "Just to show 'em that he doesn't care?"

"That noise you heard is a phonograph," said Keogh. "I sold him that. Mellinger had a graft in this country that was the only thing of its kind in the world. The tooting machine saved it for him once, and he always carried it around with him afterward."

"Tell me about it," demanded Johnny, betraying interest.

"I'm no disseminator of narratives," said Keogh. "I can use language for purposes of speech; but when I attempt a discourse the words come out as they will, and they may make sense when they strike the atmosphere, or they may not."

"I want to hear about that graft," persisted Johnny. "You've got no right to refuse. I've told you all about every man, woman and hitching post in Dalesburg."

"You shall hear it," said Keogh. "I said my instincts of narrative were perplexed. Don't you believe it. It's an art I've acquired along with many others of the graces and sciences."

LXXXVII: PHONOGRAPH AND GRAFT

"WHAT was this graft?" asked Johnny, with the impatience of the great public to whom tales are told.

"'Tis contrary to art and philosophy to give you the information," said Keogh calmly. "The art of narrative consists in concealing from your audience everything it wants to know until after you expose your favourite opinions on topics foreign to the subject. A good story is like a bitter pill with the sugar coating inside of it. I will begin, if you please, with a horoscope located in the Cherokee Nation; and end with a moral tune on the phonograph.

"Me and Henry Horsecollar brought the first phonograph to this country. Henry was a quarter-breed, quarter-back Cherokee, educated East in the idioms of football, and West in contraband whisky, and a gentleman, the same as you and me. He was easy and romping in his ways; a man about six foot, with a kind of rubber-tyre movement. Yes, he was a little man about five foot five, or five foot eleven. He was what you would call a medium tall man of average smallness. Henry had quit college once, and the Muscogee jail three times—the last-named institution on account of introducing and selling whisky in the territories. Henry Horsecollar never let any cigar stores come up and stand behind him. He didn't belong to that tribe of Indians.

"Henry and me met at Texarkana, and figured out this phonograph scheme. He had $360 which came to him out of a land allotment in the reservation. I had run down from Little Rock on account of a distressful scene I had witnessed on the street there. A man stood on a box and passed around some gold watches, screw case, stem-winders, Elgin movement, very elegant. Twenty bucks they cost you over the counter. At three dollars the crowd fought for the tickers. The man happened to find a valise full of them handy, and he passed them out like putting hot biscuits on a plate. The backs were hard to unscrew, but the crowd put its ear to the case, and they ticked mollifying and agreeable. Three of these watches were genuine tickers; the rest were only kickers. Hey? Why, empty cases with one of them horny black bugs that fly around electric lights in 'em. Them bugs kick off minutes and seconds industrious and beautiful. So, this man I was speaking of cleaned up $288; and then he went away, because he knew that when it came time to wind watches in Little Rock an entomologist would be needed, and he wasn't one.

"So, as I say, Henry had $360, and I had $288. The idea of introducing the phonograph to South America was Henry's; but I took to it freely, being fond of machinery of all kinds.

" 'The Latin races,' says Henry, explaining easy in the idioms he learned at college, 'are peculiarly adapted to be victims of the phonograph. They have the artistic temperament. They yearn for music and colour and gaiety. They give wampum to the hand-organ man and the four-legged chicken in the tent when they're months behind with the grocery and the bread-fruit tree.'

" 'Then,' says I, 'we'll export canned music to the Latins; but I'm mindful of Mr. Julius Cæsar's account of 'em where he says: "*Omnia Gallia in tres partes divisa est*"; which is the same as to say, "We will need all of our gall in devising means to tree them parties." '

"I hated to make a show of education; but I was disinclined to be overdone in syntax by a mere Indian, a member of a race to which we owe nothing except the land on which the United States is situated.

"We bought a fine phonograph in Texarkana—one of the best make—and half a trunkful of records. We packed up, and took the T. and P.

for New Orleans. From that celebrated centre of molasses and disfranchised coon songs we took a steamer for South America.

"We landed at Solitas, forty miles up the coast from here. 'Twas a palatable enough place to look at. The houses were clean and white; and to look at 'em stuck around among the scenery they reminded you of hard-boiled eggs served with lettuce. There was a block of skyscraper mountains in the suburbs; and they kept pretty quiet, like they had crept up there and were watching the town. And the sea was remarking 'Sh-sh-sh' on the beach; and now and then a ripe coconut would drop kerblip in the sand; and that was all there was doing. Yes, I judge that town was considerably on the quiet. I judge that after Gabriel quits blowing his horn, and the car starts, with Philadelphia swinging to the last strap, and Pine Gully, Arkansas, hanging on to the rear step, this town of Solitas will wake up and ask if anybody spoke.

"The captain went ashore with us, and offered to conduct what he seemed to like to call the obsequies. He introduced Henry and me to the United States consul, and a roan man, the head of the Department of Mercenary and Licentious Dispositions, the way it read upon his sign.

" 'I touch here again a week from to-day,' says the captain.

" 'By that time,' we told him, 'we'll be amassing wealth in the interior towns with our galvanized prima donna and correct imitations of Sousa's band excavating a march from a tin mine.'

" 'Ye'll not,' says the captain. 'Ye'll be hypnotized. Any gentleman in the audience who kindly steps upon the stage and looks this country in the eye will be converted to the hypothesis that he's but a fly in the Elgin creamery. Ye'll be standing knee deep in the surf waiting for me, and your machine for making Hamburger steak out of the hitherto respected art of music will be playing "There's no place like home." '

"Henry skinned a twenty off his roll, and received from the Bureau of Mercenary Dispositions a paper bearing a red seal and a dialect story, and no change.

"Then we got the consul full of red wine, and struck him for a horoscope. He was a thin, youngish kind of man, I should say past fifty, sort of French-Irish in his affections, and puffed up with disconsolation. Yes, he was a flattened kind of a man, in whom drink lay stagnant, inclined to corpulence and misery. Yes, I think he was a kind of Dutchman, being very sad and genial in his ways.

" 'The marvellous invention,' he says, 'entitled the phonograph, has never invaded these shores. The people have never heard it. They would not believe it if they should. Simple-hearted children of nature, progress has never condemned them to accept the work of a can-opener as an overture, and ragtime might incite them to a bloody revolution. But you can try the experiment. The best chance you have is that the populace may not wake up when you play. There's two ways,' says the consul, 'they take it. They may become inebriated with attention, like an Atlanta colonel listening to "Marching Through Georgia," or they will get excited and transpose the key of the music with an axe and yourselves into a dungeon. In the latter case,' says the consul, 'I'll do my duty by cabling to the State Department, and I'll wrap the Stars and Stripes around you when you come to be shot, and threaten them with the vengeance of the greatest gold export and financial reserve nation on earth. The flag is full of bullet holes now,' says the consul, 'made in that way. Twice before,' says the consul, 'I have cabled our government for a couple of gunboats to protect American citizens. The first time the Department sent me a pair of gum boots. The other time was when a man named Pease was going to be executed here. They referred that appeal to the Secretary of Agriculture. Let us now disturb the *señor* behind the bar for a subsequence of the red wine.'

"Thus soliloquized the consul of Solitas to me and Henry Horsecollar.

"But, notwithstanding, we hired a room that afternoon in the Calle de los Angeles, the main street that runs along the shore, and put our trunks there. 'Twas a good-sized room, dark and cheerful, but small. 'Twas on a various street, diversified by houses and conservatory plants. The peasantry of the city passed to and fro on the fine pasturage between the sidewalks. 'Twas, for the world, like an opera chorus when the Royal Kafoozlum is about to enter.

"We were rubbing the dust off the machine and getting fixed to start business the next day; when a big, fine-looking white man in white clothes stopped at the door and looked in. We extended the invitations, and he walked inside and sized us up. He was chewing a long cigar, and wrinkling his eyes, meditative, like a girl trying to decide which dress to wear at the party.

" 'New York?' he says to me finally.

" 'Originally, and from time to time,' I says. 'Hasn't it rubbed off yet?'

" 'It's simple,' says he, 'when you know how. It's the fit of the vest. They don't cut vests right anywhere else. Coats, maybe, but not vests.'

"The white man looks at Henry Horsecollar and hesitates.

" 'Injun,' says Henry; 'tame Injun.'

" 'Mellinger,' says the man—'Homer P. Mellinger. Boys, you're confiscated. You're babes in the wood without a chaperon or referee, and it's my duty to start you going. I'll knock out the props and launch you proper in the pellucid waters of this tropical mud puddle. You'll have to be christened, and if you'll come with me I'll break a bottle of wine across your bows, according to Hoyle.'

"Well, for two days Homer P. Mellinger did the honours. That man cut ice in Anchuria. He was It. He was the Royal Kafoozlum. If me and Henry was babes in the wood, he was a Robin Redbreast from the topmost bough. Him and me and Henry Horsecollar locked arms, and toted that phonograph around, and had wassail and diversions. Everywhere we found doors open we went inside and set the machine going, and Mellinger called upon the people to observe the artful music and his two lifelong friends, the *Señors* Americanos. The opera chorus was agitated with esteem, and followed us from house to house. There was a different kind of drink to be had with every tune. The natives had acquirements of a pleasant thing in the way of a drink that gums itself to the recollection. They chop off the end of a green coconut, and pour in on the juice of it French brandy and other adjuvants. We had them and other things.

"Mine and Henry's money was counterfeit. Everything was on Homer P. Mellinger. That man could find rolls of bills concealed in places on his person where Hermann the Wizard couldn't have conjured out a rabbit or an omelette. He could have founded universities, and made orchid collections, and then had enough left to purchase the coloured vote of his country. Henry and me wondered what his graft was. One evening he told us.

" 'Boys,' said he, 'I've deceived you. You think I'm a painted butterfly; but in fact I'm the hardest worked man in this country. Ten years ago I landed on its shores; and two years ago on the point of its jaw. Yes, I guess I can get the decision over this ginger cake commonwealth at the end of any round I choose. I'll confide in you because you are my countrymen and guests, even if you have assaulted my adopted shores with the worst system of noises ever set to music.

" 'My job is private secretary to the president of this republic; and my duties are running it. I'm not headlined in the bills, but I'm the mustard in the salad dressing just the same. There isn't a law goes before Congress, there isn't a concession granted, there isn't an import duty levied but what H. P. Mellinger he cooks and seasons it. In the front office I fill the president's inkstand and search visiting statesmen for dirks and dynamite; but in the back room I dictate the policy of the government. You'd never guess in the world how I got my pull. It's the only graft of its kind on earth. I'll put you wise. You remember the old top-liner in the copy-book—"Honesty is the Best Policy"? That's it. I'm working honesty for a graft. I'm the only honest man in the republic. The government knows it; the people know it; the boodlers know it; the foreign investors know it. I make the government keep its faith. If a man is promised a job he gets it. If outside capital buys a concession it gets the goods. I run a monopoly of square dealing here. There's no competition. If Colonel Diogenes were to flash his lantern in this precinct he'd have my address inside of two minutes. There isn't big money in it, but it's a sure thing, and lets a man sleep of nights.'

"Thus Homer P. Mellinger made oration to me and Henry Horsecollar. And, later, he divested himself of this remark:

" 'Boys, I'm to hold a *soirée* this evening with a gang of leading citizens, and I want your assistance. You bring the musical corn sheller and give the affair the outside appearance of a function. There's important business on hand, but it mustn't show. I can talk to you people. I've been pained for years on account of not having anybody to blow off and brag to. I get homesick sometimes, and I'd swap the entire perquisites of office for just one hour to have a stein and a caviare sandwich somewhere on Thirty-fourth Street, and stand and watch the street cars go by, and smell the peanut roaster at old Giuseppe's fruit stand.'

" 'Yes,' said I, 'there's fine caviare at Billy Renfrow's café, corner of Thirty-fourth and——'

" 'God knows it,' interrupts Mellinger, 'and if you'd told me you knew Billy Renfrow I'd have invented tons of ways of making you happy. Billy was my side-kicker in New York. There is a man who never knew what crooked was. Here I am working Honesty for a graft, but that man loses money on it. *Carrambos!* I get sick at times of this country. Everything's rotten. From the executive down to the coffee pickers, they're plotting to down each other and skin their friends. If a mule driver takes off his hat to an official, that man figures it out that he's a popular idol, and sets his pegs to stir up a revolution and upset the administration. It's one of my little chores as private secretary to smell out these revolutions and affix the kibosh before they break out, and scratch the paint off the government property. That's why I'm down here now in this mildewed coast town. The governor of the district and his crew are plotting to uprise. I've got every one of their names, and they're invited to listen to the phonograph tonight, compliments of H. P. M. That's the way I'll get them in a bunch, and things are on the programme to happen to them.'

"We three were sitting at table in the cantina of the Purified Saints. Mellinger poured out wine, and was looking some worried; I was thinking.

" 'They're a sharp crowd,' he says, kind of fretful. 'They're capitalized by a foreign syndicate after rubber, and they're loaded to the muzzle for bribing. I'm sick,' goes on Mellinger, 'of comic opera. I want to smell East River and wear suspenders again. At times I feel like throwing up my job, but I'm d——n fool enough to be sort of proud of it. "There's Mellinger," they say here. "*Por Dios!* you can't touch him with a million." I'd like to take that record back and show it to Billy Renfrow some day; and that tightens my grip whenever I see a fat thing that I could corral just by winking one eye—and losing my graft. By ——, they can't monkey with me. They know it. What money I get I make honest and spend it. Some day I'll make a pile and go back and eat caviare with Billy. To-night I'll show you how to handle a bunch of corruptionists. I'll show them what Mellinger, private secretary, means when you spell it with the cotton and tissue paper off.'

"Mellinger appears shaky, and breaks his glass against the neck of the bottle.

"I says to myself. 'White man, if I'm not mistaken there's been a bait laid out where the tail of your eye could see it.'

"That night, according to arrangements, me and Henry took the phonograph to a room in a 'dobe house in a dirty side street, where the grass was knee high. 'Twas a long room, lit with smoky oil lamps. There was plenty of chairs, and a table at the back end. We set the phonograph on the table. Mellinger was there, walking up and down, disturbed in his predicaments. He chewed cigars and spat 'em out, and he bit the thumb nail of his left hand.

"By and by the invitations to the musicale came sliding in by pairs and threes and spade flushes. Their colour was of a diversity, running from a three-days' smoked meerschaum to a patent-leather polish. They were as polite as wax, being devastated with enjoyments to give *Señor* Mellinger the good evenings. I understood their Spanish talk—I ran a pumping engine two years in a Mexican silver mine, and had it pat—but I never let on.

"Maybe fifty of 'em had come, and was seated, when in slid the king bee, the governor of the district. Mellinger met him at the door, and escorted him to the grand stand. When I saw that Latin man I knew that Mellinger, private secretary, had all the dances on his card taken. That was a big, squashy man, the colour of a rubber overshoe, and he had an eye like a head waiter's.

"Mellinger explained, fluent in the Castilian idioms, that his soul was disconcerted with joy at introducing to his respected friends America's greatest invention, the wonder of the age. Henry got the cue and run on an elegant brass-band record and the festivities became initiated. The governor man had a bit of English under his hat, and when the music was choked off he says:

" 'Ver-r-ree fine. *Gr-r-r-r-racias*, the American gentleemen, the so esplendeed moosic as to playee.'

"The table was a long one, and Henry and me sat at the end of it next the wall. The governor sat at the other end. Homer P. Mellinger stood at the side of it. I was just wondering how Mellinger was going to handle his crowd, when the home talent suddenly opened the services.

"That governor man was suitable for uprisings and policies. I judge he was a ready kind of man, who took his own time. Yes, he was full of attention and immediateness. He leaned his hands on the table and imposed his face toward the secretary man.

" 'Do the American *señors* understand Spanish?' he asks in his native accents.

" 'They do not,' says Mellinger.

" 'Then listen,' goes on the Latin man, prompt. 'The musics are of sufficient prettiness, but not of necessity. Let us speak of business. I well know why we are here, since I observe my compatriots. You had a whisper yesterday, *Señor* Mellinger, of our proposals. To-night we will speak out. We know that you stand in the president's favour, and we know your influence. The government will be changed. We know the worth of your services. We esteem your friendship and aid so much that ——' Mellinger raises his hand, but the governor man bottles him up. 'Do not speak until I have done.'

"The governor man then draws a package wrapped in paper from his pocket, and lays it on the table by Mellinger's hand.

" 'In that you will find fifty thousand dollars in money of your country. You can do nothing against us, but you can be worth that for us. Go back to the capital and obey our instructions. Take that money now. We trust you. You will find with it a paper giving in detail the work you will be expected to do for us. Do not have the unwiseness to refuse.'

"The governor man paused, with his eyes fixed on Mellinger, full of expressions and observances. I looked at Mellinger, and was glad Billy Renfrow couldn't see him then. The sweat was popping out on his forehead, and he stood dumb, tapping the little package with the ends of his fingers. The colorado-maduro gang was after his graft. He had only to change his politics, and stuff five fingers in his inside pocket.

"Henry whispers to me and wants the pause in the programme interpreted. I whisper back: 'H. P. is up against a bribe, senator's size, and the coons have got him going.' I saw Mellinger's hand moving closer to the package. 'He's weakening,' I whispered to Henry. 'We'll remind him,' says Henry, 'of the peanut-roaster on Thirty-fourth Street, New York.'

"Henry stooped down and got a record from the basketful we'd brought, slid it in the phonograph, and started her off. It was a cornet solo, very neat and beautiful, and the name of it was 'Home, Sweet Home.' Not one of them fifty odd men in the room moved while it was playing, and the governor man kept his eyes steady on Mellinger. I saw Mellinger's head go up little by little, and his hand came creeping away from the package. Not until the last note sounded did anybody stir. And then Homer P. Mellinger takes up the bundle of boodle and slams it in the governor man's face.

" 'That's my answer,' says Mellinger, private secretary, 'and there'll be another in the morning. I have proofs of conspiracy against every man of you. The show is over, gentlemen.'

" 'There's one more act,' puts in the governor man. 'You are a servant, I believe, employed by the president to copy letters and answer raps at the door. I am governor here. *Señors*, I call upon you in the name of the cause to seize this man.'

"That brindled gang of conspirators shoved back their chairs and advanced in force. I could see where Mellinger had made a mistake in massing his enemy so as to make a grand-stand play. I think he made another one, too; but we can pass that, Mellinger's idea of a graft and mine being different, according to estimations and points of view.

"There was only one window and door in that room, and they were in the front end. Here was fifty odd Latin men coming in a bunch to obstruct the legislation of Mellinger. You may say there were three of us, for me and Henry, simultaneous, declared New York City and the Cherokee Nation in sympathy with the weaker party.

"Then it was that Henry Horsecollar rose to a

point of disorder and intervened, showing, admirable, the advantages of education as applied to the American Indian's natural intellect and native refinement. He stood up and smoothed back his hair on each side with his hands as you have seen little girls do when they play.

" 'Get behind me, both of you,' says Henry.

" 'What's it to be, chief?' I asked.

" 'I'm going to buck centre,' says Henry, in his football idioms. 'There isn't a tackle in the lot of them. Follow me close, and rush the game.'

"Then that cultured Red Man exhaled an arrangement of sounds with his mouth that made the Latin aggregation pause, with thoughtfulness and hesitations. The matter of his proclamation seemed to be a co-operation of the Carlisle war-whoop with the Cherokee college yell. He went at the chocolate team like a bean out of a little boy's nigger shooter. His right elbow laid out the governor man on the grid-iron, and he made a lane the length of the crowd so wide that a woman could have carried a step-ladder through it without striking against anything. All Mellinger and me had to do was to follow.

"It took us just three minutes to get out of that street around to military headquarters, where Mellinger had things his own way. A colonel and a battalion of bare-toed infantry turned out and went back to the scene of the musicale with us, but the conspirator gang was gone. But we recaptured the phonograph with honours of war, and marched back to the *cuartel* with it playing 'All Coons Look Alike to Me.'

"The next day Mellinger takes me and Henry to one side, and begins to shed tens and twenties.

" 'I want to buy that phonograph,' says he. 'I liked that last tune it played at the *soirée.*'

" 'This is more money than the machine is worth,' says I.

" ' 'Tis government expense money,' says Mellinger. 'The government pays for it, and it's getting the tune-grinder cheap.'

"Me and Henry knew that pretty well. We knew that it had saved Homer P. Mellinger's graft when he was on the point of losing it; but we never let him know we knew it.

" 'Now you boys better slide off further down the coast for a while,' says Mellinger, 'till I get the screws put on these fellows here. If you don't they'll give you trouble. And if you ever happen to see Billy Renfrow again before I do, tell him I'm coming back to New York as soon as I can make a stake—honest.'

"Me and Henry laid low until the day the steamer came back. When we saw the captain's boat on the beach we went down and stood in the edge of the water. The captain grinned when he saw us.

" 'I told you you'd be waiting,' he says. 'Where's the Hamburger machine?'

" 'It stays behind,' I says, 'to play "Home, Sweet Home." '

" 'I told you so,' says the captain again. 'Climb in the boat.'

"And that," said Keogh, "is the way me and Henry Horsecollar introduced the phonograph into this country. Henry went back to the States, but I've been rummaging around in the tropics ever since. They say Mellinger never travelled a mile after that without his phonograph. I guess it kept him reminded about his graft whenever he saw the siren voice of the boodler tip him the wink with a bribe in its hand."

"I suppose he's taking it home with him as a souvenir," remarked the consul.

"Not as a souvenir," said Keogh. "He'll need two of 'em in New York, running day and night."

LXXXVIII: MONEY MAZE

THE new administration of Anchuria entered upon its duties and privileges with enthusiasm. Its first act was to send an agent to Coralio with imperative orders to recover, if possible, the sum of money ravished from the treasury by the ill-fated Miraflores.

Colonel Emilio Falcon, the private secretary of Losada, the new president, was dispatched from the capital upon this important mission.

The position of private secretary to a tropical president is a responsible one. He must be a diplomat, a spy, a ruler of men, a bodyguard to his chief, and a smeller-out of plots and nascent revolutions. Often he is the power behind the throne, the dictator of policy; and a president chooses him with a dozen times the care with which he selects a matrimonial mate.

Colonel Falcon, a handsome and urbane gentleman of Castilian courtesy and debonair manners, came to Coralio with the task before him of striking upon the cold trail of the lost money. There he conferred with the military authorities, who had received instructions to co-operate with him in the search.

Colonel Falcon established his headquarters in one of the rooms of the Casa Morena. Here for a week he held informal sittings—much as if he were a kind of unified grand jury—and summoned before him all those whose testimony might illumine the financial tragedy that had accompanied the less momentous one of the late president's death.

Two or three who were thus examined, among whom was the barber Estebán, declared that they had identified the body of the president before its burial.

"Of a truth," testified Estebán before the mighty secretary, "it was he, the president. Consider!—how could I shave a man and not see his face? He sent for me to shave him in a small house. He had a beard very black and thick. Had I ever seen the president before? Why not? I saw him once ride forth in a carriage from the *vapor* in Solitas. When I shaved him he gave me a gold piece, and said there was to be no talk. But I am a Liberal—I am devoted to my country—and I spake of these things to *Señor* Goodwin."

"It is known," said Colonel Falcon, smoothly, "that the late President took with him an American leather valise, containing a large amount of money. Did you see that?"

"*De veras*—no," Estebán answered. "The light in the little house was but a small lamp by which I could scarcely see to shave the President. Such a thing there may have been, but I did not see it. No. Also in the room was a young lady—a *señorita* of much beauty—that I could see even in so small a light. But the money, *señor*, or the thing in which it was carried—that I did not see."

The *comandante* and other officers gave testimony

that they had been awakened and alarmed by the noise of a pistol-shot in the Hotel de los Estranjeros. Hurrying thither to protect the peace and dignity of the republic, they found a man lying dead, with a pistol clutched in his hand. Beside him was a young woman, weeping sorely. *Señor* Goodwin was also in the room when they entered it. But of the valise of money they saw nothing.

Madame Timotea Ortiz, the proprietress of the hotel in which the game of Fox-in-the-Morning had been played out, told of the coming of the two guests to her house.

"To my house they came," said she—"one *señor*, not quite old, and one *señorita* of sufficient handsomeness. They desired not to eat or to drink—not even of my *aguardiente*, which is the best. To their rooms they ascended—*Numero Nueve* and *Numero Diez*. Later came *Señor* Goodwin, who ascended to speak with them. Then I heard a great noise like that of a *canon*, and they said that the *pobre Presidente* had shot himself. *Está bueno*. I saw nothing of money or of the thing you call *veliz* that you say he carried it in."

Colonel Falcon soon came to the reasonable conclusion that if anyone in Coralio could furnish a clue to the vanished money, Frank Goodwin must be the man. But the wise secretary pursued a different course in seeking information from the American. Goodwin was a powerful friend to the new administration, and one who was not to be carelessly dealt with in respect to either his honesty or his courage. Even the private secretary of His Excellency hesitated to have this rubber prince and mahogany baron haled before him as a common citizen of Anchuria. So he sent Goodwin a flowery epistle, each word-petal dripping with honey, requesting the favour of an interview. Goodwin replied with an invitation to dinner at his own house.

Before the hour named the American walked over to the Casa Morena, and greeted his guest frankly and friendly. Then the two strolled in the cool of the afternoon, to Goodwin's home in the environs.

The American left Colonel Falcon in a big, cool, shadowed room with a floor of inlaid and polished woods that any millionaire in the States would have envied, excusing himself for a few minutes. He crossed a *patio*, shaded with deftly arranged awnings and plants, and entered a long room looking upon the sea in the opposite wing of the house. The broad jalousies were opened wide, and the ocean breeze flowed in through the room, an invisible current of coolness and health. Goodwin's wife sat near one of the windows, making a water-colour sketch of the afternoon seascape.

Here was a woman who looked to be happy. And more—she looked to be content. Had a poet been inspired to pen just similes, concerning her favour, he would have likened her full, clear eyes, with their white-encircled, grey irises, to moonflowers. With none of the goddesses whose traditional charms have become coldly classic would the discerning rhymester have compared her. She was purely Paradisaic, not Olympian. If you can imagine Eve, after the eviction, beguiling the flaming warriors and serenely re-entering the Garden, you will have her. Just so human, and still so harmonious with Eden seemed Mrs. Goodwin.

When her husband entered she looked up, and

her lips curved and parted; her eyelids fluttered twice or thrice—a movement remindful (Poesy forgive us!) of the tail-wagging of a faithful dog—and a little ripple went through her like the commotion set up in a weeping willow by a puff of wind. Thus she ever acknowledged his coming, were it twenty times a day. If they who sometimes sat over their wine in Coralio, reshaping old, diverting stories of the madcap career of Isabel Guilbert, could have seen the wife of Frank Goodwin that afternoon in the estimable aura of her happy wifehood, they might have disbelieved, or have agreed to forget, those graphic annals of the life of the one for whom their president gave up his country and his honour.

"I have brought a guest to dinner," said Goodwin. "One Colonel Falcon, from San Mateo. He is come on government business. I do not think you will care to see him, so I prescribe for you one of those convenient and indisputable feminine headaches."

"He has come to inquire about the lost money, has he not?" asked Mrs. Goodwin, going on with her sketch.

"A good guess!" acknowledged Goodwin. "He has been holding an inquisition among the natives for three days. I am next on his list of witnesses, but as he feels shy about dragging one of Uncle Sam's subjects before him, he consents to give it the outward appearance of a social function. He will apply the torture over my own wine and provender."

"Has he found anyone who saw the valise of money?"

"Not a soul. Even Madama Ortiz, whose eyes

are so sharp for the sight of a revenue official, does not remember that there was any baggage."

Mrs. Goodwin laid down her brush and sighed.

"I am so sorry, Frank," she said, "that they are giving you so much trouble about the money. But we can't let them know about it, can we?"

"Not without doing our intelligence a great injustice," said Goodwin, with a smile and a shrug that he had picked up from the natives. "*Americano* though I am, they would have me in the *calaboza* in half an hour if they knew we had appropriated that valise. No; we must appear as ignorant about the money as the other ignoramuses in Coralio."

"Do you think that this man they have sent suspects you?" she asked, with a little pucker of her brows.

"He'd better not," said the American, carelessly. "It's lucky that no one caught a sight of the valise except myself. As I was in the rooms when the shot was fired, it is not surprising that they should want to investigate my part in the affair rather closely. But there's no cause for alarm. This colonel is down on the list of events for a good dinner, with a dessert of American 'bluff' that will end the matter, I think."

Mrs. Goodwin rose and walked to the window, Goodwin followed and stood by her side. She leaned to him, and rested in the protection of his strength, as she had always rested since that dark night on which he had first made himself her tower of refuge. Thus they stood for a little while.

Straight through the lavish growth of tropical branch and leaf and vine that confronted them had been cunningly trimmed a vista, that ended at the cleared environs of Coralio, on the banks of the mangrove swamp. At the other end of the aerial tunnel they could see the grave and wooden headpiece that bore the name of the unhappy President Miraflores. From this window when the rains forbade the open, and from the green and shady slopes of Goodwin's fruitful lands when the skies were smiling, his wife was wont to look upon that grave with a gentle sadness that was now scarcely a mar to her happiness.

"I loved him so, Frank!" she said, "even after that terrible flight and its awful ending. And you have been so good to me, and have made me so happy. It has all grown into such a strange puzzle. If they were to find out that we got the money, do you think they would force you to make the amount good to the government?"

"They would undoubtedly try," answered Goodwin. "You are right about its being a puzzle. And it must remain a puzzle to Falcon and all his countrymen until it solves itself. You and I, who know more than anyone else, only know half of the solution. We must not let even a hint about this money get abroad. Let them come to the theory that the president concealed it in the mountains during his journey, or that he found means to ship it out of the country before he reached Coralio. I don't think that Falcon suspects me. He is making a close investigation, according to his orders, but he will find out nothing."

Thus they spake together. Had anyone overheard or overseen them as they discussed the lost funds of Anchuria there would have been a second puzzle presented. For upon the faces and in the bearing of each of them was visible (if countenances are to be believed) Saxon honesty and pride and honourable thoughts. In Goodwin's steady eye and firm lineaments, moulded into material shape by the inward spirit of kindness and generosity and courage, there was nothing reconcilable with his words.

As for his wife, physiognomy championed her even in the face of their accusive talk. Nobility was in her guise; purity was in her glance. The devotion that she manifested had not even the appearance of that feeling that now and then inspires a woman to share the guilt of her partner out of the pathetic greatness of her love. No, there was a discrepancy here between what the eye would have seen and the ear have heard.

Dinner was served to Goodwin and his guest in the *patio*, under cool foliage and flowers. The American begged the illustrious secretary to excuse the absence of Mrs. Goodwin, who was suffering, he said, from a headache brought on by a slight *calentura*.

After the meal they lingered, according to the custom, over their coffee and cigars. Colonel Falcon, with true Castilian delicacy, waited for his host to open the question that they had met to discuss. He had not long to wait. As soon as the cigars were lighted, the American cleared the way by inquiring whether the secretary's investigations in the town had furnished him with any clue to the lost funds.

"I have found no one yet," admitted Colonel Falcon, "who even had sight of the valise or the money. Yet I have persisted. It has been proven in the capital that President Miraflores set out from San Mateo with one hundred thousand dollars belonging to the government, accompanied by *Señorita* Isabel Guilbert, the opera singer. The government, officially and personally, is loath to believe," concluded Colonel Falcon, with a smile, "that our late President's tastes would have permitted him to abandon on the route, as excess baggage, either of the desirable articles with which his flight was burdened."

"I suppose you would like to hear what I have to say about the affair," said Goodwin, coming directly to the point. "It will not require many words.

"On that night, with others of our friends here, I was keeping a lookout for the president, having been notified of his flight by a telegram in our national cipher from Englehart, one of our leaders in the capital. About ten o'clock that night I saw a man and a woman hurrying along the streets. They went to the Hotel de los Estranjeros, and engaged rooms. I followed them upstairs, leaving Estebán, who had come up, to watch outside. The barber had told me that he had shaved the beard from the president's face that night; therefore I was prepared, when I entered the rooms, to find him with a smooth face. When I approached him in the name of the people he drew a pistol and shot himself instantly. In a few minutes many officers and citizens were on the spot. I suppose you have been informed of the subsequent facts."

Goodwin paused. Losada's agent maintained an attitude of waiting, as if he expected a continuance.

"And now," went on the American, looking steadily into the eyes of the other man, and giving each word a deliberate emphasis, "you will oblige me by attending carefully to what I have to add. I saw no valise or receptacle of any kind, or any money belonging to the Republic of Anchuria. If President Miraflores decamped with any funds belonging to the treasury of this country, or to himself, or to anyone else, I saw no trace of it in the house or elsewhere, at that time or at any other. Does that statement cover the ground of the inquiry you wished to make of me?"

Colonel Falcon bowed, and described a fluent curve with his cigar. His duty was performed. Goodwin was not to be disputed. He was a loyal supporter of the government, and enjoyed the full confidence of the new president. His rectitude had been the capital that had brought him fortune in Anchuria, just as it had formed the lucrative "graft" of Mellinger, the secretary of Miraflores.

"I thank you, *Señor* Goodwin," said Falcon, "for speaking plainly. Your word will be sufficient for the president. But, *Señor* Goodwin, I am instructed to pursue every clue that presents itself in this matter. There is one that I have not yet touched upon. Our friends in France, *señor*, have a saying '*Cherchez la femme*,' when there is a mystery without a clue. But here we do not have to search. The woman who accompanied the late President in his flight must surely——"

"I must interrupt you there," interposed Goodwin. "It is true that when I entered the hotel for the purpose of intercepting President Miraflores I found a lady there. I must beg of you to remember that that lady is now my wife. I speak for her as I do for myself. She knows nothing of the fate of the valise or of the money that you are seeking. You will say to his excellency, that I guarantee her innocence. I do not need to add to you, Colonel Falcon, that I do not care to have her questioned or disturbed."

Colonel Falcon bowed again.

"*Por supuesto*, no!" he cried. And to indicate that the inquiry was ended he added: "And now, *señor*, let me beg of you to show me that sea view from your *galeria* of which you spoke. I am a lover of the sea."

In the early evening Goodwin walked back to the town with his guest, leaving him at the corner of the Calle Grande. As he was returning homeward one "Beelzebub" Blythe, with the air of a courtier and the outward aspect of a scarecrow, pounced upon him hopefully from the door of a *pulperia*.

Blythe had been re-christened "Beelzebub" as an acknowledgment of the greatness of his fall. Once in some distant Paradise Lost, he had forgathered with the angels of the earth. But Fate had hurled him headlong down to the tropics, where flamed in his bosom a fire that was seldom quenched. In Coralio they called him a beachcomber; but he was, in reality, a categorical idealist who strove to anamorphosize the dull verities of life by the means of brandy and rum. As Beelzebub, himself, might have held in his clutch with unwitting tenacity his harp or crown during his tremendous fall, so his namesake had clung to his gold-rimmed eyeglasses as the only souvenir of his lost estate. These he wore with impressiveness and distinction while he combed beaches and extracted toll from his friends. By some mysterious means he kept his drink-reddened face always smoothly shaven. For the rest he sponged gracefully upon whomsoever he could for enough to keep him pretty drunk, and sheltered from the rains and night dews.

"Hallo, Goodwin!" called the derelict, airily. "I was hoping I'd strike you. I wanted to see you particularly. Suppose we go where we can talk. Of course you know there's a chap down here looking up the money old Miraflores lost."

"Yes," said Goodwin, "I've been talking with him. Let's go into Espada's place. I can spare you ten minutes."

They went into the *pulperia* and sat at a little table upon stools with rawhide tops.

"Have a drink?" said Goodwin.

"They can't bring it too quickly," said Blythe. "I've been in a drought ever since morning. Hi —*muchacho!—el aguardiente por acá.*"

"Now, what do you want to see me about?" asked Goodwin, when the drinks were before them.

"Confound it, old man," drawled Blythe, "why do you spoil a golden moment like this with business? I wanted to see you—well, this has the preference." He gulped down his brandy, and gazed longingly into the empty glass.

"Have another?" suggested Goodwin.

"Between gentlemen," said the fallen angel, "I don't quite like your use of that word 'another.' It isn't quite delicate. But the concrete idea that the word represents is not displeasing."

The glasses were refilled. Blythe sipped blissfully from his, as he began to enter the state of a true idealist.

"I must trot along in a minute or two," hinted Goodwin. "Was there anything in particular?"

Blythe did not reply at once.

"Old Losada would make it a hot country," he

remarked at length, "for the man who swiped that grip-sack of treasury boodle, don't you think?"

"Undoubtedly he would," agreed Goodwin calmly, as he rose leisurely to his feet. "I'll be running over to the house now, old man. Mrs. Goodwin is alone. There was nothing important you had to say, was there?"

"That's all," said Blythe. "Unless you wouldn't mind sending in another drink from the bar as you go out. Old Espada has closed my account to profit and loss. And pay for the lot, will you, like a good fellow?"

"All right," said Goodwin. "*Buenas noches.*"

"Beelzebub" Blythe lingered over his cups, polishing his eyeglasses with a disreputable handkerchief.

"I thought I could do it, but I couldn't," he muttered to himself after a time. "A gentleman can't blackmail the man that he drinks with."

LXXXIX: THE ADMIRAL

SPILLED milk draws few tears from an Anchurian administration. Many are its lacteal sources; and the clock's hands point for ever to milking time. Even the rich cream skimmed from the treasury by the bewitched Miraflores did not cause the newly-installed patriots to waste time in unprofitable regrets. The government philosophically set about supplying the deficiency by increasing the import duties and by "suggesting" to wealthy private citizens that contributions according to their means would be considered patriotic and in order. Prosperity was expected to attend the reign of Losada, the new president. The ousted office-holders and military favourites organized a new "Liberal" party, and began to lay their plans for a re-succession. Thus the game of Anchurian politics began, like a Chinese comedy, to unwind slowly its serial length. Here and there Mirth peeps for an instant from the wings and illumines the florid lines.

A dozen quarts of champagne in conjunction with an informal sitting of the president and his cabinet led to the establishment of the navy and the appointment of Felipe Carrera as its admiral.

Next to the champagne the credit of the appointment belongs to Don Sabas Placido, the newly confirmed Minister of War.

The president had requested a convention of his cabinet for the discussion of questions politic and for the transaction of certain routine matters of state. The session had been signally tedious; the business and the wine prodigiously dry. A sudden, prankish humour of Don Sabas, impelling him to the deed, spiced the grave affairs of state with a whiff of agreeable playfulness.

In the dilatory order of business had come a bulletin from the coast department of Orilla del Mar reporting the seizure by the custom-house officers at the town of Coralio of the sloop *Estrella del Noche* and her cargo of dry goods, patent medicines, granulated sugar and three-star brandy. Also six Martini rifles and a barrel of American whisky. Caught in the act of smuggling, the sloop with its cargo was now, according to law, the property of the republic.

The Collector of Customs, in making his report,

departed from the conventional forms so far as to suggest that the confiscated vessel be converted to the use of the government. The prize was the first capture to the credit of the department in ten years. The collector took opportunity to pat his department.

It often happened that government officers required transportation from point to point along the coast, and means were usually lacking. Furthermore, the sloop could be manned by a loyal crew and employed as a coast-guard to discourage the pernicious art of smuggling. The collector also ventured to nominate one to whom the charge of the boat could be safely entrusted—a young man of Coralio, Felipe Carrera—not, be it understood, one of extreme wisdom, but loyal and the best sailor along the coast.

It was upon this hint that the Minister of War acted, executing a rare piece of drollery that so enlivened the tedium of executive session.

In the constitution of this small, maritime banana republic was a forgotten section that provided for the maintenance of a navy. This provision—with many other wiser ones—had lain inert since the establishment of the republic. Anchuria had no navy and had no use for one. It was characteristic of Don Sabas—a man at once merry, learned, whimsical and audacious—that he should have disturbed the dust of this musty and sleeping statute to increase the humour of the world by so much as a smile from his indulgent colleagues.

With delightful mock seriousness the Minister of War proposed the creation of a navy. He argued its need and the glories it might achieve with such gay and witty zeal that the travesty overcame with its humour even the swart dignity of President Losada himself.

The champagne was bubbling trickily in the veins of the mercurial statesmen. It was not the custom of the grave governors of Anchuria to enliven their sessions with a beverage so apt to cast a veil of disparagement over sober affairs. The wine had been a thoughtful compliment tendered by the agent of the Vesuvius Fruit Company as a token of amicable relations—and certain consummated deals—between that company and the republic of Anchuria.

The jest was carried to its end. A formidable, official document was prepared, encrusted with chromatic seals and jaunty with fluttering ribbons, bearing the florid signatures of state. This commission conferred upon *el Señor* Don Felipe Carrera the title of Flag Admiral of the Republic of Anchuria. Thus within the space of a few minutes and the dominion of a dozen "extra dry" the country took its place among the naval powers of the world, and Felipe Carrera became entitled to a salute of nineteen guns whenever he might enter port.

The southern races are lacking in that particular kind of humour that finds entertainment in the defects and misfortunes bestowed by Nature. Owing to this defect in their constitution they are not moved to laughter (as are their northern brothers) by the spectacle of the deformed, the feeble-minded or the insane.

Felipe Carrera was sent upon earth with but half his wits. Therefore, the people of Coralio called him "*El pobrecito loco*"—"the poor little crazed one"—saying that God had sent but half of him to earth, retaining the other half.

A sombre youth, glowering, and speaking only at the rarest times, Felipe was but negatively "loco." On shore he generally refused all conversation. He seemed to know that he was badly handicapped on land, where so many kinds of understanding are needed; but on the water his one talent set him equal with most men. Few sailors whom God had carefully and completely made could handle a sail-boat as well. Five points nearer the wind than the best of them he could sail his sloop. When the elements raged and set other men to cowering, the deficiencies of Felipe seemed of little importance. He was a perfect sailor, if an imperfect man. He owned no boat, but worked among the crews of the schooners and sloops that skimmed the coast, trading and freighting fruit out to the steamers where there was no harbour. It was through his famous skill and boldness on the sea, as well as for the pity felt for his mental imperfections, that he was recommended by the collector as a suitable custodian of the captured sloop.

When the outcome of Don Sabas' little pleasantry arrived in the form of the imposing and preposterous commission, the collector smiled. He had not expected such prompt and overwhelming response to his recommendation. He despatched a *muchacho* at once to fetch the future admiral.

The collector waited in his official quarters. His office was in the Calle Grande, and the sea-breezes hummed through its windows all day. The collector, in white linen and canvas shoes, philandered with papers on an antique desk. A parrot, perched on a pen rack, seasoned the official tedium with a fire of choice Castilian imprecations. Two rooms opened into the collector's. In one the clerical force of young men of variegated complexions transacted with glitter and parade their several duties. Through the open door of the other room could be seen a bronze babe, guiltless of clothing, that rollicked upon the floor. In a grass hammock a thin woman, tinted a pale lemon, played a guitar and swung contentedly in the breeze. Thus surrounded by the routine of his high duties and the visible tokens of agreeable domesticity, the collector's heart was further made happy by the power placed in his hands to brighten the fortunes of the "innocent" Felipe.

Felipe came and stood before the collector. He was a lad of twenty, not ill-favoured in looks, but with an expression of distant and pondering vacuity. He wore white cotton trousers, down the seams of which he had sewn red stripes with some vague aim of military decoration. A flimsy blue shirt fell open at his throat; his feet were bare; he held in his hand the cheapest of straw hats from the States.

"*Señor* Carrera," said the collector, gravely, producing the showy commission, "I have sent for you at the president's bidding. This document that I present to you confers upon you the title of Admiral of this great republic, and gives you absolute command of the naval forces and fleet of our country. You may think, friend Felipe, that we have no navy—but yes! The sloop the *Estrella del Noche*, that my brave men captured from the coast smugglers, is to be placed under your command. The boat is to be devoted to the services of your country. You will be ready at all times to convey officials of the government to points along the coast where they may be obliged to visit. You will also act as a coast-guard to prevent, as far as you may be able, the crime of smuggling. You will uphold the honour and prestige of your country at sea, and endeavour to place Anchuria among the proudest naval powers of the world. These are your instructions as the Minister of War desires me to convey them to you. *Por Dios!* I do not know how all this is to be accomplished, for not one word did the letter contain in respect to a crew or to the expenses of this navy. Perhaps you are to provide a crew yourself, *Señor* Admiral—I do not know—but it is a very high honour that has descended upon you. I now hand you your commission. When you are ready for the boat I will give orders that she shall be made over into your charge. That is as far as my instructions go."

Felipe took the commission that the collector handed to him. He gazed through the open window at the sea for a moment, with his customary expression of deep but vain pondering. Then he turned without having spoken a word, and walked swiftly away through the hot sand of the street.

"*Pobrecito loco!*" sighed the collector; and the parrot on the pen racks screeched "Loco!—loco!—loco!"

The next morning a strange procession filed through the streets to the collector's office. At its head was the admiral of the navy. Somewhere Felipe had raked together a pitiful semblance of a military uniform—a pair of red trousers, a dingy blue short jacket heavily ornamented with gold braid, and an old fatigue cap that must have been cast away by one of the British soldiers in Belize and brought away by Felipe on one of his coasting voyages. Buckled around his waist was an ancient ship's cutlass contributed to his equipment by

Pedro Lafitte, the baker, who proudly asserted its inheritance from his ancestor, the illustrious buccaneer. At the admiral's heels tagged his newly-shipped crew—three grinning, glossy, black Caribs, bare to the waist, the sand spurting in showers from the spring of their naked feet.

Briefly and with dignity Felipe demanded his vessel of the collector. And now a fresh honour awaited him. The collector's wife, who played the guitar and read novels in the hammock all day, had more than a little romance in her placid, yellow bosom. She had found in an old book an engraving of a flag that purported to be the naval flag of Anchuria. Perhaps it had so been designed by the founders of the nation; but, as no navy had ever been established, oblivion had claimed the flag. Laboriously with her own hands she had made a flag after the pattern—a red cross upon a blue-and-white ground. She presented it to Felipe with these words: "Brave sailor, this flag is of your country. Be true and defend it with your life. Go you with God."

For the first time since his appointment the admiral showed a flicker of emotion. He took the silken emblem, and passed his hand reverently over its surface. "I am an admiral," he said to the collector's lady. Being on land he could bring himself to no more exuberant expression of sentiment. At sea with the flag at the masthead of his navy, some more eloquent exposition of feelings might be forthcoming.

Abruptly the admiral departed with his crew. For the next three days they were busy giving the *Estrella del Noche* a new coat of white paint trimmed with blue. And then Felipe further adorned himself by fastening a handful of brilliant parrot's plumes in his cap. Again he tramped with his faithful crew to the collector's office and formally notified him that the sloop's name had been changed to *El Nacional.*

During the next few months the navy had its troubles. Even an admiral is perplexed to know what to do without any orders. But none came. Neither did any salaries. *El Nacional* swung idly at anchor.

When Felipe's little store of money was exhausted he went to the collector and raised the question of finances.

"Salaries!" exclaimed the collector, with hands raised; "*Valgame Dios!* not one *centavo* of my own pay have I received for the last seven months. The pay of an admiral, do you ask? *Quién sabe?* Should it be less than three thousand *pesos*? *Mira!* you will see a revolution in this country very soon. A good sign of it is when the government calls all the time for *pesos*, *pesos*, *pesos*, and pays none out."

Felipe left the collector's office with a look almost of content on his sombre face. A revolution would mean fighting, and then the government would need his services. It was rather humiliating to be an admiral without anything to do, and have a hungry crew at your heels begging for *reales* to buy plantains and tobacco with.

When he returned to where his happy-go-lucky Caribs were waiting they sprang up and saluted, as he had drilled them to do.

"Come, *muchachos*," said the admiral; "it seems that the government is poor. It has no money to give us. We will earn what we need to live upon. Thus we will serve our country. Soon—his heavy eyes almost lighted up—"it may gladly call upon us for help."

Thereafter *El Nacional* turned out with the other coast craft and became a wage-earner. She worked with the lighters freighting bananas and oranges out to the fruit steamers that could not approach nearer than a mile from the shore. Surely a self-supporting navy deserves red letters in the budget of any nation.

After earning enough at freighting to keep himself and his crew in provisions for a week, Felipe would anchor the navy and hang about the little telegraph office, looking like one of the chorus of an insolvent comic opera troupe besieging the manager's den. A hope for orders from the capital was always in his heart. That his services as admiral had never been called into requirement hurt his pride and patriotism. At every call he would inquire, gravely and expectantly, for dispatches. The operator would pretend to make a search, and then reply:

"Not yet, it seems, *Señor el Almirante—poco tiempo!*"

Outside in the shade of the lime-trees the crew chewed sugar-cane or slumbered, well content to serve a country that was contented with so little service.

One day in the early summer the revolution predicted by the collector flamed out suddenly. It had long been smouldering. At the first note of alarm the admiral of the navy force and fleet made all sail for a larger port on the coast of a neighbouring republic, where he traded a hastily collected cargo of fruit for its value in cartridges for the five Martini rifles, the only guns that the navy could boast. Then to the telegraph office sped the admiral. Sprawling in his favourite corner, in his fast-decaying uniform, with his prodigious sabre distributed between his red legs, he waited for the long-delayed, but now soon expected, orders.

"Not yet, *Señor el Almirante*," the telegraph clerk would call to him—"*poco tiempo!*"

At the answer the admiral would plump himself down with a great rattling of scabbard to await the infrequent tick of the little instrument on the table.

"They will come," would be his unshaken reply; "I am the admiral."

XC: THE FLAG PARAMOUNT

AT the head of the insurgent party appeared that Hector and learned Theban of the southern republics, Don Sabas Placido. A traveller, a soldier, a poet, a scientist, a statesman and a connoisseur—the wonder was that he could content himself with the petty, remote life of his native country.

"It is a whim of Placido's," said a friend who knew him well, "to take up political intrigue. It is not otherwise than as if he had come upon a new *tempo* in music, a new bacillus in the air, a new scent, or rhyme, or explosive. He will squeeze this revolution dry of sensations, and a week afterward will forget it, skimming the seas of the world in his brigantine to add to his already world-famous collections. Collections of what? *Por Dios!* of everything from postage stamps to prehistoric stone idols."

But, for a mere dilettante, the æsthetic Placido seemed to be creating a lively row. The people admired him; they were fascinated by his brilliancy and flattered by his taking an interest in so small a thing as his native country. They rallied to the call of his lieutenants in the capital, where (somewhat contrary to arrangements) the army remained faithful to the government. There was also lively skirmishing in the coast towns. It was rumoured that the revolution was aided by the Vesuvius Fruit Company, the power that for ever stood with chiding smile and uplifted finger to keep Anchuria in the class of good children. Two of its steamers, the *Traveler* and the *Salvador*, were known to have conveyed insurgent troops from point to point along the coast.

As yet there had been no actual uprising in Coralio. Military law prevailed, and the ferment was bottled for the time. And then came the word that everywhere the revolutionists were encountering defeat. In the capital the president's forces triumphed; and there was a rumour that the leaders of the revolt had been forced to fly, hotly pursued.

In the little telegraph office at Coralio there was always a gathering of officials and loyal citizens, awaiting news from the seat of government. One morning the telegraph key began clicking, and presently the operator called, loudly: "One telegram for *el Almirante*, Don *Señor* Felipe Carrera!"

There was a shuffling sound, a great rattling of tin scabbard, and the admiral, prompt at his spot of waiting, leaped across the room to receive it.

The message was handed to him. Slowly spelling it out, he found it to be his first official order—thus running:

"Proceed immediately with your vessel to mouth of Rio Ruiz; transport beef and provisions to barracks at Alforan.

"MARTINEZ, *General*."

Small glory, to be sure, in this, his country's first call. But it had called, and joy surged in the admiral's breast. He drew his cutlass belt to another buckle hole, roused his dozing crew, and in a quarter of an hour *El Nacional* was tacking swiftly down-coast in a stiff landward breeze.

The Rio Ruiz is a small river, emptying into the sea ten miles below Coralio. That portion of the coast is wild and solitary. Through a gorge in the Cordilleras rushes the Rio Ruiz, cold and bubbling, to glide, at last, with breadth and leisure, through an alluvial morass into the sea.

In two hours *El Nacional* entered the river's mouth. The banks were crowded with a disposition of formidable trees. The sumptuous undergrowth of the tropics overflowed the land, and drowned itself in the fallow waters. Silently the sloop entered there, and met a deeper silence. Brilliant with greens and ochres and floral scarlets, the umbrageous mouth of the Rio Ruiz furnished no sound or movement save of the sea-going water as it purled against the prow of the vessel. Small chance there seemed of wresting beef or provisions from that empty solitude.

The admiral decided to cast anchor, and, at the chain's rattle, the forest was stimulated to instant and resounding uproar. The mouth of the Rio Ruiz had only been taking a morning nap. Parrots and baboons screeched and barked in the trees; a whirring and a hissing and a booming marked the awakening of animal life; a dark-blue bulk was visible for an instant as a startled tapir fought his way through the vines.

The navy, under orders, hung in the mouth of the little river for hours. The crew served the dinner of shark's-fin soup, plantains, crab gumbo and sour wine. The admiral, with a three-foot telescope, closely scanned the impervious foliage fifty yards away.

It was nearly sunset when a reverberating "hallo-o-o!" came from the forest to their left. It was answered; and three men, mounted upon mules, crashed through the tropic tangle to within a dozen yards of the river's bank. There they dismounted; and one, unbuckling his belt, struck each mule a violent blow with his sword scabbard, so that they, with a fling of heels, dashed back again into the forest.

Those were strange-looking men to be conveying beef and provisions. One was a large and exceedingly active man, of striking presence. He was of the purest Spanish type, with curling, grey-besprinkled, dark hair, blue, sparkling eyes, and the pronounced air of a *caballero grande*. The other two were small, brown-faced men, wearing white military uniforms, high riding-boots and swords. The clothes of all were drenched, bespattered and rent by the thicket. Some stress of circumstance must have driven them, *diable à quatre*, through flood, mire and jungle.

"*O-hé! Señor Almirante*," called the large man. "Send to us your boat."

The dory was lowered, and Felipe, with one of the Caribs, rowed toward the left bank.

The large man stood near the water's brink, waist

deep in the curling vines. As he gazed upon the scarecrow figure in the stern of the dory a sprightly interest beamed upon his mobile face.

Months of wageless and thankless service had dimmed the admiral's splendour. His red trousers were patched and ragged. Most of the bright buttons and yellow braid were gone from his jacket. The visor of his cap was torn, and depended almost to his eyes. The admiral's feet were bare.

"Dear admiral," cried the large man, and his voice was like a blast from a horn, "I kiss your hands. I knew we could build upon your fidelity. You had our dispatch—from General Martinez. A little nearer with your boat, dear admiral. Upon these devils of shifting vines we stand with the smallest security."

Felipe regarded him with a stolid face.

"Provisions and beef for the barracks at Alforan," he quoted.

"No fault of the butchers, *Almirante mio*, that the beef awaits you not. But you are come in time to save the cattle. Get us aboard your vessel, *señor*, at once. You first, *caballeros—à priesa!* Come back for me. The boat is too small."

The dory conveyed the two officers to the sloop, and returned for the large man.

"Have you so gross a thing as food, good admiral?" he cried, when aboard. "And, perhaps, coffee? Beef and provisions! *Nombre de Dios!* a little longer and we could have eaten one of those mules that you, Colonel Rafael, saluted so feelingly with your sword scabbard at parting. Let us have food; and then we will sail—for the barracks at Alforan—no?"

The Caribs prepared a meal, to which the three

passengers of *El Nacional* set themselves with famished delight. About sunset, as was its custom, the breeze veered and swept back from the mountains, cool and steady, bringing a taste of the stagnant lagoons and mangrove swamps that guttered the lowlands. The mainsail of the sloop was hoisted and swelled to it, and at that moment they heard shouts and a waxing clamour from the bosky profundities of the shore.

"The butchers, my dear admiral," said the large man, smiling, "too late for the slaughter."

Further than his orders to the crew, the admiral was saying nothing. The topsail and jib were spread, and the sloop glided out of the estuary. The large man and his companions had bestowed themselves with what comfort they could about the bare deck. Belike, the thing big in their minds had been their departure from that critical shore; and now that the hazard was so far reduced their thoughts were loosed to the consideration of further deliverance. But when they saw the sloop turn and fly up-coast again they relaxed, satisfied with the course the admiral had taken.

The large man sat at ease, his spirited blue eye engaged in the contemplation of the navy's commander. He was trying to estimate this sombre and fantastic lad, whose impenetrable stolidity puzzled him. Himself a fugitive, his life sought, and chafing under the smart of defeat and failure, it was characteristic of him to transfer instantly his interest to the study of a thing new to him. It was like him, too, to have conceived and risked all upon this last desperate and madcap scheme—this message to a poor, crazed *fanatico* cruising about with his grotesque uniform and his farcical title. But his companions had been at their wits' end; escape had seemed incredible; and now he was pleased with the success of the plan they had called crack-brained and precarious.

The brief tropic twilight seemed to slide swiftly into the pearly splendour of a moonlit night. And now the lights of Coralio appeared, distributed against the darkening shore to their right. The admiral stood, silent, at the tiller; the Caribs, like black panthers, held the sheets, leaping noiselessly at his short commands. The three passengers were watching intently the sea before them, and when at length they came in sight of the bulk of a steamer lying a mile out from the town, with her lights radiating deep into the water, they held a sudden voluble and close-headed converse. The sloop was speeding as if to strike midway between ship and shore.

The large man suddenly separated from his companions and approached the scarecrow at the helm.

"My dear admiral," he said, "the government has been exceedingly remiss. I feel all the shame for it that only its ignorance of your devoted service has prevented it from sustaining. An inexcusable oversight has been made. A vessel, a uniform and a crew worthy of your fidelity shall be furnished you. But just now, dear admiral, there is business of moment afoot. The steamer lying there is the *Salvador*. I and my friends desire to be conveyed to her, where we are sent on the government's business. Do us the favour to shape your course accordingly."

Without replying, the admiral gave a short command, and put the tiller hard to port. *El Nacional* swerved, and headed straight as an arrow's course for the shore.

"Do me the favour," said the large man, a trifle restively, "to acknowledge, at least, that you catch the sound of my words." It was possible that the fellow might be lacking in senses as well as intellect.

The admiral emitted a croaking, harsh laugh, and spake.

"They will stand you," he said, "with your face to a wall and shoot you dead. That is the way they kill traitors. I knew you when you stepped into my boat. I have seen your picture in a book. You are Sabas Placido, traitor to your country. With your face to a wall. So, you will die. I am the admiral, and I will take you to them. With your face to a wall. Yes."

Don Sabas half turned and waved his hand, with a ringing laugh, toward his fellow-fugitives. "To you, *caballeros*, I have related the history of that session when we issued that O! so ridiculous commission. Of a truth our jest has been turned against us. Behold the Frankenstein's monster we have created!"

Don Sabas glanced toward the shore. The lights of Coralio were drawing near. He could see the beach, the warehouse of the *Bodega Nacional*, the long, low *cuartel* occupied by the soldiers, and, behind that, gleaming in the moonlight, a stretch of high adobe wall. He had seen men stood with their faces to that wall and shot dead.

Again he addressed the extravagant figure at the helm.

"It is true," he said, "that I am fleeing the country. But, receive the assurance that I care very little for that. Courts and camps everywhere are open to Sabas Placido. *Vaya!* what is this molehill of a republic—this pig's head of a country—to a man like me? I am a *paisano* of everywhere. In Rome, in London, in Paris, in Vienna, you will hear them say: 'Welcome back, Don Sabas.' Come!—*tonto*—baboon of a boy—admiral, whatever you call yourself, turn your boat. Put us on board the *Salvador*, and here is your pay—five hundred *pesos* in money of the *Estados Unidos*—more than your lying government will pay you in twenty years."

Don Sabas pressed a plump purse against the youth's hand. The admiral gave no heed to the words or the movement. Braced against the helm, he was holding the sloop dead on her shoreward course. His dull face was lit almost to intelligence by some inward conceit that seemed to afford him joy, and found utterance in another parrot-like cackle.

"That is why they do it," he said—"so that you will not see the guns. They fire—boom!—and you fall dead. With your face to the wall. Yes."

The admiral called a sudden order to his crew. The lithe, silent Caribs made fast the sheets they held, and slipped down the hatchway into the hold of the sloop. When the last one had disappeared Don Sabas, like a big, brown leopard, leaped forward, closed and fastened the hatch and stood smiling.

"No rifles, if you please, dear admiral," he said. "It was a whimsey of mine once to compile a dictionary of the Carib *lengua*. So I understood your order. Perhaps now you will——"

He cut short his words, for he heard the dull "swish" of iron scraping along tin. The admiral had drawn the cutlass of Pedro Lafitte, and was darting upon him. The blade descended, and it was only by a display of surprising agility that the large man escaped, with only a bruised shoulder, the glancing weapon. He was drawing his pistol as he sprang, and the next instant he shot the admiral down.

Don Sabas stooped over him, and rose again.

"In the heart," he said briefly. "*Señores*, the navy is abolished."

Colonel Rafael sprang to the helm, and the other officer hastened to loose the mainsail sheets. The boom swung round; *El Nacional* veered and began to tack industriously for the *Salvador*.

"Strike that flag, *señor*," called Colonel Rafael. "Our friends on the steamer will wonder why we are sailing under it."

"Well said," cried Don Sabas. Advancing to the mast he lowered the flag to the deck, where lay its too loyal supporter. Thus ended the Minister of War's little piece of after-dinner drollery, and by the same hand that began it.

Suddenly Don Sabas gave a great cry of joy, and ran down the slanting deck to the side of Colonel Rafael. Across his arm he carried the flag of the extinguished navy.

"*Mire! mire! señor*. Ah, *Dios!* Already can I hear that great bear of an *Oestreicher* shout, '*Du hast mein herz gebrochen!*' *Mire!* Of my friend, Herr Grunitz of Vienna, you have heard me relate. That man has travelled to Ceylon for an orchid—to Patagonia for a headdress—to Benares for a slipper—to Mozambique for a spearhead to add to his famous collections. Thou knowest, also, *amigo* Rafael, that I have been a gatherer of curios. My collection of battle flags of the world's navies was the most complete in existence until last year. Then

Herr Grunitz secured two, O! such rare specimens. One of a Barbary state, and one of the Makarooroos, a tribe on the west coast of Africa. I have not those, but they can be procured. But this flag, *señor*—do you know what it is? Name of God! do you know? See that red cross upon the blue-and-white ground! You never saw it before? *Seguramente no.* It is the naval flag of your country. *Mire!* This rotten tub we stand upon is its navy—that dead cockatoo lying there was its commander—that stroke of cutlass and single pistol shot a sea battle. All a piece of absurd foolery, I grant you—but authentic. There has never been another flag like this, and there never will be another. No. It is unique in the whole world. Yes. Think of what that means to a collector of flags! Do you know, *Coronel mio*, how many golden crowns Herr Grunitz would give for this flag? Ten thousand, likely. Well, a hundred thousand would not buy it. Beautiful flag! Only flag! Little devil of a most heaven-born flag! *O-hé!* old grumbler beyond the ocean. Wait till Don Sabas comes again to the Königin Strasse. He will let you kneel and touch the folds of it with one finger. *O-hé!* old spectacled ransacker of the world!"

Forgotten was the impotent revolution, the danger, the loss, the gall of defeat. Possessed solely by the inordinate and unparalleled passion of the collector, he strode up and down the little deck clasping to his breast with one hand the paragon of a flag. He snapped his fingers triumphantly toward the east. He shouted the pæan to his prize in trumpet tones, as though he would make old Grunitz hear in his musty den beyond the sea.

They were waiting, on the *Salvador*, to welcome

them. The sloop came close alongside the steamer, where her sides were sliced almost to the lower deck for the loading of fruit. The sailors of the *Salvador* grappled and held her there.

Captain McLeod leaned over the side.

"Well, *señor*, the jig is up, I'm told."

"The jig is up?" Don Sabas looked perplexed for a moment. "That revolution—ah, yes!" With a shrug of his shoulders he dismissed the matter.

The captain learned of the escape and the imprisoned crew.

"Caribs?" he said; "no harm in them." He slipped down into the sloop and kicked loose the hasp of the hatch. The black fellows came tumbling up, sweating but grinning.

"Hey! black boys!" said the captain, in a dialect of his own; "you sabe, catchy boat and vamos back same place quick."

They saw him point to themselves, the sloop and Coralio. "Yas, yas!" they cried, with broader grins and many nods.

The four—Don Sabas, the two officers and the captain—moved to quit the sloop. Don Sabas lagged a little behind, looking at the still form of the late admiral, sprawled in his paltry trappings.

"*Pobrecito loco*," he said softly.

He was a brilliant cosmopolite and a *cognoscente* of high rank; but, after all, he was of the same race and blood and instinct as this people. Even as the simple *paisanos* of Coralio had said it, so said Don Sabas. Without a smile, he looked, and said, "The poor little crazed one!"

Stooping, he raised the limp shoulders, drew the priceless and induplicable flag under them and over the breast, pinning it there with the diamond star of the Order of San Carlos that he took from the collar of his own coat.

He followed after the others, and stood with them upon the deck of the *Salvador*. The sailors that steadied *El Nacional* shoved her off. The jabbering Caribs hauled away at the rigging; the sloop headed for the shore.

And Herr Grunitz's collection of naval flags was still the finest in the world.

XCI: THE SHAMROCK AND THE PALM

ONE night when there was no breeze, and Coralio seemed closer than ever to the gratings of Avernus, five men were grouped about the door of the photograph establishment of Keogh and Clancy. Thus, in all the scorched and exotic places of the earth, Caucasians meet when the day's work is done to preserve the fullness of their heritage by the aspersion of alien things.

Johnny Atwood lay stretched upon the grass in the undress uniform of a Carib, and prated feebly of cool water to be had in the cucumber-wood pumps of Dalesburg. Dr. Gregg, through the prestige of his whiskers and as a bribe against the relation of his imminent professional tales, was conceded the hammock that was swung between the door jamb and a calabash-tree. Keogh had moved out upon the grass a little table that held the instrument for burnishing completed photographs. He was the only busy one of the group. Industriously from between the cylinders of the burnisher rolled the finished depictments of Coralio's citizens.

Blanchard, the French mining engineer, in his cool linen, viewed the smoke of his cigarette through his calm glasses, impervious to the heat. Clancy sat on the steps, smoking his short pipe. His mood was the gossip's; the others were reduced, by the humidity, to the state of disability desirable in an audience.

Clancy was an American with an Irish diathesis and cosmopolitan proclivities. Many businesses had claimed him, but not for long. The roadster's blood was in his veins. The voice of the tintype was but one of the many callings that had wooed him upon so many roads. Sometimes he could be persuaded to oral construction of his voyages into the informal and egregious. To-night there were symptoms of divulgement in him.

" 'Tis elegant weather for filibusterin'," he volunteered. "It reminds me of the time I struggled to liberate a nation from the poisonous breath of a tyrant's clutch. 'Twas hard work. 'Tis strainin' to the back and makes corns on the hands."

"I didn't know you had ever lent your sword to an oppressed people," murmured Atwood, from the grass.

"I did," said Clancy; "and they turned it into a ploughshare."

"What country was so fortunate as to secure your aid?" airily inquired Blanchard.

"Where's Kamchatka?" asked Clancy, with seeming irrelevance.

"Why, off Siberia, somewhere in the Arctic regions," somebody answered, doubtfully.

"I thought that was the cold one," said Clancy, with a satisfied nod. "I'm always gettin' the two names mixed. 'Twas Guatemala, then—the hot one—

I've been filibusterin' with: Ye'll find that country on the map. 'Tis in the district known as the tropics. By the foresight of Providence, it lies on the coast, so the geography man could run the names of the towns off into the water. They're an inch long, small type, composed of Spanish dialects, and, 'tis my opinion, of the same system of syntax that blew up the *Maine*. Yes, 'twas that country I sailed against, single-handed, and endeavoured to liberate it from a tyrannical government with a single-barrelled pickaxe, unloaded at that. Ye don't understand, of course. 'Tis a statement demandin' elucidation and apologies.

" 'Twas in New Orleans one morning about the first of June; I was standin' down on the wharf lookin' about at the ships in the river. There was a little steamer moored right opposite me that seemed about ready to sail. The funnels of it were throwin' out smoke, and a gang of roustabouts were carryin' aboard a pile of boxes that was stacked up on the wharf. The boxes were about two feet square, and somethin' like four feet long, and they seemed to be pretty heavy.

"I walked over, careless, to the stack of boxes. I saw one of them had been broken in handlin'. 'Twas curiosity made me pull up the loose top and look inside. The box was packed full of Winchester rifles. 'So, so,' says I to myself; 'somebody's gettin' a twist on the neutrality laws. Somebody's aidin' with munitions of war. I wonder where the popguns are goin'?'

"I heard somebody cough, and I turned round. There stood a little, round, fat man with a brown face and white clothes, a first-class-looking little man, with a four-carat diamond on his finger and his eye full of interrogations and respects. I judged he was a kind of foreigner—maybe from Russia or Japan or the archipelagos.

" 'Hist!' says the round man, full of concealments and confidences. 'Will the *señor* respect the discoveryments he has made, that the mans on the ship shall not be acquaint? The *señor* will be a gentleman that shall not expose one thing that by accident occur.'

" 'Monseer,' says I—for I judged him to be a kind of Frenchman—'receive my most exasperated assurances that your secret is safe with James Clancy. Furthermore, I will go so far as to remark, Veev la Liberty—veev it good and strong. Whenever you hear of a Clancy obstructin' the abolishment of existin' governments you may notify me by return mail.'

" 'The *señor* is good,' says the dark, fat man, smilin' under his black moustache. 'Wish you to come aboard my ship and drink of wine a glass.'

"Bein' a Clancy, in two minutes me and the foreigner man were seated at a table in the cabin of the steamer, with a bottle between us. I could hear the heavy boxes bein' dumped into the hold. I judged that cargo must consist of at least 2,000 Winchesters. Me and the brown man drank the bottle of stuff, and he called the steward to bring another. When you amalgamate a Clancy with the contents of a bottle you practically instigate secession. I had heard a good deal about these revolutions in them tropical localities, and I begun to want a hand in it.

" 'You goin' to stir up things in your country, ain't you, monseer?' says I, with a wink to let him know I was on.

" 'Yes, yes,' said the little man, pounding his fist on the table. 'A change of the greatest will occur.

Too long have the people been oppressed with the promises and the never-to-happen things to become. The great work it shall be carry on. Yes. Our forces shall in the capital city strike of the soonest. *Carrambos!*'

" '*Carrambos* is the word,' says I, beginning to invest myself with enthusiasm and more wine, 'likewise veeva, as I said before. May the shamrock of old—I mean the banana-vine or the pie-plant, or whatever the imperial emblem may be of your down-trodden country, wave for ever.'

" 'A thousand thank-yous,' says the round man, 'for your emission of amicable utterances. What our cause needs of the very most is mans who will the work do, to lift it along. Oh, for one thousands strong, good mans to aid the General De Vega that he shall to his country bring those success and glory! It is hard—oh, so hard to find good mans to help in the work.'

" 'Monseer,' says I, leanin' over the table and graspin' his hand, 'I don't know where your country is, but me heart bleeds for it. The heart of a Clancy was never deaf to the sight of an oppressed people. The family is filibusterers by birth, and foreigners by trade. If you can use James Clancy's arms and his blood in denudin' your shores of the tyrant's yoke they're yours to command.'

"General De Vega was overcome with joy to confiscate my condolence of his conspiracies and predicaments. He tried to embrace me across the table, but his fatness, and the wine that had been in the bottles, prevented. Thus was I welcomed into the ranks of filibustery. Then the general man told me his country had the name of Guatemala, and was the greatest nation laved by any ocean whatever anywhere. He looked at me with tears in his eyes, and from time to time he would emit the remark, 'Ah! big, strong, brave mans! That is what my country need.'

"General De Vega, as was the name by which he denounced himself, brought out a document for me to sign, which I did, makin' a fine flourish and curly-cue with the tail of the 'y.'

" 'Your passage money,' says the general, businesslike, 'shall from your pay be deduct.'

" ' 'Twill not,' says I haughtily. 'I'll pay my own passage.' A hundred and eighty dollars I had in my inside pocket, and 'twas no common filibuster I was goin' to be, filibusterin' for me board and clothes.

"The steamer was to sail in two hours, and I went ashore to get some things together I'd need. When I came aboard I showed the general with pride the outfit. 'Twas a fine Chinchilla overcoat, Arctic overshoes, fur cap and earmuffs, with elegant fleece-lined gloves and woollen muffler.

" '*Carrambos!*' says the little general. 'What clothes are these that shall go to the tropic?' And then the little spalpeen laughs, and he calls the captain, and the captain calls the purser, and they pipe up the chief engineer, and the whole gang leans against the cabin and laughs at Clancy's wardrobe for Guatemala.

"I reflects a bit, serious, and asks the general again to denominate the terms by which his country is called. He tells me, and I see then that 'twas the t'other one, Kamchatka, I had in mind. Since then I've had difficulty in separatin' the two nations in name, climate and geographic disposition.

"I paid my passage—twenty-four dollars, first

cabin—and ate at table with the officer crowd. Down on the lower deck was a gang of second-class passengers, about forty of them, seemin' to be Dagoes and the like. I wondered what so many of them were goin' along for.

"Well, then, in three days we sailed alongside that Guatemala. 'Twas a blue country, and not yellow as 'tis miscoloured on the map. We landed at a town on the coast, where a train of cars was waitin' for us on a dinky little railroad. The boxes on the steamer were brought ashore and loaded on the cars. The gang of Dagoes got aboard, too, the general and me in the front car. Yes, me and General De Vega headed the revolution, as it pulled out of the seaport town. That train travelled about as fast as a policeman goin' to a riot. It penetrated the most conspicuous lot of fuzzy scenery ever seen outside a geography. We run some forty miles in seven hours, and the train stopped. There was no more railroad. 'Twas a sort of camp in a damp gorge full of wildness and melancholies. They were gradin' and choppin' out the forests ahead to continue the road. 'Here,' says I to myself, 'is the romantic haunt of the revolutionists. Here will Clancy, by the virtue that is in a superior race and the inculcation of Fenian tactics, strike a tremendous blow for liberty.'

"They unloaded the boxes from the train and begun to knock the tops off. From the first one that was open I saw General De Vega take the Winchester rifles and pass them around to a squad of morbid soldiery. The other boxes was opened next, and, believe me or not, divil another gun was to be seen. Every other box in the load was full of pickaxes and spades.

"And then—sorrow be upon them tropics—the proud Clancy and the dishonoured Dagoes, each one of them, had to shoulder a pick or a spade, and march away to work on that dirty little railroad. Yes; 'twas that the Dagoes shipped for, and 'twas that the filibusterin' Clancy signed for, though unbeknownst to himself at the time. In after days I found out about it. It seems 'twas hard to get hands to work on that road. The intelligent natives of the country was too lazy to work. Indeed, the saints know, 'twas unnecessary. By stretchin' out one hand, they could seize the most delicate and costly fruits of the earth, and by stretchin' out the other, they could sleep for days at a time without hearin' a seven-o'clock whistle or the footsteps of the rent man upon the stairs. So, regular, the steamers travelled to the United States to seduce labour. Usually the imported spade-slingers died in two or three months from eatin' the over-ripe water and breathin' the violent tropical scenery. Wherefore they made them sign contracts for a year, when they hired them, and put an armed guard over the poor divils to keep them from runnin' away.

"'Twas thus I was double-crossed by the tropics through a family failin' of goin' out of the way to hunt disturbances.

"They gave me a pick, and I took it, meditatin' an insurrection on the spot; but there was the guards handlin' the Winchesters careless, and I come to the conclusion that discretion was the best part of filibusterin'. There was about a hundred of us in the gang startin' out to work, and the word was given to move. I steps out of the ranks and goes up to that General De Vega man, who was smokin' a cigar and gazin' upon the scene with satisfactions and glory. He smiles at me polite and devilish. 'Plenty work,' says he, 'for big, strong mans in Guatemala. Yes. T'irty dollars in the month. Good pay. Ah, yes. You strong, brave man. Bimeby we push those railroad in the capital very quick. They want you go work now. *Adios*, strong mans.'

" 'Monseer,' says I, lingerin', 'will you tell a poor little Irishman this: When I set foot on your cockroachy steamer, and breathed liberal and revolutionary sentiments into your sour wine, did you think I was conspirin' to sling a pick on your contemptuous little railroad? And when you answered me with patriotic recitations, humping up the star-spangled cause of liberty, did you have meditations of reducin' me to the ranks of the stump-grubbin' Dagoes in the chain-gangs of your vile and grovellin' country?'

"The general man expanded his rotundity and laughed considerable. Yes, he laughed very long and loud, and I, Clancy, stood and waited.

" 'Comical mans!' he shouts, at last. 'So you will kill me from the laughing. Yes; it is hard to find the brave, strong mans to aid my country. Revolutions? Did I speak of r-r-revolutions? Not one word. I say, big, strong mans is need in Guatemala. So. The mistake is of you. You have looked in those one box containing those gun for the guard. You think all boxes is contain gun? No.

" 'There is not war in Guatemala. But work? Yes. Good. T'irty dollars in the month. You shall shoulder one pickaxe, *señor*, and dig for the liberty and prosperity of Guatemala. Off to your work. The guard waits for you.'

" 'Little, fat, poodle dog of a brown man,' says I, quiet, but full of indignations and discomforts, 'things shall happen to you. Maybe not right away, but as soon as J. Clancy can formulate somethin' in the way of repartee.'

"The boss of the gang orders us to work. I tramps off with the Dagoes, and I hears the distinguished patriot and kidnapper laughin' hearty as we go.

" 'Tis a sorrowful fact, for eight weeks I built railroads for that misbehavin' country. I filibustered twelve hours a day with a heavy pick and spade, choppin' away the luxurious landscape that grew upon the right of way. We worked in swamps that smelled like there was a leak in the gas mains, trampin' down a fine assortment of the most expensive hothouse plants and vegetables. The scene was tropical beyond the wildest imagination of the geography man. The trces was all sky-scrapers; the underbrush was full of needles and pins; there was monkeys jumpin' around and crocodiles and pink-tailed mockin'-birds, and ye stood knee-deep in the rotten water and grabbled roots for the liberation of Guatemala. Of nights we would build smudges in camp to discourage the mosquitoes, and sit in the smoke, with the guards pacin' all around us. There was two hundred men workin' on the road—mostly Dagoes, nigger-men, Spanish-men and Swedes. Three or four were Irish.

"One old man named Halloran—a man of Hibernian entitlements and discretions, explained it to me. He had been workin' on the road a year. Most of them died in less than six months. He was dried up to gristle and bone, and shook with chills every third night.

" 'When you first come,' says he, 'ye think ye'll leave right away. But they hold out your first month's pay for your passage over, and by that time the tropics has its grip on ye. Ye're surrounded by a ragin' forest full of disreputable beasts—lions and baboons and anacondas—waiting to devour ye. The sun strikes ye hard, and it melts the marrow in your bones. Ye get similar to the lettuce-eaters the poetry-book speaks about. Ye forget the elevated sintiments of life, such as patriotism, revenge, disturbances of the peace and the dacint love of a clane shirt. Ye do your work, and ye swallow the kerosene ile and rubber pipe-stems dished up to ye by the Dago cook for food. Ye light your pipeful, and say to yoursilf, "Nixt week I'll break away," and ye go to sleep and call yersilf a liar, for ye know ye'll never do it.'

" 'Who is this general man,' asks I, 'that calls himself De Vega?'

" ' 'Tis the man,' says Halloran, 'who is tryin' to complete the finishin' of the railroad. 'Twas the project of a private corporation, but it busted, and then the government took it up. De Vegy is a big politician, and wants to be prisident. The people want the railroad completed, as they're taxed mighty on account of it. The De Vegy man is pushin' it along as a campaign move.'

" ' 'Tis not my way,' says I, 'to make threats against any man, but there's an account to be settled between the railroad man and James O'Dowd Clancy.'

" ' 'Twas that way I thought, mesilf, at first,' Halloran says, with a big sigh, 'until I got to be a lettuce-eater. The fault's wid these tropics. They rejuices a man's system. 'Tis a land, as the poet says, "Where it always seems to be after dinner." I does me work and smokes me pipe and sleeps. There's little else in life, anyway. Ye'll get that way yersilf, mighty soon. Don't be harbourin' any sintiments at all, Clancy.'

"'I can't help it,' says I; 'I'm full of 'em. I enlisted in the revolutionary army of this dark country in good faith to fight for its liberty, honours and silver candlesticks; instead of which I am set to amputatin' its scenery and grubbin' its roots. 'Tis the general man will have to pay for it.'

"Two months I worked on that railroad before I found a chance to get away. One day a gang of us was sent back to the end of the completed line to fetch some picks that had been sent down to Port Barrios to be sharpened. They were brought on a hand-car, and I noticed when I started away that the car was left there on the track.

"That night, about twelve, I woke up Halloran and told him my scheme.

"'Run away?' says Halloran. 'Good Lord, Clancy, do ye mean it? Why, I ain't got the nerve. It's too chilly, and I ain't slept enough. Run away? I told you, Clancy, I've eat the lettuce. I've lost my grip. 'Tis the tropics that's done it. 'Tis like the poet says: "Forgotten are our friends that we have left behind; in the hollow lettuce-land we will live and lay reclined." You had better go on, Clancy. I'll stay, I guess. It's too early and cold, and I'm sleepy.'

"So I had to leave Halloran. I dressed quiet, and slipped out of the tent we were in. When the guard came along I knocked him over, like a ninepin, with a green coconut I had, and made for the railroad. I got on that hand-car and made it fly.

'Twas yet awhile before daybreak when I saw the lights of Port Barrios about a mile away. I stopped the hand-car there and walked to the town. I stepped inside the corporations of that town with care and hesitations. I was not afraid of the army of Guatemala, but me soul quaked at the prospect of a hand-to-hand struggle with its employment bureau. 'Tis a country that hires its help easy and keeps 'em long. Sure I can fancy Missis America and Missis Guatemala passin' a bit of gossip some fine, still night across the mountains. 'Oh, dear,' says Missis America, 'and it's a lot of trouble I'm havin' ag'in with the help, *señora*, ma'am.' 'Laws, now!' says Missis Guatemala, 'you don't say so, ma'am! Now, mine never think of leavin' me—te-he! ma'am,' snickers Missis Guatemala.

"I was wonderin' how I was goin' to move away from them tropics without bein' hired again. Dark as it was, I could see a steamer ridin' in the harbour, with smoke emergin' from her stacks. I turned down a little grass street that run down to the water. On the beach I found a little brown nigger-man just about to shove off in a skiff.

" 'Hold on, Sambo,' says I, 'savve English?'

" 'Heap plenty, yes,' says he, with a pleasant grin.

" 'What steamer is that?' I asks him, 'and where is it going? And what's the news, and the good word and the time of day?'

" 'That steamer the *Conchita*,' said the brown man, affable and easy, rollin' a cigarette. 'Him come from New Orleans for load banana. Him got load last night. I think him sail in one, two hour. Verree nice day we shall be goin' have. You hear some talkee 'bout big battle, maybe so?

You think catchee General De Vega, *señor*? Yes? No?'

"'How's that, Sambo?' says I. 'Big battle? What battle? Who wants catchee General De Vega? I've been up at my old gold mines in the interior for a couple of months, and haven't heard any news.'

"'Oh,' says the nigger-man, proud to speak the English, 'verree great revolution in Guatemala one week ago. General De Vega, him try be president. Him raise armee—one—five—ten thousand mans for fight at the government. Those one government send five—forty—hundred thousand soldier to suppress revolution. They fight big battle yesterday at Lomagrande—that about nineteen or fifty mile in the mountain. That government soldier wheep General De Vega—ah, most bad. Five hundred—nine hundred—two thousand of his mans is kill. That revolution is smash, suppress—bust—very quick. General De Vega, him r-r-run away fast on one big mule. Yes, *carrambos!* The general, him r-r-run away, and his armee is kill. That government soldier, they try find General De Vega verree much. They want catchee him for shoot. You think they catchee that general, *señor*?'

"'Saints grant it!' says I. ''Twould be the judgment of Providence for settin' the warlike talent of a Clancy to gradin' the tropics with a pick and shovel. But 'tis not so much a question of insurrections now, me little man, as 'tis of the hired-man problem. 'Tis anxious I am to resign a situation of responsibility and trust with the white wings department of your great and degraded country. Row me in your little boat out to that steamer, and I'll give ye five dollars—sinker pacers—sinker pacers,' says I, reducin' the offer to the language and denomination of the tropic dialects.

" '*Cinco pesos*,' repeats the little man. 'Five dollee, you give?'

" 'Twas not such a bad little man. He had hesitations at first, sayin' that passengers leavin' the country had to have papers and passports, but at last he took me out alongside the steamer.

"Day was just breakin' as we struck her, and there wasn't a soul to be seen on board. The water was very still, and the nigger-man gave me a lift from the boat, and I climbed on to the steamer where her side was sliced to the deck for loadin' fruit. The hatches were open, and I looked down and saw the cargo of bananas that filled the hold to within six feet of the top. I thinks to myself, 'Clancy, you better go as a stowaway. It's safer. The steamer men might hand you back to the employment bureau. The tropic'll get you, Clancy, if you don't watch out.'

"So I jumps down easy among the bananas, and digs out a hole to hide in among the bunches. In an hour or so I could hear the engines goin', and feel the steamer rockin', and I knew we were off to sea. They left the hatches open for ventilation, and pretty soon it was light enough in the hold to see fairly well. I got to feelin' a bit hungry, and thought I'd have a light fruit lunch, by way of refreshment. I creeped out of the hole I'd made and stood up straight. Just then I saw another man crawl up about ten feet away and reach out and skin a banana and stuff it into his mouth. 'Twas a dirty man, black-faced and ragged and disgraceful of aspect. Yes, the man was a ringer for the pictures of the fat Weary Willie in the funny papers. I looked again, and saw it was my general man—De Vega, the great revolutionist, mule-rider and pickaxe importer. When he saw me the general hesitated with his mouth filled with banana and his eyes the size of coconuts.

" 'Hist!' I says. 'Not a word, or they'll put us off and make us walk. "Veev la Liberty!" ' I adds, copperin' the sentiment by shovin' a banana into the source of it. I was certain the general wouldn't recognize me. The nefarious work of the tropics had left me lookin' different. There was half an inch of roan whiskers coverin' me face, and me costume was a pair of blue overalls and a red shirt.

" 'How you come in the ship, *señor*?' asked the general as soon as he could speak.

" 'By the back door—whist!' says I. ' 'Twas a glorious blow for liberty we struck,' I continues: 'but we was overpowered by numbers. Let us accept our defeat like brave men and eat another banana.'

" 'Were you in the cause of liberty fightin', *señor*?' says the general, sheddin' tears on the cargo.

" 'To the last,' says I. ' 'Twas I led the last desperate charge against the minions of the tyrant. But it made them mad, and we was forced to retreat. 'Twas I, general, procured the mule upon which you escaped. Could you give that ripe bunch a little boost this way, general? It's a bit out of my reach. Thanks.'

" 'Say you so, brave patriot?' said the general, again weepin'. 'Ah, *Dios*! And I have not the means to reward your devotion. Barely did I my life bring away. *Carrambos!* what a devil's animal was that mule, *señor*! Like ships in one storm was I dashed about. The skin on myself was ripped away with the thorns and vines. Upon the bark of a hundred trees did that beast of the infernal bump, and cause outrage to the legs of mine. In the night to Port Barrios I came. I dispossess myself of that mountain of mule and hasten along the water shore. I find a little boat to be tied. I launch myself and row to the steamer. I cannot see any mans on board, so I climbed one rope which hang at the side. I then myself hide in the bananas. Surely, I say, if the ship captains view me, they shall throw me again to those Guatemala. Those things are not good. Guatemala will shoot General De Vega. Therefore, I am hide and remain silent. Life itself is glorious. Liberty, it is pretty good; but so good as life I do not think.'

"Three days, as I said, was the trip to New Orleans. The general man and me got to be cronies of the deepest dye. Bananas we ate until they were distasteful to the sight and an eyesore to the palate; but to bananas alone was the bill of fare reduced. At night I crawls out, careful, on the lower deck, and gets a bucket of fresh water.

"That General De Vega was a man inhabited by an engorgement of words and sentences. He added to the monotony of the voyage by divestin' himself of conversation. He believed I was a revolutionist of his own party, there bein', as he told me, a good many Americans and other foreigners in its ranks. 'Twas a braggart and a conceited little gabbler it was, though he considered himself a hero. 'Twas on himself he wasted all his regrets at the failin' of his plot. Not a word did the little balloon have to say about the other misbehavin' idiots that had been shot, or run themselves to death in his revolution.

"The second day out he was feelin' pretty braggy

and uppish for a stowed-away conspirator that owed his existence to a mule and stolen bananas. He was tellin' me about the great railroad he had been buildin', and he relates what he calls a comic incident about a fool Irishman he inveigled from New Orleans to sling a pick on his little morgue of a narrow-gauge line. 'Twas sorrowful to hear the little, dirty general tell the opprobrious story of how he put salt upon the tail of that reckless and silly bird, Clancy. Laugh, he did, hearty and long. He shook with laughin', the black-faced rebel and outcast, standin' neck deep in bananas, without friends or country.

" 'Ah, *señor*,' he snickers, 'to the death you would have laughed at that drollest Irish. I say to him: "Strong, big mans is need very much in Guatemala." "I will blows strike for your down-pressed country," he say. "That shall you do," I tell him. Ah! it was an Irish so comic. He sees one box break upon the wharf that contain for the guard a few gun. He think there is gun in all the box. But that is all pickaxe. Yes. Ah! *señor*, could you the face of that Irish have seen when they set him to the work!'

" 'Twas thus the ex-boss of the employment bureau contributed to the tedium of the trip with merry jests and anecdote. But now and then he would weep upon the bananas and make oration about the lost cause of liberty and the mule.

" 'Twas a pleasant sound when the steamer bumped against the pier in New Orleans. Pretty soon we heard the pat-a-pat of hundreds of bare feet, and the Dago gang that unloads the fruit jumped on the deck and down into thc hold. Me and the general worked awhile at passin' up the bunches, and they thought we were part of the gang. After about an hour we managed to slip off the steamer on to the wharf.

" 'Twas a great honour on the hands of an obscure Clancy, havin' the entertainment of the representative of a great foreign filibusterin' power. I first bought for the general and myself many long drinks and things to eat that were not bananas. The general man trotted along at my side, leavin' all the arrangements to me. I led him up to Lafayette Square and set him on a bench in the little park. Cigarettes I had bought for him, and he humped himself down on the seat like a little, fat, contented hobo. I look over him as he sets there, and what I see pleases me. Brown by nature and instinct, he is now brindled with dirt and dust. Praise to the mule, his clothes is mostly strings and flaps. Yes, the looks of the general man is agreeable to Clancy.

"I asks him, delicate, if, by any chance, he brought away anybody's money with him from Guatemala. He sighs and humps his shoulders against the bench. Not a cent. All right. Maybe, he tells me, some of his friends in the tropic outfit will send him funds later. The general was as clear a case of no visible means as I ever saw.

"I told him not to move from the bench, and then I went up to the corner of Poydras and Carondelet. Along there is O'Hara's beat. In five minutes along comes O'Hara, a big, fine man, red-faced, with shinin' buttons, swingin' his club. 'Twould be a fine thing for Guatemala to move into O'Hara's precinct. 'Twould be a fine bit of recreation for Danny to suppress revolutions and uprisin's once or twice a week with his club.

" 'Is 5046 workin' yet, Danny?' says I, walkin' up to him.

" 'Overtime,' says O'Hara, lookin' over me suspicious. 'Want some of it?'

"Fifty-forty-six is the celebrated city ordinance authorizin' arrest, conviction and imprisonment of persons that succeed in concealing their crimes from the police.

" 'Don't ye know Jimmy Clancy?' says I. 'Ye pink-gilled monster.' So, when O'Hara recognized me beneath the scandalous exterior bestowed upon me by the tropics, I backed him into a doorway and told him what I wanted, and why I wanted it. 'All right, Jimmy,' says O'Hara. 'Go back and hold the bench. I'll be along in ten minutes.'

"In that time O'Hara strolled through Lafayette Square and spied two Weary Willies disgracin' one of the benches. In ten minutes more J. Clancy and General De Vega, late candidate for the presidency of Guatemala, was in the station house. The general is badly frightened, and calls upon me to proclaim his distinguishments and rank.

" 'The man,' says I to the police, 'used to be a railroad man. He's on the bum now. 'Tis a little bug-house he is, on account of losin' his job.'

" '*Carrambos!*' says the general, fizzin' like a little soda-water fountain, 'you fought, *señor*, with my forces in my native country. Why do you say the lies? You shall say I am the General De Vega, one soldier, one *caballero*——'

" 'Railroader,' says I again. 'On the hog. No good. Been livin' for three days on stolen bananas. Look at him. Ain't that enough?'

"Twenty-five dollars or sixty days, was what the recorder gave the general. He didn't have a cent, so he took the time. They let me go, as I knew they would, for I had the money to show, and O'Hara spoke for me. Yes; sixty days he got. 'Twas just so long that I slung a pick for the great country of Kam—Guatemala."

Clancy paused. The bright starlight showed a reminiscent look of happy content on his seasoned features. Keogh leaned in his chair and gave his partner a slap on his thinly-clad back that sounded like the crack of the surf on the sands.

"Tell 'em, ye divil," he chuckled, "how you got even with the tropical general in the way of agricultural manœuvrings."

"Havin' no money," concluded Clancy, with unction, "they set him to work his fine out with a gang from the parish prison clearing Ursulines Street. Around the corner was a saloon decorated genially with electric fans and cool merchandise. I made that me headquarters, and every fifteen minutes I'd walk around and take a look at the little man filibusterin' with a rake and shovel. 'Twas just such a hot broth of a day as this has been. And I'd call at him 'Hey, monseer!' and he'd look at me black, with the damp showin' through his shirt in places.

" 'Fat, strong mans,' says I to General De Vega, 'is needed in New Orleans. Yes. To carry on the good work. *Carrambos!* Erin go bragh!' "

XCII: THE REMNANTS OF THE CODE

BREAKFAST in Coralio was at eleven. Therefore the people did not go to market early. The little wooden market-house stood on a patch of short-trimmed grass, under the vivid green foliage of a bread-fruit tree.

Thither one morning the venders leisurely convened, bringing their wares with them. A porch or platform six feet wide encircled the building, shaded from the mid-morning sun by the projecting, grass-thatched roof. Upon this platform the venders were wont to display their goods—newly-killed beef, fish, crabs, fruit of the country, cassava, eggs, *dulces* and high, tottering stacks of native tortillas as large around as the sombrero of a Spanish grandee.

But on this morning those whose stations lay on the seaward side of the market-house, instead of spreading their merchandise formed themselves into a softly jabbering and gesticulating group. For there upon their space of the platform was sprawled, asleep, the unbeautiful figure of "Beelzebub" Blythe. He lay upon a ragged strip of coco matting, more than ever a fallen angel in appearance. His suit of coarse flax, soiled, bursting at the seams, crumpled into a thousand diversified wrinkles and creases, inclosed him absurdly, like the garb of some effigy that had been stuffed in sport and thrown there after indignity had been wrought upon it. But firmly upon the high bridge of his nose reposed his gold-rimmed glasses, the surviving badge of his ancient glory.

The sun's rays, reflecting quiveringly from the rippling sea upon his face, and the voices of the market-men woke "Beelzebub" Blythe. He sat up, blinking, and leaned his back against the wall of the market. Drawing a blighted silk handkerchief from his pocket, he assiduously rubbed and burnished his glasses. And while doing this he became aware that his bedroom had been invaded, and that polite brown and yellow men were beseeching him to vacate in favour of their market stuff.

If the *señor* would have the goodness—a thousand pardons for bringing to him molestation—but soon would come the *compradores* for the day's provisions—surely they had ten thousand regrets at disturbing him!

In this manner they expanded to him the intimation that he must clear out and cease to clog the wheels of trade.

Blythe stepped from the platform with the air of a prince leaving his canopied couch. He never quite lost that air, even at the lowest point of his fall. It is clear that the college of good breeding does not necessarily maintain a chair of morals within its walls.

Blythe shook out his wry clothing, and moved slowly up the Calle Grande through the hot sand. He moved without a destination in his mind. The little town was languidly stirring to its daily life. Golden-skinned babies tumbled over one another in the grass. The sea-breeze brought him appetite, but nothing to satisfy it. Throughout Coralio were its morning odours—those from the heavily fragrant tropical flowers and from the bread baking in the outdoor ovens of clay and the pervading smoke of their fires. When the smoke cleared, the crystal air, with some of the efficacy of faith, seemed to remove the mountains almost to the sea, bringing them so near that one might count the scarred glades on their wooded sides. The light-footed Caribs were swiftly gliding to their tasks at the waterside. Already along the bosky trails from the banana grove files of horses were slowly moving, concealed, except for their nodding heads and plodding legs, by the bunches of green-golden fruit heaped upon their backs. On doorsills sat women combing their long, black hair and calling, one to another, across the narrow thoroughfares. Peace reigned in Coralio—arid and bald peace; but still peace.

On that bright morning when Nature seemed to be offering the lotus on the Dawn's golden platter "Beelzebub" Blythe had reached rock bottom. Further descent seemed impossible. That last night's slumber in a public place had done for him. As long as he had had a roof to cover him there had remained, unbridged, the space that separates a gentleman from the beasts of the jungle and the fowls of the air. But now he was little more than a whimpering oyster led to be devoured on the sands of a Southern sea by the artful walrus, Circumstance, and the implacable carpenter, Fate.

To Blythe money was now but a memory. He had drained his friends of all that their good-fellowship had to offer; then he had squeezed them to the last drop of their generosity; and at the last, Aaron-like, he had smitten the rock of their hardening bosoms for the scattering, ignoble drops of Charity itself.

He had exhausted his credit to the last *real*. With the minute keenness of the shameless sponger he was aware of every source in Coralio from which a glass of rum, a meal or a piece of silver could be wheedled. Marshalling each such source in his mind, he considered it with all the thoroughness and penetration that hunger and thirst lent him for the task. All his optimism failed to thresh a grain of hope from the chaff of his postulations. He had played out the game. That one night in the open had shaken his nerves. Until then there had been left to him at least a few grounds upon which he could base his unblushing demands upon his neighbour's stores. Now he must beg instead of borrowing. The most brazen sophistry could not dignify by the name of "loan" the coin contemptuously flung to a beachcomber who slept on the bare boards of the public market.

But on this morning no beggar would have more thankfully received a charitable coin, for the demon thirst had him by the throat—the drunkard's matutinal thirst that requires to be slaked at each morning station on the road to Tophet.

Blythe walked slowly up the street, keeping a watchful eye for any miracle that might drop manna upon him in his wilderness. As he passed the popular eating house of Madama Vasquez, Madama's boarders were just sitting down to freshly-baked bread, *aguacates*, pines and delicious coffee that sent forth odorous guarantee of its quality upon the breeze. Madama was serving; she turned her shy, stolid, melancholy gaze for a moment out of the window, she saw Blythe, and her expression turned more shy and embarrassed. "Beelzebub" owed her twenty *pesos*. He bowed as he had once bowed to less embarrassed dames to whom he owed nothing and passed on.

Merchants and their clerks were throwing open the solid wooden doors of their shops. Polite but cool were the glances they cast upon Blythe as he lounged tentatively by with the remains of his old jaunty air; for they were his creditors almost without exception.

At the little fountain in the plaza he made an apology for a toilet with his wetted handkerchief. Across the open square filed the dolorous line of friends to the prisoners in the *calaboza*, bearing the morning meal of the immured. The food in their hands aroused small longing in Blythe. It was drink that his soul craved, or money to buy it.

In the streets he met with many with whom he had been friends and equals, and whose patience and liberality he had gradually exhausted. Willard Geddie and Paula cantered past him with the coolest of nods, returning from their daily horseback ride along the old Indian road. Keogh passed him at another corner, whistling cheerfully and bearing a prize of newly-laid eggs for the breakfast of himself and Clancy. The jovial scout of Fortune was one of Blythe's victims who had plunged his hand oftenest into his pocket to aid him. But now it seemed that Keogh, too, had fortified himself against further invasions. His curt greeting and the ominous light in his full, grey eye quickened the steps of "Beelzebub," whom desperation had almost incited to attempt an additional "loan."

Three drinking shops the forlorn one next visited in succession. In all of these his money, his credit and his welcome had long since been spent; but Blythe felt that he would have fawned in the dust at the feet of an enemy that morning for one draught of *aguardiente*. In two of the *pulperias* his courageous petition for drink was met with a refusal so polite that it stung worse than abuse. The third establishment had acquired something of American methods; and here he was seized bodily and cast out upon his hands and knees.

This physical indignity caused a singular change in the man. As he picked himself up and walked away, an expression of absolute relief came upon his features. The specious and conciliatory smile that had been graven there was succeeded by a look of calm and sinister resolve. "Beelzebub" had been floundering in the sea of improbity, holding by a slender life-line to the respectable world that had cast him overboard. He must have felt that with this ultimate shock the line had snapped, and have experienced the welcome ease of the drowning swimmer who has ceased to struggle.

Blythe walked to the next corner and stood there while he brushed the sand from his garments and repolished his glasses.

"I've got to do it—oh, I've got to do it," he told himself, aloud. "If I had a quart of rum, I believe I could stave it off yet—for a little while. But there's no more rum for—'Beelzebub,' as they call me. By the flames of Tartarus! if I'm to sit at the right hand of Satan somebody has got to pay the court expenses. You'll have to pony up, Mr. Frank Goodwin. You're a good fellow; but a gentleman must draw the line at being kicked into the gutter. Blackmail isn't a pretty word, but it's the next station on the road I'm travelling."

With purpose in his steps Blythe now moved rapidly through the town by way of its landward environs. He passed through the squalid quarters of the improvident negroes and on beyond the picturesque shacks of the poorer *mestizos*. From many points along his course he could see, through the umbrageous glades, the house of Frank Goodwin on its wooded hill. And as he crossed the little bridge over the lagoon he saw the old Indian, Galvez, scrubbing at the wooded slab that bore the name of Miraflores. Beyond the lagoon the lands of Goodwin began to slope gently upward. A grassy road, shaded by a munificent and diverse array of tropical flora, wound from the edge of an outlying banana grove to the dwelling. Blythe took this road with long and purposeful strides.

Goodwin was seated on his coolest gallery, dictating letters to his secretary, a sallow and capable native youth. The household adhered to the American plan of breakfast; and that meal had been a thing of the past for the better part of an hour.

The castaway walked to the steps, and flourished a hand.

"Good morning, Blythe," said Goodwin, looking up. "Come in and have a chair. Anything I can do for you?"

"I want to speak to you in private."

Goodwin nodded at his secretary, who strolled out under a mango tree and lit a cigarette. Blythe took the chair that he had left vacant.

"I want some money," he began, doggedly.

"I'm sorry," said Goodwin, with equal directness, "but you can't have any. You're drinking yourself to death, Blythe. Your friends have done all they could to help you to brace up. You won't help yourself. There's no use furnishing you with money to ruin yourself with any longer."

"Dear man," said Blythe, tilting back his chair, "it isn't a question of social economy now. It's past that. I like you, Goodwin; and I've come to stick a knife between your ribs. I was kicked out of Espada's saloon this morning; and Society owes me reparation for my wounded feelings."

"I didn't kick you out."

"No; but in a general way you represent Society; and in a particular way you represent my last chance. I've had to come down to it, old man—I tried to do it a month ago when Losada's man was here turning things over; but I couldn't do it then. Now it's different. I want a thousand dollars, Goodwin; and you'll have to give it to me."

"Only last week," said Goodwin, with a smile, "a silver dollar was all you were asking for."

"An evidence," said Blythe, flippantly, "that I was still virtuous—though under heavy pressure. The wages of sin should be something higher than a *peso* worth forty-eight cents. Let's talk business. I am the villain in the third act; and I must have my merited, if only temporary, triumph. I saw you collar the late president's valiseful of boodle. Oh, I know it's blackmail; but I'm liberal about the price. I know I'm a cheap villain—one of the regular saw-mill-drama kind—but you're one of my particular friends, and I don't want to stick you hard."

"Suppose you go into the details," suggested Goodwin, calmly arranging his letters on the table.

"All right," said "Beelzebub." "I like the way you take it. I despise histrionics; so you will please prepare yourself for the facts without any red fire, calcium or grace notes on the saxophone.

"On the night that His Fly-by-Night Excellency arrived in town I was very drunk. You will excuse the pride with which I state that fact; but it was quite a feat for me to attain that desirable state. Somebody had left a cot out under the orange trees in the yard of Madama Ortiz's hotel. I stepped over the wall, laid down upon it, and fell asleep. I was awakened by an orange that dropped from the tree upon my nose, and I laid there for awhile cursing Sir Isaac Newton, or whoever it was that invented gravitation, for not confining his theory to apples.

"And then along came Mr. Miraflores and his

true-love with the treasury in a valise, and went into the hotel. Next you hove in sight, and held a pow-wow with the tonsorial artist who insisted upon talking shop after hours. I tried to slumber again; but once more my rest was disturbed—this time by the noise of the popgun that went off upstairs. Then that valise came crashing down into an orange tree just above my head; and I arose from my couch, not knowing when it might begin to rain Saratoga trunks. When the army and the constabulary began to arrive, with their medals and decorations hastily pinned to their pyjamas, and their snickersnees drawn, I crawled into the welcome shadow of a banana plant. I remained there for an hour, by which time the excitement and the people had cleared away. And then, my dear Goodwin—excuse me—I saw you sneak back and pluck that ripe and juicy valise from the orange tree. I followed you, and saw you take it to your own house. A hundred-thousand-dollar crop from one orange tree in a season about breaks the record of the fruit-growing industry.

"Being a gentleman at that time, of course I never mentioned the incident to anyone. But this morning I was kicked out of a saloon, my code of honour is all out at the elbows, and I'd sell my mother's prayer-book for three fingers of *aguardiente*. I'm not putting on the screws hard. It ought to be worth a thousand to you for me to have slept on that cot through the whole business without waking up and seeing anything."

Goodwin opened two more letters, and made memoranda in pencil on them. Then he called "Manuel!" to his secretary, who came, spryly.

"The *Ariel*—when does she sail?" asked Goodwin.

"*Señor*," answered the youth, "at three this afternoon. She drops down coast to Punta Soledad to complete her cargo of fruit. From there she sails for New Orleans without delay."

"*Bueno!*" said Goodwin. "These letters may wait yet awhile."

The secretary returned to his cigarette under the mango tree.

"In round numbers," said Goodwin, facing Blythe squarely, "how much money do you owe in this town, not including the sums you have 'borrowed' from me?"

"Five hundred—at a rough guess," answered Blythe, lightly.

"Go somewhere in the town and draw up a schedule of your debts," said Goodwin. "Come back here in two hours, and I will send Manuel with the money to pay them. I will also have a decent outfit of clothing ready for you. You will sail on the *Ariel* at three. Manuel will accompany you as far as the deck of the steamer. There he will hand you one thousand dollars in cash. I suppose that we needn't discuss what you will be expected to do in return."

"Oh, I understand," piped Blythe, cheerily. "I was asleep all the time on the cot under Madama Ortiz's orange trees; and I shall shake off the dust of Coralio for ever. I'll play fair. No more of the lotus for me. Your proposition is O.K. You're a good fellow, Goodwin; and I let you off light. I'll agree to everything. But in the meantime—I've a devil of a thirst on, old man——"

"Not a *centavo*," said Goodwin, firmly, "until you are on board the *Ariel*. You would be drunk in thirty minutes if you had money now."

But he noticed the blood-streaked eyeballs, the relaxed form and the shaking hands of "Beelzebub"; and he stepped into the dining-room through the low window, and brought out a glass and a decanter of brandy.

"Take a bracer, anyway, before you go," he proposed, even as a man to the friend whom he entertains.

"Beelzebub" Blythe's eyes glistened at the sight of the solace for which his soul burned. To-day for the first time his poisoned nerves had been denied their steadying dose; and their retort was a mounting torment. He grasped the decanter and rattled its crystal mouth against the glass in his trembling hand. He flushed the glass, and then stood erect, holding it aloft for an instant. For one fleeting moment he held his head above the drowning waves of his abyss. He nodded easily at Goodwin, raised his brimming glass and murmured a "health" that men had used in his ancient Paradise Lost. And then so suddenly that he spilled the brandy over his hand, he set down his glass, untasted.

"In two hours," his dry lips muttered to Goodwin, as he marched down the steps and turned his face toward the town.

In the edge of the cool banana grove "Beelzebub" halted, and snapped the tongue of his belt buckle into another hole.

"I couldn't do it," he explained, feverishly, to the waving banana fronds. "I wanted to, but I couldn't. A gentleman can't drink with the man that he blackmails."

XCIII: SHOES

JOHN DE GRAFFENREID ATWOOD ate of the lotus, root, stem, and flower. The tropics gobbled him up. He plunged enthusiastically into his work, which was to try to forget Rosine.

Now, they who dine on the lotus rarely consume it plain. There is a sauce *au diable* that goes with it; and the distillers are the chefs who prepare it. And on Johnny's menu card it read "brandy." With a bottle between them, he and Billy Keogh would sit on the porch of the little consulate at night and roar out great, indecorous songs, until the natives, slipping hastily past, would shrug a shoulder and mutter things to themselves about the "*Americanos diablos*."

One day Johnny's *mozo* brought the mail and dumped it on the table. Johnny leaned from his hammock, and fingered the four or five letters dejectedly. Keogh was sitting on the edge of the table chopping lazily with a paper knife at the legs of a centipede that was crawling among the stationery. Johnny was in that phase of lotus-eating when all the world tastes bitter in one's mouth.

"Same old thing!" he complained. "Fool people writing for information about the country. They want to know all about raising fruit, and how to make a fortune without work. Half of 'em don't even send stamps for a reply. They think a consul hasn't anything to do but write letters. Slit those envelopes for me, old man, and see what they want. I'm feeling too rocky to move."

Keogh, acclimated beyond all possibility of ill-humour, drew his chair to the table with smiling compliance on his rose-pink countenance, and began to slit open the letters. Four of them were from citizens in various parts of the United States who seemed to regard the consul at Coralio as a cyclopædia of information. They asked long lists of questions, numerically arranged, about the climate, products, possibilities, laws, business chances, and statistics of the country in which the consul had the honour of representing his own government.

"Write 'em, please, Billy," said the inert official, "just a line, referring them to the latest consular report. Tell 'em the State Department will be delighted to furnish the literary gems. Sign my name. Don't let your pen scratch, Billy; it'll keep me awake."

"Don't snore," said Keogh, amiably, "and I'll do your work for you. You need a corps of assistants, anyhow. Don't see how you ever get out a report. Wake up a minute!—here's one more letter—it's from your own town, too—Dalesburg."

"That so?" murmured Johnny, showing a mild and obligatory interest. "What's it about?"

"Postmaster writes," explained Keogh. "Says a citizen of that town wants some fact and advice from you. Says the citizen has an idea in his head of coming down where you are and opening a shoe store. Wants to know if you think the business would pay. Says he's heard of the boom along this coast, and wants to get in on the ground floor."

In spite of the heat and his bad temper, Johnny's hammock swayed with his laughter. Keogh laughed too; and the pet monkey on the top shelf of the bookcase chattered in shrill sympathy with the ironical reception of the letter from Dalesburg.

"Great bunions!" exclaimed the consul. "Shoe store! What'll they ask about next, I wonder? Overcoat factory, I reckon. Say, Billy—of our three thousand citizens, how many do you suppose ever had on a pair of shoes?"

Keogh reflected judicially.

"Let's see—there's you and me and——"

"Not me," said Johnny, promptly and incorrectly, holding up a foot encased in a disreputable deerskin *zapato*. "I haven't been a victim to shoes in months."

"But you've got 'em, though," went on Keogh. "And there's Goodwin and Blanchard and Geddie and old Lutz and Doc Gregg and that Italian that's agent for the banana company, and there's old Delgado—no; he wears sandals. And, oh, yes; there's Madama Ortiz, 'what kapes the hotel'—she had on a pair of red kid slippers at the *baile* the other night. And Miss Pasa, her daughter, that went to school in the States—she brought back some civilized notions in the way of footgear. And there's the *comandante's* sister that dresses up her feet on feast-days—and Mrs. Geddie, who wears a two with a Castilian instep—and that's about all the ladies. Let's see—don't some of the soldiers at the *cuartel*—no: that's so; they're allowed shoes only when on the march. In barracks they turn their little toeses out to grass."

"'Bout right," agreed the consul. "Not over twenty out of the three thousand ever felt leather on their walking arrangements. Oh, yes; Coralio is just the town for an enterprising shoe store—that doesn't want to part with its goods. Wonder if old Patterson is trying to jolly me! He always was full of things he called jokes. Write him a letter, Billy. I'll dictate it. We'll jolly him back a few."

Keogh dipped his pen, and wrote at Johnny's dictation. With many pauses, filled in with smoke and sundry travellings of the bottle and glasses, the following reply to the Dalesburg communication was perpetrated:

MR. OBADIAH PATTERSON,
Dalesburg, Ala.

DEAR SIR,—In reply to your favour of July 2nd, I have the honour to inform you that, according to my opinion, there is no place on the habitable globe that presents to the eye stronger evidence of the need of a first-class shoe store than does the town of Coralio. There are 3,000 inhabitants in the place, and not a single shoe store! The situation speaks for itself. This coast is rapidly becoming the goal of enterprising business men, but the shoe business is one that has been sadly overlooked or neglected. In fact there are a considerable number of our citizens actually without shoes at present.

Besides the want above mentioned, there is also a crying need for a brewery, a college of higher mathematics, a coal yard, and a clean and intellectual Punch and Judy show. I have the honour to be, sir,

Your Obt. Servant,
JOHN DE GRAFFENREID ATWOOD,
U.S. Consul at Coralio.

P.S.—Hello! Uncle Obadiah. How's the old burg racking along? What would the government do without you and me? Look out for a green-headed parrot and a bunch of bananas soon, from your old friend,

JOHNNY.

"I throw in that postscript," explained the consul, "so Uncle Obadiah won't take offence at the official tone of the letter! Now, Billy, you get that correspondence fixed up, and send Pancho to the post office with it. The *Ariadne* takes the mail out to-morrow if they make up that load of fruit to-day."

The night programme in Coralio never varied. The recreations of the people were soporific and flat. They wandered about, barefoot and aimless, speaking lowly and smoking cigar or cigarette. Looking down on the dimly lighted ways one seemed to see a threading maze of brunette ghosts tangled with a procession of insane fireflies. In some houses the thrumming of lugubrious guitars added to the depression of the *triste* night. Giant tree-frogs rattled in the foliage as loudly as the end man's "bones" in a minstrel troupe. By nine o'clock the streets were almost deserted.

Nor at the consulate was there often a change of bill. Keogh would come there nightly, for Coralio's one cool place was the little seaweed porch of that official residence.

The brandy would be kept moving; and before midnight sentiment would begin to stir in the heart of the self-exiled consul. Then he would relate to Keogh the story of his ended romance. Each night Keogh would listen patiently to the tale, and be ready with untiring sympathy.

"But don't you think for a minute"—thus Johnny

would always conclude his woeful narrative—"that I'm grieving about that girl, Billy. I've forgotten her. She never enters my mind. If she were to enter that door right now, my pulse wouldn't gain a beat. That's all over long ago."

"Don't I know it?" Keogh would answer. "Of course you've forgotten her. Proper thing to do. Wasn't quite O.K. of her to listen to the knocks that—er—Dink Pawson kept giving you."

"Pink Dawson!"—a world of contempt would be in Johnny's tones—"Poor white trash! That's what he was. Had five hundred acres of farming land, though; and that counted. Maybe I'll have a chance to get back at him some day. The Dawsons weren't anybody. Everybody in Alabama knows the Atwoods. Say, Billy—did you know my mother was a De Graffenreid?"

"Why, no," Keogh would say; "is that so?" He had heard it some three hundred times.

"Fact. The De Graffenreids of Hancock County. But I never think of that girl any more, do I, Billy?"

"Not for a minute, my boy," would be the last sounds heard by the conqueror of Cupid.

At this point Johnny would fall into a gentle slumber, and Keogh would saunter out to his own shack under the calabash tree at the edge of the plaza.

In a day or two the letter from the Dalesburg postmaster and its answer had been forgotten by the Coralio exiles. But on the 26th day of July the fruit of the reply appeared upon the tree of events.

The *Andador*, a fruit steamer that visited Coralio regularly, drew into the offing and anchored. The beach was lined with spectators while the quarantine doctor and the custom-house crew rowed out to attend to their duties.

An hour later Billy Keogh lounged into the consulate, clean and cool in his linen clothes, and grinning like a pleased shark.

"Guess what?" he said to Johnny, lounging in his hammock.

"Too hot to guess," said Johnny, lazily.

"Your shoe-store man's come," said Keogh, rolling the sweet morsel on his tongue, "with a stock of goods big enough to supply the continent as far down as Terra del Fuego. They're carting his cases over to the custom-house now. Six barges full they brought ashore and have paddled back for the rest. Oh, ye saints in glory! won't there be regalements in the air when he gets on to the joke and has an interview with Mr. Consul? It'll be worth nine years in the tropics just to witness that one joyful moment."

Keogh loved to take his mirth easily. He selected a clean place on the matting and lay upon the floor. The walls shook with his enjoyment. Johnny turned half over and blinked.

"Don't tell me," he said, "that anybody was fool enough to take that letter seriously."

"Four-thousand-dollar stock of goods!" gasped Keogh, in ecstasy. "Talk about coals to Newcastle! Why didn't he take a shipload of palm-leaf fans to Spitzbergen while he was about it? Saw the old codger on the beach. You ought to have been there when he put on his specs and squinted at the five hundred or so barefooted citizens standing around."

"Are you telling the truth, Billy?" asked the consul, weakly.

"Am I? You ought to see the buncoed gentleman's daughter he brought along. Looks! She makes the brick-dust *señoritas* here look like tar-babies."

"Go on," said Johnny, "if you can stop that asinine giggling. I hate to see a grown man make a laughing hyena of himself."

"Name is Hemstetter," went on Keogh. "He's a—— Hello! what's the matter now?"

Johnny's moccasined feet struck the floor with a thud as he wriggled out of his hammock.

"Get up, you idiot," he said, sternly, "or I'll brain you with this inkstand. That's Rosine and her father. Gad! what a drivelling idiot old Patterson is! Get up, here, Billy Keogh, and help me. What the devil are we going to do? Has all the world gone crazy?"

Keogh rose and dusted himself. He managed to regain a decorous demeanour.

"Situation has got to be met, Johnny," he said, with some success at seriousness. "I didn't think about its being your girl until you spoke. First thing to do is to get them comfortable quarters. You go down and face the music, and I'll trot out to Goodwin's and see if Mrs. Goodwin won't take them in. They've got the decentest house in town."

"Bless you, Billy!" said the consul. "I knew you wouldn't desert me. The world's bound to come to an end, but maybe we can stave it off for a day or two."

Keogh hoisted his umbrella and set out for Goodwin's house. Johnny put on his coat and hat. He picked up the brandy bottle, but set it down again without drinking, and marched bravely down to the beach.

In the shade of the custom-house walls he found Mr. Hemstetter and Rosine surrounded by a mass of gaping citizens. The customs officers were ducking and scraping, while the captain of the *Andador* interpreted the business of the new arrivals. Rosine looked healthy and very much alive. She was gazing at the strange scenes around her with amused interest. There was a faint blush upon her round cheek as she greeted her old admirer. Mr. Hemstetter shook hands with Johnny in a very friendly way. He was an oldish, impractical man—one of that numerous class of erratic business men who are for ever dissatisfied, and seeking a change.

"I am very glad to see you, John—may I call you John?" he said. "Let me thank you for your prompt answer to our postmaster's letter of inquiry. He volunteered to write to you on my behalf. I was looking about for something different in the way of business in which the profits would be greater. I had noticed in the papers that this coast was receiving much attention from investors. I am extremely grateful for your advice to come. I sold out everything that I possess, and invested the proceeds in as fine a stock of shoes as could be bought in the North. You have a picturesque town here, John. I hope business will be as good as your letter justifies me in expecting."

Johnny's agony was abbreviated by the arrival of Keogh, who hurried up with the news that Mrs. Goodwin would be much pleased to place rooms at the disposal of Mr. Hemstetter and his daughter. So there Mr. Hemstetter and Rosine were at once conducted and left to recuperate from the fatigue of the voyage, while Johnny went down to see that the cases of shoes were safely stored in the customs warehouse pending their examination by the officials. Keogh, grinning like a shark, skirmished about to find Goodwin, to instruct him not to expose to Mr. Hemstetter the true state of Coralio as a shoe market until Johnny had been given a chance to redeem the situation, if such a thing were possible.

That night the consul and Keogh held a desperate consultation on the breezy porch of the consulate.

"Send 'em back home," began Keogh, reading Johnny's thoughts.

"I would," said Johnny, after a little silence; "but I've been lying to you, Billy."

"All right about that," said Keogh, affably.

"I've told you hundreds of times," said Johnny, slowly, "that I had forgotten that girl, haven't I?"

"About three hundred and seventy-five," admitted the monument of patience.

"I lied," repeated the consul, "every time. I never forgot her for one minute. I was an obstinate ass for running away just because she said 'No' once. And I was too proud a fool to go back. I talked with Rosine a few minutes this evening up at Goodwin's. I found out one thing. You remember that farmer fellow who was always after her?"

"Dink Pawson?" asked Keogh.

"Pink Dawson. Well, he wasn't a hill of beans to her. She says she didn't believe a word of the things he told her about me. But I'm sewed up now, Billy. That tomfool letter we sent ruined whatever chance I had left. She'll despise me when she finds out that her old father has been made the victim of a joke that a decent schoolboy wouldn't have been guilty of. Shoes! Why, he couldn't sell twenty pairs of shoes in Coralio if he kept store here for twenty years. You put a pair of shoes on one of these Caribs or Spanish brown boys and what'd he do? Stand on his head and squeal until he'd kicked 'em off. None of 'em ever wore shoes, and they never will. If I send 'em back home, I'll have to tell the whole story, and what'll she think of me? I want that girl worse than ever, Billy, and now when she's in reach, I've lost her for ever because I tried to be funny when the thermometer was at 102."

"Keep cheerful," said the optimistic Keogh. "And let 'em open the store. I've been busy myself this afternoon. We can stir up a temporary boom in footgear anyhow. I'll buy six pairs when the doors open. I've been around and seen all the fellows and explained the catastrophe. They'll all buy shoes like they was centipedes. Frank Goodwin will take cases of 'em. The Geddies want about eleven pairs between 'em. Clancy is going to invest the savings of weeks, and even old Doc Gregg wants three pairs of alligator hide slippers if they've got any tens. Blanchard got a look at Miss Hemstetter; and as he's a Frenchman, no less than a dozen pairs will do for him."

"A dozen customers," said Johnny, "for a $4,000 stock of shoes! It won't work. There's a big problem here to figure out. You go home, Billy, and leave me alone. I've got to work at it all by myself. Take that bottle of three-star along with you—no, sir; not another ounce of booze for the United States consul. I'll sit here to-night and pull out the think stop. If there's a soft place on this proposition anywhere I'll land on it. If there isn't, there'll be another wreck to the credit of the gorgeous tropics."

Keogh left, feeling that he could be of no use. Johnny laid a handful of cigars on a table and stretched himself in a steamer chair. When the sudden daylight broke, silvering the harbour ripples, he was still sitting there. Then he got up, whistling a little tune, and took his bath.

At nine o'clock he walked down to the dingy little cable office and hung up for half an hour over a blank. The result of his application was the following message, which he signed and had transmitted at a cost of $33:

To Pinkney Dawson,
Dalesburg, Ala.

Draft for $100 comes to you next mail. Ship me immediately 500 pounds stiff, dry cockleburrs. New use here in arts. Market price twenty cents pound. Further orders likely. Rush.

XCIV: SHIPS

WITHIN a week a suitable building had been secured in the Calle Grande, and Mr. Hemstetter's stock of shoes arranged upon their shelves. The rent of the store was moderate; and the stock made a fine showing of neat white boxes, attractively displayed.

Johnny's friends stood by him loyally. On the first day Keogh strolled into the store in a casual kind of way about once every hour, and bought shoes. After he had purchased a pair each of extension soles, congress gaiters, button kids, low-quartered calfs, dancing pumps, rubber boots, tans of various hues, tennis shoes and flowered slippers, he sought out Johnny to be prompted as to the names of other kinds that he might inquire for. The other English-speaking residents also played their parts nobly by buying often and liberally. Keogh was grand marshal, and made them distribute their patronage, thus keeping up a fair run of custom for several days.

Mr. Hemstetter was gratified by the amount of business done thus far; but expressed surprise that the natives were so backward with their custom.

"Oh, they're awfully shy," explained Johnny, as he wiped his forehead nervously. "They'll get the habit pretty soon. They'll come with a rush when they do come."

One afternoon Keogh dropped into the consul's office, chewing an unlighted cigar thoughtfully.

"Got anything up your sleeve?" he inquired of Johnny. "If you have it's about time to show it. If you can borrow some gent's hat in the audience, and make a lot of customers for an idle stock of shoes come out of it, you'd better spiel. The boys have all laid in enough footgear to last 'em for ten years; and there's nothing doing in the shoe store but dolcy far nienty. I just came by there. Your venerable victim was standing in the door, gazing through his specs at the bare toes passing by his emporium. The natives have got the true artistic temperament. He and Clancy took eighteen tintypes this morning in two hours. There's been but one pair of shoes sold all day. Blanchard went in and bought a pair of fur-lined house-slippers because he thought he saw Miss Hemstetter go into the store. I saw him throw the slippers into the lagoon afterwards."

"There's a Mobile fruit steamer coming in to-morrow or next day," said Johnny. "We can't do anything until then."

"What are you going to do—try to create a demand?"

"Political economy isn't your strong point," said the consul, impudently. "You can't create a demand. But you can create a necessity for a demand. That's what I am going to do."

Two weeks after the consul sent his cable, a fruit steamer brought him a large, mysterious brown bale of some unknown commodity. Johnny's influence with the custom-house people was sufficiently strong for him to get the goods turned over to him without the usual inspection. He had the bale taken to the consulate and snugly stowed in the back corner.

That night he ripped open a corner of it and took out a handful of the cockleburrs. He examined them with the care with which a warrior examines his arms before he goes forth to battle for his lady-love and life. The burrs were the ripe August product, as hard as filberts, and bristling with pines as tough and sharp as needles. Johnny whistled softly a little tune, and went out to find Billy Keogh.

Later in the night, when Coralio was steeped in slumber, he and Billy went forth into the deserted streets with their coats bulging like balloons. All up and down the Calle Grande they went, sowing the sharp burrs carefully in the sand, along the narrow sidewalks, in every foot of grass between the silent houses. And then they took the side streets and byways, missing none. No place where the foot of man, woman or child might fall was slighted. Many trips they made to and from the prickly hoard. And then, nearly at the dawn, they laid themselves down to rest calmly, as great generals do after planning a victory according to the revised tactics, and slept, knowing that they had sowed with the accuracy of Satan sowing tares and the perseverance of Paul planting.

With the rising sun came the purveyors of fruits and meats, and arranged their wares in and around the little market-house. At the end of the town near the seashore the market-house stood; and the sowing of the burrs had not been carried that far. The dealers waited long past the hour when their sales usually began. None came to buy. "*Qué hay?*" they began to exclaim, one to another.

At their accustomed time, from every 'dobe and palm hut and grass-thatched shack and dim *patio* glided women—black women, brown women, lemon-coloured women, women dun and yellow and tawny. They were the marketers starting to purchase the family supply of cassava, plantains, meat, fowls, and tortillas. *Décolleté* they were and bare-armed and bare-footed, with a single skirt reaching below the knee. Stolid and ox-eyed, they stepped from their doorways into the narrow paths or upon the soft grass of the streets.

The first to emerge uttered ambiguous squeals, and raised one foot quickly. Another step and they sat down, with shrill cries of alarm, to pick at the new and painful insects that had stung them upon the feet. "*Qué picadores diablos!*" they screeched to one another across the narrow ways. Some tried the grass instead of the paths, but there they were also stung and bitten by the strange little prickly balls. They plumped down in the grass, and added their lamentations to those of their sisters in the sandy paths. All through the town was heard the plaint of the feminine jabber. The venders in the market still wondered why no customers came.

Then men, lords of the earth, came forth. They, too, began to hop, to dance, to limp, and to curse. They stood stranded and foolish, or stooped to pluck at the scourge that attacked their feet and ankles. Some loudly proclaimed the pest to be poisonous spiders of an unknown species.

And then the children ran out for their morning romp. And now to the uproar was added the howls of limping infants and cockleburred childhood. Every minute the advancing day brought forth fresh victims.

Doña Maria Castillas y Buenventura de las Casas stepped from her honoured doorway, as was her daily custom, to procure fresh bread from the *panaderia* across the street. She was clad in a skirt of flowered yellow satin, a chemise of ruffled linen, and wore a purple mantilla from the looms of Spain. Her lemon-tinted feet, alas! were bare. Her progress was majestic, for were not her ancestors hidalgos of Aragon? Three steps she made across the velvety grass, and set her aristocratic sole upon a bunch of Johnny's burrs. Doña Maria Castillas y Buenventura de las Casas emitted a yowl even as a wild-cat. Turning about, she fell upon hands and knees, and crawled—ay, like a beast of the field she crawled back to her honourable door-sill.

Don Señor Ildefonso Federico Valdazar, *Juez de la Paz*, weighing twenty stone, attempted to convey his bulk to the *pulperia* at the corner of the plaza in order to assuage his matutinal thirst. The first plunge of his unshod foot into the cool grass struck a concealed mine. Don Ildefonso fell like a crumpled cathedral, crying out that he had been fatally bitten by a deadly scorpion. Everywhere were the shoeless citizens hopping, stumbling, limping, and picking from their feet the venomous insects that had come in a single night to harass them.

The first to perceive the remedy was Estebán Delgado, the barber, a man of travel and education. Sitting upon a stone, he plucked burrs from his toes, and made oration:

"Behold, my friends, these bugs of the devil! I know them well. They soar through the skies in swarms like pigeons. These are dead ones that fell during the night. In Yucatan I have seen them as large as oranges. Yes! There they hiss like serpents, and have wings like bats. It is the shoes—the shoes that one needs! *Zapatos—zapatos para mi!*"

Estebán hobbled to Mr. Hemstetter's store, and bought shoes. Coming out, he swaggered down the street with impunity, reviling loudly the bugs of the devil. The suffering ones sat up and stood upon one foot and beheld the immune barber. Men, women and children took up the cry: "*Zapatos! zapatos!*"

The necessity for the demand had been created. The demand followed. That day Mr. Hemstetter sold three hundred pairs of shoes.

"It is really surprising," he said to Johnny, who came up in the evening to help to straighten out the stock, "how trade is picking up. Yesterday I made but three sales."

"I told you they'd whoop things up when they got started," said the consul.

"I think I shall order a dozen more cases of goods, to keep the stock up," said Mr. Hemstetter, beaming through his spectacles.

"I wouldn't send in any orders yet," advised Johnny. "Wait till you see how the trade holds up."

Each night Johnny and Keogh sowed the crop that grew dollars by day. At the end of ten days two-thirds of the stock of shoes had been sold; and the stock of cockleburrs was exhausted. Johnny cabled to Pink Dawson for another 500 pounds, paying twenty cents per pound as before. Mr. Hemstetter carefully made up an order for $1,500 worth of shoes from Northern firms. Johnny hung about the store until this order was ready for the mail, and succeeded in destroying it before it reached the post office.

That night he took Rosine under the mango tree by Goodwin's porch, and confessed everything. She looked him in the eye, and said: "You are a very wicked man. Father and I will go back home. You say it was a joke? I think it is a very serious matter."

But at the end of half an hour's argument the conversation had been turned upon a different subject. The two were considering the respective merits of pale blue and pink wallpaper with which the old colonial mansion of the Atwoods in Dalesburg was to be decorated after the wedding.

On the next morning Johnny confessed to Mr. Hemstetter. The shoe merchant put on his spectacles, and said through them: "You strike me as being a most extraordinary young scamp. If I had not managed this enterprise with good business judgment my entire stock of goods might have been a complete loss. Now, how do you propose to dispose of the rest of it?"

When the second invoice of cockleburrs arrived Johnny loaded them and the remainder of the shoes into a schooner, and sailed down the coast to Alazan.

There, in the same dark and diabolical manner, he repeated his success; and came back with a bag of money and not so much as a shoestring.

And then he besought his great Uncle of the waving goatee and starred vest to accept his resignation, for the lotus no longer lured him. He hankered for the spinach and cress of Dalesburg.

The services of Mr. William Terence Keogh as acting consul, *pro tem.*, were suggested and accepted, and Johnny sailed with the Hemstetters back to his native shores.

Keogh slipped into the sinecure of the American consulship with the ease that never left him even in such high places. The tintype establishment was soon to become a thing of the past, although its deadly work along the peaceful and helpless Spanish Main was never effaced. The restless partners were about to be off again, scouting ahead of the slow ranks of Fortune. But now they would take different ways. There were rumours of a promising uprising in Peru; and thither the martial Clancy would turn his adventurous steps. As for Keogh, he was figuring in his mind and on quires of Government letter-heads a scheme that dwarfed the art of misrepresenting the human countenance upon tin.

"What suits me," Keogh used to say, "in the

way of a business proposition is something diversified that looks like a longer shot than it is—something in the way of a genteel graft that isn't worked enough for the correspondence schools to be teaching it by mail. I take the long end; but I like to have at least as good a chance to win as a man learning to play poker on an ocean steamer, or running for governor of Texas on the Republican ticket. And when I cash in my winnings, I don't want to find any widows' and orphans' chips in my stack."

The grass-grown globe was the green table on which Keogh gambled. The games he played were of his own invention. He was no grubber after the diffident dollar. Nor did he care to follow it with horn and hounds. Rather he loved to coax it with egregious and brilliant flies from its habitat in the waters of strange streams. Yet Keogh was a business man; and his schemes, in spite of their singularity, were as solidly set as the plans of a building contractor. In Arthur's time Sir William Keogh would have been a Knight of the Round Table. In these modern days he rides abroad, seeking the Graft instead of the Grail.

Three days after Johnny's departure, two small schooners appeared off Coralio. After some delay a boat put off from one of them, and brought a sunburned young man ashore. This young man had a shrewd and calculating eye; and he glanced with amazement at the strange things that he saw. He found on the beach some one who directed him to the consul's office; and thither he made his way at a nervous gait.

Keogh was sprawled in the official chair, drawing caricatures of his Uncle's head on an official pad of paper. He looked up at his visitor.

"Where's Johnny Atwood?" inquired the sunburned young man, in a business tone.

"Gone," said Keogh, working carefully at Uncle Sam's necktie.

"That's just like him," remarked the nut-brown one, leaning against the table. "He always was a fellow to gallivant round instead of 'tending to business. Will he be in soon?"

"Don't think so," said Keogh, after a fair amount of deliberation.

"I s'pose he's out at some of his tomfoolery," conjectured the visitor, in a tone of virtuous conviction. "Johnny never would stick to anything long enough to succeed. I wonder how he manages to run his business here, and never be 'round to look after it."

"I'm looking after the business just now," admitted the *pro tem.* consul.

"Are you?—then, say!—where's the factory?"

"What factory?" asked Keogh, with a mildly polite interest.

"Why, the factory where they use them cockleburrs. Lord knows what they use 'em for, anyway! I've got the basements of both them ships out there loaded with 'em. I'll give you a bargain in this lot. I've had every man, woman and child around Dalesburg that wasn't busy pickin' 'em for a month. I hired these ships to bring 'em over. Everybody thought I was crazy. Now, you can have this lot for fifteen cents a pound, delivered on land. And if you want more I guess old Alabam' can come up to the demand. Johnny told me when he left home that if he struck anything down here that there was any money in he'd let me in on it. Shall I drive the ships in and hitch?"

A look of supreme, almost incredulous, delight dawned in Keogh's ruddy countenance. He dropped his pencil. His eyes turned upon the sunburned young man with joy in them mingled with fear lest his ecstasy should prove a dream.

"For God's sake tell me," said Keogh, earnestly, "are you Dink Pawson?"

"My name is Pinkney Dawson," said the cornerer of the cockleburr market.

Billy Keogh slid rapturously and gently from his chair to his favourite strip of matting on the floor.

There were not many sounds in Coralio on that sultry afternoon. Among those that were may be mentioned a noise of enraptured and unrighteous laughter from a prostrate Irish-American, while a sunburned young man, with a shrewd eye, looked on him with wonder and amazement. Also the "tramp, tramp, tramp," of many well-shod feet in the streets outside. Also the lonesome wash of the waves that beat along the historic shores of the Spanish Main.

XCV: MASTERS OF ARTS

A TWO-INCH stub of a blue pencil was the wand with which Keogh performed the preliminary acts of his magic. So, with this he covered paper with diagrams and figures, while he waited for the United States of America to send down to Coralio a successor to Atwood, resigned.

The new scheme that his mind had conceived, his stout heart indorsed, and his blue pencil corroborated, was laid around the characteristics and human frailties of the new president of Anchuria. These characteristics, and the situation out of which Keogh hoped to wrest a golden tribute, deserve chronicling contributive to the clear order of events.

President Losada—many called him Dictator—was a man whose genius would have made him conspicuous even among Anglo-Saxons, had not that genius been intermixed with other traits that were petty and subversive. He had some of the lofty patriotism of Washington (the man he most admired), the force of Napoleon, and much of the wisdom of the sages. These characteristics might have justified him in the assumption of the title of "The Illustrious Liberator," had they not been accompanied by a stupendous and amazing vanity that kept him in the less worthy ranks of the dictators.

Yet he did his country great service. With a mighty grasp he shook it nearly free from the shackles of ignorance and sloth and the vermin that fed upon it, and all but made it a power in the council of nations. He established schools and hospitals, built roads, bridges, railroads and palaces, and bestowed generous subsidies upon the arts and sciences. He was the absolute despot and the idol of his people. The wealth of the country poured into his hands. Other presidents had been rapacious without reason. Losada amassed enormous wealth, but his people had their share of the benefits.

The joint in his armour was his insatiate passion for monuments and tokens commemorating his glory. In every town he caused to be erected statues of himself bearing legends in praise of his greatness. In the walls of every public edifice, tablets were fixed reciting his splendour and the gratitude of his subjects. His statuettes and portraits were scattered throughout the land in every house and hut. One of the sycophants in his court painted him as St. John, with a halo and a train of attendants in full uniform. Losada saw nothing incongruous in this picture, and had it hung in a church in the capital. He ordered from a French sculptor a marble group including himself with Napoleon, Alexander the Great, and one or two others whom he deemed worthy of the honour.

He ransacked Europe for decorations, employing policy, money and intrigue to cajole the orders he coveted from kings and rulers. On state occasions his breast was covered from shoulder to shoulder with crosses, stars, golden roses, medals and ribbons. It was said that the man who could contrive for him a new decoration, or invent some new method of extolling his greatness, might plunge a hand deep into the treasury.

This was the man upon whom Billy Keogh had his eye. The gentle buccaneer had observed the rain of favours that fell upon those who ministered to the president's vanities, and he did not deem it his duty to hoist his umbrella against the scattering drops of liquid fortune.

In a few weeks the new consul arrived, releasing Keogh from his temporary duties. He was a young man fresh from college, who lived for botany alone. The consulate at Coralio gave him the opportunity to study tropical flora. He wore smoked glasses, and carried a green umbrella. He filled the cool, back porch of the consulate with plants and specimens so that space for a bottle and chair was not to be found. Keogh gazed on him sadly, but without rancour, and began to pack his gripsack. For his new plot against stagnation along the Spanish Main required of him a voyage overseas.

Soon came the *Karlsefin* again—she of the trampish habits—gleaning a cargo of coconuts for a speculative descent upon the New York market. Keogh was booked for a passage on the return trip.

"Yes, I'm going to New York," he explained to the group of his countrymen that had gathered on the beach to see him off. "But I'll be back before you miss me. I've undertaken the art education of this piebald country, and I'm not the man to desert it while it's in the early throes of tintypes."

With this mysterious declaration of his intentions Keogh boarded the *Karlsefin*.

Ten days later, shivering, with the collar of his thin coat turned high, he burst into the studio of Carolus White at the top of a tall building in Tenth Street, New York City.

Carolus White was smoking a cigarette and frying sausages over an oil stove. He was only twenty-three, and had noble theories about art.

"Billy Keogh!" exclaimed White, extending the hand that was not busy with the frying pan. "From what part of the uncivilized world, I wonder!"

"Hallo, Carry," said Keogh, dragging forward a stool, and holding his fingers close to the stove. "I'm glad I found you so soon. I've been looking for you all day in the directories and art galleries. The free-lunch man on the corner told me where you were, quick. I was sure you'd be painting pictures yet."

Keogh glanced about the studio with the shrewd eye of a connoisseur in business.

"Yes, you can do it," he declared with many gentle nods of his head. "That big one in the corner with the angels and green clouds and band-wagon is just the sort of thing we want. What would you call that, Carry—scene from Coney Island, ain't it?"

"That," said White, "I had intended to call 'The Translation of Elijah,' but you may be nearer right than I am."

"Name doesn't matter," said Keogh, largely; "it's the frame and the varieties of paint that does the trick. Now, I can tell you in a minute what I want. I've come on a little voyage of two thousand miles to take you in with me on a scheme. I thought of you as soon as the scheme showed itself to me. How would you like to go back with me and paint a picture? Ninety days for the trip, and five thousand dollars for the job."

"Cereal food or hair-tonic posters?" asked White.

"It isn't an ad."

"What kind of a picture is it to be?"

"It's a long story," said Keogh.

"Go ahead with it. If you don't mind, while you talk I'll just keep my eye on these sausages. Let 'em get one shade deeper than a Vandyke brown and you spoil 'em."

Keogh explained his project. They were to return to Coralio, where White was to pose as a distinguished American portrait painter who was touring in the tropics as a relaxation from his arduous and remunerative professional labours. It was not an unreasonable hope, even to those who trod in the beaten paths of business, that an artist with so much prestige might secure a commission to perpetuate upon canvas the lineaments of the president, and secure a share of the *pesos* that were raining upon the caterers to his weaknesses.

Keogh had set his price at ten thousand dollars. Artists had been paid more for portraits. He and White were to share the expenses of the trip and divide the possible profits. Then he laid the scheme before White, whom he had known in the West before one declared for Art and the other became a Bedouin.

Before long the two machinators abandoned the rigour of the bare studio for a snug corner of a café. There they sat far into the night, with old envelopes and Keogh's stub of blue pencil between them.

At twelve o'clock White doubled up in his chair, with his chin on his fist, and shut his eyes at the unbeautiful wallpaper.

"I'll go you, Billy," he said, in the quiet tones of decision. "I've got two or three hundred saved up for sausages and rent; and I'll take the chance with you. Five thousand! It will give me two years in Paris and one in Italy. I'll begin to pack to-morrow."

"You'll begin in ten minutes," said Keogh. "It's to-morrow now. The *Karlsefin* starts back at four p.m. Come on to your painting shop, and I'll help you."

For five months in the year Coralio is the Newport of Anchuria. Then only does the town possess life. From November to March it is practically the seat of government. The president with his official family sojourns there; and society follows him. The pleasure-loving people make the season one long holiday of amusement and rejoicing. *Fiestas*, balls, games, sea bathing, processions and small theatres contribute to their enjoyment. The famous Swiss band from the capital plays in the little plaza every evening, while the fourteen carriages and vehicles in the town circle in funereal but complacent procession. Indians from the interior mountains, looking like prehistoric stone idols, come down to peddle their handiwork in the streets. The people throng the narrow ways, a chattering, happy, careless stream of buoyant humanity. Preposterous children, rigged out with the shortest of ballet skirts and gilt wings, howl, underfoot, among the effervescent crowds. Especially is the arrival of the presidential party, at the opening of the season, attended with pomp, show and patriotic demonstrations of enthusiasm and delight.

When Keogh and White reached their destination, on the return trip of the *Karlsefin*, the gay winter season was well begun. As they stepped upon the beach they could hear the band playing in the plaza. The village maidens, with fireflies already fixed in their dark locks, were gliding, barefoot and coy-eyed, along the paths. Dandies in white linen, swinging their canes, were beginning their seductive strolls. The air was full of human essence, of artificial excitement, of coquetry, indolence, pleasure—the man-made sense of existence.

The first two or three days after their arrival were spent in preliminaries. Keogh escorted the artist about town, introducing him to the little circle of English-speaking residents, and pulling whatever wires he could to effect the spreading of White's fame as a painter. And then Keogh planned a more spectacular demonstration of the idea he wished to keep before the public.

He and White engaged rooms in the Hotel de los Estranjeros. The two were clad in new suits of immaculate duck, with American straw hats, and carried canes of remarkable uniqueness and inutility. Few *caballeros* in Coralio—even the gorgeously uniformed officers of the Anchurian army—were as conspicuous for ease and elegance of demeanour as Keogh and his friend, the great American painter, *Señor* White.

White set up his easel on the beach and made striking sketches of the mountain and sea views. The native population formed at his rear in a vast, chattering semicircle to watch his work. Keogh, with his care for details, had arranged for himself a pose which he carried out with fidelity. His rôle was that of friend to the great artist, a man of affairs and leisure. The visible emblem of his position was a pocket camera.

"For branding the man who owns it," said he, "a genteel dilettante with a bank account and an easy conscience, a steam yacht ain't in it with a camera. You see a man doing nothing but loafing around making snapshots, and you know right away he reads up well in 'Bradstreet.' You notice these old millionaire boys—soon as you get through taking everything else in sight they go to taking photographs. People are more impressed by a kodak than they are by a title or a four-carat scarf-pin." So Keogh strolled blandly about Coralio, snapping the scenery and the shrinking *señoritas* while White posed conspicuously in the higher regions of art.

Two weeks after their arrival, the scheme began

to bear fruit. An aide-de-camp of the president drove to the hotel in a dashing victoria. The president desired that *Señor* White come to the Casa Morena for an informal interview.

Keogh gripped his pipe tightly between his teeth. "Not a cent less than ten thousand," he said to the artist—"remember the price. And in gold or its equivalent—don't let him stick you with this bargain-counter stuff they call money here."

"Perhaps it isn't that he wants," said White.

"Get out!" said Keogh, with splendid confidence. "I know what he wants. He wants his picture painted by the celebrated young American painter and filibuster now sojourning in his downtrodden country. Off you go."

The victoria sped away with the artist. Keogh walked up and down, puffing great clouds of smoke from his pipe, and waited. In an hour the victoria swept again to the door of the hotel, deposited White, and vanished. The artist dashed up the stairs, three at a step. Keogh stopped smoking, and became a silent interrogation point.

"Landed," exclaimed White, with his boyish face flushed with elation. "Billy, you are a wonder. He wants a picture. I'll tell you all about it. By heavens! that dictator chap is a corker! He's a dictator clear down to his finger-ends. He's a kind of combination of Julius Cæsar, Lucifer, and Chauncey Depew done in sepia. Polite and grim—that's his way. The room I saw him in was about ten acres big, and looked like a Mississippi steamboat with its gilding and mirrors and white paint. He talks English better than I can ever hope to. The matter of the price came up. I mentioned ten thousand. I expected him to call the guard and have me taken out and shot. He didn't move an eyelash. He just waved one of his chestnut hands in a careless way and said, 'Whatever you say.' I am to go back to-morrow and discuss with him the details of the picture."

Keogh hung his head. Self-abasement was easy to read in his downcast countenance.

"I'm failing, Carry," he said, sorrowfully. "I'm not fit to handle these man's-size schemes any longer. Peddling oranges in a push-cart is about the suitable graft for me. When I said ten thousand, I swear I thought I had sized up that brown man's limit to within two cents. He'd have melted down for fifteen thousand just as easy. Say—Carry—you'll see old man Keogh safe in some nice, quiet idiot asylum, won't you, if he makes a break like that again?"

The Casa Morena, although only one story in height, was a building of brown stone, luxurious as a palace in its interior. It stood on a low hill in a walled garden of splendid tropical flora at the upper edge of Coralio. The next day the president's carriage came again for the artist. Keogh went out for a walk along the beach, where he and his "picture box" were now familiar sights. When he returned to the hotel White was sitting in a steamer chair on the balcony.

"Well," said Keogh, "did you and His Nibs decide on the kind of a chromo he wants?"

White got up and walked back and forth on the balcony a few times. Then he stopped, and laughed strangely. His face was flushed, and his eyes were bright with a kind of angry amusement.

"Look here, Billy," he said, somewhat roughly, "when you first came to me in my studio and mentioned a picture, I thought you wanted a Smashed Oats or a Hair Tonic poster painted on a range of mountains or the side of a continent. Well, either of those jobs would have been Art in its highest form compared to the one you've steered me against. I can't paint that picture, Billy. You've got to let me out. Let me try to tell you what that barbarian wants. He had it all planned out, and even a sketch made of his idea. The old boy doesn't draw badly at all. But, ye goddesses of Art! listen to the monstrosity of his idea. He wants himself in the centre of the canvas, of course. He is to be painted as Jupiter sitting on Olympus, with the clouds at his feet. At one side of him stands George Washington, in full regimentals, with his hand on the president's shoulder. An angel with outstretched wings hovers overhead, crowning him—Queen of the May, I suppose. In the background is to be cannon, more angels and soldiers. The man who would paint that picture would have to have the soul of a dog, and would deserve to go down into oblivion without even a tin can tied to his tail to sound his memory."

Little beads of moisture crept out all over Billy Keogh's brow. The stub of his blue pencil had not figured out a contingency like this. The machinery of his plan had run with flattering smoothness until now. He dragged another chair upon the balcony, and got White back to his seat. He lit his pipe with apparent calm.

"Now, sonny," he said, with gentle grimness, "you and me will have an Art to Art talk. You've got your art and I've got mine. Yours is the real Pierian stuff that turns up its nose at bock-beer signs and oleographs of the Old Mill. Mine's the art of Business. This was my scheme, and it worked out like two-and-two. Paint that president man as Old King Cole, or Venus, or a landscape, or a fresco, or a bunch of lilies, or anything he thinks he looks like. But get the paint on the canvas and collect the spoils. You wouldn't throw me down, Carry, at this stage of the game. Think of that ten thousand."

"I can't help thinking of it," said White, "and that's what hurts. I'm tempted to throw every ideal I ever had down in the mire, and steep my soul in infamy by painting that picture. That five thousand meant three years of foreign study to me, and I'd almost sell my soul for that."

"Now it ain't as bad as that," said Keogh, soothingly. "It's a business proposition. It's so much paint and time against money. I don't fall in with your idea that that picture would so everlastingly jolt the art side of the question. George Washington was all right, you know, and nobody could say a word against the angel. I don't think so bad of that group. If you was to give Jupiter a pair of epaulettes and a sword, and kind of work the clouds around to look like a blackberry patch, it wouldn't make such a bad battle scene. Why, if we hadn't already settled on the price, he ought to pay an extra thousand for Washington, and the angel ought to raise it five hundred."

"You don't understand, Billy," said White, with an uneasy laugh. "Some of us fellows who try to paint have big notions about Art. I wanted to paint a picture some day that people would stand before and forget that it was made of paint. I wanted it to creep into them like a bar of music and mushroom there like a soft bullet. And I wanted 'em to go away and ask, 'What else has he done?' And I didn't want 'em to find a thing; not a portrait nor a magazine cover nor an illustration nor a drawing of a girl—nothing but *the* picture. That's why I've lived on fried sausages, and tried to keep true to myself. I persuaded myself to do this portrait for the chance it might give me to study abroad. But this howling, screaming caricature! Good Lord! can't you see how it is?"

"Sure," said Keogh, as tenderly as he would have spoken to a child, and he laid a long forefinger on White's knee. "I see. It's bad to have your art all slugged up like that. I know. You wanted to paint a big thing like a panorama of the battle of Gettysburg. But let me kalsomine you a little mental sketch to consider. Up to date we're out $385·50 on this scheme. Our capital took every cent both of us could raise. We've got about enough left to get back to New York on. I need my share of that ten thousand. I want to work a copper deal in Idaho, and make a hundred thousand. That's the business end of the thing. Come down off your art perch, Carry, and let's land that hatful of dollars."

"Billy," said White, with an effort, "I'll try. I won't say I'll do it, but I'll try. I'll go at it, and put it through if I can."

"That's business," said Keogh, heartily. "Good boy! Now, here's another thing—rush that picture—crowd it through as quick as you can. Get a couple of boys to help you mix the paint if necessary. I've picked up some pointers around town. The people here are beginning to get sick of Mr. President. They say he's been too free with concessions; and they accuse him of trying to make a dicker with England to sell out the country. We want that picture done and paid for before there's any row."

In the great *patio* of Casa Morena, the president caused to be stretched a huge canvas. Under this White set up his temporary studio. For two hours each day the great man sat to him.

White worked faithfully. But, as the work progressed, he had seasons of bitter scorn, of infinite self-contempt, of sullen gloom and sardonic gaiety. Keogh, with the patience of a great general, soothed, coaxed, argued—kept him at the picture.

At the end of a month White announced that the picture was completed—Jupiter, Washington, angels, clouds, cannon and all. His face was pale and his mouth drawn straight when he told Keogh. He said the president was much pleased with it. It was to be hung in the National Gallery of Statesmen and Heroes. The artist had been requested to return to Casa Morena on the following day to receive payment. At the appointed time he left the hotel, silent under his friend's joyful talk of their success.

An hour later he walked into the room where Keogh was waiting, threw his hat on the floor, and sat upon the table.

"Billy," he said, in strained and labouring tones, "I've a little money out West in a small business that my brother is running. It's what I've been living on while I've been studying art. I'll draw out my share and pay you back what you've lost on this scheme."

"Lost!" exclaimed Keogh, jumping up. "Didn't you get paid for the picture?"

"Yes, I got paid," said White. "But just now there isn't any picture, and there isn't any pay. If you care to hear about it, here are the edifying details. The president and I were looking at the painting. His secretary brought a bank draft on New York for ten thousand dollars and handed it to me. The moment I touched it I went wild. I tore it into little pieces and threw them on the floor. A workman was repainting the pillars inside the *patio*. A bucket of his paint happened to be convenient. I picked up his brush and slapped a quart of blue paint all over that ten-thousand-dollar nightmare. I bowed and walked out. The president didn't move or speak. That was one time he was taken by surprise. It's tough on you, Billy, but I couldn't help it."

There seemed to be excitement in Coralio. Outside there was a confused, rising murmur pierced by high-pitched cries. "*Bajo el traidor—Muerte el traidor!*" were the words they seemed to form.

"Listen to that!" exclaimed White, bitterly; "I know that much Spanish. They're shouting 'Down with the traitor!' I heard them before. I felt that they meant me. I was a traitor to Art. The picture had to go."

" 'Down with the blank fool' would have suited your case better," said Keogh, with fiery emphasis. "You tear up ten thousand dollars like an old rag because the way you've spread on five dollars' worth of paint hurts your conscience. Next time I pick a side-partner in a scheme the man has got to go before a notary and swear he never even heard the word 'ideal' mentioned."

Keogh strode from the room, white-hot. White paid little attention to his resentment. The scorn of Billy Keogh seemed a trifling thing beside the greater self-scorn he had escaped.

In Coralio the excitement waxed. An outburst was imminent. The cause of this demonstration of displeasure was the presence in the town of a big, pink-cheeked Englishman, who, it was said, was an agent of his government come to clinch the bargain by which the president placed his people in the hands of a foreign power. It was charged that not only had he given away priceless concessions, but that the public debt was to be transferred into the hands of the English, and the custom-houses turned over to them as a guarantee. The long-enduring people had determined to make their protest felt.

On that night, in Coralio and in other towns, their ire found vent. Yelling mobs, mercurial but dangerous, roamed the streets. They overthrew the great bronze statue of the president that stood in the centre of the plaza, and hacked it to shapeless pieces. They tore from public buildings the tablets set there proclaiming the glory of the "Illustrious Liberator." His pictures in the government offices were demolished. The mobs even attacked the Casa Morena, but were driven away by the military, which remained faithful to the executive. All the night terror reigned.

The greatness of Losada was shown by the fact that by noon the next day order was restored, and he was still absolute. He issued proclamations denying positively that any negotiation of any kind had been entered into with England. Sir Stafford Vaughan, the pink-cheeked Englishman, also declared in placards and in public print that his presence there had no international significance.

He was a traveller without guile. In fact (so he stated), he had not even spoken with the president or been in his presence since his arrival.

During this disturbance, White was preparing for his homeward voyage in the steamship that was to sail within two or three days. About noon, Keogh, the restless, took his camera out with the hope of speeding the lagging hours. The town was now as quiet as if peace had never departed from her perch on the red-tiled roofs.

About the middle of the afternoon, Keogh hurried back to the hotel with something decidedly special in the air. He retired to the little room where he developed his pictures.

Later on he came out to White on the balcony, with a luminous, grim, predatory smile on his face.

"Do you know what that is?" he asked, holding up a 4 by 5 photograph mounted on cardboard.

"Snapshot of a *señorita* sitting in the sand—alliteration unintentional," guessed White, lazily.

"Wrong," said Keogh with shining eyes. "It's a slung-shot. It's a can of dynamite. It's a gold-mine. It's a sight-draft on your president man for twenty thousand dollars—yes, sir—twenty thousand this time, and no spoiling the picture. No ethics of art in the way. Art! You with your smelly little tubes! I've got you skinned to death with a kodak. Take a look at that."

White took the picture in his hand, and gave a long whistle.

"Jove!" he exclaimed, "but wouldn't that stir up a row in the town if you let it be seen. How in the world did you get it, Billy?"

"You know that high wall around the president man's back garden? I was up there trying to get a bird's-eye of the town. I happened to notice a chink in the wall where a stone and a lot of plaster had slid out. Thinks I, I'll take a peep through to see how Mr. President's cabbages are growing. The first thing I saw was him and this Sir Englishman sitting at a little table about twenty feet away. They had the table all spread over with documents, and they were hobnobbing over them as thick as two pirates. 'Twas a nice corner of the garden, all private and shady with palms and orange-trees, and they had a pail of champagne set by handy in the grass. I knew then was the time for me to make my big hit in art. So I raised the machine up to the crack, and pressed the button. Just as I did so them old boys shook hands on the deal—you see they took that way in the picture."

Keogh put on his coat and hat.

"What are you going to do with it?" asked White.

"Me," said Keogh in a hurt tone, "why, I'm going to tie a pink ribbon to it and hang it on the whatnot, of course. I'm surprised at you. But while I'm out you just try to figure out what ginger-cake potentate would be most likely to want to buy this work of art for his private collection—just to keep it out of circulation."

The sunset was reddening the tops of the coconut palms when Billy Keogh came back from Casa Morena. He nodded to the artist's questioning gaze, and lay down on a cot with his hands under the back of his head.

"I saw him. He paid the money like a little man. They didn't want to let me in at first. I told 'em it was important. Yes, that president man is on the plenty-able list. He's got a beautiful business system about the way he uses his brains.

All I had to do was to hold up the photograph so he could see it, and name the price. He just smiled, and walked over to a safe to get the cash. Twenty one-thousand-dollar brand-new United States Treasury notes he laid on the table, like I'd pay out a dollar and a quarter. Fine notes, too—they crackled with a sound like burning the brush of a ten-acre lot."

"Let's try the feel of one," said White, curiously. "I never saw a thousand-dollar bill." Keogh did not immediately respond.

"Carry," he said, in an absent-minded way, "you think a heap of your art, don't you?"

"More," said White, frankly, "than has been for the financial good of myself and my friends."

"I thought you were a fool the other day," went on Keogh, quietly, "and I'm not sure now that you wasn't. But if you was, so am I. I've been in some funny deals, Carry, but I've always managed to scramble fair, and match my brains and capital against the other fellow's. But when it comes to —well, when you've got the other fellow cinched, and the screws on him, and he's got to put up—why, it don't strike me as being a man's game. They've got a name for it, you know; it's—confound you, don't you understand? A fellow feels—it's something like that blamed art of yours—he—well, I tore that photograph up and laid the pieces on that stack of money, and shoved the whole business back across the table. 'Excuse me, Mr. Losada,' I said, 'but I guess I've made a mistake in the price. You get the photo for nothing.' Now, Carry, you get out the pencil, and we'll do some more figuring. I'd like to save enough out of our capital for you to have some fried sausages in your joint when you get back to New York."

XCVI: DICKY

THERE is little consecutiveness along the Spanish Main. Things happen there intermittently. Even Time seems to hang his scythe daily on the branch of an orange-tree while he takes a siesta and a cigarette.

After the ineffectual revolt against the administration of President Losada, the country settled again in quiet toleration of the abuses with which he had been charged. In Coralio old political enemies went arm-in-arm, lightly, eschewing for the time all differences of opinion.

The failure of the art expedition did not stretch the cat-footed Keogh upon his back. The ups and downs of Fortune made smooth travelling for his nimble steps. His blue pencil stub was at work again before the smoke of the steamer on which White sailed had cleared away from the horizon. He had but to speak a word to Geddie to find his credit negotiable for whatever goods he wanted from the store of Brannigan & Company. On the same day on which White arrived in New York, Keogh, at the rear of a train of five pack mules loaded with hardware and cutlery, set his face toward the grim, interior mountains. There the Indian tribes wash gold-dust from the auriferous streams; and when a market is brought to them trading is brisk and *muy bueno* in the Cordilleras.

In Coralio, Time folded his wings and paced wearily along his drowsy path. They who had most cheered the torpid hours were gone. Clancy had sailed on a Spanish barque for Colon, contemplating a cut across the isthmus and then a further voyage to end at Callao, where the fighting was said to be on. Geddie, whose quiet and genial nature had once served to mitigate the frequent dull reaction of lotus eating, was now a home-man, happy with his bright orchid, Paula, and never even dreaming of or regretting the unsolved, sealed and monogramed Bottle whose contents, now inconsiderable, were held safely in the keeping of the sea.

Well may the Walrus, most discerning and eclectic of beasts, place sealing-wax midway on his programme of topics that fall pertinent and diverting upon the ear.

Atwood was gone—he of the hospitable back porch and ingenuous cunning. Dr. Gregg, with his trepanning story smouldering within him, was a whiskered volcano, always showing signs of imminent eruption, and was not to be considered in the ranks of those who might contribute to the amelioration of ennui. The new consul's note chimed with the sad sea waves and the violent tropical greens—he had not a bar of Scheherezade or of the Round Table in his lute. Goodwin was employed with large projects; what time he was loosed from them found him at his home, where he loved to be. Therefore it will be seen that there was a dearth of fellowship and entertainment among the foreign contingent of Coralio.

And then Dicky Maloney dropped down from the clouds upon the town, and amused it.

Nobody knew where Dicky Maloney hailed from or how he reached Coralio. He appeared there one day; and that was all. He afterward said that he came on the fruit steamer *Thor*; but an inspection of the *Thor's* passenger list of that date was found to be Maloneyless. Curiosity, however, soon perished, and Dicky took his place among the odd fish cast up by the Caribbean.

He was an active, devil-may-care, rollicking fellow with an engaging grey eye, the most irresistible grin, a rather dark or much sunburned complexion, and a head of the fieriest red hair ever seen in that country. Speaking the Spanish language as well as he spoke English, and seeming always to have plenty of silver in his pockets, it was not long before he was a welcome companion whithersoever he went. He had an extreme fondness for *vino blanco*, and gained the reputation of being able to drink more of it than any three men in town. Everybody called him "Dicky"; everybody cheered up at the sight of him—especially the natives, to whom his marvellous red hair and his free-and-easy style were a constant delight and envy. Wherever you went in the town you would soon see Dicky or hear his genial laugh, and find around him a group of admirers who appreciated him both for his good nature and the white wine he was always so ready to buy.

A considerable amount of speculation was had concerning the object of his sojourn there, until one day he silenced this by opening a small shop for the sale of tobacco, *dulces* and the handiwork of the interior Indians—fibre-and-silk-woven goods, deerskin *zapatos* and basketwork of *tule* reeds. Even then he did not change his habits; for he was drinking and playing cards half the day and night with the *comandante*, the collector of customs, the *Jefe Politico* and other gay dogs among the native officials.

One day Dicky saw Pasa, the daughter of Madama Ortiz, sitting in the side door of the

Hotel des los Estranjeros. He stopped in his tracks, still, for the first time in Coralio; and then he sped, swift as a deer, to find Vasquez, a gilded native youth, to present him.

The young men had named Pasa "*La Santita Naranjadita*." *Naranjadita* is a Spanish word for a certain colour that you must go to more trouble to describe in English. By saying "The little saint, tinted the most beautiful-delicate-slightly-orange-golden," you will approximate the description of Madama Ortiz's daughter.

La Madama Ortiz sold rum in addition to other liquors. Now, you must know that the rum expiates whatever opprobrium attends upon the other commodities. For rum-making, mind you, is a government monopoly; and to keep a government dispensary assures respectability if not preeminence. Moreover, the saddest of precisians could find no fault with the conduct of the shop. Customers drank there in the lowest of spirits and fearsomely, as in the shadow of the dead; for Madama's ancient and vaulted lineage counteracted even the rum's behest to be merry. For, was she not of the Inglesias, who landed with Pizarro? And had not her deceased husband been *comisionado de caminos y puentes* for the district?

In the evening Pasa sat by the window in the room next to the one where they drank, and strummed dreamily upon her guitar. And then, by twos and threes, would come visiting young *caballeros* and occupy the prim line of chairs set against the wall of this room. They were there to besiege the heart of "*La Santita*." Their method (which is not proof against intelligent competition) consisted of expanding the chest, looking valorous, and consuming a gross or two of cigarettes. Even saints delicately oranged prefer to be wooed differently.

Doña Pasa would tide over the vast chasms of nicotinized silence with music from her guitar, while she wondered if the romances she had read about gallant and more—more contiguous cavaliers were all lies. At somewhat regular intervals Madama would glide in from the dispensary with a sort of drought-suggesting gleam in her eyes, and there would be a rustling of stiffly starched white trousers as one of the *caballeros* would propose an adjournment to the bar.

That Dicky Maloney would, sooner or later, explore this field was a thing to be foreseen. There were few doors in Coralio into which his red head had not been poked.

In an incredibly short space of time after his first sight of her he was there, seated close beside her rocking chair. There were no back-against-the-wall poses in Dicky's theory of wooing. His plan of subjection was an attack at close range. To carry the fortress with one concentrated, ardent, eloquent, irresistible *escalade*—that was Dicky's way.

Pasa was descended from the proudest Spanish families in the country. Moreover, she had had unusual advantages. Two years in a New Orleans school had elevated her ambitions, and fitted her for a fate above the ordinary maidens of her native land. And yet here she succumbed to the first red-haired scamp with a glib tongue and a charming smile that came along and courted her properly.

Very soon Dicky took her to the little church on the corner of the plaza, and "Mrs. Maloney" was added to her string of distinguished names.

And it was her fate to sit, with her patient, saintly eyes and figure like a bisque Psyche, behind the sequestered counter of the little shop, while Dicky drank and philandered with his frivolous acquaintances.

The women, with their naturally fine instinct, saw a chance for vivisection, and delicately taunted her with his habits. She turned upon them in a beautiful, steady blaze of sorrowful contempt.

"You meat-cows," she said, in her level, crystal-clear tones; "you know nothing of a man. Your men are *maromeros*. They are only fit to roll cigarettes in the shade until the sun strikes and shrivels them up. They drone in your hammocks and you comb their hair and feed them with fresh fruit. My man is of no such blood. Let him drink of the wine. When he has taken sufficient of it to drown one of your *flaccitos* he will come home to me more of a man than one thousand of your *pobrecitos*. *My* hair he smooths and braids; to me he sings; he himself removes my *zapatos*, and there, there, upon each instep leaves a kiss. He holds—Oh, you will never understand! Blind ones who have never known a *man*."

Sometimes mysterious things happened at night about Dicky's shop. While the front of it was dark in the little room back of it Dicky and a few of his friends would sit about a table carrying on some kind of very quiet *negocios* until quite late. Finally he would let them out of the front door very carefully, and go upstairs to his little saint. These visitors were generally conspirator-like men with dark clothes and hats. Of course, these dark doings were noticed after awhile, and talked about.

Dicky seemed to care nothing at all for the

society of the alien residents of the town. He avoided Goodwin, and his skilful escape from the trepanning story of Dr. Gregg is still referred to, in Coralio, as a masterpiece of lightning diplomacy.

Many letters arrived, addressed to "Mr. Dicky Maloney," or "*Señor* Dickee Maloney," to the considerable pride of Pasa. That so many people should desire to write to him only confirmed her own suspicion that the light from his red head shone around the world. As to their contents she never felt curiosity. There was a wife for you!

The one mistake Dicky made in Coralio was to run out of money at the wrong time. Where his money came from was a puzzle, for the sales of the shop were next to nothing; but that source failed, and at a peculiarly unfortunate time. It was when the *comandante*, Don Señor el Coronel Encarnaciòn Rios, looked upon the little saint seated in the shop and felt his heart go pit-a-pat.

The *comandante*, who was versed in all the intricate arts of gallantry, first delicately hinted at his sentiments by donning his dress uniform and strutting up and down fiercely before her window. Pasa, glancing demurely with her saintly eyes, instantly perceived the resemblance to her parrot, Chichi, and was diverted to the extent of a smile. The *comandante* saw the smile, which was not intended for him. Convinced of an impression made, he entered the shop, confidently, and advanced to open compliment. Pasa froze; he pranced; she flamed royally; he was charmed to injudicious persistence; she commanded him to leave the shop; he tried to capture her hand, and—Dicky entered, smiling broadly, full of white wine and the devil.

He spent five minutes in punishing the *comandante*

scientifically and carefully, so that the pain might be prolonged as far as possible. At the end of that time he pitched the rash wooer out the door upon the stones of the street, senseless.

A barefooted policeman, who had been watching the affair from across the street, blew a whistle. A squad of four soldiers came running from the *cuartel* around the corner. When they saw that the offender was Dicky, they stopped, and blew more whistles, which brought out reinforcements of eight. Deeming the odds against them sufficiently reduced, the military advanced upon the disturber.

Dicky, being thoroughly imbued with the martial spirit, stooped and drew the *comandante's* sword, which was girded about him, and charged his foe. He chased the standing army four squares, playfully prodding its squealing rear and hacking at its ginger-coloured heels.

But he was not so successful with the civic authorities. Six muscular, nimble policemen overpowered him and conveyed him, triumphantly but warily, to jail. "*El Diablo Colorado*" they dubbed him, and derided the military for its defeat.

Dicky, with the rest of the prisoners, could look out through the barred door at the grass of the little plaza, at a row of orange-trees and the red-tile roofs and 'dobe walls of a line of insignificant stores.

At sunset along a path across this plaza came a melancholy procession of sad-faced women bearing plantains, cassava, bread and fruit—each coming with food to some wretch behind those bars to whom she still clung and furnished the means of life. Twice a day—morning and evening—they were permitted to come. Water was furnished to her compulsory guests by the republic, but no food.

That evening Dicky's name was called by the sentry, and he stepped before the bars of the door. There stood his little saint, a black mantilla draped about her head and shoulders, her face like glorified melancholy, her clear eyes gazing longingly at him as if they might draw him between the bars to her. She brought a chicken, some oranges, *dulces* and a loaf of white bread. A soldier inspected the food, and passed it in to Dicky. Pasa spoke calmly, as she always did, briefly, in her thrilling, flutelike tones. "Angel of my life," she said, "let it not be long that thou art away from me. Thou knowest that life is not a thing to be endured with thou not at my side. Tell me if I can do aught in this matter. If not, I will wait—a little while. I come again in the morning."

Dicky, with his shoes removed so as not to disturb his fellow-prisoners, tramped the floor of the jail half the night condemning his lack of money and the cause of it—whatever that might have been. He knew very well that money would have bought his release at once.

For two days succeeding Pasa came at the appointed times and brought him food. He eagerly inquired each time if a letter or package had come for him, and she mournfully shook her head.

On the morning of the third day she brought only a small loaf of bread. There were dark circles under her eyes. She seemed as calm as ever.

"By Jingo," said Dicky, who seemed to speak in English or Spanish as the whim seized him, "this is dry provender, *muchachita*. Is this the best you can dig up for a fellow?"

Pasa looked at him as a mother looks at a beloved but capricious babe.

"Think better of it," she said, in a low voice; "since for the next meal there will be nothing. The last *centavo* is spent." She pressed closer against the grating.

"Sell the goods in the shop—take anything for them."

"Have I not tried? Did I not offer them for one-tenth their cost? Not even one *peso* would anyone give. There is not one *real* in this town to assist Dickee Malonee."

Dick clenched his teeth grimly. "That's the *comandante*," he growled. "He's responsible for that sentiment. Wait, oh, wait till the cards are all out."

Pasa lowered her voice to almost a whisper. "And, listen, heart of my heart," she said, "I have endeavoured to be brave, but I cannot live without thee. Three days now——"

Dicky caught the faint gleam of steel from the folds of her mantilla. For once she looked in his face and saw it without a smile, stern, menacing and purposeful. Then he suddenly raised his hand and his smile came back like a gleam of sunshine. The hoarse signal of an incoming steamer's siren sounded in the harbour. Dicky called to the sentry who was pacing before the door: "What steamer comes?"

"The *Catarina*."

"Of the Vesuvius line?"

"Without doubt, of that line."

"Go you, *picarilla*," said Dicky joyously to Pasa,

"to the American consul. Tell him I wish to speak with him. See that he comes at once. And look you! let me see a different look in those eyes, for I promise your head shall rest upon this arm to-night."

It was an hour before the consul came. He held his green umbrella under his arm, and mopped his forehead impatiently.

"Now, see here, Maloney," he began, captiously, "you fellows seem to think you can cut up any kind of row, and expect me to pull you out of it. I'm neither the War Department nor a gold-mine. This country has its laws, you know, and there's one against pounding the senses out of the regular army. You Irish are for ever getting into trouble. I don't see what I can do. Anything like tobacco, now, to make you comfortable —or newspapers——"

"Son of Eli," interrupted Dicky, gravely, "you haven't changed an iota. That is almost a duplicate of the speech you made when old Koen's donkeys and geese got into the chapel loft, and the culprits wanted to hide in your room."

"Oh, heavens!" exclaimed the consul, hurriedly adjusting his spectacles. "Are you a Yale man too? Were you in that crowd? I don't seem to remember anyone with red—anyone named Maloney. Such a lot of college men seem to have misused their advantages. One of the best mathematicians of the class of '91 is selling lottery tickets in Belize. A Cornell man dropped off here last month. He was second steward on a guano boat. I'll write to the department if you like, Maloney. Or if there's any tobacco, or newspa——"

"There's nothing," interrupted Dicky, shortly,

"but this. You go tell the captain of the *Catarina* that Dicky Maloney wants to see him as soon as he can conveniently come. Tell him where I am. Hurry. That's all."

The consul, glad to be let off so easily, hurried away. The captain of the *Catarina*, a stout man, Sicilian born, soon appeared, shoving, with little ceremony, through the guards to the jail door. The Vesuvius Fruit Company had a habit of doing things that way in Anchuria.

"I am exceeding sorry—exceeding sorry," said the captain, "to see this occur. I place myself at your service, Mr. Maloney. What you need shall be furnished. Whatever you say shall be done."

Dicky looked at him unsmilingly. His red hair could not detract from his attitude of severe dignity as he stood, tall and calm, with his now grim mouth forming a horizontal line.

"Captain De Lucco, I believe I still have funds in the hands of your company—ample and personal funds. I ordered a remittance last week. The money has not arrived. You know what is needed in this game. Money and money and more money. Why has it not been sent?"

"By the *Cristobal*," replied De Lucco, gesticulating, "it was dispatched. Where is the *Cristobal*? Off Cape Antonio I spoke her with a broken shaft. A tramp coaster was towing her back to New Orleans. I brought money ashore thinking your need for it might not withstand delay. In this envelope is one thousand dollars. There is more if you need it, Mr. Maloney."

"For the present it will suffice," said Dicky, softening as he crinkled the envelope and looked down at the half-inch thickness of smooth dingy bills.

"The long green!" he said, gently, with a new reverence in his gaze. "Is there anything it will not buy, Captain?"

"I had three friends," said De Lucco, who was a bit of a philosopher, "who had money. One of them speculated in stocks and made ten million; another is in heaven, and the third married a poor girl whom he loved."

"The answer, then," said Dicky, "is held by the Almighty, Wall Street and Cupid. So, the question remains."

"This," queried the captain, including Dicky's surroundings in a significant gesture of his hand, "is it—it is not—it is not connected with the business of your little shop? There is no failure in your plans?"

"No, no," said Dicky. "This is merely the result of a little private affair of mine, a digression from the regular line of business. They say for a complete life a man must know poverty, love and war. But they don't go well together, *capitân mio*. No; there is no failure in my business. The little shop is doing very well."

When the captain had departed Dicky called the sergeant of the jail squad and asked:

"Am I *preso* by the military or by the civil authority?"

"Surely there is no martial law in effect now, *señor*."

"*Bueno*. Now go or send to the alcalde, the *Juez de la Paz* and the *Jefe de los Policios*. Tell them I am prepared at once to satisfy the demands of justice." A folded bill of the "long green" slid into the sergeant's hand.

Then Dicky's smile came back again, for he knew that the hours of his captivity were numbered; and he hummed, in time with the sentry's tread:

> "*They're hanging men and women now,*
> *For lacking of the green.*"

So, that night Dicky sat by the window of the room over his shop and his little saint sat close by, working at something silken and dainty. Dicky was thoughtful and grave. His red hair was in an unusual state of disorder. Pasa's fingers often ached to smooth and arrange it, but Dicky would never allow it. He was poring, to-night, over a great litter of maps and books and papers on his table until that perpendicular line came between his brows that always distressed Pasa. Presently she went and brought his hat, and stood with it until he looked up, inquiringly.

"It is sad for you here," she explained. "Go out and drink *vino blanco*. Come back when you get that smile you used to wear. That is what I wish to see."

Dicky laughed and threw down his papers. "The *vino blanco* stage is past. It has served its turn. Perhaps, after all, there was less entered my mouth and more my ears than people thought. But, there will be no more maps or frowns to-night. I promise you that. Come."

They sat upon a reed *silleta* at the window and watched the quivering gleams from the lights of the *Catarina* reflected in the harbour.

Presently Pasa rippled out one of her infrequent chirrups of audible laughter.

"I was thinking," she began, anticipating Dicky's question, "of the foolish things girls have in their minds. Because I went to school in the States I used to have ambitions. Nothing less than to be the president's wife would satisfy me. And, look, thou red picaroon, to what obscure fate thou hast stolen me!"

"Don't give up hope," said Dicky, smiling. "More than one Irishman has been the ruler of a South American country. There was a dictator of Chili named O'Higgins. Why not a President Maloney, of Anchuria? Say the word, *santita mia*, and we'll make the race."

"No, no, no, thou red-haired, reckless one!" sighed Pasa; "I am content"—she laid her head against his arm—"here."

XCVII: ROUGE ET NOIR

IT has been indicated that disaffection followed the elevation of Losada to the presidency. This feeling continued to grow. Throughout the entire republic there seemed to be a spirit of silent, sullen discontent. Even the old Liberal party, to which Goodwin, Zavalla and other patriots had lent their aid, was disappointed. Losada had failed to become a popular idol. Fresh taxes, fresh import duties and, more than all, his tolerance of the outrageous oppression of citizens by the military, had rendered him the most obnoxious president since the despicable Alforan. The majority of his own cabinet were out of sympathy with him. The army, which he had courted by giving it licence to tyrannize, had been his main, and thus far, adequate support.

But the most impolitic of the administration's moves had been when it antagonized the Vesuvius Fruit Company, an organization plying twelve steamers and with a cash capital somewhat larger than Anchuria's surplus and debt combined.

Reasonably, an established concern like the Vesuvius would become irritated at having a small retail republic with no rating at all attempt to squeeze it. So, when the government proxies applied for a subsidy they encountered a polite refusal. The president at once retaliated by clapping an export duty of one *real* per bunch on bananas—a thing unprecedented in fruit-growing countries. The Vesuvius Company had invested large sums in wharves and plantations along the Anchurian coast, their agents had erected fine homes in the towns where they had their headquarters, and heretofore had worked with the republic in goodwill and with advantage to both. It would lose an immense sum if compelled to move out. The selling price of bananas from Vera Cruz to Trinidad was three *reales* per bunch. This new duty of one *real* would have ruined the fruit growers in Anchuria and have seriously discommoded the Vesuvius Company had it declined to pay it. But for some reason, the Vesuvius continued to buy Anchurian fruit, paying four *reales* for it; and not suffering the growers to bear the loss.

This apparent victory deceived His Excellency; and he began to hunger for more of it. He sent an emissary to request a conference with a representative of the fruit company. The Vesuvius sent Mr. Franzoni, a little, stout, cheerful man, always cool, and whistling airs from Verdi's operas. *Señor* Espirition, of the office of the Minister of

Finance, attempted the sandbagging in behalf of Anchuria. The meeting took place in the cabin of the *Salvador*, of the Vesuvius line.

Señor Espirition opened negotiations by announcing that the government contemplated the building of a railroad to skirt the alluvial coast lands. After touching upon the benefits such a road would confer upon the interests of the Vesuvius, he reached the definite suggestion that a contribution to the road's expenses of, say, fifty thousand *pesos* would not be more than an equivalent to benefits received.

Mr. Franzoni denied that his company would receive any benefits from a contemplated road. As its representative he must decline to contribute fifty thousand *pesos*. But he would assume the responsibility of offering twenty-five.

Did *Señor* Espirition understand *Señor* Franzoni to mean twenty-five thousand *pesos*?

By no means. Twenty-five *pesos*. And in silver; not in gold.

"Your offer insults my government," cried *Señor* Espirition, rising, with indignation.

"Then," said Mr. Franzoni, in warning tone, "*we will change it*."

The offer was never changed. Would Mr. Franzoni have meant the government?

This was the state of affairs in Anchuria when the winter season opened at Coralio at the end of the second year of Losada's administration. So, when the government and society made its annual exodus to the seashore it was evident that the presidential advent would not be celebrated by unlimited rejoicing. The tenth of November was the day set for the entrance into Coralio of the gay company from the capital. A narrow-gauge railroad runs twenty miles into the interior from Solitas. The government party travels by carriage from San Mateo to this road's terminal point, and proceeds by train to Solitas. From here they march in grand procession to Coralio where, on the day of their coming, festivities and ceremonies abound. But this season saw an ominous dawning of the tenth of November.

Although the rainy season was over, the day seemed to hark back to reeking June. A fine drizzle of rain fell all during the forenoon. The procession entered Coralio amid a strange silence.

President Losada was an elderly man, grizzly bearded, with a considerable ratio of Indian blood revealed in his cinnamon complexion. His carriage headed the procession, surrounded and guarded by Captain Cruz and his famous troop of one hundred light horse "*El Ciento Huilando*." Colonel Rocas followed, with a regiment of the regular army.

The president's sharp, beady eyes glanced about him for the expected demonstration of welcome; but he faced a stolid, indifferent array of citizens. Sightseers the Anchurians are by birth and habit, and they turned out to their last able-bodied unit to witness the scene; but they maintained an accusive silence. They crowded the streets to the very wheel ruts; they covered the red-tile roofs to the eaves, but there was never a "*viva*" from them. No wreaths of palm and lemon branches or gorgeous strings of paper roses hung from the windows and balconies as was the custom. There was an apathy, a dull, dissenting disapprobation, that was the more ominous because it puzzled. No one feared an outburst, a revolt of the discontents, for they had no leader. The president and those loyal to him had never even heard whispered a name among them capable of crystallizing the dissatisfaction into opposition. No, there could be no danger. The people always procured a new idol before they destroyed an old one.

At length, after a prodigious galloping and curveting of red-sashed majors, gold-laced colonels and epauletted generals, the procession formed for its annual progress down the Calle Grande to the Casa Morena, where the ceremony of welcome to the visiting president always took place.

The Swiss band led the line of march. After it pranced the local *comandante*, mounted, and a detachment of his troops. Next came a carriage with four members of the cabinet, conspicuous among them the Minister of War, old General Pilar, with his white moustache and his soldierly bearing. Then the president's vehicle, containing also the Ministers of Finance and State; and surrounded by Captain Cruz's light horse formed in a close double file of fours. Following them, the rest of the officials of state, the judges and distinguished military and social ornaments of public and private life.

As the band struck up, and the movement began, like a bird of ill-omen the *Valhalla*, the swiftest steamship of the Vesuvius line, glided into the harbour in plain view of the president and his train. Of course, there was nothing menacing about its arrival—a business firm does not go to war with a nation—but it reminded *Señor* Espirition and others in those carriages that the Vesuvius Fruit Company was undoubtedly carrying something up its sleeve for them.

By the time the van of the procession had reached the government building, Captain Cronin, of the *Valhalla*, and Mr. Vincenti, member of the Vesuvius Company, had landed, and were pushing their way, bluff, hearty and nonchalant, through the crowd on the narrow sidewalk. Clad in white linen, big, debonair, with the air of good-humoured authority, they made conspicuous figures among the dark mass of unimposing Anchurians, as they penetrated to within a few yards of the steps of the Casa Morena. Looking easily above the heads of the crowd, they perceived another that towered above the under-sized natives. It was the fiery poll of Dicky Maloney against the wall close by the lower step; and his broad, seductive grin showed that he recognized their presence.

Dicky had attired himself becomingly for the festive occasion in a well-fitting black suit. Pasa was close by his side, her head covered with the ubiquitous black mantilla.

Mr. Vincenti looked at her attentively.

"Botticelli's Madonna," he remarked, gravely. "I wonder when she got into the game. I don't like his getting tangled with the women. I hoped he would keep away from them."

Captain Cronin's laugh almost drew attention from the parade.

"With that head of hair! Keep away from the women! And a Maloney! Hasn't he got a licence? But, nonsense aside, what do you think of the prospects? It's a species of filibustering out of my line."

Vincenti glanced again at Dicky's head and smiled.

"*Rouge et noir*," he said. "There you have it.

Make your play, gentlemen. Our money is on the red."

"The lad's game," said Cronin, with a commending look at the tall, easy figure by the steps. "But 'tis all like fly-by-night theatricals to me. The talk's bigger than the stage; there's a smell of gasolene in the air, and they're their own audience and scene-shifters."

They ceased talking, for General Pilar had descended from the first carriage and had taken his stand upon the top step of Casa Morena. As the oldest member of the cabinet, custom had decreed that he should make the address of welcome, presenting the keys of the official residence to the president at its close.

General Pilar was one of the most distinguished citizens of the republic. Hero of three wars and innumerable revolutions, he was an honoured guest at European camps and courts. An eloquent speaker and a friend to the people, he represented the highest type of the Anchurians.

Holding in his hand the gilt keys of Casa Morena, he began his address in a historical form, touching upon each administration and the advance of civilization and prosperity from the first dim striving after liberty down to the present times. Arriving at the regime of President Losada, at which point, according to precedent, he should have delivered a eulogy upon its wise conduct and the happiness of the people, General Pilar paused. Then he silently held up the bunch of keys high above his head, with his eyes closely regarding it. The ribbon with which they were bound fluttered in the breeze.

"It still blows," cried the speaker, exultantly.

"Citizens of Anchuria, give thanks to the saints this night that our air is still free."

Thus disposing of Losada's administration, he abruptly reverted to that of Olivarra, Anchuria's most popular ruler. Olivarra had been assassinated nine years before while in the prime of life and usefulness. A faction of the Liberal party led by Losada himself had been accused of the deed. Whether guilty or not, it was eight years before the ambitious and scheming Losada had gained his goal.

Upon this theme General Pilar's eloquence was loosed. He drew the picture of the beneficent Olivarra with a loving hand. He reminded the people of the peace, the security and the happiness they had enjoyed during that period. He recalled in vivid detail and with significant contrast the last winter sojourn of President Olivarra in Coralio, when his appearance at their *fiestas* was the signal for thundering *vivas* of love and approbation.

The first public expression of sentiment from the people that day followed. A low, sustained murmur went along them like the surf rolling along the shore.

"Ten dollars to a dinner at the Saint Charles," remarked Mr. Vincenti, "that *rouge* wins."

"I never bet against my own interests," said Captain Cronin, lighting a cigar. "Long-winded old boy, for his age. What's he talking about?"

"My Spanish," replied Vincenti, "runs about ten words to the minute; his is something around two hundred. Whatever he's saying, he's getting them warmed up."

"Friends and brothers," General Pilar was saying, "could I reach out my hand this day across the lamentable silence of the grave to Olivarra 'the Good,' to the ruler who was one of you, whose tears fell when you sorrowed, and whose smile followed your joy—I would bring him back to you, but—Olivarra is dead—dead at the hands of a craven assassin!"

The speaker turned and gazed boldly into the carriage of the president. His arm remained extended aloft as if to sustain his peroration. The president was listening, aghast, at this remarkable address of welcome. He was sunk back upon his seat, trembling with rage and dumb surprise, his dark hands tightly gripping the carriage cushions.

Half rising, he extended one arm toward the speaker, and shouted a harsh command at Captain Cruz. The leader of the "Flying Hundred" sat his horse, immovable, with folded arms, giving no sign of having heard. Losada sank back again, his dark features distinctly paling.

"Who says that Olivarra is dead?" suddenly cried the speaker, his voice, old as he was, sounding like a battle trumpet. "His body lies in the grave, but to the people he loved he has bequeathed his spirit—yes, more—his learning, his courage, his kindness—yes, more—his youth, his image—people of Anchuria, have you forgotten Ramon, the son of Olivarra?"

Cronin and Vincenti, watching closely, saw Dicky Maloney suddenly raise his hat, tear off his shock of red hair, leap up the steps and stand at the side of General Pilar. The Minister of War laid his arm across the young man's shoulders. All who had known President Olivarra saw again the same lion-like pose, the same frank, undaunted expression, the same high forehead with the peculiar line of the clustering, crisp black hair.

General Pilar was an experienced orator. He seized the moment of breathless silence that preceded the storm.

"Citizens of Anchuria," he trumpeted, holding aloft the keys to Casa Morena, "I am here to deliver these keys—the keys to your homes and liberty—to your chosen president. Shall I deliver them to Enrico Olivarra's assassin, or to his son?"

"Olivarra! Olivarra!" the crowd shrieked and howled. All vociferated the magic name—men, women, children and the parrots.

And the enthusiasm was not confined to the blood of the plebs. Colonel Rocas ascended the steps and laid his sword theatrically at young Ramon Olivarra's feet. Four members of the cabinet embraced him. Captain Cruz gave a command, and twenty of *El Ciento Huilando* dismounted and arranged themselves in a cordon about the steps of Casa Morena.

But Ramon Olivarra seized the moment to prove himself a born genius and politician. He waved those soldiers aside, and descended the steps to the street. There, without losing his dignity or the distinguished elegance that the loss of the red hair brought him, he took the proletariat to his bosom—the barefooted, the dirty, the Indians, Caribs, babies, beggars, old, young, saints, soldiers and sinners—he missed none of them.

While this act of the drama was being presented, the scene-shifters had been busy at the duties that had been assigned to them. Two of Cruz's dragoons had seized the bridle reins of

Losada's horses; others formed a close guard around the carriage; and they galloped off with the tyrant and his two unpopular Ministers. No doubt a place had been prepared for them. There are a number of well-barred stone apartments in Coralio.

"*Rouge* wins," said Mr. Vincenti, calmly lighting another cigar.

Captain Cronin had been intently watching the vicinity of the steps for some time.

"Good boy!" he exclaimed suddenly, as if relieved. "I wondered if he was going to forget his Kathleen Mavourneen."

Young Olivarra had reascended the steps and spoken a few words to General Pilar. Then that distinguished veteran descended to the ground and approached Pasa, who still stood, wonder-eyed, where Dicky had left her. With his plumed hat in his hand, and his medals and decorations shining on his breast, the general spoke to her and gave her his arm, and they went up the stone steps of the Casa Morena together. And then Ramon Olivarra stepped forward and took both her hands before all the people.

And while the cheering was breaking out afresh everywhere, Captain Cronin and Mr. Vincenti turned and walked back to the shore where the gig was waiting for them.

"There'll be another '*presidente proclamada*' in the morning," said Mr. Vincenti, musingly. "As a rule they are not as reliable as the elected ones, but this youngster seems to have some good stuff in him. He planned and manœuvred the entire campaign. Olivarra's widow, you know, was wealthy. After her husband was assassinated she went to the States, and educated her son at Yale.

The Vesuvius Company hunted him up, and backed him in the little game."

"It's a glorious thing," said Cronin, half jestingly, "to be able to discharge a government, and insert one of your own choosing, in these days."

"Oh, it is only a matter of business," said Vincenti, stopping and offering the stump of his cigar to a monkey that swung down from a lime-tree; "and that is what moves the world of to-day. That extra *real* on the price of bananas had to go. We took the shortest way of removing it."

XCVIII: TWO RECALLS

THERE remains three duties to be performed before the curtain falls upon this patched comedy. Two have been promised; the third is no less obligatory.

It was set forth in the programme of this tropic vaudeville that it would be made known why Shorty O'Day, of the Columbia Detective Agency, lost his position. Also that Smith should come again to tell us what mystery he followed that night on the shores of Anchuria, when he strewed so many cigar stumps around the coconut palm during his lonely night vigil on the beach. These things were promised; but a bigger thing yet remains to be accomplished—the clearing up of a seeming wrong that has been done according to the array of chronicled facts (truthfully set forth) that have been presented. And one voice, speaking, shall do these three things.

Two men sat on a stringer of a North River pier in the City of New York. A steamer from the tropics had begun to unload bananas and oranges on the pier. Now and then a banana or two would fall from an over-ripe bunch, and one of the two men would shamble forward, seize the fruit and return to share it with his companion.

One of the men was in the ultimate stage of deterioration. As far as rain and wind and sun could wreck the garments he wore, it had been done. In his person the ravages of drink were as plainly visible. And yet, upon his high-bridged, rubicund nose was jauntily perched a pair of shining and flawless gold-rimmed glasses.

The other man was not so far gone upon the descending Highway of the Incompetents. Truly, the flower of his manhood had gone to seed—seed that, perhaps, no soil might sprout. But there was still cross-cuts along where he travelled through which he might yet regain the pathway of usefulness without disturbing the slumbering Miracles. This man was short and compactly built. He had an oblique, dead eye, like that of a sting-ray, and the moustache of a cocktail-mixer. We know the eye and the moustache; we know that Smith of the luxurious yacht, the gorgeous raiment, the mysterious mission, the magic disappearance, has come again, though shorn of the accessories of his former state.

At his third banana, the man with the nose glasses spat it from him with a shudder.

"Deuce take all fruit!" he remarked, in a patrician tone of disgust. "I lived for two years where these things grow. The memory of their taste lingers with you. The oranges are not so bad.

Just see if you can gather a couple of them, O'Day, when the next broken crate comes up."

"Did you live down with the monkeys?" asked the other, made tepidly garrulous by the sunshine and the alleviating meal of juicy fruit. "I was down there once, myself. But only for a few hours. That was when I was with the Columbia Detective Agency. The monkey people did me up. I'd have my job yet if it hadn't been for them. I'll tell you about it.

"One day the chief scnt a note around to the office that read: 'Send O'Day here at once for a big piece of business.' I was the crack detective of the agency at that time. They always handed me the big jobs. The address the chief wrote from was down in the Wall Street district.

"When I got there I found him in a private office with a lot of directors who were looking pretty fuzzy. They stated the case. The president of the Republic Insurance Company had skipped with about a tenth of a million dollars in cash. The directors wanted him back pretty bad, but they wanted the money worse. They said they needed it. They had traced the old gent's movements to where he boarded a tramp fruit steamer bound for South America that same morning with his daughter and a big gripsack—all the family he had.

"One of the directors had his steam yacht coaled and with steam up, ready for a trip; and he turned her over to me, cart blongsh. In four hours I was on board of her, and hot on the trail of the fruit tub. I had a pretty good idca where old Wahrfield—that was his name, J. Churchill Wahrfield—would head for. At that time we had a treaty with about every foreign country except Belgium and that banana republic, Anchuria. There wasn't a photo of old Wahrfield to be had in New York—he had been foxy there—but I had his description. And besides, the lady with him would be a dead-give-away anywhere. She was one of the high-flyers in Society—not the kind that have their pictures in the Sunday papers—but the real sort that open chrysanthemum shows and christen battleships.

"Well, sir, we never got a sight of that fruit tub on the road. The ocean is a pretty big place; and I guess we took different paths across it. But we kept going toward this Anchuria, where the fruiter was bound for.

"We struck the monkey coast one afternoon about four. There was a ratty-looking steamer off-shore taking on bananas. The monkeys were loading her up with big barges. It might be the one the old man had taken, and it might not. I went ashore to look around. The scenery was pretty good. I never saw any finer on the New York stage. I struck an American on shore, a big, cool chap, standing around with the monkeys. He showed me the consul's office. The consul was a nice young fellow. He said the fruiter was the *Karlsefin*, running generally to New Orleans, but took her last cargo to New York. Then I was sure my people were on board, although everybody told me that no passengers had landed. I didn't think they would land until after dark, for they might have been shy about it on account of seeing that yacht of mine hanging around. So, all I had to do was to wait and nab 'em when they came ashore. I couldn't arrest old Wahrfield without extradition papers, but my play was to get the cash. They generally give up if you strike 'em when they're tired and rattled and short on nerve.

"After dark I sat under a coconut-tree on the beach for awhile, and then I walked around and investigated that town some, and it was enough to give you the lions. If a man could stay in New York and be honest, he'd better do it than to hit that monkey town with a million.

"Dinky little mud houses; grass over your shoe-tops in the streets; ladies in low-neck-and-short-sleeves walking around smoking cigars; tree frogs rattling like a hose cart going to a ten blow; big mountains dropping gravel in the back yards, and the sea licking the paint off in front—no, sir—a man had better be in God's country living on free lunch than there.

"The main street ran along the beach, and I walked down it, and then turned up a kind of lane where the houses were made of poles and straw. I wanted to see what the monkeys did when they weren't climbing coconut-trees. The very first shack I looked in I saw my people. They must have come ashore while I was promenading. A man about fifty, smooth face, heavy eyebrows, dressed in black broadcloth, looking like he was just about to say, 'Can any little boy in the Sunday school answer that?' He was freezing on to a grip that weighed like a dozen gold bricks, and a swell girl—a regular peach, with a Fifth Avenue cut—was sitting on a wooden chair. An old black woman was fixing some coffee and beans on a table. The light they had came from a lantern hung on a nail. I went and stood in the door, and they looked at me, and I said:

" 'Mr. Wahrfield, you are my prisoner. I hope, for the lady's sake, you will take the matter sensibly. You know why I want you.'

" 'Who are you?' says the old gent.

" 'O'Day,' says I, 'of the Columbia Detective Agency. And now, sir, let me give you a piece of good advice. You go back and take your medicine like a man. Hand 'em back the boodle; and maybe they'll let you off light. Go back easy, and I'll put in a word for you. I'll give you five minutes to decide.' I pulled out my watch and waited.

"Then the young lady chipped in. She was one of the genuine high-steppers. You could tell by the way her clothes fit and the style she had that Fifth Avenue was made for her.

" 'Come inside,' she says. 'Don't stand in the door and disturb the whole street with that suit of clothes. Now, what is it you want?'

" 'Three minutes gone,' I said. 'I'll tell you again while the other two tick off.

" 'You'll admit being the president of the Republic, won't you?'

" 'I am,' says he.

" 'Well, then,' says I, 'it ought to be plain to you. Wanted, in New York, J. Churchill Wahrfield, president of the Republic Insurance Company.

" 'Also the funds belonging to said company, now in that grip, in the unlawful possession of said J. Churchill Wahrfield.'

" 'Oh-h-h-h!' says the young lady, as if she was thinking, 'you want to take us back to New York?'

" 'To take Mr. Wahrfield. There's no charge against you, miss. There'll be no objection, of course, to your returning with your father.'

"Of a sudden the girl gave a tiny scream and grabbed the old boy round the neck. 'Oh, father, father!' she says, kind of contralto, 'can this be true? Have you taken money that is not yours? Speak, father!' It made you shiver to hear the tremolo stop she put on her voice.

"The old boy looked pretty bughouse when she first grappled him, but she went on, whispering in his ear and patting his off shoulder till he stood still, but sweating a little.

"She got him to one side and they talked together a minute, and then he put on some gold eyeglasses and walked up and handed me the grip.

" 'Mr. Detective,' he says, talking a little broken, 'I conclude to return with you. I have finished to discover that life on this desolate and displeased coast would be worse than to die, itself. I will go back and hurl myself upon the mercy of the Republic Company. Have you brought a sheep?'

" 'Sheep!' says I; 'I haven't a single——'

" 'Ship,' cut in the young lady. 'Don't get funny. Father is of German birth, and doesn't speak perfect English. How did you come?'

"The girl was all broke up. She had a handkerchief to her face, and kept saying every little bit, 'Oh, father, father!' She walked up to me and laid her lily-white hand on the clothes that had pained her at first. I smelt a million violets. She was a lulu. I told her I came in a private yacht.

" 'Mr. O'Day,' she says. 'Oh, take us away from this horrid country at once. Can you? Will you? Say you will.'

" 'I'll try,' I said, concealing the fact that I was dying to get them on salt water before they could change their mind.

"One thing they both kicked against was going through the town to the boat landing. Said they dreaded publicity, and now that they were going to return, they had a hope that the thing might yet be kept out of the papers. They swore they wouldn't go unless I got them out to the yacht without anyone knowing it, so I agreed to humour them.

"The sailors who rowed me ashore were playing billiards in a bar-room near the water, waiting for orders, and I proposed to have them take the boat down the beach half a mile or so, and take us up there. How to get them word was the question, for I couldn't leave the grip with the prisoner, and I couldn't take it with me, not knowing but what the monkeys might stick me up.

"The young lady says the old coloured woman would take them a note. I sat down and wrote it, and gave it to the dame with plain directions what to do, and she grins like a baboon and shakes her head.

"Then Mr. Wahrfield handed her a string of foreign dialect, and she nods her head and says, 'See, *señor*,' maybe fifty times, and lights out with the note.

" 'Old Augusta only understands German,' said Miss Wahrfield, smiling at me. 'We stopped in her house to ask where we could find lodging, and she insisted upon our having coffee. She tells us she was raised in a German family in San Domingo.'

" 'Very likely,' I said. 'But you can search me for German words, except *nix verstay* and *noch einst*. I would have called that "See, *señor*" French, though, on a gamble.'

"Well, we three made a sneak around the edge of town so as not to be seen. We got tangled in vines and ferns and the banana bushes and tropical scenery a good deal. The monkey suburbs was as wild as places in Central Park. We came out on the beach a good half-mile below. A brown chap was lying asleep under a coconut-tree, with a ten-foot musket beside him. Mr. Wahrfield takes up the gun and pitches it into the sea. 'The coast is guarded,' he says. 'Rebellion and plots ripen like fruit.' He pointed to the sleeping man, who never stirred. 'Thus,' he says, 'they perform trusts. Children!'

"I saw our boat coming, and I struck a match and lit a piece of newspaper to show them where we were. In thirty minutes we were on board the yacht.

"The first thing, Mr. Wahrfield and his daughter and I took the grip into the owner's cabin, opened it up, and took an inventory. There was one hundred and five thousand dollars, United States treasury notes, in it, besides a lot of diamond jewellery and a couple of hundred Havana cigars. I gave the old man the cigars and a receipt for the rest of the lot, as agent for the company, and locked the stuff up in my private quarters.

"I never had a pleasanter trip than that one. After we got to sea the young lady turned out to be the jolliest ever. The very first time we sat down to dinner, and the steward filled her glass with champagne—that director's yacht was a regular floating Waldorf-Astoria—she winks at me and says, 'What's the use to borrow trouble, Mr. Fly Cop? Here's hoping you may live to eat the hen that scratches on your grave.' There was a piano on board, and she sat down to it and sung better than you give up two cases to hear plenty times. She knew about nine operas clear through. She was sure enough *bon ton* and swell. She wasn't one of the 'among others present' kind; she belonged on the special mention list!

"The old man, too, perked up amazingly on the way. He passed the cigars, and says to me once, quite chipper, out of a cloud of smoke, 'Mr. O'Day, somehow I think the Republic Company will not give me the much trouble. Guard well the gripvalise of the money, Mr. O'Day, for that it must be returned to them that it belongs when we finish to arrive.'

"When we landed in New York I 'phoned to the chief to meet us in that director's office. We got in a cab and went there. I carried the grip, and we walked in, and I was pleased to see that the chief had got together the same old crowd of moneybugs with pink faces and white vests to see us march in. I set the grip on the table. 'There's the money,' I said.

" 'And your prisoner?' said the chief.

"I pointed to Mr. Wahrfield, and he stepped forward and says:

" 'The honour of a word with you, sir, to explain.'

"He and the chief went into another room and stayed ten minutes. When they came back the chief looked as black as a ton of coal.

" 'Did this gentleman,' he says to me, 'have this valise in his possession when you first saw him?'

" 'He did,' said I.

"The chief took up the grip and handed it to the prisoner with a bow, and says to the director crowd: 'Do any of you recognize this gentleman?'

"They all shook their pink faces.

" 'Allow me to present,' he goes on, '*Señor* Miraflores, president of the republic of Anchuria. The *señor* has generously consented to overlook this outrageous blunder, on condition that we undertake to secure him against the annoyance of public comment. It is a concession on his part to overlook an insult for which he might claim international redress. I think we can gratefully promise him secrecy in the matter.'

"They gave him a pink nod all round.

" 'O'Day,' he says to me. 'As a private detective you're wasted. In a war, where kidnapping governments is in the rules, you'd be invaluable. Come down to the office at eleven.'

"I knew what that meant.

" 'So that's the president of the monkeys,' says I. 'Well, why couldn't he have said so?'

"Wouldn't it jar you?"

XCIX: THE VITAGRAPHOSCOPE

VAUDEVILLE is intrinsically episodic and discontinuous. Its audiences do not demand dénouements. Sufficient unto each "turn" is the evil thereof. No one cares how many romances the singing comédienne may have had if she can capably sustain the limelight and a high note or two. The audiences reck not if the performing dogs get to the pound the moment they have jumped through their last hoop. They do not desire bulletins about the possible injuries received by the comic bicyclist who retires head first from the stage in a crash of (property) chinaware. Neither do they consider that their seat coupons entitle them to be instructed whether or no there is a sentiment between the lady solo banjoist and the Irish monologist.

Therefore, let us have no lifting of the curtain upon a tableau of the united lovers, backgrounded by defeated villainy and derogated by the comic, osculating maid and butler, thrown in as a sop to the Cerberi of the fifty-cent seats.

But our programme ends with a brief "turn" or two; and then to the exits. Whoever sits the show out may find, if he will, the slender thread that binds together, though ever so slightly, the story that, perhaps, only the Walrus will understand.

Extracts from a letter from the first vice-president of the Republic Insurance Company, of New York City, to Frank Goodwin, of Coralio, Republic of Anchuria.

My dear Mr. Goodwin,—Your communication per Messrs. Howland and Fourchet, of New Orleans, has reached us. Also their draft on N.Y. for $100,000, the amount abstracted from the funds of this company by the late J. Churchill Wahrfield, its former president. . . . The officers and directors unite in requesting me to express to you their sincere esteem and thanks for your prompt and much appreciated return of the entire missing sum within two weeks from the time of its disappearance. . . . Can assure you that the matter will not be allowed to receive the least publicity. . . . Regret exceedingly the distressing death of Mr. Wahrfield by his own hand, but . . . Congratulations on your marriage to Miss Wahrfield . . . many charms, winning manners, noble and womanly nature and envied position in the best metropolitan society. . . .

Cordially yours,

Lucius E. Applegate,

First Vice-President the Republic Insurance Company.

The Vitagraphoscope

(Moving Pictures)

The Last Sausage

Scene.—*An Artist's Studio.* The artist, a young man of prepossessing appearance, sits in a dejected attitude, amid a litter of sketches, with his head resting upon his hand. An oil stove stands on a pine box in the centre of the studio. The artist rises, tightens his waist-belt to another hole, and lights the stove. He goes to a tin bread-box, half-hidden by a screen, takes out a solitary link of sausage, turns the box upside-down to show that there is no more, and chucks the sausage into a frying-pan, which he sets upon the stove. The flame of the stove goes out, showing that there is no more oil. The artist, in evident despair, seizes the sausage, in a sudden access of rage, and hurls it violently from him. At the same time a door opens, and a man who enters receives the sausage forcibly against his nose. He seems to cry out; and is observed to make a step dance or two, vigorously. The new-comer is a ruddy-faced, keen-looking man, apparently of Irish ancestry. Next he is observed to laugh immoderately; he kicks over the stove; he claps the artist (who is vainly striving to grasp his hand) vehemently upon the back. Then he goes through a pantomime which to the sufficiently intelligent spectator reveals that he has acquired large sums of money by trading pot-metal hatchets and razors to the Indians of the Cordillera Mountains for gold dust. He draws a roll of money as large as a small loaf of bread from his pocket and waves it above his head, while at the same time he makes a pantomime of drinking from a glass. The artist hurriedly secures his hat, and the two leave the studio together.

The Writing on the Sands

SCENE.—*The Beach at Nice.* A woman, beautiful, still young, exquisitely clothed, complacent, poised, reclines near the water, idly scrawling letters in the sand with the staff of her silken parasol. The beauty of her face is audacious; her languid pose is one that you feel to be impermanent—you wait, expectant, for her to spring or glide or crawl, like a panther that has unaccountably become stock-still. She idly scrawls in the sand; and the word that she always writes is "Isabel." A man sits a few yards away. You can see that they are companions, even if no longer comrades. His face is dark and smooth, and almost inscrutable—but not quite. The two speak little together. The man also scratches on the sand with his cane. And the word that he writes is "Anchuria." And then he looks out where the Mediterranean and the sky intermingle, with death in his gaze.

The Wilderness and Thou

SCENE.—*The Borders of a Gentleman's Estate in a Tropical Land.* An old Indian, with a mahogany-coloured face, is trimming the grass on a grave by a mangrove swamp. Presently he rises to his feet and walks slowly toward a grove that is shaded by the gathering, brief twilight. In the edge of the grove stand a man who is stalwart, with a kind and courteous air, and a woman of a serene and clear-cut loveliness. When the old Indian comes up to them the man drops money in his hand. The grave-tender, with the stolid pride of his race, takes it as his due, and goes his way. The two in the edge of the grove turn back along the dim pathway, and walk close, close—for, after all, what is the world at its best but a little round field of the moving pictures with two walking together in it?

CURTAIN

C: OUT OF NAZARETH

OKOCHEE, in Georgia, had a boom, and J. Pinkney Bloom came out of it with a "wad." Okochee came out of it with a half-million-dollar debt, a two and a half per cent. city property tax, and a city council that showed a propensity for travelling the back streets of the town. These things came about through a fatal resemblance of the river Cooloosa to the Hudson, as set forth and expounded by a Northern tourist. Okochee felt that New York should not be allowed to consider itself the only alligator in the swamp, so to speak. And then that harmless, but persistent, individual so numerous in the South—the man who is always clamouring for more cotton mills, and is ready to take a dollar's worth of stock, provided he can borrow the dollar—that man added his daily work to the tourist's innocent praise, and Okochee fell.

The Cooloosa River winds through a range of small mountains, passes Okochee, and then blends its waters trippingly, as fall the mellifluous Indian syllables, with the Chattahoochee.

Okochee rose, as it were, from its sunny seat on the post-office stoop, hitched up its suspender, and threw a granite dam two hundred and forty feet long and sixty feet high across the Cooloosa one mile above the town. Thereupon, a dimpling, sparkling lake backed up twenty miles among the little mountains. Thus in the great game of municipal rivalry did Okochee match that famous drawing card, the Hudson. It was conceded that nowhere could the Palisades be judged superior in the way of scenery and grandeur. Following the picture card was played the ace of commercial importance. Fourteen thousand horsepower would this dam furnish. Cotton mills, factories, and manufacturing plants would rise up as the green corn after a shower. The spindle and the fly-wheel and turbine would sing the shrewd glory of Okochee. Along the picturesque heights above the lake would rise in beauty the costly villas and the splendid summer residences of capital. The naphtha launch of the millionaire would spit among the romantic coves; the verdured hills would take formal shapes of terrace, lawn, and park. Money would be spent like water in Okochee, and water would be turned into money.

The fate of the good town is quickly told. Capital decided not to invest. Of all the great things promised, the scenery alone came to fulfilment. The wooded peaks, the impressive promontories of solemn granite, the beautiful green slants of bank and ravine did all they could to reconcile Okochee to the delinquency of miserly gold. The sunsets gilded the dreamy draws and coves with a minting that should charm away heart-burning. Okochee, true to the instinct of its blood and clime, was lulled by the spell. It climbed out of the arena, loosed its suspender, sat down again on the post-office stoop, and took a chew. It consoled itself by drawling sarcasms at the city council which was not to blame, causing the fathers, as has been said, to seek back streets and figure perspiringly on the sinking fund and the appropriation for interest due.

The youth of Okochee—they who were to carry into the rosy future the burden of the debt—accepted failure with youth's uncalculating joy. For here was sport, aquatic and nautical, added to the meagre round of life's pleasures. In yachting caps and flying neckties they pervaded the lake to its limits. Girls wore silk waists embroidered with anchors in blue and pink. The trousers of the young men widened at the bottom, and their hands were proudly calloused by the oft-plied oar. Fishermen were under the spell of a deep and tolerant joy. Sailboats and rowboats furrowed the lenient waves, popcorn and ice-cream booths sprang up about the little wooden pier. Two small excursion steamboats were built, and plied the delectable waters. Okochee philosophically gave up the hope of eating turtle soup with a gold spoon, and settled back, not ill content, to its regular diet of lotus and fried hominy. And out of this slow wreck of great expectations rose up J. Pinkney Bloom with his "wad" and his prosperous, cheery smile.

Needless to say, J. Pinkney was no product of

Georgia soil. He came out of that flushed and capable region known as the "North." He called himself a "promoter"; his enemies had spoken of him as a "grafter"; Okochee took a middle course, and held him to be no better nor no worse than a "Yank."

Far up the lake—eighteen miles above the town—the eye of this cheerful camp-follower of booms had spied out a graft. He purchased there a precipitous tract of five hundred acres at forty-five cents per acre; and this he laid out and subdivided as the city of Skyland—the Queen City of the Switzerland of the South. Streets and avenues were surveyed; parks designed; corners of central squares reserved for the "proposed" opera house, board of trade, lyceum, market, public schools, and "Exposition Hall." The price of lots ranged from five to five hundred dollars. Positively, no lot would be priced higher than five hundred dollars.

While the boom was growing in Okochee, J. Pinkney's circulars, maps, and prospectuses were flying through the mails to every part of the country. Investors sent in their money by post, and the Skyland Real Estate Company (J. Pinkney Bloom) returned to each a deed, duly placed on record, to the best lot, at the price, on hand that day. All this time the catamount screeched upon the reserved lot of the Skyland Board of Trade, the opossum swung by his tail over the site of the Exposition Hall, and the owl hooted a melancholy recitative to his audience of young squirrels in opera house square. Later, when the money was coming in fast, J. Pinkney caused to be erected in the coming city half a dozen cheap box houses, and persuaded a contingent of indigent natives to occupy them, thereby assuming the rôle of "population" in subsequent prospectuses, which became, accordingly, more seductive and remunerative.

So, when the dream faded and Okochee dropped back to digging bait and nursing its two and a half per cent. tax, J. Pinkney Bloom (unloving of cheques and drafts and the cold interrogatories of bankers) strapped about his fifty-two-inch waist a soft leather belt containing eight thousand dollars in big bills and said that all was very good.

One last trip he was making to Skyland before departing to other salad fields. Skyland was a regular post office, and the steamboat, *Dixie Belle*, under contract, delivered the mail bag (generally empty) twice a week. There was a little business there to be settled—the postmaster was to be paid off for his light but lonely services, and the "inhabitants" had to be furnished with another month's homely rations, as per agreement. And then Skyland would know J. Pinkney Bloom no more. The owners of these precipitous, barren, useless lots might come and view the scene of their invested credulity, or they might leave them to their fit tenents, the wild hog and the browsing deer. The work of the Skyland Real Estate Company was finished.

The little steamboat *Dixie Belle* was about to shove off on her regular up-the-lake trip, when a rickety hired carriage rattled up to the pier, and a tall, elderly gentleman, in black, stepped out, signalling courteously but vivaciously for the boat to wait. Time was of the least importance in the schedule of the *Dixie Belle*; Captain MacFarland gave the order, and the boat received its ultimate two passengers. For, upon the arm of the tall, elderly gentleman, as he crossed the gangway, was a little elderly lady, with a grey curl depending quaintly forward on her left ear.

Captain MacFarland was at the wheel; therefore it seemed to J. Pinkney Bloom, who was the only other passenger, that it should be his to play the part of host to the boat's new guests, who were, doubtless, on a scenery-viewing expedition. He stepped forward, with that translucent, child-candid smile upon his fresh, pink countenance, with that air of unaffected sincerity that was redeemed from bluffness only by its exquisite calculation, with that promptitude and masterly decision of manner that so well suited his calling—with all his stock in trade well to the front, he stepped forward to receive Colonel and Mrs. Peyton Blaylock. With the grace of a grand marshal or a wedding usher, he escorted the two passengers to a side of the upper deck, from which the scenery was supposed to present itself to the observer in increased quantity and quality. There in comfortable steamer chairs, they sat and began to piece together the random lines that were to form an intelligent paragraph in the big history of little events.

"Our home, sir," said Colonel Blaylock, removing his wide-brimmed, rather shapeless black felt hat, "is in Holly Springs—Holly Springs, Georgia. I am very proud to make your acquaintance, Mr. Bloom. Mrs. Blaylock and myself have just arrived in Okochee this morning, sir, on business—business of importance in connection with the recent rapid march of progress in this section of our state."

The Colonel smoothed back, with a sweeping gesture, his long, smooth, grey locks. His dark eyes, still fiery under the heavy, black brows, seemed inappropriate to the face of a business man. He looked rather to be an old courtier handed down from the reign of Charles, and reattired in a modern suit of fine, but ravelling and seam-worn, broadcloth.

"Yes, sir," said Mr. Bloom, in his heartiest prospectus voice, "things have been whizzing around Okochee. Biggest industrial revival and waking up to natural resources Georgia ever had. Did you happen to squeeze in on the ground floor in any of the gilt-edged grafts, Colonel?"

"Well, sir," said the Colonel, hesitating in courteous doubt, "if I understood your question, I may say that I took the opportunity to make an investment that I believe will prove quite advantageous—yes, sir, I believe it will result in both pecuniary profit and agreeable occupation."

"Colonel Blaylock," said the little elderly lady, shaking her gay curl and smiling indulgent explanation at J. Pinkney Bloom, "is so devoted to business. He has such a talent for financiering and markets and investments and those kind of things. I think myself extremely fortunate in having secured him for a partner on life's journey—I am so unversed in those formidable but very useful branches of learning."

Colonel Blaylock rose and made a bow—a bow that belonged with silk stockings and lace ruffles and velvet.

"Practical affairs," he said, with a wave of his hand toward the promoter, "are, if I may use the comparison, the garden walks upon which we tread through life, viewing upon either side of us the flowers which brighten that journey. It is my pleasure to be able to lay out a walk or two. Mrs. Blaylock, sir, is one of those fortunate higher spirits whose mission it is to make the flowers grow. Perhaps, Mr. Bloom, you have perused the lines of Lorella, the Southern poetess. That is the name above which Mrs. Blaylock has contributed to the press of the South for many years."

"Unfortunately," said Mr. Bloom, with a sense of the loss clearly written upon his frank face, "I'm like the Colonel—in the walk-making business myself—and I haven't had time even to take a sniff at the flowers. Poetry is a line I never dealt in. It must be nice, though—quite nice."

"It is the region," smiled Mrs. Blaylock, "in which my soul dwells. My shawl, Peyton, if you please—the breeze comes a little chilly from yon verdured hills."

The Colonel drew from the tail pocket of his coat a small shawl of knitted silk and laid it solicitously about the shoulders of the lady. Mrs. Blaylock sighed contentedly, and turned her expressive eyes—still as clear and unworldly as a child's—upon the steep slopes that were slowly slipping past. Very fair and stately they looked in the clear morning air. They seemed to speak in familiar terms to the responsive spirit of Lorella. "My native hills!" she murmured dreamily. "See how the foliage drinks the sunlight from the hollows and dells."

"Mrs. Blaylock's maiden days," said the Colonel, interpreting her mood to J. Pinkney Bloom, "were spent among the mountains of northern Georgia. Mountain air and mountain scenery recall to her those days. Holly Springs, where we have lived for twenty years, is low and flat. I fear that she may have suffered in health and spirits by so long a residence there. That is one potent reason for the change we are making. My dear, can you not recall those lines you wrote—entitled, I think, 'The Georgia Hills'—the poem that was so extensively copied by the Southern press and praised so highly by the Atlanta critics?"

Mrs. Blaylock turned a glance of speaking tenderness upon the Colonel, fingered for a moment the silvery curl that drooped upon her bosom, then looked again toward the mountains. Without preliminary or affectation or demurral she began, in rather thrilling and more deeply pitched tones, to recite these lines:

"The Georgia hills, the Georgia hills!—
Oh, heart, why dost thou pine?
Are not these sheltered lowlands fair
With mead and bloom and vine?
Ah! as the slow-paced river here
Broods on its natal rills
My spirit drifts, in longing sweet,
Back to the Georgia hills.

"And through the close-drawn, curtained night
I steal on sleep's slow wings
Back to my heart's ease—slopes of pine—
Where end my wanderings.
Oh, heaven seems nearer from their tops—
And farther earthly ills—
Even in dreams, if I may but
Dream of my Georgia hills.

"The grass upon their orchard sides
Is a fine couch to me;
The common note of each small bird
Passes all minstrelsy.
It would not seem so dread a thing
If, when the Reaper wills,
He might come there and take my hand
Up in the Georgia hills."

"That's great stuff, ma'am," said J. Pinkney Bloom, enthusiastically, when the poetess had concluded. "I wish I had looked up poetry more than I have. I was raised in the pine hills myself."

"The mountains ever call to their children," murmured Mrs. Blaylock. "I feel that life will take on the rosy hue of hope again in among these beautiful hills. Peyton—a little taste of the currant wine, if you will be so good. The journey, though delightful in the extreme, slightly fatigues me."

Colonel Blaylock again visited the depths of his prolific coat, and produced a tightly corked, rough, black bottle. Mr. Bloom was on his feet in an instant. "Let me bring a glass, ma'am. You come along, Colonel—there's a little table we can bring, too. Maybe we can scare up some fruit or a cup of tea on board. I'll ask Mac."

Mrs. Blaylock reclined at ease. Few royal ladies have held their royal prerogative with the serene grace of the petted Southern woman. The Colonel, with an air as gallant and assiduous as in the days of his courtship, and J. Pinkney Bloom, with a ponderous agility half professional and half directed by some resurrected, unnamed, long-forgotten sentiment, formed a diversified but attentive court. The currant wine—wine home-made from the Holly Springs fruit—went round; and then J. Pinkney began to hear something of Holly Springs life.

It seemed (from the conversation of the Blaylocks) that the Springs was decadent. A third of the population had moved away. Business—and the Colonel was an authority on business—had dwindled to nothing. After carefully studying the field of opportunities open to capital he had sold his little property there for eight hundred dollars and invested it in one of the enterprises opened up by the book in Okochee.

"Might I inquire, sir," said Mr. Bloom, "in what particular line of business you inserted your coin? I know that town as well as I know the regulations for illegal use of the mails. I might give you a hunch as to whether you can make the game go or not."

J. Pinkney, somehow, had a kindly feeling toward these unsophisticated representatives of bygone days. They were so simple, impractical, and unsuspecting. He was glad that he happened not to have a gold brick or a block of that western Bad Boy Silver Mine stock along with him. He would have disliked to unload on people he liked so well as he did these; but there are some temptations too enticing to be resisted.

"No, sir," said Colonel Blaylock, pausing to arrange the queen's wrap. "I did not invest in Okochee. I have made an exhaustive study of business conditions, and I regard old settled towns as unfavourable fields in which to place capital that is limited in amount. Some months ago, through the kindness of a friend, there came into my hands a map and description of this new town of Skyland that has been built upon the lake. The description was so pleasing, the future of the town set forth in such convincing arguments, and its increasing prosperity portrayed in such an attractive style that I decided to take advantage of the opportunity it offered. I carefully selected a lot in the centre of the business district, although its price was the highest in the schedule—five hundred dollars—and made the purchase at once."

"Are you the man—I mean, did you pay five hundred dollars for a lot in Skyland?" asked J. Pinkney Bloom.

"I did, sir," answered the Colonel, with the air

of a modest millionaire explaining his success; "a lot most excellently situated on the same square with the opera house, and only two squares from the board of trade. I consider the purchase a most fortuitous one. It is my intention to erect a small building upon it at once, and open a modest book and stationery store. During past years I have met with many pecuniary reverses, and I now find it necessary to engage in some commercial occupation that will furnish me with a livelihood. The book and stationery business, though a humble one, seems to me not inapt nor altogether uncongenial. I am a graduate of the University of Virginia; and Mrs. Blaylock's really wonderful acquaintance with belles-lettres and poetic literature should go far toward insuring success. Of course, Mrs. Blaylock would not personally serve behind the counter. With the nearly three hundred dollars I have remaining I can manage the building of a house, by giving a lien on the lot. I have an old friend in Atlanta who is a partner in a large book store, and he has agreed to furnish me with a stock of goods on credit, on extremely easy terms. I am pleased to hope, sir, that Mrs. Blaylock's health and happiness will be increased by the change of locality. Already I fancy I can perceive the return of those roses that were once the hope and despair of Georgia cavaliers."

Again followed that wonderful bow, as the Colonel lightly touched the pale cheek of the poetess. Mrs. Blaylock, blushing like a girl, shook her curl and gave the Colonel an arch, reproving tap. Secret of eternal youth—where art thou? Every second the answer comes—"Here, here, here." Listen to thine own heartbeats, O weary seeker after external miracles.

"Those years," said Mrs. Blaylock, "in Holly Springs were long, long, long. But now is the promised land in sight. Skyland!—a lovely name."

"Doubtless," said the Colonel, "we shall be able to secure comfortable accommodation at some modest hotel at reasonable rates. Our trunks are in Okochee, to be forwarded when we shall have made permanent arrangements."

J. Pinkney Bloom excused himself, went forward, and stood by the captain at the wheel.

"Mac," said he, "do you remember my telling you once that I sold one of those five-hundred-dollar lots in Skyland?"

"Seems I do," grinned Captain MacFarland.

"I'm not a coward, as a general rule," went on the promoter, "but I always said that if I ever met the sucker that bought that lot I'd run like a turkey. Now, you see that old babe-in-the-wood over there? Well, he's the boy that drew the prize. That was the only five-hundred-dollar lot that went. The rest ranged from ten dollars to two hundred. His wife writes poetry. She's invented one about the high grounds of Georgia, that's way up in G. They're going to Skyland to open a book store."

"Well," said MacFarland, with another grin, "it's a good thing you are along, J. P.; you can show 'em around town until they begin to feel at home."

"He's got three hundred dollars left to build a house and store with," went on J. Pinkney, as if he were talking to himself. "And he thinks there's an opera house up there."

Captain MacFarland released the wheel long enough to give his leg a roguish slap.

"You old fat rascal!" he chuckled, with a wink.

"Mac, you're a fool," said J. Pinkney Bloom,

coldly. He went back and joined the Blaylocks, where he sat, less talkative, with that straight furrow between his brows that always stood as a signal of schemes being shaped within.

"There's a good many swindles connected with these booms," he said presently. "What if this Skyland should turn out to be one—that is, suppose business should be sort of dull there, and no special sale for books?"

"My dear sir," said Colonel Blaylock, resting his hand upon the back of his wife's chair, "three times I have been reduced to almost penury by the duplicity of others, but I have not yet lost faith in humanity. If I have been deceived again, still we may glean health and content, if not worldly profit. I am aware that there are dishonest schemers in the world who set traps for the unwary, but even they are not altogether bad. My dear, can you recall those verses entitled, 'He Giveth the Increase,' that you composed for the choir of our church in Holly Springs?"

"That was four years ago," said Mrs. Blaylock; "perhaps I can repeat a verse or two.

"The lily springs from the rotting mould;
Pearls from the deep sea slime;
Good will come out of Nazareth
All in God's own time.

"To the hardest heart the softening grace
Cometh, at last, to bless;
Guiding it right to help and cheer
And succour in distress.

"I cannot remember the rest. The lines were not ambitious. They were written to the music composed by a dear friend."

"It's a fine rhyme, just the same," declared Mr. Bloom. "It seems to ring the bell, all right. I guess I gather the sense of it. It means that the rankest kind of a phony will give you the best end of it once in a while."

Mr. Bloom strayed thoughtfully back to the captain, and stood meditating.

"Ought to be in sight of the spires and gilded domes of Skyland now in a few minutes," chirruped MacFarland, shaking with enjoyment.

"Go to the devil," said Mr. Bloom, still pensive.

And now, upon the left bank, they caught a glimpse of a white village, high up on the hills, smothered among green trees. That was Cold Branch—no boom town, but the slow growth of many years. Cold Branch lay on the edge of the grape and corn lands. The big country road ran just back of the heights. Cold Branch had nothing in common with the frisky ambition of Okochee with its impertinent lake.

"Mac," said J. Pinkney suddenly, "I want you to stop at Cold Branch. There's a landing there that they made to use sometimes when the river was up."

"Can't," said the captain, grinning more broadly. "I've got the United States mails on board. Right to-day this boat's in the government service. Do you want to have the poor old captain keelhauled by Uncle Sam? And the great city of Skyland, all disconsolate, waiting for its mail? I'm ashamed of your extravagance, J. P."

"Mac," almost whispered J. Pinkney, in his danger-line voice, "I looked into the engine-room of the *Dixie Belle* a while ago. Don't you know of somebody that needs a new boiler? Cement and black Japan can't hide flaws from me. And then, those shares of building and loan that you traded for repairs—they were all yours, of course. I hate to mention these things, but——"

"Oh, come now, J. P.," said the captain. "You know I was just fooling. I'll put you off at Cold Branch, if you say so."

"The other passengers get off there, too," said Mr. Bloom.

Further conversation was held, and in ten minutes the *Dixie Belle* turned her nose toward a little, cranky wooden pier on the left bank, and the captain relinquishing the wheel to a roustabout came to the passenger deck and made the remarkable announcement: "All out for Skyland."

The Blaylocks and J. Pinkney Bloom disembarked and the *Dixie Belle* proceeded on her way up the lake. Guided by the indefatigable promoter, they slowly climbed the steep hillside, pausing often to rest and admire the view. Finally they entered the village of Cold Branch. Warmly both the Colonel and his wife praised it for its homelike and peaceful beauty. Mr. Bloom conducted them to a two-story building on a shady street that bore the legend, "Pinetop Inn." Here he took his leave, receiving the cordial thanks of the two for his attentions, the Colonel remarking that he thought they would spend the remainder of the day in rest, and take a look at his purchase on the morrow.

J. Pinkney Bloom walked down Cold Branch's main street. He did not know this town, but he knew towns, and his feet did not falter. Presently he saw a sign over a door: "Frank E. Cooly, Attorney-at-Law and Notary Public." A young man was Mr. Cooly, and awaiting business.

"Get your hat, son," said Mr. Bloom, in his breezy way, "and a blank deed, and come along. It's a job for you."

"Now," he continued, when Mr. Cooly had responded with alacrity, "is there a book store in town?"

"One," said the lawyer. "Henry Williams's."

"Get there," said Mr. Bloom. "We're going to buy it."

Henry Williams was behind his counter. His store was a small one, containing a mixture of books, stationery, and fancy rubbish. Adjoining it was Henry's home—a decent cottage, vine-embowered and cosy. Henry was lank and soporific, and not inclined to rush his business.

"I want to buy your house and store," said Mr. Bloom. "I haven't got time to dicker—name your price."

"It's worth eight hundred," said Henry, too much dazed to ask more than its value.

"Shut that door," said Mr. Bloom to the lawyer. Then he tore off his coat and vest, and began to unbutton his shirt.

"Wanter fight about it, do yer?" said Henry Williams, jumping up and cracking his heels together twice. "All right, hunky—sail in and cut yer capers."

"Keep your clothes on," said Mr. Bloom. "I'm only going down to the bank."

He drew eight one-hundred-dollar bills from his money belt and planked them down on the counter. Mr. Cooly showed signs of future promise, for he already had thc deed spread out, and was reaching across the counter for the ink bottle. Never before or since was such quick action had in Cold Branch.

"Your name, please?" asked the lawyer.

"Make it out to Peyton Blaylock," said Mr. Bloom. "God knows how to spell it."

Within thirty minutes Henry Williams was out of business, and Mr. Bloom stood on the brick sidewalk with Mr. Cooly, who held in his hand the signed and attested deed.

"You'll find the party at the Pinetop Inn," said J. Pinkney Bloom. "Get it recorded, and take it down and give it to him. He'll ask you a hell's mint of questions; so here's ten dollars for the trouble you'll have in not being able to answer 'em. Never run much to poetry, did you, young man?"

"Well," said the really talented Cooly, who even yet retained his right mind, "now and then."

"Dig into it," said Mr. Bloom, "it'll pay you. Never heard a poem, now, that run something like his, did you?—

> "A good thing out of Nazareth
> Comes up sometimes, I guess,
> On hand, all right, to help and cheer
> A sucker in distress."

"I believe not," said Mr. Cooly.

"It's a hymn," said J. Pinkney Bloom. "Now, show me the way to a livery stable, son, for I'm going to hit the dirt road back to Okochee."

Ella's Accident.
Nov. 3rd 1942

Tuesday night. 7.30. Fell off bike
Taken to Dr. then to Larne
in ambulance. unconscious.
Wed. I went to see her. Still
unconscious. But I think
she knew me for a second
& so at the time.
Thurs. Mr. Pierce came from
R.V.H. to see her. No
immediate danger, he said
but paralysed in right side &
voice gone. May need an
operation.
Friday. Ella taken to R.V.H.
Sat. I went to see her, She
was quite conscious & knew
Sun. Daddy & James to see Ella
Wed. I went to see her
thought her much better.
Sun. Daddy & James went
... She had operation